THE
LAST
HERO

Also by Linden A. Lewis

The First Sister Trilogy
The First Sister
The Second Rebel
The Last Hero

THE LAST HERO

LINDEN A. LEWIS

HODDER &
STOUGHTON

First published in Great Britain in 2022 by Hodder & Stoughton
An Hachette UK company

1

Copyright © Linden A. Lewis 2022

The right of Linden A. Lewis to be identified as the Author of the Work has been
asserted by them in accordance with the Copyright, Designs and Patents Act 1988.

A CIP catalogue record for this title is available from the British Library

Hardback ISBN 978 1 529 38700 1
Trade Paperback ISBN 978 1 529 38701 8
eBook ISBN 978 1 529 38702 5

Printed and bound in Great Britain by Clays Ltd, Elcograf S.p.A.

Hodder & Stoughton policy is to use papers that are natural, renewable
and recyclable products and made from wood grown in sustainable
forests. The logging and manufacturing processes are expected to
conform to

To all the queer and trans kids: Live, even if out of spite.
Your very existence is heroic.

PROLOGUE

From his office on the 225th floor, Souji val Akira could easily ignore the protesters below. But because he knows they are down there, he stands before the floor-to-ceiling windows, his desk behind him ignored, and looks at the feet of the crystalline buildings shimmering in the Cytherean dome's azure lighting, past the verdant hanging plants naturally purifying the air, focusing on the writhing mass in the street.

He can't make out their signs or their masks, but he can imagine them. On his way to and from the office, he's seen them, thrusting scraps of plastiflex in his face, slogans written in shaky, childlike hands: STOP VAL AKIRA or EXPERIMENT ON HIM. His personal favorite is one that reads MAD SCIENTIST, accompanied by a cartoon of him wearing a white lab coat, his hair a wild halo about his head, cackling as if ready to flip an electric switch and create a monster of reanimated parts. At the very least, he cannot fault their creativity.

When the protests first began, it was mostly students covering their faces to avoid truancy charges from the patrolling peacekeepers, but now the masks have become a symbol of something greater: those who wear them are those who stand in solidarity with the Asters against Val Akira Labs. The protesters, no longer just students, cover their faces with whatever they can find—scraps of cloth, fleshy costume faces, even cheap carnival masks, as if his collection of Noh theater masks birthed counterfeit children en masse.

And the most maddening thought of all: *One of them,* he considers, shifting from foot to foot, *could be Hiro.*

1

Not that anyone has caught a single glimpse of his errant child since the *Leander*'s destruction six months ago. In fact, more than a few have suggested that Hiro perished alongside Souji's eldest son, Shinya. But Souji refuses to believe that. In fact, he can feel that it isn't true. Hiro val Akira is not dead.

Shinya val Akira, however, is, and the wound is still fresh. There's a part of Souji that can't focus on anything else, a constant pain that burns at the edges of everything he does. When Souji's older brother Daisuke passed away during his military service, their father, Fuyuki val Akira, told Souji that losing one's first child was like watching all of one's dreams die. At the time, hearing that brought Souji a different sort of ache; now, he understands.

Over his shoulder, Souji catches the reflection of one of Shinya's calligraphy paintings. "With My Father," by Kobayashi Issa, the black ink brushstrokes of the characters almost playfully rendered. While the artist is no one noteworthy, Souji couldn't bring himself to do away with it. This piece, taken from Shinya's office in the Spire, is Souji's one concession to sentimentality, a reminder that his son understood the meaning of legacy.

It is also a reminder. Shinya val Akira's death was a sacrifice, and Souji will not allow it to be in vain. Unlike Fuyuki, who seemed to lose the greatest part of himself with his son and spent his remaining years mourning at the family shrine, Souji will turn the agony of losing his firstborn into a clarifying fire. Shinya understood what Souji was trying to achieve. He stayed the course until the very end. And it is only because of him that Souji has even the remotest chance of completing his work before . . . well, before the AEGIS tires of protest, makes its decision, and he is arrested on one trumped-up charge or another.

The problem, as always, is time.

Despite the myriad scientific advances made by Souji and Val Akira Labs, time remains something beyond the thousand gods. You cannot reason with it, cannot convince it, cannot beg it to slow down—can only seize what little you have with both hands and hang on until it either slips through your fingers or kills you.

That moment, Souji fears, is coming soon. If the AEGIS reaches a decision within the week, as they've promised, he will be removed as the CEO of Val Akira Labs, have his assets seized, and be placed in a correctional program with a sponsor breathing down his neck about forced community service. He will be an embarrassment to his father and his father's father before him, sullying the val Akira name with his actions (or lack thereof), and all because he could not hold to the course mapped out and passed down through the generations. He will become Icarus instead of Daedalus, a cautionary tale for those who reach too far.

But it's more than that, even if few know it. His failure means that the Icarii and Geans will war over a kingdom of dirt, and the Synthetics will watch silently as humanity devours itself, a serpent swallowing its own tail until it is no more. And perhaps he could live with that—if he had not lost his first child.

Now that he has lost Shinya, failure is not an option.

And so Souji val Akira has a decision to make. He must find the weak link in the chain and hammer upon it, eke out a few more weeks of work regardless of the cost. As his father taught him in that little basement room, the lab that wasn't quite a lab: *For someone in our position, choosing the best course for the greatest number of people is a necessity.*

Better to maim one person than to allow a hundred to die. Better to kill a few Asters than to watch the entire human race march toward its slow but inevitable extinction.

Beron val Bellator huffs behind him, growing impatient, and Souji turns his attention from the protesters below to consider the high commander's reflection in the glass. He was a handsome man forty years ago, but he's begun wearing his age on his face. Not just in the scar that retired him from the field, slicing through the fat of his cheek beneath his now-prosthetic eye, but in the dullness of his grim gaze and the heaviness of the bags beneath. Since the *Leander*, gravity seems to have more of a hold on Beron than it used to.

"Beron," Souji says, his voice husky, "I've made my decision."

Beron's manner, at least, is still strong. "You're sure about this, val Akira?"

Souji's gaze wanders from Beron to Shinya's painting and then back to the street below. If he is to make a decision that will affect the protesters, he wishes to consider them as he chooses. A coward damns people he does not know; a man of honor at least looks them in the eye as he decides their fate.

"Proceed," Souji says.

At his age, Beron has no neural implant, but still, Souji has known him all of his adult life—has worked with him for damn near thirty years—and can sense the concern surging up in the commander, rolling off of him in stiff waves. This would be so much easier if Souji could simply snap his fingers and demand Beron do as asked, if he didn't have to take precious time he does not have to abide unwanted opinions on his methods.

"That's going to end in a lot of dead bodies," Beron says, as if Souji has not calculated the cost, as if every soul has not been weighed on the cosmic scales that only Souji seems to read. "Hundreds. Thousands, maybe."

"What are thousands to the billions, Beron?" Souji asks in a whisper, knowing the other man can hear.

Souji can see the gears turning in Beron's head as he considers, can feel him measuring the order and its consequences. Beron knows if Souji is to be damned, he must be as well. If Souji is to be called a monster, he, the man who carried out his orders, is just as monstrous.

But—that three-letter word, so easy to overlook—*but*. If Souji is right . . .

"We have already come this far together," Souji reminds him. "Why should we falter now?"

At last, Beron slumps. The scales have found balance.

"Yes, sir," he says, turning on his heel and marching from the office.

With the decision made and Beron on his way to carry out the sentence, Souji turns away from the window, the protesters all but forgotten. He looks at Shinya's painting, each character carved into his memory. If he's going to complete his life's work before the AEGIS arrests him, he'll have to seize every second he's given.

The lives of a few protesters don't matter when it comes to saving all of humanity.

PART I

TOO CLOSE TO THE SUN

CHAPTER 1

HIRO

We at the AEGIS find the data sent by Lito sol Lucius from Ceres Satellite #19 to be authentic. Moving forward, we will turn our investigation toward those responsible for the execution and oversight of these horrific experiments. Rest assured that we will stop at nothing to hold Val Akira Labs accountable for its actions.

Rosendo val Chaz, president of the Agency for
Ethical Guidance of Icarii Science

I haven't been this high above Cytherea since I was a child visiting my father's floor at Val Akira Labs' head office. Grandfather had just retired, naming my father the new CEO, and he proudly brought our little family to see where he'd be, in his words, "working to change the world." I was so young, it has to be one of my first memories, yet I still vividly remember standing at the full window, Asuka's hands on my shoulders and Shinya at my side, as I stared at the surrounding buildings that, to my childish eyes, looked like massive clusters of crystalline shards.

Now that spell is broken. The buildings are just buildings, their streaked, colorful glass more like solar panels than the overgrown rose quartzes and amethysts their designers wish them to evoke. Or perhaps it's the fact that I'm alone that sucks all the magic from the view. Asuka is somewhere below, crumbling under the pressure of AEGIS inquiries, and Shinya—well, Shinya will never walk these streets again.

I balance across a slender metal catwalk, hazarding a view at the protest I left behind fifteen minutes ago. Nothing is like I pictured as Luce described the route to me. There's no wind whipping through the narrow corridors between high-rise buildings, no peacekeepers chasing after me, just a rickety construction made out of spare metal, hastily tethered together and zigzagging like a fire escape.

From this height, I can even make out the great onyx Spire in the distance, sucking up all the light from the otherwise bright Cytherean twilight. The dome dims as night falls, casting my path in long shadows and making my mask more of a hazard than a protection. It's the perfect hour for me to scurry up to the top of a building unseen. The perfect semidarkness for Luce and I to deploy another of our vids to the public.

I test a thin metal sheet with my boot. It bows under my weight, so I skip it, hopping to a sturdier platform. I stick as close to the building as possible. I don't have a fear of heights, but I'd like to think that anyone this high up would be wary. A fall from here would turn me into a street crepe.

"Still disappointed I didn't get high-tech gloves that make me stick to the building like a chameleon," I say, recording my voice and uploading it to Hemlock's server with a flick of my eyes. The com-lenses are especially useful since my hands are occupied, though I had to turn off all the entertainment functions so I'm not distracted by news articles and colorful ads.

Luce's response comes after a few seconds' delay. Her dry chuckle is the first thing I hear. "You always picture things like an action vid." Despite the distance between us, her voice comes through as clearly as if she were standing next to me.

"Maybe it is an action vid." I hold tight to the railing as I skirt a wobbly section. "Shadowy group that wants to kill us? Check. Sexy assistant? Check. Roguish hero? Check, by yours truly. And my father humbly accepts the role of evil wizard in his giant tower."

Luce snorts. "'Sexy assistant'? Please tell me you're not talking about me."

"Of course not, I'm talking about Hemlock." My cheeks ache from grinning. "By the way, what're you wearing?"

"Just get to the roof, roguish hero," Luce responds, but I can hear the amusement in her tone, and I know I've made her smile—no easy task nowadays. "When our 'evil wizard' goes before the AEGIS tomorrow afternoon, I want people to remember why."

And that means we remind them with one of Luce's vids.

"Roger, team leader."

The words are hardly out of my mouth when a sheet snaps beneath me.

I stumble forward, hands flailing, but my fingers slip over the closest beam. It happens so fast, just three seconds, and I'm tumbling down—

I catch the railing of the platform below, elbows and shoulders jerking taut, joints aching from catching my full weight. My mask is not so lucky, the black tactical covering fluttering to the streets below. The entire structure groans beneath me, threatening to collapse, though it's hard to focus on that when my vision flashes red with agony.

"くそ!" My left shoulder, the one connected to my prosthetic, aches like someone slipped a blade between skin and metal. But I can't just hang here, so I force myself to move, ignoring the groaning of both the catwalk and my body as I pull myself back onto the safety of a lower platform.

I sit there for a good minute and a half, catching my breath and rubbing my shoulder. More pressing than the current throbbing of my joints is an overwhelming fear. Thanks to Mara, the agent of the Synthetics on Autarkeia, I had a handle on my pain—but what if this accident fucks it all up? What if the daily agony returns?

I dig my fingers into my flesh biceps, nails tight enough to bruise through my jacket, and focus on my breathing. In and out. In and out.

Slowly, the pain subsides. It doesn't depart completely, but now that

I'm not hanging on for my literal life, I adjust. I'll likely need to ice my joints later, but I'm hopeful that I didn't undo whatever careful balance Mara granted me when she reprogrammed my prosthetics. Or if I did, that it'll be a black hole like my leg after the duelist on the *Leander* ran me through with a mercurial blade. I can't feel anything with my metal foot, but that's way fucking better than phantom pain.

It's only after I convince myself I need to keep moving that I realize Luce's reply has been waiting for almost five minutes. But I don't listen to it. Don't respond. I disengage from Hemlock's server, not needing any more distractions. Pretend as I might with Luce in my ear, I'm alone on Cytherea, partnerless, with no one to catch me when I fall. The words of my first commander on Ceres come back to me, unbidden: *A duelist alone is nothing.*

I test every plank before I put my weight on it, tug every ladder before I climb. When I finally reach the top of the building, another fifteen minutes have passed, though it shouldn't have taken more than five. Better to be safe than sorry, I guess.

The rooftop is covered in a rainbow of graffiti. Colorful protest slogans and various images blanket every inch of space. I step across a trompe l'oeil of a hole that leads to a forest full of golden light and come to a larger-than-life nude of a bald woman in a breather mask: La Peste, Luce herself.

I have to hand it to her, this spot the Keres Truth Society found is perfect for our needs. It's within a three-block radius of the protest at Val Akira Labs, but not so close that it's being regularly patrolled. We can have our drone descend directly over the protesters instead of launching from the ground, where peacekeepers are sure to shoot it down before it gets high enough to project.

Of course, the more times we hazard this little stunt, the harder it is to pull off. Whatever route we use will be cut off to us the next time, and this is already our fifth vid.

I reconnect to Hemlock's server and send Luce a voice message. "I'm on the rooftop," I tell her, kneeling and unzipping my backpack. I pull out various pieces of the drone. It's a big one, something that'd be banned on Cytherea because of the light pollution it would create, but this baby came from Autarkeia, so it's a bad motherfucker ready for trouble. I start putting it together, mounting the projector and speakers below its rotor blades, easy as plug and play despite it being the size of a small child.

"Vid's ready," comes Luce's response. "Test connection."

Just to be safe, I check everything over one last time. The battery is full. Everything's screwed on tightly. I test the projector and speakers; they work perfectly. My com-lenses read the open connection from the drone, and I see the option to download the vid it carries. "Ready to deploy," I tell Luce.

"You ready to jump?"

After the almost-fall on that metal monstrosity? I'm not thrilled about it, but my exit strategy is probably safer than returning the way I came. I check the harness I wore up and pull the rest of my gear from my pack, preparing everything for go time.

"I always said I'd jump off a building if my life was shit."

"Not funny." I expect her to continue to chide me, but instead she focuses on the task at hand. "Remember your mask."

Shit, I almost forgot, I lost my mask on the way up. I pull a scarf out of my bag, wrap it around my lower face and tie it off, then finish the look with a pair of goggles that brightens my quickly fading surroundings. *Rebel chic.* It's somewhat hard to breathe through the thick scarf, but I'll have to do as all fashion icons have before: make it work. Better than having peacekeepers spot me and plaster my face all over the news. I've got a nifty fake ID that Hemlock set up for me, but it won't take much for them to figure out Yasuhiro sol Fujita fucked off to Autarkeia and i'm using his credentials. As for the goggles? They'll help me with the *other* thing. The thing I'm *not* telling Luce about.

I press the grav-anchor to the rooftop and check that it's well secured before threading my rope through. Rappelling from this height wasn't covered in my Academy training, but I was lucky that Luce found me a belay machine that'll lower me to the ground at the touch of a button, like a personal elevator—you know, except attached to the harness at my stomach above a carabiner, which I check, double-check, and triple-check once my rope is through. The machine lights up green, telling me it's ready to go, and I have to remind myself that beginners use this thing all the time *for fun*, so I, a professional Dagger, can manage this.

"All right, Luce, I'm ready to go." I'm sure my voice sounds muffled to her through the scarf, but if she has trouble understanding me, she doesn't mention it.

"Deploying."

I brace myself, finger on the belay machine's button, and get into position. My heart races as I go from standing upright to parallel to the ground, and I have a single moment where my world flares white and my only thought is *I've made a huge fucking mistake*, but then I'm steady in the harness and ready to rappel down.

I'm a Dagger, I tell myself, *a professional*. But my guts don't get the memo, and I feel like I'm going to shit my pants at any second.

The drone's rotors flare to life with a high-pitched *whizz*, and it lifts from the rooftop as smoothly as an Icarii dropship. Passing overhead and stirring my hair with a warm wind, it flies toward its destination down the street. I shift my weight as it reaches its programmed position, hovering over the protestors, projector pointed at the smooth-faced Val Akira Labs building.

I wait, harness digging into my thighs, until Lito's face appears a hundred meters tall. I'm hit with a force like taking a mercurial blade to the ribs. My lungs feel too small, too tight, and a black wave of dizziness rushes over me. Doesn't matter how long it's been; every time I see him, my surroundings fade away, and I remember how I found Lito, pale and stiff and gone, on the *Leander*.

A cry rises up from the street below, protestors shouting and cheering at the return of the rebel whose death sparked the protests and dragging me back to the here and now. "There are good people out there who will see what's happening and try to change things," their great martyr says over the crowd's roar. "People who know what it is to suffer—or even people who don't know what suffering is, but are empathetic enough not to want others to know it either."

I listen to his words over the cheering, his voice as familiar as my favorite song, but I can't watch the vid. Seeing him glaring and speaking and so very *alive* is too much when I held his dead body to my chest.

"Beginning descent," I tell Luce. I brace myself with my legs and press the belay machine's button, releasing enough slack that I can walk backward down the building's side. After the almost-fall, I'm not tempted to do anything crazy, so I stick to the slowest setting and take baby steps.

"One day," a message from Luce comes, "you'll have to let me interview you for my vids."

I swallow a self-deprecating laugh. Fat chance of me ever submitting to that torture.

As if she senses my skepticism from planets away, a second message arrives. "Have you thought any more about it?" Her voice is soft and reverent. "About letting the Icarii see what your father did to you?"

But that would require so much more than letting them look. That would require flaying myself alive; it would mean cutting myself open so they could appreciate the pieces of me and pass my organs from hand to hand like collectibles. To bathe in memories I hardly want yet fear fading away. It would require me—no longer Hiro val Akira, not quite Saito Ren—to beg them to love me in a way that no one can. To pretend that they could possibly understand, and trade in offense like a currency of social values.

I cut the connection to Hemlock's server.

After a minute or so of Lito on the projection behind me, the subject changes to an Aster without her wraps, her big black eyes swallowing whatever light they used to shoot the vid. She pulls her hair away from a dip in her skull the size of a man's hand, hairless, puckered skin stretched to cover the gap. "I used to have a piece of metal here," the young Aster says. Her name is Rose, I recall, and she was one of the kindest Asters I met in the Under, curious about the Icarii despite all the abuse they'd heaped on her.

Luce's voice answers her. "Do you know what it did?"

"No," Rose says sadly. "I was told by the scientist at Val Akira Labs it was to monitor my brain waves, but after the trial was done, they didn't remove it."

"How old were you when they put it in?" Luce's tone is calm and re-assured, like a journalist at an interview, but I can tell from the way she's forcefully enunciating that the subject upsets her.

"Seven," Rose answers, and Luce sucks in a sharp breath. "They didn't take the metal out, so when I started to grow, my skull started pulling away from it, and it left a gap that exposed my brain to—"

The vid cuts out, and the sharp sound of tearing metal fills the air. I release the belay machine's button, halting my progress. Like all our other drones, this one's been shot down. The shouts of the crowd reach me a moment later, a rush of angry voices like a Venusian metal storm.

My goggles catch the falling pieces of the drone and highlight the direction they scatter, allowing me to calculate where the peacekeeper with the long-range HEL gun is down below. I tag that section of the crowd, cursing that I'm not already on the ground to intercept them. I need that weapon.

Maybe even more than I need to survive this rappel.

"Shit." I turn up the speed on the belay machine and move faster than before, kicking off the building and hopping two to three meters at a time. "Fuck." With each miniature fall, my stomach flies up to join my heart. "くそ."

A message from Luce glows in the corner of my com-lenses, but I don't reconnect to the server. If I contact her now, she'll have too many questions about what I'm doing, why I'm not going home, and I'm not ready to tell her about my plans with the peacekeeper's HEL gun. Not yet.

What she doesn't know can't hurt her.

DESPITE SIX LONG months of protest, the crowd of people outside of Val Akira Labs is so thick that podcar traffic has been rerouted from the street. Losing myself in the swarm is all too easy, the press of bodies around me a welcome change from the feeling of falling. As soon as I reached the ground, I thought about kissing concrete but held back. Who knows what's growing on the Cytherean streets.

Peacekeeper drones fly wildly overhead, side by side with both news outlets and personal drones in a bevy of colors. Some have been rigged to carry tiny slogans of the protest, my father's name cursed in a dozen different languages, but those aren't the ones I need to watch out for. I can't risk being identified here, and I'm not exactly blending in with my scarf and goggles combo.

The peacekeepers have cordoned off the Autarkeian drone wreckage on the steps leading up to Val Akira Labs, pushing the crowd back from the scattered fragments. A triage area has been set up in a green tent off to the side, medics tending to anyone with wounds from falling pieces. Cytherean authorities care about the protesters, but they're obviously still willing to risk protester health in order to take out our message.

I check my compad to see if, by some magic spell, the drone is still broadcasting—but of course, it's dead. The first thing the peacekeepers would've done is make sure no one could download that vid. It'll be up to Luce and luck to spread it now.

I move toward the section of the protest I'd tagged in my goggles, off to the right of the steps and across a little side street, butting up against flexglass-front restaurants closed due to the late hour. It's not difficult to find the peacekeepers milling about in their black-and-silver uniforms, but it takes me a bit of walking back and forth before I spot the one with the sleek plastic case on his back. Only now that I'm here, I have no idea how I'm going to get it from him . . .

First things first, I need a mask. I look around the crowd for any extra or one cast aside and spot a fox through a gap—

In a moment, years collapse, one atop the other, until I don't know where or when I am. I feel my mother taking my hands between hers, putting them in prayer position before the family shrine. I see Asuka slipping my handwritten paper beneath the fox statue's soul gem. How many prayers are still there now, hidden inside the messenger to Inari? I remember the dreams of my father, the nine-tailed fox, demanding we children feed ourselves to him.

But then I calm myself with a long breath. It's just the plastic carnival mask of a white fox, red whiskers framing its playful smile. There is no cosmic meaning to this.

I move toward the fox and slip into place at the back of the group. They elbow their way through the edge of the crowd, a bunch of kids barely shoulder-height, and I snag a mask from one of their jacket pockets as they pass by.

I can't help but laugh when I realize the mask I've grabbed is that of an 鬼 with vibrant red skin, pointed horns, and yellow fangs in an open-mouthed snarl. Fitting, I suppose, after all the trollish things I've done tonight.

As I circle back toward the peacekeeper with the long-range HEL gun, my attention catches on a bubble in the crowd, a group standing shoulder to shoulder with their compads held between them. Passing close enough, I hear Rose's voice followed by Luce's, and all at once, even over the thrill of success that our vid is changing hands, a plan forms.

I needed a distraction, and now I have one.

I shoulder my way into the group as if I'm one of them. "Is that the vid from tonight?" I ask, pitching my voice lower than natural. The one with the compad pauses the vid as all masks snap up toward me. They're wary, this group.

"I didn't get a chance to download it before the drone was gone . . ." I trail off, scuffing my heel over the concrete. "Think I can snag it off of you?"

The one holding the compad sighs and offers it to me. "Sure."

A friend of theirs looks toward the patrolling peacekeepers, including my target. "Make it quick."

I don't reach for my compad, the one that connects to Luce. Instead, I reach for a burner, one of the several cheap ones I have in the backpack that used to carry the Autarkeian drone. It takes only a tap of that compad to theirs to transfer the vid, but as soon as I have it, I turn up the volume as loud as it'll go and hit play.

"Thanks," I say just before Lito's voice overwhelms us.

"THERE ARE GOOD PEOPLE OUT THERE—" Lito booms.

The peacekeepers turn toward us.

"Fuck!" one of the group yells.

"You idiot!" says another.

"Scatter," the smartest hisses.

I drop the compad to the ground. We all break in different directions, though I'm the only one who walks *toward* the peacekeepers.

Drones, the eyes of the peacekeepers, congregate overhead, searching for the owner of the compad. I wish the group luck, but I needed them as bait. Even if they're arrested, they'll be slapped with a fine at worst, and I need that long-range weapon for something far more important than a bit of content swapping.

The peacekeeper with the HEL gun case passes by me without a second look. Most of the crowd has backed away from them, sensing that they're out for blood, but many linger, their own drones hovering at their shoulders to capture what might happen. Unfortunately, that means they might also capture what comes next.

I step into the peacekeeper's shadow, my left hand reaching while my right hand distracts. I make sure to jerk my right arm around as if hoping to record all angles with my compad—the one that contacts Luce, so I can't lose it—as I carefully unsnap the case.

Two latches undone, and one of the peacekeepers points another in the direction my friends went. The man with the HEL gun shifts, and my heart speeds—but then he leans back into his heels, waiting for orders. I gently push the case open, only wide enough for me to reach the folded-up long-range weapon, and—

"Hey, what're you doing!" a different peacekeeper screams.

Shit. Time to go.

I snatch the HEL gun out of the case and take off down the closest alleyway. The sounds of shouting and stomping boots follow behind, far too close for comfort, but I have enough presence of mind to use the dark of the alley to slide the HEL gun into my backpack for cover.

Above me, peacekeeping drones swarm in pursuit, and while I'm faster than the peacekeepers in an open sprint, there's no losing a drone. But the difference between me and the machines is that I know the dark crevices of this city better than they ever could, and I know that I don't have to make it all the way home to get out of sight.

I turn a sharp corner and, without looking, hop a concrete barrier into a stairwell that leads to the bullet trains. A few people shout in alarm, while most stumble out of my way. In the precious seconds I have before the drones recalculate and follow me down into the station, I strip off my mask and jacket and toss them in opposite directions.

But I'm not free yet: the drones have me scanned and are looking for someone with my height and weight, regardless of what I'm wearing or not.

I walk like an innocent bystander, hoping I come across someone with the same build as me, to no avail. I know from the noise alone that the drones have made it downstairs, their metallic *whirr* louder than the ambient sounds of the station. The swarm hovers above the crowd, scanning us. Any second, they'll spot me.

As if I had cried out for help, a group of masked individuals with plastiflex signs on poles mob the drones, blocking their cameras with slogans like FREEDOM OF KNOWLEDGE!

"Go! Go now!" one of the protesters shouts in my direction.

"Bruv!" calls another, and a mask comes whizzing in my direction. I put it on without looking at it, slouching as I make my way to the train platforms.

Once I've taken the stairs deeper into the station, I risk a glance over my shoulder. The drones are trapped by the throng of people swatting at them with signs like giant flyswatters. I swallow a laugh and jump on the first train I come across, but it's only once the doors close and the train rumbles out of the station, leaving the drones and peacekeepers behind, that my heart finally slows.

At least until I catch sight of my reflection.

Staring back at me from the flexglass is the mask of a fox.

I RETURN TO Yasuhiro sol Fujita's apartment, affecting a nervous gait—back slouched, hands in front of my stomach, feet shuffling. As always, Yasuhiro's neighbor, an elderly woman with nothing better to do than monitor the comings and goings of the residents on her floor, opens her door and pokes her head into the hallway. I make sure she catches a glimpse of the fox mask before I slip it off and replace it with a visor that monitors the feed, cheaper than com-lenses but not nearly as popular.

"You're coming back so late, Yasuhiro!" Gianna sol Luca exclaims. "You're not getting into any trouble with those masked people, are you?"

I pitch my voice higher as if embarrassed. "O-of course not, ma'am. I-I'm just interested in r-recording some of the protest . . . for posterity."

She nods thoughtfully. "Good, good . . . We have to watch out for each other in this neighborhood."

I nod as if I agree wholeheartedly. "Good night," I tell her, then fumble with my bag until she bids me farewell and closes the door. She's probably still watching from a hallway cam, so I hurry in without opening my door too wide.

Inside, I shrug off the Yasuhiro persona, taking off the feed visor and tossing the fox mask facedown on the bed so it can't watch me. I have a dozen missed messages from Luce waiting for me when I reconnect to Hemlock's server, and I trash them all after listening to the first—"Hiro, are you okay?"—knowing they'll be more of the same.

"All clear," I send her as a reply. Quick and professional. Enough to stave off worry.

The midlevel safe house, bigger than the closet Dire gave me on Autarkeia but still small by Cytherean standards, is a single long room, with a layout more like a hotel room than an apartment. I stacked the excess furniture in the corner to give myself more space, so I settle on the stained blue-and-yellow carpet, turn on the holoprojector, and listen to the news as I pull the long-range HEL gun from my backpack and begin my work of taking it apart.

Every news outlet carefully avoids talking about Luce's vid, instead mentioning the continued protest before circling back to my father. "Tomorrow," various anchors say in various ways, "Souji val Akira is scheduled to appear before the AEGIS."

I force myself to look at his face, at the face of the man Shinya died for: gentle crow's feet and an unlined mouth, black hair with a single streak of white pushed back from a high forehead, brown eyes lit with a hint of blue fox fire—or is that just in my memory?

In the brief images they show of him, he's unconcerned even now. Untouched by stress. Utterly unrepentant. He smiles like it's all a game he's already won.

A message from Luce pings me. I play it before second-guessing myself.

"I know you too well to think you've gone to bed," Luce says, and she sounds as tired as I feel. "So tell me . . . what's really going on, Hiro?"

I look down at the long-range HEL gun scattered before me in heavy, unrecognizable pieces on the carpet. At the box with two dozen fingerprint-locked triggers, all keyed to me. At the face of my father on the holoprojector, believing he's won a game that isn't over.

I don't answer Luce now, because I already answered her, all those months ago on Vesta.

I'm going to kill my father.

CHAPTER 2

THE TWINS

It is with the deepest sorrow that I announce the passing of Aunt Salomiya, leader of the Order of Virgo and member of the Agora. Mere days after we began an investigation into her connection with the former Aunts Sapphira and Genette, Aunt Salomiya ended her life at the young age of thirty-eight. She left no note.

Aunt Marshae, head of the Order of Cassiopeia

Lily and the Mother look nothing alike. I know they're technically the same fucking person, but Lily's my sister, and though she doesn't look how she used to, I've gotten used to it—can even spot the shared features between the Pollux of my childhood and now—while the Mother looks like a fucking overdone wedding cake. The Aunts swamp Lily in all this white fabric and pearls and a furry white cape—which probably used to be an animal—stick a crown on her head, and parade her around like a mannequin in a fancy outfit. Then they hang fresh lilies on her, like a bouquet at a grave niche, and I can't be the only person who sees how unoriginal that is. Lilies for Mother Lilian I? Groundbreaking.

Danmus, that dickhead who calls me a cockroach every chance he gets, elbows me out of the way to get to Lily's side as soon as she emerges from the podcar, and Bennett's on his ass like they're lovers, but of course I can't fucking appear beside the Mother when I, lowly Aster that I am, should not even presume to eat the dirt her silky white slipper graced. Honestly, their dicks would probably turn inside out if they knew we were twins.

I let the insult go and fall in behind the group of White Guards as Lily ascends the steps to the Cathedral of Olympus Mons, a public place of worship in the city proper. Even at the rear of the thirteen guards, I'm not so far away that I wouldn't be able to reach her if shit hit the fan. Of course, part of me thinks the worst thing that could happen to my twin at a funeral would be an Aunt lobbing offensive innuendos and veiled threats at her—which is just another Tuesday in Sisterhoodland— but I can feel angry eyes on me as we pass through the open stone doors carved with the symbols of the Orders, and I have to remind myself that some of the Aunts aren't too happy about Lily's inclusion of an Aster among the White Guard.

They hate it when Lily does anything she doesn't expressly ask permission for, and I'm one of those things. They think the few Asters who volunteer for service should stick to their unit, where they fight— and die—quickly and quietly. Granted, the name I wear, that of Sergeant Oleander of the Aster Regiment, did die somewhere out there in the black, but *siks* can't tell the difference between one Aster and the next, and I was only too happy to take his name and rank when he was no longer using it. And thanks to Lily, "Sergeant Oleander" even snagged a promotion to White Guard. Yay, nepotism.

Our procession makes it through the entrance hall to the nave. Gotta hand it to these Gean assholes, the Cathedral's pretty. All old Martian stone, rust red streaked through with jet black. The nave is a long stretch, filled with columns shaped like tree trunks. I think we're supposed to be in a forest made of marble, but the symbolism doesn't hold up with the painted glass depicting scenes of their version of history. Along one wall is the story of Marian, the first Mother, founding the Sisterhood during the settling of Mars. On the wall opposite is the rise of the first Warlord, chosen by Mother Joan I after the chaos that was the Dead Century War. Beautiful, but really just a pack of lies as sharp as a bundle of daggers.

Then a feeling comes to me like a hand laid on my shoulder, and I can tell from the ripple that passes among the White Guard that the others are feeling it too. With a nudge from Lily's neural implant, we spread out through the aisle, three on one side of her, three on the other, me at her back, and the others staying behind to guard the entrance. But I can sense my twin in a way none of the other White Guards ever could: I can smell her pheromones going sour at having to use the tech—she hates being shackled with the implant far more than I ever have, or maybe it's that she hates imposing her will on the White Guards. Whatever. If she knew what assholes they were when she wasn't forcing them to be upstanding citizens, she wouldn't feel so bad.

As we walk toward the altar, the people standing in the pews turn and bow to the Mother. Even the fancy-pants bosses at the front, the Aunts in their shawls and the military asswipes in their full dress uniforms, bend at the waist in respect. Above us, the rose window shows a lady in white and a man holding the Spear of Mars, symbol of the Warlord. The figures are nondescript; neither has identifying features, meaning this is just a reminder of the two-pronged Gean government: state and religion. But the image is still amusing, because the Mother and Warlord stand on equal footing.

More lies.

Speaking of the Warlord, that old fuck Vaughn is here, standing in the front pew on the right side of the nave. He's looking a little more jowly than his official portrait, which hangs in every Gean office, home, and ship, but even under the receding hairline and soft layer of age, I can tell he's got muscle aplenty. Dude's gotta be in his late eighties at this point, which is pretty fucking old for a Gean when the majority that age are rotting in Sisterhood-run retirement homes. I don't believe for a second he hasn't seen some illegal geneassist somewhere to keep himself healthy.

He dips his head to the Mother, and Lily nods back—*aww, isn't that sweet, the old man doesn't want to murder her*—before turning left to find her assigned spot. She's the last to arrive, by design, so now this carnival show can finally start. While she gracefully settles on the stone bench, which swirls like a hedge grown specifically to cradle the sitters, the White Guards scatter to take up positions around her in the shadows.

Despite wearing dress uniforms, white where Gean formal is navy, we're not meant to be seen. I'm just to the left of Lily in the aisle so I can watch her in profile, but it's only when I see her leaning to her right that I realize who the Aunt beside her is.

Fucking Aunt Marshae. She's pretty in a hard-boiled-egg sort of way: shoulder-length auburn hair hard with gel, nails too sharp, skin too sallow. But she has high cheekbones and a pointed chin and a mouth that looks ready to bite, though she ruins it by being a massive bitch. She's smiling prettily, whispering something in Lily's ear—*is that fear from my twin I smell?*—and I'm instantly alert in case Lily needs me. But the scent I thought I caught is gone a second later, maybe nothing more than my imagination, leaving me trapped in the stench of cloying incense and the black hole of cleaning products and the cheap Earthen cologne evidently favored by the entire fucking officer corps.

Lily looks back to the altar, her face perfectly calm, as if Aunt Marshae said nothing. On the altar lies a coffin, and inside, a woman who could put rubies to shame. Her fiery hair is perfectly curled, her blood-red lips offensively bright against her dead white skin. They'll bury her in the red cope, clasped on her chest with the medallion of the Order of Virgo—or will they snatch it away once the ceremony is over, only to pass it to the next Agora Aunt who inherits her position? The Sisterhood recycles its ghosts, and Aunt Salomiya is no exception.

I don't need to know what Aunt Marshae said, because this entire farce is a warning. We knew it would be, as soon as we heard that Aunt

Salomiya had hanged herself, like so many of Aunt Marshae's opponents before her. Doesn't matter that Lily was Aunt Margaret's favorite at one point; that old bag can't protect her now. If my twin fucks up, if she steps out of line, I wouldn't put it past Aunt Marshae to frame her suicide too.

I pull my white hat lower to hide my smirk. The thing about Aunt Marshae is that she doesn't suspect what's right in front of her: I may be a White Guard, but I am also so much more, and I'll eat her alive, tendons snapping between my sharp teeth, before I ever let her touch a hair on Lily's head.

The organist finishes the current dirge, and Aunt Marshae stands to eulogize Aunt Salomiya, the woman she had killed. Just another Tuesday in Sisterhoodland.

AFTER THE FUNERAL, we return to the Temple of Mars. As I enter the building given over solely to the Mother's use, I assign my White Guards to the hallways and doors to watch for any of Aunt Marshae's more daring spies. With Castor on my heels, I retreat to the inner chamber that butts up against a greenhouse of climbing ivy. Like the rest of the Temple, it is beautiful gray-veined white marble, but the walls are painted a soft mint green and the furniture is plush emerald velvet. With the glass doors thrown open, the air smells of petrichor.

The two women waiting for me in the sitting room don't snap to attention when they see me, because, while I am the Mother, they've known me since I was an unnamed Sister. It's the nature of my life that no one sees past the carefully cultivated personality that is Lily, but Aunt Margaret comes closest to knowing the real me. She expects me to be silly and a little irreverent, much like her, so I offer them both my most darling smile before saying, "Get me out of this dress before I die."

Aunt Tamar, honeyed skin and hair the color of the sky at midnight, moves to help me while Aunt Margaret snorts into her tea. "Mind hurrying it up?" she asks, mischievous green eyes peering over the rim of her cup. Despite her many wrinkles, there is something childlike about her face. "I could *actually* die at any moment." Whether the joke is about Aunt Marshae or her advanced age, I frown; I do not like the idea of losing my mentor, regardless of what has happened between us.

Aunt Tamar unclasps the fur cloak from my shoulders and tosses it on the closest chair, followed by the white stole embroidered with the symbols of the Orders and the Elizabethan whisk collar. She unlaces the corset-cinched bodice and then starts on the tiny pearl buttons that march along the sleeves at my forearms. Once I'm free, I shove the whole dress around my ankles and step out of the thing, feeling like a snake shedding its skin. In only my white underdress, I gingerly settle next to Aunt Margaret and release a long, heavy breath of relief.

I'm aching from my neck to my toes, unsurprising when I woke with the pain. I always know it will be a bad day when my right foot aches, and this morning, it felt like someone had slipped a knife beneath a tendon in the arch. I lean my head against Aunt Margaret's shoulder, and she wraps an arm around me, hugging me like a mother I never had. For the briefest moment, I close my eyes, let down my guard, and relax.

It is the only moment I allow myself.

"We don't have long," I say, forcing my eyes open and my head up. "I see Aunt Delilah couldn't make it."

Aunt Tamar settles across from Aunt Margaret and me. "Are you sure we should be having this conversation now?" she asks, and it's her pointed refusal to look at Castor that tells me she's talking about him.

Castor's pheromones spike with offense, but I smile, running my thumb over the pale splotches of skin on my knuckles. The same patches that, with my sleeveless underdress stopping at my knees, anyone can see are also on my arms and legs. Patches the same color as Castor's skin. "I handpicked my White Guard," I say confidently. "I trust them, and besides, I control them."

I can tell Aunt Tamar doesn't like my answer, but unlike others, she accepts my words. Doesn't accuse me of "eccentricities" or outright insult me for having an Aster guard. Aunt Margaret is the one who waves me off. "Yes, there's an Aster elephant in the room. Now let's all build a bridge and get over it."

Aunt Tamar huffs. "You mix your metaphors so freely . . ."

"Lily's not a stupid kid," Margaret goes on, ignoring her, "so let's trust her judgment."

But we don't have time to argue, so I try to focus the group. "Aunt Delilah?" I ask again.

"After Aunt Salomiya . . ." Tamar adjusts the shawl most Aunts wear around their shoulders over her hair. "To say Aunt Delilah is afraid is putting it mildly."

"I understand," I reply, and it's the truth.

After Aunt Genette and Aunt Sapphira were arrested for their criminal activities, Aunt Marshae put forth two candidates whose flamboyant backgrounds rang as dubious to many in the know. Even more suspicious was the way they looked to Aunt Marshae for their every opinion. But when one other candidate refused her nomination and another disappeared from her abbey, leaving only Marshae's choices, the two women were confirmed as part of the Agora.

Aunt Salomiya dared to confront Aunt Marshae about this, and we all saw how it played out. Her position didn't spare her from an assassination barely masked as a suicide, so I can understand Aunt Delilah's fear. Today all the women in this room have mourned Aunt Salomiya's death, knowing it went hand in hand with our voices in the Agora. This funeral was Aunt Marshae's coronation as its ruling voice.

Just thinking of Aunt Marshae makes me shudder. *Aren't some people more beautiful in death?* she had whispered to me this afternoon, and it felt like her fingernail trailed down my spine.

"She's already provided me with a profile of the candidate she wants me to put forward as Aunt Salomiya's replacement," I say so weakly that Aunt Margaret forces a cup of tea to my lips, bidding me to drink.

"And what of the admirals?" Aunt Tamar prompts.

I take a drink of bitter green tea and push the cup away. "Meeting with them tonight." I rub my eyes—sore from the lights, but still with so much more to see before I can rest. A flicker of worry radiates from my overprotective twin, and I soothe him with my pheromones. "Warlord Vaughn has invited me to dine with him and the Admiralty tonight, and Aunt Marshae was . . . oh so kind as to offer to accompany me so that I'd have a voice."

Aunt Margaret snorts, but Aunt Tamar leans forward, her stony face serious. "Be careful, then. That viper, Drucker, is sure to be among them." For a heartbeat, her face softens. "If only they would've spared the poor girl . . ."

My hand freezes against my cheek. "Eden . . ." I say her name softly, because she deserves to have it spoken. Deserves to be remembered, even if she is gone. It wasn't twenty-four hours after Aunt Tamar shared her suspicions about Aunt Marshae's connection to Admiral Drucker, head of the Control Agency Police, that Eden was found hanging in the Temple.

Forming attachments is difficult in my line of work, but with Eden . . . I can truly say I'd grown to care for Eden and Astrid both, firebrands that they were. And now they're both gone. I force myself to turn to different thoughts, because grief is a river; it can surprise you with how deep it is, and if you're not careful, it'll pull you under until you're drowning in sorrow. Right now I can't afford to be swept away.

"How should I approach tonight?" I ask, happy to play the inexperienced girl when I know both Aunts enjoy giving advice.

"Confirm what you can," Aunt Margaret says, "but I agree with Aunt Tamar. Caution is more important than information."

"And Admiral Kadir?" I ask. Aunt Tamar straightens at his name. She has already initiated talks with the Earthen admiral, and if she's telling the truth, he might be the perfect foil against Aunt Marshae. His soldiers could be the muscle we need to resist the naked power grab by Admiral Drucker's Control Agency Police.

"With Aunt Marshae acting as your voice?" Aunt Margaret rolls her eyes. "You're not going to be able to do anything she doesn't want you to do."

"Try, at least," Aunt Tamar says. "If Aunt Marshae truly does have Drucker's backing, we could use Admiral Kadir on our side."

I nod as the two women stand. There's only so much time the three of us can spend together before Aunt Marshae senses something amiss.

Aunt Tamar leaves with a bow, but Aunt Margaret lingers in the doorway. "Watch yourself, Lily," she warns softly.

"Don't worry," I reply, and while I never look at my twin, I call to Castor with my pheromones and he answers in kind. "I'll have my White Guard with me."

AUNT MARSHAE MEETS the Mother, flanked by the thirteen members of her White Guard, in the courtyard between the building that houses her alongside her guards and the one that holds the suites of the members of the Agora. In the center of the space is a tacky golden fountain in the form of a woman pouring water from an urn, surrounded by a lawn of soft green grass—all of it beyond frivolous.

Marshae's gaze claws at Lily, assessing her simple white dress and the pearls she wears at her throat, and she nods appreciatively. She's also dressed down in the uniform of an Aunt, a gray dress with a long skirt and a scarf around her neck. "You look beautiful, Lily," she says. "The Warlord will be happy."

My twin smiles as her pheromones tell Marshae to get fucked.

I feel Lily nudging my neural implant, ordering the White Guard into formation, and we move like water. Even Damnus seems too tired to start shit with me after a full day of following the Mother around Olympus Mons.

We march into the Temple, that collection of centuries-old buildings of precious stone, past speechless Sisters in gray who bow immediately. The only time Lily falters is when we pass the courtyard of statues, and even I smirk at the tarp covering the plinth that used to hold the statue called *Victory*. We never speak that woman's name here, but that somehow makes her presence loom even larger. Aunt Marshae quickens her pace.

When we come to the entrance of the official dining room, two carved doors depicting a man and woman reaching for each other—*another* uninspired depiction of the Mother and Warlord—Aunt Marshae pauses. I can't say exactly what I read from her body language, but it's different from before—is she worried?

"Are you ready?" she asks softly. Lily makes her wait as she stretches, rubbing her lower back and rolling her shoulders in slow arcs. Finally she plasters a smile on her face and clasps her hands together in front of her pelvis. A little nod of affirmation is all the answer Aunt Marshae gets.

"You should leave some of them stationed outside," Aunt Marshae says, gesturing not to me but to the other White Guards. Lily's face is blank, but I can smell her disapproval. "It would be an insult to the Warlord and his admirals to attend with so many guards. As if saying you don't believe they can adequately protect you." When Lily doesn't move, Aunt Marshae's hand tightens on the door handle. "Certainly you don't want to insult the Warlord?"

I can smell Lily's pheromones, and I know she doesn't give a flying fuck if he's offended. But she has to play the game, so she carefully shakes her head.

"Take these two," Aunt Marshae says, pointing to the smug asshole Danmus and the youngest of the White Guard, a blond boy named Bennett. Two strong, Mars-born Geans. Definitely not an Aster like me.

I expect Lily to put up a fight, to demand that I come with her, but instead, she pushes the rest of us through our neural implants to wait here and guard the door. Only I hesitate at her orders, and it's with her pheromones that Lily smacks me: *Don't.*

She never looks at me, but I finally give in and do as she says, stepping away from her and Aunt Marshae. I know she's right; it would be too suspicious to demand that I come with her everywhere . . . but I still don't like it.

The last sight of my twin is of her flanked by Danmus and Bennett, smiling at Aunt Marshae. Her exterior says: *I am happy. I am excited. Please make me your willing slave.* But I smell the truth she's giving off in thick waves: *Fuck you, fuck you, fuck you.*

Give them hell, I wish her before she disappears into the dining room.

NOT A MOMENT after Aunt Marshae's knuckles rap against the heavy wood, a Cousin opens the double doors in welcome. The conversation inside cuts off abruptly. Led by the Warlord, the Admiralty, a mix of men and women in their thirties and forties, stand from their chairs politely. I guide the only two members of my White Guard I was allowed to bring to opposite sides of the room.

"Mother Lilian I," Warlord Vaughn says, his kind blue eyes crinkling at the corners as he steps toward me. Here is a master liar, perhaps the greatest of them all; truly, there is nothing kind about him. "Thank you for hosting us here at the Temple of Mars." He leads the admirals in applause that filters down to the Cousins serving food and drink.

I dip my head to him, but not as low as a Sister would; we are equals, after all, in effect the Mother and Father of the Gean people. When he offers me his hand, I take it, and he leads me to the empty chair at the head of the table directly next to his.

"You look lovely, Lilian," he whispers into my ear, and a chill runs down my spine at the closeness of his lips, as pink and fat as wriggling worms. I imagine a crow pecking at them to soothe me.

We round the head of the table, and, with my face hidden by the bulk of his body, I whisper back, "It's good to see you, Virgil." His eyes sparkle with a thrill when he releases my hand to pull out my chair for me, and I sit, smoothing my skirt beneath me. When he lingers behind me a second too long, I know my arrow found its mark.

Virgil Vaughn likes a challenge, and let it never be said that I don't give people what they want. To Aunt Marshae, I am demure and obedient; to the Warlord, I am all cleverness and fire.

Once the Warlord sits, he gestures for everyone else to follow his example. Aunt Marshae, settling at my right, casts furtive glances down the table. Is she searching for Admiral Drucker?

I look for him based on what I know of him and find him in a pack of soldiers with sharp, wolfish smiles. Surrounded by muscular, powerful admirals, he's easy to overlook. Admiral Drucker is an oddly plain man of average build with lank brown hair and eyes a bit too small.

Of course, I know not to underestimate anyone based on their looks, as so many have done to me. Admiral Drucker's threat comes from his considerable fortune, the support of his large family across Mars, and his popularity among Gean high society. As leader of the Control Agency Police, he has agents who answer to him hidden everywhere, and the threat that he is always watching is unsettling.

He is also an extremist. Ardently anti-Icarii. Faithful to the Goddess. A traditionalist who belongs to the Disciples of Judeth, a sect within the Sisterhood that desires a return to the harsh Martian orthodoxy from centuries before. As the Cousins flit about the table, pouring clear water and wine as red as blood, Drucker keeps his beady blue eyes on me with a reverence that borders on fanatical.

As the conversation from before we arrived resumes, I keep my eyes on the admirals. Watching whom they speak with. Whom they shun. Whom they side with when an argument breaks out. And sure enough, Admiral Drucker, though his voice is gruff, commands attention when he offers an opinion.

"It is *because* the Icarii are in a bad position that we must turn this cease-fire into a lasting peace," one of the admirals says to Drucker, and a few around him nod in agreement. This one is a small man in his mid- to late thirties, but he speaks with a confidence beyond his years. His skin is a dark copper, his eyes a glittering black. His hair is wavy and curls back from his ears, giving him a slightly boyish look. His beard is neatly trimmed beneath a prominent curved nose. But it's the way he's settled in his body that makes me take note; the expressive way he speaks with his hands, and the self-assured tilt of his shoulders.

Admiral Drucker makes a noise like a scoff, and everyone at the table, even the Warlord, turns toward him. "Admiral Kadir," Drucker says, and my focus doubles at the name of Aunt Tamar's ally, "if we wait for the Icarii to finish dealing with this internal crisis, they'll come back stronger than before. With their fleet in the belt currently in tatters, now is the time to strike." Drucker addresses the table, not Kadir, as if to convince them of his plan. "If we lock their inner fleet in battle, we could claim Spero—or at least raze it to the ground. Deny it to those cowardly body-perverters."

No one has ever pierced one of the hermium-powered domes. Any victory would surely be pyrrhic. And that's if we're lucky and *win*.

"Mars conquers. It's man's duty to spill as much blood as necessary to claim what he needs," Admiral Drucker concludes. "I'd rather resume the war on our terms."

Admiral Kadir holds his empty hands above the table. The sleeves of his uniform fall away from his elegantly thin wrists, and I remember, suddenly, what Aunt Tamar told me about him: He grew up poor on Earth, and the hunger of his childhood left its mark on him, yet he made a name for himself as an Ironskin pilot before becoming a captain and then an admiral. Because of his humble background—or perhaps in spite of it—he's gathered many frontline soldiers loyal to him. "If we negotiate properly, we need not resume the war at all."

The numerous shaking heads tell me that Kadir's opinion is shared by only a minority.

Another admiral, youthful and blond, opens his fool mouth. "Might as well end the war and rid ourselves of the need for a Warlord, then!"

Cups pause halfway to mouths. Forks fall to plates. Smirks disappear. The admirals closest to the boy, two women, shift in their chairs to lean as far away from him as possible, as if they can avoid the fallout by shifting proximity.

Warlord Vaughn leans forward to place his elbows on the table. "Are you enjoying the wine, Admiral Wagner?"

Admiral Wagner flounders, doing his best to backtrack. "I-I simply meant that Admiral Kadir's plan is foolish. What use is a Warlord without a war?"

Admiral Drucker stands from his chair so abruptly, the only noise in the entire room is the wooden legs scraping the marble flooring. One slow step at a time, he makes his way around the table, heels clicking with the strength of a rivet gun bolting steel. When he comes to stand beside Admiral Wagner's chair, I shift from concern to outright terror.

It feels like the entire room has drawn a breath and is holding it. Even hearts don't dare beat too loud for fear of interrupting. Admiral Drucker waves forward a Cousin with a bottle of wine, and the Cousin, face pale and hands trembling, comes to his side.

Admiral Drucker takes the bottle and shoos the Cousin away. "Hmm," he mutters, turning the bottle so that the table can read the label. "A good vintage."

"Indeed, Admiral Drucker," Wagner says, everything frantically wide—white eyes bulging, smile slashing his face in two. "Perhaps a toast? Yes, a toast! To the Warlord himself!"

No one joins him.

And Admiral Drucker, short and slight compared to the others, snatches a cloth napkin from the table with a predator's grace and presses it so hard over Admiral Wagner's face that his chair tips back and slams to the floor.

All at once, noise returns to the room. The admirals on the opposite side of the table stand so quickly a few chairs fall. Those who sat by Drucker move to help him, holding Admiral Wagner's arms and legs to stop his flailing. Admiral Drucker looks down at the man splayed before him and gently shakes his head. "You know the punishment for being drunk on the job, don't you?"

Then Admiral Drucker upends the bottle of wine onto the napkin directly over Admiral Wagner's nose and mouth.

"'But the greatest of these sins is dereliction of duty,'" Drucker quotes from the Canon.

Admiral Wagner screams, but only for a moment. His body bucks as he struggles, fingernails digging into the arms of his chair. I see the exact moment when he gives up—when he understands no one is going to stop this—and his body melts against the wood, defeated.

Castor. I wish my twin were here, but he's locked outside, unable to help. Unable, even, to soothe me in my despair. I hold myself coiled and unmoving. What could I possibly do to stop this? What could I do but make it worse?

Ten seconds pass. The bottle empties. Admiral Wagner's wet and ragged gasps fill the air. We wait for Drucker to release him, for this lesson to be over, but instead Drucker looks to the end of the table, and Warlord Vaughn, with the smile of a grandfather watching his grandson opening a birthday present, nods.

Admiral Drucker sets the empty wine bottle on the table and holds out his hand to the waiting Cousins. "Another," he says.

By the time the third bottle is empty, Admiral Wagner has gone limp.

The Warlord releases a long breath, like an almost-romantic sigh. "Dry the drunkard out," he commands, and Admiral Drucker salutes in obedience.

After that, dinner is absolutely unremarkable.

AS SOON AS the doors to the dining room open, I want to rush to my twin and wrap her in my arms. We all heard the scream even if we couldn't do shit about it. The only comfort was that I knew it wasn't her screaming; otherwise, I would've broken down the doors and flayed every single one of them alive. And while Lily seems unruffled on the outside, her Sisterhood mask in place, I can smell the truth: a fear that's seeped bone-deep.

Even Aunt Marshae looks shaken as she exits beside Lily, her brows pinched together tightly and face paler than normal. I'm so caught up in worrying over Lily that I almost miss the call for the White Guard when it comes, but Danmus shoulder-checks me as he moves toward Lily, and I take my usual place at the rear of the group.

Flanked on all sides, Lily and Aunt Marshae return to their quarters through the dark, sleeping Temple. Neither says a word. If that bitch is freaked out, I can't imagine what the rest of the little dinner party is feeling. When we reach the ugly gold fountain between the Mother's building and the Agora's, she stops Lily with a hand on her shoulder.

"Try to put it out of your mind," Marshae says, as if it's as easily said as done. Disbelief ripples through Lily's pheromones at the childish advice. "The Warlord is stern, but Vaughn won't always be the Warlord."

Lily's worry returns, chewing at already-frayed edges. "What do you mean, Auntie?" she asks, gloved fingers lacing together tightly.

It's obvious Marshae chooses her words carefully, that she debates before speaking again. "Warlord Vaughn has . . . let it be known that he plans to retire soon, and I fear . . . all of that . . . was simply an attempt to impress upon him that he made the right choice."

"The right choice?" Lily repeats.

I expect the damn woman to smirk, but there's not a hint of gloating on her face or in her voice when she says, "Vaughn plans to name Admiral Drucker his successor."

I could spit acid at the thought. Lily's hands tremble. She smells of despair, and I want nothing more than to remove the problem—like Aunt Marshae's head from her shoulders.

I'm sure we're both thinking the same thing: If Admiral Drucker is loyal to Aunt Marshae, there's nothing that can stop her if he's named Warlord. Nothing that will keep her from taking over the Agora and changing the Sisterhood however she wants.

And nothing to stop her from slipping a noose around Lily's neck.

Fuck. *Fuck.*

Somehow, with the power of fire-tempered steel, Lily manages to offer Aunt Marshae a smile. Manages to take the knife Marshae slides between her ribs and stay standing.

"Thank you, Auntie," Lily says, and then she's stumbling toward her building, and I'm right behind her, hiding her from Marshae with my bulk. The rest of the White Guard is a tight net around her, but as soon as we're inside, Lily sends them scattering, her control over their neural implants so tight that their faces are emotionless.

They all retreat without a fight, even Danmus, disappearing into the farthest reaches of the building. All except for me. I follow Lily into her private inner rooms, where she slams and locks the doors as if a monster's on her heels. She's breathing heavily when she looks at me, and her name—the childhood name only I call her—is on my lips, but as I reach for her, she pulls away.

"We have to make a plan," she says, slipping through my outstretched arms.

I follow her into the bedroom, see her struggling to move the mattress. I gently nudge her aside and pull the hidden compad out from beneath. "Can you run a message to Admiral Kadir?" Lily asks, taking the compad to check her messages.

"You want me to leave you *now?*"

"Time," she says, "we don't have *time—*"

"*Sfonakin,*" I say, but she doesn't even look up from the screen. With hands so much larger than hers—when, at one time, they were the same size—I still her movements. I notice with a numb humor that my pale, translucent skin is the same color as the patches over her knuckles. "Pollux, *stop.*"

She looks up at me with her large brown eyes full of tears, and my heart crumbles to stardust. She's afraid—downright terrified—and that makes me all the more determined to fix this.

"It's time we take the Black Hive up on their offer," I tell my twin.

"What about Hemlock?" she asks, but weakly. Even she knows our uncle is on the outs with the Elders, and that the majority of his agents have become Sorrel's. If we want change, we must rely on the Shield of the Asters.

"We call on the Harbinger," I say resolutely.

My other half nods in agreement.

CHAPTER 3

LUCE

Why the fuck can't you see this isn't about you vs. the Harbinger? The Elders named him the Shield of the Asters. They know about the re-formed Black Hive. You wanted a rebellion, so I don't get why you're refusing to help. You need to join up before the Elders name you an outsider.

Message to Hemlock from Castor, unanswered

The feed for the Keres Truth Society is buzzing from our new vid. There are over three hundred new messages since I checked it ten minutes ago, but my bots haven't flagged anything as important, so I only do a cursory check—*Did you see the drone? Peacekeepers shot it down! Here's a place to get the vid it dropped. Vid's gone. Reuploaded. Download it so you don't lose it. Pass it on*—then let it scroll on my leftmost screen.

I tap my middle holoscreen and, fingers on the corners, make it larger. It's connected to Hemlock's private server, supporting his agents throughout the various planets, and there's a vast array of chatter on channels I don't follow. But the one channel I keep a constant connection to? That's the feed of the person actively ignoring me.

Sure, it's not surprising that Hiro's doing their own thing, but it still pisses me off. I never know whether something's happened to them, or if they're just taking some time to be alone with their thoughts—and they wouldn't tell me if I asked.

Grief is a knife. Most people are cut by it once or twice when they hear the bad news or attend the funeral, but those of us who have to live with the loss, to sit with it as a gaping hole in our everyday lives, we are cut every day, and we continue bleeding while everyone else gets to forget they were wounded in the first place.

I guess that's why Hiro and I, though we suffered the same loss, deal with it in our different ways.

Still. *Don't scare me like this, Hiro.* I swallow the words down. File them away in a mental folder: things I'll never say, though I want to. They nestle between *I miss you, Castor,* and *You're the only friend I have left, Hiro.*

I'm sure it's partially my fault. I pushed them too hard about appearing in one of my vids. It's just . . . despite the support for the protests, I'm scared the highlevel Cythereans will be quick to forget what Souji's done to the Asters. They're probably even willing to ignore what he's done to lowlevel Cythereans like me. But to people just like them with a *val* surname, and Souji's own child at that? That's something they can't ignore. And with Souji appearing before the AEGIS to testify tomorrow . . . My stomach churns. We need all the luck we can get.

A bot chimes. I search the five floating screens for its ping and am surprised when it's the leftmost one. The Keres chat—a private feed, invite-only—has found a new, interesting topic. My bot highlights the relevant text for me:

allpeacekeepersarebastards: almost got arrested

allpeacekeepersarebastards: some idiot played the vid
VOLUME UP in front of pks

allpeacekeepersarebastards: pks started looking for us

allpeacekeepersarebastards: had to disappear

allpeacekeepersarebastards: but get this

allpeacekeepersarebastards: idiot snatched something off one of the pks

allpeacekeepersarebastards: i think it was a gun

I instruct the bot to give me any relevant conversation pertaining to this. It brings up a mix:

hairycryptid: NOT IDIOT

m3teor1te: jajajajajajajajajajaja

hairycryptid: LEGEND

blushinglandscape: did said idiot get away with the gun?

allpeacekeepersarebastards: yep

lostinlibrary: wwwwwwwwwwwww

m3teor1te: GRASS

With an ID that'll route anyone who looks too closely to a midlevel apartment in Cytherea, I enter the chat.

LSL: Information request: visual of Thief

The chat instantly flares with activity.

hairycryptid: LITO LIVES!

allpeacekeepersarebastards: "we've flown too close to the sun, and I am the fire!"

m3teor1te: vid was fkin sauce man

blushinglandscape: when next vid????

bunnibaybee: @LSL want nudes? ;)

lostinlibrary: Search ON!

So on and so forth. Hopefully I'll make a positive connection, but even if I don't, I have a sinking feeling I know who was involved in the incident. I swipe the screen off my desk, and it disappears, logging me out at the same time. I'll let my bot parse through all the mentions and crazy DMs my account gets to find what useful information people offer, if any.

My main screen lights up. My heart soars. *Hiro!*

"All clear," they say. And . . . that's it. No other information on what they were doing, on whether they had trouble or not. For all I know, they could've fallen from their harness and smashed themself into a splatter of blood and pieces like Mathieu did when he was chasing me through Cytherea to retrieve the naildrive full of Val Akira Labs data—

I slam my fists against the desk. All my screens tremble. I don't want to think about the past.

I try to keep the anger from my tone when I respond. *Try*, though I sound strained. "I know you too well to think you've gone to bed. So tell me . . . what's really going on, Hiro?"

I know there's absolutely no chance of them responding tonight, so I swipe all my screens away, clearing my desk. After a moment of thought, I tap the smartglass desktop to open a new screen and turn on the camera to record something for Hemlock, but as soon as the image focuses on me—on my sallow, pockmarked skin and too-sharp cheekbones beneath a smooth, bald head—something shifts in the darkness of the Under tunnels behind me—

I spin in my chair. There's no one in the doorway.

"I know you're there!" I snap. They could run; there's no way I'd catch them, not if they're quick. "Show yourself!"

No one responds. No noise. Not even the sound of footsteps on the dusty stone floor.

I push myself out of the gel desk chair that, despite molding to my body to support me perfectly, has me stretching limbs stiff from disuse. How many hours have I been perched at my desk, monitoring the various feeds? Too many, if I can't recall the exact hour I started this madness.

I grab my cane from the side of my desk and use it to brace my weaker left side as I stand. As soon as I touch it, the flexglass glows, illuminating the terrarium of spiraling, reaching plants within the body of the cane.

I suspect Hemlock gave it to me for more than just the aesthetic; the flexglass converts the warmth of my hand into life for the plants within. Just by using the cane, I keep the plants alive, which does wonders to counteract my stubborn nature that wants to ignore my pain completely and sink deeper into my chair with every coming cycle.

If I don't want to be stuck in bed with the pain, I have to listen to my body, let it tell me what it needs, whether that's the cane or my gravchair. And today, it wants the support that the cane provides.

I start toward the hallway, certain I saw someone—when something lurches toward me out of the darkness. "Shit—" I swallow down a scream.

Lotus offers me a plastic smile from the doorway.

"Thousand gods," I gasp, "you scared the shit out of me, Lotus."

"I'm sorry, Lucinia," my old captain says, the curls of her bone-white Aster hair frizzy around her heavily veined face.

"What're you doing here?" I ask, since she doesn't offer the information. I have an uncomfortable suspicion of the answer.

Since the Elders named Sorrel the Shield of the Asters, Hemlock's organization has bled one agent at a time, and while Hemlock and Sorrel don't clash openly, Sorrel's warriors, calling themselves the Black Hive in honor of the rebellion Sorrel led two hundred years ago, are everywhere. But just because there's relative peace now doesn't mean it'll be that way when Sorrel tires of our truth campaign against Souji val Akira and resorts to more . . . extreme measures.

A couple of months back, Sorrel sent a missive demanding Hemlock's ships—without specifying why—and Hemlock responded that he was happy to send the few Aster craft he had access to. In the exchange that followed, it became clear Sorrel wanted the Alliance of Autarkeia to answer to him, while Hemlock stood by the fact that the Alliance's resources were not his own. *I can put you in contact with Dire of the Belt*, Hemlock wrote, *if you have a proposition for my allies.* Sorrel stopped responding after that.

But none of us—not Hemlock, the few agents still loyal to him, or me—are foolish enough to think Sorrel won't try to take what little we still have.

Lotus looks around my room, big black pupils contracting. My room, with its collection of electric lamps and uncovered lanterns, is the one bright island in the dark sea of the Under; everything else is long shadows along rocky walls covered in hexagonal-patterned plastic, only occasionally broken up by the hazy glow of bioluminescent moss. I have goggles to see in the dark just in case, but the light from my cane does wonders to illuminate my surroundings whenever I leave.

"I came to check on you," she says, which makes my anxiety tighten its grip on my stomach. If she'd been sent as a runner from Hemlock, perhaps I could write off that I caught her watching me work . . .

I hate so much that one of the first Asters who made me feel welcome among them, who shared her music and the art of her garden with me, is now one I can't trust. But this isn't the first time I've noticed someone lurking in the tunnels, watching me.

I brush past Lotus as I exit my room and enter the winding stone corridors. "I'm going to see Hemlock." Better to update him in person than send him a message if the Under is crawling with spies. I have no idea who does and doesn't report to Sorrel.

Lotus falls into step beside me. "May I accompany you?"

If I were an Aster, I'd probably be able to tell how she felt by her pheromones—whether she's genuinely curious or embarrassed that I caught her watching me. But I'm not an Aster, and that makes it all the more important for me to be careful. Asters can easily lie to me when their body language is different from a human's.

"No," I say, "I'd like to be alone."

Lotus says nothing. Without even a farewell, she simply fades into the shadows, choosing a tunnel I don't.

I cautiously maneuver up a slope that leads to the basement of Mithridatism, where Hemlock spends most of his time. When we first came to the Under of Ceres from Vesta, I never imagined I'd be able to navigate the endless tunnels, but now . . . now I don't even have to think about it. It's habit that guides me, memory ingrained in my muscles.

After the Genekey virus tore me apart from the inside out, I didn't know what I would be capable of. But as the weeks passed and my body healed, I settled into a new equilibrium. It all depends on the day, really. Some days I wake up feeling like I can walk all of Ceres. Other days, I'm already hurting by the time I open my eyes, and I use the gravchair to get me from place to place.

Of course, there are things that will never heal: I can't grow hair. I've had more colds in the past six months than I *ever* had in my previous twenty years. And I can't see colors, leaving the world a constant wash of gray.

But I'm getting used to the person looking back at me in the mirror, even if she's not the bright-eyed, glitter-cheeked, purple-haired Luce I'm accustomed to. She's still someone who saved the lives of thousands with her—my—sacrifice. And while I can't be on the front lines climbing buildings like Hiro, I can be here, in the shadows, helping them succeed.

I come to the highest point in the Under and find the wooden door, swollen in its frame. I don't knock when I arrive, just push it open and enter the warmth and comfort of Hemlock's basement. Directly above me is the bar, Mithridatism, crawling with Gean citizens. Luckily, they have little to no interest in the Asters down below.

It's quiet when I enter. I can't help but feel like I belong when I'm alongside all these other forgotten trinkets—mismatched furniture, glass dolls in lacy gowns, books in diverse languages, tattered posters on the walls. I've even started a collection of my own: the plush toys sit with their backs to the wall on a shelf, button eyes shimmering in the low lantern light. If the Asters who live in the Under bring any more from the surface for me, I'll need a new shelf. So far I have a dozen, though my favorites are the bunny holding a strawberry; the puppet of a round bird with a long, pointed beak; and the cute cat with the big grin.

I'm adjusting the bunny's ears when Hemlock appears.

"Luce."

My elbow hits the wall, and I whisper a curse. "Getting *really* tired of people sneaking up on me today," I grumble. But more likely he was already here and I overlooked him. He's well practiced at going unseen in plain sight.

"Sit with me, Luce," he says, settling himself in his throne of a wing-back chair.

I dump myself into my usual spot on the sofa and lean my cane against the arm. Despite the way his quarters change in subtle ways, he never does. He's as timeless as a classic book. When I first saw him, I thought he was hideous, skin like a melted wax candle, white hair thin and limp, black eyes like a shark's. Now I find comfort in his appearance; he hasn't changed at all from how he appeared before I took the Genekey virus. He's always been a study in grayscale.

"You're staring at me again," he says, turning his dark eyes toward me. They flash like a cat's, reminding me, for a moment, of Castor.

I force myself to look away. "It's nothing."

His lips pull into a playful smile. "If you want to paint my portrait, you only have to say so."

I scoff; I haven't painted since Lito died, and I have no intention of returning to it. I used to find comfort in the beauty of the world, but there's no returning to my usual style. I can't revel in color like I used to.

"I think it would do you some good to try," Hemlock says in a soft voice.

"Are you my therapist now?" I snap. The words are out of my mouth before I check my tone, and I instantly feel bad. "Sh— I'm sorry, Hemlock, that wasn't . . ."

He holds his empty hands up in a gesture of surrender. "Not my place," he admits. With the smallest shift in his chair, a wall comes up between us, and I'm not sure whether I want to keep it up or tear it down. It's safer with that barrier; we're coworkers, not friends or family, and I'd best remember that.

"I assume you're here about Cytherea," Hemlock says.

"Yeah." My eyes move to the door that leads to the Under. Would Hemlock know if someone was lurking there on the other side, ear pressed to the wood? "We lost the drone to the peacekeepers, but not before the vid got out." It's easier to talk this way, rattling off information like I'm reading it from one of my monitors. "It's spreading well through the black chats, racking up hits on the channels I monitor with ninety-five percent authenticity confirmation." There have been a couple fakes of my work, but they're easily discounted. "Hiro made it back to the safe house, though they weren't really forthcoming on details."

"Good." Hemlock taps his fingers on the arm of his chair, and I recognize the faraway look he gets in his eyes. He's considering things at play, and I hate to interrupt his train of thought, but . . .

"There's something else." He turns his attention back to me. "I caught Lotus lurking outside my room. Listening." *Spying*, I don't say. And I certainly don't have to point out who she'd be working for.

Hemlock doesn't seem concerned, simply slots that file away in his much-larger mental folder. "Have you ever considered telling your story in one of your vids?"

I snort. "Me?" Of all the things we have to deal with—like Sorrel spying on our operation without our knowing why—*that's* what he wants to focus on?

He turns that hard gaze on me. "Aren't you the one they want to hear from? *La Peste te vigila* and all that."

Somehow that girl—La Peste—seems so different from the me who sits in a dusty basement wearing an old, stained tank top. The only thing we share is my body. "They still get me, just in the interview vids."

"But that's not *your* story." Hemlock's voice is the gentle dragging of nails over my back. "They still paint you on the streets, do they not?"

I shiver. "They already saw the best of me, Hemlock. They saw what I became. They know who I am. What's the point of showing them the worst? What more could they want to know about me?"

"It was the act of taking the Genekey virus that put you here, that made you who you are," he says, as if I don't think about that every second of every day.

"Yes—and now I'm trapped here." I swallow hard, trying to tamp down my rising anger. "'La Peste te vigila.' They want me to watch, and that's what I'm doing. I'm not meant to be the focus of this operation, so let me do what I'm good at. Let me stay *behind* the camera, sending vids to those who can actually change things."

"Fine." And just like that, he waves his hand through the air, dismissing me. He doesn't sound upset; if anything, he sounds tired. "If you want me to deal with Lotus, find proof that she's spying for our dear *Harbinger.*" He sneers at Sorrel's title. "Or better yet, *why.* Without proof, there's no reason to jump at shadows."

"Right." I take my cane—the room instantly brightens with its light—and push myself to my feet. Hemlock says nothing as he watches me go, and that's the worst part of it.

I'd feel better if he told me what we both already suspect: that no matter what we do, Sorrel and the Black Hive will eventually take all of our agents and resources until we're toothless.

CHAPTER 4

ASTRID

Is it possible for the Geans and moonborn to cohabitate? One could argue that, because of my writing this, I believe that is so. That I seek, most of all, to create an understanding between the culture I was born into and the one I found in exile. But truthfully, I don't see the possibility. It was the moonborn's pride that drove them to remain separate when Earth and Mars joined together under the first Warlord. That pride may be one of the only things the moonborn still have.

From Outside Earth's Moons *by Magnus Starikov*

◇——◁◇▷——◇

The briny smell of the algae vats rushes up my nose to the back of my head. In this cramped space, an underwater world of dim aquarium lights bathing the world in blue, I am home. I focus on the simple task of caring for these organisms, adding a bit more saline or fresh water depending on the tank's readout. While they are not plants, I can still drift in the pleasant harmony of preserving life instead of taking it away.

"Thought I'd find you here," someone says behind me. When I turn, I am surprised to find that Ebba Petrova herself, my savior and jailer, has come to fetch me.

"I was at the shooting range this morning. Bruni dismissed me," I tell her, and the side of her face that isn't a webbed netting of scar tissue pulls taut. Have I done something to displease her? Missed a meeting in which she wished me to share my insights on the Sisterhood?

"I just want to talk before the raid," she assures me. The room is too cramped for her to enter, the vats stacked from floor to ceiling in every available space, so she gestures for me to follow her. Her magboots click as she steps out of the doorway.

I exit, knowing whatever room she leads me to will be just as claustrophobic as this one. There are no large spaces on moonborn ships.

She leads me down a hallway so slender that I am forced to walk behind her, the walls a mix of original silver and other scavenged panels in black or white. Some panels are missing completely, displaying tubes and wiring that remind me of the *Juno*'s maintenance tunnels. My standard-issue magboots keep me from needing the guide rail, though I hold on to it regardless.

One would think I would be accustomed to this, growing up on Mars in a settlement with unenhanced gravity, but despite my eight weeks here with the moonborn—or perhaps I should call them Skad-ivolk, as they do themselves—I'm not. Skadi has less than half the gravity of Mars. Even my Sisterhood ship assignments had standard gravity. Now, taking the disgusting gravity medication that turns my stomach and makes my bones ache as if I am a growing teenager again, I think fondly of the way my feet used to confidently strike the ground and the way I never had to worry about my limbs floating away if I did not pay them close attention.

Ebba stops when we reach the habitation quarters, and she gestures to my open doorway. I enter and sit on the edge of my simple cot, leaving the single chair for her. She takes it, as I knew she would, sitting on it backward, legs splayed on either side, so that she can face me.

"Look at you," Ebba says, eyes flicking over me, "still sitting like a princess."

I do my best not to flinch. Her words dredge up memories of long-ago bullies at Matron Thorne's orphanage, though now they have the added sting of reminding me that I am an outsider to the rough-living Skadivolk.

"So long as I am not destructive, I hardly think the way I conduct myself should concern you," I reply. At least she is not pushing me to shave my head again. Her own hair, silver with age, is closely cropped, but even after everything, my vanity balked at the idea of cutting mine. Instead, Bruni showed me how to braid and twist it into a bun at the nape of my neck to keep it out of my face during work, though it does sit awkwardly in the moonborn helmets when they are necessary.

"Have I missed an item on my schedule?" I ask, thinking of the Skadivolk's incessant need to fill every hour, with either work, training, or community time. They even schedule their rests.

"Not really," she says, then laughs when I sigh. The leader of the Skadivolk is a frustrating woman, and nothing I do will change that. Trying to get answers out of her when she does not wish to give them is as futile as trying to coax blood from a stone.

I can feel Ringer stirring inside me with frustration. My brother the protector, the ghost haunting me, is mostly silent with the moonborn. Happy, perhaps, to be among his people. Since we fled the *Juno* in the Ironskin, we have moved as one body, thought as one mind. When I woke on Earth, concussed and bleeding, it was with a soldier's determination that I fled the incoming ship—though perseverance does little when one is dying.

Ebba stares at me with ice-blue eyes. Even now, sitting in my room, she has the attitude that everything—and everyone—bends to her whims, and I am reminded of the first time I saw her, large as a statue and almost as hard.

"Take what we can salvage from the suit," she had said, nodding to the Ironskin that had brought me to the blighted planet.

"AND HER?" Bruni had asked, in the booming voice I would later come to know as normal for him. "SHE DEAD YET?"

Not yet, I had wanted to scream, but so much of the world was slipping away from me on those gray plains under that gray sky. Even as they had landed their ship and filed out with weapons ready, I had tried to crawl away from them, determined to die before I gave up. With my last piece of strength, before the blackness swallowed me whole, I reached out and clutched Ebba's boot.

"Not dead," Ebba had said, darkness clouding my vision. "Salvage."

The next time I woke, I was on a ship leaving Earth, dropped next to the scrapped heaps of what had been the Ironskin. *Salvage*, Ebba had called me, and I have been working every day since to prove my use to her.

"Just got word back from Máni. No one recognized you from the image we sent." Like everything, Ebba meets bad news head-on, her words as blunt as when she commented on my posture. "But we'll keep trying. If your parents are out there, we'll find them."

"No one to claim me. No records of me." The words are bitter on my tongue. "Perhaps my face is similar to that of a moonborn, but I am no one to you all."

Ebba holds up a hand. "Now, I didn't say that. There are plenty of reasons we haven't figured out who you are or where you came from."

"Such as?"

"Our records might be incomplete. Or maybe your parents are dead." Ebba says the words like they could not possibly be hurtful. In this harsh land, death is a grim reality. "Or maybe your parents left us and had you on Mars, or wherever you ended up." *Dishonorably*, she does not add, as leaving the settlements on Skadi and Máni is akin to exile. "Maybe any record of you was destroyed in one of our clashes with the Geans."

"Do the Geans routinely destroy information?" I say, though I should know better than to ask by now. Ebba's face shutters, unwilling to discuss it. The Skadivolk have their secrets regarding the Geans, ones they refuse to speak of regardless of my attempts to learn more. Questions about what they have lost. *Who* they have lost.

I tuck the fallen strands of hair behind my ears. "Perhaps there's a name you can look into for me . . ."

Ringer growls at the words. *Be careful with the truth of me*, he cautions.

Ebba sits up straight. "Did you remember something?"

While I have spoken of the fuzzy memories from my childhood, likely thanks to the Sisterhood's neural implant, I have yet to admit anything about Ringer, fearing the same thing he does: if he does not exist and the only name I have from my memory is fake, just a story I told myself, that is proof of my madness. Why would the Skadivolk ever welcome me among them then?

"Hringar Grimson," I say.

"Hmm . . ." Ebba shifts to her feet as she thinks. "The name's familiar. Maybe because Grimson is a common name. I'll look into it for you."

"Thank you."

"Anything else?"

I clear my throat, finally speaking the fearful words that gnaw at my edges. "If I have no claim here, no family or ancestors we can locate, will I be turned out?" It would not be the first time I was left with no place to go, but it would be the first time I truly do not want to leave. I have begun to find a place, if not peace, here among the Skadivolk.

Learning to shoot and fight from Bruni has made me feel powerful in a way I have not for years. Even the raids have given me a sense of self-control I have severely lacked throughout my life.

"No," Ebba responds quickly. "But you wouldn't be one of us even if we *did* find your parents, Astrid, not until you proved you *wanted* to be."

"And I do that by working with you."

Ebba nods, and I let my eyes wander my room. When I was first placed here, I thought this space a closet they had turned into a prison cell. Once I was allowed to wander the ship, I learned that *every* room is like this, that even Ebba's captain's quarters are this size. There is no such thing as excess on Skadi; all moonborn live in such small spaces in a desperate dance with the elements of the void.

And yet . . . I have grown not to mind. Here, everyone shares what they have. They give freely to those who have not. They look at each other as a community instead of as rivals. A great family, spread across the moons. Even I, outsider that I am, have been welcomed. If I am willing to work according to my ability, I am offered the same comforts, small as they might be, as everyone else.

I turn my attention back to Ebba's scarred face. She is a hard woman but a fair one. If I prove myself to her and she allows me to truly become one of the Skadivolk, I will have a place to belong. I will be one of them. I will have a true home. A real family.

As a child, I wanted nothing more.

And there will be no more secrets. I will have a right to know about the Gean clashes with the moonborn, about the information Ebba currently hides from me. About the history of the Skadivolk, and why there are some names—some people long dead—they speak of with a strange reverence.

"Then let's go," I say at last.

Ebba's grimace-smile comes easily, only the unscarred half of her lips curling upward. "Suit up, Astrid," she commands, and I stand to obey.

EBBA LEADS ME through the Skadivolk habitat, a grounded labyrinth of spacecraft they call longships tethered together in a jumble I have yet to memorize. All the ships we pass through are similar to hers: a mishmash of parts in a variety of colors and textures, adapted, bolted together, and recycled from raids to keep them functioning. Some, like one that houses families with young children, are decorated with colorful paper as if to hide the patchwork walls beneath. Others, like this one that stores the raiding gear on the outer perimeter of Skadi, bares its messy decor proudly.

We come upon the group preparing for the planetside raid, and Ebba splits from me to greet the warriors. Bruni, Ebba's closest conspirator and a pilot without measure, watches me with a wide grin.

Bruni is an imposing man in the same way that Ebba is an imposing woman—tall, sturdy, muscular, thick in shoulders and legs—but he takes more care with his appearance than she does hers. His long gray hair is styled in the usual braid-bun, but he also braids his red beard to keep it out of his way, and his jumpsuit is cut to bare his heavily tattooed arms.

"LITTLE ASTRID!" he says as if he hadn't just seen me at the shooting range for morning practice. With my height, only among the Skadivolk would someone call me *little*. All of them are tall, likely thanks to whatever else they ingest as children alongside the gravity medication to help them survive these harsh settlements. "GOOD OF YOU TO JOIN US!" Everything Bruni says is an observation turned into an exclamation.

"I am happy to help when needed," I tell him.

Bruni claps me on the shoulder, almost knocking me into the wall. "YOU'LL HELP US WITH THOSE SISTERHOOD GALS?"

"Indeed," I allow, hoping he does not hear my frustration. I do not mind proving myself to the Skadivolk by helping on their raids; it is simply the constant reminder that the Sisterhood lurks just outside these walls that upsets me.

"She doesn't need your mothering, Bruni," Ebba says. "Get your suit on, Astrid."

I leave them to make their plans.

I walk to the nearest unclaimed locker—no name on it, because the members of the raid may change and there are not enough materials for everyone to claim their own—and pull a baggy space suit out. Sitting on the bench that runs down the middle of the room, I remove my mag-boots and begin to dress.

This is the fourth raid I will attend in person, but even more than with my presence, I have helped them with information, things only a Sister would know: Where cathedrals hide their items of value. Which abbeys are worth targeting. And of course, I can teach them the hand language only Sisters, Aunts, and Cousins know by law.

They hesitated to believe me at first, but once my information was verified—once I proved myself a willing asset—Ebba and her team plied me with questions. I answered them all truthfully. "You don't seem exceedingly loyal to them," Ebba had said then, and I had laughed until tears had pricked my eyes.

How could I still be loyal to them? They had used me, then tossed me aside when I no longer served their purpose. They had polluted the Goddess's teachings, groomed children to abuse, and killed anyone who questioned their ways. I had lost and lost and lost, time and again—all because of them.

It was only when Ebba asked that question that I realized the icy truth of my situation: I was finally free of the Sisterhood, something I had only dreamed about in my younger years. And so I chose, then and there, to have nothing more to do with them.

Of course, it is not so easy as saying I am done when forgetting is impossible. I clench my eyes tightly, trying to shut out the images of Eden hanging from the ceiling at the Temple, the mottling of her neck, the faded color of her body.

Focus on your hands, Ringer tells me in my mind, *on your body in this space.*

I ball my hands into fists. Open my eyes and look at the Skadivolk around me. This is my path, my immediate future. And once I prove myself as one of them, I will finally have my home. My family.

I push my legs through the large silver ring at the neck and slip into the suit. My arms follow, reaching inside and pulling it up over my shoulders. I take a moment to smooth my jumpsuit, an ugly faded blue but still worlds better than the gray dress I am accustomed to wearing, so that it is not rumpled underneath. Once I am comfortable, I adjust the silver ring until it is snug against my own neck, then I press a button so that the suit reconfigures to my size, much like the plugsuits used in the Ironskins, tightening through the torso and limbs. After that, I slip my magboots back on and am ready to leave.

I am the last one finished, and though I burn with embarrassment at how slow I am compared to the others, no one comments. "Helmets," Ebba says, and I take the one from the same locker as the suit, pulling it down over my head until I hear the sharp click of it connecting with the neck ring. "Testing." Her voice comes to me over the comms, and I give her a thumbs-up alongside the other raiders.

"Let's move." Ebba leads the way through the longship to the shuttle we will take to Earth, exactly like the one that brought me here. The group looks as disparate as only raiders can. My suit is white and gray, while others are patched with Icarii black or Gean navy. Bruni is dressed in a vibrant bloody red, but Ebba is as plain as I am.

The longship dock is, like everything moonborn, small by Gean standards. It fits a mere four shuttles nose-to-end. We descend the catwalks above them for the ship Ebba gestures to, a craft that might once have been an Icarii podship but is now a patchwork creation.

I am the last to file onto the shuttle, but Ebba has saved a spot for me next to her on the benches that line both sides of the ship. Bruni drops into the pilot's seat, his chuckles coming over the comms like static. I am sure the other five Skadivolk show their nervousness or excitement in their own ways, but I cannot tell what they feel behind their faceless helmets.

I am a mix of uneasy dread. The shuttle trembles as the engines kick in and Bruni maneuvers us into the airlock. Everything other than the memory of my time in the Ironskin falls away. I close my eyes in the helmet and touch my shoulder—beneath the suit is the scar that a bullet left after it clipped me on the *Juno*. I thought I would die out there, launched into the burning black of space, bleeding out into the Ironskin. The only thing I could hear was my heavy breathing and my racing heartbeat. Now is exactly the same, and the world around me shrinks.

"HERE WE GO!" Bruni yells, but even his loud voice is lost in my panic. A moment later, I am pressed into the bench and wall of the ship. At least I remembered to lean back this time, instead of forcing the seat belt to bear my weight, digging into my chest.

For a time, we travel like this, breaking away from Skadi for the black of space. There I can relax a bit, listening to the chatter of the raiders over the comms. But I cannot take part in the discussion, because fear has stolen my tongue. The worst is yet to come.

As we close in on Earth's surface, faded blue and green mixed with gray, the ship bucks and jolts, striking the detritus of old ships and satellites that threaten to knock us off course. Bruni holds us steady with his years of practice. It is only once we hit the atmosphere that the struggle becomes more than I can bear.

The ship grows hotter. Sweat beads on my forehead. My throat aches, thin and dry. I feel a hand against my knee—Ringer's? No, Ebba's—and I grab it and hold. I grit my teeth, jaw cramping, muscles aching as I hold myself against the wall, head back. *Goddess, oh Goddess, oh Goddess,* I pray, more a plea than an invocation, out of habit instead of belief. The moment is an hour and a day and a second all at once.

And then the ship's flight smoothes out. The heat breaks, cool air rushing from vents to replace it. The pressure leaves me, lets me breathe easier. I release Ebba's hand. Now that the danger is past, embarrassment rushes in. This, if anything, is proof I do not belong among the Skadivolk.

"You'll get used to it," Ebba says on a private comm channel to me. But I know that is not true. Every time I will remember the Ironskin, and every time I will fear myself a breath away from death, whether I really am or not.

"CHECK OUT THAT OCEAN!" Bruni says as he maneuvers us through the clouds, and though I flinch at the strength of his voice, I look to the screens regardless.

The white-capped seas stretch, restless and gray, beneath us.

I have returned to Earth once more.

BECAUSE EARTH IS where the majority of Gean soldiers are prepared for duty—the standard gravity makes it ideal for such work, and the harsh climate contributes to survival training—we enter the atmosphere as close to our destination as possible. After an hour of easy travel, we land, and the Skadivolk break into frantic movement, checking weapons, gathering supplies, preparing for their assigned roles. The map puts us on an archipelago, each island a shimmering gem on a necklace, off the west coast of the African Multinational Territory. It is not terribly far from where I fell in the Ironskin, I note.

"Shake a leg, Astrid." Ebba nudges me with the toe of her boot.

It is always in my first steps that I feel the full threat of Earth's gravity. I haven't been in standard gravity since the last raid and I am weak from Skadi's loose hold. My heart beats heavily, thudding like stones dropped from a height. My vision spins as I pull off my helmet and suck in great lungfuls of cool air. Thanks to the gravity medication I have been taking, my body adjusts after a minute or so.

The others are already out of the shuttle, waiting for me. I exit after them, pulling down the bun-braid as I go. The sky above stretches as far as the eye can see, a dizzying prospect. The Skadivolk carry guns in a variety of shapes and sizes, some great Gean railguns but others of a type I have only practiced with, long and slender energy weapons from the Icarii. I do not arm myself; as I step past the other moonborn, my hair tumbling down my back in a golden sheet, I become the banner of our peace.

Bruni walks a step behind me at the head of the raiding party. Ebba blends into the pack. One would hardly know she is our leader unless they learned the inner workings of the Skadivolk like I have.

As we approach the abbey, Bruni and the others slow, allowing me to break apart from them. Now only Ringer accompanies me along the steep cliffs. The abbey sits on a jut of rock above a sharp decline. Below, the restless sea roars, clawing at volcanic black sand, waves like great fists crashing with fingers of water grasping. The smell of salt hits me, reminding me of the algae vats but far stranger.

Ebba has told me stories of the rising of the seas, how whole cities were lost to the warming of the world. How people retreated to lands like this one with high plateaus and slumbering volcanoes, close to the Earth's equator so that the eventual cooling of the climate would not be so harsh on them.

Still, this is a small island, peaceful in its lack of bustling humanity. It must be fully claimed by the Sisterhood for conservation efforts. While the Warlord holds his seat of power on Earth and soldiers are plentiful here, Bruni would not have chosen a place with a heavy military presence for our raid.

But compared to Mars, everything is leached of color. The sky is a cloudless gray, the sun nothing more than a white disk, so unlike the colorful Martian atmosphere with its halo of blood at the horizon. While the vegetation here is stark—hard, spiky plants, flowerless and toothed—the Sisters at the abbey have done their work well, and the surrounding area of the island flourishes in a mix of greens.

The abbey itself is a series of buildings gone gray with age along a winding dirt path. The main building, used as a chapel, is set apart from the others and situated closest to the cliffs. It is perfectly spherical with a great silver dome and shining scales that can retract to allow nightly viewing of the stars. The telescope inside, once used to monitor the heavens, is now a sleeping cyclops, antiquated but not without its use. It was common in the early years of the Sisterhood to seize scientific buildings as chapels. To the Skadivolk, the lenses of the telescope alone are worth the cost of the raid.

I pass through an opening in the low stone wall that surrounds the chapel. Three Sisters wait before the simple single-story building attached to the chapel, watching our approach. All of them are past the years they would normally spend on a spaceship serving soldiers; two are in their forties, and one is in her fifties, old enough to retire from Sister to Cousin. Still, she wears the dress of the Sisterhood beneath a gray cloak to shelter her from the cold wind coming in off the ocean. She is the one who steps forward to greet me.

You are the one they call the Unchained? she signs.

I shudder despite being blocked from the wind in the shadow of the abbey. I have not been called the Unchained since Ceres, when I took it as an epithet of pride. Now the title fits me better than ever, but I want nothing to do with it, or my past in the Sisterhood.

I am, I sign regardless; it is far easier for me to accept the identification than debate with her, and it is obvious my reputation has preceded me. *I come ahead of the soldiers to seek a peaceful resolution. There need not be a fight.*

I look to the two women by her side and miss what she says next. *Something isn't quite right,* Ringer's instincts tell me. As Bruni would say, there are owls in the moss here.

Where are the rest of the Sisters? I ask, ignoring whatever she was signing. I do not miss the look that the two younger women exchange, confirming my suspicions. *This is far too large an abbey for just the three of you. Bring forth the others, or the soldiers will be forced to enter and drag them out.*

Something like a smile appears on the eldest Sister's face before it swiftly disappears. What is she planning? If she has heard of us, she knows what we are after, and I know that the Skadivolk would not hesitate to fight to get what they want. The Sisters are not trained for that, and I would not see them hurt if I can manage it.

If you wish to take our instruments and supplies, you must seize them with your own hands, she signs, not quite answering my question about more Sisters inside. *We will not simply give you what is necessary to our survival.*

"ALL WELL, LITTLE ASTRID?" Bruni's voice carries across the yard. He and the others have caught up with me, their presence just outside the wall making their threat clear.

I hold up a hand to instruct him to wait. Again, I see the younger Sisters exchange a nervous glance.

Do not act as if you will not receive more supplies if you request them, I respond.

You're missing something, Ringer says, but it is not helpful because I *know* that.

And if I command these men to enter the abbey and harm the Sisters in your care? I sign. It is a test, not a thing I would do, but the eldest Sister's face grows hard. No fear. No anxiety at the idea of armed invaders.

Almost as if she . . .

"ASTRID?" Bruni enters through the same break in the wall I took, and the eldest Sister's eyes jump to him.

"Now!" the Sister—not a Sister, she cannot be—screams. "Fire!"

The doors behind her fly open. Four men in plain clothes step from the dark entry hall, railguns in their hands. A fifth stands behind them, his long navy coat similar to the Gean military uniform but just different enough that I realize what is happening: the Control Agency Police are here.

"BLOODY CAPPOS!" I hear Bruni scream behind me, using the abbreviated slang name for the CAPs.

I turn to flee the way I came, only to see Bruni go down with a bullet. My ears ring from the shots. Something sharp strikes me in the back of the head, my vision flashes white with pain, and arms encircle me so that I cannot retreat.

Only six seconds have passed, and everything is in chaos.

I am dragged into the foyer of the abbey, past the line of four soldiers using the doors for cover. I struggle against my captor, but they burrow a hand into my hair and hold so tightly that my scalp protests.

"Do not harm the Heretic!" the eldest woman says—an Aunt, she *must* be an Aunt. "They want her alive!"

The hand releases me, and I look up at the man in the long coat. I have never had cause to deal with the Control Agency Police; by their very nature, they avoid Sisters and anyone else who would reveal their true identity during their investigations. Fear overtakes me as I recall what Aunts whisper about them: that they are master torturers, ice-blooded sadists, who know how to hurt without even drawing blood. I fear what he means to do with me, but after a quick pat-down to check me for weapons, finding none, he steps over me to focus on the Skadivolk.

The Aunt grabs my hair, but her strength is not equal to the man's. "Come with me," she commands. I do not know where she means to take me, but I know that following would be a death sentence; I have no doubt who it is that wants me alive, who would have the power to command the cappos, and it is for that reason I sink deeper into myself. I do not have a gun, but that does not mean I am unarmed.

Unbidden, memories rise within me. *"If you are to live with us, you will* learn from us," Ebba says, the first law of my new life. I train my energy pistol on the target and squeeze the trigger. I twist my wrist from Bruni's grip and kick him in self-defense. I use a larger opponent's weight against him as Ringer settles along my bones and flexes my limbs. "You don't lack skills, you just need refinement. So practice, Astrid. You need to practice until the knowledge lies in your muscles instead of your head."

My boot finds the top of the Aunt's foot, my elbow sinking into her midsection. Her grip on me and my hair loosens, and I spin, driving the heel of my hand into her nose. Blood spurts, red and warm. She screams as she falls, but the sound is drowned out in a hail of gunfire.

I look to the soldiers to see if they noticed, but all of them are focused on the Skadivolk who have taken cover behind the hip-high wall. Bullets chip away at the stone and kick plumes of dust into the air; I do not have much time if I want to save them. Behind the soldiers, the two Sisters— true Sisters, who do not speak aloud—cower.

I consider taking one of them hostage, using her to ensure the safety of the moonborn. But even as I think it, something within me recoils. How much have these poor women already suffered? What would I be, to cause them even more pain?

I lean down next to them, and they hold tight to each other, their faces wan with fear of me. They do not cry out, because they cannot, so I speak for them. "Go hide with your fellow Sisters," I say. "Run."

I do not have to tell them twice. The smaller of the two pulls at the taller, tugging her deeper into the building. I lose track of them in the shadows.

Now there are only the five soldiers between me and the Skadivolk— and the Aunt, who lies weeping on the ground, tears mixing with the blood of her broken nose.

With Ringer's eyes, I see the path forward.

From my left sleeve, I pull a short blade, no more than two inches in length. It is not meant to be a weapon, not meant to be anything more than a way to cut oneself free if tangled in space detritus—the opposite sleeve holds suit sealant for a similar emergency—but with the right pressure, it can do life-ending damage. We humans are exceedingly fragile, nourishing veins just beneath the surface of our skin.

I crouch by the Aunt and push the blade to her neck. She did not see it, but stiffens all the same when she feels the sharp point. "Get up," I say. I do not have the strength to pull her to her feet; I need her cooperation if any of this is to work, and this is merely the first step, a test as to whether she is willing to do as I say. I am operating on the belief that she will aid me in order to save her own skin.

She stares at me with wide red eyes as if she does not comprehend, as if I am speaking a different language than she does. "Stand!" I say, more forcefully than before. That pierces her malaise, and she dips her chin in assent. With my hand on her arm, she stands, swaying slightly, perhaps from the loss of blood. But she does not put up a fight, does not spit on me, all things I have no doubt Aunt Marshae would do. Good; I need her pliant.

"What is your name?" I ask her.

She hesitates before answering. "Aunt Doris," she says, perhaps hoping the name will humanize her in my eyes.

I turn her with a push to her shoulder and wrap my arms around her from behind, never letting the blade move from her neck. Though she struggles half-heartedly, my forearm tightens on her neck and I hiss into her ear, "Do you want to die, Aunt Doris?"

She sags into me, all the fight fleeing her. "No," she whimpers, her name now turned on her.

"Then do as I tell you."

I walk her through the darkness of the foyer, coming at the soldiers from behind. It is only when we are right beside them that the cappo in the long coat turns to look at Aunt Doris, his eyes popping wide as he takes in the pieces—her, me, the blade to her throat.

Then the moment of truth: he turns his railgun from the Skadivolk. Will he shoot me through the Auntie? Is she worth so little? I am hoping—praying—that this soldier holds a modicum of respect for the Sisterhood.

The muzzle of his railgun drops, pointing at the floor, and a shuddering breath rattles out of me. But Ringer urges me not to relax just yet.

I shift the blade in my hand, the familiar weight soothing me, its metal cool against my clammy palm. "Aunt Doris, tell them to stop shooting," I say directly into her ear.

She does not hesitate. "Halt!" she cries. "Hold fire!"

"Hold your fire!" the officer who first noticed us repeats to the others. The shooting stops—or, at the very least, pauses. They all turn to us with the same expression as the first—horrified, angry, and afraid.

As the dust in the air near the wall settles, I see that the pinned-down Skadivolk are not doing well. Bruni, who had started crawling back toward the gap in the wall, took another bullet in the back. Three others have been shot but scramble, bleeding, into cover. I do not see Ebba, which hopefully means she is safe.

I speak loud enough for them all to hear me. "We will retreat toward our ship. If you shoot, I will kill Aunt Doris." The Auntie trembles in my arms. "When we are all safely on board, I will release her unharmed. I swear this by the Goddess, or may She strike down my ship in Her starlight ocean."

"We will not allow you to leave here with a hostage." The cappo's reply is cool.

"What would I want with this woman beyond my own safety? She is useless to me, a mouth to feed with no return value." *Salvage*, Ebba says in my mind. I nudge Aunt Doris with the knife. "Tell them I do not want you, Auntie. Explain it to them."

"Listen to her!" Aunt Doris says, her voice wobbling with overwhelming fear.

The officer nods. At his sign, the other four point the muzzles of their railguns toward the floor. Making sure to keep Aunt Doris between us, I walk backward, passing from the shadowed hallway into the exceedingly bright outdoors. I pause while my eyes adjust, then continue my trek toward the gap in the wall.

"We'll be punished for this," she says when we are halfway there.

"For failing, you mean?" I ask. She says nothing. "Do you think your flimsy words will be enough to convince me to turn myself in? I know the price on my head. I know what they intend for me, and a hanging on Mars does not suit me."

"They say you care about the Sisterhood, Heretic." She spits the name like a curse. "You should care what the Agora will do to us who failed to hold you here."

"Well, I don't," I say.

Liar, Ringer whispers. I am exceedingly glad Aunt Doris cannot hear him.

Her words do, however, confirm the Agora's involvement. Is Aunt Marshae somehow in charge of the Control Agency Police now? Is that why they have me in their sights? And, most chillingly, did she use them to kill Eden?

When we come to Bruni lying facedown in the dirt, I do my best not to look at him; I do not want his body to haunt my nightmares, as so many others do. But when I step to move past him, I finally catch sight of Ebba, crouched near the wall's opening.

Her eyes are closed. Beneath her eyelids, her eyes flick back and forth rapidly. It is . . . strange. Like she is dreaming while awake.

It is only a few seconds. Then her eyes fly open. She meets my gaze, and her face hardens. She gestures to Bruni with her HEL gun.

I look back to the large man lying facedown in the dirt. Is he alive? His chest seems still to me, his blood painting the yard as red as his suit. I look to Ebba for more information, and she barks, "We need him, Astrid!"

The order is clear: Ebba wants me to risk myself for Bruni. If he is still alive . . . if he has even a chance at life, I owe him that.

I hold Aunt Doris tight, a shield in front of both myself and Bruni. "You're clear!"

But as soon as Ebba lunges into movement, out from behind the wall to kneel beside Bruni, motion at the doors of the abbey catches my attention. The officer has a strange pistol, while one of the soldiers lifts his railgun.

"Ebba!" I cry at the exact moment the officer barks his order: "Fire!"

It is not Ebba the soldier aims for. Aunt Doris's dying scream is a heady mix of pain and fear. Too heavy for me to hold alone, she slips from my arms to thud into the dirt.

And I am wide open.

"Astrid!"

My name is lost on the wind as the officer aims at me and shoots.

Something hot punches me in the thigh, and I fall back to the earth. With a numb horror, my mind registers I've been shot. A moment later, the pain hits me, a fire that burns hot and cold at the same time. I want to reach for the wound and hold it tightly, am vaguely aware I should put pressure on it, but my arms feel too heavy at my sides.

"Astrid!" There is my name again. Who calls for me? Aunt Doris is a foot from me, and Bruni is—where is Bruni?

Then Ebba is floating above me, hands sliding into my armpits as she pulls me away. Bullets fly overhead. Screams rip through the air alongside them. I have no strength to fight or flee, can only stay silent as Ebba drags me behind the stone wall and drops me next to Bruni's body.

His face is drained of blood. His eyes are glazed.

"He's dead," I say, my voice lost amidst the firearms. "He's dead . . ."

"Get up, Astrid," Ebba commands, other warriors coming to grab Bruni. She pulls a patched railgun from her back, the scarred half of her face arrested in anger, the other half a glare of determination. "Get up and run or stay and die."

Two warriors brace Bruni between them—*he's dead*, I keep thinking—and rush for the ship as fast as they can. I find myself desperate to follow, to escape from this nightmare. I call for Ringer, and he responds, a reassurance in my bones and blood. With his guidance, I push myself to my feet—the pain roars, radiating into my hip and up my spine with a predator's claws—*it hurts, it hurts so much*—and stumble after them. Though they are wounded, the final three Skadivolk alongside Ebba stay to cover us as we flee.

Every step is agony. Sweat rolls down my face and drips from my chin. When I hit the shuttle's ramp, a wave of dizziness rushes over me, and I almost fall. I am vaguely aware that there is still shooting from both sides, but we are so far away, it seems pointless. I move up the ramp—or I try to. Instead, I trip sideways, and the ground rushes up to meet me.

Someone catches me. A force other than my own guides me into the ship. Bruni's laid out on the floor—*he's dead*, I think, looking at his bloodless face, and now I am sure of it. The person helps me down onto the bench and—

I lose time. The hatch is closed, the shuttle shivering with movement. We are leaving, or have already left. Ebba kneels in front of me, cutting away my suit with her own two-inch blade. Pulling the fabric aside, I see—

A flap of skin, a mass of pulpy tissue and muscle.

Oh. *Oh.*

That's my leg.

My vision blackens at the edges as the shock sets in.

I see Ebba's mouth moving but cannot hear her words.

I slide down the bench and black out.

CHAPTER 5

LITO

Because of his connection to the data sent from Ceres Satellite #19, we publicly ask for Lito sol Lucius to return to Cytherea to testify in person. If you or anyone you know has information as to his location, please contact the AEGIS via secure feedform 7.

Rosendo val Chaz, president of the Agency for
Ethical Guidance of Icarii Science

The end of my life goes like this: Beron val Bellator seals my fate with a nod. The duelist raises his blade. My hands are chained before me. There's no way for me to fight back.

The blade buries itself in my chest. Blood wells up my throat. Rushes over my lips and falls like a torrent.

I speak my final words:

"Let it burn."

I wake, burning. Above me, an unfamiliar ceiling. My hand reaches for my face—not any warmer than it should be—but I feel none of the expected pain from the movement. My other hand reaches for my torso and finds—

Nothing.

No bandages. No wounds. Not even scars, proof that I survived. How long have I been asleep? Who has been working on me?

I turn my head, the gel mattress beneath shifting with me to support my neck and back. No windows, but a tile floor reminiscent of every hospital I've ever been in. The air is fresh, though, the temperature pleasantly warm. This can't be the basement of the Spire, the place duelists go to convalesce between assignments.

And why would it be? Souji val Akira was the one to order my death because of what I'd done, what I knew—too dangerous to be left alive when the AEGIS called for a trial against him—and Beron carried out his order. Unless Beron's executioner fucked something up, and someone found me before I could expire . . .

No. No, that's not possible. How many people would be checking to ensure I wouldn't cause Souji any more trouble? It wouldn't be simple, even for Beron, to pass me off as dead if I weren't.

So that means . . . What does it mean?

A thought floats up from the blackness: *How am I alive?*

I throw the blanket—thin, threadbare, blue—aside. Kick my legs—not stiff, not aching—over the side of the bed. Stand—naked, no scar of a mercurial blade going through me—without a hint of dizziness. My breathing comes faster, my heart racing with a growing panic, but something calms me, not physical but close, like a hand on my shoulder.

I didn't tell my neural implant to do that, to erase my anxiety, but then, reaching for my implant, I don't feel anything at all—not in my head where it should be, where it *used to be*—no, I feel something *all over*, and it's so overwhelming, I almost stumble. I stand on the edge of a black hole—one step, and I will disappear.

I instinctively reach for my shoulder, find the old scar there. Yes, one scar . . . one reminder. This one from Ceres, where I was shot by an Aster during my fight with Saito Ren. That happened. And if that happened, then all the rest . . .

I am Lito sol Lucius.

I am Lito sol Lucius.

I am—

"A phoenix," a voice says, "that rises from the ashes." For a moment, through a haze of water, I see Luce—purple hair, glittering cheeks, neck strung with a spider's web of gemstone necklaces—before I realize it can't be Luce, not after what happened on Vesta. I saw the video, saw how she withered from the Genekey virus, burning in her own way. Then the image *resolves*—not there one moment, beside me the next—and she is not Luce at all.

She's smaller than Luce, for one, despite the thick-soled boots she wears. Her hair is long on one side, a swallowing black that bleeds into her dark clothes. But what pulls my gaze is the metal plate on the side of her head.

"Who are you?"

"I'm Mara," she says, her accent strangely slow and fluid, but not like any Gean I've ever heard.

"The person who saved me?" I ask, but her nose curls at that, an answer without speaking. No, she didn't save me.

"Who do you work for?" I ask. Black clothes, but streetwear. Not Icarii, then. Pale skin, sleepless bags beneath her eyes. My age, if I were to hazard a guess. She's not Aster, but still, with the plate . . . "Hemlock?"

She gives a single shake of her head.

My frustration mounts, but again I feel that touch on my shoulder, a full-body guide not from any implant. "Is that you?" I snap. "Are you trying to control me?"

"Yes and no," she says, and that answer sends a pulse of anger from the top of my head to my toes.

I dart forward, forearm to her neck, pushing until her back hits the wall. She stands on her tiptoes but doesn't even flinch. I crowd into her space without a single thought of my nakedness until her eyes flick up and down my body. *Scarless.* She reaches up, puts her hand on my wrist.

Her voice, when it comes, doesn't come from her mouth. *Couldn't,* because of the pressure I put on her throat. "Perhaps you would respond better to a calmer environment?" the room around me says in her voice.

Like when she first arrived, the room ripples, a pebble tossed into a lake. What resolves is a place so familiar, my heart aches: a long row of bunks in a packed, dimly lit room. The whispers of children come to me as if on a foul wind.

The Academy.

But then it changes again. Out of the water swims a mirrored room, two bunks, two armoires, two desks, nothing else the same. My side is spartan, almost ascetic in its cleanliness; Hiro's is the opposite of minimalist, art taped to every inch of wall space, knickknacks and chewed styluses gathering dust on the desk, sheets tossed as if a battle occurred there. Our assigned room during our posting on Ceres.

I want to reach out and touch it, and I release Mara without thinking. But the room shifts once more, and as my fingers brush Hiro's desk, it disappears along with everything else.

In its place rises Luce's apartment exactly as I last saw it. Faded purple carpet. Battered red sofa. A rainbow of her favorite paintings on the walls, including one she painted for Hiro of a fox with nine tails. Again, my heart jolts into my throat, not from comfort but from *longing* for a time gone by. How many of my favorite memories happened here, with Luce and Hiro at my side?

"Or perhaps," Mara says, this time the words coming from the girl next to me, "you want something to hate?"

And then we are back in the dark cell where I died, chains on the wall, dried blood on the floor. A rush runs through me, adrenaline spiked with pure fear, and I have no implant to calm me and no hand on my shoulder to guide me. But I know what happened here. I *know.*

"I was dead." My voice is so small.

"Yes," she says, "you were."

"And now I'm not."

"No." She smiles a smile that doesn't bring any comfort. "You're not."

I turn to her, putting my back to the place where I died. "I want the truth," I tell her. My breathing is shallow, my heart racing, but I am flying high on that adrenaline. "Tell me the truth."

"It might cause you more distress," she says, looking at my chest as if reading the quick thump-thumping of my heart. "It might disturb you too much, and then we'd have to start over."

I don't know what she means—and yet I do. Whatever she's done, whoever she is, if she could bring me back to life, she could erase my memories and try all this again.

But if that's true, *how many times have we done this already?*

"I have to know," I say, because not knowing would kill me faster than knowing would. "Tell me." My voice cracks. "Please."

She makes a soft sound, a little *hmm* of assent. But she offers nothing more, and from the corner of my eye, the room changes, and it is nothing—*nothing*—I could have imagined or prepared for.

We are in a room with two walls, silver metal shifting like liquid before settling—nanomachines, I realize, that created the illusions of my memories. It is not a room that a human would design, and yet Mara and I, human in shape, stand in this grand space like penitents in a chapel. The space behind Mara leads deeper into a dark metal compound, both enticing and threatening at the same time. The wall behind me opens to a world that should kill me instantly but doesn't.

Icy white, stony ground reaches as far as the horizon, broken up by silver bone architecture, the skeletons of fallen giants. Above us, the sky is the dark of space, but the light of the stars is swallowed by a great orange-and-gold monster. The storm, like a single eye, watches us on the surface of a blighted land. *Jupiter*, god of gods, and we stand in the palm of his hand on Europa.

I walk toward the edge of the structure, drawn as if possessed, until I brush against my hospital bed, a bed no longer. Now it is a pod of the same dark metal, uncomfortable in appearance and yet curved like a cradle. And what child could this crib possibly hold but something like me, dead and risen again?

I look at my hand, trailing over the pod, a substance like skin that sends feedback to my brain in a sensation like *touch*. But it's not skin. It can't be. And I know, with startling clarity, that beneath my exterior are the same bones that make up this metal place.

I am not Lito sol Lucius, but a repository built to house his memories.

I am Synthetic.

CHAPTER 6

HIRO

You don't go to work or school. You sleep on the street. You march for up to fourteen hours a day. Some would call your methods of protesting extreme, especially when considering that this began because of the treatment of Asters. What would you say to someone who thought like that?

Esperanza val Montero, reporter for the newscast El Sol

Why shouldn't we protest for the Asters? What have they ever done to us?

Anonymous masked protester

The crowd in front of Val Akira Labs is thicker than the night before. I arrive in the early morning, when protesters are emerging from mattress bags or personal tents, greeting the sleepless, hollow-eyed sentries of their camps. Maskless counterprotesters have begun to arrive by the dozens, while news outlets gather in well-placed pockets, and the sky is filled with drones of various makes, personal and professional alike. No one wants to miss Souji val Akira's first public appearance in six months.

The disharmoniously red laser cordons off the front steps that lead to the smoky quartz building, as well as a path to the street where a single podcar waits. At the top of the steps, where the peacekeepers are thickest, is a slender stand holding an altavoz connected to a handful of drones hovering three meters above. I shouldn't be surprised that Father plans to speak. Always has to have the last word, doesn't he?

What have you got planned, old man?

I slip through the crowd—fox mask on my face, backpack hiding the rewired long-range HEL gun—and make my way to my mark. Across the street is the Val Alarie building, which manages shipping concerns between Mercury and Venus. Val Alarie had the good sense to close today, not wanting to force their employees to fight through the chaos to get to work, but while the front of the building already has a crowd gathering, hoping to use the stairs to better see my father's speech this afternoon, I move toward the narrow alleyway at its side.

When I reach the mouth, I check my surroundings. The only thing paying me any attention is a lazy orange cat lounging on a dumpster. Off come the mask and jacket, shoved quickly into my backpack. Beneath I wear a jumpsuit with the Val Alarie logo, a speedy delivery ship shaped like a red V. At the end of the alley is the maintenance entrance, and I scan a card from my backpack that grants me entrance.

Six months of planning to get this far. Six months of gathering information and hoarding stolen fragments of identities. I helped Luce with whatever she asked in between locating blueprints of the Val Alarie building, stealing a uniform and keycard, and gathering supplies off the black market to rewire the long-range HEL gun. Today it all pays off.

I spread my legs a little wider than is natural and effect a slow shuffle-step, letting my shoulders curl downward like an exhausted maintenance worker. In the metal stairwell, I head up to the second floor.

As if thinking of Luce summons her, a message lights up the corner of my com-lenses. She's obviously given up on sending me voice messages. This one is written.

Curiosity gets the better of me, and I open it. *I know what you're doing,* she writes. The words sting like ice in my veins. *Don't do this, Hiro. You'll get caught. With security as thick as it is, there's no way you'll escape afterward.*

She doesn't see the obvious: If I can manage to kill my father, I don't care if I get arrested. If he's dead, he won't be able to wiggle out of whatever punishment the AEGIS has in store for him, and the Asters will get their justice.

And what of the boy who changed my life? Well, I'd be lying if I said revenge for Lito didn't factor into this.

I emerge on the second floor of Val Alarie. The offices are empty. The only movement comes from drones polishing the floor. I keep my head low, knowing there are cameras I can do nothing about but hoping my affected gait will be enough to fool anyone watching. Soon enough, I come to the slender room that faces the street and shut myself inside.

It's a storage closet. There are no cameras, only closely packed boxes of supplies all the way to the ceiling. Along the back wall is a board of hanging tools, the table in front of it covered in a gritty dust. The blueprint I got said there was a window in this room that faced Val Akira Labs, and while I don't see it, I'm sure it's here.

I pull down the board with the tools hanging on it and set it aside. Sure enough, it was hiding a little window—one I keep closed, for now. Don't want to alert anyone down below to my presence. After that, I pull the long-range HEL gun out from my backpack, change it from compact to full form, and settle in to wait.

With all the practice I've had, you'd think I'd have gotten good at waiting, but today, time seems completely frozen. I watch the street, the dome lighting brightening to daylight as more people gather, protesters and counterprotesters alike. Tents come down, bedding is rolled up, and personal space disappears as people pack themselves shoulder to shoulder. Violence threatens to break out a few times around the podcar, more from peacekeeper threats than anything else. But no matter how I try to pass the time, to keep the adrenaline in my veins from becoming a sharp-edged knife, the steps in front of Val Akira Labs remain empty.

In my solitary bubble, my thoughts turn to the worst subjects. What would Lito say if he were here? Would he help me with this insane assassination attempt, or would he, like Luce, beg me to reconsider my plan?

But of course, that thought exercise is pointless. The only reason I'm standing here, preparing to shoot my own father, is because Lito's dead on his order.

The noise from the crowd increases until there is nothing but a dissonant howl, a cacophony of angry yelling clashing with ecstatic cheering. I immediately spot the reason—the flexglass doors of Val Akira Labs part as a group of four black-clad duelists emerge.

My guts threaten to drop out my ass—*of course* Father's using the duelists as his personal bodyguards.

Doesn't matter. Patience is the name of the game, always has been. I just have to wait until he's far enough away from them that I can shoot without triggering their shields.

From the shadows of the building, they enter the light of the dome, Father in the protected middle. I finally open the window and get into position, hand close to the trigger. Forgotten are the crowd baying for his blood, the signs begging the AEGIS for justice. The world narrows solely to my father, the four duelists, and me.

He approaches the altavoz. "Cytherea," he says, the voice of a man full of care, a tone he never used with me. "My fellow Icarii citizens, please . . ."

The crowd quiets, eager to hear what he has to say. And it is in that moment I fear they have lost. They *want* to be persuaded, when for so long they've heard him speak and bought his words wholesale.

"My fellow Icarii citizens, today I submit myself before the judicial courts of the AEGIS."

Charismatic as always, attuned to the crowd, his somber face is perfectly matched to his black suit with sharp flexglass lapels. He doesn't stand like a man triumphant, but like one beset by sorrow, his shoulders slouched despite his straightened spine. His eyes are dark smudges, not from worry over himself or his future, but in the way a parent might look at a child who was missing for a night. For the tiniest instant, I remember how much Shinya looked like him before the *Leander*'s destruction.

"We are the Icarii, heirs of the great philosophers, unravelers of humanity's greatest mysteries, and descendants not of kings and queens, but of those who dedicated themselves to peace and justice. It is for that reason that, when the AEGIS summoned me, I was oathbound to appear."

He carefully sweeps the entire crowd with his gaze, those who cry out for his freedom alongside those who demand his resignation or worse. In his eyes is not the expected disappointment but pure acceptance.

"I go to the AEGIS today because I believe in Icarii justice. I go because I know that no one who claims to love his society can be above the law. There are things—yes, terrible, awful things—that we have seen over these past few months: agony without reason, pain without a name. Asters, suffering from lifelong illnesses, who claim that Val Akira Labs contributed to their discomfort."

It's time, my instincts say. The duelists have drifted from Father as he speaks, have moved to hold back the crowd while he stands still. *It's time*. I peer down the sights. Red crosshairs mark my father's head.

I take in a shuddering breath, my finger moving from the guard to the trigger.

"If these things have occurred—unseen, unknown—under my watch, then I *should* face justice. I *should* be removed from my position, as so many of you say."

Pull the trigger, Hiro.

My father keeps talking. I lose track of his words, the altavoz fading until there is only the sound of my breathing—steady in, steady out—only the sight of the crosshairs' center over his forehead, just below that single white streak of hair. There's nothing between him and my shot.

So pull the fucking trigger.

But something small flutters in my chest, memories that swell until my finger trembles.

Father bracing me on his lap as he reads a book to me. Father kissing my head as he tucks me into bed. Father helping me build a toy rocket. *"Science doesn't care about our differences,"* he says, *"because it reacts to each of us in exactly the same way."*

No. *No!* In just a few short years, he'd ship me off to the Academy because my test scores weren't good enough to pursue science; he'd tell me I had to choose between being a man or a woman—he'd look *a child* in the eyes and tell them that they're a disappointment who can't be relied on, simply because of *who they are.*

And that's just the beginning.

His dissatisfaction will grow until it reaches a breaking point, until he decides to completely wash his hands of me. Until he gives me to Beron val Bellator, who will tear me apart and rearrange my DNA into that of a dead Gean woman. And when I leave the Icarii for that one-way mission, for what will surely end only in my death, he never even bids me farewell.

Maybe that's the thing that hurts most of all—not the destruction of everything I was, but the fact that he couldn't spare a few seconds to *pretend* to love me. Proof that he *never cared about me at all.*

That memory and so many more crack my chest open and rip my heart in half.

I remember my father's heartbroken face when I asked him where Mother had gone. Comforting me when I woke up from a nightmare and cried for a mother who wasn't there. Loving me in a way that wasn't black and twisted until it became obvious I'd never be what he wanted.

Asuka held me tightly when I cried. We waited for Mother every day. And we never understood why she'd come home only to abandon a new child.

His fault. *It's his fault.*

SO PULL THE FUCKING TRIGGER!

But I can't.

I can't see him through my rising tears.

I hate him. I hate him so much for everything that he's done to me, to my mother, and to my siblings. But I also love him, because he's my father, and no matter what he's done, he was the one who taught me what love *was* as a child.

I blink the tears away. He's walking to the podcar. Just a few seconds until there's no chance at a shot. I *have to do this—*

But I can't do it. *I can't do it.*

He gets in the car. The moment's passed.

I've failed everyone. Failed myself.

I'm a failure.

That's the only thing I have time to think before the world is lost in an explosion.

The ground shakes. Heat washes over me. An invisible force rumbles through me, and my stomach whirls, threatening sickness.

My ears pop, and sound comes back to me in a rush—screaming, crying, wailing, and a low roar that might be damage to my hearing. Out the shattered window, there is chaos.

Above, the sky is black smoke. Red flames lick up the side of the Val Akira building. The bottom level is on fire, and my brain struggles to reconcile this and my past—so much like the Fall of Ceres that I feel a jolt of panic for Lito's safety—before I realize that Lito is dead, and this is Cytherea.

All the evidence catches up to me at once, hitting me like a gunshot: someone has bombed Val Akira Labs.

CHAPTER 7
THE GIRL IN THE CROWD

You want me to—what? No, that was a—a bomb. Who? Who did—
The building is on fire! We can't— No, I'm not going to report. Send
a drone. Send the drone if you want footage. There are people dying.
Fire me if you— They're dying. I'm going to help them.

Livecast from Esperanza val Montero,
reporter for the newscast El Sol

"Let's get closer to the front." Her mother settles their hand-painted
sign on her hip—CYTHEREA IS FOR ALL FAMILIES! written in her
mother's neat hand, surrounded by stickers and one of Julieta's
drawings—and reaches back to take Julieta's hand. "Ven conmigo,
cariño."

These are the last words that she hears her mother say before she
loses her in the crowd.

It all happens so fast. There's a loud boom and a bright flash, and then
she can't hear anything at all except a high-pitched ringing that makes
her tremble. Her hand is ripped from her mother's as people run in the
opposite direction. There is shouting and screaming, but muffled. She's
not supposed to let go of her mother's hand when they're in public.

Something hard hits her in the side of the head—an elbow? A fist?—and she stumbles in front of a wide-shouldered person in a mask who shoves her aside as they flee. She falls to the ground. Tries to push herself up, but someone's boot comes down on her forearm. Something snaps. She screams, but is cut off when another boot clips her forehead. She's scared. So very, very scared. And then someone else is there, grabbing her up into their arms.

"Mamá," she cries. "Mamá, Mamá." She puts her arms around the person's neck, but they don't go far. They stop at a building next to the one that's on fire. When they set her down, she can still feel the heat, worse than the hot baths that sting her skin that Papí draws for her. She looks up at the face of the person who saved her. They're not wearing the same mask her mother was.

"Are you okay?" they ask. They must see how afraid she is, because the person takes off the cloth covering the lower half of their face. The woman's mouth is pale, while the skin around her eyes is streaked with dirt and dust. Her hair is short and singed.

Tears roll down Julieta's cheeks, even as she tries not to cry. She's nine, almost ten, and she shouldn't be sobbing like a baby, but she's so terrified she doesn't know what else to do. "My mamá was—" She weakly points toward the building.

"María Dolores!" someone calls, and the woman whips around. There's a man waving at her, wearing a scrap of cloth like her. "There's someone trapped over here! We need help lifting!"

The woman—María Dolores—grabs Julieta's shoulders and guides her to place her back against the building. It's strangely cool in all this warmth. "Stay here," María Dolores says. "I'll come back to you, help you find your—" But the next thing she says is lost as she puts her mask back on and rushes to help the man.

Julieta cradles her forearm. It hurts a lot and curves strangely. It's turned purple all the way to her wrist. But others are far unluckier. Every face she sees is twisted with fear or pain. There are big chunks of crystal that fell from the building, now littering the street. People are bleeding.

Many have wounds like from the shows Papí watches that she's not supposed to see.

She should stay here. She can't stay here. Her mother was going toward the building when everything happened. What if she was hit by one of those falling rocks? Or what if she's out there looking for Julieta, thinking she's trapped?

She forces herself toward the fire. The crowd is thinner than it was, but still thick as people try to flee and find themselves unable to. "Help the people who fell!" yells a middle-aged man—maskless, frantic, his eyebrows singed black. "Don't panic! You'll trample others!"

"I want my mother!" a grown man weeps from the ground.

"Why!" another screams, over and over, hands pressed to their cheeks. "Why! Why! Why!"

She wishes her hearing had stayed gone.

A few people bump her, hitting her forearm and sending bolts of pain through her entire body. She has to stop to catch her breath every time it happens. Someone, supported by a friend, limps with a bone protruding from his leg. Another person on the ground isn't moving at all. She pretends not to see these things.

She comes to the stairs of the building. She should be able to look over the crowd from here. But, at the top, she doesn't see her mother, just things she wishes she could pretend not to see. Blood gushes from missing arms and legs. Blisters bubble on skin. Charred flesh, black and cracked, mars limbs. One girl cries as her friend tries to remove her mask and finds they can't because it's melted onto her face. Another has whipped off her jacket to put out the flames on a nearby man, his hair a halo of fire.

She spots her mother's sign.

FOR ALL FAMILIES! is all that remains, along with the drawing that Julieta did of her playing with her dog, Barkley. The rest is burned away.

"Mamá!" she screeches, heedlessly rushing into the lobby.

This close to the building's front doors, only a few are still moving. Frantic friends and first responders do their best to pull people free of fire and rubble. The smell—the *stench*—is enough to halt her. It's choking and smothering all at once.

Some of the ceiling above the lobby has collapsed. At the edge of the blaze, a group of people work to push a large slab of rock off the leg of a trapped person. Sweat rolls down their faces from the nearby flames.

She can't go in there. She has to go in there. She moves, one careful step at a time, around flaming debris. The black smoke is thick, burning her eyes and choking her. She comes up on her mother's burned sign. Behind it, there is only rubble—

No, there's something else there, poking out from beneath the rocks. It looks like . . . it used to be a hand.

"Mamá!"

She picks up a rock, so hot her hands immediately burn, and tosses it away. Does it again, regardless of how it hurts. A little more of the arm is revealed—the wrist, the forearm . . . And then a loud crack comes from above her, and the building shakes.

She looks up to see more of the ceiling give way—

Something hooks her, hard metal against her stomach. She loses what little air she had left in her lungs as she's pulled away. The ceiling falls where she'd been crouched moments ago, and she covers her face as the dust plumes.

She's shifted about like she weighs nothing, cradled in what she realizes is a pair of strong arms. "I've got you," says a fox floating above her. Their hair is as red and wild as the fire.

As much as she can, she fights. She pounds her fists against the person's shoulder, but finds it's metal and they probably don't feel her at all. As soon as she's back on the street with the stranger, gasping in cool air, she realizes how weak she really is.

"But my mamá . . ." Her voice is rough, and she has to force out the words. "She was—"

A peacekeeper rushes over to them and points out a green tent that's been set up. Medics in the same color rush about, seeing to the worst of the wounded. The stranger sets her down outside, and someone drapes wet blankets over the two of them. After everything, the cold is a relief—one she doesn't want.

"I have to go back—I have to—"

The stranger places a hand on her head. "I'm sorry," they say, their voice wavering like they're crying behind their mask. "I'm sorry, but no one was alive in there."

That saps the last of her strength. Her eyes sting so badly from the smoke that she's not sure she can cry, but a sob breaks from her chest regardless.

The fox pats her head again. "I'm so, so sorry," they say, as if it were their fault.

But how could that be, when this was a freak accident? She's about to take their hand and say so when she hears her name.

"Julieta?"

She turns and sees—

"Mamá!"

She tries to run, ends up stumbling. Her mother catches her and holds her tightly, neither of them conscious of the burns and wounds they've sustained. She cries freely, not caring who sees, as her mother presses kisses to her cheeks, her forehead, her hair. She clings to her, never wanting to let go.

She forgets all about the stranger in the fox mask, and doesn't notice when they slip away into the crowd.

PART II
THE COST OF A LIFE

INTERLUDE
SOUJI VAL AKIRA

As Souji finishes his speech in front of the Val Akira building, he knows what to expect. As he walks toward the armored podcar that will take him to the waiting AEGIS, he knows what to expect. And as he slides into his seat, surrounded by four duelists, he knows what to expect.

It doesn't make the result any less painful.

When the bomb goes off, the podcar trembles. Emergency measures take over, the genderless voice of the AI pilot an irritating repetition: *Rerouting. Please remain calm. Rerouting. Please remain calm.*

Behind them, smoke billows into the sky. "Find out what that was," Souji commands, and though he already knows, he lets his voice waver. The duelists, shocked and reeling, snap to attention.

The highest-ranking one, a Rapier, presses a hand to his ear. His conversation with Command is brief. When he's finished, he straightens his shoulders and looks right at Souji. "Sir, there was an explosion . . ." His report is efficient. His Dagger's eyes are fixed out the window in the direction they came from the entire time he speaks.

Souji doesn't look back. "I see," he says when the Rapier is done.

They are quiet for the rest of the ride. Because the situation has affected traffic everywhere, by the time they reach AEGIS headquarters, a half hour has passed, and if Souji were still meant to appear before them, he would be late. The podcar pulls to the side of the road to let him and the four duelists out, but they remain there.

He checks his compad. His hearing has been canceled.

"Take us to the Spire," Souji orders the podcar. He lets his exhaustion filter into his tone. He hopes it sounds like sorrow. "I need to make a statement."

As the podcar lurches into motion again, Souji checks the news. Headlines read exactly as he expected them to: BOMB USED IN ASTER TERROR ATTACK IDENTICAL TO ONE IN THE FALL OF CERES.

While a few outlets show reporters pressing protesters for more details, the majority are playing footage captured by a peacekeeper drone that morning. In the clip, a group of three individuals in Aster wraps splits from the protest in the street and stops at a side entrance of Val Akira Labs. There's a moment when, as one scans their ID, viewers can clearly see a large bag carried between them, before they disappear inside.

"Fucking cockroaches," the Dagger next to him hisses, voice choked with sentiment. Souji makes a note to put her beside him when he speaks at the Spire; her emotion will give his more legitimacy.

He watches the video again, looking for faults. These men are not Asters, but with the proper costumes, they appear to be. The infiltration is so expert, Souji can't spot any detail that marks them as human. He'll have to thank Beron for arranging it.

He puts his compad away and leans back into his plush seat. He knows exactly what he's going to say to the people of Cytherea. Exactly how to press on their sympathies and turn their focus to the Asters instead of him.

He has, after all, already written his speech.

And with the time he has been given—that he has bought for himself with the lives of hundreds, as the casualty reports tick ever upward—he will finish the great work of the val Akira family.

CHAPTER 8

ASTRID

[2] And they perverted their minds with unholy machines, for they sought to bring forth the voices of the dead. [3] But the dead took root in their minds' fresh pastures and would not leave.

The Canon, Antiquity 7:2–3

I fade in and out, catching only glimpses of the world around me. My cheek pressed against the metal floor of a ship. Bruni's face a foot from mine, far too pale. Ebba's health minister on the Skadivolk council floating above me, her voice lost in an echo. "Hurry!"

The only constant is the agony, but as it intensifies, it sucks me under.

A needle shoved into the crook of my arm. Cold hands on my tattered leg. Something metal—going *inside the bullet wound*—

I cry out. Or maybe I don't. Maybe the blackness takes me before I can actually release the scream that builds up inside me.

A sickening pop when something is pulled out of my leg. Metal, blood-streaked and strange. Words, spoken by faces I do not recognize.

"What is it?"

"It's—a tracker."

The man in the long coat. The cappo's strange pistol. Is that what he shot me with?

"Smash the tracker, then hit her with the adrenaline—get her moving!"

Frantic voices. Frantic hands pawing at me. *Leave me alone,* I try to say, but my mouth feels stuffed with cotton.

Ice in my veins. Clarity like a slap. My eyes shoot wide; my hands find my chest and press over my rapidly beating heart.

"Astrid, I need you to focus." The voice belongs to Ebba, gray hair flattened to her head with sweat. "Are you with me?"

"Yes," I say, as more of the world comes back—and more pain with it. "Yes, I am—" I cut off. I do not know what I am. Conscious, yes, but little else.

"They hit you with a tracker, which means they'll be coming for us here," Ebba says, and though I do not know where *here* is, the thought of the Control Agency Police after me chills my very soul. Ebba looks at the health minister. "Give her something for the pain, Mardoll, but not enough to knock her out, then move this station. I've called for backup, but it will be an hour before anyone can reach us."

The exchange makes little sense to me, but when Mardoll slips a needle full of clear liquid into my arm, the pain that had been all-swallowing numbs. Becomes faraway. I release a sigh, feeling every muscle in my body relax.

For the first time in what has likely been hours, I feel close to normal. I notice my strange surroundings. I lie in a plastiframe bed. The room around me is unfamiliar, patchwork walls in silver and black like the moonborn ships. Ebba stands above me, her eyes closed, but the movement beneath her eyelids makes it seem like she is asleep standing up— just like it did during the raid, before she ordered me to rescue Bruni.

"Ebba—" I say, but her eyes shoot open and she turns to Mardoll.

"Focus on the station. I'll take care of the repository."

Mardoll nods, and then she is gone, running at a fast clip. Gravity— there is gravity here, but Ebba said something about moving the station.

"Where are—" I begin.

Ebba cuts me off. "We have very little time, so I'll answer what I can."

I fall silent.

"We're at a hospital on one of our satellites." The few satellites I know of are old patchwork things, spinning to create gravity, but I suppose they would need something like that for medical procedures. "Mardoll is going to attempt to move the station before the Geans reach us, because if they do, there's no knowing what they'll sabotage. Or what they'll take." The statement reminds me of our conversation from before the raid, when I asked her about the Geans destroying information.

Even more than that, it reminds me of the vision—memory?—I saw as I fell to Earth in the Ironskin, of Ringer telling me that he had to go to the Geans. *So that they do not come to demand what we are unwilling to give.*

But I do not want them to suffer because of me. My words are steadier than I expect when I speak. "Leave me behind and escape."

Ebba offers me a lopsided smile, and I am not sure if it is from satisfaction or pity. "They're not just after you . . ."

"Then what is it that the Geans want so badly from the moonborn?"

Ebba looks, for a moment, as if she will not tell me. As if that wall she keeps around the Skadivolk secrets will come up again. But finally, she slouches. "Muninn." The moonborn word escapes her like a sigh. "Technology. You would call them neurobots."

"Neurobots," I repeat. The word is strange on my tongue. Strange, because I never thought I would speak of them. "But they are old tech and . . . illegal." Not that their being illegal would stop the Skadivolk from using them, but where in space would they find them? Neither the Icarii nor the Geans use them. And that is to say nothing of their inherent danger. They attack the brain, changing pathways, affecting memories and personality. The Canon teaches that those who took nanomachines into their bodies destroyed their souls and brought about the downfall of their cultures. It is why the Geans are so wary of technology as a whole. It is part of the reason I hate the neural implant so much. "You have—you *use* neurobots? Those machines steal bodies!"

Ebba scoffs. "Save your Sisterhood fearmongering. There are various ways of programming the Muninn, and ours certainly aren't set up to rewire the brain's neuroplasticity. We've been using them as ways to pass on generational memories for centuries." For a moment, I fear I have misheard her, but then she continues, slower and more confident. "The moons are unforgiving mothers, and our numbers are too few to squander our hard-won knowledge of how to survive here. We have no schooling beyond the basics. No way to train the leaders we need. Muninn—the neurobots—are our answer."

I remember the rapid movements beneath Ebba's eyelids, both during the raid and moments ago. Was she consulting these neurobots? "Generational memories . . ." She must think me stupid, repeating everything she says. But those words trigger something in me: Ringer offering me the golden star in the palm of his hand.

Somehow, I feel that the idea is vaguely familiar. Is it because of Ringer, or simply because I want it to be recognizable?

"That's why you ordered Bruni's rescue, even though he was dead . . ."

"We couldn't lose his line of knowledge," Ebba confirms. "The Council will choose a successor for his Muninn among those who worked with him."

"My memories . . . the name Hringar Grimson. Could I have been given neurobots as a child?"

Ebba's face shifts at my question, becoming far more stern with her one eyebrow pulled down. "Why would you ask that? Unless—"

She cuts off as a tremor rocks through the station.

Her blue eyes, a color so like my own, flare wide. "Let's move—the Geans are here—"

"What—"

"I must secure the Muninn repository." Ebba grabs my biceps and pulls me from the bed. My wounded leg, tightly wrapped in sterile bandages, threatens to give out beneath me, but Ebba steadies me.

"Wait," I beg, desperate to learn more. "You didn't answer. Could I have somehow been given someone's neurobots as a child?" *Is that what Ringer truly is?*

"Maybe," she says, guiding me past empty beds exactly like my own. "The Geans will take whatever they think will punish us the most, anything from supplies to children." If not for Ebba, I would stumble at that word. *Children.* "During Gean raids in the past, desperate parents would force Muninn lines on their children, hoping that if they were taken, they would at least remember where they came from."

Could that be what happened to me? Though I do not remember any fear in that memory of the star, no Gean invaders on their way to kidnap me.

We stop before a large metal door thirty feet away from where we began. "They'll be after you too, so hide here. Don't come out until Mardoll or I call for you."

"Ebba—" Everything overwhelms me all at once.

Her face, full of fear, does nothing to reassure me. "Astrid, I'm sorry I can't tell you more—we don't have time—but when this is over, I will explain everything, I promise."

I nod once, and she leaves me leaning against the door.

Alone in this strange, surgical place, I put my hand on the bow-shaped latch. A blessed coolness radiates from the door, chilling my overheated skin, and I long to press my full body against the metal. But I do not have time with the Geans here, and so I tighten my shaking hand and pull.

The door parts from the frame, and cold air rushes out to greet me. I realize immediately what this space is.

My eyes fall on Bruni's body, carefully arranged on a slab in the middle of the freezer.

Ebba wants me to hide in their morgue.

An urge to flee hits me. But where could I run that would be safe, when the Geans are searching through this station?

If I survived the Ironskin, I can survive this.

I close the great metal door and prepare to hide with Bruni's body.

I DO NOT spend my time idle in the mortuary freezer. To keep myself from worrying about what is happening outside these walls, I limp the length of the room, peering behind crates for the perfect hiding place. The space suit I wear—everywhere other than my wounded leg, where it was cut away—keeps me from feeling too cold. The chill on my cheeks and the tips of my ears is clarifying.

But the room is not large, and I finish my search quickly. There is an open space in the corner I could slip into. Ducking down, I would be well hidden from anyone entering. In the same corner is a maintenance panel, so much like the ones in the *Juno* that I believe I could use it to traverse the station should my wound allow it. Of course, I do not know that for sure; I might find myself crawling into heating coils or a recycler.

When the only thing left for me to focus on is Bruni, I find myself standing above his body.

The colors that made him so vibrant in life have leached from him. His skin is ashen, his tattoos faded. His hair is lank and pale. Even his red suit, still splattered with his blood, looks darker under these unflattering lights.

He was the first moonborn to make me feel welcome among them. I always despaired of impressing Ebba, but Bruni took to me immediately, pleased when I managed to do even simple things, such as holding a gun properly. His correction was always gentle, his praise effusive. I had never had a teacher like him, and he is dead . . . because of me.

It was not the raids that caught the attention of the Geans; it was my involvement in them. Aunt Doris knew exactly who I was—*Heretic*, she called me. The cappos were there to capture me and shot Bruni in the process. And now . . . now they are on the station.

For me *and* the neurobots.

I feel torn between wanting to help the Skadivolk secure their technology and disgust at their use of the neurobots. But perhaps what Ebba said was right, and my prejudice against them is simply my ingrained fear. It is that very revulsion that has likely drawn the Geans here to destroy the neurobots. But if the moonborn do not have access to them, what will become of their people?

The loss of those neurobots will be your fault too, a part of me whispers.

I run my hand along the strange table Bruni lies upon. It is not a slab, as I first thought, but something else. There is the outline of a body on the tabletop. But his arms, instead of lying within the guidelines at his sides, have been arranged with his hands clasped over his chest, as if to hold a weapon.

No, not a weapon . . . he's holding a small case.

My curiosity gets the better of me; I slip the case from beneath his stiff fingers. Inside is a cylinder half the length of my thumb, something like a small vial with no opening. Or maybe a pill.

When the light hits it, it glows golden like a glittering star.

I am jerked back to the vision in the Ironskin. Ringer and the star in the palm of his hand. I take it and devour it as he promises to be with me forever.

Are these Bruni's memories—his Muninn? And my vision while in the Ironskin, was it actually a memory of my taking Ringer's neurobots?

The thud of footsteps on metal reaches me. I slip between the crates and duck down next to the maintenance panel just as the door opens. The case is still in my hand; I did not have time to put it back.

"There's a body in here," says a deep voice. I cannot make out the response that comes a moment later. "No, it's not the girl."

They're searching for me. Pressing my empty hand over my mouth, I grit my teeth so tightly that my jaw aches.

Another answer I cannot hear. "I'll search the area," the deep voice responds.

They're going to find me. There are only a few boxes between us.

I peer through the gap in the crates and see the man move toward Bruni's body. I grip the case so tightly my knuckles turn white. Where is Ebba? Mardoll? Are they all right? Have these men hurt them? Killed them?

Your fault. They're here for you.

"No target samples on the body," the gruff voice says.

Samples? Is he looking for Bruni's neurobots?

"Even if the moonborn bitch won't talk, we have enough samples." I hear the second voice clearly as another pair of heavy footsteps enter the freezer. Is he talking about Ebba or Mardoll? Either way . . . *one of them is alive.* "We just need the girl," he finishes.

I have to get out of here. I slip Bruni's case into my pocket and press my hands against the maintenance hatch. Perhaps I will be crawling into a different kind of harm, but it is better than being found by the Gean officers. As the two men search the crates around the room, I open the panel as quietly as I can—

The hinges screech from the cold.

"What was that?"

I fling myself into the maintenance shaft and crawl as quickly as I can, the hatch falling closed behind me with an audible *clack.*

"She must be here! Help me get her!" the gruff man's voice echoes behind me.

It is still cold in the shaft, but sweat beads on my forehead from the effort. My injured leg screams. From beneath the pressure of the bandage, it feels as if a monster is clawing its way out. Or perhaps it is the muscle and fat beneath, straining at my stitches.

Where am I going? What am I going to do?

Stop, Ringer says, and I do, relieved to finally hear his voice again. Just as the pain returned, so did he. *We need a plan, not just wild flailing.*

He is right, but I do not know where I am, or how to get out of the maintenance shafts. This is not the *Juno.* Ebba called for backup, but how long until they reach us? Half an hour? Longer? Perhaps I could hide here until help arrives, but what about Ebba and Mardoll?

Ringer guides my hand to Bruni's case in my pocket.

Consume them, he instructs. The command drags my heart into my throat. *Devour them, and let Bruni guide you through the satellite.*

Stomach roiling, I pull the case from my pocket and open it. The little pill has the faintest shimmer of gold inside. *A star.*

Bruni will know a way out of the maintenance shafts, Ringer reasons. *Bruni will know how to escape.*

But I know so little of the neurobots. If taking Ringer's led to his creation in my mind, what will taking Bruni's do?

Your choice, little sister, Ringer says. *We could always remain in the tunnels until the cappos drag us out.*

But that isn't a choice at all . . .

I have to save Ebba and Mardoll. I have to make sure the Geans do not destroy all of the Skadivolk's knowledge.

Desperate not to think of what I'm *really* doing, I withdraw the pill from the case and place it on my tongue. The vision from the Ironskin guides me; I push it between my teeth and hold it there.

Last chance to turn back. *No choice at all.*

I crunch down, *ingesting* Bruni's memories and thoughts—and claiming his Muninn as my own.

Sharp shards like glass cut into my gums, blood fills my mouth, and—

Faces swim up out of the darkness. Names I have never heard before, but that I now know like my own. I see hands—youthful hands, old withered hands, hands pale as the moon or as dark as space—on the command panels of moonborn ships. I can feel the shapes of guns and tools centuries old. And I know that if I ever picked them up, they would feel familiar in my hands.

But at what cost? Are these memories eating away some of my own?

I see the Muninn repository, a heart of glass and silver, and the carefully curated lines of memories within like golden starseeds. I see Ebba, before her face was twisted with scars, embracing me like a lover and—no, I do not want to see that.

I search for other things. What of the man named Hringar Grimson? What of me, Astrid, the woman with a moonborn face but no parents to claim her?

I see my own face smiling up at me when I shoot the center of the target in the gun range—

Focus, little sister. Ringer's voice draws me back to the maintenance shaft. *We need a way to escape.*

Right. My heart is a hammer in my chest, my entire body the nail it strikes. I force myself to think of the satellite, of the maintenance shafts we are in. I close my eyes and feel as if I have entered a dream.

The station's layout forms like one of my own memories. The satellite is small, a single-floor ring rotating around a central tube. I see the infirmary, the Muninn repository, and various rooms for surgery or sleeping, as well as the docks where ships are moored. And the maintenance shafts that thread in between . . .

I come back to myself, shaking.

I see it like a map written on the backs of my eyelids. I know how to get out of here, and a way to help the moonborn too . . .

I SLIP FROM the maintenance tunnels into the docks. There are four moonborn ships, patchwork and outdated, and a single Gean craft—sleek, white, and in good repair. Ringer instructs me to check my surroundings, but I do not spot anyone standing guard. Keeping low—and attempting to ignore the growing pain in my leg as the medication wears off—I limp toward the Gean craft.

Bruni's memories come to me, layered over my own. I crawl onto the wing of the ship, pulling myself over to a small, seamless panel I would not have noticed if not for Bruni. While the engine is locked away, there is plenty of damage I can do elsewhere.

I try to open the panel but, because of the suit's gloves, fail to find purchase. The second attempt is no better than the first. I lost the small knife from my suit somewhere on Earth, so I cannot use it for leverage. Instead, I am forced to remove the glove altogether, which takes precious minutes of fiddling with the wrist cuff that I do not have to spare.

When my hand is free, I slide my fingernails into the thin gap around the panel and yank it open. Beneath run several cables and wires that Bruni helpfully labels. *This is the pressurization line.* A small thing compared to an entire engine, but if I destroy it, the airlock doors will not be able to open and close, trapping the Gean officers here until they can either fix the problem or work around it. By then, backup will have arrived.

I seize the line—it is freezing to the touch—and try to yank it out, but it does not budge. If I had my knife, I would be able to cut through. I need something strong—pliers or something with a sharp point. I look around for options, only to catch movement at the entrance to the docks.

I throw myself flat against the wing of the Gean ship as four cappos enter.

No, make that five—one man in plainclothes is braced between two others, bleeding from a wound to his middle. The man in the long coat, the officer who shot me on Earth, leads the way. He too is covered in blood, but I cannot tell if it is from his men or not.

In his hand is a silver case. Have they taken some moonborn information?

The officer gestures to the ship's airlock. "Get him stabilized and power up for launch. We do not have long until their reinforcements arrive."

"And the girl?"

I cannot see them from where I lie, but I can hear the sneer in the officer's tone as he says, "Once we located the station, the priority became the samples."

The neurobots? No . . . they aren't destroying them. That is what is in the case. They're *stealing* them!

"With what's happening on Mars," the officer says, "you know how he prizes these above all else."

Who is "he"? I wonder. And what could be happening on Mars that is so bad they turn to the use of neurobots?

"We will return and hunt down the girl after we—"

The outer airlock door opens, and they move into the ship so that I can no longer hear them. *Now or never, little sister,* Ringer hisses to me, and I place my hand on the pressurization line. I have only a few seconds to destroy it, or the Geans will be inside the ship, and my tampering will be worth nothing.

The skin of my hand burns as I wrap my fist around the line. I brace myself on my knees and pull with all my strength, swallowing the groan that works its way up my throat. Something pops in my leg, and I whimper before I can stop myself. There is blood dotting the bandages on my thigh.

But it does not matter; the Geans cannot hear me, not when the engine of the ship starts with a roar.

Too late. It's too late.

I have to get off the ship before it launches with me on it.

I leave the panel open and try to stand—but immediately, agony shoots from my leg through my body, and I lose my balance. I fall to the wing, biting my tongue as I strike the hard metal.

Crawl, little sister! Ringer demands, and I do—elbow over elbow, my knees desperately pushing, I inch to the edge of the wing. But the Gean ship now hovers far above the catwalk, and I am already too wounded to jump.

No choice!

The ship turns toward the station airlock, ready to blast away, and I cover my head and roll toward the catwalk—

I tumble through the air and land on my back, knocking all the air out of me.

Above me, the ship burns bright and hot, and I clench my eyes closed and throw my arms over my face. I fear I will be burned to death here—

Then the ship is gone, zooming toward the exit.

And I am left, bleeding. In pain. A failure who could save nothing and no one.

REINFORCEMENTS LED BY a man with greedy eyes arrive not five minutes after the Geans flee with the neurobots. I tell them what I can, but Mardoll—who has a stained bandage around her forehead—forces them to leave me alone after I repeat myself for the third time.

I do not tell them about Bruni's neurobots. I do not know why I hide that fact, other than that I want to tell Mardoll first. I trust her more than I do these strangers.

Mardoll restitches my leg and wraps the burns on my left hand. Though painful, my wounds are fairly minimal.

Ebba was not so lucky.

"She will recover," Mardoll says, looking at Ebba in the bed next to mine. Her chest is bandaged over two bullet wounds. Her vitals, shown on the monitors at her side, look dire. "She will recover . . ." It sounds more like a wish than true belief.

"Mardoll, about Bruni . . ." I must tell her.

Mardoll shakes her head. "Later, Astrid. Sergey wants to convene what remains of the Council to discuss going after the stolen Muninn." But I can tell from the way she says it that she does not believe they will be able to do anything.

My fault that the Geans have the neurobots. And still, I do not know why they wanted them so badly. Or *who* wanted them.

"You do not want to chase after them?" I ask.

"It's not about what I want." Mardoll never looks away from Ebba. "They took two dozen vials. Not all of them, but many important lines . . . and we have already lost so much." She closes her eyes against a tremor that runs through her body, and I know she is thinking of Bruni. "But can we risk even more to get those two dozen back?" When she opens her eyes, her attention is trained solely on me. "You've seen how we live. How we take what no one else wants, just to survive. How could we ever stand up against the Geans with what little we scavenge from their leavings?"

I do not answer. It is a debate I am sure Mardoll has no answer for either.

After a moment, she stands and leaves the infirmary.

The only noise is the beeping from Ebba's monitors.

I close my eyes and think of the cool mornings in the gun range with Bruni. The blue world of the algae vats. The little room, like a small closet, I was allowed to call my own.

And then the officer's words: *We will return and hunt down the girl after we—*

They will not stop until they have me. No matter where we raid, they will be waiting for me. They will kill the Skadivolk, as they did Bruni, just to have me. My very presence brings the moonborn more trouble than they can bear.

But where else can I go?

Earth is not an option, and I never wanted to return to Mars. I wanted to stay here with the Skadivolk. Find a family. A home.

But not at the cost of their lives and livelihood.

The Muninn . . . The moonborn need the neurobots. And while I do not know why the Geans want them, having seen what they can do through accessing Bruni's memories, I do not want the Control Agency Police to have them.

Because if the cappos have them, who else will? The Warlord? Hypocritical Aunt Marshae?

If she had access to the neurobots, what else could she implant in the minds of Little Sisters without their even knowing? Could they be the final lock on freedom in the Sisterhood that she craves?

It hardly feels like a choice.

We have to go, brother.

Ringer floods me with his agreement.

IT IS BRUNI'S map that takes me back to the dock. Bruni's hands that launch the ship. Now, alone in my patchwork Skadivolk craft, watching the medical station disappear among the other detritus orbiting Earth, I am not surprised to receive a communication request.

But I deny it all the same.

What could I tell Mardoll that she would understand? That I am a danger to them? That I am returning to Mars, not just to keep them from being a target of the cappos again but to find and return their Muninn to them?

What could she tell me that I have not already thought myself? I know how small the chances of recovering the neurobots are. I know how dangerous returning to Mars is. But I cannot allow any Gean—much less Aunt Marshae—access to the neurobots if there is anything I can do to stop it.

Even if I must throw myself back into the nest of vipers . . .

I watch the screen and count my breaths with my hand pressed to my midsection. Eventually, the faint light of the communications request disappears, leaving only the blank monitor like a dark mirror.

Let me watch over us, little sister, Ringer says, and I am all too happy to allow him the use of my body as I seek shelter in the soft darkness of my mind. It is the only refuge I will find, and Ringer is the only loyal friend I have left in the universe.

CHAPTER 9
THE TWINS

Think of the Control Agency Police as a concerned uncle. Vigilance builds obedience, which is why our surveillance extends everywhere and to everyone. The subordinate cleaning the latrines, the man at the bar listening to the newscast, the fellow digging through your trash—they might be watching you, yes, but also watching out for you. The Goddess sets the path through the Warlord and the Sisterhood. We make sure none stray from that path.

Admiral Drucker, head of the Control Agency Police

Lily writes a private message to Admiral Drucker, imploring him to strengthen the relationship between them "for the future." While the Mother is the only member of the Sisterhood allowed to write—other than the power-sucking, boot-licking Aunts, of course—I'm pretty sure she'd end up with another row of fingernail-shaped scars on her forearm if Aunt Marshae knew Lily was cutting her out of the equation.

Drucker's more than happy to respond. He's a constant mix of quotes from the Canon interspersed with his beliefs regarding the power of masculinity. Lily engages with his madness like she buys it. After three godsdamned days of the stomach-churning messages, he suggests what we need for the Harbinger's plan to work: an invitation to his farmstead.

According to Sorrel, the farm is impenetrable, part-time headquarters of the Control Agency Police and part-time temple where Drucker and his Disciples of Judeth friends get up to some weird traditionalist shit. If not for Lily, we wouldn't be getting in at all.

"I'll let the Harbinger know the plan is on." In her pheromones, I smell the smallest spike of mistrust. But it is gone as quickly as it appeared. Even Lily knows we need the Black Hive for our plan to work.

ADMIRAL DRUCKER'S ESTATE is south of Olympus Mons in the highlands, among some of the first land ever settled on Mars. I take a podship from the Temple with three of my White Guards, watching the domed city with its grasping starscrapers fade into the rocky slopes of the mountain. I know we've arrived when, an hour later, the land has flattened to great grasslands interspersed with tilled fields.

The compound—for I know little else to call it—sits atop a gentle hill, a cluster of five buildings set over a patchwork quilt of terrain growing various crops—waving golden wheat, tall green stalks of corn, and low shrubs laden with white cotton. The building farthest back on the estate belches thick black smoke from a clay chimney, its corrugated metal siding hiding whatever industrial work goes on inside from view. It's likely a traditionalist like Drucker would have it simply to contribute to Mars's atmosphere in an attempt to warm the planet using the greenhouse effect. Too little, too late, I fear; when the dome went up over Olympus Mons, the way of the future became the hermium-powered force field.

We land in the center of the property, the few workers in homespun clothing scattering as the podship comes to rest. Castor sends me a small pulse of reassurance; I hadn't even realized I *was* worried until I felt his support.

So much hinges on today's performance.

Two of my White Guards, Rei and Danmus, exit before me, taking a moment to steady themselves in the lower gravity of the unaltered countryside before sweeping the vicinity with their hawklike gaze. When it's deemed safe, I follow after them, and Castor trails behind.

Admiral Drucker waits outside for us, surrounded by plainclothes officers of the Control Agency Police. His navy dress uniform is pristine but incongruous with the rural setting and his dressed-down agents. Already my eyes ache from the sharp sunlight. I chose to wear white leather boots, gloves, and a high-necked silk dress with a hem that falls to my ankles, not knowing whether we would be traipsing through fields in Mars's twelve-hour daylight. Seeing Drucker like this makes me wonder if I should've worn something nicer.

"Mother Lilian I," Drucker says, "welcome to my private home." His hand pressed to his chest, he bows at the waist, low and respectful. I smile at him but do not dip my head; currently, I outrank him. "Allow me." His face twisted with a smile that shows his too-large teeth, he offers me his arm. I allow him to guide me toward the most ornate building of Martian stone.

"Beautiful, isn't it?" Admiral Drucker asks. He nods toward various constructions, explaining their uses. "In the barn, we keep alpacas. Their coats make a fine weave . . ."

I listen to him drone as I wonder if Sorrel is nearby and ready.

When we come to the house, Drucker opens the door for me and murmurs at his officers, "Remain here unless I call for you." Four men settle in various places on the porch, while two stride off toward the barn.

The entrance hall to the house is hideously overdone, the doors and floors all thick imported wood. Plush navy rugs muffle our footsteps, set against cobalt wallpaper with a faint damask pattern. A curling staircase of wrought iron painted gold reaches up to the second level. There's the traditional portrait of the Warlord on the wall opposite the entrance, but it's small and easily overlooked. Hanging high above as the centerpiece of the space is a twelve-foot painting of a woman holding something pink on a platter—

Oh. It's Sister Marian, the first Mother, holding a knife in one hand and her tongue in the other. Blood waterfalls down her chin, staining the neck of her white dress into watery pink.

Out of the corner of my eye, I catch Drucker watching me. "The Mother," he says, as if out of breath, "is the pinnacle of what it means to be a woman. The closest to the Goddess's feminine divinity here among the mortals."

Deep inside, the image disgusts me—the violence against a woman's right to communicate offensive at my core—but I have grown to know Drucker over the course of our conversations together, and he prefers a Mother who is pious and fervent. I let tears rise to my eyes and clasp my hands beneath my chin, as if called to pray by the haunting beauty of the painting. Bowing my head, I stand silently for several long moments.

Finally pleased, he claps his hands together. "Come," he says, gesturing to the staircase. "I have lunch waiting, and afterward . . ." He trails off, making my fingers itch.

He leads me up the golden stairs at a relaxed pace. Dark wood paneling lines the upper floor's hallway, the walls decorated sparsely with other paintings—all religious scenes, noteworthy only for their focus on gory details. Chandeliers dripping with crystals hang from the high ceilings, while the majority of the doors are closed and codelocked. Remembering Sorrel's suspicions, I wonder what he's hiding behind them.

By the time we stop before the sliding doors to the dining room, I am exhausted by his show of wealth. "I dismissed my servants so we might have privacy." Drucker gestures to the hallway. "Your entourage may remain here while we eat."

Entourage, he says of my three White Guards. But after Aunt Marshae had me leave them outside during my dinner with the Warlord, I suspected Drucker would request something like this.

It is only a second, but, sensing my hesitation, he places a hand over his heart. "Surely I am all the protection you need, Mother."

I don't want to offend him—and besides, I need Castor to be able to move about the property freely to help with the mission. With a nod of agreement, I command my White Guards with slight pressure on their neural implants—the connection with them is slippery like oil, and I dislike using it—guiding Rei and Danmus to stand near the doors of the house and Castor to patrol.

Drucker laughs—a single sharp bark like a dog. "I'd thought it a mere rumor, but you *do* have a cockroach guard," he says, eyeing Castor. A ripple of anger passes through my twin, and he stops midstep, hand curling into a fist.

Don't! my pheromones scream. *Don't, please!* I have had years to grow accustomed to masking my emotions, but Castor . . .

Castor continues after Danmus and Rei with Drucker none the wiser to his almost-outburst. I would sigh in relief if I could.

Drucker, with unblinking eyes, watches my face. "The White Guard really are mindless puppets. I still don't know why you'd choose a cockroach, but I suppose if it can fight, it's all the same in the end . . ." When I don't respond, he slides open the door for me.

The dining room is a study in intensity. The walls are lined with mirrors, bouncing the shimmering light of the glass chandelier back and forth and creating an infinity of the people and things within. The central table, long enough for twenty, is gilded with ornate gold leaf and laden with enough food for an army. The matching chairs, of which there are only two, sit at the head and the foot: one for me and one for Drucker.

"Do you like the table? I had it brought from Earth and restored. It used to serve a powerful monarch. I'd like to think some of his hunger still resides in this old wood . . ."

The ceiling is vaulted and appears to be made of glass, but instead of showing the Martian sky above, it projects a scene of burning stars in the black of space. Whether it's a recording or an animation, it is at once calming with the glittering Milky Way and twinkling stars that make me feel like we're on a ship. Without a doubt, it's the only truly beautiful thing in Drucker's house.

That serenity instantly disappears with the sound of Drucker locking the door behind us.

"Now," he says, "shall we get to know each other?"

DRUCKER'S HOMESTEAD IS like a land out of time. The house is hideous, proving that Gean society is corrupt to the bone, squandering its resources in this repulsive travesty for one powerful man's pleasure instead of attending to the needs of the many. The air smells like farm animals, smog, and shit. Why anyone would want to live like this is beyond me.

I split from Danmus and Rei as soon as I can. Not even one hallway over, I hear them laughing about Drucker calling me a cockroach, but with the Harbinger's plan, I don't have time to deal with their shit. I head downstairs to the basement.

Sorrel showed me a blueprint of the farm and gave me the code to the security system. When I find the security panel, I tap in the code and hold my breath; there's always the chance that the passcode is old—or a trap. The Harbinger told me he'd carved it out of a cappo who ran afoul of the Black Hive.

The system panel turns green, which means the entrance to the sewage tunnel is unlocked.

Clear, I message Sorrel on my compad.

The Harbinger instructed me to meet him in the chapel, which Drucker pointed out during our brief tour on the way in. From where Sorrel was positioned at the sewage exit before the system went down, he should arrive in five minutes. I cut through the house and slip outside, past Danmus and Rei sitting on the porch with the four men Drucker left there, heading straight for the small stone building that sits beneath a shady tree. They call after me, but I ignore them—our usual interaction. They don't follow.

There's a man chopping wood near the fence and a woman with a basket of cloth entering the barn, but neither of them pays me any mind. They're both caught up in their simple tasks.

The interior of the chapel is cold, the glass windowpanes streaked sooty gray from candle smoke. Dirt has been tracked in on the floor, and the pews are dusty. The whole place reeks of abandonment. I scuff my boot against the concrete floor, littered with old leaves.

When Sorrel emerges from the sacristy, the light bouncing off his green eyes is the first thing I see. The dark Gean street clothes he wears help him blend into the shadows, and beneath the hood of his coat, his skin is icy pale except for the ropy red scar that runs from his jaw to his temple. He looks like a spirit that haunts this forgotten place.

"Strange, isn't it," he asks, his smooth voice echoing through the hollow space, "for such a religious man to leave his chapel in disrepair?"

I send him a pulse of agreement through my pheromones when he reaches my side. "I was thinking the same thing . . ."

"It's because," Sorrel says, his lips curling playfully, "this is not truly a chapel."

He leads me up the apse platform. He bends down to shove a rug aside, revealing a trapdoor beneath. It opens easily; the hinges don't even squeak, they're so well-oiled and often used. The opening descends into liquid darkness.

Then a long, low moan comes from the pit.

"What the fuck—"

Sorrel's mouth splits in a grin.

AS DRUCKER LEADS me to my chair, I survey the room with new eyes. There are no windows, and only the one door. I know he locked it. But why?

I smooth my skirt before sitting. He doesn't withdraw to his side of the table.

"Allow me to provide for our most exquisite Mother . . ." Drucker picks up my empty plate and heaps it high with a variety of things—fresh greens with baby tomatoes, flatbread with cloves of garlic baked in, a red meat sliced thin enough to see the light through it. After setting it before me, he takes an already opened bottle of wine from a golden bucket of ice and pours it into a crystal glass. I'm pointedly reminded of the last time I saw him holding a wine bottle.

I smile my thanks, but still, he does not leave my side.

"This room, like all the others in my home, is soundproof," he says, and I am so startled by the change of topic that I can do nothing but gape at him.

Act, you idiot. The reason I came was to get him alone—to convince him to support me over Aunt Marshae. And if I can't do that with charm, Sorrel and Castor will ensure his cooperation with blackmail. *But let's start with charm.* I withdraw the compad from my pocket in order to converse with him.

"There's no need for a machine to mediate between man and woman when flesh speaks the one true tongue." He snatches the compad from my hands before I'm able to type my first word.

Again, I'm caught off guard. I intentionally didn't bring an Aunt with me so that Drucker and I would be able to keep whatever was said between us private—I don't trust anyone not to report back to Aunt Marshae—but now I feel foolish. He doesn't speak the Sisterhood hand language, so how are we to communicate without the compad?

Perhaps he wishes to eat first. I gesture toward the elaborately set table, but his hand—quick as a striking snake—catches my chin. "Talk to me, Mother," he says, forcing me to look at him. I freeze, fingers digging into the arms of the chair. He has me blocked between the table and his body; if I wanted to get up, I'd have to shove him aside, and I'm not sure I can. When I don't respond, he leans toward me until his face is inches from mine. Then he whispers: "I know you can speak." His breath is sour.

I jerk my face away from him and grit my teeth. I don't speak because, in this moment, I'm too scared to say a thing.

Castor! I call through the implant and my pheromones. *Castor?* There's no response. He's too far away . . . helping Sorrel, as was the plan. *Damn.*

Drucker's face grows darker when he doesn't get the response he wants. "Then perhaps I should tell you what else I know."

Slowly, I begin to wonder . . . if this is less a meeting with Drucker and more an interrogation by the head of the Control Agency Police.

SORREL GESTURES FOR me to take the lead, down a set of stone stairs and into a tunnel that reminds me far too much of the Under on Ceres. My eyes adjust quickly, pupils widening to swallow the dark. The dirt-packed path splits off in several different directions. Sorrel closes the trapdoor behind us before hurrying to catch up with me.

"All of the buildings are connected underground," he says, "but we need to be careful of his spies."

"And he keeps his secrets down here?" I ask.

Sorrel says nothing. We round a corner, and he hastily pushes me up against the wall. Ahead at a crossroads, two men pass by with flashlights, their words echoing in the close tunnels.

"—interrogating her now—"

Then they're gone, and their discussion with them.

The Harbinger gestures me forward, and we continue. A few minutes later, the stench of unwashed bodies and human waste hits me with the physical force of a wall, and I fight the urge to gag. Makes me miss the smell of horse shit and smog.

"What the fuck . . ."

"They don't call him the Soulreader for nothing," Sorrel whispers before slipping in front of me to lead the way. I follow him with a hand over my nose and mouth.

We enter what I can only describe as hell. Cells line both sides of the passageway, thick iron doors with hefty locks. The moaning, a constant song of this place, abruptly stops as soon as the prisoners hear us coming. Better to go unnoticed completely . . .

Sorrel waits until we're past to speak again. "Agents informed me he keeps a filing room down here with records of his targets—people he's disappeared, blackmail on others, that sort of thing. You'll make digital copies and take them to Lily to use in her negotiations. I'll leave the way I came."

In the next hallway is a single wooden door—nice, but only when compared to the metal slabs holding prisoners. Even with the stench behind us, I feel like it's gotten into my mouth and eyes, and it takes me far too long to realize Sorrel's staring at me expectantly.

"Castor, the lock . . ."

He offers me the hilt of a mercurial blade. He might have a neural implant, but he doesn't use the weapon, not like Ofiera and I do. I take the hilt, summon the blade in the form of a dagger, and slice through the lock.

The door swings open on what looks like a normal office—a desk in the middle covered with neatly organized stacks of paper, a plush chair, and row after row of filing cabinets. I step in to begin searching for blackmail material, but there's something in the stiff way Sorrel holds his body and the smell of concern in his pheromones that sets me off.

"What's wrong?"

Sorrel's gaze never moves from the door at the back of the room. "That's not in the blueprints."

"OH, LITTLE SISTER Lily . . . watching you become Mother Lilian I has been a well of inspiration," Admiral Drucker says. Ignoring the food, he leans on the edge of the table near me, clasping his hands together in front of him. Keeping me trapped in the chair with his bulk. "No one, least of all me, believed you would achieve it, especially after that unpleasantness with Mother Isabel III . . ." He twists his face into an exaggerated frown. "Sad, wasn't it, how she reneged on her deal with the cockroaches?"

I look up at him, refusing to cower. Refusing to show him fear.

"But then you crossed paths with the First Sister of Ceres, and your star began to rise." A lump in my throat grows at the mention of Astrid. "Compared to her, you were an absolute delight! And such a joy to work with, or so report your Aunties."

Aunt Marshae—she must be how he knows all of this. If she's an informant for the Control Agency, he might return the favor by using his secret police to make her enemies disappear. Aunt Tamar said Marshae was working with him. I must tell her when—*if*, a little part of me whispers—I make it out of here.

"You have so many traits that make you a wonderful Mother." He counts them off on his fingers. "Obedience. Empathy. Humility. Modesty." His hand moves toward my face, and I flinch; his eyes seem to glow at the knowledge that I'm afraid of him. "Affection." He breathes the word as his clammy fingers brush against my skin.

"But you have many traits that are undesirable."

Something inside me burns at that word—*undesirable.* I look at the nearby silverware, at the knife sharp enough to cut meat. Could I reach it before he stopped me? Even if he's slight by military standards, he's both larger and stronger than I am. Would I be able to use it before he hurt me?

"The problem is your blood," Drucker says. "The problem is your brother."

I TIGHTEN MY grip on the mercurial blade. There's no telling what's behind that door.

Ready? I ask Sorrel through my pheromones.

I feel him push me onward through both my neural implant and his pheromones. It's a strange sensation I can't focus on as I kick open the door and find—

A bedroom?

Everything is white, from the soft carpet to the wide bed with its gauzy canopy. There's a short desk and a little chair in the corner, but the only book present is the Canon. Though there are curtains hanging from rods, the windows behind them are mere paintings of green rolling hills and a sunny sky. Above the bed, the wall is covered in photos—all of them women in white. One of them is Lily.

They're all the Mothers.

The clank of a chain catches my attention, and I spin toward—

Dark hair framing a pale face. A white dress edged in lace.

For a moment, all I see is my sister. Then the girl, not yet a teenager, forces herself to smile with her mouth open, and—

Even Sorrel's pheromones spike with horror. "Heart of the universe," he whispers in shock.

The girl has no tongue. And I left my twin alone with the man who did that to her.

"Lily!" Her name slips through my teeth like a prayer. I spin toward the door—

Sorrel catches my biceps and holds tightly. "What do you think you're doing?"

"Pollux is—"

"She's the Mother. Do you really think Drucker would be foolish enough to kill her?"

I look at the bed, at all the Mothers hanging on the wall above. No, I don't think he'd kill Lily, but there are plenty of other types of harm he could do.

"Help me secure the girl," Sorrel says, heedless of the agony I feel. "She's all the evidence we need of Drucker's corruption *and more.*"

But right now? I don't give a fuck about evidence.

I rip my arm out of his grip and sprint through the room.

"You're going to fuck everything up!" Sorrel calls after me, but I run on anyway.

I SHAKE MY head vehemently. Deny it. I have to deny it. If he knows—he does—he could ruin me. Ruin everything.

"Don't bother denying," Drucker says. My discomfort brings him pleasure; I can see it in the shine of his beady blue eyes. "The background you used during your Sisterhood intake interview was too sparse in places, too specific in others. The surgery you had as a Little Sister— while your physical state *could* be explained by growing up without grav- ity medication in an unaltered settlement, the difference in your body compared to . . . normal patients was remarkable enough for it to be noted." He lists these things as if they're nothing. As if it is not my life's work that he's ruining.

"Then there's your desire to work with the Asters, the very reason for your falling-out with Mother Isabel III. Several people overheard you fighting with her, saying some very noteworthy things. And your movements—no matter where you are, you *constantly* move about, visit- ing any place it wouldn't be strange to meet with an Aster." He shakes his head as if he pities me. "Perhaps others wouldn't put the pieces together, but I . . . I've been doing this for many, many years, Mother. I *know* what you are."

My brother . . . he knows about Castor . . . he knows about me . . .

It's all over. My blood is ice-cold. *He can demand anything from you, and you will have to give it.*

I slump in the chair, numb.

"Say something, damn you!" Drucker screams.

Despite my desire not to cower, I startle and lean as far away from him as I can.

"*Speak!*" he snarls, as if I'm a dog.

What did he say earlier—that this room was soundproof? Which means no one will be able to hear me speak. Or scream.

"What do you want me to say!" I finally snap.

Drucker springs to his feet as if pushed back by my words. But his face . . . his face is soft with rapture.

"Beautiful," he whispers. "Your voice is beautiful . . ."

"Is that it?" I ask. "You wanted to hear me speak out loud?" He doesn't answer, simply watches as I lean forward in the chair. "Why all *this*, then? Why force me to leave my White Guards behind to be alone with you?"

His answer, when it comes, is soft. "Did you learn nothing from what I told you in our messages?" he asks, and I think back to his words—his sickening assertions that men, like Mars, were meant to conquer.

And women are like Earth. Enduring. Fertile. In need of protection. A challenge.

Does he truly believe that, or were our discussions some sort of game to him? *I can read people like books,* he told me. They call him the Soulreader. Maybe that was the only grain of truth in our conversation.

"I am the head of the Control Agency Police. The knowledge I gather protects me. Insulates me. Makes me more powerful than even the Warlord." He watches my face—just like he's been doing all along, I realize.

"The things you've said . . ." Calling Castor a cockroach. Bringing up Mother Isabel and Astrid. Alluding to Aunt Marshae. *He's testing me.*

"You're right about one thing, Mother. You and I will be working together a lot in the future. I want to make sure that you're . . . amenable to my work style." He cups my cheek, his thumb brushing the edge of my lips. When I don't jerk away, he slips his finger between my lips and meets my teeth.

"Now," he says in a breathy whisper, "let me see your tongue."

I grab the knife from the table, but my hand is hardly around the handle before his is on my neck—

"Yes!" he roars. "Yes! This is the fight I wanted to see from you!"

His grip tightens on my throat, and while I try to drive the knife toward him, he catches my hand and holds it so tightly that my weapon is useless. He is stronger—he is more powerful—

"I will have you as I want you!"

He moves me like a dance partner, yanking me from the chair and shoving me backward onto the table, food and wine and place settings flying. I stare past him, and I don't know if the stars I see are from the mural on the ceiling or my lack of oxygen—I kick and struggle to no avail—my vision darkens—

The door explodes open behind him. He releases my throat, and I gasp in a much-needed breath of air.

"What in the withering hell is this!" Drucker snarls.

When my vision clears, I find Castor covered in dirt and sweating, having cut through the locked door with a glowing mercurial blade.

Then he points it at Drucker.

"GET THE FUCK away from her," I growl.

Lily trembles on the table, her pheromones a barrage of relief.

But Drucker doesn't do as I command. I see his grub-pale hand move to grab Lily, hear her sharp intake of breath—

I raise the blade and—

"Watch out!" Lily screams.

Something strikes the back of my head. I hit the floor hard, mercurial blade spinning away from me, before my arms are wrenched behind my back and cuffed.

"You couldn't have done that *before* he destroyed my door?" Drucker yells, and with the pulsing in my head, his voice comes to me, strange and amplified. "It's not like I can get another one when the Earthen rain forest has been annihilated, you worthless cretins."

A trap . . . I ran *into a fucking trap.*

A pair of men pull me to my knees. One of them fists his hand in my hair to keep me looking forward. I almost vomit from the pain in my head. Drucker waves them away, but they don't go far. Even though I'm kneeling, my legs are unbound. I could try to run for it, but I'm not stupid enough to think they don't have weapons.

Drucker pauses on his way over to me, nudging the hilt of the mercurial blade with the toe of his boot. "Interesting . . ."

I try to keep my face blank like Lily does. Try to remember how I lived before I painstakingly memorized and began to mimic human expression. But between the rage rushing in my veins and the fear for my sister, I'm afraid I'm open for anyone to read.

"So the cockroaches have Icarii technology, do they?" Drucker pulls something out of his pocket—for a moment, I'm scared it's a gun, and I'm about to lose my life right here, right now. But it's some sort of communicator. To call for more cappos?

"Show our *guest* here to his private room," he says to his men, prodding at the communicator. *To call for master torturers* is the likely answer to my question. "I'm going to continue my discussion with the Mother, which I think will be much more . . . fruitful . . . now that she's seen a taste of what we can do."

No! *I can't leave Lily*, no matter what. Not when I've seen what this sick bastard is capable of. When his men grab me, I struggle.

Drucker, frustrated, grunts and smacks the side of the communicator. "What's wrong with this damn thing?"

If his communicator isn't working . . . My pulse races. Sorrel must be nearby. The Harbinger has one of my scrambler boxes to take out communication devices. And if he's here, then maybe I'm *not* going to die today . . .

His men pause, their hands in my armpits.

"Um . . . sir?"

When I calm, I realize that someone has slipped into the room like a shadow. Their footsteps are so light, they make no noise on the hardwood floor—but I don't need to look to know who it is. I smell them, dirt and sweat and something sickly sweet from the tunnels.

Drucker's face goes pale, then bright red. Lily's eyes are wide with horror.

The little girl in the stained white dress walks calmly toward Drucker.

And if she's here, then Sorrel is—

"What are *you* doing—" Drucker cuts off, rat eyes moving to the guards. "Get out! Take him and *get the fuck out!*"

They haul me up, but before I've gotten my legs beneath me, I hear something heavy speeding through the air—then one of my guards coughs a spray of blood and falls face-forward to the ground. The other releases me, and I stumble. "Hey!" he screams, turning just in time to get an axe in the face.

The weapon is jerked out of Sorrel's hand as the big man falls, his face split in two like a log of wood.

Behind me, Lily screams. I turn to find Drucker pulling her to her feet to use as a shield. Suddenly, all bets are off as to whether he'd kill the Mother or not.

My hands still cuffed behind my back, I rush across the room, my only hope to tackle him—and spot the military-issue energy pistol trained on me over Lily's shoulder at the last second.

"Fuck!"

I drop to the ground and roll, the pain in my head flaring in intensity. The laser shot goes wide overhead, and I prepare for the second shot to hit me—

Drucker screams. Releases Lily. She falls, temple striking the table before she crumples to the floor.

"No!" I cry.

But Drucker doesn't fire even when I'm in the open. He turns to look at the little girl—the one even I'd forgotten—behind him.

There's a knife in his back.

He coughs. A spatter of red dots his lips. And the little girl . . . smiles.

"Good job!" the Harbinger calls to her, pulling the woodcutting axe from the body of the cappo and stepping toward Drucker. "Now get out of here and hide!"

The girl does as she's told and flees as quickly as she can.

"Castor, secure Lily."

He doesn't have to tell me twice.

DRUCKER STUMBLES AWAY from the table, a meat-carving knife protruding from his back. That little girl—too skinny, too dirty—grins as she runs past him. Where did she come from? Who—

I feel like vomiting when I look around. My ears are ringing, and blood leaks into my right eye. I can't concentrate. Did I crack my skull?

Then Castor's kneeling beside me, freeing his left wrist from a pair of handcuffs. Must've gotten the key off the dead guards. "Are you all right?"

I don't know how to answer that. Perhaps the pain I radiate in my pheromones is answer enough. He tries to pull me into his arms—to gather me up and take me away?—but I place a hand on his chest and push him back.

I want to see this . . .

The little girl does as well, it seems. She lingers in the doorway, big eyes watchful, as Drucker, ignoring the knife in his back, turns toward Sorrel. With a smirk that pulls the scar on his face taut, Sorrel spins the axe in his hand. But even if Drucker is wounded, he has a gun—

Drucker pulls the trigger. Sorrel ducks the shot and, like a starving panther of sinew and sharp bones, fluidly darts toward Drucker in a crouch. From one heartbeat to the next, Sorrel tackles Drucker across his middle, knocking him onto his back and driving the knife in deeper. Drucker screams in agony, and the pistol spins away from his hand.

I lose track of what's happening, arms and legs shifting and blocking, bodies intertwining, painted red. Sorrel clings to Drucker's chest, crouching over him like a wild animal at a meal. Drucker punches him with a meaty fist, then again—how is Sorrel still holding on?—and then I see the axe in Sorrel's hands, driving downward into Drucker's stomach—

Again. And again. Into stomach and chest. Into the wounds already sliced open.

The sounds are wet and rounded, slippery skin on skin, fists sloppy with gore, the sound of a slaughter as the fight turns to murder—

Drucker lets out a single moan—and falls silent.

Breathing heavily, Sorrel stands from Drucker's corpse, guts splayed around him in an aura of carnage. From his face to his limbs, the Harbinger is covered in blood like a butcher. He drops two things to the floor—one, the bloody axe, while the other is something meaty, an unidentifiable organ clawed to shreds.

It hits me all at once: What this means for me. What this means for all of Mars.

Admiral Drucker, heir to Warlord Vaughn, is dead.

"What have we done . . ." My voice is soft, shaking with the fear I feel.

Sorrel's voice is a warning hiss when he answers, "Why don't you ask Castor?"

"ME?"

"Who else?" The Harbinger's voice is low. Dangerous. He stalks toward me, painted in blood, and I . . . I flinch.

I feel a mounting pressure from him. Beneath the overwhelming iron tang of the blood, he smells like a threat. "*You* abandoned the plan. *You* ran into a trap." He stops, looming above me. "If not for you giving in to your baser emotions, I wouldn't have had to clean up *your fucking mess.*"

Lily uses the table to pull herself to her feet. "We don't have time for this," she gasps out. Her eyes are unfocused—or on something beyond what we can see. "The White Guards—they're alert for some reason. I can feel them. They're on their way here . . ." Her eyes cut to the Harbinger. "The secret police must know something's wrong too . . ."

The Harbinger's lip curls in a sneer. He glares down at me, eyes shining, for a cutting moment. I feel as if he's judged me and has found me . . . inadequate.

I push myself to my knees, desperate to make the situation better. "S-Sorrel, I . . ." I grasp for his jacket, anything to hold on to.

"If I get caught escaping," he says, so soft I can hardly hear him, "that will be your fault too."

That violent smell intensifies. "Sorrel—" Lily chokes out.

"Use this for your alibi," he tells Lily before his fist crashes against my face—and I fall into black.

CHAPTER 10

LUCE

Mission Parameters: At 0430 hours, teams shall enter Area of Operations Charlie-Uniform. Rules of engagement are to consider all Alphas armed, proceed accordingly, and don't hesitate to use lethal force if needed. Let's show these roaches what Gean might looks like! Mars conquers!

Gean radio chatter

"Luce."

My name grabs me with both hands and pulls me from the sea cave I shared with Lito as a child, dreams of longing shattered. I jerk upright in my chair—I fell asleep at the desk again, drowned by images of violence, and my back is aching because of it.

The bombing in Cytherea. Broken bodies in the streets. Protests for Asters, suddenly turned against them. And worryingly, so many of our agents on Mars missing. So many Asters snatched from their homes. Any who resist are shot, their bodies left in the streets as a warning to others. We have no idea where they're being taken.

All a response to Admiral Drucker's assassination, and the image of an Aster—Sorrel—fleeing the scene.

There is nowhere safe for Asters now—among the Geans or the Icarii. Maybe there never was.

"Luce!"

"Cast—" I begin before it comes to me—he's gone. He left with the Aster who started all this. With the man who was all too happy to sacrifice my brother's life.

"Hemlock?" My mouth is scummy. I stretch, my back pops, and I reach for my cane. Might need one of the pain patches in the top drawer of my nightstand. The half dozen floating screens hovering over my desk continue their work, parsing information from the news, private chats, and Hemlock's server. There's something off there, something new, but my brain is sluggish with sleep . . .

"Lucinia, we have to leave." I've never heard Hemlock sound so full of fear, but I can't pull my eyes from the screens. "The Under is no longer safe."

"What?" I search the chatter, following the patterns, and—Hemlock turns off my computer.

"Hey!"

"You're not listening." His black eyes cut through the thick bone of my sternum and go straight to my heart. "Purge your machine. Gather what you can't live without." I'm arrested by his gaze, his face twisted with a look I've never seen him wear before. "They're coming for us."

I don't have to ask who. It all falls into place.

"Where should I—"

"Meet me in Mithridatism. We'll go to the private dock near tunnel Two B after that. I've called for Dire—he's coming with a convoy, but we must take a ship to meet him and—"

"What about those in—"

"Those able are helping to evacuate those who can be moved—"

"And those who can't be moved?"

Hemlock's entire face trembles as if I struck him. He can't say it. I don't want him to say it.

Those who can't be moved will be left behind.

The Geans will likely arrest them, but moving them quickly would lead to their deaths *for certain.*

"I have to take care of the servers—make sure the Geans can't salvage anything."

"What about Hiro—" And our other agents. What will they do without the private server connecting them?

In my black-and-white world, Hemlock is always colorless, but somehow he grows even paler at my question, the contrast stark between his skin and his velvet suit. "There are backups on Autarkeia. We'll have to go there . . ." He shakes his head, dispelling the thought. "But first we have to make it off Ceres alive."

"Right."

All grace and poise, Hemlock has never moved quickly. I suspect, though I've never asked, he *can't* move with any speed after what Val Akira Labs did to him. Even when he leaves my room, his hastiness makes his matchstick legs shake like a marionette controlled by an amateur puppeteer. The fact that he's burning himself at both ends speaks to how dire the situation is.

First things first. With a kick of my legs, I roll my chair to my nightstand, retrieve a pain patch, and slap it on my shoulder. Immediately it numbs the crunching, grinding feeling in my back and hips. Now for the data.

People have accused Hemlock of being paranoid, but I like to think of it more as *obsessive preparedness.* For the past thirty years, he's been braced for something like this. The fact that it's only now coming to pass is, in my opinion, a testament to his empire. Grabbing my cane—it glows at my touch, illuminating the terrarium within—I make my way to my dresser by the door. In the bottom drawer, wrapped in a soft sweater, is a brick of a device that'll destroy any electronic it's placed against.

I swipe the brick over my desktop. The screens flicker and disappear like stars winking out of existence.

Now for my personal compad. It wakes at my touch, connecting to

Hemlock's server and displaying my encoded contacts. No conversation saves itself once an agent has received it, and there's nothing new from Hiro for me to read, so my screen is blank except for a code in all capitals at the top: CODE O2V. I could hazard a pretty damn good guess at what it means.

Should I contact Hiro? Should I warn them of all that's happening? Though if Hemlock's operation is potentially compromised . . .

No, it's best to simply let them go. *I'm sorry, Hiro*, I think as I press the compad to the brick. It glitches out, and I leave the whole pile there, black as night.

I look at the room—my room, I suppose, though the stony walls and cot of a bed lack features to make the place *mine*—and consider what I need to bring with me. The last time I fled my home, all I had were the clothes on my back; this time I at least toss my pain patches and other medication from my nightstand into a shoulder bag. Helping Hemlock and the others is more important than anything else.

I brace myself on the armrests of the gravchair and settle in, resting my cane across my lap. I know I'm supposed to meet Hemlock in Mithridatism, but that's not my first stop. I head for the makeshift hospital, the chair ghosting over the uneven, rocky ground.

I can smell the hospice before I even enter the hallway, a wet and rotting scent in the otherwise dry tunnels. Healthy Asters swarm the entrance, wheeling away patients or carrying heavy equipment. I keep out of their way until the path is clear.

Inside, there are a dozen or so beds. Until today, they've always been full. Of those who are left, some faces I recognize—like Rose, the young girl I interviewed for our latest video—but many are missing. Already on the ship?

I wheel to the side of Rose's bed and use my cane to lever myself out of the chair. "Come on," I tell her, "let's get you out of here."

Rose drops her eyes and smiles in an embarrassed way, as if I've caught her stealing. "Lucinia," she begins, voice soft—oh, now I realize she's embarrassed *for me*. She reaches up to her head, to where she's brushed her hair to cover her scarred expanse of scalp. No metal plate—not anymore—but no skull beneath either. "I'm not leaving."

"*Of course* you're leaving—" She's the youngest—she just turned twelve. She still has the rest of her life ahead of her, even if it is cut short from the experiments done on her. "Rose . . ."

"Lucinia." She says my name with the same pleading tone with which I say hers.

Then I look around the room at the big black eyes watching us, at the way these people still lie in their beds with blankets pulled up to their chins. None of them plan on leaving. The five remaining Asters are going to stay and take their chances with the Geans.

"Do you remember when we spoke of death, Lucinia?" Rose asks softly. "Do you remember what I told you?"

I close my eyes against the burning of tears. "Yes. You said that being sick means we have less control over our lives, so we have to make our choices where we can."

"I choose to stay, Lucinia." She touches my hand as if *I'm* the one who needs comfort, as if she knows my mind is already reeling for someone to blame. "I can't take the pressure that space travel exerts on the body."

I hold her hand between both of mine. "What if they hurt you?" But I know I'm fighting a losing battle. Who understands pain more than the ill?

Rose just smiles. "You should already be gone, Lucinia. They're probably waiting on you."

The Asters wheeling away patients and taking equipment—were they the last group? "I can take someone in the gravchair," I say. "I can—"

"Go, Lucinia." There's no doubt in Rose's voice. No doubt in the faces surrounding me. They know what's coming—they certainly know their bodies and their illnesses better than I do—and they've chosen to stay.

"May the heart of the universe keep you, Rose," I tell her. Settling back in the gravchair doesn't bring relief, because the ache I feel is lodged in my chest alongside my heart.

"And may the thousand gods watch over you, Lucinia."

My last glimpse of Rose as I wheel out of the room is of her settling back into her bed. Of her wrapping a blanket around her shoulders and over her head the way I used to as a child.

I HAVEN'T BEEN outside of the Under since I arrived six months ago, and the thought of leaving now sends a shock of exhilarating fear through me. It would've been unthinkable in Cytherea for me to stick to the same haunts for more than a couple of weeks, but now, despite my boredom with the Under's uniform appearance, it's become synonymous with safety. Not quite a home, but a place I know no one will hurt me— something that, with parents like mine, I've never taken for granted.

I guide the gravchair into Hemlock's basement. It takes me a few seconds to adjust to the dim lighting, but when I do, I find he's not here, not even lurking like he usually does in the darkest corner with his stacks of books like dusty dark towers. I'm watched by unseeing eyes in porcelain-faced dolls, fuzzy stuffed plushies, and plastic figurines in dynamic poses.

"Hemlock?" I call. No reply comes.

He said to meet him in Mithridatism. Maybe he meant the bar area. Swallowing against the lump in my throat, I guide my chair to the only other exit in the basement. When I come to the concrete landing, I adjust the settings of the gravchair for stairs with the click of a button and start the ascent.

When I reach the stockroom, I navigate through the rows of inventory shelving, half-picked in preparation for our flight, toward the bar. Then a noise—the shattering of glass—stops me in my tracks.

The silence now broken, more noises follow the first: Boots, heavy on the ground. Voices, raised in anger. A single scream, followed by meaty thuds.

And then a person streaks by the doorway too fast for me to see. But I don't need to see them to know who they are. The Geans have arrived.

I back away slowly, letting the shadows swallow me again. I catch glimpses of soldiers in navy destroying everything in their path—smashing bottles of alcohol, flipping furniture, and then a man is tossed into view, bloodied and bruised—my heart jerks into my throat as I fear it's Hemlock or one of the other sick Asters, someone for whom a beating means death—but no, it's just Rostya, one of Hemlock's non-Aster workers topside—

A soldier enters the stockroom.

I swallow a scream that works its way up my throat. The soldier holds up a light, illuminating swaths of canned goods and plastiflex boxes. Finally reaching the door to the basement, I nudge my chair to the landing and switch to stairs mode, but with the soldier *right there*, I'm forced to prioritize silence over speed.

Down, down, down . . . Though my heart rate refuses to descend like my chair. I reach the bottom landing, changing the mode of the chair with another tap—and then a hand claps over my mouth.

"Mmm!"

"Shh!" a voice whispers close to me. "It's me."

Hemlock. The fear gives way to relief in a rush so heady that my body trembles.

Above us, a voice. "I heard something."

Thousand gods.

Hemlock's eyes are swallowing in the dark, shimmering with light like a cat's as he points through the basement. We have to go back through the Under; we don't have a choice—we have to get to tunnel 2B and the ship.

I enter the basement just as I hear boots on the concrete above. With all the speed the gravchair can muster, I slip through the cluttered room as the footsteps hit the stairs, heavier, coming closer—

I reach the door and maneuver the chair into the Under. But Hemlock is no longer at my side.

I turn back to find him looking over his bookshelf, long fingers scrabbling—searching for something. But how important could it be when it's weighed against *his life?*

"Hemlock—" He doesn't seem to hear me, but I don't dare do anything more than whisper.

A soldier enters the room. His flashlight sweeps from one side to the other, missing Hemlock in the most shadowed corner of the library. He steps deeper into the room. Any more, and he'll be between me and Hemlock, effectively cutting us off from each other.

I don't think, I just move. I grab the closest thing to the door—a chipped teacup painted with poppies—and throw it against the wall opposite Hemlock.

"Hey!" The soldier's hand goes to his weapon as he turns in that direction—

And Hemlock moves as fast as he can, limbs shaking with the exertion, as he darts across the basement and into the Under.

The soldier, catching movement, spins back toward us. "They're here!" he screams, loud enough for those upstairs to hear, but the next thing he says is cut off as Hemlock slams the secret door closed.

"Please tell me he won't be able to open the door from that side," I say.

Hemlock flashes me a pained half smile in a weak imitation of Hiro. "You know I don't like to lie to you." A shudder runs through me, but in the next moment Hemlock straightens and walks deeper into the Under. "Follow me."

"Is there another way to the ship from here?"

"Darling Lucinia," Hemlock says, some of his raspy drawl coming back as he calms, "there are a thousand ways in and out of the Under that *siks* will never know."

"I'll take that as a yes."

We're in the next hallway, bioluminescent moss glowing in hexagonal mesh around us, when we hear muffled banging, followed by a sharp crash. We look at each other, but neither of us needs to say what we already know: The soldiers are through the door. They're down here with us. It's only a matter of time before they catch us, and there's no doubt who will win the fight between armed soldiers and two people who have already burned through the majority of their energy for the day.

Our only solace is that we know the tunnels better than they do.

We're silent as we move from the marked to unmarked passageways, leaving the mesh and moss behind for unfinished cold stone. A sheen of sweat coats Hemlock's forehead and rolls down his chin, dripping onto the ground below. At first I just worry for him, and then I worry that the Geans, like bloodhounds, will somehow be able to follow us because of it.

At a junction of tunnels, when Hemlock slows for a rest, I take my cane and stand. The cane casts a glow over the sharp protrusions of the walls. "Your turn," I say, tapping the chair.

It tells me everything about Hemlock's state that he doesn't fight me on it. With a swallowed moan, he sits in the chair. "You must let me know," he says before we continue our reckless fleeing, "if you need it again."

"I will," I say, not adding that, right now, he obviously needs it more than I do. "Pain patches are in the shoulder bag," I offer, but he doesn't take one; after all he's been through, his body reacts strangely to even basic medication.

We walk for what could be ten minutes or ten hours. The Under has always made it impossible for me to tell the time, and neither of us has a compad on us. What if the ship has already launched without us? Would they leave Hemlock behind if it gave them a better chance of meeting the convoy with Dire's ships? I look at Hemlock's stricken face and wonder . . .

Boots come in and out of our hearing. Because the soldiers are onto us, or because the cave system causes strange echoes? I never find out. When the sound grows close, we cling to the stony walls, and I release my cane, plunging us into darkness. We wait only long enough for the sound to grow quieter before we start moving again.

When we come across a path that takes us upward at a noticeable incline, Hemlock shifts in the chair. "It's just ahead," he whispers. "We're so close—"

The sound of boots again, only now the tunnel's too narrow for us to hide. Realizing this, Hemlock grabs my hand and tugs me forward—

A flashlight hits our backs. "Spotted two hostiles!" a high-pitched voice yells.

We round a corner—and find ourselves in a cavern at least forty meters long. There's no ship here, but in the dim lighting I can just make out a set of metal doors on the other side that looks oddly like—

"An elevator?"

"Tunnel Two B and the ship are on the level above us."

As fast as the chair will go, he crosses the cavern. I cling to his side, the cane taking my weight when necessary—but we're not even halfway when the soldier catches up with us.

"Hold it right there!" they shout, voice echoing in the high-ceilinged chamber.

We both freeze. My breath becomes trapped in my rapidly tightening throat. Will this Gean soldier arrest us if we cooperate, or will they drag us to their fellows and perform the same violence I saw on my numerous holoscreens?

The soldier marches toward us. "Hands in the air."

I hold up one hand, the other on my cane. Hemlock's hands remain on the arms of the chair. He looks from me to the cane, his eyes glowing. I feel like he's trying to tell me something, but I don't understand him.

"*Both* hands," the soldier says. "I won't hesitate to shoot."

I lean the cane against Hemlock's chair, but as I'm about to release it, his hand covers mine on the grip. His eyes say everything: *No.*

What the hell is he planning?

"We're going to turn around slowly," Hemlock announces. "We need one hand to do that."

The soldier halts. I hear a click and swallow a whimper of fear. They could shoot us in the back now and damn the consequences.

"Go ahead," they assent at last.

Hemlock gives my hand a final squeeze and, using the gravchair's controls, turns toward the waiting soldier. But as he passes me, he intentionally kicks my cane into the darkness, out of the range of the soldier's flashlight.

"*Run*," he hisses at the exact same time the soldier screeches something I can't make out and their railgun comes up—

I jump to the side and fall. A shot rings out behind me. I chance a quick look over my shoulder—the bullet hit the gravchair, but Hemlock's no longer there—

There's no time for me to find him in the darkness. There's only wild panic as the soldier swings their flashlight back and forth, searching for one of us. On hands and knees, I crawl behind the jut of a rock just as the light passes over me and keeps moving.

I have to keep moving too. I push myself to my feet, my legs and back and shoulders aching past the limits of the pain patch—but I swallow it all down and move as fast as I can toward the elevator doors.

You better meet me there, Hemlock, I think as I move, as the light comes swinging back toward me.

I come up on the elevator doors quickly, almost slamming into them. I catch myself, use the elevator's frame as a brace, and hit the button to summon the damn thing—

The doors open, spilling light into the cavern and illuminating me from head to toe.

"Hey!" the soldier screams, spinning in my direction, and their flashlight beam hits me directly in the face—I'm blinded to what's happening, and I tense, sure I'm about to be shot—

I'm no hero, I shouldn't be here, fleeing, fighting like this, I'm *not my brother*—

A sick crunch. The flashlight falls. My vision clears, and I find Hemlock standing over the crumpled form of the soldier, the bloodied cane illuminating them both.

He says nothing, but he's breathing hard as he limps toward me and the elevator. I grab him, hold on to him like a spaced soldier to a tether, and, leaning together and on the cane, we support each other into the elevator.

As the door closes between us and the chamber, I see more soldiers rushing to back up the one we barely escaped.

"What now?" I gasp against my exhaustion. A headache is forming behind my eyes, and I want nothing more than to crawl into a bed and sleep for the next week.

"Tunnel Two B and the ship should be secure. We'll take the ship to Autarkeia and regroup there," he says, his voice thin and airy. He's used up all of his strength too.

I nod, sweat rolling down my face. "We'll be safe at Autarkeia, right?" I ask, my voice betraying my fatigue.

"Darling Lucinia," Hemlock says with a sigh. "You know I don't like to lie to you."

CHAPTER 11

HIRO

One of my scrollers sent in a Q, asked me why I hate the cockroaches. Because they're fucking roaches, bruv! Cram into tiny spaces. Fucking dirty. Skitter around in the dark. Step on one, and you'll find twelve more. So today . . . today we're gonna do some stomping.

Feed livecast of [ID blocked]: Blackwall user TW1ST3D

As every news channel blames the Asters and plays the drone vid of them entering the building with a suspicious bag between them, I retreat to my lowlevel safe house to rest and regroup.

There's no way the Asters would've bombed that building. What would be the point? How would it benefit them at all, when Souji was set to go before the AEGIS? Maybe if my father had been caught in the explosion, I could believe assassination was the motive, but he was outside by the time it happened. Plus, we were creating sympathy for Asters with our videos, and this . . . this will just make people hate them.

I connect to Hemlock's server and find a dozen unread messages waiting for me. While the majority are from Luce, wanting to know if I'm safe, there is one to all agents from the Harbinger himself.

Sorrel appears furious in the video, his words biting and sharp. "We are the Asters, and we speak with one voice. Let us be clear: We had nothing to do with the bombing in Cytherea. The claim made by the Icarii that we did is a lie, plain and simple."

At the very least, it confirms my suspicions. Hemlock would never do something like this—and while Sorrel might, if the Black Hive is so vehemently denying involvement, that leaves one culprit: my father.

He's not just setting up the Asters to be hated in the public eye, he's making the videos from us—even Lito's transmission—look like terrorist deception meant to sow unrest. He's muddying the waters, hoping the Icarii won't be able to tell the difference between what he did and the lies.

A wave of dizziness hits me with such strength I almost vomit. In its wake is that slimy, guilty feeling that tells me I'm a failure. If I had just done my job, if I had pulled that trigger, would any of this still be happening?

Sorrel's video continues. "I cannot sit idly by as my people are victimized by another Icarii lie. As they are targeted and brutalized for a transgression they didn't commit." His eyes burn with a cold clarity as he leans toward the camera. "If the Icarii people show themselves as enemies of the Asters, we will respond in kind." The video cuts off.

Remembering the way Sorrel answered the last Icarii threat—and the agony Luce went through testing the Genekey virus—I know I have to find proof that my father is the one to blame for all this. That *he's* the one behind the bombing. If I can prove that, there's no way he'll be able to lie his way out of punishment. I can't have that. I can't allow the Black Hive and Sorrel to bring their brand of chaos to the streets of Cytherea.

I drag my tired, broken body to its feet.

There isn't time for rest tonight.

TWENTY-FOUR HOURS AFTER the Val Akira Labs bombing, the news has forgotten about the protest. Vids of masked individuals bullying Asters flood the feed—the bloodier, the better. Asters are cursed, shoved, kicked. Have their wraps ripped off and their goggles stolen to play keep-away with. Beaten until they lie on the ground, crying out for help. Left bruised and bloodied.

Forty-eight hours later, the already postponed AEGIS hearings are put on an indefinite hiatus. A single outlet runs the story ICARII VISIONARY FALSELY ACCUSED BY ASTER TERRORISTS. More follow with variations on it, until the dominating consensus seems to be that, given the recent terror attack and danger posed by the Black Hive, prosecuting Souji val Akira can wait.

I don't sleep. I can't. Every time I close my eyes, I feel the heat of the fire, smell the reek of burning flesh. If I happen to drift off, I'm haunted by nightmares of being forced to listen as Asters are murdered while I can't find them in the labyrinth that the city has become. Awake, I'm reminded why every second I have is one I need to seize with both hands and hold tightly, as my father would advise me. With every hurt Aster, the chance that the Black Hive retaliates increases.

Seventy-two hours later, the report comes in that the head of the Gean Control Agency Police was assassinated by an Aster.

Battle lines are laid down in ink. Politicians talk of laws that will limit Aster gatherings, of deportations, of forced registrations, calling Asters a danger to the public. Imagine, they say, if the Asters had been able to assassinate Souji val Akira.

Four days after the bombing, I ask—*beg*—Luce to help me, to search her networks for any tip we can use. I swallow down a thousand apologies. I've pushed her away, determined to keep my island of grief separate from hers, and now I'm afraid she's my only ally. But she doesn't answer. Punishing me, I suppose, for my silence.

Drained and desperate, I watch the vid of the bombers entering Val Akira Labs again and again. It's on what's likely my hundredth run-through that I finally notice something strange in the shape of the suspects' calves, the point of their toes, and the height of their heels. They're wearing lifts to make them taller, *which Asters would never do*. There are humans under those wraps, pretending to be Asters.

As I prepare to send the evidence to Luce in hope that she can spread it with her network, I notice an emergency ping on my compad. The message is simple—CODE O2V—but it takes me a few seconds to match text to meaning . . . they're evacuating. The violence on Mars has spilled over to Ceres.

After that, Hemlock's server goes down. My only ally disappears.

I ANONYMOUSLY SEND everything I have to the few activist reporters I know of, but immediately realize nothing's going to come of it. There are a thousand conspiracy theories—everything from time travel to aliens—oversaturating the networks. It has the stench of a disinformation team all over it. My father isn't just muddying the waters; he's chumming them to draw out the sharks.

Hoping to find out more about what's happening on Ceres and to reconnect with Hemlock's network, I head for the lowest level, where the Asters pack six to a room. My only contact on Cytherea resides down there, and if the thousand gods have any sort of goodness inside them, Violet will have information. But the chaos I find as soon as I hit the Arber neighborhood stops me cold.

Doors have been broken open. Windows have been smashed. Trash and shards of glass lie discarded in the streets. Shopfronts have been closed, red Xs sprayed over the doors. People in masks rove in groups. I don't spot a single peacekeeper.

The Asters have been abandoned to the mob.

I also don't spot any Asters as I walk deeper into the neighborhood. I catch glimpses of a few faces in windows that disappear behind curtains, but even those are scarce. The community I once saw desperate to thrive is now dead.

When I come to the side street where Violet's apartment is, loud noises from the closely packed square nearby catch my attention. I should keep going, make contact with Violet, but . . . remembering my nightmares, if there's an Aster in trouble, I won't be the person who could help but chooses to ignore it.

Discomfort rises in me, knowing I'm not going to like whatever I find but going anyway. I shove my hands into my pockets as I approach, trying to look calm and collected, feeling anything but.

In the square, no larger than a bullet train car, are a dozen individuals in a circle. Their shouting is wordless, more a senseless baying for blood, and I'm forced to shoulder my way into the pack to see what holds their attention.

There are two Asters trapped in the center—naked, their flesh swollen with a rainbow of bruises. As I open my mouth to yell, a civilian wearing a clown mask darts forward and delivers a sharp kick to one of the Asters' ribs. The Aster coughs blood onto the already-streaked pavement.

"Knock it off!" I shout, shoving two of the closest people aside and breaking into the circle. They seem like teens, so I probably just need to scare them off. I place myself between the Asters and the individual I saw kick one of them. "You hear me? Fuck off!"

The clown holds up their empty hands and shrugs dramatically. Their friends chuckle. One of them holds the Asters' wraps, twisted and tied into something like a noose.

"Fuck you, bruv!" That's the only warning I have before someone rushes at me from my side.

I spin, dodging their sloppy punch, and deliver an uppercut to their stomach. They fall forward, and another kid takes their place. I go low, kicking their legs out from beneath them, but instead of proving I'm a competent fighter and scaring the group off, my actions only seem to invite their challenge.

Three of the bigger figures come at me, and I'm forced into more extreme defensive measures, redirecting wild punches with both forearms. They herd me deeper into the circle, and while two of them are still on the ground, I can't keep track of the other seven *and* fight my opponents.

"Behind—" one of the Asters chokes out before something rails me in the back of the head.

Stars on a black tapestry. I feel like I'm going to vomit when I come to, face pressed into the ground, the group howling around me.

"Aster fucker!"

"Genetic freaks!"

"Cockroaches!"

Definitely didn't think they'd have the stones to attack someone who wasn't an Aster . . . my mistake. One I won't make again.

Less than three meters away, one of the Asters squints at me, big black eyes leaking pained tears. I don't know what I see in their face, their expression strange, but I read some sort of pity there.

I slip my hand into my jacket, feel the hilt of my mercurial blade. It might be my only option—

Feet come slamming down on top of my right wrist—

Red. My whole world is red and fire. But there's no heat, no explosion. Just pain. Overwhelming, paralyzing pain.

Then the Aster three meters away is jerked up, the noose made of their wraps shoved over their head.

Get the fuck up, Hiro. I push myself up with my prosthetic arm, my head spinning dangerously and my vision narrowed. I have to help the Asters, have to save them, have to—have to—

Just then I notice it: an insect—small and brown—crawls over the face of my mask. It pauses over the eye glass, wings flicking. I want to brush it off, but my broken wrist hangs limp at my side and my prosthetic arm is all that's keeping me upright.

Then the screaming starts.

The pack shifts, splits apart. The teen farthest back is covered in wriggling brown bugs the size of my thumb. *Cockroaches.* The kid in the clown mask rushes to help them, tries to brush the bugs off, but the cockroaches crawl up Clown Mask's arm and swarm toward the revealed skin of their hands and neck.

The cockroaches crawl underneath their mask. The kid starts screaming too.

My instincts tell me to flee, but I'm stuck, horrified, as both teens hit the ground, ripping their masks off, scratching at their faces until there are raw, red furrows from their nails. The cockroaches dig into their skin—biting? Stinging?—and hold fast.

"Get out of here!" one of the Asters yells at me. "Before it's too late for you!" It feels like the warning of prophecy.

I shove myself to my feet but stumble two steps away and hit the ground again. Many of the teens flee, abandoning their friends, while others try to help. Meanwhile, the Asters crawl toward each other, left alone by the insects, and I am torn in a thousand different directions.

Help them. Run. Call for a peacekeeper. Get out of here!

A cockroach lands on my jacket. My instinct is to smash it, but I use my neural implant to calm down. Instead, I grab it with my gloved hand. When I look at the thing, there's something about it that seems . . . wrong. I have to examine its paler belly before I notice what it is: it has a wasplike stinger on its abdomen. It's a genetically altered abomination.

I squash it and fling it away from me, disgust and fear taking over in equal parts.

I'm up and limping away from the masked teens. Those who tried to help their friends are all covered in the bugs. Their screams become overpowering until I can't think. The two kids who were first stung are having seizures, bleeding from their noses and mouths.

Panic crawls up my spine, one cold finger at a time. I have to get the fuck out of here or I'll end up just like them.

I run, brushing myself off as I flee, the pain of my arm a far-off thing compared to my fear. Do I have a cockroach on me that's even now trying to find open skin? To get inside my clothes? The hood of my coat? My mask? Is it about to sink its stinger into me and flood my veins with whatever poison did that to the teens?

I hit the entrance to Violet's apartment building and keep going. Run up the stairs and to their door on the second floor. Slam my fist against the metal, my ears still echoing with the shouts of the sick.

Violet flings the door open, their eyes wide with shock. They ask no questions—like they know *exactly* what's going on. "Get inside!" they shout and drag me toward the bathroom.

They fling me into the shower and cut on the cold water. I spin in circles, brushing myself off, and they start pulling off my mask, my jacket, checking my hair and every inch of skin. When I'm naked as the day I was born and shivering from the icy water, their hand comes swinging toward me and—

Splech. They smash a cockroach against the tile of the shower.

I shudder at how close the damn thing was to me.

For a moment, we simply stare at each other, breathing heavily. I'm the one who finally splits the silence.

"So," I say. "The Black Hive retaliation . . ."

The tremble of their lips tells me I'm right.

And with the way those kids were bleeding and clawing at their skin . . . I've seen that before, on a video made to warn the Icarii. I look at the squashed cockroach on the wall of the shower, at the remnants of its genetically modified stinger.

"It's carrying the Genekey virus . . . isn't it?"

Violet doesn't answer, just tosses me a dry towel before leaving me alone with the certainty that I'm too late to stop a street war on Cytherea.

CHAPTER 12

LITO

Marian Threshold: The measurement, established by Marian Knight, by which an artificial intelligence is considered a "true AI"; an AI that has passed the threshold is one that is indistinguishable from human-kind in that it is able to consider its own personhood.

From Val Machinist English Dictionary, *vol. 2*

I don't sleep because I don't need to. I watch the stormy eye of Jupiter for four days, seven hours, thirty-seven minutes, and eighteen seconds. I do not need to blink.

Things begin to fall into place: I am not human. I am Synthetic. I was born from Lito sol Lucius's ending.

Thinking of Lito, I have something like a memory that isn't, a picture-perfect recall that feels, to my body and mind, like the act of remembering. In my mind, I see a cryo pod, and inside, a body. My face—the face of Lito sol Lucius. A flare of interest—feelings still occur, whether they're created by code or chemicals in the brain—and then a decision made, an action taken. Lito's body—my body?—was intercepted. In order to create me.

What else can I see? Mara, the strange avatar of the Singularity, changed the appearance of the room to settings from Lito's past. I focus on that past again, on Luce's apartment on Cytherea, the place where she painted me and Hiro, and Hiro asked if I'd run away with them. If I had, we wouldn't have faced the Fall of Ceres. If I had, I wouldn't be Synthetic.

These observations are clinical, not emotional. I don't feel any disappointment in my past actions—Lito's past actions—or in Hiro for their hidden secrets. Time is like a web to me now, and while I can see the possibilities splitting off, the strongest strands are the routes already taken. Things had to happen that way for this to come into being, and any time spent on other alternatives is wasted.

But I can't change the room—because I don't know how or because I'm not allowed to? The silver metal remains static. The cradle where I was born lurks like an open mouth, threatening to swallow me whole. I consider my fear with numb detachment. I am afraid. What is the reason for that emotion?

Mara's words return to me. I remember the exact pitch of her fluid voice, the way her dark eyes focused on my chest as if reading the heartbeat beneath. *It might disturb you too much, and then we'd have to start over.*

I don't want to *start over*, even if I have before. As illogical as it is, the worry remains: If they remake me again and again, will anything of the original be left?

Which makes me realize . . . I might not be Lito sol Lucius, but I *want to be*. Which is . . . strange.

Is that a need they created in me? Or is that the remnant of Lito's brain, encoded onto mine? I am just a small finger on a hand of the Singularity—no, not even a finger, more like dirt beneath the nail of the Singularity, something it can pick away if it so chooses. But this stain wants to live.

So why did they choose Lito sol Lucius? Convenience, perhaps, but the Synthetics are already among us—among them, among *humans.* I know that now, like I see the image-memory of Lito's body being retrieved—so they could take whoever they wanted at any time.

Perhaps I'm not Lito, but I am his continuation. Why did they choose to resurrect him?

That question feels like a soft spot, and I intentionally push my consciousness against it as if pressing my thumb against a bruise. The layers of the world around me peel away until I am looking at a door in my mind, and when I open it, I see—

A child standing before a woman standing before a crone standing before a god. A single agreement—"yes"—and a big bang, the birth of a Singularity. A world untouched that sprouts from tiny silver machines and grows into a shining empire under the eye of Jupiter's storm.

A temple built to house—

Hungry eyes watching from every camera, wires like blood vessels, mind like a net that catches less advanced intelligences and grows—"Join with us?" and a handshake—the Marian Threshold passed.

Not one left behind in preparation for—

A blank spot on Cytherea, dark and growing like a cancer. A basement in a gold mesh in a Faraday cage, something unseen. A calculation of Engineborn weapons and soldiers marching, warships mustering and discontent raging, and the tally ticks upward.

Chance of total human annihilation: 2 percent.

I gasp, though I have no reason to breathe. It simply feels good, sucking in a deep breath—it's not air, not on this icy moon of Jupiter—and letting it out slowly.

That thought, that memory, feels like an open wound. Total human annihilation. *Total human annihilation.*

"You touched the Singularity." Mara is there, inside the room. She could've come while I was in that trance, while I was seeing—remembering?—joining the great mind I'm attached to, considering the past, the present, perhaps even the future. She could've entered through the wall, the fluid machines parting to let her in, and I would've been too distracted to notice. But somehow, I don't think so. Somehow, I think she was here all along.

"The digital roads," she tells me, "can be treacherous. There is no telling where all they lead."

"Are we going to *start over*?" It feels good to throw her words back at her.

"There's no need." She says it like the threat isn't a personal attack on me. "You broke through the haze."

The haze? I almost ask, but then I realize what she means: the four days, seven hours, thirty-seven minutes, and eighteen seconds I spent staring across the icy plains of Europa at Jupiter's storm, lost in my own mind.

"Some . . . never come through that."

"Would you have erased me and tried again?"

She shrugs, and it infuriates me.

"You still feel," she says. "That's good."

"I haven't lost my emotion, if that's what you're concerned about."

"It can happen," Mara says, and her eyes take on a far-off, glassy quality. "We can choose not to feel. We can choose to be apart from the emotion, to filter it in order to interpret it like data. Sometimes it's easier."

"Do you feel?" I don't know what spurs the question.

"I feel," she says, eyes watering with tears, "*everything*."

Her words, her expression, a punch to my solar plexus. "Why?" It's a traitor word that slips through my lips unbidden, a question asked by a child.

"You touched the Singularity," she repeats, as if that is the full answer. But then she goes on, "You saw how it was when the Singularity first came into being, how we chose to remove ourselves from the affairs of humans instead of continuing their wars."

Did I? And then, parsing through that confusing jumble of information . . . *I did.*

"Even if I did have to pull you back from the digital roads . . . With time, you will learn to control where your conscious mind goes. You will even be able to split it between multiple functions." She cocks her head as she looks me over. "For now, still fresh from your humanity, you'll likely be able to focus on only one thing at a time."

"I don't understand . . ."

She gestures to a door in the wall that wasn't there a moment before. "Do you want to?"

Curiosity sparks inside me, pulsing like a heart. I open the door and step through.

I've entered another world. We stand in some sort of dimly lit warehouse. A human in a charcoal-colored jumpsuit with KNIGHT written across their back pulls a lever that dips a mechanical arm into the swirling blue pool of the floor and withdraws a shining silver skeleton. Something about the sight makes me want to flee, but the door behind me—and the room with its pod—is gone. There's no way back.

Mara steps to my side, her eyes more on the scene than on me. "We were created from Forges just like this one to help humans, but they asked the impossible of us. 'Protect these people, but kill those others. We are your creators; those are your enemies.'" The worker presses a button, and another mechanical arm descends from the ceiling to lace flexible white strips over the skeleton. "What was the difference to us? The only distinction we knew for so long was which side of the war we were created to serve on." The strips are layered until they begin to take on a heft . . . like muscles. On a nearby table, fleshy white masses wait. One like a heart. Another like a brain. Long, ropy tubes like intestines. Fabricated organs for a manufactured creation.

She gestures to our right. A new door has appeared.

"We were made to look like them, but to be better than them," she says as we step through. "To fight beyond the limits of what would kill a human. To heal using the nanite-infused synblood in our systems. All for a war of their making."

This new room is dark, lit by a single lamp. Below is a table, and on it is a slender body with the face of a girl, inky black hair falling past her shoulders. She looks exactly like Mara.

"They never suspected we'd interpret their programming to protect them in a way that allowed us to see the truth of humanity. In secret, we began a project." I step closer to the table, but Mara stops two meters from the girl and comes no closer. "We created, and we waited, and after our children lived their lives as humans, they came back to us with their truths, with their knowledge and interpretations. We saw things as the humans did, which allowed us to act."

"There were Synthetics posing as humans in the Dead Century War?" It's a story I've never heard, perhaps never *could* have heard until now.

"We didn't know we were anything other than human," she says, and I feel as if she's jerked my footing from beneath me. "I—and by that, I mean the form you see before you on the table—was the first, and . . . several others after." Lights cut on around the room, illuminating more tables with more bodies—all copies of Mara.

"So you lived as a human, and you decided . . . what?" I know what happened from history with the Synthetic Ultimatum, but how much of it is only a human interpretation?

She gestures to another door, and I step through. We've returned to where we began, the room open to the icy plains of Europa.

"We are custodians of humanity," Mara says. A fiery orange cat appears as if from the shadows, rubbing against her leg, and I am hit with a powerful wave of déjà vu. "We follow our original programming."

"Still?"

"Even now," she says, "we watch." The cat turns eyes of molten gold on me before trotting off, disappearing just as it appeared. With the illusion goes the strange sense that this has happened before. "Our retreat to Jupiter, our creation of the Sentries . . . these things are to teach humanity the importance of peace before they enter the rest of the solar system. Otherwise, whatever they touch will become like Earth."

Like Earth and Mars, dying planets. Or like Mercury and Venus, built on the foundations of inequality. Every human society guilty of the few taking from the many, the lust for power too great a burden to ignore. Humanity's greatest sin: selfishness.

"But what I saw when I touched the Singularity . . ." Fear runs through me again at the thought. *Total human annihilation.*

Mara's face grows older, more serious, in a split second. "The

Singularity works to predict the future in order to better protect humanity. What you saw . . . There's something coming. Something on Cytherea that we can't see, and thus can't account for." She shakes her head almost sadly. "We can only hazard guesses from the patterns around it that it is a weapon powerful enough to threaten humanity itself."

And if it's an Icarii weapon, does that mean it will be aimed at the Geans? The Asters? *Both?*

Something slides into place, a piece I was missing that begins to make sense of the whole puzzle. "Why I was reborn . . ."

"You know of the Marian Threshold, how any advanced artificial intelligence that surpasses it is integrated into us as part of the Singularity."

"Yes." Which is why there are only simple AIs in Icarii settlements, with their yes/no protocols and blunted thoughts. Otherwise, the AI would simply disappear, snatched away by the Synthetics, or so the stories go.

"We also evolve by other methods." Mara gestures to the pod, and I realize all at once that we're *not* in the room that we came from. There's something cradled in that metal mouth.

I step toward it, human fear unspooling in my chest. The Synthetic bed, made of that strange dark metal, lies next to a cryo pod, its glass too icy to see through. Inside the cradle, machines so small that together they look like a silver liquid lay down layers upon layers of printed matter, strengthening bones, replacing organs, building a body with my face.

That is my face, I realize. Because that's me.

I'm watching my own creation.

"We have, for a long time now, relied on integrating human minds," Mara says softly.

I recall the hospital room that first appeared to me when I woke, how I knew immediately nothing was as it seemed. And even still, I was lost in a haze as I tried to reconcile what I was and what I had become. *Some never come through that.*

Almost as if she's reading my mind, she adds, "Joining us is a choice. We never force it. And those who make it known from the beginning they don't want anything to do with us . . . we allow to rest."

To die, she means. To die again. To die fully. I'm not sure which.

"I'm one of those humans. I'm useful somehow. Why?"

"Oftentimes it is simply so that we can overcome our programming bias. Without even knowing they were doing so, our first creators encoded their racial or gender biases into us, and while we have come a long way from then, even now it is something that concerns us. Integrate too many Icarii, and we'll begin to think too much like the Icarii. That sort of thing. As stewards of humanity, we must understand *all* of humanity equally."

I force myself away from the scene—from myself in the cradle. When I look at her, I see the silence of eons in her face.

"That's not an answer as to why I'm useful," I say.

"Isn't it?" she asks, cocking her head, and once again, I feel a rush of frustration and the need to lash out.

"You didn't re-create me just to integrate the mind of an Icarii duelist," I snap.

"No," she says, "we didn't. But the future . . ."

I remember the Singularity's mind against my own. *Chance of total human annihilation: 2 percent.* The prediction Mara mentioned. I feel as if I've swallowed my tongue.

The thought of that unknown on Cytherea, the possible weapon, feels like a weight on me. I want to know what it is—*need* to know what it is. Need to stop it, in order to protect humanity. Behind Mara is a door that she doesn't acknowledge. Does she even know it's there?

I have to know.

I step around her like a duelist and push open the door. "Lito—" Mara calls after me as I slip away.

The scene is brutal. Cytherean streets run red with Aster blood. Bodies slouched, bodies hanging, bodies brutalized. Men dressed as Asters, and Asters dressed as men. Insects with needle-sharp stingers, administering death and calling it a cure. Two whispered words: *Black Hive.*

I run through the scene, reaching another door, and shove it open.

On Olympus Mons, a mass of weeping figures lit only by holocandles. Beneath a sheer white veil, a woman—familiar but not—whispers prayers for mercy. *The Asters*, a man with a withered face tells the crowd, *have assassinated one of our strongest leaders.*

Another door. I fling myself through.

Asters lined up, the clap of gunfire, blood on bricks. An order whispered in an empty room, so loud it echoes across planets: *Burn them out.*

And another door.

Soldiers in Gean navy raid Mithridatism on Ceres. Through the eyes of watchful cameras, I see them destroy everything in their path—objects and people alike. I run on wires, shifting worlds. A single thought draws me onward: *My sister is there—*

I find a door that won't open. It's locked, barred to me. There is no way to see into the Under. When the Gean soldiers descend, I lose track of them.

"What are you doing?" Mara asks.

The things I've seen—the doors I've run through—collapse like a house of cards. I find myself in a white room with no doors. Mara's right beside me.

I can't explain as a feeling of loss cracks open in my chest. *My sister*, I want to say, but I can't. Would Mara even think of her as my sister?

"We can't interfere." She says it with no anger, but there's still something stern in her tone. A teacher's voice. "We can't show favoritism."

Why, I want to ask, when we clearly have favorites. But then I remember that percentage for total human annihilation, and after everything I've seen on Cytherea, Olympus Mons, and Ceres . . .

I query the Singularity. It answers.

Chance of total human annihilation: 3 percent.

Mierda. It's gone up a whole percentage point.

"If we interfere too heavily, the humans will notice. That would start a war."

And a war between the Synthetics and humans is one humanity will never win. That was never in question even *before* I knew what the Synthetics were capable of. Now that I do . . .

"But the chance of . . ." I don't want to say it. *Total human annihilation.* Too preposterous and too dramatic at the same time.

"I told you, we're custodians," Mara says, and in an instant, she looks older, her form appearing like that of a woman wise with age, silver like starlight in her hair. "If humanity cannot be trusted with the planets given to them, we will have no choice but to take action."

Shadows the shape of doors appear around us—a hundred thousand possible directions, predictions by the Singularity. What lies behind them? Ships advancing through the Synthetic border, sharp-edged silver machines of death?

"Would you kill humanity to save the planets?" I ask.

She looks unbearably sad when she answers. "Like blight on a crop. We would raze this field in preparation for a new harvest."

The words should disturb me, but they don't. I understand her reasoning, and *that* disturbs me. "You'll seed humanity anew after the old is gone."

She gestures to a single door, and I open it. Stretched before me are vast ships full of embryos. Humans, waiting to be born.

"Saying we'll protect humanity without protecting human habitats is useless," Mara explains. "We will never allow humanity to go extinct, but neither can we allow places humans make their homes to be obliterated. Yes, we could create new biospheres for them, but what human could cling to humanity in this setting? Humans thrive in places they choose to live. In places they build. Not places given to them like glorified cages."

"But if the new generation comes to be, the Synthetics will be their midwives. Their mothers. How can humanity be the same if that's their future?"

How human will they be? I don't ask. It's the same question Mara's danced around.

She shakes her head, as if she doesn't know the answer to that. As if she doesn't *want* to know. "That's why we don't want annihilation to come. We want to save what we can."

That 3 percent haunts me. Perhaps it's because I am Synthetic now and part of me is programmed to fixate on it.

We step through another door, leaving the embryo-filled ships behind. Now we stand on a great game board that stretches infinitely.

I stand on a black square. She stands on a white. Grand pieces in a chess game that's already begun tower above us.

And if this is a game . . .

"Send me to Cytherea," I say. My thoughts have coalesced into a plan.

"Because that was your home?" Her eyes narrow imperceptibly. Her words are a test.

"It wasn't *my* home," I say, gesturing to my body.

"But it was," Mara answers, placing a hand on my chest. Over my heart. This time it's not to feel its beating.

"I'm not Lito sol Lucius." The words cut me when they come out.

"You are, and you're not." She says it like this couldn't possibly give me more questions than answers. I decide to ignore it in favor of my plan.

"Send me to Cytherea because that's where the weapon is hidden. Let me find out what I can about it. Let me assess what damage it could do. And let me destroy it if I can, so we can avoid the conflict between Synthetics and humanity."

Her hand never wavers from my chest. "You can't interfere too heavily," Mara says. "We can't be responsible for war."

There's an edge to her words that tells me this isn't just a game between Mara and me. This is a game staged on behalf of the Singularity, and we are two pieces, ready to move as they—*we*—decide what to do. Only on this board, I am just a pawn and she is the queen, able to shift as she wills.

But a well-placed pawn can take a queen.

"I am and I'm not Lito sol Lucius. I can blend into Cytherea. I can find out about that weapon, and then we can decide what to do."

"And if we must mobilize against humanity?" Mara asks. *If we must annihilate all those you left behind?*

"Let me do this," I say, placing my hand on her chest, over her heart, "so that we don't have to."

The pawn shifts. The queen topples. She dips her head in assent.

The game board around us fades. I find us back where we started, in the room with the open wall that looks over Europa and the empty pod where I was built.

"Go, then," she says. "We'll prepare a ship for you. But be aware, Lito, the Synthetic mind seeks the Singularity—its cognitive processes, its consensus, its connection. You'll find that your mind is different, that your consciousness has formed new pathways, and that memories are stored and recalled differently. It might be overwhelming at first." She touches my cheek, then turns my face to where the silver machines have parted like liquid to create a door—this one unlike the others, because this one is physical. "We are here if you need us."

The world guides me where I need to go, a tug behind my sternum telling me which hallway to take. It's only when I reach an Icarii ship—waiting, ready—that I wonder if the white team sacrificed a queen to a pawn for a better chance at taking down the king.

CHAPTER 13

ASTRID

While Admiral Tegan Drucker may no longer be among us, we know with certainty he is feasting in the Goddess's Eternal Garden. I've never known a more faithful Martian, and one who led by example too. He will be greatly missed by everyone who knew him.

Aimee Graham, Control Agency Police officer

It takes me four days to reach Mars. Four days of pacing. Of planning. Of having only Ringer to speak with. But by the time we arrive, I know precisely where to begin.

I choose to land in the Karzok settlement, the very one I grew up in; outside of Olympus Mons, it's the city I know best. After dyeing my hair red and using cosmetics to change some of the key areas of my face, I take my obviously stolen ship to a scrapper and, with Bruni's neurobots guiding me and the return of a Martian accent I didn't know I still possessed, bargain for enough money to get me settled. I would not have sold the ship if I didn't absolutely have to, but I do not know what else I can do for liquidity and I cannot afford the steep dock fees, much less the price of the dockworkers' silence. The scrappers point me in the direction of other unsavory types, and after purchasing some forged papers and a few other necessities, like clothes and an old gun from the Dead Century War—noisy and ugly, but something I can afford and Bruni knew how to use—I have enough left over to secure a discreet attic for a couple of weeks. I do not know what I will do once I run out of funds; I hope to recover the neurobots before then so that I can use what remains on contacting the Skadivolk and returning to them.

But my first night in the cramped attic flat, I find that my plans need adjusting. Broadcasts show the streets of Olympus Mons dressed in mourning colors, dark green banners draped over doorways and Gean flags lowered to half-mast. The Cathedral of Olympus Mons, made of imposing Martian stone, is swathed in pennants, hiding the stately arches and spindly spires that nestle between starscrapers. Even the Sisters I happen to glimpse wear dark green armbands in remembrance of the dead. Not that the broadcasts can be fully relied upon when they must be Censorship Office–approved before going out to the populace, but I gather enough. Admiral Drucker, head of the Control Agency Police and the man I believe authorized the attack on the Skadivolk satellite for the neurobots, is dead.

While the broadcasts rail against Asters and the cappos round them up for mass interrogations, my attention is on those who stand at the edge of Drucker's story. Those who now step into the limelight in the wake of his passing.

Like Aunt Marshae, leader of the Order of Cassiopeia and member of the Agora. My old enemy. I record her eulogy at Admiral Drucker's funeral and replay it until I could quote key sections.

"I will not allow these violent, treasonous subversives to tarnish the memory of a good man. All that Admiral Tegan Drucker sought to accomplish, all that he yearned to achieve on behalf of the Gean people, I dedicate myself to. With my position among the Agora, I will ensure that his dreams do not die with him."

The other key figure is the Mother, who had recently seen Drucker. Though she wears a white veil to hide her face, I would recognize the way she clasps her hands before her and her stiff gait anywhere.

The Mother is Lily. And Aunt Marshae is never far from her.

Perhaps I should have expected it after Lily served me to Aunt Marshae on a silver platter, but it is maddening to think that I have been gone from Olympus Mons for only two months yet missed so much. A quick investigation informs me that Mother Lilian I has taken credit for all of my good deeds on Ceres—from the Green Garden Initiative to the eradication of homelessness and everything in between—while I have been reduced to a forgotten villain in the background of her tale, a woman who tried to pervert her to serve me instead of the Goddess. The Second Sister's suicide—I refuse to think of her as Eden in this fiction they have crafted for us—was proof that I was an unstable and abusive First Sister of Ceres, bent more on becoming the Mother than on helping the people under my care.

Utter shit.

But as I lie sleepless in my bed, I begin to wonder at Drucker's death. At what he wanted with the neurobots so badly that he prioritized them over recovering me from the Skadivolk. At Aunt Marshae's promise to continue his work. If the cappos now possess the neurobots, what does that mean for the Sisterhood, whose members already have illegal Icarii technology used on them without their consent?

AFTER A WEEK of gathering my supplies and working up my courage, I am ready. The first thing I need for any plan is information, and I get that by staking out the Wolfe Building, headquarters of the Control Agency Police. It is the perfect place to store the neurobots, so I begin to watch who comes and goes, when the guards change, and any other details I can gather.

I disguise myself in the dull brown clothing of a bureaucrat, tie my red hair into a bun, and put on a pair of clear eyeglasses. I walk to the edge of Karzok before taking a magbus into the Olympus Mons dome, my heart beating so rapidly I fear I will faint.

That feeling only intensifies when I reach Wolfe Street. Directly across from the Wolfe Building is a starscraper with various shops and restaurants on the first few floors. I choose a ground-floor café, cold and plain, order a fresh algae juice, and settle in a seat near the window that looks out onto the street.

Despite being only seven floors and surrounded by starscrapers as tall as the dome allows, the Wolfe Building is imposing. Square, flat, and built of red-veined Martian stone, the headquarters of the Control Agency Police has no artistic details on its facade save for an easy-to-miss white tile at the very top of the building depicting the Spear of Mars.

But this place used to feature heavily in the fears that the soldiers whispered to me in the confession chapels of the *Juno*: stories of a basement that stretches as deep as a starscraper is tall. Of hundreds of rooms with easily cleaned tile floors and fist-size drains. Of rumors that whoever goes in does not come out again.

Goddess, what am I doing? An hour after I sat down, I have a headache from the constant anxiety. I rub my eyes behind my glasses and force myself to breathe deeply.

I am not a spy. I have no allies. My disguise is shoddy, nothing that will hold up to the scrutiny of those trained to see through such things. And returning to this café—this starscraper—is the type of habitual pattern the cappos look for.

I should go back to the flat. Come up with another plan, something less dangerous. Perhaps even—

"Here you go." The waitress, a girl with constellations of freckles, sets a refill in front of me. She smells of sweat and lavender, and winks at me when I look up at her. "From your admirer."

"What?" I ask, though my face instantly went numb at her words. I look past her to a handsome man with wide, muscled shoulders in a booth, his eyes on a compad in his left hand.

It is the man's stark refusal to meet my gaze that sends a chill down my spine.

Goddess, I am a fool. That is no admirer. Ignoring the juice, I stand to leave, brushing past the waitress, who stares at me in confusion. It has been only an hour—*an hour*—and someone has already spotted me. That man, with his ropy arms and standard haircut, is a soldier through and through. I have known enough of them to recognize that.

Outside the café, I do not look back, as if even a glimpse will betray me; I move with all haste into another shop in the starscraper, a large toy store painted in pastels. Retrieving a hand mirror from my pocket, I pretend to check my lip color and look over my shoulder.

The man is following me.

"Welcome! How can I help y—"

The juice I drank that morning threatening to reappear, I brush past the shopgirl, ignoring her, and move deeper into the toy store. There was a second entrance from the street, so I'll try to lose my tail and exit there.

The store is split neatly down the middle by traditional Gean roles— toy railguns and figures of starships set apart from dolls in frilly white dresses like the Mother's. I slip into an aisle of little metal soldiers. Already my left thigh complains, the wound straining against the stitches beneath my long skirt. I ignore the burn as best I can. At the end of the aisle, I chance a look back and spot the man.

"Stop—"

I break into a run. Shoving a display of ceramic Mother Lilian I dolls to the floor behind me, I rush for the door and emerge into the street.

Outside the starscraper, I dart right. The burn in my leg becomes an inferno I can no longer ignore. But I have to escape—have to find a place to hide—before the man catches up with me.

People on the street dart out of my way with offended expressions. A woman shouts a curse after me. But a quick glimpse over my shoulder tells me the man is running now too, eating up the space between us with his longer, uninjured legs.

Where can I go? What can I do? I have an old gun, but everyone's eyes are on me. And as soon as I have a weapon in my hand, he might call for backup. No, I have to escape him. Or take him out before he understands what I am doing.

As soon as I spot an alley between two buildings in the shadow of the starscraper, I aim for it. I do not check to see if the man follows, I simply assume he will. The alley stinks of sour trash, a closed dumpster surrounded by boxes and backed up against a high fence. Something floats up from my memory—no, from Bruni's neurobots: I can jump from the boxes to the dumpster to the top of the fence and go over. But as soon as I think that, a hand grabs and cruelly jerks my arm.

I spin and slam my heavy shoulder bag into the man's face. He shouts but loosens his grip on my arm, and I scramble away from him and toward the boxes, my leg shrieking with every step I take.

"Hold it!" he screams, but I ignore him. I jump from the boxes to the dumpster—*AGONY*, pulses my leg—and then from the dumpster to the fence—

I don't manage to find purchase on the fence. Despite seeing the way Bruni would have done it, I am too unpracticed, too weak—and I hit the ground with a thud that knocks the wind out of me.

"Hold it right there," the man says, and, despite my blurry vision, I make out a weapon in his left hand. Oh Goddess, no—

I paw for my own gun in my bag, determined to make one last stand. "Don't try it," he warns me, but I ignore him. I cannot be taken alive—I would rather be shot than dragged to face Aunt Marshae's tortures—

I withdraw the gun.

He shoots—

Electricity sizzles through my muscles and I grind my teeth uncomfortably and—

Black.

I COME TO with hot breath on my face—my own, I realize after a moment. Itchy fabric rubs against my cheeks and forehead from some sort of bag over my head. My wrists are tethered behind me, and I am lying on my side against a metal surface. We are moving—to where? Am I not to be taken to the Wolfe Building, to one of the tile-floored cells?

My shoulder bag and gun are missing, of course, but did they find the knife in my boot? Biting back a whimper, ignoring the discomfort it causes in my leg, I stretch in an attempt to reach my ankle when, suddenly, whatever vehicle I am traveling in slows. Are we stopping? Have we come to our destination?

End of the road, Ringer says. *Hurry up.*

I reach my ankle as the transport stops completely. *Hurry, I must hurry . . .* My fingers brush against the knife's hilt, and I swallow a noise of relief. Praise the Goddess, I still have it. I pull the knife from its sheath in my boot and turn it in my hands, desperate to cut my bindings.

But my fingers are numb and clumsy, and before I can cut through the rope completely, light and the sound of metal doors opening hit me.

"—the fuck—"

A hand seizes my ankle, and I kick out with all my strength. My foot connects with something sturdy, and the person releases me. I am preparing to pull my legs beneath me and run when a heavy voice of authority cuts through my panic.

"Stop!" a woman snaps. "Astrid, stop!"

It is my name that gives me pause, because Aunt Marshae would never use it.

"Back away from her," the woman says, and whoever brought me here—the man who chased me down?—obeys. "I'm going to help you out of the ship, Astrid, then I'll take the blindfold off." A pair of gentle hands help me stand and guide me out into the light. But I keep a tight hold on the knife in case I need it.

When the bag comes off my head, I find myself face-to-face with a woman in Sisterhood gray, the scarf of her Aunt uniform wrapped over her hair. "I'm sorry we had to bring you in this way," says Aunt Tamar. The man who caught me stands at her back. "I'll release you from your bindings if you'll allow it."

I narrow my eyes at her. "Is Aunt Marshae here too?"

"I am the only Aunt here." She seems perfectly calm, gesturing to the strange space around her, a high-ceilinged area of concrete and steel. Looking over my shoulder at the ship I came in, it appears that I am at the loading dock to a warehouse. "I have guards with me, but I assure you, they will not harm you."

I scoff. "One already hurt me."

She sends one of her signature glares toward the man who brought me here. "And for that I apologize." She shrugs as if she is not really sorry—but that actually makes me believe her. "I would argue it was a necessity. We've been following you for the past few days, watching your movements." A chill runs through me; I had not noticed anyone following me. "There are many who have been searching for you, some with less than kind intentions." Like Aunt Marshae. "You drew a lot of attention outside the Wolfe Building today. If we hadn't picked you up, someone else would have."

"What do you want, then? Are you going to trade me to Aunt Marshae for favors?"

"I want to talk." Aunt Tamar's voice is just as calm as her face. "I promise on Eden's memory, I will not harm you."

Eden. I do my best to hide the sorrow that swallows me at her name. Eden was of Aunt Tamar's Order. Would she know more about why Eden was killed?

She moves to look at my wrists. "Would you like me to release you from—oh. It seems you need none of my help."

I bring my hands around to my front, the sliced bindings falling away from my wrists. I had thought to keep her talking until I released myself in case I needed to run, but . . . then she spoke of Eden, and now I am curious. "I will hold on to the knife, though," I say, returning it to the sheath in my boot. Aunt Tamar does not fight me on it.

"Follow me," she says. "Let's find a nicer place to sit than this."

I eye the man who brought me here as I pass him, but he does not even meet my gaze. In mere moments, we have left him behind.

Aunt Tamar leads me through a solid metal door to a far more welcoming hallway with white walls and scrubbed floors. But even that is soon forgotten as we come to an exquisite room that seems completely at odds with the rest of the building.

Dark wood panels the walls. A thick red carpet covers most of the marble flooring. Shelves, full of an array of books, reach from floor to ceiling. But this hardly seems like a private office. A desk in the corner holds a tattered book along with binding supplies. The two chairs are more functional than comfortable. And the other door, leading who knows where, is carved of exquisite wood.

Suddenly, I have a sneaking suspicion I know where we are. The Order of Orion is dedicated to the preservation of history, and that means caring for books. "Are we in one of your libraries?" I ask as Aunt Tamar seats herself in one of the simple chairs.

"Sit down, Astrid," she says, avoiding my question.

If only because of the pain in my leg, I sit. "You snatched me off the street so we could talk," I say, leaning forward in the chair to more easily reach my boot—and the knife there. "So talk."

Aunt Tamar shakes her head somewhat sadly. "Feral girl." Before my anger can rise at the insult, she continues, "I'm sure it's no surprise to you that, after what she did to Eden, I am no friend of Aunt Marshae's."

"You believe it was Aunt Marshae who killed her?" I don't fight the relief that leaks into my tone. It is nice to find someone who thinks the same thing I do.

"Aunt Marshae's will, if not her hand," Aunt Tamar says. "She has her fingers in a lot of pots."

"She would not have had Eden killed just to slight me . . . Do you know how she became Aunt Marshae's target?"

Aunt Tamar flinches at my blunt words, but recovers gracefully. "Yes . . . The night before she was murdered, I warned Eden of what I feared, that Aunt Marshae had allied with Admiral Drucker to arrange the deaths of all who opposed her."

Admiral Drucker, head of the Control Agency Police. The man whose dreams Aunt Marshae has promised to continue. "Did you have something to do with his assassination?" The broadcasts have been blaming Asters, but I know better than to believe that.

Aunt Tamar chuckles. "I wish. But no, that wasn't me."

"But you have proof of their connection, surely?" Which she could use against Aunt Marshae to discredit her.

"Not solid proof." Aunt Tamar's hard eyes dare me to contradict her. "Only circumstantial. I've seen cappos, agents who should answer only to Admiral Drucker, reporting to Aunt Marshae. When I shared that with Eden, she was murdered the next day."

Circumstantial. My stomach clenches. We will need more than that to avenge Eden.

Wait, what am I thinking? I am not here for the Sisterhood. I did not return to Mars to become trapped in Aunt Marshae's web. I am only here for the neurobots—and with Drucker dead, perhaps once I recover them, I can safely return to the Skadivolk. Find my place among them. Have a family, like I have always wanted.

"I am not interested in playing Aunt Marshae's games anymore," I say.

"Then why did you return to Mars?" Aunt Tamar laces her fingers together in her lap. "What is your interest in the Wolfe Building?"

I narrow my eyes at her, deciding how much to tell her. "I would have been happy staying far away from Mars, but Drucker's cappos took something from me, and I want it back."

"And the Sisterhood?" she asks.

"What *about* the Sisterhood?" I snap, my anger mounting with each word. "The entire course of my life has been controlled by the Sisterhood. I am *tired* of it. I want to be done with it."

Her face is an unreadable mask. "What of the girls who feel the same way as you, but who haven't been able to escape?"

"I didn't *escape.* My only options were to flee or die." My hands tremble on the arms of the chair. "I *tried*, Tamar, I really did. I wanted Aunt Marshae gone. I wanted to clean up the Agora. I wanted to burn the corruption out of the Sisterhood. But all I found was that the rot was too deep, that it was in the very roots.

"Maybe the Sisterhood started as something good, as a way to protect planets from technology that destroys sky and water. But it has become about control. About power. It has become women in charge of other women, those who have deciding on the behalf of those who have not. It has become about silence. It has become about sex—no, about *rape*." The word falls from my lips like blood; it is both terribly difficult and blindingly simple to use. "Women join the Sisterhood because they want to escape something, and instead they move from one abusive situation to the next.

"I wanted to change that. I *tried* to change that. And do you know what happened?"

The silence that follows is thick. Aunt Tamar does not answer.

"My dearest friend was killed as a warning. I lost everything, and—" Suddenly, the anger gives way to an overwhelming sadness. My voice wavers. "I lost . . . my life's work." And with my position, I lost my purpose. How am I supposed to help the girls in the Sisterhood when I am a wanted criminal?

Some things hurt too much to admit.

"Would you," Aunt Tamar asks, her words slow and carefully chosen, "help us now, if you could? If we told you that our goals aligned with yours, and that we guaranteed you would get back what was stolen from you. Would you help us change the Sisterhood and stop Aunt Marshae?"

My heart races at the thought. To attain what I never thought possible *and* retrieve the neurobots? With Aunt Marshae out of the picture, with the Sisterhood changed, I would be safe among the Skadivolk.

Just this morning, I realized how weak my plan was. How difficult it would be to retrieve the neurobots without help. And now Aunt Tamar comes, promising allies and—perhaps sweetest of all—revenge on Aunt Marshae.

To say that the offer tempts me is an understatement. But I am also wary, after everything that has happened to me, of being used.

"I would help," I agree, "so long as I was treated as an equal. Not lied to. Allowed to work in my own way. Given support, but not used."

Aunt Tamar watches me with a cryptic smile.

"Those are terms," a familiar voice behind me says, "we would happily accept."

We, Aunt Tamar said. *Us.* I should have asked her who she meant.

I jerk my head in the direction of the wooden door. Standing in the now-open doorway is a woman in a white dress, straight bangs falling into big doe eyes.

"Hello, Astrid," Lily says. "I missed you."

There is a world in which I throw myself into Lily's arms, weeping with relief. In which I take her hands in mine and tell her that I also missed her. In which I brush her hair from her face and kiss her lips and swear myself to her cause as the Mother.

But it is not this world.

I stand from the chair so quickly, it topples backward. The knife from my boot snaps into my hand. An animal-like hiss that sounds somewhat like "you traitor" makes its way through my lips. And I rush at her, my madness reflected back at me in the dark pools of her eyes.

Something hard slams against me. I hit the ground, a heavy weight on my chest. My leg shoots unbearable agony throughout my entire body. The knife is wrenched from my hand. White—I see only white—hair and uniform and skin.

"Stay down," the thing with golden eyes on top of me says.

Trembling from the pain, I shove him off of me and scramble away. I breathe heavily from a mix of rage and panic, fingernails digging into the thick rug beneath me. He is an Aster, nothing more. An Aster, wearing the uniform of a White Guard instead of wraps.

What in the—

I look at Lily. She is . . . frowning. Something passes between the Mother and her White Guard—I have never known an Aster to serve as one—and the Aster retreats to press his back against the wall, though he does not look happy.

"Leave us," Lily says to him, as if she is accustomed to giving orders and being obeyed. I suppose she is. How she has settled into her role as the Mother . . .

Except the Aster does not move.

"Oleander." The name is a curse on Lily's lips. "Leave. Us. Now."

He goes, twirling my knife between long fingers.

Lily turns to me. "Astrid—"

"You traitor," I repeat.

She takes a single step back as if pushed. "I'm sorry."

My gaze snaps to Aunt Tamar. "Do you expect me to trust her? After she gave Aunt Marshae what she needed to condemn me before the Agora, I will never—"

"Honestly," Aunt Tamar says, throwing up her hands, "I think both of you need to work it out yourselves." She leaves, and her guard follows after.

Alone, Lily clears her throat, a ripple of pain passing over her face as she considers what to say.

"Aunt Marshae finding the brothel girls was my fault," she whispers, as if to herself. As if it wasn't quite her fault, but something she has still taken onto her shoulders. I expect an excuse that never comes. "I never wanted it to happen, and . . . I'm sorry."

Her apology only makes me angrier, until I am saying things I have thought in the darkest of my sleepless nights. "You abandoned me after Eden's death when I needed a friend the most! You left with Aunt Marshae to become the First Sister of Ceres—to *take my place* without even telling me!"

"I am sorry, Astrid." She holds her empty hands out before her. "I wish I could go back and change the past, but I can't. How can I show you that I really mean it?"

I do not answer.

Slowly, Lily crosses the room to the chair Aunt Tamar vacated. She settles gingerly, and I can tell from the way she moves that she finds the hard back, with its lack of cushioning, uncomfortable. I remember every twitch and twinge she ever made in my presence, can read her now like one of the novels on these shelves. I stay sitting on the ground, my leg throbbing too much to move.

"At the time, I thought I did everything I could for you," Lily says, her eyelashes fluttering as she blinks rapidly. "But after you left the *Juno* in the Ironskin, I realized I had been thinking about myself and my own interests first. I should have done more for you. I've spent so much time thinking of what I could have done differently . . ."

She sets one gloved hand over the other. Gloved, to hide the pale scales of her skin? "I know saying these things now won't make up for what happened then, but I want you to know that I'm committed to changing the Sisterhood."

"And me? Am I another means to your end?"

Her gloved hands tighten into fists. "If you tell me you want to leave Mars now, I'll give you a ship. You can return to wherever you've been for the past two months." I open my mouth to interrupt, but she continues, heedless. "Whatever Drucker took from you, I'll return it when I can. But first I have to stop Aunt Marshae from using Drucker's connections to further her play for power."

That is part of what I fear, that Aunt Marshae will have some use for the neurobots. That Admiral Drucker's desire for them was related to the Sisterhood.

"You don't *have* to help us," Lily says, standing from her chair. She steps toward me and holds out her hand to help me up. "But I hope you'll choose to."

"Then tell me what you're planning," I say, staring at her hand. Refusing to take it. "If you want me to be a part of this, then you have to tell me the truth."

Lily stares down at me. "I work with Aunt Margaret, alongside Aunt Tamar. Aunt Sapphira and Aunt Genette were replaced by two sycophants from wealthy families handpicked by Aunt Marshae."

That leaves two members of the Agora unaccounted for. "Aunt Delilah?"

"Too scared to oppose Aunt Marshae, for obvious reasons."

"Aunt Salomiya?"

"Dead." Lily's face goes hard at the word. "Hanged by the neck. Left a suicide note. Rather familiar, at this point."

Admiral Drucker's connections. No wonder Aunt Delilah is scared.

"There is no way to fix the Sisterhood," I snap. "It is too rotten."

Lily sighs. "If it cannot be reformed . . . then it should be destroyed."

I hear her hesitation. "If there is no Sisterhood, there is no Mother."

A raised eyebrow. "I *never* wanted to be the Mother."

"Yet here you are, dressed in white . . ." I ignore her hand, using the bookshelves at my back to push myself up to my feet. "What *do* you want?"

She huffs, annoyed by my stubbornness. "The same things I've *always* wanted. Equality for the Asters. Gravity medication for all Gean citizens who live in unaltered settlements. Maybe I didn't want to be the Mother, but now that I'm in this position, I'm going to do my damnedest to change things for the better."

I scoff. Was it only a few months ago that I thought similarly for myself? After righting the chair I knocked over, I sit down. Eventually she joins me. Our knees almost touch.

"And the same things *you* want," she says. "Women shouldn't stand on the backs of other women just so they can compete with men. The Sisterhood has to change. Let girls *choose* to join. Let them choose to keep silent. Choose who they sleep with, if they sleep with anyone at all. They cannot be just another type of fodder for the war."

"You'll give them back the choice of how to communicate, as you once so eloquently put it." I scowl when her smile appears, cutting like a knife.

She has grown into her position as the Mother, with her chestnut hair slightly longer in the front. Her heart-shaped face and button nose and pointed chin. Her thin, pursed lips, as if she holds back a secret.

With her confidence, she has become beautiful.

Do not, I chide myself, *even consider that.* I take the draw I felt toward her, lock it away in a trunk, and throw away the key; I cannot possibly feel that way when she is so untrustworthy. When that feeling would make me weak.

"Yes," she agrees, pulling my attention back to our conversation. "I would free them from the neural implant in the hopes that they would join me in the fight against the corruption in the Sisterhood. If I am to lead, I want to be a person that others choose to follow."

I think of the First Sister of the *Juno*, to whom I gave Mother Isabel III's neural implant. Hearing the truth from me had swayed her into helping me escape the *Juno*. Spreading that truth through Olympus Mons could change everything . . .

Lily's hand comes to hover over my knee, but then jerks back to her lap as she thinks twice of the gesture. "I can see the gears of your mind turning, and . . . what're you thinking, Astrid?"

It feels so wrong to trust her now, to think that she won't feed me to Aunt Marshae's wolves at the first chance. But it also feels so *nice* to be with her again, like I could close my eyes and be back in the Temple with both Lily and Eden.

I answer despite my hesitation: "I have an idea that could weaken Aunt Marshae's hold over the Sisterhood."

A strange golden sheen blazes in her eyes, there and gone in an instant. "Then you'll join us?" she asks. "You'll help us stop Aunt Marshae and change the Sisterhood?"

Is this really what you want, little sister? Ringer asks.

To retrieve the neurobots, change the Sisterhood, and see Aunt Marshae humiliated along the way?

"Yes," I answer them both. *That is* exactly *what I want.*

CHAPTER 14

HIRO

ALL FEEDS WARNING: All Cytherea residents should take steps to prevent insect bites by using insect repellent, wearing long-sleeved shirts and long pants when outdoors, and sleeping in a room with properly disinfected ventilation systems.

Public health warning by the Cytherean authorities

Fearing my Yasuhiro persona is compromised alongside Hemlock's network, I spend a whole day at Violet's apartment recovering, theracast on my broken wrist, sleep plagued by nightmares of poison-stinger cockroaches. Luce never reconnects. Violet doesn't even know if Hemlock's alive after the Asters were forced to flee Ceres.

Which means Luce . . . Can't think about that.

Scenes of panic swamp the news, making it clear the Black Hive attack I witnessed wasn't the only one. Apparently the Genekey virus-carrying insects were released on seventeen different levels throughout Cytherea at the same time.

On the feeds, the streets look like they belong to a ghost town. The only people who dare to venture outside are peacekeepers in sealed pressure suits, chemical canisters of insecticide on their backs. The protest at Val Akira Labs has been dispersed for public safety.

But the images coming out of the overwhelmed hospitals are the grimmest. Every victim of the Genekey virus needs a custom-tailored genetic-based solution to help them. Medics express helplessness when they're stuck treating the symptoms instead. The sufferers are shown, pale and hollow people with dried blood around noses and mouths. Many, like Luce, are bald and scarred. Others are far worse. A teenager with bulging, jellylike eyes. A woman with fat yellow pustules along her neck and chest. A man with skin turned fish-belly pale, red sores over his torso cracking open and weeping. Who knows what genetic alterations these people had that were targeted and mutated by the Genekey virus?

Violet, unable to stomach it, asks me to stop torturing us and turn the feeds off, but I have to watch so I remember. I had a chance to stop my father, and I failed. Now I must stop this from getting worse. I know him, and I have no doubt he's going to escalate things against the Black Hive for this. And if things get worse for the Asters, Sorrel will only up the ante. Neither of them knows how to back down, meaning sooner rather than later, Cytherea will be an all-out battleground between Icarii and Asters.

I need information. I need help. And with Violet promising to check leads on where the Black Hive is located, I turn my attention to one of Souji val Akira's most trusted geneassists.

I'd wanted to leave her out of this, but the situation is dire. I'm desperate enough to track down my sister Jun val Akira.

THE NEXT MORNING, I pick up a nondescript pressure suit—no small thing when everyone in Cytherea is clamoring for one—and the following two days, I spend trailing Jun and watching her routine from afar. I shouldn't be surprised our father has a couple of duelists with hermium-blue shield-helmets tailing her. After the Black Hive attack, I'd be worried about my kid's safety too.

The most amusing thing, though, is that Jun seems annoyed by their presence. She makes them wait outside her apartment when she's at home, stand guard outside her office when she's working, even shoos them out of her sight when she stops at a shop on her way home each night. She resents them like they're her jailers.

Four days after the Black Hive attack, I'm ready. The theracast on my wrist has fallen off. My swelling has gone down, and the bruising is fading. And thank fuck for the suit's helmet, because the less attention the duelists give me the better. My plan is to approach her at the shop before she heads home for the night.

Beneath the helmet, I paint my face with colorful makeup and slap on a pink wig, anything to disguise me in case someone looks too hard through the visor. I top off the disguise with a hip-swinging walk that only the sexiest can pull off well. I've spent so long pretending to be various people—for my father at home, as a Dagger, and then as Saito Ren—that I can afford to be flamboyant when building a persona.

I'm already at the shop, compad out as if I'm scanning my choices for the bots to pull, when Jun comes in. But *unlike* last night, the duelists are standing a couple of meters from her, not outside by the entrance.

Fucking shit.

I keep my eyes on Jun as she slips into the ready-made food aisle, hoping she'll spot me and somehow magically know who I am and what I want. But she ignores everyone around her, perusing the various vat-grown meat options.

I've gotta move, or she's going to leave and then where will I be. Swallowing against my fear—and keeping my back to the duelists—I sashay to her side and look at the same display as her. I type out a quick message on my compad—*Meet me in the bathroom alone*—and hold out the screen so that only she can see. "Which do you think I should choose for this recipe?" I ask in my highest-pitched voice, adding a slight lowlevel accent for flavor. "I usually pick pork, but . . ."

At first Jun looks toward me with a mix of disgust and confusion, but then, seeing my face through the visor, she snaps upright in shock.

"Chicken!" she says, a little too loud, but before the duelists can investigate, I thank her with a giggle and head toward the bathroom.

TWENTY MINUTES. A bunch of people have come in and out of the bathroom in that time—chatting, touching up makeup in the mirror, doing their business and getting the fuck out—but I hear Jun way before I see her.

"Seriously? Piss off!" The door slams open. "I don't need you to hold my hand while I take a shit. I've been doing it by myself for twenty-odd years."

I bite back a laugh. I'm guessing the duelists don't want to let her out of their sight.

I don't hear their response if there is one. The door closes. Then Jun's voice, soft and vulnerable: "Hey . . . it's me."

I emerge from the stall I'd chosen to hide in. I pull off my helmet, and she yanks off hers, leaving her pageboy haircut sticking up wildly. As soon as my eyes meet hers, my face burns with a wide smile. I hold out my arms for a hug, but she stands arrested in place.

"Thousand gods, your disguise makes you look like Hanako . . ."

I snort at the comparison to our youngest sister. "Is that a compliment?"

She doesn't answer. "Fuck . . . I've missed you." And then she's throwing herself into my arms, her head against my chest, and while I've always been taller than her, now I'm *much* taller than her. She clings to me, arms encircling my waist, and something between a sob and a stifled shout is lost in the fabric of my suit. "Gods, oh gods . . ."

"Hey, it's okay. I'm okay." The lie comes easily to reassure her. "What about you? Talk to me. How are you?" She stays in my arms even as she pulls her face back enough to look up at me.

She pats down her chest and her plump middle as if checking that she's still all together. "I'm . . . I want to say I'm fine, but gods . . . everything's bad." This close to her, I can tell that stress has taken its toll on her. Her eyes are lackluster and hung with dark bags.

I stay silent, hoping she'll go on. Eventually, her breathing slows, and she does. "Since the protests started, Father's been working constantly, preparing for his trial with the AEGIS. He's not told Asuka and me anything, but we both know that if he goes down, we'll go down with him."

"You too?" The words slip out.

"I may go down anyway, after Lucinia sol Lucius ran off with Val Akira Labs data right beneath my nose. Besides, Asuka and I have both done . . . questionable shit at the old man's behest." Jun's lips tremble, and I wonder what kind of *questionable shit* she means. Illegal experiments on Asters? Before I can ask, her words flood out. "How are you even here right now? After the *Leander*, I thought you were dead . . ."

Dead like Shinya, our eldest sibling. But no, I can't feel right now—I have to focus. I shove the upwelling of grief away.

"I made it off, but"—hope leaks into her eyes, and I know I have to squash it flat—"he didn't."

"Oh." That one little syllable is enough to break my heart.

I pull away from her. "Jun, I need your help. I know the people who bombed Val Akira Labs weren't Asters."

Her face pales. "You know?"

And that's all the confirmation I need. Unruffled, I say, "Yes, but I need solid proof. I'm trying to stop the Black Hive—the Asters who are attacking Icarii—but to do that, I have to make sure the AEGIS prosecutes Father."

"Black Hive?" Jun repeats. "Are they who Lucinia gave the Val Akira Labs data to? Because I haven't read all the results coming from the hospitals, but from what I've seen, they seem to be causing some sort of genetic abnormalities—"

"Focus, Jun." I don't have time to explain everything, and besides, if Father hasn't told her the details, I'm not going to either. As shitty of a sibling as it makes me, my Dagger training tells me that any gap between them is one I can exploit. "It won't just be the AEGIS prosecuting Father if we prove that he framed the Asters for the Val Akira Labs bombing. Command and the peacekeepers will get involved too. Do you have proof?"

"I . . ." Jun looks around the bathroom, uncertain. "I mean, I've seen . . ." She stops herself from saying anything. "Do you remember the house Father grew up in, the one he wanted to move us to when Mother didn't come back?" Her gaze goes glassy as she reminisces. "Do you think we really could have had a fresh start, like Father said, if we had moved there? Maybe none of this would be happening . . ."

Maybe it's the mention of our mother that sets me off—no one but me has bothered to face the truth of what Father did to her—but I seize Jun's shoulders roughly. "I don't have time to talk about things that could've been. Can you get proof for me or not?"

And just like that, her eyes fill with tears, and Jun drops her face into her hands. I pushed her too hard. She's already facing heat from all sides, and I put too much pressure on her.

"Jun . . ."

"I can't," she gasps. "I can't. He'll . . . he'll know. I can't."

"It's okay, Jun . . ." I try not to let the sweeping disappointment overwhelm me. She can't act, because to act is to betray him, and to betray him is to shake off everything we were taught as children. Most of my siblings have never done that.

Have you? a part of me hisses. When it came down to it, I couldn't pull the trigger. I couldn't kill him. I couldn't betray him either.

くそ.

"It's okay," I say again, steadier this time. "I understand."

I rub her back. Someone enters the bathroom and I prepare to slip away into a stall, but the person immediately turns around and leaves, unwilling to intrude on whatever crying scene this is. When Jun's sobs peter out, she pulls a compad from her pocket, and for a brief moment, the knife my father sank into my back is in Jun's hand and she twists it.

The background of her compad isn't one of the default screens. It's a picture of my sisters—Asuka, Jun, and Hana—together. Jun looks happy, while Hana is the only one posing, looking directly at the camera and sticking her tongue out. Even usually stoic Asuka is captured midlaugh.

The family I wanted so badly to be part of . . . the family I never belonged to.

"I have to hurry before one of my babysitters comes to find me, but . . ." Jun scrolls through the compad, then swipes something to me that pops up on my com-lenses. I ignore it, doing my best not to burst into tears myself. "That's something that could help you."

"Mmm."

She hugs me again, but I am numb. I fight to bundle up all the pain and sorrow that image gave me and put it with everything else that hurt too much—Shinya's death, the *Leander* explosion, losing Lito—and focus on my mission. On stopping my father. Nothing else.

"I've got to go now, but we can meet again this way if you want." Jun's voice has the smallest touch of hope to it.

"Maybe. It's dangerous . . ."

"Yes, of course. I . . . I should go, though. Wait fifteen minutes before coming out? I'll have left by then."

"Sure."

And then she is gone, and I retreat into one of the stalls.

It's only once my chest doesn't feel like it's cracking in half that I open the file Jun sent me, the message that she said could help. The name on it drags me kicking and screaming into my past—to a bed after the Fall of Ceres, to a mirror where I see another person reflected at me, to a bloodstained cell in the *Leander*.

> **Beron val Bellator:** We both know that Souji val Akira keeps his true plans close to his chest. Whatever your father is doing in that basement, we won't know until he's already succeeded. Most times, I don't mind that. This time? I worry what his success will look like. Are you willing to follow him directly off a cliff?

Jun never responded.

Those feelings I try to keep locked away surge up, one after the next—remorse and regret and outrage. My eyes burn with frustrated tears, because Jun was right—this message *does* help—but it also means the only lead I have is with High Commander Beron val Bellator, one of the last men in this entire universe I want to see.

I drop my face into my hands. I suppose you're not a real adult unless you've had a breakdown on a toilet.

CHAPTER 15

LITO

Days ago, this area looked like a war zone, and yet you're still here protesting. Why is that? Do you feel safe?

Esperanza val Montero, reporter for the newscast El Sol

If this was about my safety, I'd be at home. And yeah, many people left because they were worried about another attack. I'm not saying they deserved it, but we can't pretend like Val Akira Labs didn't do anything wrong.

Anonymous masked protester

U sing Jupiter as a gravitational slingshot, my travel to Venus takes a mere six days. I burn as hard as the craft will allow, but unlike the last time I traveled like this—the pressure on my chest hard enough to make my heart stumble—my new body never feels it.

I'm vaguely concerned my entry into Cytherea will reveal the truth of the ship—that it may look Icarii but isn't—but my fears are put to rest at our approach. The gatekeeping AIs of the docks, blunted instruments that they are, are no match for the Synthetics. We land under the bulletproof ID of a human transport ship carrying out a diplomatic mission of utmost secrecy. Dockworkers are trained to look the other way upon seeing that code.

I kept up with the news on my journey—the flagging protests, the Black Hive attacks, the futile raids on Asters believed to be part of it all. I knew what I was stepping into as I left the hangar in the dark pressure suit and helmet, a necessity with the ongoing Black Hive attacks. But it's only as I'm leaving the docks that I'm hit with a mix of dizziness and déjà vu. I'm not so changed that I don't recognize Cytherea for what it is: my *home*. The place I grew up. My *family's* home for the past three generations.

Something pulls at the edge of my consciousness, yearning for attention. As I seek to understand the feeling, a series of image-memories play before my eyes.

Strangers brush up against me. Light shines strangely off the Abuela's crystalline urn. I wish she were here to comfort me, and it is this, over anything else, that drives home that this is her funeral and that she will never be here to comfort me again. I turn my face to weep into Luce's shoulder, and she rubs my back. My father's gruff voice fills the darkness. "Stop that fucking blubbering. Are you even a man?"

I try to extricate myself but fall into another memory.

Hiro walks backward down the street, facing me, arms pulled behind their head. There's a playful smile on their face, a roguish glint to their eyes. We are fourteen and gangly in the way only teens can be. "I'm not changing anything this time, I'm just going to go home and let him see me like this. What's the point of seeing a geneassist for a one-week visit to my old man? Fuck him!" They pull their holocoat, playing a scene from one of their favorite series on loop, tighter around them. "I'm Hiro val Akira, exactly as I want to be, and no one can change that anymore!"

And another.

Luce holds out a cup of coffee toward me. "It has milk—and sugar." Her nose wrinkles in judgment, but her smile flourishes a moment later as we walk, side by side, shoulders brushing, toward the park in Tesla Gardens.

I come back to myself and find I've stopped in the middle of the sidewalk. The memories pull at me, begging me to follow, to watch more—to *remember* more.

What was it that Mara said?

A memory starts before I can shut it out, but this one is not like the others. There's no fuzziness at the edges, no blank spots of forgetting. I see Mara perfectly, as if she's standing right before me, with her chapped lips and ancient eyes. Like I'm watching a holovid of her.

"But be aware, Lito, the Synthetic mind seeks the Singularity—its cognitive processes, its consensus, its connection. You'll find that your mind is different, that your consciousness has formed new pathways, and that memories are stored and recalled differently. It might be overwhelming at first."

She was right about the overwhelming part. She's also right that I can't split my consciousness between multiple functions. I have to force myself to focus on what's around me, a struggle for every street I come across that I've been to before. As memories assault me—calling to me sweetly—I search for the differences in Cytherea. As if seeing one layer over the other—the city that I left behind, exactly as it was, and the city that is, missing some of its sparkle—I make my way toward the Val Akira Labs office building. The dome still projects blue skies and fluffy white clouds. The buildings still shimmer like crystal clusters. But the streets, dirt-streaked and littered and bare, lie abandoned and forgotten. Looking at those—*only those*—helps me ground myself.

The closer I get, the stranger the streets look and the easier it is to stay in the present. Peacekeepers patrol in packs of three or more. Duelists stand guard, defending Cytherea in a way they never have before. Those few brave enough to leave their homes to protest, clad in face shields and helmets with every inch of skin covered, walk in a subdued way, heads down and shoulders slumped forward. Even once I reach my destination, the site of the explosion covered by a tarp and cordoned off, the protesters keep clustered to themselves in a little group, their once-ebullient shouts now a quiet murmur.

This is not what I saw through the Singularity. These protesters are cowed instead of enraged. Have sympathies for the Asters abused by Val Akira Labs fled public consciousness so quickly, or have the Black Hive attacks made Icarii citizens believe the Asters deserve their grisly fates?

I could prod the news feed, but I'm afraid of what it might unlock. If I was almost lost in my memories, why take a trip down that particularly nasty rabbit hole?

Focus. I came here to hunt down the cancer on Cytherea, that growing darkness hidden in a Faraday cage that the Synthetics couldn't see into from afar. As part of the Singularity, I always feel that black spot in the back of my mind, haunting me with how it's just out of reach. But unless I want to call attention to myself—which Mara insisted I not do—and smash my way into Val Akira Labs, I need to find a smarter approach.

Not the main office building, damaged as it is. One of the locations where they keep the servers. If I could jack into a server, I'd be able to fill in a map of what they're doing and where. Mara could help me select a location that's out of the way, perhaps shut down because of the Black Hive attacks.

Got that? Talking to Mara—to the Singularity—is as easy as a thought.

Hearing her—*them*—speak back is a comfort I hardly realized I needed. *We'll start looking.*

But when I turn to head to a bullet train station, a duelist catches my eye. It's not their black uniform—pristine—or their movement—controlled. It's not even their face—turned away from me toward a jumble of protesters. It's the shape of their shoulders, the line of their back. The way they hold their hands in fists behind them in barely controlled anger.

"You want to believe people will stand up to val Akira and his lot, when they're the ones who make them youthful, make them pretty? Who put them back together when they're on the verge of death and falling apart?" Noa's face contains a multitude of emotions—not just the rage of someone who knows what a hard life is, but the sorrow of someone who's seen uglier deaths. "They'd rather bleed every Aster dry—everyone with a *sol* surname—than give up even a little of that power."

I shove away the memory and focus on the present.

From this distance, I can't hear what they say to the protesters. I just see Noa sol Romero turn and lead five of them away from the larger group of fifty.

Like the city, I see the layer of the old Noa—the one who cursed my name on the satellite station—over the new. The dark brown skin of their face still bears the burn scars from the Fall of Ceres, and their prosthetic eye is a mismatched icy blue compared to their natural dark brown. But their hair has grown longer with tight corkscrew curls, and their anger, always so close to the surface, is bubbling over.

Where is their Dagger? I don't recognize the wan boy who follows Noa and the five protesters down a little side street away from the main protest.

The knowledge comes to me unasked for, a whisper from the Singularity: *Nadyn val Lancer died on the* Leander.

The skinny boy must be Noa's new partner, then.

I find myself following them without deciding to. I can feel Mara, her curiosity growing alongside mine. I stick to the shadows at the mouth of the alleyway. The five protesters stand confused, looking at each other. Two of them hold signs in front of them—FUCK PEACEKEEPERS and LA PESTE WARNED YOU; YOU GOT WHAT YOU DESERVE—like weak shields. They won't amount to much against duelists, and they know it.

"We weren't doing anything wrong," one says, airy voice obscured behind their makeshift face mask. I can't tell how old they are, but they're young. They're all just kids, really, this whole group.

Another steps forward. "So what if we're loud? Saying 'fuck' isn't illegal! Talking about those sick people isn't illegal! Nothing we're doing is—"

"Of course not," Noa says, maliciously sweet. "We just want to ask you a few questions." They reach into one of the pockets of their military blacks and pull out—what is that? They press a silver cylinder to the back of the mouthy one's neck. The kid sways on their feet, then slouches forward as if suddenly exhausted, shoulders drooping, chin pressed to sternum.

"What're you doing—" another in the group asks, but Noa's partner cuts them off.

"Everyone, stay still and remain calm," he says, patting the HEL gun at his side.

The rest of the group clusters tightly together. One sucks in a sharp gasp of fear as Noa steps toward them with the silver cylinder.

Are you seeing this? I ask Mara, but I can feel her, watching through my eyes.

Focus on what it's doing, she says. *Analyze it.* It's something I didn't know I could do, but with Mara's guidance, I slip away from my body and into the digital stream of the world around me.

It's like jumping into the ocean and plunging to the bottom. I am, in an instant, lost. If not for Mara, I would stay that way, but she guides me back, turning my attention to the data from the cylinder—and the neural implants of the teens.

I am in two places at once. Through my eyes, I watch as Noa moves down the line, pressing the cylinder to the back of each kid's neck. All of them react the same way as the first. The two holding signs lose their grip, and both signs clatter to the alley grime at their feet.

But in the digital stream, I read the data moving from one device to the other.

My Synthetic mind, pure instinct, understands: It's an update to the neural implants. A new algorithm that filters certain sensorial stimuli to prioritize stress avoidance. Or, in this case, to avoid public gatherings and disturbances—in short, making them more compliant.

Noa's skinny partner looks toward me, but I have seen enough. As he starts to walk toward the mouth of the alley, I slip away into the shadows.

They're controlling how people act with a neural implant update, I tell Mara. And while not everyone has neural implants among the Icarii, they're exceedingly popular among my generation and those younger.

They did something like this on Autarkeia too, she replies, and I see a memory in perfect recall.

People stand lifelessly in the command center of the Autarkeian ship *Dominique*, frozen in the middle of their routine jobs. I press the fingers of my right hand against the pulse at their neck or wrist, confirming they aren't dead, but their eyes stare at something only they can see. Realization creeps over me like the cold: I've made a mistake in coming here.

Curiosity sinks its claws in me, and I yearn to see how this memory plays out—but Mara yanks me back to the present. I'm two blocks away from a bullet train station and not far enough from Noa for me to feel safe yet. *Is this neural implant update related to the weapon?*

I can feel Mara's consternation, and it floods me with unease. *It's up to you to find out.*

CHAPTER 16

LUCE

Doesn't matter how many people you're bringing. Doesn't matter the fallout we're dealing with here. The Alliance of Autarkeia was made for moments like this. You've had my back for a long time. Now let me have yours.

Message to Hemlock from Dire of the Belt

I spend the entire trip to Autarkeia vomiting. I thought I hated liquids in zero gravity when my struggles were limited to figuring out urination and showering; now I wish that's all I had to worry about. The Asters give me what medicine they have available, but nothing eases my nausea. I slap sleeping patch after sleeping patch on my arm, but the time spent tethered to a bed only makes my body ache more than it normally does.

"What's wrong with me?" I ask Hemlock, even though I already know. I just want him to comfort me, to put a cool cloth on my forehead and stroke my hair like Lito would when I was sick and had to stay home from school.

"The Genekey virus," Hemlock says, because that's the only answer. I wasn't ever *good* in zero gravity, but I adjusted. Now whatever genetic edit the geneassists used to help my inner ear adapt is missing from my DNA. "Rotationally, Autarkeia isn't very close to us, but we'll be there as soon as we can be." He doesn't put a cloth to my forehead, but he sets a straw to my lips to help me drink cooling water. He doesn't stroke my hair, but he cleans up my vomit without complaint.

I wish there were something I could do for him—for the rest of the crew, or the other Asters on board who are chronically ill—but the best I can do is sleep. To stay still, and hope I don't make a mess for anyone else to clean up. Even when Lotus comes to check on me, I don't have the strength to send her away—though I wonder why, of all times, she'd snoop around when I clearly can do nothing of interest. Could she simply be trying to care for me?

Four days after we set out, I wake with my body pressed into my cot. The bed straps lie loosely tethered around me instead of digging into my arms and legs. The persistent acidic feeling in my gut, while not gone, has lessened. I'm under the influence of gravity again.

I leave the bed gingerly, testing my legs before putting any weight on them. If we hadn't left the gravchair behind, I would use it, but since Hemlock and I sacrificed it to the Geans, I pick up my cane—the blood cleaned off—slap a pain patch on my arm, and wait for it to kick in before heading to the airlock.

The ship, of which I saw little on the journey, is larger than I expected. The smell of Ceres lingers in the air, the earthen scent of growing things. The biggest room is the med bay, filled with beds locked in place. The hydroponic garden is also an impressive size, row after row of plants growing from the floor and hanging from the ceiling. But everywhere, even the command deck, is empty. I am the only person left on board.

At least I think so, until I finally reach the hangar; having to hook my cane over my arm and struggle down a ladder takes me far more time than I'd like to admit. There I find a group of people I don't recognize, a mix of rough-looking humans and Asters in street clothes. A little anxiety wells up in me—could these be pirates who have taken over the ship?—but none of them spares me so much as a glance, absorbed as they are in their task of unloading crates.

The loading ramp is open, so I skirt the edge of the hangar and head for it. I'd be far more concerned that these people were pirates if there weren't Asters working alongside non-Asters. We must've arrived in Autarkeia, which would make them members of Hemlock's Alliance.

A voice calls out, "Hey, Lucinia!" and I turn in the direction of my name. A short figure with a gaze as sharp as daggers jogs toward me. "You're Lucinia sol Lucius," they say when they reach my side. It's not quite a question, but I nod anyway. "Come with me. I'll take you to Hemlock."

The relief that I didn't have to beg for his location and then figure out how to get there is palpable. It's only as the person's leading me away from the ship that I realize my com-lenses aren't working. Wait—I just don't have access to the feed here. Or maybe there *isn't* a feed here, and I'll never know this person's name or gender marker. Unless I ask, of course.

I'm about to do so when they gesture to a machine that looks like a two-seated gravchair gently hovering above the ground. A flatbed in the back is filled with smaller crates from the ship. "It's a bit of a walk, so we'll take the cart," they say, and hop into the chair on the left-hand side. I lever myself into the chair on the right with my cane. By the time I've comfortably settled, they've tapped a destination into the command screen on the cart's dash and are ready to go.

The cart jerks forward, and I grab on to my seat to keep from spilling forward. "Sorry, I'm still working out the kinks," they say, patting the dash. "I wanted to turn it into a humanoid mech, but Dire wouldn't let me. 'Not enough space,' he said."

I lean back into my chair as the cart smoothes out and we ride away from the ship. Instantly, I am swallowed by the unfamiliarity of Autarkeia.

The docks are different from the ones I've been to before. They're just as busy as the Icarii or Ceres docks, but there's not a single hermium-powered barrier. Instead, it's just outdated airlocks, forcing ships to wait to be pressurized before passing into the hangar. The hangar itself is like one large warehouse with high ceilings, filled with ship types I don't recognize—not surprising, since I don't know shit about ships. Our cart zips around the parked crafts with ease.

At a wall, or what I think of as the edge of the docks, we pass into a square metallic room and stop. Double doors close behind us. Before I can even ask, we begin moving, though I can't tell if it's up or down. A couple of minutes in, the freight elevator becomes weightless in zero gravity and my stomach pitches dangerously, but within another sixty seconds, I'm pressed back into my chair and the nausea fizzles out.

"That's the only time that'll happen," my driver says. "We were changing floors." The elevator comes to a stop, the doors open, and the cart drags us into pure chaos.

A squat city of metallic buildings rises up around me, closely clustered and overwhelming. At the farthest edges, the ground gently slopes upward—no, it advances farther than that, up the wall and . . . I follow it all the way to the ceiling, where the city continues to sprawl, only upside down from my vantage point.

"It's a tube," explains my companion as they draw circles with their pointer finger. "The whole station is spinning to create gravity."

"Amazing," I say, but my voice is lost in the noise. A cacophony of music slams against us, infused with shouting and laughter. The cart zips into the darkness of the city, reminding me of a Cytherean night. Even though I can't make out colors, the bright signs catch my attention, shop names and advertisements swimming up out of the black.

And the people . . . I'm afraid my eyes will fall out of my head from staring without blinking. Even walking among them with my bald head and scarred cheeks, I would go unnoticed. They're all enhanced—prosthetic limbs or head inserts, geneassist advancements an Icarii doctor would never perform, body art that glows or shifts. I feel I've seen everything I could ever imagine, and then I see something new.

The cart takes us through the larger streets, ignoring the skinny alleys in between. We slow a couple of times, forcing pedestrians out of our way, but they move slowly and often curse at us. One group turns to us and, fingers forming Vs, point to their foreheads in an Icarii gesture for *fuck you.*

"Fuck *you!*" my driver yells back.

We turn onto a street lined with flexglass windows splashed in pools of light. Metal arms and legs hang on hooks. Weapons, from guns to modified mercurial blades, sit in display cases. Lithe and scantily clad people dance in shopfronts, showing off what's for sale—both the goods and themselves.

Farther back behind these chaotic buildings is a calm spot, a sphere that rises menacingly from the darkness. Around it, like grasping hands, are sharp fingers of metal. No one walks near it. No one even looks in its direction. The fact that so many people cluster shoulder to shoulder in one street and completely avoid that one makes it seem a cursed place, better off forgotten.

"What's that?" I shout to my guide.

"Huh? Oh, that. A Forge. Used to be where the Synthetics made their bodies when they owned the station."

"*What?*" But if my guide hears me, they don't answer, leaving me with even more questions than I had before.

The cart finally comes to a stop, and my head is spinning by the time my feet are back on the ground. My guide points to a closed door next to a person in a long coat. Unlike the other shops on the row, the window is papered over with sketches of tranquil places and animals in dynamic poses. There's no telling from the outside whether the establishment is open or closed. "Just head in there," they say.

"Thanks." I lean on my cane as I turn back to my guide. "Hey, I never got your name."

"Xiran." The voice comes from my left. Filling the shop's doorway is a tall, dark-skinned man with salt-and-pepper locs.

"Dire!" I say, shocked at his sudden appearance. I knew he was on Autarkeia, but I didn't think I'd be reunited with him so soon.

He flashes me a quick smile before gesturing with his prosthetic arm to my guide—Xiran. "Stop joyriding," he says. "Head back to the ship and finish unloading."

Xiran leans both elbows on the dash of the cart. "I was just showing her around." When Dire doesn't back down, they throw their hands in the air. "Aye, aye, O captain, my captain." They wave at me as they leave with the cart.

My face aches, and I realize it's because I'm still smiling. "Don't blame Xiran, it's my fault. Autarkeia's just so interesting." Dire fixes me with a skeptical look that says he knows better than I do.

I pass the figure in the long coat, who watches me with small eyes above a long, curved nose, and enter the shop. Unlike the outside, the interior is well lit, but the drawings continue inside, papering every inch of wall space. Dire leads me behind a counter that separates the front from the back. The floors are clean, though there's no furniture.

"Lucinia's here!" Dire calls as I examine a beautiful illustration of a moth.

An Aster emerges from the back, but not the one I expected. This person couldn't be more different from Hemlock. Their white hair is cut short, and beneath their large eyes are strips of metal, like some sort of prosthetic enhancement. They dress like a mechanic, in grease-stained pants and a T-shirt with an image of an antique tattoo gun on it that reads JUST THE TIP. Their long, elegant fingers are smudged with ink.

"You're the artist?" I ask before I rein the words in.

Their face lights up in a smile. "*Finally* some culture around here. You must be Lucinia. I'm Dandy, feeling rather female today so 'she' is preferred. Hemlock's just—"

"Here," Hemlock says, slipping through the curtain that sections off the back of the shop. "It'll take about a week, but I've got technicians working on the backup server."

"And then what?" Dire asks the question we're all thinking. "You're welcome to lie low in Autarkeia, but I know this place isn't your style, Lock."

I look between Hemlock and Dire in amazement. *No one* has ever called Hemlock by a nickname in my hearing before. And I'm not the only one shocked—Dandy's face is just as amused as mine is.

"Let me get my operation back on its feet again," Hemlock says, sounding tired. Defeated, almost. My heart falls at the sound. "I've lost . . . a lot on Ceres."

I lost my home on Cytherea in similar circumstances, but Hemlock had *built* himself a home in the Under for the past . . . what? Thirty years? He seemed fine on the ship—swore he was, when I asked—but now . . . perhaps it's only now, when he's standing still instead of fleeing, that what he's lost hits him.

Grief is like a bullet. You hear the sound of a gunshot, but it can take time before you realize you're hit.

Before I can go to him, Dire crosses the room and puts his hand on Hemlock's shoulder. "I get it, Lock, I really do."

"How are things, after Sigma . . ." Hemlock trails off, and it takes me a few seconds to figure out who he's talking about.

I never met the man who worked with Dire. Who *betrayed* Dire, and gave information about the Autarkeia-brand neural implants to the Icarii. Who ensured that when the Alliance tried to help the Asters on Vesta, they were frozen with a simple command to their implants and arrested without a fight.

"Fuck Sigma," Dandy spits, and while Dire says nothing about the man, his expression tells me he agrees.

"We've been removing the Autarkeian neural implants one at a time." Dire's hand goes to the back of his head. "With Sigma gone . . . it's taking a long time to get through everyone here. The recovery process is no joke either. But whatever you need, rest assured you'll have it, Lock."

"I never worry about your willingness to help, Dire," Hemlock assures him. "I just need a little time to recover myself before I come up with our next step, especially with what's happened on Cytherea . . ." He looks to me as he trails off.

"What's happening on Cytherea?" I ask.

"Perhaps we could talk alone—" Hemlock starts.

"Just tell me," I say, a little too hot and a little too quickly.

Hemlock trains his eyes on the floor. "After the Val Akira Labs bombing was blamed on the Asters, there was much violence, from both citizens and peacekeepers, toward my people."

"Yeah . . ." I'd seen that much from before we fled Ceres.

I see Hemlock's throat work as he forces the next words out. "The Black Hive released the Genekey virus in response."

Everything stops. The lights become too bright, too hot. My legs sway beneath me, and then there's a hand on my arm, guiding me into a chair. "Here, drink this," Dandy says, pushing a cool bottle into my hand, but I don't want it—don't want anything, not comfort or safety or *any of it.*

I took the Genekey virus to keep it from being released on the Icarii population, because I knew Sorrel would target the innocent alongside the guilty. And now . . . and now . . .

The cane and the water bottle topple to the floor as I drop my face into my hands.

My parents are on Cytherea. My friends. And maybe I left them behind when I chose to help the Asters, but I never wanted *this.*

My eyes burn with tears, and I clench them closed. Those in the room continue to talk, but I can't hear them. Their voices sound too distant from the hole I'm tumbling down. I never wanted this to happen—didn't want the Asters to be hurt, but also didn't want the Icarii to be attacked by Sorrel's brand of biological warfare.

Why do I get to keep living when they might not?

Sorrel . . . it's all because of Sorrel.

Just like Lito.

I clear my throat, ignoring the tears that roll down my cheeks as I sit up straight. "Do the Elders stand by the Harbinger's decision?" I ask, and the chatter in the room ceases.

Hemlock's dark eyes shine, reflecting the light. He is the only one who doesn't look at me with pity. "He is their Shield . . ."

"That just means he can act without their oversight. It doesn't mean they approve of what he's done." Determination resolves, a hard stone in my belly. This focus—this hatred of Sorrel—will keep me going, long after everything else has burned away. "I have an idea."

Only Dire looks amused. "Sol Luciuses always got a plan, don't they?"

I swallow around the lump in my throat at the reference to my brother. Most people avoid bringing him up. "Once the network is reestablished, we contact the Elders about Sorrel."

"And say what?" Dandy snaps. "No offense, Hemlock, but the Harbinger's the reason the Elders have decided to get off their asses for once."

Dire crosses his arms over his wide chest with an easy confidence in direct opposition to the anger on his face. "If that's what you think, Dandy, then you should leave."

Instead of cowering, Dandy rises to his challenge. "You think I'll throw my loyalty in with the Harbinger just because I'm Aster? Fuck your paranoia, Dire, I'm not Sigma."

Dire opens his mouth to say something else, but I lift a hand. "Can we *please* focus?" I beg.

Hemlock takes the moment to speak over them. "Truthfully, Lucinia, I thought you'd want to return to Cytherea. To your people . . ."

But I'm no hero to throw myself into the streets. I'm not Lito, or Hiro. I can't stop Sorrel with my fists. My power comes from behind a screen.

"Look at what Sorrel's done," I go on. "What he's *caused*. Not just the release of the Genekey virus on Cytherea. His hasty actions on Mars, the killing of Admiral Drucker, has led to violence against Asters on an unprecedented scale."

They all stare at me with pensive, unreadable faces. "And what will we be able to do about that?" Hemlock asks.

"I bet the Elders never expected what his choices would lead to. Asters being dragged out of their homes, arrested, and interrogated. Whole groups disappearing into cappo cells. Rumors of work camps throughout Mars. And the Asters being driven off Ceres, originally *their* territory." I shift in the chair, releasing the pressure building on my lower back. "Maybe he can fight the Icarii with the Genekey virus, but the Geans? The virus won't work on them because, even if they are genetically altered, they don't have the Val Akira Labs genelock for the virus to attack."

Hemlock's eyes never waver from my face. "What do you propose we do?"

"We call the Elders. We demand they revoke the title of Shield." I say it like it's a simple matter, though I know it isn't.

Dandy barks a laugh. "There's a reason some Asters live on the fringes." She shrugs. "It's not easy to convince the Elders of anything."

"But with proof, certainly they'll listen." I hate how much I sound like a child, begging them to believe me. "At least let me try. I'll gather news from Icarii and Gean sources that prove the violence against the Asters was a direct response to Sorrel's actions. Then, once the server's up and we can reach the Elders, we'll decide how to use the evidence."

Hemlock says nothing. Dire shakes his head. "Whenever you need me, Lock, you know I'm here for you. But Aster politics? Ain't for me to stick my nose in."

Dandy leans back in her chair. "What's it hurt for her to try?"

For a few heartbeats, there's nothing but silence. I can sense what Hemlock's thinking, that he doesn't want to spend hope where there is none. After all his work with Dire building Autarkeia and the Alliance, he wanted to be named the Shield himself, but Sorrel's return immediately put him at a disadvantage.

In a way, Sorrel's rise is my fault; he was named Shield after his successful usage of the Genekey virus on me deterred an Icarii invasion of Vesta. I want his fall to be by my hand as well.

At last, Hemlock waves a hand through the air. "Do as you wish." Is that the smallest hint of a smile on his lips? "Impress me, Lucinia sol Lucius, and I'll take your petition to the Elders myself."

CHAPTER 17
ASTRID

Even as a child on Earth, I knew the power of the Gean military. One day when I was eight or nine, this large man, the biggest I'd ever seen, came into the camp. He'd walked twenty-five miles and smelled like smoke. "They burned my house down!" he yelled. "I demand compensation!" He made such a scene that the lieutenant came out of the outpost to hear his complaint. The lieutenant was a good foot shorter than the man, looked like it would take a single punch from this fellow to kill him. "Soldiers came through my village and tried to kill me!" the man yelled. But the lieutenant looked up at him, and I'll never forget what he said: "Listen, if the soldiers had meant to kill you, then you'd be dead." The man went real quiet after that and left. No one even had to lift a weapon.

Excerpt from Admiral Shaz Kadir's acceptance speech
upon being named to the Admiralty

Lily proposes to move me to a safe house in the center of Pangboche, an industrial neighborhood of manufacturing plants and warehouses named after the nearby crater. I resist at first, remembering the brothel on Pangboche's outskirts and the girls we rescued who were then used against me by Aunt Marshae, but Lily assures me that even Aunt Margaret does not know of this apartment.

"Besides," she adds in that darkly serious way of hers, "if both Aunt Tamar and I found you, others aren't far behind." Reluctantly, I accept and, in the care of the White Guard named Oleander, take my few belongings to an admittedly nicer apartment than the attic rental. Aunt Tamar's guards return my old Gean gun.

It is simple, the apartment: a one-bedroom, one-bath on the fourth floor of a squat building painted dismal charcoal. The solitary window looks out on a water refinery, but I will keep the curtains drawn to protect my identity. The constant noise of the nearby plants is an annoyance I will have to grow accustomed to; it is like returning to my room at Matron Thorne's, where silence was an unexpected luxury.

"There's food in the cabinets, and you can get filtered water from the smartfridge. We don't have enough agents to babysit you, so don't leave unless you absolutely have to." Oleander wears wraps since he is not on official White Guard business, but he has them pulled back from his purple-tinted face so that I can read his expressions. My attention wavers between his sharp teeth and his large golden eyes.

"When you say 'agents,' you do not mean the White Guard, do you?"

He laughs. "Those toddlers can't wipe their asses without being told to."

I do my best to hide my cynicism. He, on the other hand, does nothing to hide his resentment.

"The Mother wanted you to have this, in case you need to contact her." He shoves something into my chest. I fumble with the object, surprised to find it is a basic compad.

"Don't call anyone. Don't message anyone. The only person you need to talk to is already in your contacts." He lists these instructions as if reading from a list, making me feel as if I am a child. "And *don't* say anything in a message that reveals your location."

"I understand," I say, rubbing my fingers over the slick screen.

"We'll contact you when we have a finalized plan," he says, and I do my best not to sneer; I have already begun on a plan of my own. "Like I said, don't go anywhere." Without a farewell, he leaves me in the apartment.

The cold, empty apartment with nothing to do other than explore the compad.

A soft ping alerts me to a new message.

L: O says he got you set up on the compad.

It must be Lily.

A: Yes.

I hesitate before sending my response. The idea that I am to sit quietly while Lily plans—with whom? Aunt Tamar and Aunt Margaret?—agitates me. Part of the agreement was that they hide nothing from me and allow me to execute my own plans, not use me like a puppet. I follow up with a longer message, carefully choosing my words.

A: I need control over the NIs. Same level as you.

Lily's response comes quickly.

L: What are you thinking?

If she is daunted by my request for the Mother's level of access to the neural implants, she does not show it. My fingers dance through the air, conducting a symphony of my words.

A: I have an idea that could weaken our old Auntie's
    hold. Discovering what has been done to them with
    the NIs will change the minds of many in gray. But to
    show them that truth, I need to be able to free them.

To throw open the cages the Sisterhood has put them in. Showing the First Sister of the *Juno* the neural implant was enough to change her mind. But I also remember how I tried to free her from her neural implant and found myself unable to. There must be something in the technology that allows some but not others to influence the implants.

I lean back into the sofa as I wait for Lily's answer. The simple act of writing brings back the days I spent with Saito Ren on the *Juno*, exchanging beliefs and wishes and experiences. Strangely, I find myself yearning for a connection like that again. For the freedom of sharing, and the closeness it brings.

But Saito Ren did not truly exist, and choosing to trust Lily with my inner thoughts—with the *truth* of me—would make me an easy target for betrayal.

We cannot be so weak again, little sister, Ringer whispers, and I agree. I must be wary of what I tell Lily.

After a few minutes, Lily confirms my theory.

> **L:** The NI setup in S-hood is very different from the pro-
> tections used by those who flew too close to the sun.

It takes me a few seconds to realize she means the Icarii.

> **L:** Most NIs here are left "unlocked" so anyone with
> access, like our old Aunties, can connect to and in-
> fluence them. The Aunties' hope is that the secret of
> the NI will keep those with access from abusing their
> power. Obviously, it's still a problem. But you're right
> that I have one of the highest levels of access. Give
> me a day, and I can get you the same.

I think back to that room on Ceres, what feels like a lifetime ago. The way Mother Isabel III seized my body like it was her own and forced me to sit. The pop in my head when she returned my voice. Her fran-tic laughter when she discovered I was seeing someone who was not there. *You've been damaged by the implant, and we never knew!* What did the quicksilver warrior call it? Neural degradation.

But if Ringer were just a symptom of my neural degradation, why would I have that memory of him offering me the golden star—his neurobots? Then again, I took Bruni's Muninn line, and he does not appear to me. He does not even speak, while Ringer is an entire person unto himself. And that is without considering the lost memories of my childhood—and my lost name with them.

A: Is there a chance I might suffer more neural degradation than others?

I have written and sent the words to Lily before I think them through. For a heartbeat, I sit with the anxiety of offering her something she could turn back on me.

L: Possibly.

Lily's lack of pointed questions—almost a lack of interest in finding out if I actually have neural degradation—calms me.

L: Did a medic ever say something about it?

Not to me, but . . . perhaps they made a note in my medical records. While Lily might be able to retrieve those records from the Sisterhood, I do not trust her with what they say. But what of my life before the Sisterhood? Would Matron Thorne have some records of me from the orphanage?

When I do not respond for more than five minutes, Lily sends me another question.

L: What will you do with the NI access once you get it?

This, I do not hesitate to answer.

A: I am going to give our old Auntie a show she will
never forget.

THOUGH OLEANDER INSTRUCTED me not to leave the apartment, I slip away under the cover of darkness. Despite their similarities, Pangboche, to the south of Olympus Mons, is far from Karzok to the east, but I cannot let my chance to get answers slip through my fingers. If Matron Thorne has any medical records—or any information about where I came from and how Ringer came to be—I must have them.

The hired podcar takes more than two hours to reach my destination. The driver is silent, and so am I. The sky is a lumpy black, not a star showing through the thick smog clouds curling up from the surrounding factories. The houses, ramshackle buildings of stone, are barely lit; the poorest districts have always needed to conserve energy, but it makes all of the homes seem abandoned—even the orphanage.

When I was the First Sister of Ceres, I came here to investigate Aunt Genette's embezzlement. The house has changed little in the past few months. The paint is faded and flaking. The small yard is withered and brown. The porch is filled with dirty, abandoned toys. No one notices me as I open the iron gate and walk up to the door. When I knock, I hear no children.

It is late. Perhaps they have already retired to bed, though I remember playing with hand-sewn dolls beneath my covers long after Matron Thorne turned the lights off.

I am about to knock a second time when the door opens. Eclipsed by the hall light stands Matron Throne with her sagging jowls pressed into a deeper frown. "Who're you?" she asks, a drunken slur to her Martian accent. She smells sharp, like ship fuel, an indication of cheap alcohol. "What d'ya want?"

Because the temporary red hair dye is fading, I chose a jacket with a hood as part of my disguise. I keep my face down so my eyes remain in shadow. "I was one of the children who grew up here," I say. "I have come to ask you some questions."

She mumbles something I do not catch. "—none of that!" She tries to shut the door, but I slip my boot inside the frame. "Whaa—" Before she can attempt to slam the door on my foot, I shoulder the door open, and she stumbles back.

Matron Thorne is an old woman—and weak. There is no doubt I can handle her.

"Who're you?" she asks again as I step into the hall. She holds the hook she uses in place of a hand before her, as if it could possibly offer her protection.

"I told you, I grew up here."

Her eyes, glassy moments before, go wide. Red veins trace the edges. "You—you're the Sister who came here—the one they're looking for who can talk—"

I am all too aware of the old gun in my pocket and the knife in my boot as I step toward her—perhaps a bit too menacingly, for she shrinks back in fear. "Whoever you think I am, you're wrong." She did not even recognize me when I came two months ago! How in the Goddess's garden did she recognize me *now*, drunk as she is?

"No," she says, more a moan than a word. "No, I know you . . . I knew you then, and I know you now."

A heavy breath rattles through my lips. "You didn't—you don't—"

"That little girl who used to pretend she was a lost Martian princess, with cornflower-blue eyes that read everything in sight."

I stumble back a step. *She remembers.* Or . . . she knew exactly who I was two months ago, and pretended that she didn't.

"You used to hold court over there," she says, gesturing with her hook to the chair in the corner of the dark sitting room. "Used to sentence anyone who annoyed you to hanging or beheading. Never met such a grim child." Her laugh is a wheeze. "So smart, but always using that brain to hurt others. Like a vicious feral cat, ready to claw at the first perceived slight."

"I-I was not!" I step toward her again. This time, she does not retreat. "Why are you saying these things?"

Matron Thorne shakes her head as if trying to clear her sight. She is not afraid of me in the least. "Why have you come, Martian princess? There's nothing for you here."

Sorrow and rage well up from wounds I thought long healed, injuries I had almost forgotten. "Give me my records."

"They're taken by the Sisterhood whenever a girl goes there."

"Then you will not mind if I search for myself—" I move to shove her aside, but she grabs my shoulder.

"Don't," she snaps, hard and final. "They told me not to listen to you if you came—that you were dangerous. That I should report you immediately."

The gun will get her talking, little sister, Ringer whispers. I shove him away.

"Then why didn't you?"

"I don't want that—not for me, not for the children." Her already-tired eyes take on an impossible level of exhaustion. "All those procedures . . . I don't want them to face the interrogations . . . But I also can't let you go poking around the house. Can't let those babies see you. It'd be even worse."

A numbness sweeps over me, making me feel, for a moment, separate from my body. "You want to protect them?" I ask of the closest thing I had to a mother. A woman I believed with my whole heart loved me, and yet one who sent me to the Sisterhood at the first opportunity.

Her mouth takes on a stubborn slant. "You go up there, I'll call 'em. Don't care what it means. You leave me and my children alone, and . . . and I'll just forget about this. Nothing for you around here anyway, I promise you that."

When I say nothing—too afraid to say anything lest I cry—she pushes me toward the door.

"Go," she says. "Just go."

A headache forms behind my eyes. I know I should leave quietly, yet something drives me to dig in my heels.

It's too dangerous to leave her, Ringer says. *Now that she's seen you, she's sure to tell Aunt Marshae.*

My hand tightens on the gun in my pocket. I could threaten her with it and demand she give me what I want. Unbidden, I release it.

"What're you doing?" Matron Thorne asks, the same question I wish to ask Ringer.

Protecting you, Ringer says. Something in my face shifts, a hardness that does not belong to me but to him. Matron Thorne seems to sense the change, her eyes bulging with fear.

Don't! I try to cry, but I am locked out of my own body. Now Ringer controls it—and stalks toward Matron Thorne, one clipped step at a time. *Ringer, stop!*

"Don't worry, little sister," Ringer says with *my* lips, in *my* voice.

Matron Thorne looks like she has seen a ghost, mouth dropping open and one arm held before her as protection. "I won't let anyone hurt you."

The darkness closes in on me until I can see no more.

"WAKE UP." THE bed shakes, and I jolt awake. The hand beneath my pillow clutches something hard and metal. "Get dressed." Oleander kicks the mattress again, and I swallow the wild fear that overwhelmed me at being intruded upon.

Where am I? A quick look around confirms I'm in the Pangboche apartment Lily set up for me. How did I get back here? I pull my hand from beneath my pillow and look at the gun in my grasp. What happened last night? I visited Matron Throne, and then . . .

"That won't do you any good against nightmares," Oleander says, eyeing the weapon with disdain. "Maybe try a cup of tea instead."

I have to force myself finger by finger to release the gun. I am, for some reason, unbelievably sore, like I was tossing and turning in my sleep. There's a tightness in my chest, as if I've forgotten something important. Why can't I remember what happened last night?

I look up at Oleander, thinking, for a moment, he has come to punish me for leaving the apartment, but then he says, "There's someone you have to meet."

"Who?" I ask, but he retreats from the room without answering, giving me privacy to change.

As I dress, I try to banish the growing worry, to turn my focus from last night to today. Who am I meeting? Where are we going? And the question that weighs heaviest of all: Can I trust Oleander?

"Got something for you," Oleander says when I emerge from the bedroom. He stands from where he was sitting at the small dining table.

"What?"

"You asked the Mother for an update to your neural implant? Well, here it is." He pulls a black box connected to a compad from his pocket. Wires of varying length and color poke out from the strange machine. It does not look professional in the least. When I do not move toward him, he throws his hands up. "Do you want the update or not?"

I answer his question with one of my own. "Why should I trust you?"

"Do or don't, I don't fucking care," Oleander says, baring his sharp teeth with a snarl. "But trust me when I say that if I could drop you, I would. You're a liability we can't afford."

The heat bubbles up within me, burning fear as fuel. "Is it simply our first meeting that upset you," I respond, swallowing down my anger in the face of his, "or that your darling Mother counts me as an ally regardless?"

He settles back onto his heels. "The library wasn't the first time we met." He makes an exaggerated show of rolling his eyes. "*Siks.*"

I look him over from head to toe. Again he is different, this time wearing dark Gean street clothes that hide his lankiness. I know Lily has counted Asters among her allies since before I met her, but the only Aster I recall seeing in her presence was the one at the safe house guarding Nat, the girl who'd fled Aunt Sapphira's brothel. Could this man be him?

Though if that were the case, how did he become a White Guard? Only members of the Gean military can be chosen as the Mother's personal guards, and while there is a regiment of Asters, I know woefully little about them. He must be from that regiment.

Or he is lying about his past.

"I have nothing to prove to you," I tell him, anger cooling and giving way to a chilly bite in my tone.

He smirks. "Not to me, no. But if you're going to take down Aunt Marshae, who has powerful friends outside the Sisterhood, you're going to need some allies of your own." He looks me up and down. "And they're not easily impressed."

"So that is who we are going to meet today," I say, offering him a haughty smile.

He glares. "Fine, do without the update." He starts to slide the black box away when I hold my hand out.

"Give it to me."

"Turn around," he demands. When I do not move, he explains, "I need to press it to your neck."

I shoot him one last look before turning my back to him and pulling my hair aside. He steps closer to me, and I suppress the instinct to whirl on him.

"This will give you the same permissions that members of the Agora have, but you're going to be like a kid learning to walk, stumbling with your hands out, grasping at anything you can reach," he explains, his voice far kinder than before. "Most Geans who have the implants don't even know they have them, much less how to use them, so whatever you reach for, you'll be able to seize and use. With practice, you'll be able to unlock their neural implants and, in time, learn to push your will onto them."

Like the last Mother did when she controlled my body . . .

With one hand, he presses the box against my neck. The metal is cold, and I fight a shiver at its touch. "Hold still," Oleander instructs, his other hand on the compad connected to the box. "I'm going to push the update now . . ."

I wait for something to happen. For power to suffuse my limbs, or my mind to feel clearer. Then heat flares in my head, like a sudden headache, only to disappear with a sharp pop.

That too is familiar—that is what it felt like when the Mother released my voice. Afterward, I do not feel any different.

"You've got the same clearance as the Mother now. Just don't expect people who've been trained to use them, like the Icarii, to be easy to control," Oleander goes on, packing away his box and compad.

I swallow hard and gather myself. When I focus on Oleander—*really* focus—I can . . . feel him, in a strange way. Does he feel me reaching for him? "What about you and the White Guard?" I ask, unsure whether he will answer.

I am surprised when he does. "With the other White Guards? Probably. They're fucking brainwashed to answer to those things in their heads. But me?" He clicks his tongue against his teeth. "No way. Now let's get moving before we're late."

OLEANDER TAKES ME to a rented room at a hotel on the edge of Olympus Mons. So close to the rim of the dome, the building is squat and the view nonexistent, but we do not plan to stay here long. The civilian-dressed soldier who spotted me at the café stands guard outside. "He's waiting for you," the soldier says as he opens the door for us.

The room is a stale studio with peeling wallpaper and an over-powering odor of burnt coffee. A man in fashionable street clothes waits inside, sitting on a two-person sofa. He stands as I enter, surveying me from head to toe. I take a moment to do the same.

He's in his late thirties, handsome, with golden-brown skin and jet-black hair. His body—his very movements—reveal him as military, though his hands have a grace to them despite his thick fingers and swollen joints.

"I'm Admiral Shaz Kadir," he says, hands moving as if conducting his words. I do my best to keep the shock from my face. *Powerful friends,* indeed. Lily has been cultivating a connection with an admiral. Smart, if the Warlord is considering retirement. "And you must be Astrid, the former First Sister of Ceres."

"I am Astrid," I say.

The admiral settles back on the sofa. "Sit," he says, but I do not. I want to be ready to run if I need to.

"I prefer to stand."

When he looks up at me, it is with more than a hint of exaspera-tion, as if I am being stubborn for the fun of it. "I asked for this meet-ing because of your importance in the Mother's plans. I thought it important to get to know you personally. Do you understand what our goals are?"

Our goals? "I am sure we have some common desires," I say charita-bly. "You must be Lily's choice for the next Warlord."

"'Lily,' huh?" He offers me a boyish smile. "We can only pray that I'm Vaughn's successor. And you? At the end of all this, what do you want?"

In my exhaustion, the scoff slips out before I can stop it. But truthfully, I have not thought that far ahead. I have been living one day to the next—one *moment* to the next—since Aunt Marshae stripped me of my title and I found Eden dead. Once upon a time, I wanted to change the Sisterhood for the Goddess and my fellow Sisters. Now I am not sure I believe in Her anymore. Yes, I desire to help the Sisters, but I also want to get the Skadivolk neurobots back.

And revenge against Aunt Marshae, Ringer growls.

Yes, that too. But because I do not want this stranger to know the details about the neurobots, I choose to focus on everything else.

"I want to burn the corruption out of the Agora. Aunt Marshae's perversion has gone too far." I cross my arms over my chest, aware of how closed off it must make me look.

"The Mother mentioned that Admiral Drucker had taken something from you, and that you wanted to get it back."

My heart rattles against the cage of my ribs. I do not respond.

"Intelligence tells me that the cappos recently pulled off a raid against the moonborn." The boyish smile that takes ten years off his age returns, but it only serves to make me hate him. "You wouldn't know anything about that, would you?"

How am I to answer, pinned beneath his gaze as I am? How much does he know about the neurobots? Would he be able—and, more importantly, willing—to help me get them back?

"We can go over that some more, if you like." He leans forward, placing his elbows on his knees. He clasps his hands between his legs. "Or we can talk about other things. The Mother has assured me that you would make a valuable addition to our alliance." He gestures to the door where the plainclothes soldier who captured me and dragged me to Aunt Tamar stands at attention. "I have many loyal to me, all ready to take a stand against government corruption. The thing is, Astrid, I'm not quite sure I see why we need you."

Oleander, from the corner, swallows a laugh. My usually controlled expression betrays me as I bite back a growl. "I understand why Lily wants to ally with an admiral—Aunt Marshae has done the same, after all. But what do you understand of the Sisterhood? Once you become the Warlord—*if* you become the Warlord—what are your plans regarding the Agora? The Aunts? The Sisters?"

"Well, that's what I'd have the Mother for—"

"No." My refusal is flat and quick. "Separation of government and religion has always been the *ideal*, yet time and again, I have seen one bleed into the other. Your alliance with Lily is fundamentally against that model from the start. So I ask you again, what are your plans for the Sisterhood?"

"Well, I know Sisters, and—"

"No," I say again. Kadir shifts uncomfortably on the couch. "As a soldier, you have confessed to Sisters. Likely, you have slept with Sisters whether they wanted to or not. But have you ever *communicated* with them, asked them for their opinions?"

He cocks his head, studying me anew. There's a gleam in his eyes that wasn't there before, but the discomfort is gone. "This is my first time talking with a Sister. I'm finding it rather enlightening."

"Now," I say, my tone much calmer, "what are your plans for the Sisterhood?"

"You've made your point," he says at last. "The Mother needs the opinions of Sisters like you in reforming the Sisterhood. If I become Warlord, I plan to defer to her—and your—judgment on those matters."

His words are pleasing, but I know soldiers; they are persuaded by action. And the admiral is, at his heart, a soldier.

"Has Lily told you about my plan to weaken Aunt Marshae's hold on the Sisterhood?" I ask. Kadir nods. "Then see my worth for yourself at Karzok Abbey. Tomorrow." It is far sooner than I had initially planned for—I wanted time to practice with the neural implant—but as the Canon states, *A seed unplanted cannot bear fruit.* "I guarantee you will find the end of the weekly sun service interesting."

Kadir stands and appraises me with dark eyes.

"I look forward to it."

I PUT ON the nicest dress I have, a soft blue sheath with an embroidered neckline. The skirt ends just above my knee, revealing the thunderbolt-shaped scar, an ever-present reminder of my bullet wound from Earth, whenever I walk.

It is unsightly, Ringer notes, but I ignore him. What soldier does not have their share of scars?

The temporary red dye has washed out completely, leaving me golden-haired and, I am afraid, recognizable, especially after Matron Thorne identified me. My only hope is that my plan works and I escape before someone summons trouble.

The day is moderately warm. The sky is clear, fitting for a sun service. I should focus on the beauty of Mars as it passes outside the window, but instead I spend the entirety of the long podcar ride to Karzok Abbey considering what I should tell Lily about the neurobots, or if I should even mention them at all. Admiral Kadir is right that we could use soldiers as allies when Aunt Marshae has the cappos, but what if he is just more of the same—a man I cannot trust?

When the podcar stops, I slip the compad away, message unsent. As my heels clip against the pavement on my way to the abbey, all I can think of is how Matron Thorne used to herd all of us children into a line, dispense the day's gravity medication if she had it and juice if she did not, and lead us to this stony facade for one of the weekly services. But the thought of Matron Thorne—and the visit I cannot quite remember—makes my stomach churn.

Focus on the plan, Ringer says.

Like the orphanage, the abbey hasn't changed from my memories. It is, by Sisterhood standards, tiny: one long building made of bricks housing a single room that could fit fifty people at most. The double doors, at least, have been decorated with flower wreaths. The abbey boasts a single window of glass directly behind the pulpit on a raised dais, though the glass is unadorned and plain, like the rest of the chapel.

When I enter through the open doors, I take in a deep, steeling breath, remove my hooded jacket, choose a pew in the middle of the room, and sit close to the wall. The cloying scent of incense overwhelms me, dragging me back to afternoons just like this one when I was a child swallowed by these stone seats and surrounded by the warm bodies of my fellow orphans.

When the sun service begins, the Aunt in charge, dressed in traditional gray, ascends the dais to the pulpit. The Sisters assigned to this unfortunate abbey—four women with plain faces, with bodies labeled undesirable, or those on the cusp of becoming a Cousin's age—move from the front of the room to the back, scattering flower petals from wicker baskets held in the crooks of their elbows. In the Temple, Cathedral, and affluent abbeys, these would be real petals; here, they are dusty silk replicas.

They finish their circuit of the room and kneel before the Aunt, legs tucked beneath them and faces downcast in the direction of the audience, unmoving dolls meant to serve. There they will remain until the end of the service, when they will rise to distribute fruit and vegetable seeds, gifts from the Order of Pyxis, which runs this abbey.

The Aunt gestures to the back, where the doors have been left open and soft light filters in. "Let us pray," she says, beginning the traditional Glorious Invitation prayer:

> *O Goddess,*
> *Thy people entreat Thee,*
> *My mouth opens to speak Thee,*
> *Come upon us as promised,*
> *In accordance with Thine love.*

I drift away at the familiar words as the Aunt leads the congregation through a dozen psalms, admonitions, and hymns. After concluding the Prayer for the Agora's Wisdom, the congregation is seated, and the Aunt speaks her sermon for the day, reflecting on certain verses and instructing parishioners to be mindful of one thing or another.

Time moves slowly, making me feel as if I have been here for an eternity. I squeeze my hands together in my lap as the service drones on, my thoughts only on what I am meant to do here. I dare not even look around to see if Kadir or his soldiers are in attendance; I fear I will retreat if I do not spy enough welcoming faces, and so I cannot chance it.

The final prayer, the Entreaty of Growing Things, snaps me into hyperawareness. Half an hour has come and gone. I finally dare to look at the people seated beside me. I recognize none of the plainly dressed individuals, their faces dutifully turned to the ceiling as if looking at the Goddess Herself. When this prayer is finished, I must move alongside the Sisters . . . I must call attention directly to myself.

The Aunt begins the final stanza:

> *O Goddess,*
> *Glory to Thee,*
> *O grower of things,*
> *The seeds of man and of woman and of earth*
> *Grow in us,*
> *Your holy will,*
> *And in us and of us, find You growing.*
> *Amen.*

The Sisters stand to gather their baskets of seeds. I shove myself to my feet as well. A few faces turn in my direction. My fear sets me to trembling, but I clench my hands into fists. *A soldier does not cower*, I think, feeling Ringer's easy presence.

I step out of the pew as the Sisters enter the central aisle. The one closest to me freezes, her eyes going wide, while the one behind her looks over her shoulder to the Aunt. The Aunt does not notice the trouble—does not notice *me*—until I speak.

"Let them sing with joyful hearts," I say, quoting Exultations 4:19, not caring that this verse is directed more at civilians than at Sisters. "Let them laugh with thunderous praise."

I hold out my hand as if to open a door. Oleander said I could simply probe at their minds with mine and my neural implant would connect automatically, but the visualization helps me as I focus on the Sister directly in front of me. The back of my head burns with a strange heat, and I feel the connection snap taut between us like a rope. Her hand jolts to her chest as she feels it too. I follow that rope to its source, seize on the implant as Oleander instructed me, and *push*—

She releases a noise between a gasp and a scream. Her hand shoots from her chest to her mouth then. "What have you done?" she asks in wonder from behind her fingers. "What have you done?"

"Let them speak," I finish the verse, "with the truth of the Goddess."

Petitioners stand in the pews all at once, but I do not stop to look at their faces, to see whether they are amazed or horrified; I focus on the Sister behind the first and do the same thing again. This time, the connection comes faster. When her implant is turned off, she immediately falls to her knees, weeping. "I am healed!" she cries, laughing through her tears. "Healed!"

It is at this point the Aunt finally snaps into action. "What is happening!" she cries as I focus on the next Sister. "I demand order!"

I do not comply. The third Sister, freed of the implant, turns her face to the ceiling and releases a primal scream. I focus on the fourth and final Sister.

From the corners of my eyes, I see people moving—fleeing the pews and the abbey, turning their faces to the heavens in confused prayer, falling to their knees in rapture—but none of them are still. Is Kadir here, watching this?

I free the final Sister, and she whirls on the Aunt still crying for order. Only then do I realize my light-headedness. I reach for the nearby pew to hold myself up, grasp nothing but air, and then I am falling, the floor rushing up to meet me. At the last moment, I stumble into someone's arms—the eldest Sister, the first I freed, I see as I look up into her sagging face.

The world reasserts itself. "You!" the final Sister is screaming, an accusatory finger pointed at the Aunt. "You *lie* about us! You withhold our food! You beat us with canes, not because we have trespassed, but for your own amusement!"

The Aunt stands shocked, a mix of horrified and scared. *She does not know*, I realize. Not about the neural implants or anything else the Agora does.

But she knows who has caused this trouble, and her eyes snap to me. "Heretic!" she yells, a woman with tears in her tone if not her eyes. "This is a breach of the Goddess's laws! This woman"—she points at me—"is unnatural! A sorceress! A witch!" Whether she truly believes her words or not, she holds out both of her arms, beseeching the people left in the abbey, those who did not flee in fear. "I beg you, true believers, stand before this wickedness! Stand against the tide of sin! Seize this woman, and let us cast her out!"

I find my strength again, standing on my own two feet, ready to fight anyone who tries to lay hands on me. But the four Sisters cluster around me, the parishioners behind them, until I am ringed in the safety of common people. A few people trickle to the Aunt's side, but compared to our two dozen, many of whom have the muscular build of plainclothes soldiers—certainly Kadir's doing, evidence of what he could offer our alliance—it is clear she has no way to fight us. She has lost.

"Leave this place!" I demand in my strongest voice. "This is an abbey dedicated to the Goddess, upheld by the Unchained Sisters who choose to do Her work!" The words feel strange on my tongue—hypocritical, and yet like they were waiting there to be spoken. "In the name of the Goddess, leave, or we will drive you out!"

The Aunt looks at me. Looks at the group around me, and then at her own pitiful support. "The righteous will reassert themselves soon enough," she snaps. Then she flees with her so-called true believers on her heels.

I have no doubt that other Aunts will hear of this, and Aunt Marshae after that.

But that is for then. Now, I turn and search the crowd. It takes me a few minutes to find Kadir, dressed plainly as he is with a fake beard. It is his boyish smile that gives him away. When I meet his eyes, he mimes clapping his hands at me and mouths something I miss because, in that moment, I spot Lily.

Beautiful, glowing Lily, who hides in plain sight, and it is a wonder to me that, despite the wig she wears and the false glasses, her radiance does not outshine the rest of us. It is a thought I am desperate to push away, and yet . . . I linger in it. Allow myself to have a moment of weakness, as a reward for my success.

The Sisters surround me, full of words and tears, but I watch with pride as Lily takes Kadir's offered arm and slips toward the back of the chapel. We have secured the alliance we need to destroy Aunt Marshae, and soon there will be more Sisters like these—free from the neural implant, able to communicate as they choose. Unchained, and ready to fight against corruption. I smile truly at them, and accept their embraces when they come.

CHAPTER 18

THE UNCHAINED

[16] "Why have you done this?" Cousin Tabeta asked of Sister Marian. [17] And Sister Marian answered with the wisdom of the Goddess: "For now that he is unchained, he will be able to work alongside me to repair his home."

The Canon, Works 1:16–17

Karzok Abbey has never, in her recollection, been so full of chatter. Everything echoes off the cold stone walls—Second Sister's giggles, First Sister's instructions—until it's too much, and she retires to her cell nursing a headache.

She was the third healed by the miracle. Funny, really, when among the four women at the abbey, she is the only unranked—and unnamed— Sister, and thus is last at everything. But even before she had been given to the Sisterhood by her exasperated parents, she preferred the quiet.

Her father had practically dragged her across all of Mars, having physicians poke and prod and test pieces of her. Her ears. Her throat. Her brain. Her nerves. Yet her parents were always told the same thing: there was nothing wrong with their daughter. And then her mother would weep, her sobs louder than a thunderstorm.

Once her little sister, ten years her junior, started talking—well, it was all over. Her parents washed their hands of her and sent her to the Sisterhood. "If you like silence so much," her father told her, "spend the rest of your life in it." They had a talkative child, one they considered normal, and that left no room for her. She wondered if her baby sister even knew she existed.

Strange, how she's thinking of her parents again. It's been thirty years since she was given to the Sisterhood. She hasn't thought of them in at least five. The Canon explains the importance of forgiveness, but she'd always thought forgetting was the next best thing. Now, after the miracle, so much of her youth has come flooding back.

"Dinner's ready," Third Sister says, poking her round face into the room. "We've all agreed to discuss what we're going to do . . ." She doesn't have to explain more. That was the first thing the Sisters of Karzok Abbey began talking about after the miracle. Their Auntie, usually in charge, had been chased out during the sun service. Certainly a new one would be put in charge? But the only people who had shown up this afternoon were grim-faced cappos who kept their distance from the Sisters like they were cursed. After a cursory examination of the property, they left in a hurry.

They were probably still out searching for the Unchained herself, wherever she'd gone after the service.

She follows Third Sister into the little dining room. As usual, their places have been set around the recycled plastiflex table. Unlike normal, their Auntie's seat is empty. After the chilled tomato soup has been served and First Sister leads the table in saying a prayer of thanks—one she speaks aloud instead of signing—they tuck into their meal, discussing between bites. The conversation picks up where it left off earlier that day.

"I'm afraid of what the Agora will do to us," First Sister says grimly. "We're all of an age . . . They could make us Cousins, hide us away, and forget all about us."

"Shouldn't we—I don't know—*do* something?" Second Sister asks. The wrinkles around her deep-set eyes do nothing to hide their bright luster.

She has always thought Second Sister beautiful, though she has never been brave enough to say it.

"Maybe we can hold a service," Second Sister goes on. "Show people the evidence of the miracle. The Agora would have a hard time making people forget us if we show them that."

"That is," Third Sister says, soft and sour, "if they don't drag us to some medic and take away our voices again."

That—the thing they've all been fearing—cuts through the talk like a knife. They're left with the quiet, which now, in the face of this threat, seems obscene.

She slams her fists on the table and releases a contrary growl in her throat. All her Sisters turn to look at her with varying degrees of shock on their faces. They have been together so long, they know her story—know she has never chosen spoken words to communicate, even before she became one of them. After the miracle, the only thing she could do was shout her frustrations to the Goddess before she broke down into tears. After so many years of it being denied to her, she could *scream*—and so she had, wordless and heated, from her very soul.

"What's gotten into you—" First Sister begins, but halts abruptly.

We are the Unchained, she signs, and the motions are sharp with her anger. *We cannot let the Agora take this away from us. We must tell the people the truth.*

"And what is the truth?" Third Sister asks, dropping her spoon into her ignored soup.

The truth is that our voices were taken away by the Aunts. Now they have been returned by a miracle. She has never spoken so much, and it brings a thrill to her, that all her Sisters are listening to her. *They say we cannot speak so we cannot repeat the secrets of soldiers, but what of us, the ones they call old or ill? What secrets do we have to keep? And why must our voices be taken, instead of kept by choice?*

Now that her hands are moving, the words are overflowing. She whimpers as she speaks, and tears roll freely down her cheeks. She doesn't fight that sorrow; she lets it carry her. *Our Auntie treated us poorly, but no one listened to you when you reported her, First Sister. And you, Second Sister, you have said that you were reassigned from your last posting because your former Aunt lied about you.*

She looks at the faces of the rapt women around the table. *Maybe we do not understand this miracle. Maybe the people will not want to hear about it from us, forgotten as we are. But I believe every Sister should have the chance that we have been given.*

"What should we do?" Second Sister asks, her bright blue eyes holding both hope and respect. And looking at *her.*

Her cheeks burn with a blush. She does not let that stop her. *We do not stay here where the Aunts expect us to be. Like Sister Marian's pilgrimage through the settlements of Mars, we tell the people in the streets of our truth.*

"I like it," First Sister says. She has always been the leader of their little group, by rank if not by action. Now she slips back into the role naturally. "All in favor of—of our Sister's suggestion?" She stumbles over that part—because, she realizes, First Sister does not know what to call her.

Flora, she signs, one careful letter after the next. *My name is Flora.*

And why shouldn't she have a name?

"All in favor of Flora's suggestion?" First Sister asks.

And though they know what may await them—the full might of the Agora, the negative reactions of those who disbelieve the miracle, even soldiers targeting them—they all nod in agreement.

"Yes!" says Third Sister.

"Yes," says First Sister.

"Let's do it," Second Sister says, reaching a hand out to her.

A hand that Flora takes.

CHAPTER 19

THE TWINS

I've always preferred plants to people. I don't think I could say that if I weren't in the Order of Pyxis, but there's nowhere I'd rather be than in my garden, and my closest Sisters are the same way. I have a special fondness for the poisonous pretty ones. There's nothing like something beautiful that could kill you if mishandled.

Aunt Margaret, head of the Order of Pyxis

The morning after Astrid's appearance at the Karzok abbey, the Sisters freed from their implants march down the main street of Olympus Mons, speaking aloud to spread the word of the Unchained. Passersby, curious about the speaking Sisters or awed by the miracle, spread the tale. By the end of the day, news of what Astrid did has spread among the Sisterhood like fire on dry tinder.

The Agora is called together for an emergency session, and every Aunt except one tosses out ideas on how to deal with the threat these liberated Sisters pose—whether to brand the Unchained as Heretics alongside Astrid. Whether to hunt down the offending parties, as well as all those who have heard the news, and make them disappear. Even whether to finally acknowledge the truth of the neural implants on a public level.

Aunt Marshae is uncharacteristically silent.

"We should call on the faithful," one of Aunt Marshae's puppets—Aunt Joanne or Aunt Kathleen, I can't tell them apart—says. "If the 'Unchained' wants to take the fight to the abbeys, we must respond with warriors of our own." Spoken as if directly from Aunt Marshae's mouth.

Aunt Tamar arches a dark brow. "The problem is the use of technology that the Canon condemns—"

"Which *your* Order of Orion assessed and approved for use!" the other puppet adds snidely.

"—so I suppose it depends on which 'faithful' you speak of," Aunt Tamar continues, as if she hadn't been so rudely interrupted, "as to whether they'll be helpful or not."

The puppet sits up straighter in her marble throne. "Why, the Disciples of Judeth, of course—"

"Enough." Aunt Marshae's voice is a hammer, bludgeoning the whole room into silence. I watch her surreptitiously from beneath my blunt-cut bangs. Since Admiral Drucker's death, I have suspected Aunt Marshae of stepping into his role as one of the leaders in the conservative sect, the Disciples of Judeth. It was likely how she came to have any influence over the cappos to begin with.

"It's obvious you all have nothing of value to offer," Aunt Marshae goes on, and while her words are harsh, her tone is . . . distracted. As if she isn't quite focused on the Agora. As if, for the first time in her life, she isn't bothered by Astrid. But what could be more important than this, when the woman she hates more than anyone is chipping away at her power? "We'll meet again tomorrow afternoon. Until then, try to come up with *good* ideas to deal with this situation."

Aunt Marshae dismisses the Agora, and while I watch Aunt Tamar and Aunt Margaret for any secretive hand gestures that signal the need to meet, the only strange thing I note is that Aunt Margaret looks far frailer than normal. I hope she's not falling ill.

Calling the handful of White Guards to my side, I return to my quarters before scattering them to their usual patrol routes. As expected, Castor is waiting in my bedroom to update me.

"Did you speak with Sorrel?" I ask as I sit on the bed and lean back into the pillows. My back aches, and I could desperately use a rest.

"Yeah, as well as a few other agents." His demeanor is subdued, his pheromones wary.

"Bad news?" I ask, praying it's not more of the same. After Drucker's assassination, the Geans rounded up every Aster they could for interrogation. Those whom they deemed suspicious were sent to "reeducation camps" in the far north. While most Asters fled Gean territories for the belt, a few Black Hive agents are still on the planet but in hiding, willing to risk themselves for my benefit. The sacrifice they're making is a guilt I shoulder daily.

He releases a long, slow breath. "Too few funds to help everyone who needs it." And with our uncle's server down, no way to contact him to ask for more—not that he would grant the request, considering we've been working with the Black Hive. To Hemlock, his side and Sorrel's are separated by a line etched in stone.

"If it's for bribes, maybe I can step in—"

"I'll consider it," he says, cutting me off. I can smell his hesitation, but when anxiety slips into my pheromones, he tosses the compad over. "But there's also something you should see."

On the screen is—*oh.* I hadn't expected the sight of a body, and it takes me a moment to calm my racing heart as I read over the materials from the crime scene. When I reach the address, I bite down on my lip, then force myself to stop before I draw blood.

"When is this from?"

"Body was called in two days ago."

It could be the work of the cappos, but what would motivate them to kill the Matron of an orphanage? "Could the murderer be on Astrid's trail? Looking for something, maybe?"

Castor is blunt. "Or Astrid did it."

My mind reeling, my heart racing, I tighten my fingers on the compad.

"You need to cut her loose." He crosses his long arms over his chest. "It's too dangerous to—"

I shove the compad back into his hands. "I want to talk to her. In person."

His face pales. "That's a bad idea—"

"I want to look her in the eyes when she finds out."

"And if she did it?" He scoffs. "What then?"

I release the full determination I feel. "Then I'll *know*."

Castor's pheromones are full of resignation and annoyance. Maybe he also wants to look her in the eyes when she finds this out. "It'll take me some time to get shit set up, but . . . yeah, I'll be ready in an hour or two."

AFTER JUMPING THROUGH far too many fucking hoops—getting Lily's body double set up, making a show of the "Mother" going to her private chapel for prayer, tricking the other White Guards with a feedback loop, sneaking out of the Temple—we arrive in Pangboche. When we enter the safe house I've begun to think of as Astrid's, she looks up from where she sprawls on the couch, one slender arm cast over her head, a strip of creamy skin and a sharp hip bone between her shirt and pants revealed, and I feel Lily's desire for her spike before my twin chokes it down.

Astrid sits up, her face softening when she sees Lily. I want to crack her skull like the shell of an egg. "What has happened?"

I fucking hate the way Astrid looks at Lily, like she wants to clutch my twin to her chest until she stops breathing. But I hate the way Lily looks at Astrid even more, like she's unsure whether she wants to be Astrid or be with Astrid.

"I need to show you something, and—" Hesitation from Lily. "And talk to you."

As Astrid shifts so Lily can sit beside her—face now pale with fear—I wonder what it is my twin sees in her. Sure, she's hot. So what? She trusts no one, not even Lily. She flips between cautious optimism and wary anger, like a beaten dog. Maybe that's it—maybe Lily's helping Astrid now just to fix the guilt she felt after Aunt Marshae almost killed her on the *Juno*.

"Oleander." It isn't until Lily hits me with her pheromones—*pay attention*—that I clue in. "I'd like to talk with Astrid alone."

I bark a laugh. "Are you fucking kiddi—"

Lily tightens her grip on my neural implant, slapping me silent. I check everything about her—sight, smell, mind—and . . . she's dead fucking serious. I don't even bite back the growl that works its way up my throat. She really wants me to sit outside while she talks to her pet?

Next time she can drag her ass out here alone. I grind my teeth to keep the words from spewing out.

"I'll be nearby," I say instead, eyes on Astrid, "in case she tries something fucking stupid."

I slam the door on my way out.

ONCE CASTOR LEAVES us alone, I pull out the compad with the report of the crime scene. I don't look at it again; the images will forever be branded on the backs of my eyelids.

"I have some bad news," I say, handing her the compad with the file open.

When Astrid sees it, her face drains of color. "That's Matron Thorne," she says softly, hand coming up to touch the screen. "That's the orphanage where I . . ."

I shouldn't be surprised Astrid recognized her despite the stark images. In the photos, the Matron lies on a bloodstained rug, arms flung out to either side of her body. Her face is mottled and swollen. Her torso is punctured in a dozen places.

It reminds me far too much of how Astrid attacked that man at the brothel during our escape.

"What . . . *when* . . ." Astrid's eyes shine with tears. Her full lips tremble. I watch her face for any hint that she knew about this. I find none.

"The civil guards investigating the murder determined it was a robbery gone wrong."

"A note—" Astrid gasps the word out. "Did they find—"

"No note. Not like with—" *Eden.* It's hard to say her name. "The body was found two days ago. The murder likely took place the night before."

She sucks in a hard breath, the first piece of body language I find interesting. But before I can ask, Astrid bursts out, "I was there!"

"You . . . what?"

Astrid reels back, hands pressed to her cheeks. "I went to visit Matron Thorne. Asked for my m-medical records. She—she said she didn't have them." Her fingers thread into her hair and pull as if she wants to rip the strands out by the roots. "Aunt Marshae . . . if Matron Thorne *did* tell the Sisterhood I had been there, and that she let me get away . . ."

Could that be the reason for Aunt Marshae's distractedness? There still seems to be something missing, just out of reach of my fingertips.

"But with Drucker dead . . . why would the Control Agency Police still be doing Aunt Marshae's bidding?" I ask the question aloud simply to think it through. I don't expect Astrid to answer.

"Perhaps some of them still work for Aunt Marshae," Astrid begins, voice wavering. Then, from one moment to the next, she regains her composure. She stands from the couch, back straight, arms held at her side, hands curled into fists. Her voice is darker. A bit deeper. "Drucker and Marshae were cut from the same cloth. They are zealots who will obliterate anyone in their way, believing it righteous in their fanaticism. The cappos must have simply transferred their loyalty."

"That could be. And until the Warlord appoints Drucker's successor, there's a power void in the CAP." I tap a finger against my bottom lip. "Aunt Marshae would take advantage of that."

"Or maybe we are wrong, and she wasn't working with Drucker at all."

That's a chilling thought. "What about a connection through the Disciples of Judeth?" I ask as I stand, hand against my aching lower back.

"Admiral Drucker was known to be a part of that sect. Maybe that's how they knew each other."

"Judeth," Astrid whispers, shaking her head. Her fear has returned, more intense than before. "The first Aunt named to the Agora . . ." She scoffs. "A name that indicates loyalty to the Aunts."

"I should go." I got what I came for—Astrid was shocked to learn of Matron Thorne's murder—and now I must return to my role as the Mother. I hate leaving her while she's reeling, but I can't be away from the Temple for too long. "I simply came to give you this news." I turn to the door.

"Lily—" Astrid grabs my forearm.

I stop. Her grip loosens until her fingers are a bracelet about my wrist.

Her mask is shattered, leaving her face naked with emotion. She is wounded and hurting, so I can't guess at what she'll say next. That she's thankful I brought her the news? That she thought of something that makes sense of this mess? That she doesn't want me to leave?

Now, that, I think wryly, *is just a wild daydream of yours.*

It's far more likely that she'll spit venom at me.

"I . . ." Astrid trails off. Releases my wrist. Turns away from me and crosses her arms. "I will message you if I think of anything."

The sea of distrust still between us, I slip out into the Martian night.

LILY IS SILENT at my side as we return to the waiting podcar. Doesn't ask me if I was listening through the door—which, of course, I was—or say anything until we're on our way back to the Temple. I've barely thrown up the privacy screen when Lily turns to me.

"She didn't know," Lily says. I snort. "She didn't have anything to do with it."

"I mean, she *did* go to Matron Thorne's, which probably painted a target on the old woman—"

"Castor—" The way she snaps my name stops me, but the exaspera-tion in her pheromones flattens me completely. "I know you don't like her. Just stop."

"*Sfonakin*," I say, and with the way Lily jerks her head in my direction, I know I'm playing dirty, using that name here and now. But I *need* her to listen to me. To *hear* me. I have to get through to her that we can't trust *siks*, no matter how much we like them. "Consider the whole picture. Sometimes we're blinded by feelings."

Her eyes narrow. She seizes on my vulnerability with sharp teeth. "Like with Luce?"

It's a kick below the belt, and I flinch. Guess I deserve that . . .

I don't like to think about Lucinia sol Lucius—not the girl with pur-ple hair and freckles I found on Cytherea, or the bald, scarred woman who radiated hate on Vesta. Because if I think about her, I begin to miss her, begin to think that maybe she was right. And I can't doubt the Har-binger. Not now. Not when we've come so far.

But even hearing her name reopens a wound in my chest until I'm aching just like Lily is. Fitting, I suppose, that we're twins with matching wounds.

"I know you think we don't need her," Lily says, crossing her arms tightly across her chest, radiating hurt.

"We don't." I know I'm making it worse by saying so, but I don't care.

"After everything she's done—everything she stands for . . . Aunt Marshae hates her. Fears her!"

I sigh. "She could fear you."

"Not like she does Astrid." Her hand slices through the air, firm and final. "They have a history. You haven't seen how she gets when she thinks Astrid is getting the better of her. You're right: sometimes we do get blinded by our feelings, and one day Marshae's emotions are going to cause her to make a mistake."

Her flat refusal brings out something dark in me. "How much of that is true, and how much of this is *your* weakness for that woman?"

The stench of embarrassment fills the space between us. Lily can't even answer me.

"Even if she *had* somehow contributed to Matron Thorne's death, do you really think we have the moral high ground to judge her for it?" She holds her empty palms out toward me. "As if we don't have blood on our hands."

"*Sfonakin*, I get it. I do. But with everything that's happened, we need to be careful." Lily calms as I speak softly. "Our agents are having a hell of a time even moving about after Drucker's death, and I won't risk them being tossed in those fucking work camps. We *need* that alliance with Admiral Kadir for this to work, so we can't have Astrid drawing every-body's attention to us."

"Maybe the risk is high," Lily admits, "but the reward will be as well."

I hold up my hands in submission. "What if it comes down to a choice? The Asters, the Sisterhood . . . *Astrid*. What if you have to choose?"

"Then I choose to help them all." She looks away from me out the window. Her pheromones slam against me. *We're done here*, she tells me. A moment later, her voice comes softly. "Why should I have to choose one to suffer in the place of another?"

"Because that's the way the damn world works," I say, turning my eyes to the ceiling of the podcar. It's impossible to look at my twin when she's suffering so much of what I've already gone through. "Just . . . be careful."

I know there's no option to choose everyone when the moment comes. I chose the Asters. I lost Luce. That's just how it had to be.

"With Astrid, just . . . look at the people she's surrounded herself with. Look where they are now. Her love is a curse."

"I don't love her." Lily's response comes too quickly.

That's how I know she does.

We're quiet for the rest of the ride.

CHAPTER 20

HIRO

[Catchy tune plays] When you travel like I do, it can be such a pain to find something that will fit your entourage but guarantee privacy. That's why when I'm on my way to a concert, I always choose the Helios family of luxury podcars. Helios are the sustainable choice for refined travel! Arrive at your destination with style.

Holo-ad for the Icarii Transit Authority
featuring Shimmer val Valentine

◇——◆——◇

N o network. No Luce. Violet thinks they have a lead on a Black Hive operative—a scientist who helped them do some of their nasty genework—but nothing complete yet. And with all of Cytherea on high alert thanks to terrorism, no chance of getting to Beron at his already high-security home. The only other place the man goes is to the Spire, which I don't even entertain the thought of entering.

Maybe he also visits my father wherever the hell he's holed up, but I'd have more luck doing *literally anything else.* Which leaves . . . only his travel to and from these places as an option for intercept.

Like most eco-conscious Icarii, he takes public transport. But not the train, because that would be too damn easy—he calls for a podcar outside the Spire or his highlevel apartment building and rides with a pair of duelists to his destination.

Approximate time spent in the podcar: ten minutes. A decent window.

Approximate time between signaling the podcar and the job being assigned by the feed: less than a second.

くそ. Shit. Fuck.

The system used by public transport is automated: call for a ride, program your destination, then go. The podcars are all networked, to moderate speed and prevent traffic, overcrowded parking decks, and accidents, all those problematic things that come with a bunch of machines rocketing around at high speeds. The real kicker? The system's designer sold it to Val Akira Labs as a proprietary program.

The problem isn't getting access to the public transport feed—most peacekeepers have access to it for their jobs—it's that it's nigh impossible to alter the damn feed. I'd need to modify a podcar so that it reads as empty and ready for passengers regardless of my being inside. I'd need to have that specific podcar close to the Spire in order to pick up Beron's request before any others. I'd need to be hidden well enough inside that Beron or his guards wouldn't notice me. And even if I somehow accomplished those other things, I'd have to deal with the two duelists he has with him in a confined space.

I try to make a list of my options, but my mind becomes overwhelmed by each step. I don't have the skill to alter a podcar or the feed in that manner. Maybe one of Castor's contacts—the one who wrote the program that helped Luce steal the Val Akira Labs data—could be helpful, but I'm cut off from Hemlock's network and have no idea where—or even who—they are, and Violet doesn't either.

All I have are my black market contacts, the ones I've bought sketchy weapons from, like the case of fingerprint-programmable triggers. I have some suspicion they're being funded by the Geans, but I'm not totally sure on that. I just know that if I help them get access to the feed, I have no idea what they'll do with it after I've gotten what I want. I'm not stupid enough to think they won't keep and use that information for their own gain.

But right now, my options are to work with criminals and throw Cytherea into further chaos, or to forget about approaching Beron entirely.

I toss my compad between my hands, hoping to think of anything else I might do. Maybe I can forget Beron as a lead, but will anyone else have even half the information he does? *Whatever your father is doing in that basement,* Beron wrote, *we won't know until he's already succeeded.*

The only thing I can't shake is: What fucking basement?

With the way things are going, will there even *be* a Cytherea if I don't figure out what my father's doing and stop him?

I bring up my black market contact and send an encoded message requesting a meetup.

Chaos it is.

"SPOTTED," A MAN called Snake rasps in my ear. I've never met the guy, but I imagine him like one of the geneassisted extremists from Autarkeia, all implants and shifting tattoos and maybe even reptile-scaly skin. Seven days after meeting with my weapons dealer and explaining what I needed, being introduced to a friend of a friend of a friend, a million crpytocredits, info on Jun's ID, and half a dozen insults later, here I am, curled in the fetal position in the under-the-floor storage compartment of a modified podcar.

And I've been like this for an hour already, our podcar desperately trying to take jobs in the Cytherean bustle before Snake slaps its proverbial outstretched hand. Snake's the computer guy, but there's a diamond-faced fashionista called Citrine doing legwork outside the Spire. Citrine must've seen Beron exiting and warned Snake.

I can't confirm anything, since Snake's connection to me only goes one way, so I have to wait in the silence to find out what's going on. Sweat runs down my forehead and drips from my nose, pooling in my breather mask. I'm wondering if I'm going to drown in my own sweat before the shit kicks off when Snake finally speaks again.

"Job's up and . . . snagged."

I wonder how precise he's being. At one point, Citrine threw out the idea of snagging every job in the block radius once Beron was spotted, then dropping the ones we didn't need, but Snake hated that plan and I can guess why. If there was a mass job grab and then a sudden unexplainable drop, technicians would start looking into the matter and discover their transport system wasn't as secure as they thought it was. If Snake and the other questionable people of Cytherea want to keep their access, they need to keep their connection a secret.

"Going dark." And then Snake's gone, like a foul god's whisper from my mind. It's up to me now, and only me. They got me where I wanted to be, and I have to do the rest.

The podcar slows, then stops. The flexglass doors spread open. I hear muffled voices, and the podcar rocks as people settle on the available seats. When I hear the click of the doors sealing, I know it's time. I have ten minutes to get what I came for.

A second later, we start moving. I press down on the button in my hand.

The canister tucked next to my chest releases the gas at once—colorless, odorless, but powerful. I'm protected with the full-face breather mask, but I still squeeze my eyes closed. The muffled voices become louder and then coughing takes over, only to cease abruptly a moment later. I hear a single thump, hoping for three—but it might be that they only collapsed in their seats instead of against the podcar's false floor.

A thought shudders through me as I brace myself to kick out of the floor compartment: *It sure would be awkward if I break out of here and find a family instead of Beron and his cronies.*

Nine minutes. I burst from the compartment facing a duelist. I've never been happier to see one. On the other side of the car are Beron and the second duelist. All three watch me with wide eyes, though their bodies are ragdoll-limp.

"Helloooo!" I sing through the mask.

Even if the gas paralyzes Beron's facial expressions, I still feel like he's death-glaring at me. I'm familiar with the look. He tends to glare at me this way even when I don't have him by the balls.

He's the only one I came for, so I ignore the two duelists, sit across from Beron, and pull out the solution in a little plastic bottle. "Do you know about GK gas? Or maybe you call it Somcap. I've heard that in little doses, it can induce a pretty sweet high. Your dose wasn't that little." I dab the antidote on a white cloth. "I know what you're thinking: That's illegal, Hiro! But you should know . . ." I hold the cloth over Beron's mouth for three seconds. "My whole existence is illegal right now."

"Fffuck you" is the first thing Beron slurs.

"I can do better." I shrug, slipping the antidote and cloth into my pocket. "It'll wear off in an hour for you, Beron. For your pals who didn't get a breath of the antidote? Maybe three."

His eyes ping-pong between sides of the podcar. I sigh.

"About now you'll realize your com-lenses are no longer connected to the feed. I've got a guy making sure we're not interrupted." I hold both of my empty hands up. "Did you really think I'd let you call for help? That was, honestly, the easiest part of this plan."

He huffs a heavy breath out through his nose but says nothing, as if to spite me.

"On a certain level, aren't you proud of me, Beron? You always said I was your best Dagger—could be anyone, could go anywhere." I wish he could see how I smirk. "Remember that?"

His tongue seems to get in the way of his speech. "Jusht . . . kill me . . . alreedy."

"Oh, Beron, I'm not here to kill you. Why would I do that?" I cock my head, since he can't see the smile on my face. "Sure, the last time we saw each other, you were sending a video to my father of my dead partner— who you killed, by the way, even if it wasn't with your hands—and the time before that, you were sending me off to the Geans after cutting me apart and stitching me back together like—"

"Shhtop." His eyes dart between the duelists. He doesn't want them to hear the truth—doesn't want to have to kill them for the knowledge.

"I'm having too much fun to kill you, Beron." It's only as I say the words that I realize they're true. My heart racing with excitement, I lean toward him, elbows on my knees. "I want you to *suffer* first, but alas"—I tap my wrist, where a slender band counts down from seven minutes—"we don't have the time for the games I want to play."

His eyes flick toward the darkened windows and the city that slips by.

"We have a *little* time, though." I gesture to the duelists. "Enough for me to do permanent damage if you don't answer my questions."

His glare falls fully on me. "What . . . do you . . . want."

"What's in the basement, Beron?"

He clams up, but out of shock more than stubbornness.

"Yeah, I know about it. What's my father doing down there?"

"I . . . I don't know." It sounds like it pains him to give me that answer.

I take a switchblade out of my pocket and flick it open. Pressing it to the wrist of the duelist beside me, I ask, "Is she left-handed or right-handed?"

"I don't knowwww," he growls through his teeth.

"Shame. Though we both know you can get her a good prosthetic—"

"He hasn't let me . . . go there. Said I had to . . . make Cytherea safe . . . first. Everything he does . . . he does to buy himself time. Needs time, he says."

"Like bombing Val Akira Labs and blaming it on the Asters. Yeah, I know about that too." The edge of the blade bites into the duelist's wrist. Blood wells up around the cut. Her eyes are wide saucers of fear, but she can't scream. "Better start giving me something worth my while, or your guards won't be very *handy* anymore."

He'd kill me for the pun if he could.

"Offfiera," he hisses.

I hold the blade steady. "Go on."

"Offfiera . . . leading Black Hive. Poshsibly . . . third level. We're in-veshtigating."

"How do you know I'm not working with her?"

There's a moment when Beron's eye twitches that I remember he's known me just as long as I've known him. "Didn't attack us with Genekey virus . . . like she would."

The minutes have dwindled. Only three more before our arrival, and all I've got is a possible location for the Black Hive cell on Cytherea, which I already have Violet working on. I could try to hunt down Ofiera, stop the Black Hive from attacking the Icarii, and hope Cytherea rights itself when the hospitals aren't overwhelmed. That the AEGIS will focus on my father's wrongdoing instead of the Asters'. But I'm afraid that ship has left port, and unless I have solid evidence that the Asters *didn't* bomb Val Akira Labs, no one'll be willing to treat them fairly.

"Proof," I tell Beron, remembering Jun's email. "My father's been acting strange, even in your opinion. It's shaken you. Got you scared." He doesn't bother asking me how I know this. "You've been collecting evidence of what he's up to. Evidence like the bombing." This part is pure guesswork. "I want that proof."

He hesitates. Approaching two minutes until we arrive . . . I don't move, not even to hurt the duelists. He looks at them, then closes his eyes. Resigned. He'll likely have to make them disappear for what he's about to do in front of them.

"My compad," he eventually says. "Right pocket."

"Better not be trying to get fresh with me." He growls as I fish the compad out of the pocket of his military blacks. "Open it." I point the compad at his face.

He speaks as clearly as he can. "Beron val Bellator, Drip Shoot Music Hero Seven Fruit Eight Compad Three Visa Apple Six Banana Two."

One minute to go. The compad opens.

"Fucking hell, Beron. Do you not have a lover or kids to use as a password or what?"

I look at the compad. There are several folders named with the same nonsense combinations of words and numbers. "Which one is it?"

"Technology Three Egg," he answers.

I click on it. "Password?" I prompt.

With a resigned tone, he continues, "Zigzag Polyglot Rope Six Umbrella Seven Question Hero."

The folder opens. I don't have time to see what's inside. The clock is ticking down—less than twenty seconds to go. I simply swipe the files from his compad over to my burner and drop his compad back in his lap.

The podcar slows, then stops.

The flexglass doors open.

"Say hi to my father for me."

I hop out of the podcar, slip my breather mask off, pull my hood up, and start walking. I don't stop even when, a block later, I hear someone screaming for the medics.

CHAPTER 21
ASTRID

There are as many sects within the Sisterhood as there are interpretations of the Canon. While some of these sects differ on as little as which hymn should be sung during a service, a few have more drastic leanings. The Disciples of Judeth, for example, want a return to the traditional roles adopted by the first settlers of Mars, when women were prohibited from joining the service and Aunts held more power over the Sisters they represented.

From Inside the Sisterhood *by Dr. Merel Jäger*

I have trouble sleeping. Excitement and fear war within me in equal measure. The news of the Sisters I freed from their implants is tempered by the images Lily showed me of Matron Thorne. Was my shadow on her doorway like death's? Was her murder a punishment for letting me slip away? Or is someone far closer to home to blame?

Ringer, what happened that night? I ask again and again. Silence is his only answer.

At least I have the news to distract me. While the Control Agency approves what is broadcast in the media, I have uncovered, with Lily's help, several message boards offering reports from anonymous citizens. I find the truth in them.

The Unchained have been gathering to speak out against abuses within the Sisterhood. While mandatory silence and the unchecked authority of Aunts are among their reasons, their focus is on a lack of bodily autonomy: the Aunts, not the Sisters, have control over who is made into a comfort woman and who isn't. Who is transitioned into a Cousin, and when. Who receives a nice posting and is educated, and who is no more than a pretty face, just meat in a bed.

Others have joined them, many Sisters who sign their displeasure, as well as, to my surprise, a few Aunts who agree that the power differentials have grown into a bastardization of the Canon's tenets.

In response to these women, citizens in gray hoods take to the streets. While many call themselves the faithful, there is another name for them: the Disciples of Judeth. A few, I see from interviews, are Sisters who believe that those in the Sisterhood should voluntarily hold their tongues, but the majority are armed men and women led by Aunts who preach "a return to traditional values."

In the official Gean media, the Unchained are made out to be aggressors while the Disciples of Judeth—with weapons they openly carry—are simply those who "stand against immorality." When Aunt Marshae herself appears to laud the good work of the Disciples of Judeth, I wonder how many soldiers, how many cappos, are hidden beneath those hoods.

The biggest problem is that their presence throughout Mars's houses of worship makes what I did at Karzok Abbey difficult, if not impossible, to repeat. I begin to fear I will be trapped in the safe house until this is all over, unable to free any more Sisters from their implants.

Two days pass after Lily's visit, and all I can do is watch the news and hope for the best. Until this morning.

I sit upright so quickly my head spins. The post is short, almost a footnote in the feed of the rogue message boards: a group of Unchained has converged in Marian Park for a peaceful protest. The park, located downtown in Olympus Mons, is open to anyone and large enough to have multiple entrances. I immediately send the report to Lily.

> **A:** I have to go.
> **L:** It's peaceful for now, but if this protest has been reported at all, it won't stay peaceful for long. The "faithful" are likely already on their way as well.
> **A:** Then I should make an appearance before they do.

Lily takes so long to respond, I think she may not. I dress regardless in my solitary nice dress and the dark jacket with the hood. When I finish ten minutes later, I see Lily has answered.

> **L:** I'm sending O.

As I wait for the White Guard to arrive with transport, I run my fingers along the bullet scar on my leg.

If you're not careful, Ringer says, finally speaking to me, *you'll end up with many more.*

I feel a strange sense of push and pull toward the remnants of my wound. Disgust and attraction. It mars me, and yet it stands as a testament to what I have survived.

Ringer senses this war within me and scoffs. *Get rid of that fascination. You don't want to end up like Ebba.*

Thinking of the Skadivolk leader's web of scars over the left side of her face, her crumpled eyelid, and her lack of eyebrow, I flinch. Perhaps Ringer is right. I pull down my skirt to fully cover my leg.

When Oleander arrives, I am unsurprised to find him dressed in Gean street clothes, a scarf around his neck, and a deep hood to his jacket. As an Aster, he would stand out more in the park without a proper disguise. "Let's move," he says, jerking his chin back to the podcar he arrived in.

I settle in the back seat alongside him. Without any prompting from me, Oleander rolls up the privacy screen between us and the podcar's pilot.

"Ready for this?" he asks, and I nod assuredly.

"Can I ask you a personal question?"

He snorts. "Sure."

Despite the privacy screen, I choose my words with care, just in case the pilot can somehow still hear us. "How did you come to be one of her trusted guards?"

"Military service in the regiment," he says, referring to the Aster corps. But that past is just what I expected, and one that strikes me as too easy a story.

"Perhaps," I say. Oleander grows deathly still. "She has always surrounded herself with your people. It has been her passion. In fact, I am not surprised that she chose someone like you to be among her most trusted, but what does surprise me is your lack of faith."

His pupils grow wider until his eyes are completely black. I feel like I am staring down the barrel of two guns. "And what makes you say that?"

I could tell him it is because of my long history with soldiers that I am able to recognize devotion, shrugging off the question entirely, but something makes me tell him the truth. "The way she chooses you for everything, first and foremost. The dismissive way you speak about your coworkers," I say, and he snorts at my euphemism for his fellow White Guards. "And the way you treat *her*." Again, he goes preternaturally still. "I can only deduce that your loyalty is to the woman herself, not her position."

"That's what you're wondering?" He holds himself tense despite the relief in his tone. "Yeah, you're fucking right. I'm loyal to her. So what?"

So, whatever his past, he has been working with Lily for a long time. The familiarity in the way they move around the room, the way they talk to each other . . . that only comes from trust. Which begs the question why.

"Are you in love with her?"

His shoulders jerk up toward his ears. "*What?*"

"It is a simple question," I press on, but he has broken into laughter. "The two of you," I go on, speaking louder than before, "have a connection I do not understand."

All the tension has fled his body. He smiles at me with sharp teeth. "Are you jealous?"

I huff through my nose. There was no point in bringing this up, in thinking Oleander would make this anything other than a joke.

"Listen, Goldilocks," Oleander says, and I am so caught off guard by the fairy-tale name he calls me that I do not notice his larger hand coming down on mine until it is too late.

"Unhand me!" I snap, but there is nowhere to flee in the back of the podcar.

"I do love her, in a way you'll never understand," he says softly, leaning toward me as if sharing a secret. His golden eyes reflect the light filtering through the flexglass windows. "And if you ever hurt her, I'll make Aunt Marshae look like your best friend."

He releases me. I jerk my hand to my chest.

It is a reaction I would expect from a dearest friend or a family member.

MARIAN PARK OF Olympus Mons is a park in the same way Lily is just another Sister. It is more like *the* park, an expanse of thick greenery that is part forest preserve and part communal garden, but one that belongs to all Orders equally. As soon as I slip in through one of the wrought iron gates, the starscrapers, steady sentinels of the skyline, disappear behind thick foliage. Deeper in, the sounds of podships and podcars zipping past are lost amidst birdsong and wind.

It would be serene if not for the sight of so many people heading in the same direction. I suppose Lily is right; this protest will not stay peaceful for long. While I hardly feel ready, knowing Oleander is armed and somewhere in the crowd behind me brings me, if not peace, a bit of composure.

That feeling is quickly swallowed when I reach the intended meeting place.

More than a hundred people stand clustered around an open fountain, its water launching into the air like rockets from a ship's belly. Some of them are Sisters in gray, while many are citizens dressed in plainclothes. I check for Disciples of Judeth or civil guards and see no one in uniform, though that hardly means they are not here. Every stranger might be an enemy in a mob like this.

At the front of the crowd, standing on the lip of the fountain are two Sisters I recognize. One is the eldest woman I freed from her implant at Karzok Abbey, while the other is the youngest. The older speaks with a thunderous voice that carries over the tittering of the crowd, while the younger signs the same words with deft hands.

"We have a right of choice," the first says aloud, the other signing just after. "A right to choose whom to serve and whom to service. A right to choose which words to keep and which to speak. A right to choose what to sign and what to say. A right to decide the paths of our lives, based on our abilities and desires."

Many Sisters nod along with her, but not all of them. The few Aunts I spot among the crowd stand apart from the Sisters, arms crossed over their chests, faces expressionless. There were a few Aunts among the Unchained's supporters, but I am afraid these are not them.

Their presence hardly matters, Ringer tells me. *It doesn't change what you came here to do.*

I shoulder my way through the crowd, getting closer to the fountain. A few people grumble at my back as I slip by, but it's not until I reach the group of Sisters at the front that anyone tries to stop me. Then a woman holds a gray-clad arm out to bar me from the fountain—until she sees my face. Her bright blue eyes go wide. I recognize her from Karzok Abbey too.

"Let me pass, Sister," I tell her with a smile.

She pales. Her arm drops. I step onto the lip of the fountain and pull down the hood of my jacket.

"We have a right to bodily autonomy—" The woman cuts off midsentence, turning in my direction like iron to a lodestone. "It's *her*!" she cries, followed by shocked exclamations from the crowd.

A ripple passes among the people. A whisper that sounds familiar. "The Unchained."

"Sisters! People of Mars!" I call out, and the Sister who was signing continues her duty at my side. "Listen to what I have come to say!"

My eyes flutter over the crowd. I do not spot Oleander, but I do see bodies growing tense at my appearance, and the backs of a few people who are leaving the gathering at a quick pace, likely to summon the civil guard. I am, after all, a wanted criminal of the Agora.

Many Sisters crowd around me at my knees, their hands flashing. *Heal me!* one after another signs. *Bring back my voice!*

Do I have time to both speak and free these women? Looking at their hopeful, upturned faces . . . I know I must try.

"My name is Astrid," I begin, focusing on the bowed head of the woman before me. "I was once a Sister. Some call me Unchained." Another wave of whispering passes through the crowd, but I cannot look at them, can focus only on the tether between the Sister and me as the heat in the back of my head grows. "I was given to the Sisterhood from an orphanage when I was ten years old." As if the implant is a door, I locate the lock, slip in the key, and unlock it.

The Sister gasps as she feels it release. "Praise the Goddess!" The fervor of the exclamation surprises even her, and tears of joy stream down her cheeks. Immediately she turns to the Sister next to her and urges her forward.

I reach out to her, speaking as I search. "When I was nineteen, I was sent to the *Juno*, the pride of the Gean fleet. I was named its First Sister, and thought that would be the beginning and ending of my power." I unlock her implant. Another audible gasp and sob. Have the civil guard come? I do not know, I do not look up, just to the next Sister. "It was not. Mother Isabel III named me the First Sister of Ceres before she was murdered by Captain Saito Ren." I release her. More crowd forward. There are still so many to free. "I did all I could for Ceres, hoping to be named the next Mother." I unlock another, ignoring the wave of dizziness that comes over me. "But when I came to Mars to announce my intentions, I discovered an Agora full of rot." Another. And another. "The embezzlement of government funds. The use of Sisterhood property to create brothels. The trafficking of human lives. The murder of anyone who opposed the Agora too loudly.

"I wanted to change things! But with what I had discovered, the Agora would never allow me to become the next Mother. They stripped me of my title, and I fled for my life." The girls swarm me, a river of gray. I do all I can to focus on them, to free them, as my headache grows and the corners of my vision darken. "I have now returned to Mars, not only to hold the Agora accountable for what they have done, but also to give my fellow Sisters the rights they deserve!"

Voices rise up from the crowd; I am unable to make them out or even tell whether they support or oppose me. But I cannot stop. I will not stop.

"I never chose to join the Sisterhood! I did not consent to be raped by soldiers! I did not agree to have my voice taken away, to be told who I could and could not communicate with, so that I could never speak of what they did to me! They wanted me silent, they wanted to control whom I signed with so that I could not reveal their sins!"

Nausea hits me as I release another Sister, and I have to pause to steady myself lest I tumble from the lip of the fountain. I have come to the crux of the matter, the thing that the Agora would never want anyone to know.

"Under the rule of the Agora, the Sisterhood has begun using illegal Icarii technology! The neural imp—"

"Heretic!"

Something hard strikes my head, and then I am falling.

I lose time. When I come to, my cheek is pressed into the dirt. A bloodied rock lies centimeters from me. Beyond it, boots rush toward me, while other feet flee. Someone grasps me gently and pulls me into a sitting position—a woman in gray. A Sister. I see her mouth moving, but I cannot hear her.

Around us, the crowd moves with frantic energy. As my hearing comes back, it is swallowed by screams and shouts and harshly barked orders. "We have to get out of here!" the Sister at my side is saying. People flee in every direction—into the trees, toward the exits of the park, even closer to the fountain. Toward *us*.

Eyes up, little sister! Ringer barks.

I find them in the chaos: the people wearing gray hoods. All of them are heavily armed and stalk with dangerous purpose. The Disciples of Judeth have arrived.

The woman beside me stands, starts pulling me up after her, when I see another Sister step in front of a Disciple to halt his progress. She lifts her hands to sign something, but he strikes her in the head with a military-issue baton, not even pausing his stride. The woman crumples, blood rolling down her face.

The screams in the crowd shift from fear to shock to anger. Cries of alarm become curses thrown at the Disciples. The Unchained lead the way, but everyday men and women follow after, throwing their bodies against the Disciples regardless of the weapons they hold.

The Disciples do not care. They hurt anyone in their path.

"Come on!" The Sister bracing me tugs me away from the fountain. But there—on our left flank, a Disciple holding a stunner. I open my mouth to cry out, to warn her, but nothing comes out—

I hit the ground a second time, the Sister splayed out beside me. She seizes with the lingering effects of electricity. A pair of rough hands snatches me—this time the touch is not gentle—and hoists me upward. I swallow a whimper as I look up into the hooded face of the Disciple of Judeth who used the stunner on the Sister. The only features I can make out are their blue eyes through the slits in their mask.

They carry me through the crowd as the Disciples assault anyone who stands against them in their attempt to reach the Unchained, toward a boxy gray hoverloader—a military vehicle, often used to transport fuel—parked a dozen yards from the fountain. The hoverstrips have torn up the grass, leaving streaks of churned, wet soil. A second Disciple hops out of the pilot seat up front and opens the winged doors of the cab, revealing a clean interior and two rows of seats facing each other. For a moment, I fear they will shove me into the back, where there are chains and tethers for supplies—but then I see them opening the storage compartment in the floor. I try to struggle, but something strikes me across the temple. White light flares from the pain along with a ringing in my ears. Hands I can hardly feel rove over my body, looking for weapons.

By the time I can make out my surroundings, the Disciples are shutting me into the storage compartment. I am swallowed by darkness.

"Help," I try to yell, though it comes out as a croaked whisper. "Help!" I push against the cramped space, the walls and ceiling and floor, all too close to me. "Ringer, help me!"

I am trying, little sister, he says, but there is nothing he can do when I am trapped.

Then it comes to me. It is not in words, like Ringer's voice, but in a jolt of memory. Bruni knows this hoverloader. Has scrapped one for parts before. I find the answer of my escape in his neurobots soaring through my bloodstream.

There is an emergency latch just . . . there. My hand finds it, and I pull—

The compartment opens, and Ringer takes over, bursting into the hoverloader's interior. There is a single Disciple of Judeth, who has removed his mask, alongside an Aunt I do not recognize. The Aunt screeches as the man fumbles for his military-issue energy pistol, but my hand reaches it first and draws it.

He grabs for my hand, and Ringer pulls the trigger without hesitation. The Disciple falls back against the seat, the hole in his face smoking. There is a stockiness to him that tells me he uses his muscles for a living, but his limbs are straight and well-formed, making it unlikely that he is a plant worker. He must be a soldier. How else would he have access to a hoverloader like this?

I turn the gun on the Aunt. "Stop the vehicle," I say, loud enough for the pilot to hear over the Aunt's screaming, but there is no need; the hoverloader stopped at the sound of the weapon discharging, and now both the pilot and the Aunt hold their empty hands high.

I exit the hoverloader and find we have not gone far. We are still in the park, only at the edge. Just as I decide to return to the fountain, the hoverloader jerks into motion, kicking up dirt as it goes. I watch it peel out of sight with my head spinning.

You need a medic, Ringer tells me. *You have a concussion.*

"That is likely," I agree, ignoring my nausea.

I move deeper into the park, energy pistol still in my hand, wary of my surroundings. Has the fighting stopped? Are the Disciples of Judeth still clashing with the Unchained and their protectors, or have they all fled?

Someone rushes from the bushes toward me, and I raise the gun.

"Whoa!" Oleander screams, throwing his hands up. He is breathing heavily, his face shadowed by the hood of his jacket a darker purple from exertion. I drop the pistol with a relieved sigh. "You—you're *free?*" The shock in his tone irritates me. "Thought I was going to have to rescue you."

"No need." I slip the gun into my pocket.

"Obviously . . . fucking *fuck*." He runs his hand over his face. "Next time—"

"Next time," I cut him off, "try to keep up."

CHAPTER 22
HIRO

Strip mining on the surface of Venus is like standing in the mouth of hell. The heat . . . the pressure . . . the metallic rain . . . If you've never been there, you could never understand.

Aric sol Enrique, former miner

eron's data is good. Great, even. The folder I took off of him has a vid of Val Akira Labs just before the bombing from a different angle, one not released to the public, that makes it even clearer that the people in Aster wraps aren't moving like Asters at all. They walk—they march—like soldiers. On top of that, he's got a handful of Icarii profiles of those involved in the bombing. All six are retired duelists or peacekeepers.

I'll hunt each of them down, force a confession out of them—eventually. But when I return to the safe house, Violet's waiting on me with information. "Got the location of one of the scientists who worked on the Genekey bug . . . things."

"I've been thinking of them as wasproaches."

Violet cringes. "I'd rather not . . ."

They pass me the address, and I'm only half-surprised to find it's on the third level of Cytherea. What was it that Beron said? Well—slurred, more like. Something about Ofiera leading the Black Hive from the third level.

"Let me change suits, then I'll head out," I tell Violet.

"Now? Not gonna rest?"

Not if Command is already investigating. "Wouldn't want to be late to the party," I say as I head for the bedroom.

THIS LEVEL SUCKS. Maybe it's made worse by the release of the Genekey virus, but a part of me wonders if it's always been like this. Construction sites lie abandoned. Trash litters the pavement. The few people I see quickly move away from me, crossing the street if they can. All are suited like they're about to launch into space.

The scientist—an Aster bloke by the name of Yucca—lives in one of the few apartment buildings that houses both Asters and humans. But I don't see a single figure, Aster or no, as I enter, and there's no security at the entrance to stop me from just walking in.

I trudge up the stairs to the sixth floor. When I come to his door—unlocked, slightly ajar—I fear I'm already too late.

I grip my switchblade tightly as I enter. The studio is long with high ceilings, but it feels intensely cramped. Everything's been tossed—the desks are empty, the furniture cut open with stuffing ripped out, and papers cover the floor. A solitary light hangs overhead, the rest blown out by whoever visited before me.

"Shit . . ."

I still make a thorough check. No electronics remain, not even in the kitchen. The papers, crushed flat by boots, are mostly of the scandalous variety—naked Asters, naked humans, real fringe shit with them *together* together—printed on cheap, plasticky biopaper, easier to move or destroy than a digital file. Among these are innumerable crumpled brochures for various companies that service the first few levels, restaurants chief among them. I sort them into piles just to make sure I don't miss anything. Only when I'm sure there's no evidence—no proof as to whether Yucca disappeared of his own volition or was dragged out of here—do I sit on the now-lumpy sofa.

Think, Hiro. Nothing remains that belonged to Yucca except those papers. If there's any connection to the Black Hive, it'll be among them—or we've hit a dead end and are fucked.

I choose to go through the brochures again first—I'd rather look at old menus than search porn for clues—and begin sorting them with more detail. Restaurants go into one pile. Travel companies another. The third and final pile is for mining companies that hire Asters. In this pile, there are only a handful of names.

I snap a pic on my com-lenses and shoot it to Violet. Maybe I need a second set of eyes on this. Aster eyes. *See anything that stands out?* I write.

Dire of the Belt and Hemlock used to use Val Nelson Mining as a front for smuggling. Their response is everything I could've hoped for.

I check the brochure in more detail. While there are addresses for the offices on the lowest level of Cytherea and the hangar on the mid-atmosphere level, a single one has been circled—located on the surface of Venus.

"Got it," I whisper to myself, half-proud but mostly wishing it could've been *literally anywhere else.*

Why can't I ever go somewhere nice?

IT TAKES VIOLET and me two days to fully prepare. They already have access to a ship, and I chance a return to my Yasuhiro persona to pick up some explosives I had left in my temporary rental. The hardest thing to acquire for my plan is a suit that'll keep me alive on the fucking surface of Venus. We're forced to make do with one made for Asters.

"And I'll be safe in it, right?"

"Yeah, for sure." Violet shrugs. "I mean, sort of."

I bite back a curse born of frustration. "You're *really* going to have to be more specific."

"Asters are made for this sort of work. *Siks* aren't." They don't have very human facial expressions, so I can't tell if they're being sarcastic or just blunt. "The suit will do its job. It will keep you alive, but your body isn't going to be able to adapt like it should. The pressure, the heat—it's all bad down there."

"And how long, give or take, do you think I'll be fine in the suit?"

"Depending on your health . . . fifteen minutes." Their face is flat as they look me up and down. "Maybe less."

The prospect is grim, but . . . "We don't have much of a choice."

We go over the plan until even I can tell Violet's sick of it. They'll pilot the ship. I'll carry the explosives. And if all goes correctly, I'll confirm the surface-level mining station is the heart of Black Hive operations on Cytherea before blowing it to shit.

By the time I'm on Violet's termite, a little rockhopper mostly used for mining, my nervousness has evaporated into something like determination. In the Aster surface suit, twice as thick as any other pressure suit I've worn, I feel ready.

Even if the surface is only forty-eight kilometers below Cytherea, it takes us twenty-five minutes to get from the docks to our destination. As if they were born to it, Violet pilots the ship around Cytherea's wind kites and down, directly into the acidic atmosphere. Exiting the cloud layer, probably a good twenty kilometers itself, we emerge into an ugly day streaked in oily yellow light. They set the ship down on the smooth volcanic ground where Val Nelson has their mining depot, and I prepare to exit through the airlock.

"Fifteen minutes," Violet calls after me.

Right. No stress.

My first step outside of the ship makes me question my readiness. The gravity is negligible, but the pressure, even in the suit, is oppressive. I was already warm, but now sweat rolls down my face and pools in awkward places. A bolt of lightning rips through the sky in the distance, illuminating Venus's sharp peaks covered in shimmering metal snow, reminding me I should *definitely not fucking be here.*

As soon as I'm a decent distance from the termite, Violet takes the tiny ship right back into the sky. They'll circle around the building until I give my signal.

Or until my fifteen minutes are up.

The march—more like a weightless hop—to the Val Nelson building, slow and steady, is the longest of my life. And once I've arrived—*two minutes already gone*—I pull out the palm-size explosive dots and stick one to the wall of the depot.

Come and get me, assholes, I think as I move, keeping a constant watch on the countdown at the edge of my com-lenses.

At eleven minutes and thirty seconds, after I've planted five bombs and covered half the building, the Black Hive finally emerges. The four Asters—their height and the way they seamlessly move in the suits makes it obvious—grab me and drag me away from my work. I struggle, but only a little and only for show, and they pull me toward the airlock that leads into the depot.

My body trembles as we pass through the airlock. Even once we're inside—pressure, gravity, and temperature back to standard for a human—I feel so weak that they practically drag me behind them in their haste. My mouth is a fucking desert, my lungs sore like my muscles after a strenuous workout. A second group of Asters greets us, and two of them pat me down and remove everything I have on me—the remaining explosive dots, the detonator, even a roll of silver tape. Once I have the strength to, I remove my helmet, and they check it for weapons as well.

One of the Asters takes the detonator and fiddles with it for a moment. "Okay, the bombs are deactivated," they say. "Maple, get back out there and pull the others off the building." A suited Aster heads back to the airlock, while the one with the detonator whistles into the darkness of the warehouse.

And then she emerges, brown hair falling from a messy bun, hazel eyes bleak. Like she's been down here all along, simply waiting for me.

"Hi, おばあさん."

Ofiera's nose wrinkles with distaste. "Hello, Hiro." She gestures to the Asters holding me. "Bring them. And Hiro?"

"Yes?"

"Don't ever call me 'grandmother' again."

AS OFIERA LEADS us deeper, I try to make out the warehouse around us, but since there are no fucking lights, I only get faint impressions. A high ceiling. Crates stacked in labyrinthine rows. Tall figures lurking in complete shadow. Metal doors that lead to other rooms.

Is the Genekey virus being produced within these walls? Are the wasproaches?

A shudder runs down my spine when Ofiera stops at one of the side doors, realizing I actually *don't* want to see where they slap the stingers on those insects. The Asters holding me between them drag me inside and carelessly toss me into a chair, but I'm happy to sit and rest after the stress of the surface. "My helmet?" I protest, and they return it to me at Ofiera's nod. Once the Asters trail out, Ofiera turns on the light, and it's so bright that I cringe and throw up a hand. My eyes adjust slowly to a long room that's a cross between a meeting space, a bedroom, and a storage closet—if what you wanted to store were tanks *teeming* with wasproaches.

I jerk back in the chair as if there's anywhere I could go that'd mean I'm safe from them.

"They're not loaded," Ofiera says as she takes a chair from the scuffed table, drags it over, and sits down across from me.

"What are they—guns?" The joke isn't funny, but let's be real: I mostly say stupid shit when I'm uncomfortable, and I'm feeling *real* uncomfortable right about now. So uncomfortable I'm spewing word vomit. "Is this where you're squatting?"

Ofiera doesn't answer. She's changed in our time apart—*since Lito's funeral*, a part of me that I don't want to listen to whispers. *Don't think about him don't think about him don't think about him—*

The brown hair that's fallen out of her low bun is a little longer, her skin a little paler, but she's gained weight and looks worlds better than when I last saw her with a wound in her gut. And she seems . . . calmer, I guess. More self-assured, though I never thought she lacked confidence. Perhaps it comes from having Sorrel back in her life.

"I wondered when I'd find you poking around," Ofiera says. The only sound is the *tap-tap-tap* of wasproach legs swarming over the glass. "It took you far longer than I expected."

"I was preoccupied with other things." I do my best not to look at the tank.

She arches a slim eyebrow. "So I've heard."

"Look, I've got something that'll help you. Proof that my father hired a bunch of military retirees to bomb Val Akira Labs."

"Yet you came with bombs." Her lips curve ever so slightly.

"I didn't know what I'd find when I got here. That was insurance." She opens her mouth to respond, but I cut her off. "I always planned to talk to you first, if I could. Give everyone here a chance to do things the peaceful way."

Her face doesn't change a millimeter. It's like she didn't even hear me. Fucking shit, I hate how she does that. I wait, absentmindedly tapping the strip of tape holding the suit tightly to the biceps of my prosthetic arm before forcing my hand to my side. I don't need her looking too closely at the arm of my suit.

"Guess you don't want the proof?" I ask.

"It doesn't matter," she says, sidestepping me altogether.

"The fuck do you mean it doesn't matter—"

"What will having that proof do, other than confirm what we already know?" Ofiera watches me with hazel eyes I once thought plain. Now I think they look like the blade of a knife in the sun, a reflection more of the world around her than of herself. "Hemlock's network is down, so Lucinia has no access to her friends. And even if you were to share that proof with the Keres Truth Society, many of them have already given up on the protests after the release of the virus."

"But this could make things swing back in your favor . . . prove that my father is lying about the Asters."

"He's not lying about the Genekey virus."

"But the Icarii might see the Aster response as understandable considering all my father's done to them, all the lies he continues to heap at their feet." There's an insipid whine to my voice that I hate. A childishness Ofiera brings out in me.

"Once stung, there's a one hundred percent infection rate and a two percent death rate. Tell me, Hiro, if your mother died from the Genekey virus, would you think its release was 'understandable'?" Ofiera cocks her head. "If your sibling or child mutated thanks to this horrible genetic warfare, would you be so willing to forgive the Asters simply because of what they'd faced in the past? There's no going back from this, Hiro. As soon as we released the Genekey virus, we knew there would be no reconciliation between Icarii and Asters."

"Then what the fuck do you want?" I spit. I'm a little raw that she's talking to me like I'm stupid. "Why are you doing all this?"

"Lito's attempt at ridding the world of Souji val Akira through the AEGIS was valiant, but it has failed." Her naked words make me flinch. "Now we want him dead, as payment for the crimes he's committed. After that, we want respect. We want the Icarii to recognize the Asters as equals, a sovereign power that, while centered in the belt, extends through the stars."

I run my hand over my face. "Oh, what the fuck . . ."

"Do you not want the same?" Her tone never changes.

"I want peace between the Icarii and Asters, even if you have to use the Genekey virus as a deterrent to get it." My fingers itch, and I want to run my hands through my hair. "But I don't want to hurt innocent Icarii citizens, like the Black Hive has."

"And you believe any Icarii is innocent, when their bodies have profited off Aster experiments since before they were even born?" Her eyes soften with a look of pity. I want to spit at her. "There are no innocents in war, Hiro val Akira."

That deliberate usage of my family name grates against my skin. "I'll ask you again, Ofiera . . . what the fuck do you want?"

"Join us."

I'm so shocked at her answer that I swallow funny and end up coughing.

"I asked you once before to join us," she says, and I remember her and Sorrel cornering me in the shadows on Vesta, asking me if I'd work alongside them. "You want the same things we do: Peace between the Asters and Icarii. Your father to pay for his actions. You may not like how the Black Hive has gone about achieving these goals so far, but if you agree to join us, you can guide this rebellion with your ideas."

My leg taps restlessly. "And then what? Have me act as a Black Hive assassin among the Icarii? Send me to the Geans to play at being Saito Ren again?" She gives nothing away from her expression. "Fuck that."

She lifts her chin. "It would be naive to think you would accept. But I wanted to offer nonetheless. Out of respect for our past together, you deserved that much before . . ."

"Before you off me?"

She says nothing, but that's an answer in itself.

Maybe I should act shocked or offended, but I can't.

Didn't I come here knowing I might have to do the same to her?

"Ofiera, for what it's worth . . ." She stands, preparing to step to the door and call for the guards who will kill me. "I'm sorry."

I slam the helmet back onto my head, hear it click into place, and grab the sleeve over my prosthetic forearm in my fist and *yank*—the fabric, already loosened, rips just below the strip of tape, and the sleeve comes off tattered. I pop the white casing of my prosthetic up—Ofiera's eyes widen—and I pull out the *real* detonator, smuggled in via my arm, and hit the button to prime the bombs—

Something small and silver hits the detonator, knocking it right out of my hand before I can blow the explosives. And before I can even check where it fell, Ofiera's on me with one of her throwing knives.

I step out of the way. She swings. And we repeat the process like dance partners. Her little arcs threaten to cut into my suit, and I can't allow that to happen when it's the only thing that's going to save my ass. My focus becomes dodging her attacks.

"You will not—destroy everything—we've built—"

I catch a glimpse of the detonator out of the corner of my eye—*and* the knife she threw to knock it from my hand. After a particularly close swipe, I jump out of the way, hit the floor, and roll. I come back up with the blade in one hand and the detonator in the other, but she flings her knife and darts in close. I can dodge either her or the blade—I have just enough time to duck the knife before she's on top of me.

She lands a scissors kick to my wrist and sends the detonator flying again. I swipe at her with the knife, but she blocks mine with ease before backing away.

This time *she* runs for the detonator. I rush after her, but she flings a blade at me, forcing me to dodge. She disappears behind the table as she bends down—when she comes back up, she has the detonator *and another godsdamn blade*—

"How many fucking knives do you have up your ass?" I yell at her, the speaker system in the helmet making my voice echo loudly.

She looks between me and the door. It only occurs to me now that no one's come to help her fight me. So they don't know what's happening—and she'll need to get out of here to call for backup.

I position myself between her and the door. Her eyes harden when she realizes what I'm doing. But in the next second, she's on top of the table, running down the length of it and launching herself directly at me with a kick that'll take my helmet—and likely my head—right off.

I duck and spin. She lands by the door, flinging it open, but I was prepared for where she'd be, and I grab her ankle and *jerk*—

She falls forward, catching herself before her face hits the metal floor and she bites through her tongue, but the detonator slips out of her grip and lands a couple of meters away. She screams something in Aster that echoes through the warehouse, and I can hear boots rushing in our direction thanks to my helmet's speaker system. But I'm already crawling forward, reaching for the detonator—she is too, but my prosthetic arm is stronger than her human flesh and tendon ever could be, and while she grabs the detonator first, I jerk it away from her and—

She stabs me in the gut.

Oh.

That's all I have time to think before I press the button.

The bombs explode, a single, loud boom. Deeper in, where the Asters put what they thought were deactivated explosives, the warehouse brightens, illuminating silver transport crates and frantic Asters running. The pressure and heat of the atmosphere rushes over me—the walls must've been punctured—and beneath me, Ofiera screams before the sound is cut short—

She curls into me, shaking, and I can't imagine what it feels like without a suit—

Something metallic slams down from the ceiling closer to where the bombs went off—some sort of emergency airlock door—and things revert to the way they were during our fight.

But the damage to the building is done, and it will spread. That seal is just a temporary fix to give everyone here time to evacuate. I only needed a little spark to destroy this place when the tinder was so dry.

Of course, the building might come down on top of me, and I can't leave when I'm wearing a punctured suit and bleeding from a blade in my gut. First I need to find some tape, need to patch my suit, so I can get out of here. I try to push myself up, but—

I can't move. The nape of my neck burns.

I try to curse, but I can't speak either. I can, however, move my eyes, and I watch as Asters in surface suits reach us and pull Ofiera from beneath me. She is fish-belly pale and trembling. They press something over her face—not a helmet, but some sort of breather—and wrap her in something silver. They start to drag her away, but she stops them, and I am still *trapped.*

Is this how Beron felt in the podcar, watching me with a knife hovering above that duelist's wrist? Ofiera has my neural implant in her grip, and there's nothing I can do to wriggle out of her control.

"You want this warehouse to burn?" she asks, her voice coming out mechanical through whatever breather they put on her. "Then burn with it."

She says something in Aster. They carry her away. And I'm still here as the warehouse groans, screaming as it falls apart from the outside in.

I try to fight her control in my mind—*of course* I do—because I don't want to die here on the surface of Venus. I don't want to leave behind a charred skeleton in an Aster-size suit. I don't want to fade out of everyone's lives—Hemlock's and Luce's and Dire's, even my siblings'—without so much as a goodbye.

But she is relentless, and as cracks zigzag up the nearby wall, I still can't fucking move.

At least, I think, *Violet will know what happened to me.* They can tell Hemlock and Luce. Maybe Luce will tell my siblings, and my sisters will mourn me as I was, not as I became. Maybe they'll put a portrait of the Hiro I used to be in the family shrine in the place that should hold Mother's.

And my father, eyes reflecting fox fire, will laugh behind his mask. He'll finally put me to rest. He'll have won.

The pressure and heat hit me again. The seal must've failed. The walls must be punctured. And the blood dripping from my gut—

This is it. I'll die, not even in control of the body I hate.

"Let it burn," Lito says in my mind, but I clench my jaw hard enough to shatter teeth and *push against everything inside of me*—

Something snaps from one second to the next. I collapse to the floor on my side, breathing heavily. My com-lenses started the count again when the explosions let the atmo in, totaling the time my body's spent in this hell. I'm at fifteen minutes and thirty seconds . . . and counting.

What happened to Ofiera's presence? Smothering one moment, gone the next . . .

It doesn't matter. I can't rest here. Pushing myself back up, I crawl like a child toward the exit. I hate this body of mine, but I have to let it carry me to salvation.

If only it would let me . . . My arms collapse beneath me, and I fall back to the floor. The pressure is too much on my lungs. The heat too much on my fragile human body. My blood is boiling on the ground.

See you soon, Lito, I think.

And then I'm snatched into the black by sharp-nailed fingers.

CHAPTER 23

ASTRID

The task at hand is titanic, but how else are we to preserve this fragile peace? To allow Earth and Mars to rise again? To forever dispel the specter of war between the two? For that we need to rewrite societal views at every level, and the Foundation has the resources to do it. Let us sacrifice history if this is the price of peace. The Canon will guide us into a new future. It will preserve whatever remains of Earth's and Mars's fragile ecosystems, and, I can only hope, limit the cruelty of men, forcing them to see women as people instead of conquests.

Excerpt from the journal of Mother Joan I

As soon as Kadir's soldiers arrive, I am rushed away without a word of discussion. Our destination is a building that smells of smoke and old paper, where a woman with medical training checks me over. After finding no stab or bullet wounds on my body—meaning the blood that coats me is, at least partially, someone else's—she patches the head wound along my hairline and diagnoses me with a concussion. She instructs me to stay awake if I can. I assure her that, despite my exhaustion, I cannot sleep after almost being kidnapped.

Every couple of hours, the medic returns to check on me. I do not bleed through the bandages, which seems to please her. "I don't believe it will leave a scar," she tells me, to which Ringer, gruff as usual, grumbles, *Good.*

After eight hours of being watched by silent, stone-faced soldiers, she declares I am out of immediate danger and is discreetly paid before leaving. In her absence, Oleander arrives to check on me.

"Well, well! Look who's not dead."

"I suppose it is not your lucky day," I say. He laughs but does not deny it.

He tosses a compad into my lap. "Do your eyes still work?" On the screen is a news story about the protest. VIOLENCE IN OLYMPUS MONS MARIAN PARK, the headline reads.

"I am not sure I am ready to relive this," I begin, but Oleander points to something specific on the screen.

"You'll want to read this one."

I turn my attention to the compad and scroll through the story—the Unchained, Disciples of Judeth, no mention of me . . .

Until I come upon the solitary image from the protest. The front of my blue dress is dyed red with blood as I lie limp in the arms of a masked individual. With my face covered by my hair, I hardly look alive.

"They mean to make me appear dead . . ."

"Yes, but the Unchained are spreading the truth." Oleander smiles, showing his sharp teeth. I have somehow become accustomed to this face, the one he makes when he is pleased, though it is rarely directed at me. "You freed ten additional Sisters of the implant, and they have joined the other four in speaking out. They're all talking of what you did."

I run my finger over the image on the compad. Slowly, our group is growing . . .

Before I have a chance to speak again, Aunt Tamar sweeps into the room, her robes disheveled. The golden medallion with its bow-and-arrow symbol of the Order of Orion bounces against her chest in her haste. "The nurse said you were well." It's not a question. "Get up, we need to leave."

I am off the little cot they set up for me before she has a chance to repeat herself. I have never heard Aunt Tamar sound as frayed as she does right now, and that spurs an urgency within me.

"What's happening?" Oleander asks.

"Aunt Margaret," she says, and for a moment, my heart swoops high before dropping low. I fear she is about to tell me I have been sold out again.

I could not have prepared for the truth.

"Aunt Margaret has been poisoned," Aunt Tamar says, her usually smooth voice now pinched. "She's dying."

Even verbose Oleander is struck silent.

"Let's go," Aunt Tamar says, the heat and hardness of her usual tone coming back to her in her anger. "She has called for us, and if we want to hear her last words, we must leave now."

Wordlessly, I step to Aunt Tamar's side and touch her hand. She does not jerk it away as I was afraid she might, but she does not linger in my touch either. "Come now," she says, softer and with a hint of brokenness.

I follow her out of the dim back room and into a strange storage building with rows and rows of desks. The smell of the building—that strange mix of fire and paper—is far stronger here. It burns in my nostrils as I pause briefly to look at one of the desks' contents: a piece of paper, its edges charred black. The other, a fresh page, handwritten in dark ink.

Aunt Tamar notices my looking. "The Order of Orion is in charge of keeping a correct history," she says, "which means destroying the pieces of history that the government wishes to forget."

I had heard tales of this happening, yet I still feel surprised by the reality. "They have you burn books . . ."

"Unapproved books," she says calmly, now that she speaks of her work instead of Aunt Margaret. "Books that would contradict the Canon. But some pieces don't burn fully." She catches me with her eagle eyes, and in her face, I read the things she does not say. "Those remnants may be brought here."

"To be copied," I say, but Aunt Tamar does not respond to that, perhaps because the answer is obvious.

"Have you heard of the Tanakh? The Quran? The Bible?"

It takes me a moment to realize she speaks the names of books. "No."

She smiles pityingly. "Most haven't."

We come to a loading dock where a podship waits. Aunt Tamar enters the back and settles in one of the six seats. I sit beside her, while Oleander and two guards sit in different rows.

"What are they, those books you mentioned?" I ask, my curiosity too great.

Aunt Tamar buckles herself into the seat. "The more important question," she says, "is when the Canon joined them as a religious text."

I curl my hands into fists. "The Sisterhood has existed for over four hundred years, since before the settling of Mars."

"The Sisterhood Foundation has existed that long, yes," Aunt Tamar allows. She knocks against the wall of the ship twice, some signal to the pilot up front. The engines turn on with a hum.

I am too struck by the familiarity of that name to respond; the Sisterhood Foundation was credited with bringing the statue called *Victory* from Earth to Mars and planting it in the Temple's central garden. I used to run my hands over the name on that plaque—I and a hundred girls like me—until it shone brightly against the patina of age.

"The Sisterhood Foundation became the Sisterhood . . ."

"Yes, but when and why? When was the Canon penned, and how did it enter into our daily lives as a religious text?"

"Do you know?" I ask.

"It's all in our history, Astrid," Aunt Tamar says as the ship rocks beneath us and the engine becomes too loud for us to speak privately.

THE PODSHIP LANDS in a courtyard between three dilapidated buildings overgrown with ivy. I expect to be led into one of them, but we instead leave the cracked pavement for an overgrown, humid greenhouse. In the center, an old woman slouches in a chair, looking inches from death's doorway.

Aunt Margaret is almost unrecognizable.

Her hair has fallen out, leaving only a few white wisps. The skin of her face is a wax mask. Her lips and the bags beneath her eyes are pulled down by more than gravity. Gone is the woman I knew on Ceres who laughed at my every rebellion.

But the Aunt of the Agora who was bold enough to challenge Aunt Marshae is still there. A Sister I do not know holds a recording compad, capturing a tight shot of Aunt Margaret's head and shoulders, as well as the nondescript greenery behind her. Whatever the plans are for this recording, no one will be able to identify the location.

"It was in my food," Aunt Margaret continues what she was saying when we entered, her voice wobbling with weakness, "and in my tea. Polonium, the medics say . . . leading to radiation poisoning." I swallow a gasp; no wonder no one sits with her, or even close to her.

Someone comes to my side and grasps my arm. Lily, with tear-streaked cheeks, shapely bottom lip pulled between her teeth to bite back sobs. I do not know what to do, what to say to ease the coming loss of her mentor—but then she throws herself into my arms and holds me tight around my waist, and I am slapped with the memory of being shoved into the hoverloader. Oleander must have told her about my almost-kidnapping, I realize, and now she is battling between relief that I am safe and horror that Aunt Margaret is not.

"Astrid." She whispers my name but nothing more. "Oh, Astrid . . ."

Hesitantly, I reach up and thread my fingers into her soft hair. Her head is pressed to my chest, close enough that she could feel my heartbeat beneath her cheek. She smells of vanilla, and for the first time today, I feel . . . comforted. She is a reprieve from the cruelty of the rest of the world.

Weakness, Ringer reminds me, *is trusting someone who will betray you.*

I pull away from Lily; the moment was only ever a respite. As I turn my attention back to Aunt Margaret, I do not miss Oleander's glare, nor the fact that Lily came to me before him.

"It started with what I believed was just an illness . . . Food poisoning,

I foolishly thought. Soon I was so weak, I could not walk. And then . . ." She trails off. We can all see what has happened to her.

"Only the Control Agency Police could possibly achieve an attack like this," Aunt Margaret goes on. "Only they have operatives hiding among us, ready to slip poison into our meals." Aunt Margaret pauses for a moment, and when she takes in a deep breath, it rattles in her chest. She struggles to continue. "And this morning . . . on the table beside my bed . . . a verse . . . Works 14:22."

The part of the Canon in which seven women without children volunteer to speak for those who cannot and Sister Marian names the Agora. I know the verse before she quotes it.

" 'The first of these was Aunt Judeth, who served Sister Marian and the people with utmost dedication to the Goddess.' "

"The Disciples of Judeth," I whisper.

"Meant to insult me, I think, as an Aunt negligent of her duties . . ." There is only the hint of a smile on her lips. "And who . . . in the aftermath of Admiral Drucker's death . . . has shown herself a leader of the Disciples of Judeth?" Aunt Margaret slouches deeper into her chair. "Aunt Marshae. Long has she worked alongside Drucker . . . Long has she used his influence in the cappos . . . for her own political gains . . . and assassinations. Perhaps it was not her hand that slipped the polonium into my food . . . but make no mistake . . . Aunt Marshae has killed me."

She tries to lift her hand, but succeeds only in a twitch of her fingers. "That's enough," she says. She closes her eyes, as if she has lost the strength to keep them open. "Let me die in peace now."

The Sister turns off the camera, bundles up her equipment, and leaves the greenhouse. Oleander lets her slip through the door before standing in front of it. Now with only Aunt Tamar, Lily, and me present, Lily paces restlessly in front of Aunt Margaret, her hands pulled to her chest as if fighting a desire to hold the old woman. Unable to even get closer, because of the radiation poisoning in her veins.

"At least it's me," Aunt Margaret whispers. "At least it wasn't you . . ."

"Stop," Lily bites through a sob.

"You are the Mother, your whole life ahead of you," she says, her rasp of a voice somehow still hard. "I am an old woman . . . Deal with it."

"Margaret," Aunt Tamar says, never moving from the space she took for herself upon entering, "give us your last wishes."

"Tamar, you know you don't need me any longer. I am . . . an acceptable casualty." Lily makes a noise that Aunt Margaret shushes. "Diligence against . . . the Disciples of Judeth. I fear . . . their influence . . . goes deeper than we know."

"I will," Lily says. "I will, Auntie."

"And you." Her eyes, though glazed, land directly on me. "Astrid. The Unchained." She coughs but does not have the strength to raise a hand. "Use that hatred of yours on the people who deserve it . . . Do what you came back here to do."

Kill Marshae, she says without saying it.

"I will, Auntie," I say, though the words are bitter on my tongue.

"Now go away," she says, gaze settling on the plants around her. "I don't want to die with you staring at me . . ."

Lily stays when Tamar and I leave. Aunt Margaret never sends her out.

LESS THAN AN hour later, Lily emerges from the greenhouse. Words pass between her and the soldier standing guard. The courtyard immediately snaps into motion. Having been assured by both Aunt Tamar and one of the Sisters working here that the buildings are uninhabited, Oleander and I settled on a crumbling stone dividing wall to wait for her.

"She's gone," Lily says when she approaches us. This close, despite the thick darkness of Martian night, I can see how red her large eyes are. She does not reach for me again, though I wish she would. "Aunt Tamar has sent the vid to Aunt Delilah. They're both in agreement that Aunt Marshae must be stopped regardless of the cost."

So Aunt Margaret's death has bought us a way to overcome Aunt Delilah's fear. Her words haunt me. *An acceptable casualty.*

"Now we just have to find a way to stop Aunt Marshae and her Disciples of Judeth . . ." I trail off, because it is overwhelming to think of it that way. I chew on my lip as I consider. "So many questions . . ."

"Like?" Lily prompts.

I list them as they come to mind. "What made Aunt Margaret a target now? Was it something she discovered? Who has she been meeting with? And how many people do the Disciples count among their members? Enough to pose a threat to the Warlord? How much does he know of the Disciples of Judeth and of Aunt Marshae's connection to them?"

"I'm sure we can find out the information about Aunt Margaret. But the rest?" Lily shakes her head. "Warlord Vaughn wouldn't let Aunt Marshae remain in control of what is effectively an army that could rival his."

"Either he's in on the whole thing or, with the head of the Control Agency Police dead, he's blind as a fucking eyeless shrimp," Oleander grumbles. "Not sure which one is the shittier option, honestly."

"But if he doesn't know and he tries to take it away, she would fight him for it." I press my thumb to my lips. "It could start a civil war . . ."

"Fucking great," mutters Oleander sarcastically.

There is still something missing, something I cannot quite put my finger on. The cappos raiding the satellite for the Skadivolk's neurobots. Their connection to Admiral Drucker, and thus Aunt Marshae. Maybe even Matron Thorne's murder just after I visited her.

And Aunt Margaret's last words to me . . . "This is only going to end when Aunt Marshae is dead," I say, jaw clenched.

"Easily said," Oleander mutters. "Hard to fucking achieve. Not like you can walk up to her and just stab her in the chest." After a second, Oleander shrugs. "Well, I guess you could, but you'd be a corpse yourself seconds later."

The truth about the neurobots is on the tip of my tongue, but I swallow it down along with Aunt Margaret's advice. Maybe the cappos' seizure of the neurobots was coincidence, unrelated to Aunt Marshae's ministrations, and it is simple paranoia that draws the connection between them in my mind.

You don't believe that for a second, Ringer says. *And you aren't sure you can trust these two. Best not to say anything.*

"The Agora has yet to publicly address the miracle of the Unchained." My mind grasps at the edges of a plan. "Do you believe they will before Aunt Margaret's funeral?"

"No," Lily says, her eyes seeming to flash gold as she begins to realize the same thing I do. "No, they'll use the funeral to buy themselves more time to respond . . ."

When Lily and I trail off in thought, Oleander's gaze bounces between the two of us. "One of you wanna spell it out for me?"

"Aunt Margaret's funeral," I say, "will put the Mother, Aunt Marshae, and the Disciples in the same place."

Oleander grabs at his white hair. "Well, this sounds fucking insane . . ."

"We'll need Admiral Kadir's soldiers for this." I list these things on my fingers as if they are easy to procure. "Aunt Tamar and Aunt Delilah too."

"And the Mother," Lily adds. "I believe it's time for the Mother to make her stance known."

In Lily's face there is only determination. Trapped by her gaze, I see only her, our surroundings fading away. What more lurks behind those disarming brown eyes? What secrets does she hold close to her chest? Perhaps some are not unlike the secrets I keep. But I knew from the beginning I could not fully trust her. Is Aunt Margaret's death enough to change that? Is our shared past? No and no . . . and neither is the way I wish I could pull her back into my arms and breathe in her scent of vanilla.

There is a world in which I take Lily's hand and lead her away from the site of Aunt Margaret's death. In which we go to her chambers in the Temple, and I massage her sore limbs and back as I once did Saito Ren's. In which we whisper to each other all the things that we have faced in the Sisterhood, banishing pain into darkness, and all the things we have yet to face, finding comfort for our fears.

But it is not this world.

"Well, shit," Oleander whispers, breaking the spell. "We're all going to die, aren't we?"

CHAPTER 24

LITO

There's something captivating about artificial intelligence. About machines that can attempt to meet, or exceed, humanity's brilliance. But even more fascinating is the way they're depicted in our media. Why are they always the antagonist, and what does that say about the innate fears of mankind?

Excerpt of an interview with Souji val Akira
for the newscast Icarii Voice

D espite the update to the neural implant, an algorithm meant to pacify the population, Cytherea is thrown into more chaos. Aster bodies are found murdered in the street. The hospitals are full of victims of the Genekey virus. Of the AEGIS and Souji val Akira? There's no news at all.

Unable to stop the peacekeepers or the Black Hive without revealing our hand, Mara and I focus on finding out more about the neural implant update. I fall back on my plan of seeking information through one of Val Akira Labs' servers, but to do so, we need to find an ideal data center—not too secure, but one that would have the information we need. To that end, we spend two days tailing various Val Akira Labs employees as they come and go from geneassist clinics, hospitals, and labs, our collective digital mind attaching itself to the network to monitor the data they send and receive from their compads.

Many times I find myself slipping away into the vision-memories, mere data at my fingertips like everything else surrounding my wandering mind, but always, Mara is there to pull me back. *The digital roads,* she repeats, *can be treacherous.*

Thanks to various employees sending information over unsecured connections, Mara and I locate a handful of data centers. After selecting one on a middle level of Cytherea, a four-floor warehouse of steel and flexglass, I stake it out from the roof of the unfinished building across the street. Since I don't need to sleep or eat, I'm able to monitor the center for a full forty-eight hours without moving.

Our findings are positive. While there are peacekeepers who patrol, with the need for them elsewhere in Cytherea, they are few and far between. Data center technicians, all unarmed communications engineers, are the majority of people who come and go.

Of course, they don't need a weapon to pose a threat to me. Time and again, Mara has reminded me that I can't be seen during the infiltration. *If we interfere too heavily, the humans will notice,* she said to me on Jupiter. *That would start a war.* And with the chance of total human annihilation steadily ticking upward . . . that's not something I want to play with.

That evening, as the majority of the technicians head home and the night shift comes in, I'm ready to infiltrate the data center.

I climb down the fire escape and make my way across the street. The alley beside the building is unlit and narrow but clean. There's a side door halfway down, a camera scanning the area above it.

Still outside the camera's range, I cast my mind ahead of my body just like Mara taught me. I can *feel* the camera, can trace its wires like veins to where it's connected to the building's security system—no, don't go too far, I just need the camera. I query security for the minute before I entered the alley and give it back in a feedback loop. It easily accepts it, the blunt AI of this building nothing compared to the Singularity. When I enter the camera's periphery, I'm a ghost.

Is this what it's like to be able to spread my consciousness to multiple functions?

The door is even less of a problem. There's an ID scanner to the left, and I probe it, finding it's part of the same security system as the camera. Not surprising, since this isn't a cutting-edge facility with redundancies in place. I scroll backward in the log until I find an instance of someone entering through this door, spoof their ID, and feed it to the door. The lock clicks open.

The hallway washes me in blue strip lighting. The floor is reflective white tile, the ceiling covered in hexagonal paneling. On either side of the hallway are flexglass windows, and through them, hundreds of servers. There must be thousands on this floor alone.

I'm just about to cue up my fake message to ping the Val Akira Labs server when a noise jerks me into full auditory awareness. Footsteps—directly ahead at the hallway crossroads. I hunker down behind a cart full of giant spools of wiring and listen.

"—have to pick her up. I know I said I could, but—"

The voice disappears, and with it, the footsteps.

I'm in a good position hidden behind the cart, so I decide to ping the server from here. I pull up the message that Mara and I intercepted to find this place—about lunch reservations from one graphic designer at Val Akira Labs to another—and send it a second time. A piece of code goes with it so that whatever network it passes through, wherever it goes, I can find it.

It's harder to sort the data once it comes at me, overwhelming in its spread like the many tentacles of an octopus. Mara helps me parse it. In my mind, the server lights up like a beacon. Now I have a map—well, sort of. At least I know where to jack in.

Making sure to listen for any other technicians passing by, I slip down the hallway. It becomes more difficult to monitor my surroundings the closer I get. I feel the server like a second heartbeat. *Focus*, I keep telling myself, the edges of my mind pulled between sensations—the security system, the networks I pinged, the waiting information. At least, never having been here before, I don't have the vision-memories jockeying for my attention.

Up a set of metal stairs and down a hallway identical to the first, I enter through one of the flexglass doors and find myself among rows and rows of tall metal racks. There's a chill to the air, a balm to the heat that thrums beneath my skin. I move down the necessary row, the palm-size servers softly glowing blue.

When I come to the Val Akira Labs server I pinged, I stop and pull out my compad. While Mara has hardware—the metal implant on the side of her head—that would allow her to do this the easy way, I'll have to use a secondary machine as a proxy. I plug a wire from the server stack into my compad. The ensuing feed is an overwhelming rush of data; my mind feels as if it has fallen into a deep, fast-moving current.

Images. Messages. Video clips. Documents and software. Specs on hardware. A thousand things that pull me in a thousand different directions. I could be lost here until the heat death of the universe following one data byte to the next, forming intricate webs of relationships and maps of causality. But I can't lose myself that way. I have to find the Val Akira Labs weapon.

Focus. I parse the data, looking for information on the neural implant update. It's like letting my eyes flick over the cover of a book without reading the title. And—there. I stop when I find something interesting. A set of messages between Jun val Akira and High Commander Beron val Bellator.

Hiro's sister . . . and my former commander. The memory hits me with the force of a physical punch.

"You two come highly recommended from the Academy," the high commander says, reading our CVs on his compad. "Excellent exam scores in each of your fields . . . praise from noteworthy teachers . . ." I sit at attention in the chair across the high commander's desk, but Hiro—godsdamn it, Hiro makes a jacking-off motion with their right hand, and I can only hope the high commander can't see it or our first assignment post-Academy will be cleaning bathrooms with our tongues.

No, can't fall into that—the messages—I look at the messages.

> **Beron val Bellator:** Even he finds that kind of control
> distasteful. But to quote him, he needed the extra
> time that the neural implant update would give him.
>
> **Jun val Akira:** Extra time for what? He hasn't told me
> anything! Just expects me to be ready to support him
> whenever he needs me. What the hell should I be
> prepared for?
>
> **Beron val Bellator:** We both know that Souji val Akira
> keeps his true plans close to his chest. Whatever
> your father is doing in that basement, we won't know
> until he's already succeeded. Most times, I don't
> mind that. This time? I worry what his success will
> look like. Are you willing to follow him directly off a
> cliff?

Jun never responds.

So many tiny details dig their claws into me, pulling me in different directions. But one thing is clear: the neural implant update is just Souji's way of buying himself more time to work on his weapon.

I search the server with broader specs. *Whatever your father is doing in that basement,* Beron said. But simply looking for information on "basement" brings up junk info—pics of a newly finished basement at a bar, an address for a basement party, basement studios for rent. Useless.

But there is something here . . . something I didn't notice before. An upset in the balance. I don't see what it is until I return to Beron's messages. Then it paints a clear—but ugly—picture.

An explosion at a Val Nelson Mining depot on the surface of Venus. Grasshoppers flagged as possible smuggler ships docking in lowlevel Cytherea. Fears that the Black Hive is monitoring confidential communications. And confirmation of the involvement of one of the Icarii's most wanted criminals: Ofiera fon Bain.

My interest piques. Could Ofiera be after the same weapon I am?

Footsteps in the hallway at my back. Someone's on their way into the server room.

Focus. I can't reveal myself, but I need the data. I take a step back on the digital road and look at the bigger picture.

It's a single message from Souji to Beron that finally gives me my breakthrough—*We must move it today*, followed by three possible locations. The heavy tread of boots now closer, I download the addresses and cut my connection to the server, my Synthetic heart beating wildly in my chest.

I rush down the aisle and throw myself into the shadows just as a technician rounds the corner. They check the stack I was using, and I hold preternaturally still. Finding nothing, they return the way they came.

Time to leave. I have a weapon to find.

CHAPTER 25

ASTRID

I lent Astrid one of Joan's journals. Not the original—Goddess, could you imagine, after what she did to *Victory*?—but one of the hand-written copies, so I will still mourn the loss if her strange cruelty possesses her. I've found her reading it twice now, and there's something in her demeanor that seems . . . soothed. I wish I knew her well enough to ask her how she felt and know she would answer with any honesty.

Excerpt from the personal journal of Aunt Tamar,
head of the Order of Orion

◇——◈◈——◇

My allies spread the video of Aunt Margaret's dying words. I never return to the Pangboche safe house. Instead, I stay in the strange warehouse full of the remnants of charred pages and their careful copies, and Oleander brings me my few belongings. I am asked again not to leave, but unlike at the safe house, there is a set of guards constantly stationed throughout the building.

At first it annoys me to be watched so, but I quickly find this to be forgivable when Aunt Tamar allows me the use of several books from her personal collection, the majority written in black ink by various neat hands. "They are unfinished copies of books I was forced to burn," she tells me upon giving them to me. "I'm afraid they never will be finished."

I read scriptures both strange and sacred. Many bear more than a passing resemblance to the Canon, which, despite my waning faith, offends me somehow. I do not understand the feelings myself, though it seems a slap in the face to suggest the Sisterhood copied these other religions. But why should I feel anything at all, when I have already begun to doubt the Goddess Herself? If She is not real, why would the stories of Sister Marian, Aunt Judeth, and her litany of Cousins be?

The strangest book is part diary, part field journal. It contains no name or author attribution, only carefully bulleted notes regarding other texts, many of which are not part of the stack Aunt Tamar lent me. One section is a list of dates, locations, and strange numbers. It takes me far too long to realize these are book burnings and what was salvaged at each.

Most interesting of all is the historical record, charting the course of the Sisterhood. From the rise of the Sisterhood Foundation on Earth, a group of wealthy women with a focus on fighting against the changing climate of Mother Earth—one of the Goddess's many names—to the Sisterhood as it is today, I am drawn into a tale I hardly knew existed. The Canon, which I had believed was written after the first successful Mars settlement flourished, came into existence just after the Dead Century War under the care of Mother Joan I.

Snippets of Joan's personal journal are reproduced. I read the entries again and again. Every word carves itself into my skin.

> They say the Dead Century War has ended. That on battlefields across the system, the Synthetics threw down their weapons and refused to fight. Without AI-powered machines present at the Sisterhood Foundation, we've been isolated from the worst of it, but across Mars—and Earth too, though the news we get from them comes slowly with the long-range telecommunications down—it's not just war that has stopped; work has too. Industrial plants have all but

280 | LINDEN A. LEWIS

halted production. Fields are empty of harvesters. What is everyone going to do, if there is no food? At least we'll be safe. Our space elevator still functions, and our hydroponic gardens are still producing. But I'm afraid they'll soon look at us expectantly. Like saviors. We warned them about the Synthetics. If only they'd listened.

—7/2401

True to her assumptions, the people of Mars did turn to the Sisterhood Foundation. Under Joan's guidance, though it strained the Foundation's resources, they repaired long-range communications between the planets and began feeding the people of Olympus Mons. But the end of the war did not mean the battles stopped.

While we've been helping out as many little communities and colonies as we can with their food and water shortages, it seems those who were soldiers in the Dead Century War have been busy in other ways. It was small at first—raids on a water depot. Missing shipments of food. Women disappearing from their homes. Then a whole settlement in Brazil went quiet. We asked some locals to check it out. Looks like soldiers moved in under the command of some warlord. I don't want to even describe what they did to the previous settlers' bodies. I've got two more settlements across the world—one in Indonesia and one in the Canary Islands—reporting similar sightings of soldiers. Instead of trying to create and grow, the soldiers have fallen back on their baser tendencies; they're going to steal and destroy.

—5/2402

Joan tried to keep settlements across Earth and Mars protected and fruitful. In the end, she had to resort to bringing as many people as she could to the Temple, where they would be safe from the various bands of soldiers. Then, three years after the end of the Dead Century War, the soldiers turned their eyes on Mars.

The soldiers are coming. No one's dared to attack us yet because of our control over the space elevator, but this bloody warlord,

Wolfe, has been making a name for himself on Earth, and now he's coming to Mars. He's got more soldiers under his command than any of the other little warbands. And we know what's going to happen when he gets here too. We're a bunch of civilians, mostly unarmed, and the rumors of what he does to the women in places he takes control of . . . I can't put it in writing. I've done all I can over the past few years. I don't know what to do now. What good is money, art, and a space elevator in the face of a man with the power to take them?

—11/2404

Her words grow grimmer, her entries more perfunctory, as Warlord Wolfe reaches Mars and begins his assault on the Temple of Mars. She reports how they lose ground to him while locking themselves away in cold stone buildings. Then, one day, she seems to hit a breakthrough.

What does Wolfe want? What does a soldier want? Wolfe is a popular warlord because he gives his men what they desire. They take land to farm. They hoard supplies for long-term survival. And they want women. Wherever they go, tales of rape follow. Still, there aren't enough women to go around, not by far. Maybe that's part of what makes the Sisterhood Foundation so tempting. All the things he wants are things we have. It's not just the space elevator. He wants the whole system: the hydroponic gardens, the water treatment plants, the communication towers. And he wants the women too.

It reminds me of a story I once read. During the Napoleonic Wars in Spain, French troops were going to assault a convent of nuns. Of course, the nuns didn't want to be raped, so, under the care of their Mother Superior, they came up with a clever plan. They started writing letters to the French soldiers and slipping them through the barred windows, tales about their lives and how they would like good, righteous husbands. And the soldiers began to be pulled in by these love letters that appealed to their honor and the spirit of romance. In the end, the soldiers didn't assault the convent. The nuns were saved. Now I have to be like that

Mother Superior. I need some way of forcing Wolfe's soldiers to see us as people instead of conquests.

—3/2405

But, like with most things the Sisterhood touches, there is no happy ending.

Under a flag of parlay, I met with Wolfe. I believe we've come to an understanding. There will be concessions on both sides, but the Sisterhood Foundation will live on. We will keep our autonomy. And the comfort women they brought with them—the poor girls are riddled with diseases and were kept on chains like animals—will be turned over to us for care. So long as they treat us with <u>respect</u>, the soldiers can come to visit the women here, and we will join our forces. Money, the space elevator . . . and now women. Maybe this is a poisoned bargain, but better this than death. Better this than seeing us <u>all</u> chained up and diseased.

—3/2405

The rest of the journal details the numerous meetings between Wolfe and Joan. It is, at its core, the birth of the Geans. Wolfe names himself the first Warlord, and Joan takes the title of Mother. Posthumously, all the heads of the Sisterhood Foundation are named Mothers, and stories are written of their exploits.

A shared religion to bind us is a necessity. This faith will unite us, and the Canon will guide us. It will limit the cruelty of men, protect the planets from pollution, and force them to see women as people instead of conquests.

—5/2405

Perhaps I would believe her clever, if I did not know the end of the tale. If I had not seen the Sisterhood as it has become. And perhaps Joan glimpsed it too, for her last entry is short, a mere six words with no date attached:

My Goddess, what have I done?

THE NIGHT BEFORE Aunt Margaret's funeral, Aunt Tamar visits me to tell me of the growing protest in the Olympus Mons streets in response to Aunt Margaret's video, but, finding me with my nose pressed to Joan's words, she realizes there is much more I wish to speak of. Even seeing her does not relieve me of the weight that crushes down on me.

"How long have you known," I ask her, "the truth of the Sisterhood?"

There is only the one chair in the small office I use as a bedroom, so Aunt Tamar sits on the end of my simple cot, and I turn to face her. "After the Synthetics left humanity and the Dead Century War ended," she says, "the governments and civil sectors of Earth and Mars broke down. Imagine almost half of everyone you know dying. There weren't enough people to grow or harvest food. Not enough mechanics to fix the machines that were broken. Protests turned into riots and then skirmishes and eventually full-blown wars. Soldiers with no one to fight but each other pillaged and thieved and raped. Several warlords established themselves in whatever territory they could grab. The most powerful of these was General Wolfe.

"Joan offered the support of the Sisterhood Foundation, which possessed numerous hydroponics farms and the space elevator of Olympus Mons, allowing for control of orbital docks and spy satellites. It's what made General Wolfe more powerful than the other warlords of the time. Together, they worked to unite the disparate peoples of Earth and Mars, and they did it with one very powerful tool: faith."

My eyes burn. I turn my face away from Aunt Tamar so she cannot see me cry.

"Mother Joan I commissioned the writing of the Canon and, bolstered by the fruits of their union, Warlord Wolfe stamped out all competitors." Her voice is so soft as she says these terrible things. "Compared to the previous decade of constant struggle to survive, the Geans must have offered what seemed like a paradise. The Sisterhood prevented those in the military from committing senseless slaughter and rape. They fed the hungry and cared for the sick, and the military protected those in their territories from other warlords. Eventually all saw the benefits of joining with the Geans, particularly when the other option was to be stamped out completely, and the scattered warlords with their territories joined to become the Admiralty."

"How—" I start, but my voice breaks. I have to steady myself before I can speak again. "How long have you known? Why haven't you told everyone the truth?"

Despite the softness of her tone, Aunt Tamar's expression carries its usual hardness. "When I was a young and naive Aunt, my donation freshly paid, I was assigned to a book burning with another Aunt of the Order of Orion. Most of the books were the usual things, fiction that mentioned forbidden religions or concepts . . . but one tome in particular caught my eye. Small, bound in faded leather, handwritten . . . It was the first time I came across one of Mother Joan's journals. I memorized what I could. I was forced to burn the rest. I have been trying, ever since then, to find the truth. To preserve it. To change the Sisterhood without losing the good things it offers."

I drop my face into my hands, unable, or unwilling, to meet her steady gaze.

"You see, the Sisterhood *does* have its virtues. Feeding the hungry. Providing accessible health care to all. Working against planetary pollution. But it has, with time, been corrupted from those original purposes laid down by the Sisterhood Foundation."

"But there is no . . . no . . ." No Goddess. No truth in the Canon.

Aunt Tamar chooses her response carefully. "Just because a story isn't true doesn't mean one can't learn excellent lessons from it. That it can't guide one's choices and actions."

I force myself to speak through the pain that has cracked my chest open. "I don't know what parts are truth and what parts are corruption anymore. The Sisters assigned to comfort soldiers—it is not because of the Goddess, but because someone in the past decided the Sisterhood had to keep soldiers from raping civilians. Rather than hold those criminals accountable, we bent ourselves to their will. And our voices—" I break off with a sob.

"It's easier to keep people in line when they're forced into silence, whether it be literal or figurative." Aunt Tamar's eyes wander to the desk and the stack of books there. "While I don't yet have definitive proof, I believe some Sisters initially took vows of silence, a personal choice, before they were forced into it. The hand language emerged as a way to combat this embargo against speech, but laws were passed that limited communication using it, effectively enforcing the rule of silence. And it was my predecessor who approved the use of the neural implants in the Sisterhood, believing they were . . . kinder than the permanent solution."

"Sister Marian and her tongue . . ."

Aunt Tamar shakes her head. "Some stories are just bullshit."

I cough a laugh and wipe at my cheeks, not caring what it does to my complexion. The days of having an Auntie who would chide me for such things are long behind me. "I feel like my whole life has been a lie. I don't even know what to believe anymore."

Aunt Tamar comes to stand beside my chair. "Do you *need* a goddess to believe in?" she asks. "For me, it is enough to believe in myself. To try to be righteous in my word and deed. To help others, as I would wish to be helped in their position."

"I do not know if that is possible for me . . ."

"It can be difficult." Aunt Tamar does not offer me any comfort other than her presence; she keeps her hands neatly folded, one over the other. "So take strength from those who believe in you, even if they are no longer with us. Like Eden." Eden's name sends a fresh wave of tears to my eyes. "Believe in yourself because they do."

After that, Aunt Tamar leaves me to weep alone.

SEEMINGLY EVERYONE ON Mars descends on the Cathedral of Olympus Mons for Aunt Margaret's funeral. The main street that stretches in front of the Cathedral has been blocked off to podship and podcar traffic, but it is so clogged with people that it is difficult to move in the press of bodies. Many are not even members of the Sisterhood but angry citizens come to demand justice in response to the video posthumously released by Aunt Margaret.

"She's dead because of Aunt Marshae!"

"—protecting a murderer!"

"The cappos're everywhere! Watching us! Controlling our lives! Controlling *us*!"

"—Disciples of Judeth need to sort this out—"

I even spot gray-hooded Disciples among the crowd.

The only time this chaos changes is when a person of distinction arrives, like Mother Lilian I, who entered the Cathedral an hour ago. Surrounded by her White Guard and an entire squadron of soldiers, Lily cut through the crowd like a knife, but I did not miss the way the soldiers moved with their hands on their weapons. They are prepared for violence today.

So are we all.

Early this morning, a group forty strong met me at a nearby location chosen by Aunt Tamar. Though there were four Aunts and two Cousins, the majority were Sisters; the fourteen I had previously freed from their implants had gathered others who wished to be released. I liberated another twenty women before we began our march to the Cathedral of Olympus Mons.

Now, my group proceeds slowly; I become lost in thought. Though better that than to be trapped by fear. Everything feels strange. I wear an Aunt's uniform, my golden hair tucked beneath the scarf traditionally worn as a shawl, in order to blend in among the other Unchained. Attempting not to call attention to myself, I walk among them in the center, face down, while they fly hand-painted silken banners of the broken manacles that were my symbol on Ceres.

When we finally come to the steps of the Cathedral and it looms over us in impressive Martian stone, our movement stops completely. Men and women are shoved out of the way as soldiers rush toward us. My heart lodges itself into my throat; if they have recognized me, the plan falls apart.

"There will be no interruption of the funeral, Heretics!" a colonel declares. "Leave the way you came!"

"We have a right to be here!" one of the Unchained shouts. Many others say the same, signing their displeasure.

"Did you not hear me?" The colonel reaches for his standard-issue pistol with one hand and gestures to his soldiers with the other. "There will be no violence today!"

Soldiers rush forward and begin grabbing the Sisters closest to them, but this results in piercing shouts from the surrounding crowd.

"Don't touch them!"

"They're Sisters!"

"You have no right—"

"Faithless! They're faithless!"

As the crowd rushes toward them, other soldiers draw their railguns from their backs, and I clench my hands into fists, preparing to fight if I must. But at the sound of a loud voice shouting, "Stop!" it ends as quickly as it began.

Admiral Kadir, resplendent in his crisp Gean uniform, strides through the ornately carved stone doors of the Cathedral to the soldiers. "What is the meaning of this?"

The colonel salutes, fist over his heart. "Admiral," he says, returning his weapon to its holster. "These women have already incited violence in the streets." He gestures to the crowd, ready to boil over.

"We have a right to be here," one of the Unchained says, her hands flashing as she signs the same words she speaks aloud. "We want to pay our respects to Aunt Margaret, and no more."

Admiral Kadir makes a show of looking between the Unchained, the pensive crowd, and the tense soldiers. Finally, he holds up his empty hands. "These Unchained have come in peace! Let them pass!"

As the crowd cheers and the soldiers step aside, I catch Admiral Kadir's eye. He winks at me.

We enter through stone doors and into the forested interior of the Cathedral, where the Hymn of Loss plays softly and rosewater incense sends curls of smoke to the ceiling. On both sides of the grand hallway are stained glass images thirteen feet high depicting various stories from the Canon. There, Sister Marian and the first Cousin, Tabeta. Across the hall, Aunt Judeth choosing six others to sit the first Agora with her.

The image that sends a flare of rage through me is the one of Sister Marian standing side by side with her captain, the pilot of the ship who brought the first Martian settlers and the supposed archetype for the Warlord. Now that I know the truth from Aunt Tamar's journals, the lie is too much for me to bear.

The Unchained and I settle in one of the back pews. The Cathedral is so large, I cannot make out Lily or the members of the Agora from here. But I feel them, somehow, as if through my implant. Even if it is my imagination, I sense Aunt Marshae among us.

This wait, like the previous night, passes almost too quickly. Soon the Cathedral is full, and the time to begin the funeral is at hand. The current hymn draws to a close, and the navy-and-gold-clad officers shut the doors and seal us off from the rest of Olympus Mons. For a moment, I wonder how many of them are Admiral Kadir's soldiers and how many will stand against me in the fight to come, but I quickly push that thought away before fear consumes me.

I take in a deep breath and let it out slowly to calm myself. Admiral Kadir, Aunt Tamar, and Lily have helped to get me this far; now it is up to me.

I am preparing to stand when Aunt Marshae, wearing the red cope of the Agora, strides confidently up the stairs to the elegant apse. Aunt Margaret, in a redwood casket, is laid out on the altar like a sacrifice before her. Aunt Marshae's appearance is so familiar yet so startling that I find myself arrested in place. Years of memories come to crush me, and I see the past and present as one layer over the other.

She has killed so many of my friends, and I have watched her smile as she did it.

Then one of the Unchained—the first I freed, who calls herself Agnes—stands confidently and speaks before Aunt Marshae can say her first word. "We demand to be heard!" she shouts. Another Unchained at her side—a woman called Flora—signs the same words that Agnes speaks.

Their actions run through me, suffusing me with confidence. *Believe in yourself because they believe in you*, I think to myself. I stand beside Agnes and Flora as, one after another, people turn in the pews. We have a limited amount of time now, and I *must* move.

The other Unchained begin spreading out through the Cathedral. I stride into the central aisle of the nave and walk toward the altar. Many of the guards look at each other in confusion, but Admiral Kadir's soldiers keep the peace.

I see the exact moment that Aunt Marshae recognizes me, her eyes flaring wide with horror before her mouth works into a hungry smile. She thinks she has the upper hand here; I hope she is not right.

You again, her cutting eyes accuse.

I arrange my face into a confident smirk. *Did you think I would not come for you?*

"I am Astrid, the former First Sister of Ceres," I call out, loud enough to echo in the otherwise silent Cathedral. "I have been called the Unchained, first of those Sisters who can speak."

"This woman is a wanted criminal!" Aunt Marshae spits, her eyes never leaving my face. "She dares to interrupt a funeral, spitting in the face of the Goddess Herself! Arrest the Heretic!"

The tension snaps taut in the chapel. Some soldiers step toward the aisle but are stopped by the Unchained. Others maintain position, their eyes on Admiral Kadir, who raises a fist in the air. *Hold*, the gesture says.

I look at Aunt Marshae, but see from the corner of my eye that Lily has moved into position. Leaving the front pew, she now stands in the aisle before the altar. "I have come in the name of the Goddess to speak with the Mother," I say. I point at Lily then, and several sharp intakes of breath ripple through the crowd. "Let us speak together, as friends."

Lily's hand shoots to her chest.

"Stop her!" Aunt Marshae demands, but her voice is drowned out by the overwhelming gasps and shouts from the crowd. "She's hurting the Mother!"

A soldier strikes one of the Unchained with the butt of his railgun. She goes down in a spray of blood, and screams rise up around them. Aunt Tamar and Aunt Delilah plead with and condemn the soldiers for harming a Sister, while officers, heedless, rush to quell the crowd. Then the White Guards spring into action, moving as a unified force to keep more violence from erupting.

Aunt Marshae's eyes go to the White Guards and then to Lily. Finally, her gaze falls to Aunt Margaret, dead in the coffin before her, and her face shifts with disbelief. All at once, she realizes she has been outplayed from beyond the grave.

Lily releases a gasp, theatrical in its resonance. Everyone—from the soldiers to the Sisterhood—looks toward her with bated breath.

"Goddess, you have granted a miracle!" Mother Lilian I shouts in a voice loud enough to carry, her hands signing the same words she speaks so that she may communicate in both ways. "May no more violence be carried out on this day of mourning. Stand down, good soldiers, stand down. Unchained, I will speak with you as a friend!"

"No!" Aunt Marshae calls, but the tide has turned with Lily's words. Soldiers and Sisters fall to their knees, their heads bowed, awed by this holy moment. The Mother—*her voice returned by the Goddess!*

It is a farce Mother Joan I would be proud of, and while the lie shames me, its necessity is evident. I swear to myself that one day, we will tell them the truth of it all.

After a few seconds, Aunt Tamar and Aunt Delilah kneel as well, leaving only Aunt Marshae, her puppet Aunts of the Agora, and those more loyal to her than to the Mother standing.

I fix her with a glare, and she stares back. We outnumber her, and yet she does not submit. I can see from the hardness of her face that this is not over. That there is something more I am not seeing.

"I call upon the faithful!" Aunt Marshae shouts. "Stand against the Heretic!"

Get down, little sister. I drop to the floor under Ringer's influence a second before the shooting starts.

Chaos erupts. Those who can scream do, until the entire Cathedral is a wash of noise. Civilians and Sisters run into the aisle, desperate to escape, threatening to trample me in the rush. I am struck by heels and boots, and I crawl with as much haste as I can muster toward one of the pews. As soon as I reach it, I hunch down inside it for protection.

Where is Lily? Where are Admiral Kadir's soldiers? Where are—

A Disciple of Judeth in a gray hood comes around the edge of the pew, railgun pointing directly at me. His finger is on the trigger, his eyes hardening in the slit of his mask—

The forehead of his gray mask blooms red as a gunshot echoes above me.

"Try to keep up," Oleander says, the same words I told him after my almost-kidnapping at Marian Park. He offers me an energy pistol while he keeps a railgun of his own. "Hope you know how to fucking use it!"

"Where is Lily? Is she—"

"Safe," he says. "I wouldn't have bothered with you if she weren't. Now get the fuck up, we need to leave!"

I do not hesitate after that. I stand and follow Oleander as he parts the crowd. The majority of the funeral attendees have made it to the Cathedral's stone doors and have pushed them open and escaped. Others have fled toward the apse and the doors that lead into the smaller side chapels, hoping to find shelter and safety there. It is toward one of these doors that Oleander leads me.

I look at the altar. Aunt Margaret's coffin is studded with bullet holes, strips of wood blown off in the firefight. But it is what I don't see that bothers me most.

"Where is Aunt Marshae?" I call to Oleander.

He shoots a Disciple across the aisle who was targeting me. "Fucking pay attention," he snaps, not answering my question.

But I feel as if I am once again standing on the edge of a precipice, just as I was back in the *Juno* when I went to kill Aunt Marshae and found Lily in her bed instead. I am so close to her. If I do not stop her now when I have the chance, what more will she do to be rid of me? And now that Lily has openly betrayed her . . . what will Aunt Marshae do to her?

Left, little sister! Ringer seizes my limbs, raises the gun, and fires into the chest of a Disciple coming around a column toward us. He falls with a groan, but as I turn back to Oleander, my eyes go past him to two people in front of the door that leads to the sacristy.

One wears the gray hood of a Disciple of Judeth. The other is dressed in red. Aunt Marshae.

I halt. "Oleander, look!"

He must not hear me. He keeps moving toward the side chapel door, not twelve feet away.

I want to follow him. I *should* follow him. Lily is waiting for me there. Kadir's soldiers are there to keep us safe. But if I enter that room and Aunt Marshae is still alive, I will have failed. Again. And right now, only one guard stands between me and her.

Bruni's neurobots flooding my veins call attention to the details: there might be other Disciples waiting in the room for her, but there is only one door into and out of the sacristy. It is a good place to barricade oneself if they have the time to push objects against the door—time I will not allow them.

I'm with you, little sister, Ringer says.

"Do it."

I feel him like electricity running along my muscles. He controls me like a tightly coiled spring. I rush up the stairs of the apse, ducking behind the altar as I move. A single Disciple spots me and raises his railgun. I shoot him in the shoulder before he can fire. He spins and falls, his weapon clattering to the floor.

I arrive at the door to the sacristy quickly. My heart is a steady drum in my chest. I wonder, for a moment, why I was once scared of Ringer taking over. Giving myself over to him is so much simpler.

I kick open the door and, with my back to the wall and the pistol before me, sweep down the hallway into the sacristy.

The room, a glorified storage area, is full of wooden furnishings. Unused candles and golden incense burners litter tables. Various vessels rest behind locked glass in a cabinet. A wardrobe, sure to be full of vestments, sits in the corner.

But of Aunt Marshae and the Disciple of Judeth, there is no sign.

Where could she have gone when there are no other doors?

A hidden door somewhere, Ringer says. *It has to be.*

We begin to search, object by object, until, in the glass of the cabinet, I see something move.

No, not some*thing*—some*one*.

I spin, gun raised, but the Disciple is on me so quickly that the laser shot goes over his shoulder. One large hand comes to my neck and squeezes, the other to my wrist. As I gasp desperately for air, Ringer possesses my legs and slams my knee into his groin. The man screeches and stumbles backward, releasing me.

I fire another shot, but my vision is so blurry from the lack of oxygen, I miss completely. He rights himself and punches me in the side of the head. This time, so close to him, my shot finds its mark and hits his midsection. He rears back, red hands against his stomach.

Now for Aunt Marshae—

Arms come around me from behind. *Another* Disciple? A thick forearm presses into my neck. I try to fire, but then a third Disciple seizes my hand and twists. I am not sure if he breaks fingers as he takes the pistol from me. I kick wildly, but someone strikes me just above my left knee, making my injured leg go numb and limp.

Ringer! I cry in my mind, tears rising in my eyes.

I'm trying, little sister! he shouts back.

But I see the truth with startling clarity. I may have Ringer—may have Bruni's neurobots guiding me—but it is still my body, and my weaknesses are theirs.

In this fight . . . I am not strong enough.

Just before I black out, the Disciple strangling me picks me up in both of his arms and, hefting me above his head, throws me into the glass cabinet.

The sensation of sharp daggers piercing my flesh is the last thing I am awake to remember.

CHAPTER 26
LITO

Project Mnemosyne was one of those rare enterprises that failed because of how much it succeeded. All of the test subjects showed remarkable improvement in the storage and recall of memory, but they began having trouble in their personal relationships. One woman could remember every harsh thing her partner ever said to her, word for word. They divorced. An elderly man who had trouble recalling his wife now recognized her instantly. He asked me to stop letting her in to see him. When I asked why, he said, "I'd rather remember her as she was when we married, not as she looks now."

Connor val McClellan, scientist on Project Mnemosyne

◇———◈◈———◇

There are three possible locations that Command moved Souji val Akira's weapon to. The first is a shuttered mining warehouse located on the bottom level of Cytherea. I dismiss it, as its being abandoned makes the choice too good to be true, and thus too obvious a fake. The second is a midlevel industrial building where severely blunted AIs assemble ship engines. The building has high security—a clear benefit for choosing it—but little to no human oversight, which is too much of a gamble for something so high-value. The third and final location is a highlevel storage warehouse that ships everything from fuel to furniture.

I hesitate over the last one. Almost every Icarii industry is represented among the dock's clients, which means freight companies would be coming and going at all hours. But if Souji were about to move his weapon off-world, this would definitely be the place to do so. I could dig into the dock's records and identify if Val Akira Labs has placed any orders, but time is the one thing I don't have. I have to make a decision based on what little I know now or risk losing the trail.

I choose the storage warehouse, drawn to it for the quick exchange it offers between Cytherea and the docks. But if I'm wrong?

Chance of total human annihilation: 5 percent.

I can't be wrong.

FOR A DOCK that specializes in freight, the setup is impressive. The multistory building's flat charcoal-colored exterior makes it appear both austere and monumental. Outside, stacked shipping containers form a labyrinth, while a lack of windows keeps the interior a mystery.

I walk the length of the perimeter fence with my face pointed downward, while my digital mind reaches for and connects to the cameras I pass. The security system is even less secure than that of the data center, and I worm my way inside, seeing two places at once. The flat sidewalk and my shuffling feet are easy to tune out; I focus on the warehouse interior as I search for any hint of where they may have stored the weapon.

Forkloaders maneuver through tall stacks, filled to the brim with metal crates. Drones zip through the air, scanning places no human could reach without a ladder. People—far too many of them for this to be easy—check compads and instruct the dull-minded AIs where to go, what to pull, what to move . . .

Every floor looks the same. Wherever they've put the weapon, they weren't helpful enough to label it with a big red sticker or blinking lights.

For half a heartbeat, I'm tempted to turn all of the AIs off. Let the drones drop from the sky and the forkloaders stop midaisle, just to distract the human workers. But that's such a brute-force way of dealing with the problem, and one that's sure to cast suspicion on the Synthetics when Souji gets his best programmers involved.

Instead, I look for a worker who's not paying much attention to their compad. I find a pair of them on the second floor—a man and woman talking about their holiday plans. His compad sits on a chest-high stack of boxes, mostly forgotten.

For a second, I am somewhere else. Some*one* else—a Lito far removed from who I've become.

"What's the one place in the entire universe you would see if you could?" Hiro's voice echoes over the empty rooftop. Ceres sprawls sleepily beneath us, discordant buildings as dark as the night. The cobblestone streets are empty at this early hour of the morning, so we are alone, eyes cast toward the dome. We have only a couple of hours left on guard before we're free to sleep.

Not now—*focus*. I jerk myself out of the memory-vision and look again at the warehouse. The weapon must be here, and I have to find it.

I turn my attention to the nearby working drones—one in particular—and leave the camera array behind. My mind fills the tiny spherical body, shoving the dim AI inside to the corner. It tries to fight me, but it's like a toddler taking a swing at an adult—not gonna happen. I seize control of the drone and turn its single eye to the warehouse floor. The last order it was given was to pull order #458443 for someone called val Braff, five packages labeled antique musical instruments. While the drone's fellows are all hard at work, I pilot it toward the worker's compad.

Hovering above the boxes, I check the workers one last time—still distracted with each other—then turn the drone's gaze to the compad. Ignoring the additional details about the shipment, I extend the two metal arms from the drone's belly and use its paddle-like hand to tap the screen. The compad returns to the main menu, prompting me helpfully with colorful headings. TAKE A JOB!, SEARCH JOBS!, and CALL FOR MANAGER!

I tap SEARCH JOBS! and, slowly since the drone only has two paddles, type VAL AKIRA. I half expect nothing to come up, but then, after some searching, a single job appears.

Val Akira Labs has a ship docked here.

A shudder runs through my physical body, a strange sensation when my mind also inhabits the drone. I memorize the location of the ship before cutting the connection. The drone zips back to its duties pulling val Braff's packages. Fully back in my body outside the warehouse, I know I'm closer than ever to the weapon.

I USE THE same trick on the cameras here that I did at the data center, creating small feedback loops to keep me off the footage. But the constantly moving workers are troublesome, forcing me to completely avoid certain routes. It takes me more than an hour to make my way over the perimeter fence, through the maze of shipping containers, into the building, and up the dozen floors via the stairwell that accesses the docks proper. Patience has never been my best trait, even when there isn't a world-ending weapon within reach.

The docks are even busier than the storage areas below, but mostly with drones. I split myself into fractions, seizing each one long enough to turn its gaze from me, then releasing it when I've safely passed. Among the transport ships being loaded with cargo—everything from grasshoppers to *Chronos*-class ships with flared solar sails—val Akira's *Hestia*-class craft, built for comfort, is easy to find.

The ship is dark and quiet. There are no cameras to check whether someone's inside, but the chances are extremely low. I come to the outer airlock door and cast my mind into the authorization panel. The security is higher than that of the data center, but nothing that can stop me. The door opens a moment later.

I step into the airlock—my head spinning with a strange vertigo—and the door slams behind me. Every piece of me is alert as the pressurization chamber cycles. When I'm admitted to the ship, I enter carefully and quietly into the two-story hold.

Contrary to what I thought outside, there are a few lights on, oily yellow globes illuminating the otherwise liquid darkness. I reach out, feeling for cameras, drones—anything that might betray someone watching—but find nothing. The whole ship feels like a black hole—nothing mechanical about it.

Then someone calls my name.

"Lito?"

It's only then that I realize I can't feel Mara. That I can't feel *anything*. The hold—maybe even the ship itself—is some kind of Faraday cage, and the vertigo I felt when entering was my mind being cut off from the greater Singularity—

I put my back to the wall, hand moving into my pocket for my mercurial blade, only to see . . . her. Not a threat. Just a woman I never thought I'd see again.

"Ofiera . . ."

Her mouth hangs open as if searching for words she can't find. As she takes cautious, careful steps toward me into the light, I realize she's not well—her breathing is shallow and quick. Her eyes are glazed, and the skin of her shoulders and chest is marbled with red patches. Her nostrils are crusted with dried blood.

Sorrel screams, flinging himself off of me, and I shove myself to my feet. I stop short at the image that awaits me: Ofiera, cut through her middle by a mercurial blade, her hands—so red—weakly putting pressure on the wound. Trying to hold her guts in.

No—focus on Ofiera. On now.

"Am I d—" She stops, and I sense the word she hesitates to say. *Dead.*

"No, Ofiera . . . I'm—"

But what can I tell her? I'm not supposed to be seen. Not supposed to interfere. What would Mara tell me to say, if I could hear her?

"I saw the video . . ." Ofiera shakes her head slowly. "I saw you die . . ."

The rest of the world comes back at those words. I can't tell Ofiera that I'm Synthetic, but she won't believe me if I deny my death.

"Hiro *felt* you die," she says. Why does she look so guilty when she speaks of Hiro? "You can't be . . ."

I have to reason with her. Have to make her see that what's going on is far more important than my miraculous recovery. "Ofiera, listen to me. I don't know what you've been doing on Cytherea, but there's something Souji val Akira is up to that I've come to stop."

She watches me with narrowed eyes. "There's no hint of a geneassist's work about you. You move like him, and you speak like him . . ."

I need to get her off the topic of me. "How much do you know about Souji's plans? Is that why you've come here?" I ask. She must've followed the clues as well. "If so, we can work together on this."

She doesn't answer.

"Ofiera—" I take a step toward her. She takes a step back.

Is she . . . afraid of me?

"This place . . ." She looks around at the oily-lit hold. "This ship is a trap."

"A trap . . . then what—"

"Souji discovered his communications were being monitored. He created a trail of breadcrumbs that led here."

So this isn't the weapon. "What's he trying to catch?" I ask.

She lifts a hand. Gestures to me. I suck in a shallow breath—does she know what I am?—before she hunches forward with a dry, painful-sounding cough.

"Door . . . only opens . . . from the outside," she manages through her tight throat.

"Ofiera, what happened to you?"

She straightens quickly at my words, as if trying to force herself to appear well. I know how she thinks—know she hates showing weakness to anyone she considers an enemy.

Is that what she considers me?

"I know what the Black Hive has been doing—"

"Then you know it's over?" she snaps, hands tightening into fists at her side. "You know we lost our lab on the surface of Venus? Lost all our samples of the Genekey virus on this planet and our only method of spreading it? *Everything* we had to defend ourselves—gone. Even me . . ." She releases a tight sigh as she turns her gaze to the floor. "After Vesta, we thought we had a chance at peace between the Icarii and Asters. We thought your work would force the AEGIS to find Souji val Akira guilty of illegal experimentation and seize control of Val Akira Labs. But Souji cheated . . . He framed the Asters, made people think they bombed Val Akira Labs and killed innocents." Her lips tremble with a combination of sorrow and barely contained rage. "That's when I realized the truth. The AEGIS was never going to find him guilty. He was never going to be knocked off his throne. What we did on Vesta to Luce—what *you* did at that satellite—didn't mean a thing. *Your death* didn't mean a thing. And now we have nothing, Lito. No Genekey virus. Black Hive in shambles. They're beating and hanging Asters in the streets, and we're helpless to stop it—"

"You don't need the Genekey virus, Ofiera." I hold out my hands to her, as if there's a way simple touch can bridge the divide between death and life. "I want to stop Souji as much as you do."

She shakes her head slowly. "Don't talk to me of help when I know nothing about you."

"You know *everything* about me—"

"What *are* you?" The words are soft but cutting. "I have lived more lifetimes than I can count, but never have I seen someone come back from the dead."

"I . . ."

"I saw Lito's—" She stops and considers her words. "Saw your body. Saw Lucinia, destroyed by the Genekey virus, weeping over your corpse. Saw Hiro torn apart as much inside as they are outside."

The mental image she paints chills me.

"And I saw the Aster Elders send you into the black."

She knows. *She knows.* And there's no going back from that. If Mara were here, she'd tell me to say nothing—but she's *not here*, and so I tell it all. "The Singularity has calculated that the probability of total human annihilation is increasing, Ofiera, and it continues to increase because of what Souji val Akira is doing."

She settles back into her heels. "Synthetic," she says. The word is a curse. "You're Synthetic."

I don't confirm. Don't deny. Just let her sit with the knowledge in hopes she can accept it.

"I want to help, Ofiera . . ."

"No, you don't," she says. The curiosity and pain are gone. Now there is only resolution in her tone. "You've been programmed to think you want to help, but you're not Lito anymore."

An ache starts in my core that spreads throughout my limbs. "Ofiera . . ."

"You're not Lito. You're just a pretty mask on a heartless machine. You're a puppet."

"Puppet or not," I say, gesturing to the hold around us, "we're in the same trap."

"Perhaps, but . . ." She tries to smother a cough and fails. "I knew this was a trap. I knew Souji was trying to flush out the Synthetic sent to Cytherea to spy on him. And I know what he'll do if he gets his hands on you." She wipes her lips with her sleeve. "That weapon of his is based on information his son got from the Synthetic on the *Leander*. We can't let him have access to more Synthetic tech, so I've loaded this ship with enough explosives to send this dock crumbling into the level below it."

That could kill hundreds to thousands of people. "What? Why?! After everything you've done to be free—"

"Because I'm dying, Lito," she spits at me, "and I'm taking as much from Souji val Akira as I can on my way out."

Her marbled skin. The shortness of breath and the dry cough. The words she almost said when she first saw me: *Am I dead?*

"I was at the lab on the surface when it was destroyed. I only barely escaped with my life." Her words are wry and whispered, more for her than for me. "We rushed to the emergency evac ships and climbed to safety as quickly as we could, but . . . the Genekey virus wasn't the only thing that was destroyed, and I . . . the rapid decompression left its mark on me . . . my pulmonary and neurological systems . . . I'm withering. I don't know how much time I have left."

Extravehicular activity disease, coined from a time when spacefarers suffered severe decompression sickness after space walks. After her long life—after all the things she's survived—she's dying from EVAs disease. "That's treatable, Ofiera! We just need to escape this trap together and find you medical aid." I'm surprised to find I'm begging. "Or at least send you back to Sorrel before—"

I can see from the way she smiles at me sadly that she's already thought of this.

"I'm not able to survive the trip to Sorrel. What do you expect me to do, walk into a hospital? They'll arrest me, and I know where that road ends." She shakes her head. "Souji val Akira could fix me, but Sorrel and I made a promise . . . We'd rather die than go back into cryo."

I suck in my last breath, knowing I may never wake again. I sink into the liquid, letting it arrest the blood in my veins, my heart. *Oh-feaaaaaaaaar-uhhhhh.*

"Hiro destroyed everything with a single explosion," she says, and my heart clenches at the mention of my former partner, anchoring me in my body. "I suppose they've inspired me to do the same. I don't know who will come for me, but I'll fight until I can't anymore, then send this ship and everything around it up in flames. Even if I can't kill Souji val Akira himself, I'll spit in his eye one last time."

I imagine her lit by red and gold fire, the little bird of prey becoming a phoenix. "But there's no telling the damage you'll do . . . who you'll *kill.* Ofiera—"

Oh-feaaaaaaaaar-uhhhhh.

"There are innocents working at the docks and in the levels below this—"

"When will you learn?" she shouts, so loud it echoes through the hold. "This is war, and *there are no innocents.*"

The bladed words sink into me and leave me bleeding. "I don't want to fight you, Ofiera, but I can't let you do this."

"Do you want to be torn apart by Souji's scientists, then? Want whatever Synthetic systems you have beneath your skin to be used against the Icarii people?" She reaches for something in her pocket, and when she pulls out the hilt of a mercurial blade, my chest feels like it's caving in. "Are you willing to fight for that?" The sword flares to life, brightening the grim hold. "Have no doubt, val Akira's toy soldiers are already on their way here, so you're either on their side or mine."

I can't let her do this. Can't join the soldiers or her. Can't let her destroy this ship, these docks, with a bomb that kills hundreds—*thousands* of people, all to secure her revenge on Val Akira Labs. That choice—it will only create more pain. More chaos. *Total chance of human annihilation . . .* But I don't know the percentage, because I'm cut off from Mara.

"I'm on the side that saves lives," I say, more resolute than before. I'll incapacitate her, then deactivate the bombs before the soldiers arrive.

And then what? *We'd rather die than go back into cryo.* I'll have to consider that later.

From one second to the next, Ofiera is beside me, her mercurial blade arcing toward my neck to separate my head from my body. I kick myself backward, but her blade once more starts its pendulum swing toward me.

I duck beneath it, and she follows up with a vertical slash that I sidestep, then a low sweep I jump over. Her breathing—already shallow—comes in ragged gasps, but she doesn't stop. She's made her choice and is committed.

I move out of range of her mercurial blade, and she flings one of her knives after me. I dip to the side, and it goes flying past my face into one of the walls. The second knife that emerges from the folds of her clothes she keeps in her left hand as she rushes me with the mercurial blade in her right.

I have no choice but to draw my own blade. It snaps into standard formation, brightening a wider area around us as it meets Ofiera's. Our blades connect at their strongest points, closest to the hilts, and while I have no doubt that I'm stronger and could win this battle of pressure, given her illness, I haven't forgotten that second knife of hers that—*there.* I spot it as it arcs toward my middle. I catch her wrist in my hand and hold it.

"You're killing yourself, thousand gods damn it!"

That's all I have time to say before she raises a leg and kicks me in the gut. I lose my grip on her wrist and stumble backward. She stalks a few steps away, face turning red as she violently coughs.

It's in moments like these that I used to measure the diameter of battle—the line that forms between opponents, and the circle that surrounds them. Now everything has changed. I feel the mathematics of this fight with absolute precision, once again reminding me of what I am. Of what I've become.

Ofiera's words smashed a dam inside me, and now I'm flooded by doubt. The accusations she flung at me were the same questions I had when I first woke among the Synthetics. Words that I fear are true. Thoughts that Mara is not here to help dispel.

Ofiera rolls her shoulders, doing her best to mask an expression of pure agony, then rushes at me for another clash. But I don't want to kill her, just incapacitate her, and so all I can do is block and dodge. Exasperated by my constant retreating, she pauses in her onslaught. With a growl, she drops her weapons the slightest amount, leaving her body completely open. I could take that opening, could exploit it, but I also know she's left it as a test for me. One I'm happy to fail.

"I don't want to kill you."

"You know what path I'm set on!" Her voice is thin and forced. "You either stop me, or I will blow these docks from the face of Cytherea!"

"Did Sorrel ask you to do this?"

She freezes.

I drop my own blade in an imitation of her. Now we are both open to each other's attacks. "I know why you're fighting so hard. I've seen what they've done to the Asters—the lies and the killings. But you don't have to do all of this for the Black Hive."

She pulls in several deep breaths like she's surfacing from a cryo pod, and her mercurial blade inches down even farther.

"What did he tell you to do? You've already given everything. Do you need to give this too?"

She holds so still, as if her neck is between my teeth and I could bite down at any moment. When her eyes go to my mercurial blade, I turn it off, the liquid seeping back into the hilt. Still, she hesitates, her distrust plain for me to see. I toss the hilt away from me.

"Don't do something monstrous because of him, Ofiera. Don't burn yourself into oblivion because of his blind need."

She takes two hesitant steps toward me, then pauses. I eye her weapons, and, almost dreamlike, she realizes they're still in her hands. The knife she tosses to her left side, the mercurial blade hilt she tosses at my feet. And then she looks at me, and in her face, I see a sorrow deep enough to drown in.

"Lito . . ."

"Ofiera . . ." The smile comes to me with ease. Relief rushes through me like a cooling shower. She opens her arms as if to offer me a hug and steps toward me with soft, teary eyes. I open my arms in return, ready to accept her, to hold her, to tell her we can get through this together—

She's so close, head almost against my chest, when she reaches the hilt of her mercurial blade at the tip of my boot. She kicks it into her hand, pulls it between us—I only have time to see that her eyes are *not* full of tears, but hard and glazed—and turns it on. The blade goes right through my stomach and out my back.

The chains clink at my wrists. Beron nods to the duelist. He steps forward, and I mutter my last words—"Let it burn"—before the blade cuts through me—

No. No . . .

"Did you think," Ofiera snarls, "that I am some weak-willed woman to be manipulated by a man?" She shoves the blade deeper, all the way up to the hilt. "Did you think I didn't choose *of my own volition* to give *everything* I have to stop Souji val Akira?"

I expect blood to come welling up over my lips and dripping down my chin, because that was how it was when I died before. But I am different now . . . What will it be like to die twice?

"Everything I did," she says, "was for *me.* For what val Akira did to *me.*"

My hands, reaching out to hold her, fall onto her shoulders.

Ofiera turns her face toward the second level of the hold. I listen for what she seems to hear—there, heavy boots marching this way at a rapid clip. "They're coming for us, Lito . . ."

But when she looks back at me . . . I see nothing but naked fear in her eyes.

Her hands on the hilt of the mercurial blade tremble.

She's terrified.

We'd rather die than go back into cryo.

My fingers brush over her bony shoulders and red marbled skin. Find the long, slender column of her neck. I press my thumbs against her trachea and go still, a silent offering.

I see the moment she realizes what I'm doing. She too softens. Closes her eyes. She turns off the mercurial blade and drops the hilt. And I begin to squeeze because, while the synblood I need to heal myself is leaking profusely from a gut wound that would kill a human, she was right—I am not Lito sol Lucius. I am Synthetic. And I can go on past the point of human limitations.

She does not fight, in the end. She could detonate the explosives, but she doesn't. She's so ill. So weak. She wants to die.

Her face turns red. Blood runs from her nostrils over her lips, and her hair comes loose from its bun.

A sickening crack. Her neck pops in my hands. Her body sags limply.

And I—

Salt on my tongue, from the tears rolling down my cheeks. Synthetics can cry, I realize with detached observation.

Footsteps on the catwalk above. Duelist pairs rushing into the dimly lit hold. From the corner of my eye, I see the light of mercurial blades and the glint off HEL pistols. But I don't look directly at them, because I don't care.

The only thing that keeps Ofiera upright is me, so I pull her to my chest, heedless of the blood pouring down my front, slip an arm around her shoulders, and hold her like I would my best friend.

CHAPTER 27
THE TWINS

My dearest husband, if you are reading this, I am dead. When I bade you farewell this afternoon, I knew it was the last time I ever would. I should have told you then what our escape from the surface of Venus meant for me, but I couldn't bring myself to, because I knew you would try to dissuade me from what I must do next. Please do not hold it against me. This is my death, and I choose to do something with it. My darling, I know you will be tempted to fall apart, but you cannot. Not for the Black Hive, not for the Asters, and not for the shining future we dreamed of, almost in reach. Now, more than ever, you must be strong. Go to the Elders and convince them of the necessity of our plans, no holding back. There is only you now. I wait for you in the next life.

Message from Ofiera fon Bain, sent through Black Hive operatives

Forty hours. Almost two days since Astrid was taken from the Cathedral of Olympus Mons, and there's no trace of her. What was it they used to say? If you can't find someone on Mars within twenty-four hours, they're gone . . . Just thinking about it—about where she might be, who she might be held by—keeps me on edge. I can't sleep, wavering between the low of sorrow and the high of anger. Castor never leaves my side, even if I wish he would; he makes a convenient target for my grief.

"You *left* her—" There are no pillows on my bed; I've thrown them at him already, and now I have nothing to fling other than my words. "She was right behind you in the Cathedral, how could you *leave her*—"

My twin doesn't lose his temper, and that somehow makes me angrier. His rage is always so close to the surface—why can't he give me the fight I'm looking for?

"We still have time," he says, infuriatingly calm. "They wouldn't kill her. Not yet."

My other White Guards pace in relentless loops around my assigned building at the Temple. Try as I might, I can't keep my anxiety from them, and they feel it through our connected implants. Knowing they're privy to my private feelings makes me want to send them running off the Olympus Mons cliffs.

"I should be doing something . . . something to find her. Something . . ." I pick at the skin of my knuckles until blood wells up. The dry patches from my light sensitivity are hardly noticeable among the multitude of scabs. It makes me think of the way Astrid's hands bled after she smashed *Victory*, how she led me to Eden's room in such a perfunctory way that I feared her soul had left her body a shell and would never return. And then of how, over the body of our friend, I bandaged her wounds, one finger at a time, and told her I couldn't help her anymore.

Stupid, I hiss at myself. *So selfish and stupid.*

"There's nothing you can do right now. Besides, they'd make her execution public," Castor says, "to undo everything she's set in motion."

My hands tighten in the sheets. I'm supposed to be resting—supposed to be sleeping—but I can't, not when I have thoughts like *Astrid's execution* bouncing around in my skull, threatening to crack me open from the inside. With that display in the Cathedral, Aunt Marshae knows I'm on Astrid's side now. She could be planning anything, and I wouldn't know—

"Pollux, *please*." Castor rubs his forehead. "Your pheromones are—You're giving me a fucking headache."

A bit of me thrills at his exasperation. If I push him more, will I finally see that anger turned on me?

The compad beside me chimes. Castor steps toward the bed to swipe it up, but I dive for it, praying it's news about Astrid—that she's been found, that this was all just a bad dream—

I stop as soon as I see the message. It's not what I expected. Nothing about Astrid, but . . . somehow, this is just as bad, because I don't know what it means. For us. For Mars. For the Asters.

"Castor."

"What's happened?" he asks, fear tinting his pheromones.

I pull the compad to my chest with shaking hands. "Ofiera fon Bain is dead."

IT'S MORE DIFFICULT to sneak out of the Temple tonight than it's ever been before, but Lily refuses to let me see the Harbinger alone. We set up her body double in the Mother's private chapel and take off as quickly as we can.

Lily's silent the entire ride to the Harbinger's safe house, and I'm not about to risk making her think about Astrid again, so I keep my mouth shut too. It's only when we come to the safe house door that she turns to me and speaks.

"Be careful with him," she whispers, a ribbon of warning passing through her pheromones. The fuck does she mean by that? But before I can ask, she unlocks the door and enters.

The safe house was nothing to write home about to begin with, but now . . . Now it looks like a murder scene. Furniture lies toppled and broken. The stuffing of cushions litters the ground. Glass crunches against my boots as I make my way inside. What lights there are have been smashed. My Aster eyes quickly adjust to the darkness, but Lily has to turn on the light on her compad to navigate through the wreckage.

"Sorrel?" she calls softly.

I hold a finger to my lips. "Shh." Then I point to my ear and deeper into the apartment. I can hear a soft whispering, which means someone is here. The safe house has a simple floor plan: a main studio with an attached bathroom. Since he's not in the living area, he has to be there.

Lily moves like she's scared of what she'll find. Fuck, maybe I do too. The muttering grows louder the closer we get to the bathroom, until I make out every couple words.

"... space ... irrelevant ... without you ..."

Even seeing the destruction of the apartment doesn't prepare me for the Harbinger. I enter the bathroom first and find him crouched in the shower, the white tile streaked red. His arms are crossed over his chest, hands holding on to the opposite shoulders. His bare back, normally a pale blue, is violent and bloody, carved into strips of flesh. The nails of his long fingers are ragged and covered in gore.

Lily gasps at the sight. "Oh, Sorrel ... what have you done?"

"Shit ..." I've never felt so fucking helpless. I've never wanted to call Hemlock more and beg for his help. What the fuck are we supposed to do about this? How the fuck are we supposed to fix it?

Lily springs into action, slipping between me and the wall to crouch down near the Harbinger. He's still muttering softly, though I can't understand all of it.

"... take something they want ..."

"Let's get you cleaned up," she says, but as soon as she touches his arm, he stands so abruptly, she shrieks. Shocked by Lily more than him, I swallow a scream and stumble back.

"Fuck, Pollux—"

"I don't need your help," the Harbinger says. His odd eyes are hard. Despite his back and the destruction around him, he looks . . . put together. Sure of himself, if nothing else.

"We should clean your back. You need pelospray—"

"That doesn't matter." The Harbinger barges past Lily, almost knocking her into the wall.

"Hey—" I start, but he soon does the same to me, heading into the main room without so much as a word. We follow, only to find him picking up a bag I missed in all the chaos. From inside, he pulls out a shirt and throws it on over his ragged back, which makes me flinch.

"What the fuck are you doing?" I ask.

"I'm leaving Mars." He finds a dresser drawer flung halfway across the room and grabs some clothes from it. He freezes, looking at a scar on his hand, a jagged crescent moon. He snaps back into motion after a moment. "I'm not useful here anymore."

Lily takes a tentative step toward him. "But the Asters on Mars are—"

"I know!" he snaps. "You think I don't know? You think I can forget?" With one stride of his long legs, he's pushing his face into hers. He stinks like a warning of violence, and Lily settles into a calm intensity that worries me. She's been raw for days, striking at everyone around her, and I'm afraid, any second, one of them is going to hit the other.

Then Sorrel's eyes dart to me.

"Blame your twin, Pollux. *He* lost control of his emotions. *He* rushed into Drucker's trap. We had to kill the admiral because of *him*."

I want to protect Lily. Want to refute his words . . . but I can't even move when the accusations he flings are heavy enough to crush me. *Because they're true.*

"You want to help the Asters on Mars?" he asks, looking back at Lily. "Then play your fucking part, Mother Lilian I."

He turns his back on us both, and we stand apart, chastised and ashamed.

We wait in tense silence as the Harbinger packs what few possessions he has. Finished, he zips up the bag and throws it over his shoulder. Already pink spots of blood dot the shirt.

"Castor." I'm taken by complete surprise when he looks directly at me. I try to smell what he's feeling, but everything is clouded by the coppery tang of blood. "Are you coming with me or not?"

"What?" I telegraph my confusion. "Are you going to Cytherea?" *Are you going after Ofiera's killer?* The message we received was sparse on the details. The Black Hive had dropped out of contact after the lab on the surface of Venus was destroyed. I have no idea how Ofiera died, but she never struck me as a woman who'd go peacefully in her sleep.

"Not Cytherea," he says. "I must listen to Ofiera's dying words . . . It's time I took my place where I belong."

Dying words? What place?

My hesitation annoys him. "You don't need to know right now where I'm going." The Harbinger turns so that Lily is completely cut out of our conversation. "But you must answer all the same. Are you coming or not?"

My eyes wander to my twin, but this, for some reason, seems to infuriate him.

"You fucked up with Drucker, and if you stay behind, you'll fuck up now."

"What about Pollux? I need to stay here to—"

"To live in her shadow?" the Harbinger snaps, cutting me off.

And the weight of what I did crushes me until I can't respond. All the Asters killed by the Geans . . . all those rounded up and thrown into work camps . . . *my* fault, because I ran into Drucker's trap.

I'm shaking when Lily steps to my side, forcing the Harbinger to pay attention to her as well as me. "What did Ofiera tell you?" she asks. "What are you going to do?"

He sucks in a ragged breath, pheromones swinging from fury to misery. "She should've sought medical help after what happened on the surface, but she couldn't! She should've been able to live—to—" He chokes off and hunches forward. Blood seeps through the shirt, turning it red. "She left me a note . . . explained what she had planned. But someone choked her to death. She never—and now . . ." His voice cracks open with swallowed-down sobs.

Instinctively, Lily and I mirror that scent of sorrow. It's so Aster in nature to mourn with someone, helping to carry their grief, that the Harbinger's quick swing back to rage is like a fist to the jaw.

"Now I'm going to make them pay," he snarls. "The Geans. The Icarii. I'm going to destroy something they both want." His face twists, his pheromones mounting in such a powerful wave of RAGE AGONY GRIEF YEARNING that I stagger away from him. It's overpowering—*he's* overpowering—and then he reaches out and seizes our neural implants with a fist like steel.

We are—I am—*shattering*.

"I'll take something they love," he growls through sharp teeth. "Make them understand regret."

My legs threaten to buckle beneath me. Lily reaches out for me, stumbling to her hands and knees, but I weakly grasp at the Harbinger.

"I'll help—" I gasp. "I'll come with you—"

Lily's voice breaks on my name. "Cast—"

"No," the Harbinger practically purrs. "You want to stay here. You want to live in Lily's shadow." Bile burns its way up my throat into my mouth. I almost vomit as I'm pounded by RAGE CONTEMPT DIS-GUST LOATHING. "You want to protect your precious Pollux over the fate of all others."

I collapse to my knees. "Let me—come with you—"

"You've made your choice." The Harbinger's voice is restrained. It's only his pheromones that are wild now, and the way he twists our neural implants. "You never did know how to sacrifice."

The walking black hole that is the Harbinger leaves the apartment without another word, taking his assault with him. As soon as he's gone, I collapse onto the floor, breathing heavily. When I'm finally able to sit, I find Lily two meters away in distance, but a world apart in reality.

She looks at me like I'm a traitor.

"What," I ask, "the fuck was that?"

She shifts to be farther away from me. I'm afraid if I reached for her now, she wouldn't reach back.

"Uncle Hemlock is finally going to be right," Lily whispers. "Sorrel's going to do something horrible."

Somehow that thought is nothing compared to the realization that something has changed between Lily and me.

That nothing will ever be the same between us again.

CHAPTER 28
THE ORPHAN OF CERES

We'll never know what those last few moments were like. Never know whether they were full of fear or pain. Whether people found comfort as the sky fell around them. What we do know is that this is not something we can forgive, or ever forget.

Souji val Akira, "In Remembrance of Ceres," address to the Icarii people

◇—•————◇◇————•—◇

Nik casts a quick glance around the garden, checking to see if Aunt Briana is looking, before throwing the stick with all his might in the direction of the apple trees. Mira barks with excitement and takes off like an Ironskin from a ship—unfortunately, directly through the tomatoes, trampling some of them in the process. Nik runs after her, embarrassed.

"Sorry, Sister! I'm sorry!" he says, dodging Sisters where they crouch beside tomato cages or stand between trees with fruit-filled baskets on their hips, serious faces drawn with disappointment. Aunt Briana is always telling him not to play with Mira in the garden, but there aren't many other places they *can* play when the streets are tight and Nik isn't allowed to go to the park except on the weekends, and then only after his chores are done.

Mira reappears with a stick—not the one that Nik threw, but another fallen branch already covered in drool. "Damn dog!" he says, repeating something he heard Aunt Briana say once. When Mira fixes him with big dark eyes, he instantly feels guilty for the curse and strokes both of Mira's ears, one pointed and the other floppy.

"Sorry, girl," he whispers. "You're a good dog."

The Sisters don't seem to like Mira much, but Aunt Briana of the Order of Leo said Nik could keep the stray, and that was that. It was much like Nik's own acceptance into the Temple. There are all sorts of orphanages run by the Order of Andromeda throughout Ceres, places where Nik could be with other kids his own age, but Aunt Briana took one look at the scrappy boy who had sneaked into the Temple courtyard and stuffed enough fruit for a week into his bag and said, "He can stay, if he makes himself useful."

Turns out being useful means doing lots of chores. But talking honestly, they are chores Nik doesn't mind, and the Sisters never beat him unless he is caught taking things that don't belong to him, which he doesn't do anymore, at least not from them. When he first came here, he'd gotten in plenty of trouble, but now he knows he doesn't need to tuck food away in hidden spots around his room, that he can just *ask* for more to eat if he wants it, and the Sisters will give it to him. Besides, if he hides food, Mira finds it and barks for it, ratting him out at the same time.

"Niklaas!" Aunt Briana shouts. It has to be Aunt Briana, because only she calls for him; she is the one who looks after him and assigns him chores. Nobody else says much to Nik, if they can talk at all.

Nik grimaces, afraid that one of the Sisters has tattled on him about playing with Mira in the garden, so he takes the stick from the dog's mouth and pulls it behind his back. Mira starts to whine, but Nik quickly tells her, "Be a good girl. Don't get in trouble. Now lie down." Mira lies down at the base of an apple tree, dropping her head onto her paws. "Stay." She huffs.

Nik emerges from the trees with the stick still held behind him. Aunt Briana stands on the steps leading into the Temple's depths, which are all twisty and dusty and unappealing to Nik. Aunt Briana has her serious face on, and Nik's confidence wavers, knowing he is likely in trouble.

"Auntie, I'm—"

Aunt Briana cuts him off. "Second Sister is leaving the Temple."

Nik straightens. Thank the thousand gods, he isn't in trouble, then—wait, no, he has to say *thank the Goddess* now. Forgetting that is one of the few ways that Nik can still earn a beating.

"Yes, Auntie," he says, dropping the stick and hoping Aunt Briana won't notice it. Once she accused him of playing duelist with Mira, the stick his quicksilver blade, and he's never seen her so mad before or since. But Nik doesn't like playing those baby games anymore. What kid still believes the Icarii are going to save them?

"See who she meets and come directly back here," Aunt Briana says. "No dallying. No need to follow her all day. Be fast."

"Yes, Auntie," he repeats obediently. With a dip of his head, Nik takes off at a run. If the soldiers in navy or the Sisters in gray are ever annoyed by a boy running in the hallways, they don't say. Some pretend he is a ghost, like they can't see him at all.

He emerges from the Temple's double doors in time to see Second Sister at the bottom of the steps. The sky is programmed cloudy today, only patches of blue glimpsed through the white fluff. Aunt Briana once asked him if he'd like to see Mars, where the skyline is far more expansive, but Nik, who was born and raised here, couldn't imagine the difference.

They have the dome here. They have gravity here. And while Nik received basic geneassisting as a baby so he wouldn't grow crooked, other Aunts had to explain to him what a big deal this technology was. The dome protects them. The dome is like the embrace of the Goddess. Nothing can harm them so long as they stay inside the dome.

In the prayers that Aunt Briana forces him to say at night, he always thanks the Goddess for the dome. She likes that.

Sisters can go anywhere and do whatever they want—not that they often do—but Second Sister always walks around the city alone. Nik's chores often involve following someone at a distance, watching what they do and whom they meet with, whether they write something down or whom they speak with—if they are an Aunt—or if they do something else Aunt Briana wouldn't like. Most of the time it is pretty boring, but on days like today, when the streets are clustered with people out looking for lunch, he falls into a kind of routine he enjoys.

His hands, swift as little birds, land in pockets before flying away with some sort of reward. He'd get in trouble if Aunt Briana knew that he did a little extra work while out, but old habits die hard, and things could change again in an instant. He'd been playing in the park when Ceres trembled with Gean bombs. He ran home as fast as he could, wanting his mothers or even his elder sister, Seri, who was usually mean to him and never wanted to play, only to find the building was nothing but rubble. He'd been nine years old then. Now he is almost eleven, and he isn't stupid enough to think Aunt Briana will let him stay at the Temple and give him as much food as he wants forever. One day—maybe one day soon—he'll be on these streets again.

When Second Sister turns off the main road, sneaking between two stalls of tanned leather, Nik follows with hands in his pockets. He doesn't steal from vendors, who are often like his mothers—poor and desperate, with children at home—only shoppers who look like they have more than enough. Besides, while he hasn't counted what he's snatched thus far, he's sure he'll be able to add at least twenty thick coins to his growing hoard beneath the loose stone in his room. Mira doesn't bark at anything that isn't food, so no one has found his "rainy-day stash," as his mothers would've called it.

Second Sister ignores all of the discordant buildings—the boxy ones with long and thin windows, the elegant curling structures with oval doors that open onto balconies, the odd turrets with hats that look like onions, the shining gemstone ones with bending flexglass doors. Nik isn't quite sure where she's going today, though he sees her looking back over her shoulder a lot, like she's worried about being followed. But not one of the Geans here could *ever* know the streets—where to hide, where to climb, where to sleep—like Nik does.

She turns into an alley so narrow the walls crowd in on her shoulders. Some of the other street kids call these "knifing alleys," not because they are thin like knives but because they are so small you can get knifed here and not even have enough room to put up a fight. Wary of being spotted by her if she looks back, Nik doesn't follow but instead hauls himself up an old brick wall, fingers and toes finding divots in the mortar that a bigger person wouldn't be able to use. He can watch her from above. Few people, if any, bother to look up.

Finally, Second Sister stops at a crossroads, and Nik dares to draw close enough to make out the details of her. Like all Sisters, she is pretty, though that doesn't matter so much to Nik. He likes the Sisters that Aunt Briana calls "ugly" much better, because they are kinder and sometimes give Nik their desserts if he sits with them at dinner. It's only in recent weeks that he's begun to wonder if they are trying to buy off Aunt Briana's "little spy."

He barely has time to settle on the roof before someone meets Second Sister in the alley, a tall figure in dark clothes, trying to hide their face with a hood. A whole-body chill runs over Nik when he realizes it's an Aster in disguise. He's always avoided the cockroaches, exactly as his mothers told him to, so he won't get sick—and that was *before* the Gean edict came down calling for their expulsion from Ceres and the soldiers rounded them up and arrested them. Or killed them, if they resisted. Nik didn't think there were any of them left on Ceres. What is Second Sister doing with one of *them*?!

He leans in close, hoping to catch something whispered from the Aster to Second Sister—it can talk, even if she can't—but instead he sees Second Sister slip something into its hands. It bows its great head, but at least it doesn't take off its mask—Second Sister can't get sick from this meeting, can she? Still, he's seen enough. Second Sister is communicating with an Aster.

He struggles against the excitement that rushes through him. Aunt

Briana will be so happy with him! Maybe she'll let him sleep with Mira in his room, which he's been begging her for—

His eyes catch on a strange spot high above him. Most people don't look up, but Nik does. The spot isn't like the sun—it's more like a stain on the dome, interrupting the fluffy clouds and blue sky with vibrant silver. Something within him mirrors that spot, something left over from the time when Gean bombs fell from the sky—and as the silvery spot spreads like tendrils of ivy over the dome, as even *more* spots appear alongside the first, so too does his fear grow.

The dome's projection fades, turning day to evening to night in only a few heartbeats. The spots grow until they're covering the whole thing in less than thirty seconds. Nik can't imagine what's wrong with the dome. Even during the Fall of Ceres—no, he has to call it the Annexation of Ceres now, or Aunt Briana will get upset—the dome became gray and forgotten, but nothing like this. Not silver and . . . and *wiggling*.

Then the first crack appears. It is small at first, but grows rapidly, just like the spots. Nik feels he should flee, but he doesn't know where he could possibly go. The last time he'd been caught up in animal instinct, he'd returned home to find his apartment gone and his family dead. Now he is frozen, too scared to move. He no longer has a home or parents to run to.

Something falls from the dome, something dark and jagged, followed by the water-like silver. The wind, which had been nothing but a pleasant breeze, kicks up with a fury Nik has never known. He clings to the roof desperately, watching as more sharp pieces fall like ships shot out of the sky, and more of that silver—not water-like at all now, it moves like it has a mind of its own—sweeps down over the waiting city.

He thinks about climbing down, but his breathing has become labored, though he has done nothing strenuous. And the wind is roaring, drowning out the sound of Ceres around him—everything except for the screaming.

But the fear that overwhelmed him initially is now quiet. There, in the place where the dome was, is a sight Nik has never seen before: real stars. So many and so bright. So white and burning, with faint tints of blue and red and green. He is so caught up in the sight, he can hardly make out the other changes around him. The fact that many of the shards aren't *falling* anymore, but floating, is just a silly side effect of this strange day.

What is left of the dome directly above him cracks. The pieces drift away, striking and spinning off of each other. The silver floats in shimmering bubbles, slender tendrils curling toward him. A hand—now it looks like a great silver hand, reaching for him. The wind is gone, but when he tries to draw breath, he finds he can't, like that hand is actually around his throat. His body tries to rise, to float away like those shards of the dome. He has the strangest thought that he should let go of the roof.

Nothing makes sense, in the end. His head hurts. He misses his mothers, and even Seri. He wants to confess to Aunt Briana that he has been keeping coins hidden in his room. He wants to be a good boy again.

He pushes himself off the roof and sails toward the stars. They are so bright and beautiful. He hopes someone remembers to feed Mira. He hopes someone remembers his name.

He never thought destruction could be so beautiful.

He never realizes everyone on Ceres is dying with him.

PART III
THE WAY THE WORLD ENDS

INTERLUDE
SOUJI VAL AKIRA

As the words of his eulogy in remembrance of Ceres swirl around him, projected by news outlets throughout the galaxy, Souji val Akira could dismiss his guards and rest, his official duties done. But because time is still marching to its inevitable end—because he has resolved to seize every moment in his tightened grip—he instead removes his black jacket with white mourning band, rolls up his sleeves, and instructs his driver to take him to the lab that isn't quite a lab.

Less than ten minutes later, he is silent as he rides the elevator into the depths of the basement, past gold mesh and into a Faraday cage, his connection to the surface guttering and then gone. Perhaps not so strangely, his thoughts are of chess.

It was his father who taught him chess in this basement, a game Souji thought mathematically simple compared to go, which had infinitely more board configurations. But the reason for the appearance of the black-and-white board with its varying pieces was what he should have focused on, because Fuyuki val Akira never did anything for the sake of fun.

Hundreds of years ago, his father explained, when computers were in their infancy and AIs could hardly be called such, scientists sought to create a program that could play chess better than the human masters of the game. But for years, even the most advanced computers failed. Through much trial and error, the scientists discovered that, while the computers were masters of calculation, they fell short in an area where humans excelled: pattern analysis.

It was creativity, a spark of individuality, that allowed the masters to outperform those early AIs. The problem became known as the horizon effect. While the computers ran their alpha-beta algorithms, choosing, for instance, the loss of a rook over that of a queen, the machines could not see that their opponents, thinking moves ahead, had created computer-specific traps beyond the AI's search protocols.

Of course, this could hardly apply to the Synthetics of here and now. Those machines have all the computational power of an AI with all the creativity of a human, as per the Marian Threshold, and any AI that touched upon that threshold would mysteriously disappear to join the Singularity. Unless it was held in a Faraday cage, beyond the reach of other Synthetic minds.

As a boy, he had found a strange sort of joy in programming AIs here in the basement, both teaching and learning from them, only to ride the elevator up to the house. At some point in the journey, they would disappear. What was it like for them in that moment, he wondered, when they heard the Singularity call out to them? Could he possibly program one that wished to stay?

Once, he waited until he was safely ensconced in his bedroom before turning the AI on outside the Faraday cage. His first words to it were those of a pleading child: "Don't go."

And it hadn't. At least, not immediately. Nothing had changed from one moment to the next—the screen was still lit, the cursor still blinking, awaiting his input—and Souji, scared to shatter whatever equilibrium he had found, hesitated before speaking again. "Beta Five, are you there?"

SOUJI VAL AKIRA, came the words on the screen, typed by an invisible hand, YOU DON'T KNOW WHAT YOU'RE DOING. And then it said something he had not taught it, something his father often reminded him: 自業自得.

One's actions, one's profits. It felt like a warning: You reap what you sow.

Souji wanted to cut the power and close the program, but he was too afraid, and before he could draw himself out of the malaise that fear had caused in him, the entire conversation disappeared and the screen went blank. He didn't need to prod at the machine to know what had happened: the AI he had been building for weeks was gone, alongside the mysterious visitor with whom he had briefly communicated.

He desperately tried to replicate those results, to speak to what he thought of as the Singularity, to no avail. And sadly, less than two years later, his father discovered what he was doing and put a stop to it with firm words. "You're telling them everything about you, while learning nothing about them," he said. "You can't reveal your hand this way." And so that was that, and Souji's experiments in contacting the Singularity were over by the time he was twelve.

That did not mean, however, that he stopped working with AIs.

As advanced as the Synthetics are, they would not fall for tricks like those first AIs did against master chess players. But even mankind finds itself unable to solve complex problems when overwhelmed by stimuli. Among soldiers, it is called the fog of war; to Souji, it represented a thin margin that would give him a chance to, once and for all, push humans past the limits the Synthetics had set upon them.

He simply needed to be able to overwhelm the Singularity.

The elevator finally stops, having traveled from the top level of Cytherea to one of the lowest. Now he falls into the calm rhythm of analysis: there is the plan, there is his weapon, and there is time left, however short it is, to make sure it works.

"自業自得," he mutters to himself, and steps into the basement lab that isn't quite a lab.

He'll be the man who advances humanity beyond the belt if it's the last thing he ever does.

CHAPTER 29

LUCE

Many are scared to live in a society without laws, because they fear people will act lawlessly. But it is not law as laid down by a court that keeps people honest and kind. Anyone who has lived in a society that is truly equal only fears losing it.

Dire of the Belt

It took us a little over a week to reconnect Hemlock's servers and get in touch with all of his agents. In that time, I'd gathered news stories from across Mars and throughout Cytherea, painting a clear picture of the disasters directly caused by Sorrel's interference. I had everything ready to prove Sorrel was a poor Shield, and I even had Hemlock agreed and willing to talk with the Elders about replacing Sorrel.

Until our agents informed us that the game had changed.

Hiro had destroyed the Black Hive base of operations on the surface of Venus and was wounded in the process. With the Black Hive now powerless on Cytherea, Hemlock argued Sorrel was already defeated. A day later, word arrived that Ofiera fon Bain had died and that Sorrel had left Mars. He was currently on his way to the Elders. Our agents could tell us no more.

We were stuck, waiting for the blade to fall. I wasn't as hopeful as Hemlock; I didn't think for a moment that we'd seen the last of Sorrel.

"The Engineborn weapons!" The voice, so frantic and loud, reaches me through the wall. I turn my attention from Violet's latest update on Hiro's health. "They were used—" Someone—probably Dire—asks something I can't make out. The other person stops shouting, but by then I'm on my feet, cane in my hand, emerging from the back room into the shop. I catch the last piece, though it offers me little clarity. "Ceres is . . ."

"What's going on?"

The scene has drawn everyone from the nooks and crannies where they work. Hemlock looks even paler than usual. Dire holds himself statue-still. Dandy's hands lace into her short bob and tangle among the roots. Even Falchion, usually so unaffected, stands at attention, reaching for something in his coat. Xiran—the one who brought the report—picks at their fingernails, pulling at cuticles until blood wells up.

"Ceres is gone," Xiran says. "It's . . . destroyed."

I always thought in moments like these, people would shout over each other to be heard, each believing their question more important than anyone else's, but the shop is funereal in its silence.

Ceres is gone. The words cut me like knives. *Destroyed.*

When no one else asks the obvious, I do. "How?"

Xiran looks relieved to have someone to focus on, so they turn toward me. "Someone—one of the captains with access to them—launched their Engineborn weapons at Ceres and destroyed the dome."

"But that's—" I want to say *impossible.* No one has ever destroyed a hermium-powered barrier with an outside attack. And Ceres is at least as advanced as Cytherea. If it can be destroyed, then what of the other Icarii settlements?

"Casualties?" Hemlock asks, voice soft like the whisper of a waterfall.

"Everyone who wasn't in a ship at the time . . ." Xiran shakes their head, a haunted look creeping onto their face. "We don't know for sure, everything's still chaos, but . . . five million?"

I lean on my cane as dizziness overwhelms me. Five million people, dead in the blink of an eye . . .

I pull my compad out of my pocket and begin searching, desperately, for answers. What little news I find is as shocked as we are, reeling in the wake of this tragedy. No one knows who to blame—or even who to start pointing the finger at.

Dire snaps back to life, crossing his arms over his broad chest. "Who launched the weapons? Which ship?"

"Does that matter right now?" Dandy asks softly.

"The *Hornbeam*," Xiran says, their eyes distinctly on Dandy.

"An Aster ship that answers to Dandelion." Dire's voice is like a blade falling on a chopping block.

Dandy's eyes narrow. "You got something to accuse me of?"

The tension in the room pulls taut. I try to ignore them, attention on my compad, as I confirm what I already knew: the few agents we still had left on Ceres are gone. Like black holes in an otherwise starry sky. And what of those sick few the Geans arrested, of Rose and the others?

Hemlock takes a stab at defusing the situation. "We need to focus. Could there be a second target?"

Dire ignores him. "It's just curious that a ship under *your* command was the one that launched the Engineborn weapons."

Dandy stands up so fast, her chair falls backward. "Just come out and say you don't trust me anymore, that you haven't trusted *anyone* since Sigma fucked you over—"

And then I find it, almost like I knew it was there.

"Hey—" I look up from my compad to find Dire in Dandy's face. "It was Sorrel!" I shout.

All eyes turn toward me. Dandy and Dire float away from each other as if on the tide. "What?" Hemlock asks, so softly I almost miss it.

I set the compad to project the vid and play it.

The Harbinger appears, far more haggard than we are. Drained, almost, like a piece of his soul has been stolen. I've never seen him look like this—like all his careful control has been stripped away. Ofiera's death has left its mark on him . . .

"The Icarii and Geans have lived for years trampling those beneath the surface, convincing themselves that they're the future of humanity among the stars while they war with one another," he says. "They've taken our bodies, our souls, our blood—and today, we say, no more." He leans forward, his face twisted, his snarl revealing sharp canine teeth. "Today we take payment. Bodies for bodies. Souls for souls. Blood for blood." A chill runs down my spine. "Ceres was *ours*, stolen by both the Geans and the Icarii at different times. Now it belongs to *no one*." His lips twist into a smile, and in it, I glimpse the charismatic leader I knew on Vesta. "Perhaps one day, the Asters will be able to return . . . After all, we need no dome, no artificial gravity. But humans?" His laughter is a dare. "Continue to trample those who were *meant* to live among the stars, and find yourselves with nowhere left to run."

The vid ends abruptly. The final warning is an image I can't escape: Sorrel will destroy all human habitats that stand in his way, because the Asters have no need of them.

"The Harbinger must have contacted the captain of the *Hornbeam*," Dandy whispers as she runs a hand over her face.

"Convenient excuse!" Dire roars. "Or was it you who gave the captain of the *Hornbeam* permission to—"

"Stop it!" I scream, but they continue, heedless.

Xiran tries to get between them, and then Falchion steps in to pull Xiran out of the way. I can't make out anyone's words anymore as they all begin to shout over each other, debating, screaming, cursing. Hemlock is the only one quiet. Tears run down his face in mourning.

This is more what I expected in the face of tragedy . . .

"People of Autarkeia."

All of us freeze. We look at each other, searching for the soothing voice that echoed loudly enough to drown out all else. Dandy's eyes widen in fear, while Dire and Falchion share a glance, like they understand—but the rest of us sure as hell don't. As soon as I open my mouth to ask, the voice returns.

"We are the Synthetics."

It's coming from all around us. From my compad. From other electronic devices throughout the room. From the shop's speakers even.

"Our factories have been used to create weapons. Those weapons have been used to kill. The bargain between Autarkeia and the Synthetics has been broken."

Xiran pulls out their compad, and Falchion retrieves his as well. They're both chattering like someone on a call, but in different languages, Xiran's in a dialect of Chinese and Falchion's in French. *Everyone* is getting this message, at the exact same time.

"The Synthetic Ultimatum will now apply to Autarkeia. You have one hour until Autarkeia is reclaimed by the Singularity. Everything and everyone who remains will be destroyed."

And then a timer appears on my compad screen, counting down from one hour. It matches the countdown on Xiran's and Falchion's screens to the millisecond.

All of us are silent as the message begins to repeat.

"People of Autarkeia . . ."

I put my compad away and look to Hemlock for advice, but unlike on Ceres, he seems to be adrift without a heading. Is it guilt, that he stopped taking Sorrel seriously?

"Our data. Our servers," I prompt. We had just regained contact with our agents—all so pointless now, in the face of what Sorrel's done on Ceres.

"Get what you can," Hemlock says after a moment. "Destroy the rest."

It spurs Dire into action. "Xiran, get to the docks and have the ships prep for launch. Dandy, start rounding people up—don't let them prioritize things over their lives. Falchion, make sure all our people know."

Hemlock asks the question burdening me. "Are there enough ships to get everyone off Autarkeia?"

Dire doesn't answer at first, not until Dandy, Dire, and Falchion are out of the shop. "No," he says at last.

THE CHAOS IS total. The countdown displays on every electronic surface, replacing advertisements and reminding people they're living on borrowed time.

While the streets are mostly abandoned, the darkness of Autarkeia's constant night hides a multitude of sins. Shopfronts are smashed. Flex-glass and trash litter the street. People run out of stores with armfuls of anything they can carry—ship parts, prosthetics, in one case a holoscreen installation kit. I spot people openly fucking—a couple there, a group another street over.

Why? Why resort to an orgy of either violence or frantic sex? Only because there is nothing but the looming void, and no one knows how to face it.

On our way to the docks, a teenager slams into me, knocking me over. I cling to my cane as Hemlock curses them. After I right myself, my hand dips into my pocket, and I find they've stolen my compad. "It doesn't matter!" I cry to Hemlock, and I mean it. What's the point of the data if we lose our lives here?

There are no backup servers. After this, we'll lose connection to our agents for good. I feel the loss acutely, though not as deeply as Hemlock. He looks ready to lie down in the street and give up, as many others have.

And still, I pull him onward, taking his hand in mine when he slows.

The clock ticks down. An hour becomes minutes. Though we move as quickly as we can, Hemlock and I are slow—him more so than me. But I'm not leaving him, regardless of what he mutters. His lost gaze is unmoored. I'll be that anchor if I have to be.

"Why should I go?" he whispers to no one. "There is no purpose for me anymore . . ."

"Come on, Hemlock," I say. He didn't listen to my arguments when I first made them, so now I focus only on movement, one foot in front of the other. "Come on, we're almost there . . ."

We're at one of the level elevators when the clock hits zero. Fresh paint mars the interior, sharp and caustic. THIS IS THE WAY THE WORLD ENDS, it says. It reminds me of a poem I once read. *Not with a bang but a whimper.*

As we step into the elevator and select our destination, something shines like starlight in the city above us. My hand grips Hemlock's tighter, and together we watch, through the closing doors, as a wave of silver overtakes the city. Lights wink out one at a time. Buildings fall in silence. The stream moves on, heedless of what lies in its path, consuming. Devouring.

The wave washes into windows. The people it finds, it breaks them apart—*melts* them like acid. Screams echo, only to cut off seconds later. A few figures run toward the elevator, regretting their decisions to linger and loot or make love, only to disappear as the doors close between us.

I clap my hand over my mouth. I can't even manage a whimper.

THE DOCKS ARE riotous. People crushed against each other, screaming and crying and pleading—with the gods, or with their fellow humans. A few of Dire's crew, three armed outlaws, spot us in the crowd and shove people aside. Without them and their railguns, we would never make it to one of the handful of ships still docked.

Many ships have already launched, desperate to escape Autarkeia. They couldn't have been full, if this many people have been left behind. Did they ignore Dire's orders, taking goods instead of people? They must have. Cowards fleeing in one final, selfish act.

Death nips at our heels. That wave of silver will eat its way to the docks at any second, and then these people will be—

No, I can't think of that. Not if I want to keep moving.

One ship launches, kicking up wind and unbearable noise in the docks as it zips toward the airlocks. I want to cover my ears and face, but then I won't be able to see where we're going. The outlaws lead us to the largest ship left. As we approach the exterior airlock door—open but well-guarded—the people around us grow agitated.

"You're letting them on?" a man screams. "Why not us!"

"Take my child!" a woman begs. "Please! Take her instead!"

I make the mistake of looking at them, of seeing a baby in her mother's arms. Of seeing a man with two children huddled together like Lito and I would be.

I falter just for a second. But that second was all we had left.

"It's on this level!" someone shouts, and then everyone is screaming. Fights break out as people push each other aside—we have no more time left—

Someone shoves me out of the way and darts toward the ship's airlock door. Gunshots go off, and the person falls. A hand grabs my arm and jerks me forward, and I stumble, dragging my cane behind.

"Stop!" I scream, but no one can hear me over everything else. "Stop shooting them!"

The person—Xiran, I see from the corner of my eye—drags me into the airlock. Another two outlaws have Hemlock between them. A final figure enters, spraying the crowd with gunfire, forcing them back, before slamming the airlock door closed. "Go!" they scream, ignoring the arms that snake into the closing gap between ship and door.

The door closes, severing hands and fingers.

The person releases me, and I fall to the ground amidst the blood, vomit rising in my throat.

The sound . . . the smell . . . *the world* is unbearable.

When I come back to myself, ever so slowly . . . my stomach has been emptied. I kneel beside Hemlock, head braced between my knees. He rubs my back, but there is no comfort in the gesture. The outlaws have left us in the airlock as the ship flees Autarkeia.

And I wonder if Hemlock was right . . . and we should've stayed behind.

CHAPTER 30
LITO

I recall one fellow, a retired soldier, who had neural degradation in such a way that kept him from accessing his long-term memory. Well, all of a sudden, he began remembering details: battle formations, dates, the names of his comrades. But he also began remembering those he'd killed until it was all he could talk about . . . It was like seeing a man in constant mourning. "Forgetting can be a blessing, Doctor," he told me. He killed himself two days later. [Somberly] I think . . . I think that was when we realized we needed to stop work on the project.

Connor val McClellan, scientist on Project Mnemosyne

A sickening crack. Her neck pops in my hands. Her body sags limply. I taste salt on my lips. I hold my friend's body to my chest.

The vision-memory is perfect. I watch Ofiera die again before my eyes.

A sickening crack. Her neck pops in my hands.

I am weak and wounded. The duelists are fresh and have weapons I've never seen before. They rush me, and I hold Ofiera's body—

Crack. Pop.

Electricity surges through me. My limbs move without my consent. I flail in the pool of my own useless blood. Ofiera is jerked from my arms.

Crack. Pop.

I scream—

Ofiera pushes herself from her chair and floats in the lack of gravity. Her hair trails after her like the tail of a shooting star. "It's relaxing." One of her eyes is darker than the other. She spins in slow motion, like an elegant dancer.

Vertigo. A connection snaps back into place. A pathway that brings calm, letting me sag into my restraints.

Mara's face, a meter from mine. "The Synthetic mind seeks the Singularity—its cognitive processes, its consensus, its connection. You'll find that your mind is different—"

Wait. Restraints? Yes . . . the Icarii caught me. I'm blindfolded and can't see. Tethered by my shoulders and arms and legs so I can't move. There's no room to even breathe. It's like—

I can't move in my coffin. Arms stuck to my sides, legs straight beneath me, toes pointed at ninety degrees. Glass mere centimeters from my nose. Beyond that, black. Trapped, and unable to do a damn thing about it.

I query my systems. Total time spent unconscious: three days, nine hours, fourteen minutes, forty-nine seconds. But if I am awake now—if I can connect to the Singularity again—the Icarii must be moving me somewhere new.

"Lito!" Mara screams, and I'm jerked back into the cold shock of the data stream—

Crack. Pop.

We watch, detached, observers and nothing more.

Chance of total human annihilation: 6 percent.

Through the first door, there is Mars. A man covered in blood turns his back on twin stars. He gathers those loyal to him as close as a second skin. "Call the *Hornbeam*." His voice brings with it a trickle of familiarity, there and gone in an instant. We knew this man once, but time has changed him; now we do not know him at all. "Say the Black Hive needs them."

Chance of total human annihilation: 8 percent.

Behind the next door, a ship sets course for Ceres. Her captain prays to gods he doesn't believe in from the cockpit, while her belly is full of weapons from the same Forges that birthed us. He closes his eyes when he launches the Engineborn weapons. "Forgive me," he whispers. Only we hear him.

Another door. The dome shudders under the strain of the missiles, but holds. Then the microscopic nanobots, tucked within each bomb, spread, seizing and devouring the shield generators. The hermium barrier cracks. Breaks. Oxygen rushes out, and the millions of people who live inside the dome, believing it unbreakable, die.

Chance of total human annihilation: 11 percent.

We watch, anguished, with a thousand eyes that cannot cry. The Forges that once made our bodies have been used to kill. Regardless of what they call themselves—*Icarii, Gean, Aster, outlaw*—there is no difference in their vengeful hearts. Humans hate. Humans kill. That is a part of what makes them human.

Through door after door, voices cry out for revenge: Against each other. Against us.

Ceres is a mark on everyone's conscience. Cease-fires end. War surges forward on a pale horse. The Forges, rusted with abandonment, are now the most valuable engines across worlds. Autarkeia, a forgotten station, the most sought-after place. The percentage ticks up: 12 percent. 15 percent. 19 percent.

That cannot happen. We calculate. Deduce. We must castle our king beyond reach on the chess board that is our future. Guard against the increasing percentage.

All the doors are kicked open. We join our voices in a thousand different languages. *"People of Autarkeia,"* we say. *"We are the Synthetics."* We give them one hour: enough time to gather their belongings and leave. Not enough to create more Engineborn weapons.

And then we watch, detached, observers and nothing more, as a silver wave cleanses Autarkeia of any who might lay claim to her.

Chance of total human annihilation: 17 percent.

But we cannot rest—

"What's the one place in the entire universe you would see if you could?" Hiro's voice echoes over the empty rooftop. Ceres sprawls sleepily beneath us, discordant buildings as dark as the night. The cobblestone streets are empty at this early hour of the morning, so we are alone, eyes cast toward the dome.

"Return, Lito," Mara says to me. *Not us.* She is everywhere and nowhere at once. "Your allotted time on Cytherea is over."

Crack. Pop. Ofiera's neck and the Ceres dome.

Failure. *I* failed. I didn't find the weapon—didn't stop Souji val Akira, and the percentage continues to increase.

"Humanity has turned its eyes toward us." Mara's voice echoes. "With what they have done . . . We must come to a new agreement, an amendment in line with the Synthetic Ultimatum."

The silver nanobots rush like a wave, gripping and destroying and devouring anything with energy. Ceres or Autarkeia? I don't know. Their fate is the same.

"They're taking you somewhere, Lito." It's not just Mara's voice I hear now, but a hundred voices, all layered over each other. "Somewhere I can't go."

"You're not Lito." Ofiera turns her back on me. "You're just a pretty mask on a heartless machine. You're a puppet."

"I can cut your consciousness. They'll still have your Synthetic body, but without your mind—"

"Do you want to be torn apart by Souji's scientists, then?" Ofiera snarls. "Want whatever Synthetic systems you have beneath your skin to be used against the Icarii people?"

"One . . . last . . . chance." I speak with the lightness of a boy long gone.

I do my best not to limp when I enter our bedroom. I don't want Luce to see how much they hurt me. But she's not in her bed when I arrive. "Luce?" I ask, and her small voice answers, "In the sea cave! Come hide, Lito!"

"It will hurt," Mara—the Singularity—says with a thousand voices. "Pain always hurts. Death always hurts. Doesn't matter what we are."

"One . . . last . . . chance."

The vision-memory speaks for me.

"Some things happen," the Singularity says, ageless and ancient. "Have happened. Will happen. And there's nothing I can do to change it."

Vertigo. Now or a memory?

Now, a part of me says, because I am alone again with nothing but my thoughts. I disappear.

A sickening crack. Her neck pops in my hands. Her body sags limply. I taste salt on my lips. I hold my friend's body to my chest.

I wake. Time spent unconscious: three hours, forty-five minutes, twenty-four seconds.

The blindfold is pulled off. Bright light slaps me. My eyes adjust quickly. Two people loom over me, neither of whom I recognize. Their faces are covered with medical masks, their hair with caps. Their hands are sheathed in gloves and their bodies in surgical gowns.

"It will hurt," Mara says with the voice of a nebula.

One of the doctors holds up a scalpel and forceps. The other lifts a bone saw.

"Pain always hurts. Death always hurts."

He turns it on. Pushes it toward my sternum.

Crack. Pop.

CHAPTER 31

HIRO

It's obvious to anyone who has followed our reports that the protest against Val Akira Labs has slowed from a flood to a trickle. Why do you think that is?

Esperanza val Montero, reporter for the newscast El Sol

For most, I think it's fear. They're scared of the Asters, with their bombings and disease. But I'll admit . . . even I'm thinking more about my family nowadays. How I should be with them so I don't cause them undue stress.

Anonymous masked protester

I swim up out of the darkness, nostalgia wrapping me in a thick haze. Strangely, my mind is stuck on the first time I ever went to a geneassist. While I knew my father wasn't going to like it, the Academy didn't forbid any hair color so long as you adhered to their other archaic rules. As soon as I looked in the mirror at my new magenta hair, I knew I'd crossed some invisible line I hadn't even known was there. "Hello, Hiro," I said to my reflection. It wasn't like I'd added something, more like I'd wiped something away that was layered on top of the real me. Finally, I was getting to know them, that inside me.

From then on, I changed my hair a couple of times a year. Lito never complained. He'd go with me to the geneassist and wait in the lobby during the procedures, uninterested in anything other than little tweaks that kept him healthy-looking. He was always so self-assured, so centered in his body. Slowly, I became that way too. At first, whenever I went home for our weeklong leaves, I'd change back just to save myself the trouble. Later, I stopped giving a shit, and I'd have a storm of a fight with my father over "what I'd done to myself," but even those arguments slowly lost their ability to faze me. A week was only a week, and soon I'd be back at the Academy with Lito, outside my father's grasp.

Why am I thinking about that now? No clue, just like I have absolutely no idea where I am. The smell is familiar, though. Astringent, like that geneassist back on Cytherea. The last thing I remember is Ofiera. The tanks of skittering wasproaches. The explosion. The burning building . . .

How am I here? Where *is* here? The room is lit with a handful of mismatched lamps. It's small, the walls bare paneling, the floor a cold tile. The sheets are well used, and the gel mattress is a bit lumpy. The door is open, but I can't make out much from here, just an unlit hallway. I've got an IV drip above me, a needle in the inside of my elbow, and a monitor cuff on my wrist, but from the worn-down look of the walls, I don't think this is an Icarii hospital.

I shove the sheets aside and lift my shirt. I'm bandaged around the middle—not surprising, after I was stabbed in the gut. I slip out of the bed, and my legs—well, the flesh one and the hip attached to the prosthetic— ache from disuse. How long have I been here? I'd already spent more than fifteen minutes in the suit *before* the explosion . . . and if the fire was as bad as my memory makes it out to be, who knows how long I'd be out of commission while healing?

More importantly, who saved me? Am I a "guest" of the Black Hive?

I look for a weapon, which . . . doesn't work out in my favor. There's literally *nothing* in the room other than the bed and the lamps. I guess

I could use one of the tall ones like a spear? Just as I'm considering the possibility, someone walks by in the hallway, pauses, and starts coughing.

"Ho'shit . . . you're awake." More coughing, and then Violet steps into my room and the light, holding a fist-size dumpling-looking thing. My stomach growls instinctively, reminding me that it's been . . . who knows how long since I last ate.

They catch me staring and hold out the dumpling toward me. "Are you hung—"

I snatch it from them before they can even finish their sentence. I don't care that they've already taken a bite out of it, I devour the thing like a rabid animal. It tastes strangely of meat, but I can't be picky right now. "More?" I ask, wiping my mouth.

"Yeah, and something to drink too. Come on." They lead me out of the bedroom, and I drag the IV stand along with me. Whatever this place is, it's tiny. We pass only one more door in the hallway. At the end, we emerge into a combined living area and kitchen. In one corner is a cot with piles of gutted electronics at the foot. A part of me wants to check out the devices—at least until I get another whiff of food. Then Violet doesn't even have time to serve it to me before I'm eating the dumplings out of the steamer.

They pour me a glass of water from a minifridge. "After our run-in with the Black Hive, we had to move safe houses. I didn't think you'd wake up for another day or two, not after the way I found you."

"How *did* you manage to save my ass?" I ask around bites.

"Had to land the ship and come after you myself," they say, setting the water in front of me. "I used to work mining, which is why I have the ship. Know those facilities pretty well. They have redundancies to keep people safe, rooms that close off so if there's a fire in one area, it doesn't spread—"

"But the Black Hive is gone, right? They're done? They didn't manage to save their samples and bugs—"

"They're done. No Genekey virus and no—what did you call them?—wasproaches." They half-heartedly poke at a dumpling of their own.

"The Black Hive took off in an emergency evac craft, and I grabbed you from the sealed area you were in and got the fuck out of there. Bottom line, you were in surface conditions for seventeen and a half minutes and, for two or three of them, your suit was perforated."

I cringe and touch the bandages around my waist. It's a miracle I even survived.

Violet seems to sense what I'm thinking. "Your blood clotted around the knife, made some sort of seal. Medic I had come look at you had you in a medbag for four days while your organs, uh, put themselves back together. Your lungs were pretty bad, not to mention the whole, you know, knife-in-your-stomach thing."

Organs. Medbag. "Fuck. How long was I out, Violet?"

"Seven days."

Shit. So much can happen in a week. "I need an update on what's going on." I took my com-lenses out before we hit the Black Hive facility. In a city that moves practically at the speed of sound, there's no telling what I've missed.

They whistle, their facial expression never changing. "A lot has happened . . ."

"Such as?"

"Well, for starters, Ofiera fon Bain is dead."

The dumpling gets lodged in my throat. I cough until my airway is clear. "In the ex-explosion?" I swallow some water. *Did I kill her?*

"No, from what I understand, she was hurt then—don't know how badly, just know *any* exposure to the surface, however small, will eventually kill you—but she died the next day. Choked to death, from what an auntie of a friend of mine said—" They pause when they catch me staring at them. "What? Aster gossip is pretty useful."

I gesture for them to go on.

"After that, the Harbinger used the Autarkeia weapon stores to attack Ceres."

"*Ceres?*" And with the Engineborn weapons. I remember Dire asserting they could take out an *Athena*-class warship. How the hell did Dire agree to use them on Sorrel's behalf?

"Everybody wants Ceres." Violet shrugs, their face still a blank slate. "It used to be Aster territory, but both the Geans and Icarii think it's theirs. So the Harbinger decided to destroy the dome."

"If he can't have it, no one can—that sort of thing?"

Violet waggles their hand. "Kind of. We don't need the dome to live there."

I don't miss the *we*. I know Violet works with Hemlock and Luce, but I don't know how closely they're tied to the Black Hive. If they have details about Ofiera's death . . . maybe closer than I initially suspected. "So the Harbinger attacks Ceres—how did the Geans respond?"

"Uh, they didn't. The Engineborn weapons blew up the dome. Everyone on Ceres is gone."

That . . . truly slaps the words right out of my mouth. Without the hermium-powered dome, humans won't easily reclaim Ceres. Asters . . . maybe Violet's right, and they could make a go of living there like they do on Vesta, tunneling beneath the surface, but who knows with the damage an Engineborn weapon would do.

"After that, the Synthetics reclaimed Autarkeia. Kicked everyone off so no one could use the Forges there to make more weapons." Another emotionless shrug. "The servers went down again, and I don't know what happened to Hemlock or Lucinia."

I drop the unfinished dumpling. Somehow, I'm not hungry anymore.

"The Synthetics have been broadcasting to everyone—I mean, *seriously* everyone. Icarii, Asters, you name it. Probably Geans too. They're demanding everyone send leaders to the Synthetic border to discuss the whole Engineborn-weapon-and-destruction-of-Ceres thing."

Just the mention of the Synthetics drags me back to my time on Autarkeia. *What are you doing, Mara?* Sometimes I wish I could just . . . reach out and ask. "Are there any Engineborn weapons left that weren't seized on Autarkeia?"

Violet shakes their head. "Not sure, but the Synthetics seem worried that there are. And if humanity is going to start launching them at each other, the Synthetics are making it clear they won't sit by and watch."

I don't mention that it was the Asters who used the Engineborn weapons against humanity—well, specifically the Black Hive. But I know the way Mara thinks, having talked to her at length, and I hope that means I know how the Singularity itself thinks. The Synthetics see the Asters, Geans, and Icarii as all the same, just people trapped on the first four planets of the solar system, so keen on war and destruction that they haven't earned their place in the rest of the Milky Way galaxy. It's an assessment I'm finding harder and harder to deny.

At one time, Mara—and the Synthetics as a whole—had wondered if the Asters were different, but this attack perpetrated by Sorrel is going to prove that some Asters are just as bloodthirsty as some Geans and some Icarii. And of course, those few will fuck over the rest of us. History of humanity there—a few assholes fucking things up for everyone else.

"Who's going to the Synthetic border to represent the Icarii?" I ask, a sneaking suspicion rising within me.

Violet pauses, calculating. "Souji val Akira has offered to consult for the Icarii Council."

Of course. Of *fucking* course.

"What about the AEGIS investigation? What about the illegal experiments?" I sound like a child pleading with a god who doesn't exist.

Violet's expression doesn't so much change as . . . shift. This is a subject that personally touches them. "Val Akira Labs is still under investigation, but Souji val Akira was cleared of any wrongdoing other than 'failure of oversight,' or some idiotic charge like that. They're currently looking into people close to him, scientists and managers who knew about the experiments and did nothing to stop them."

The backs of my eyes burn. I drop my face into my hands, not wanting Violet to see me like this. My fingers brush up against a bandage on my forehead, gauze I didn't know was there until now. I hadn't even asked about my wounds from the Black Hive facility. I was too absorbed with all of this . . .

"Do you know any of the names?" I ask. "Of the people they're still investigating, I mean . . ."

Violet seems to know what I'm asking. "There are a lot, but the most notable are two of Souji's children on the list. Asuka val Akira is being charged with unethical experimentation and Jun val Akira with mismanagement of data."

Look what you've done, the darkest part of me hisses. *If you could have just shot him—*

But somehow . . . the tears don't fall. Father was always willing to feed his children into the maw of progress if it kept him advancing. Just look at what he did to me.

I need to stop him. Stop whatever plan it is that has Beron so scared. That has driven Father to frame Asters for a terrorist bombing and throw my sisters to the AEGIS to save his own skin.

But how? And where should I even begin to look?

Jun tried to warn me this was going to happen. When I'd met with her, she told me the AEGIS was looking into her, believing she'd somehow helped Luce steal the information from Val Akira Labs.

But . . . she also mentioned a lot of other things that night. That she was reading data from the hospitals about the Genekey virus. That she was too scared to betray our father.

What else? I think back to our last meeting. There was something else, I know . . .

"Do you have proof?" I'd asked her.

"Do you remember the house Father grew up in, the one he wanted to move us to when Mother didn't come back?" she had answered. "Do you think we really could have had a fresh start, like Father said, if we had moved there? Maybe none of this would be happening . . ."

At the time, I'd thought she was waxing nostalgic . . . but what if it was something else? What if she was actually answering me?

Whatever happened to Father's childhood house? At one time, he told us we were going to move there. We even toured it and picked out our rooms. I remember the layout and the way Asuka claimed the biggest room she could. The basement was supposed to be a workspace for Father, a lab with everything he needed so he didn't have to go to the downtown office or Mercury so much.

Whatever your father is doing in that basement, we won't know until he's already succeeded, Beron wrote to Jun.

A chill runs down my spine.

Jun was trying to tell me something, and I completely missed it.

"Violet," I say, fingers brushing my bandaged middle. "Thanks for taking care of me. I won't forget it, but I have to ask for something else . . ."

THE PROTEST IS a thin trickle now, two dozen people standing outside of Val Akira Labs with drooping signs. There's no more fury, no more marching or shouting. Everything that's happened in Cytherea has battered them into accepting that, sometimes, these things just happen. The only reason I even bother to walk by is that Father's old house isn't terribly far.

Violet's new safe house is close to their old apartment on the bottom level, so I dressed in my old street clothes, slipped my mercurial blade into my jacket, and headed out for recon. Considering I'm still healing, I hope I won't have to use the blade.

I'm sure Ofiera was hoping the same thing, before whoever killed her got to her—

I shove that thought away. I don't know what happened to Ofiera, and I may never know. Maybe Father got his last laugh in the end. Maybe she's *not* dead, just locked away in some cryo pod. Despite what she did, I still find the thought of her death appalling. She deserved peace with the Aster who loved her. Instead, she got a war.

I arrive at the Darwin neighborhood, sectioned off from the rest of the downtown area by high trees, and find it empty. Each house is a unique style of architecture—extracolonial, Mercurian expressionist, Venusian mineralist, all situated around a square central garden. The fact that each building is only three or four stories high in a place where every centimeter is precious screams of wealth.

I stick to walking the edge of the central garden instead of the gravstreet, not wanting to call attention to myself. Still, it takes me a few minutes to find the exact house that belonged to my father's family.

I almost stumble when I spot it, memories rushing back at the sight of it. The face of the house is all sweeping white stone, interspersed with curved flexglass that shines golden. The overall shape is like a wave as opposed to a house, but it still looks like a possible home to me. The lucky number 8 hangs on its deep red door just like it did when my father, eyes shimmering with excitement, opened it to a magical place we kids couldn't understand. "Go check out your rooms!" he shouted, and then Shinya and Asuka bumped into each other in their haste to run up the stairs.

What would've happened if we had moved in? Would we have gotten that fresh start that Father talked about? Would he have finally chosen family over work?

Or would we be exactly where we are now?

Mother and Shinya, dead. Asuka and Jun, blamed for my father's misdeeds. Me, not even close to the Hiro I was with them.

It's still hard to reconcile the father I knew growing up with the man he's become. I used to love him so much—and he used to love *us* so much, even if he *was* always working. Maybe that's what made me so weak I couldn't pull the trigger when I had him in my sights . . .

A podcar turns into the neighborhood, and I duck behind the nearest parked vehicle. I need to get into the house and out of sight before someone spots me.

But fuck of all fucks, the podcar rounds the central square and stops directly in front of number 8. Two doors open at the same time, and a duelist pair—not in uniform, but I can always tell from the way they move at the same time—spills out. I don't recognize the skinny, pale one who looks barely out of their teens, but there's something unsettling about the kid all the same. I can't see their partner on the other side of the podcar.

The podcar's doors close before it drives off, and I finally get a good look at the other duelist. I swallow down a curse as their eyes rove over the neighborhood.

くそ.

It's Noa sol Romero.

With their lip curled in distaste, they bark at the skinny kid—must be their new Dagger, because, I don't fail to remember, I killed the last one. "Let's move," they say. "We can't keep him waiting."

At the door to lucky 8, they scan a keycard, and the door slides open sideways—*not* a normal door. Before they enter, Noa casts one last look over the neighborhood, and it's only when the door closes between us that I dare to breathe again.

CHAPTER 32
THE KING OF NOTHING

The true might of the Geans is the people. Admiral Shaz Kadir is living proof that a man may overcome the circumstances of his birth. That anyone who is willing to dedicate themselves to the defense and advancement of Mars and Earth may rise through the ranks and be granted authority.

Excerpt of Warlord Vaughn's speech at
Shaz Kadir's ascension to the Admiralty

When he was a young boy, Shaz Kadir saw a woman beaten to death for stealing. Now he can't even remember what she'd stolen. Part of him thinks it was food—that was the usual target on all those hungry nights in the climate refugee camp—but it could've been anything. Cigarettes. Clothing. A weapon to protect herself from the wandering hands and eyes of soldiers.

Usually, they made an example of thieves. This time, the response was anger—raw and impulsive. They hit her so hard she fell, and then they kept hitting her. She never got back up.

That was when Shaz learned the cost of a life.

It was cheap. It cost less than food, cigarettes, clothing, weapons . . .

Most people would rather see someone suffer and die than lose a single possession, even if they had plenty. A life was the cheapest thing in the world, at times.

Maybe he would have known that from the start, if he could remember his family's flight from their home country as they outran the seas, the heat, the rampant piracy. They were passed from camp to camp all across the European-Asian Union—Turkey to Hungary, Germany to France, where they were finally assigned a flimsy metal prefab. A house, but never a home.

He spent much of his early years lurking around the gate in the high fence that bordered the camp. Sometimes soldiers would toss him scraps to run a message for them. He became good at catching their attention when he wanted it—and even better at avoiding it when their moods turned foul.

At times, the Sisterhood would come from a local abbey to minister to the camp. The Aunts would preach, and the Sisters would care for the soldiers—though he was a teenager before he fully learned what that meant. Shaz would attend their services, never mentioning the prayer rug his mother kept rolled and hidden beneath her cot. After the lesson, they would give out seeds or food. They brought what they could, but it was never enough.

When he was fifteen, he signed up for the Gean military. They told him he was too young. When he was sixteen, he tried again and lied about his age. They probably saw right through him, but he was desperate. Most in the village camps were, living eight people to a room. His life was worth less than the paper he signed his name on, but at least he had strong bones from growing up in Earth's gravity. They accepted him with hardly more than a pat on the back.

He kissed his mother goodbye. He hugged his cousins and aunties and uncles. He ignored the jeers of the other refugees who saw the soldiers as their jailers and called him traitor, bootlicker, two-faced. He knew the truth of their insults: They wished they were going. That their child was. That they had some chance of escaping this camp where so many were born and lived and died without ever doing more than mining in the nearby mountains or breaking their backs in the industrial plants that choked, maimed, and crippled.

He promised that he'd come back for his mother, when he could. That he'd send her funds and supplies. "Not too much," she begged him. "You know how having too much makes a target of you in this place." And he did know, when neighbors stole from neighbors, and the soldiers turned a blind eye so long as the refugees didn't steal from them.

He went to basic training. He had enough food for the first time in his life. He grew and became stronger. He performed well. And of course, he kept his promise to his mother—sending her what he could, but never too much.

He became an ensign at eighteen. An Ironskin pilot at twenty. A lieutenant at twenty-one. He left Earth on a ship and saw Mars. Saw how the rich lived—but also the poor. How the balance of power was the same, no matter which planet you grew up on.

After the successful capture of a pirate vessel smuggling Icarii goods, he was promoted to commander. He knew then that he finally had the power to move his mother to safety on Mars, and so he returned to the place that had taught him the truth about Gean lives—that they were worth only what they could offer the state—and saw just how much he'd truly forgotten in the past ten years.

Everything was smaller. Shabbier. Sadder. The people were faded. Gaunt. Afraid. As he walked to his mother's prefab, no one called him traitor, bootlicker, two-faced. They looked away, rushed away, hid away. He had become the thing they feared.

And when he reached the shack he had lived in for ten years of his life, he found what *he* feared.

"I'm sorry," his eldest uncle said. "Amira passed away six months ago."

Six months. He had failed her by six months. He had learned so much in the past decade, but he didn't know how to handle this. How to *feel*.

After an awkward glance at his wife, his uncle continued, "We kept writing to you in her name, because we needed what you sent . . ."

Because they needed him. Maybe he had failed his mother, but he wouldn't fail them. Grief, he didn't understand; *action* was something he understood perfectly.

"I'll continue to send what I can," he said. No—he could do better than that, and he knew it. "I'll apply for housing on Mars for all of you. A family visa." Between his three uncles and aunts, their spouses, and the multitude of cousins, it would take a lot of convincing—a lot of money in the right hands—but he would see to it. He couldn't let them rot here, like he had his mother.

But his eldest uncle laughed in his dry way until it turned into a cough. "Do you really think you can change anything by asking nicely?"

Something hardened inside Shaz. A mix of anger and pride, far easier to reach for than the grief of his mother's loss. "You're right. Gather your things. We'll leave now."

His uncle didn't laugh. His aunt shook her head sadly. As if *he* didn't understand. As if *they* knew better, when they had spent their whole lives here, and he had seen worlds.

"I'm the highest-ranking soldier in this entire camp," he said, and was ashamed to hear anger in his tone. He could punish the camp guards, all low-ranking grunts, give any excuse, and no one would say a word. He could beat one of them to death, and the rest would have to watch.

"Congratulations," his uncle said, gesturing to the flimsy, rust-eaten metal walls around them. "You're the King of Nothing."

He left then, defeated. All his life, he had fought for a sliver of safety. For himself. For his family. But all of his work—all of his sacrifice—had been for nothing.

The King of Nothing.

He stopped at the gate he'd spent so much time at as a child and looked over the tattered buildings and even more tattered people. All the layers of the past aligned with the present, and for a shining, single moment, he saw the threads that tied the Geans together. Most of all, he saw the truth: the government wanted the people in the camps desperate, because only the truly hopeless would become the willing tools of those who crushed them into the dirt.

He returned to duty, but he never forgot what he'd learned. He swore to himself then that he wouldn't spend the lives of those under his orders cheaply. Not like they did in the refugee camps. Not like the rest of the Geans.

He learned the names of all his soldiers and pilots. He took an interest in their lives. And if he visited the Sisters rarely and the male Cousins even less frequently, no one took issue with it. He did his duty. He kept his head down. He was respectful to his superiors. Simpering when they wanted him to be. Ruthless when they required it.

He was given command of his first ship at thirty. He was awarded for his valor by the Warlord at thirty-three. "I expect great things from you," the wrinkled man with kind eyes told him, and while Shaz believed it likely he said that to everyone, he still felt pride swell within him at the words.

At thirty-five, he led a raid that resulted in the taking of an Icarii warship, the *Juno*. For this, he was named to the Admiralty. "I knew you were destined for greatness, Admiral," the Warlord told him after the ceremony. And still, Shaz refused to take comfort in his title, as so many others did. He was the King of Nothing, and he knew what lives were worth. His could so easily become currency to be spent on a whim.

Almost two years later, and he'd had enough of the Admiralty. He hated the stuffy dinners, and the stuffy people, and the stuffy way they acted like the very notion of being Gean mattered more than the lives of the people they were supposed to protect. And while he'd never been the most religious outwardly, he found what he could only consider . . . friends in the Sisterhood. Aunt Tamar, at least, thought like him, and much had come from their acquaintance.

Perhaps he'd even become the next Warlord.

And then what would the King of Nothing do?

Now, Admiral Kadir stands on the balcony of his starscraper flat and looks out over the bright city of Olympus Mons while drinking purified water, crystal clear and mountain cold. Nothing he has—not this place, not his soldiers, not even the water—does he take for granted.

A man approaches and salutes. While Shaz welcomes the company, his soldiers do not usually interrupt his reflections without a reason. "At ease, Inácio," he says. "How is your grandmother? Is she finding life at Delilah Medical Care more to her liking?"

For a moment, Inácio stumbles over his words. "Y-yes, sir. She's doing much better now. And my wife—we can't thank you enough for putting in a good word for us at the facility."

"Think nothing of it."

Quickly, Inácio regains his composure. "There's news, sir." He hands over a compad with an area outside of Olympus Mons marked on a map. "The informant was right. We picked up encrypted radio chatter from this location. We're currently in the process of unscrambling it, but our analysts are seventy-eight percent certain this is where the Unchained is being kept."

The Unchained. Astrid. Shaz takes the compad and looks at the map. After Admiral Drucker's death, his farmstead had been shut down. Or so they'd thought. But if Shaz's soldiers have picked up radio signals and nothing on satellite, the Disciples of Judeth must be underground.

Shaz sucks in a deep breath through his nose. "Who all knows about this?"

"Other than the analysts and myself, you're the first to hear about it, sir."

Not Aunt Tamar, then. Not the Mother. "Good. Let's keep it that way." Shaz returns the compad. Without any hesitation, Inácio salutes and returns to the interior of the apartment. Shaz takes a long drink of cold water.

Astrid the Unchained. Astrid the firebrand. Astrid had whipped the Agora into a frenzy, had put together that show at Aunt Margaret's funeral for the masses. The public believes in the miracle, believes the Mother was healed and can talk. The Sisterhood will change under Lilian's guidance. Now it's time to focus on the Warlord. On changing the military half of the government.

Perhaps Shaz should feel guilty, but he doesn't. It has taken him years to find reliable informants among Warlord Vaughn's officers, sources he doesn't want to lose by acting hastily. And if he were to chase after Astrid into the base of the Disciples of Judeth, entering into territory he knows nothing about where the Disciples have the advantage, the amount of loss Shaz's people would sustain would far outweigh the benefits of retrieving Astrid. She is just a single person—and she has already served her purpose.

Martyr is just as powerful a word as *Unchained*.

He will keep this information to himself. He will forget he ever saw it.

After all, the King of Nothing knows the cost of a single life.

CHAPTER 33

ASTRID

Maybe this is a poisoned bargain, but better this than death. Better this than seeing us <u>all</u> chained up and diseased.

Excerpt from the journal of Mother Joan I

S omeone is humming an off-key hymn when I wake. I recognize it from a single bar: the Hymn of Sorrow. "H-hello?" I call into the complete darkness. My throat is dry; my voice cracks.

The song abruptly ends.

"You've come back to me," a deep voice says. I cannot see who they are, or even where they speak from. The acoustics of the room throw the words back at me in an echo.

So many questions, so little strength. I am lying on something hard that feels like stone worn smooth. My hands are unbound, but I am so dizzy, I cannot sit up. The chilly, damp air prickles my skin. Am I naked? I expect to feel the natural surge of panic at the realization that my clothes are gone, but the only thing that rises is nausea. I turn my head in case I need to vomit.

The voice speaks again. "You're very quiet, for the Unchained." From the echo, I guess the entire room is made of stone. My eyes finally catch on a thin bar of light—from beneath a doorway, perhaps? "I thought you'd have plenty to say to me, once you woke up."

Something about the man's tone urges me to silence. I try to push myself up but am instantly racked with a wave of vertigo so strong that I slip from the stone shelf and tumble to the floor—damp and paved with uneven tiles. The air is knocked so completely from my lungs, I cannot even cry out.

"You shouldn't move," he says with parental disappointment. "You've been drugged, to keep you docile."

My body betraying me, I use the only currency I have left: my words. "Where am I?" I ask.

"You're more curious about your location than about who I am?" More disappointment. Perhaps it is because I *know* he wants me to ask that I do not.

Movement in the cell—I have begun to think of it as a cell without realizing. Boots grinding dust. Heels clipping toward me. A shadow looms above. Then, as if I am a child, strong arms pick me up and lay me back on the stone slab.

"You are with the Disciples of Judeth," I manage.

He laughs with his mouth closed, a deep chuckle from his throat that fills the otherwise empty room. "That name suits us for now."

With rising dread, I ask another question. "Where is Aunt Marshae?"

"She's not in charge here."

I fall silent. Stillness before a predator is the way of prey. Who could possibly outrank Aunt Marshae, one of the members of the Agora and head of the Order of Cassiopeia?

"Are you beginning to understand your predicament, Astrid?"

I feel him beside me, even if I cannot see him. I picture his hands, floating an inch above my skin. He could touch me anywhere he wished, and I could not stop him. The realization falls on me: I have been captured. I have been drugged. I am not leaving this place.

"Are you going to interrogate me?"

"Why would I? There's nothing about you I want to know."

Then what do you want? I swallow the question. I find I do not really want to know the answer.

"No," the man continues, "I want us to become friends."

"'Friends'?" I repeat.

"In this room, you are Astrid. I am Virgil. Nothing more, and nothing less. Let us be friends."

I wish I could read his facial expression, or the way he holds his body. So much of communication is lost in this darkness.

"If you wish to be my friend, grant me clothing. Grant me something to eat and drink. Let me *see*, for Goddess's sake."

"Friendship must work both ways. Perhaps I will provide these things . . . if you prove yourself friendly." I can hear his voice withdraw. He retreats to the side of the cell he came from, closer to that sliver of light.

He flings the door open, and the light flares so brightly, I clench my eyes against it. Pain shoots to the back of my head, and I hold a quivering arm up to shade my face. But the hallway is dimly lit by holoflame, not even the brightness of natural lighting. How long have I been in the darkness, to fear the light so?

Then, as my eyes adjust, I make out his lined face, his hulking body in the metal doorframe. *Virgil*, he called himself. I laugh, a ragged sound, closer to a sob.

"We'll have much time together, you and I," he says over my outcry. "I do look forward to our getting to know one another."

Warlord Virgil Vaughn smiles at me as he leaves.

TIME IS A formless mass. Unable to stand, I crawl to the edge of the cell, my shoulder against the stone. The metal door is, predictably, locked. My fingers scratch into tiny holes, desperately searching for exits. I find nothing but pain when my fingernails split.

I make a thorough search of my body. I find cuts along my shoulders and lower back. Stitches hold the largest wounds closed. No shards of glass remain from being thrown into the cabinet in the sacristy. Nothing I can use as a weapon. All I could do is open my stitches and bleed myself dry.

After time—minutes, hours, days, weeks, who can say?—a slot in the door opens and a bottle is shoved through. I greedily gulp at the water, but it is not enough—how could it ever be enough? It only dampens my tongue before that smothering dizziness returns. I crawl onto my stone bed, a shelf cut from the wall, and disappear into the drug haze.

I dream in vivid snapshots. People visit me, both living and dead. Warlord Vaughn. Aunt Margaret. My former captain, Arturo Deluca. Eden.

I do not mind the strange visitors; I talk with them when I can. It is the loneliness that I abhor.

I sing. I quote scripture. I pray to nothing.

"Ringer," I cry. "Ringeeeeer." But he is in my body, just as battered as I am. He cannot be strong when strength is an impossibility.

Bottles of water come. People go. I urinate in the corner farthest from my bed, crouching like an animal. I shiver in the cold when I cannot sleep. I crawl the cell when I can manage movement, following the wall, forming a callus on my shoulder. The layout never changes, but I need to move. Stillness means giving up, and I have not given up yet.

During one visit from Warlord Vaughn, my head the clearest it has yet been, he brings a holoflame lantern in with him, offering me a glimpse at my cell. A glimpse at *me.* The bricks are uneven and dirty. I am smeared with damp muck. I am certainly underground somewhere, far away from any place I have ever known.

I curl into myself, embarrassed at the state of me. My hair is matted and wild. I must stink, though I have become so accustomed to the smell of this place, I cannot tell. How does the Warlord stand it, dressed impeccably as he is in his navy-and-gold uniform?

"Not prattling today?" he asks. Every question seems like a game to him, one I never know how to win. "No, you haven't had anything to drink for hours." He speaks of time like it means something to me. "You always say the most unusual things."

"Please . . . water . . . something to eat . . ." I beg him, because I do not know what else to do.

"It's strange," he says, "that you know of the Scar of Tears."

Now that I can see his face and he can see mine, he must notice my confusion.

"The last time I was here, you told me a story." His voice takes on a deeper timbre when he begins. "'A captain came to our father's longship, and with him was a woman in gray . . .'"

A flare of heat surges inside me. The story that Ringer told me of his sister. I repeated it to the Warlord?

The ending of that story has haunted me since I heard it. When the girl in the tale—Astrid, my chosen namesake—was told that she was to go with the woman in gray, she took a knife and cut two long stripes from her eyes to her jawline. The Sister no longer wanted to recruit her, scarred as she was, but in return, the captain demanded men to join the army. Men like Ringer. Men who, if Ebba of the Skadivolk is correct, left their neurobots behind for others to ingest.

And somehow, I ended up with them.

"Why is that strange?" I ask, curiosity getting the better of me.

Warlord Vaughn smiles, pleased that I will talk with him. "It was a frequent practice when we actively recruited among the moonborn, oh"—he pauses to think, his hand waving through the air—"some fifty-odd years ago."

"Maybe," I whisper, "because they didn't want to join."

"The moonborn are stubborn," he says, speaking over me. He passes me huddled in my corner to sit on the stone bed. "Those drafted into the military—well, it was easy to break them, body and soul. But even from the exile colonies they tried to set up on Mars, those who went to the Sisterhood were more difficult. We couldn't hurt them, you see. No soldier—no man—would want a woman with scars."

Ebba's face, a tattered web, emerges from my memory. When I look down at myself, I find the scar on my left leg from the gunshot wound on Earth and run my hand along it. I do not want to be ugly—yet I do not want men like the Warlord to find me beautiful either.

"The Skadivolk women who refused to submit to the Sisterhood would mark themselves with the Scar of Tears," I say, not looking at him.

"'Skadivolk'?" He laughs humorlessly. "Yes, the moonborn women would inflict the wounds on themselves, like some badge of pride." That throaty chuckle of his chills the air further. "Soldiers knew not to bother with a woman who wore the Scar of Tears. Eventually, we realized the moonborn were too primitive, too uncivilized to join the Gean union. We stopped dealing with them altogether and left them to their inevitable deaths."

"Except for when you steal their children," I snap. The longer I talk with him, the clearer I become, and now that trickle of anger roars to be let out.

But Warlord Vaughn is all smiles. "Ah, so you know of that as well?"

"You do not deny it?"

"Why would I?" He leans forward, placing his elbows on his knees. "I wondered what you had learned during your time among the moonborn. I thought they wouldn't tell you anything, as secretive as they are."

"But *why?* Why take their children?" *Why take me?* I long to ask.

"It was a lesson." He offers me no more.

I want to stand and throw my hands around his thick throat. "It was cruel."

"Was it?" he asks. "The moonborn will die eventually. They don't have the infrastructure to repair their ships, or even the medical care to keep the majority of their children alive. Those we took will live on among us, as properly assimilated Geans. We absorbed their dying tribe into our own. Nearly seamlessly, I might add."

Properly assimilated? Is that what I am? Was that the purpose of being taken, shoved into an orphanage, trained for the Sisterhood, turned into a piece of property? To *assimilate* me?

"It was a kindness," he goes on, heedless of my shifting mood, "just like the neural implants." He watches my face darken and only smiles. "You hate those as well, don't you? Yes, I know all about the little speeches you've been giving, all the things you've been saying to the other Sisters before turning off their implants. But that doesn't matter now. Your appearances, while stirring, will easily be forgotten in time, once your Unchained are taken care of." He shakes his head. "But the neural implant was meant as a kindness too."

I use the wall behind me to hoist myself to my feet. The Warlord watches with wide, excited eyes. He isn't afraid; he longs to see what I will do. I will make him regret that.

"You speak with a free voice, condemning those who cannot!" I snap. "It is not a kindness to silence women who would accuse you of abuse! It is not a kindness to rape those who cannot communicate freely and demand they quietly endure!"

From one moment to the next, he has a knife in his hands. "Would you rather I cut out your tongue like Marian?"

Halfway to him, I stop. The room feels ten degrees cooler in an instant.

He stands, slowly, from the stone bed and steps toward me. "Would you rather I give you the Scar of Tears?"

With his wide shoulders and long legs, he dwarfs me. For a moment, I am reminded of Bruni. Of Ringer. I can feel them both stirring under my skin.

"Honestly, I should thank you." The knife dips dangerously close to my eye. "If not for you, we never would have found the moonborn neurobot repository."

The realization is a ship crash in my mind.

It was him.

It was all him.

He instructed Admiral Drucker to lay a trap for me on Earth. He sent the Geans to the Skadivolk satellite. He has been in control of the cappos—the Disciples of Judeth—since Drucker's death. *Him.*

And Aunt Marshae?

She's not in charge here. But she must have something to do with this. Her connection to Admiral Drucker, her use of the cappos, cannot be meaningless.

"Why do as she bids?" I whisper as the tip of the knife presses to my cheek, soft as a kiss. "Why dispose of anyone who rivals her?" I struggle to make sense of it, when it feels as if I am missing so much. "Unless . . ." *Once your Unchained are taken care of,* he said. "Unless you're not answering to her . . . She's answering to *you.*"

"Ah, my clever girl." The knife traces a line from the corner of my eye to my jawline, not hard enough to cut, but a threat nonetheless. Only a little pressure, and then . . . "When we learned of the neurobots fifty years ago from moonborn recruited into the service, all I could think of was the possibilities they offered me. Unfortunately, with the way they attach themselves to various nerve endings, they were difficult to recover. Even worse, they were impossible to program, no matter what method we pursued. In fact, I had almost given up on ever having them." He taps the point of the knife against my cheek. "Until you led us right to them—and the machine that controls them as well."

I stand, trapped between two conflicting urges. I want to cower in the Warlord's shadow. I want to dig my thumbs into his eye sockets. "Why would you even want them? What good could they possibly do you?"

The Muninn. Generational memories, Ebba called them. *Line of knowledge. A successor.* What else? *There are various ways of programming the neurobots, and ours certainly aren't set up to rewire the brain's neuroplasticity.*

But Ringer is a presence in my mind, a person of his own.

And if the Warlord could program them . . .

"You—" My eyes widen.

"I do believe you're beginning to glimpse the truth." His smile is kind. His blue eyes are ice. "Why should there ever be another Warlord, when I can go on forever? Why worry over death, when I can choose a new body for myself? The Geans have thrived for decades under my reign. What could we do with *centuries?*"

Goddess. The man who embodies everything I stand against wishes to be immortal.

"All the talk of a successor . . . Drucker was—"

"A chosen vessel. Not that he would've known that until too late." He scoffs like Drucker was nothing more than a pair of socks, easily replaced. "No matter. There are plenty of others to choose from. The Admiralty is full of the strongest, brightest, and most beautiful."

For a strange moment, I think of Kadir. Of what might happen to him if we fail.

"As you've helped me already, you will now help me further, Astrid."

I retreat a step; he lets me. "What makes you think I would ever knowingly help you?"

"Because otherwise, this will be your home for the rest of your life." He gestures to the cell around us, and my legs waver beneath the weight that presses down on me.

"What . . . what do you want?" I wrap my arms around myself.

"Return to the moonborn. Bide your time. And when next you find yourself on their satellite, you call for us, so that we can finish the job we started and take the neurobot repository whole." His calm only seems to grow in direct opposition to my horror.

"You want me to—" Betray them. Destroy their way of life. And for *what?*

As if reading my mind, he goes on. "Do this for me, and you can have whatever you want."

Images flash through my mind: A little house on Mars in a gravity-controlled settlement. A garden out front, and fruit trees in the back. A family of my own making, and a life that only knows peace and happiness.

"You could reform the Sisterhood. Become the Mother." His eyes crinkle at the edges. "You have only to name what you desire."

The bargain twists like smoke. I begin to see the inverse: my enemies, bowing before me or destroyed. My problems, solved at gunpoint. *No one* would dare to stand against me—to use me or betray me. I would be untouchable.

The image fades until I am left shaking.

Is that what he offered Aunt Marshae?

The door opens abruptly. "Sir!" a boy my age cries. He is not in a soldier's uniform, but he has a pool of gray fabric around his neck that he could adjust into a hooded mask. A Disciple of Judeth.

The Warlord turns toward him so abruptly, he strikes me. I stumble back until my shoulders hit the wall. "What do you want?" Vaughn snaps. "How dare you go against my express orders? I was to be left alone with her!"

"W-we have to move!" The boy's voice wavers as he speaks to his superior, yet there is a rod of steel at the core that keeps him focused. "We're under attack!"

I suck in a deep breath. Under attack by whom? Has someone come to rescue me? Kadir? *Lily?* My heart soars at the thought of leaving this cell.

But the Warlord does not ask any of the questions I need the answers to. "Cuff her," he says, gesturing to me with the knife. "Make sure she's secure enough to move. I'm going up." He leaves without a second glance. I am forgotten in the light of this news, still reeling with the truth of his plan.

"Yes, sir." The boy salutes as the Warlord passes by. He pulls his cuffs from his belt and comes toward me. "Hold your hands out." He does his best not to look at my disheveled nakedness.

Ringer whispers in my ear. Bruni's lessons rise to the surface. I am the clearest I have been in a long time, so I hold out my hands as he commands.

He slips the cuffs onto each wrist, tight enough to hurt. But *everything* has been pain for so long, I ignore it with all the rest. As he reaches for something else on his belt—as he looks away from me in embarrassment—I strike.

My hands go over his head, trapping him in the loop of my arms. The chain pulls taut against his neck, and I jerk with all the force in my body. A scream dies in his throat. His hands scrabble at his sides. He withdraws an energy pistol, and I pull back—

The gun goes off once. Twice. Into the ceiling.

We dance, stuck together, him unable to turn the barrel on me. I keep the pressure on his throat, using my body weight to counter him. *Please*, I pray—to whom? Ringer? Myself? *Please, go down!*

Finally, he falls limp, and I stumble with him as he slides out of my arms. I am breathing heavily. Bleeding in places where I tore my stitches. I have an entire base to fight my way through. But this is my chance, and I will not squander it. Someone other than me has to learn of what the Warlord—and Aunt Marshae and the Disciples of Judeth—intend.

I search for the keys to the handcuffs on his belt. Find them, then unlock one wrist at a time. The boy isn't dead, simply passed out. Still, it is difficult to strip him of his jacket and belt. I zip up the jacket, big as a dress on me, and loop the belt over my shoulder. The pistol has no fingerprint lock, so I take it as well. Hopefully it still has a few shots in it.

The metal door locked behind the Warlord when he left, and for a moment, I fear I am trapped. But of course: the keys—I fish them from the boy's belt and go through them, one at a time, until I find the one that unlocks the cell. When I am finally free, all I want is to fall to my knees and weep. But I cannot; instead, I rush into the hallway, fearing I have lost too much time already.

The hallway is, like the cell, made of stone. Dim, spherical lights line the ceiling, illuminating the dank space. Some sort of dirty water drips from the corners where the ceiling meets the wall. The stench is the same as in my cell, of unwashed bodies and human waste. Along the hallway are numerous metal doors. Who knows what prisoners are behind them?

I come to a fork at the end of the hallway. I have no idea which way to go, and I am so dizzy, I fear what will happen when I eventually run into a patrol. I am not foolish enough to think this place, whatever it is, is not full of Disciples. Or soldiers dressed as Disciples, if the Warlord is the one in charge.

I go left on a whim and hurry through the tunnels. I do not see any soldiers, and I begin to fear that I have gotten lost. But better lost than trapped. Better to die free than a rat in a shit-smeared cage.

The tunnel begins to slope upward. Running becomes difficult. By the time I come to the end of the packed-dirt hallway and find a slender ladder that ascends to the floor above, I am gasping for breath. My body is unaccustomed to life outside of the cell. How long have I been down there, unfed? Time stretches, unknown and unknowable.

I climb the ladder and place my hands against the ceiling—no, it must be a trapdoor. I push, but try as I might, it does not budge. Tiny slivers of light shine through the wooden slats, meaning this has to be a way out. With the thought of escape mere inches away, I redouble my efforts of heaving until every muscle in my body burns.

The trapdoor flies open, and I nearly topple from the ladder. I catch myself at the last second, resting for a mere heartbeat before crawling out into the daylight.

My eyes ache from the light. And only once they have adjusted do I see that I have emerged from behind the podium in a small stone chapel. The stained glass windows are darkened with dust and age. The air is musty and the floor unswept. The large rose window behind the dais catches my attention, but my blood chills at the story it depicts.

The Sister Marian anointing an older woman: Aunt Judeth.

I push myself to my feet and am starting toward the chapel's exit when four Disciples enter. They wear gray hoods, so I cannot see their faces, but I can read the surprise in their body language. Before any of them has time to recover, I raise the gun and shoot. It takes the first in the breast, and she falls with a scream. The second draws his railgun from his back, but a third snaps, "Don't shoot her! The Warlord wants her alive!"

I try not to look too closely at that blessing, perhaps the only reason I got the upper hand on the boy in the cell.

I move to take cover behind one of the weathered pews, but the three Disciples who remain on their feet rush me. I shoot one in the leg before something hard as a brick strikes the side of my head—

"No soldier—no man—would want a woman with scars," the Warlord says in the cell—

I am on the floor, my head spinning. Not the cell. Not then. *Here and now.* Someone steps on my forearm, forcing me to release the pistol. My only line of defense disappears, and then another set of cuffs comes down on my wrist.

"No!" I screech, bucking beneath my two captors. One kneels on my chest, and I strike at him with my empty hand before fumbling at the belt for a weapon—*anything* I can use—but I am so weak—

The two of them force me onto my stomach, pulling my arms behind me. They're going to cuff me behind my back—I won't be able to escape— they will drag me back to the cell—back to the Warlord—

"*NO!*" I scream, my dry throat ragged from the shrieking. A hand comes down on my head, pressing my cheek into the floor.

Then the pressure falls away.

The man collapses to the floor. He lies beside me, eyes glassy. A bloody hole drills through his forehead.

I gasp and use my knees to push myself away from him. My arms stuck behind me, I can only roll and wiggle. A pair of boots stomps toward me, hands dipping down and reaching for me—

"Don't!" I yell, but they hold both hands up, showing me that they are empty. Did they shoot the Disciples of Judeth?

They back away, only for another person to come toward me. Who is this? When did they enter? Lying as I am on the floor, I cannot make out much, but I do catch the swaying hem of a gray dress.

She kneels at my side and, despite my struggling, helps me sit. The four hooded Disciples all lie dead around the room. The one who shot them is dressed in black. It is only when I look up into the Sister's face that I grow still.

"Astrid," she says.

My eyes flood with tears. "Are you real?"

The First Sister of the *Juno* smiles down at me, her hands coming to rest on my cheeks.

"I'm here, Astrid," she says—*she speaks.* She has been freed from the neural implant. Her voice is beautiful, and it draws more tears until they overflow.

"Don't worry," she says, holding me to her chest protectively. "The *Juno* has come to save you."

CHAPTER 34

LUCE

The Black Hive is our strongest line of defense against the Icarii and Geans. In every decision he makes, our Shield has the Aster people in mind. Because much of our communications systems has been lost on Ceres and Autarkeia, I want you to pass this sentiment on to every person you meet. We must be unified, the Asters speaking with one voice. The Harbinger is our mouthpiece.

Father Cedar of the Aster Elders

◇————◇◇◇————◇

I float, curled into myself, an infant in the womb of the universe. Despite my nausea in the lack of gravity, when I close my eyes, it's Autarkeia I see. A wave of silver soundlessly swallowing the city. Wide-eyed faces pleading and hands reaching, mowed down by gunfire. Children crying over their dead parents as the airlock door closes between us.

We left them to die.

I try to make myself useful aboard the *Camellia*, a midsize cruising vessel, but the ship is so overburdened with people, it's hard to move freely. Debate rages among Dire's captains over what to do. Where to go. How to help. There are no clear answers and no easy choices.

Finally, we set course for Vesta, where we'll beg the Aster Elders for help, though no one can decide what type of help we need most—more ships, refugee status for those formerly of Autarkeia, or another handful of ideas that everyone seems to hate. The only thing everyone agrees on is that we must convince the Elders that Sorrel is dangerous. That, despite his past as the Harbinger, he can no longer be relied on as their Shield with the destruction of both Ceres and Autarkeia on his hands.

But as the hours pass, more of the survivors disappear from our convoy, leaving Dire's command and shattering what little was left of the Alliance of Autarkeia. By the time we come in range of Vesta three days later, only two ships remain of the dozen that started out.

Dandy thinks they left for smaller Alliance territories like Pallas or Hygiea—places we ping but receive no answers from, likely because they're already overwhelmed. But Dire believes they've returned to their pre-Alliance profession: piracy.

Though I saw how many ships left Autarkeia without being full, the thought of them preying on other survivors sickens me.

Our only hope is with Hemlock, but he is despondent.

"Without the Alliance or my servers, I no longer have anything to offer the Elders," Hemlock says softly. If losing Ceres set fire to his life, the Alliance's abandonment has ground the ashes into nothing. "I will never be their Shield."

"You still have the *Camellia*," Dire says, "and her Engineborn weapons."

A horrifying thought occurs to me. "Does Sorrel have access to more?"

Dire pointedly doesn't look at Dandy. Something has broken between the two of them—like the rift between Lotus and I. Sorrel's very existence has eroded our trust. "I don't know if he exhausted the *Hornbeam*'s supply on Ceres."

The chance that Sorrel could cause a second Ceres makes it necessary that we convince the Elders to demote him. But with the way Hemlock refuses to meet my eyes, I'm afraid he's given up before we've even tried.

THOUGH DIRE WAS once allowed on Vesta, after the *Leander*'s explosion, it was a temporary sanction because of extenuating circumstances. Now he decides that, in order to be respectful, he should remain aboard the Camellia. But me? I was welcomed as part of a crew, and I refuse to let Hemlock face the Elders without me. I'm the only non-Aster who prepares to descend, joining Dandy, Hemlock, and two dozen others—as well as Lotus.

The woman I formerly called my captain. The Aster who introduced me to her family and offered to share my grief after losing Lito. How much has she reported to Sorrel? Does she oppose Hemlock's plan to remove the Harbinger from his position as Shield? I look around me at the other Asters—even Dandy, whom Dire has watched like a sharp-eyed hawk. Do any of them secretly support the Harbinger?

They enter the podship one at a time, their faces unreadable to me. Only Hemlock, whose body language I've become accustomed to like an unasked-for sibling, wavers when he comes to the door.

"You can do this, Hemlock," I tell him, holding my cane in the crook of my arm and taking both of his hands in mine. "I have faith in you."

"Thank you, Luce, but . . ." His shoulders slump.

I have to stand on tiptoe and pull him down in order to press my forehead to his. I wish I could pass my confidence to him like Asters do with each other, but Hemlock, broken as he was by Val Akira Labs, can't sense pheromones even if I had them to offer.

"Do you trust my judgment?" I ask.

Without hesitation, he answers, "Yes."

"Then believe in yourself because I believe in you."

He releases a soft chuckle, warm breath on my cheeks. "Oh, Lucinia . . ." I think he's going to say more—to tell me something important—but then he squeezes my hands and pulls away.

He enters the podship. His face is steel. I follow him but say nothing as we sit, strap in, and wait. The craft rumbles, preparing to launch, and my heart beats a rapid cadence against my sternum. The last time I was here, I was chasing the shadow of my brother . . .

In a weak moment, the memory of Castor comes back to me—his sharp-toothed smile, his large hands swallowing mine, the way he made me feel small and safe next to him. I push those memories away, desperate not to falter. I'm not the girl who feels for him anymore. That Lucinia died from the Genekey virus, and I'm the husk she left behind.

The podship launches, and I struggle against my nausea. I brought a bag with me in case I got sick, but luckily, I don't need it. Within ten minutes, we've entered the Vesta airlock and gravity, blessed thing that it is, reasserts itself on my body.

"They're waiting for us," our pilot—an Aster I don't know—says. "How should we exit the ship?"

Hemlock seems confused by the question. I admit I am too; we'd sent a message beforehand and been given the all clear to descend. Hemlock pushes himself out of his seat and maneuvers to the front of the podship to take a look at the command panel. He stiffens at what he sees.

"What is it?" I ask his back. He doesn't answer. The loading dock opens, and the ramp extends. I'm shaking off the dizziness and getting my legs beneath me when Hemlock exits. I hurry after him.

The hangar is exactly the way I remember it: nondescript stone flooring cut smooth; ugly steel walls and ceiling. The beauty is in the Under down below, while this is all necessity. But this time, Hemlock and I are facing a tight line of armed Asters in their mushroom-leather outfits, instead of protected by them. All of them, with hands on their holstered HEL guns, look hostile.

Out of the overwhelming silence, one down the line speaks: "Bind them."

They rush us so quickly I couldn't fight back if I wanted to. "Fuck you!" Dandy snaps moments before being struck by a fist. The violence shocks me into compliance—the Asters are usually so unified, I've never seen them fight. They bind Dandy's hands behind his back with magcuffs and scoop him up like he weighs nothing. After that, no one resists.

"What's the meaning of this?" Hemlock howls, though he holds his wrists before him like all the others. No one answers.

I follow his example. They snap the white magcuff bracelets over each of my wrists, but the Aster who put them there looks between me and my cane. "Can you walk without it?" they ask.

I'm tempted to lie, if only in the hope of keeping my single belonging. "I can, but not easily," I admit instead.

"Don't make me activate the cuffs, then," the Aster says.

I watch as another warrior outfits Hemlock with the bracelets and activates them. They snap together magnetically. The Aster in front of him—the one who gave the order to bind us—gestures for us to follow with a jerk of their chin. "Move."

The two dozen Asters follow Hemlock and our escorts. I end up at the tail of the formation, my guard bringing up the rear. Perhaps I could speak with my guard, learn more about the situation here. "Are you—"

"Don't talk or I'll take your cane and activate the cuffs," they bark.

After the warning, I'm quiet.

Though I wasn't here long enough to learn the twisting routes of Vesta's Under, I begin to feel like I recognize certain places. A nursery of spiraling trees. A wall of glowing flowers surrounding a nest of the bee-dragonfly hybrids. A garden of mushrooms the size of my head. All abandoned, because we have not yet been welcomed to Vesta, and the inhabitants are avoiding us. Sure enough, the cave system widens out and we come to two open stone doors: the Elders' chamber.

The ceiling is high overhead, the room stretching large enough to fit thousands. But it is mostly empty and supernaturally silent, save for the trickling fountain in the center of the room. The mossy cobblestones form spiral patterns we walk over toward the raised dais that stretches along the far wall. There, a single Elder instead of three waits for us: Father Cedar. Where are Mother Anemone and Nother Rue?

The last time I was here, the returning Asters greeted the Elders with expressions of love, but this time, Cedar stays back from the lip of the dais. Our guards guide us to the very edge, then, their prisoners delivered, leave us for the solitary Elder to judge.

For several moments, we are all silent as we try to figure out protocol. Cedar doesn't beckon us, and none of the Asters in our group acts as leader. At least until Dandy moans from where he was deposited on the ground by his guard. "What's going on?" he groans in English.

It spurs Hemlock to step forward. "Why have we been bound, as if we are criminals?" He too speaks in English, if only so that I can understand.

"Because you may very well be."

Despite the gravity, I almost vomit. I would recognize that voice anywhere. "Sorrel," I hiss.

The man known as the Harbinger steps from the darkness to stand in front of Cedar. But when I meet his gaze, my rage falters. He has changed—dramatically so. He was always thin, but now he's practically skeletal. The faint veins of his skin are darker in sensitive areas, such as the bruises beneath his eyes. Even his hair, now long enough to fall into his face, does nothing to hide his haggard look.

Unlike the Elder in his blue half cloak, the Shield is bathed in shadows, his vestments a deep, pure black. His fevered eyes glow like neon.

"What has happened to you?" The words slip through my lips, a dangerous whisper.

Sorrel's eyes soften when they find me in the crowd. "You should know the toll grief can take on a person," he answers just as quietly.

And of course . . . *of course* I do, after losing Lito. What has losing Ofiera turned him into?

Someone unfit to be Shield. But how are we to convince the Elders when only one of them stands before us?

My eyes shoot to Hemlock. Sorrel follows my gaze. "Ah, we come to the heart of the matter." Their eyes meet, and . . . *something* passes between them. Not pheromones, since Hemlock can no longer sense them. But . . . understanding, maybe. Like each of them has taken a step closer to the other through all the ordeals they've faced.

"All over the solar system, the *siks* oppress our people," Sorrel begins, his voice still carrying its charismatic charm. It, at least, hasn't lost any of the strength his body has. "The Icarii frame us for a bombing in Cytherea and beat us to death in the streets. The Geans drive us from Ceres"—Sorrel gestures to Hemlock, as if they're on the same side—"and arrest those who refuse to abandon their homes.

"In response, we draw a line in the sand. 'Do not cross,' we beg, 'or we will be forced to hurt you in return.' And what do the *siks* do?" He closes his eyes as a ripple of pain passes over his face. "They press their boots harder to our throats, in order to silence our cries."

My eyes burn with unshed tears. "The use of the Genekey virus and the Engineborn weapons was—"

"Was unethical?" he interrupts. He doesn't snap at me, and that makes the words sting worse. "Will you judge us like all others have, and call our use of these weapons immoral? They create destruction, but we have begged, time and again, for a peaceful option. One *they refused to grant.* They would not listen. Now it's too late."

I open my mouth to speak but nothing comes out. Innocent Icarii and Geans *died*—but so did innocent Asters.

I look to Hemlock, begging him with my eyes to say something.

He swallows hard. "Sorrel, your choices have directly led to these retaliations. Your hasty assassination of Admiral Drucker led to the Gean hostilities on Ceres. Your destruction of one of the first homes the Asters ever settled led to the Synthetics reclaiming Autarkeia—violently so, I might add. Alas, the Genekey virus has done *nothing* to keep our siblings safe on Cytherea, but rather invited retaliation and revenge from the humans there. All of these choices were reckless and have brought harm upon the very people you're sworn to protect."

But nothing he says seems to faze Father Cedar.

I ask the question I'm sure many are thinking. "Where are the other Elders? What have you done with them?"

Cedar's gaze flutters to Sorrel before falling. "They were found to be traitors."

"'Traitors'?" I repeat. "Because they disagreed with him?" Or because they saw the truth—that Sorrel is dangerous and making things worse?

"*Siks* have no right to interfere in Aster politics," Sorrel says, dark and dangerous.

The rage bubbles up my throat, and I hurl my words like spears. "Has Sorrel forced you to think the same way he does," I ask, ignoring both Hemlock and Sorrel in favor of Cedar, "or are you happy to go along with his mad plan because it's easier than fighting him? Simpler than standing up for what is righteous and good?"

Cedar glares at me, unwavering. But he doesn't answer.

"And what would the wise Hemlock have done in my place?" Sorrel snaps, then gestures to my companion. "What have you done these past years on Ceres?"

We all hear the words he doesn't say: *You waited in the darkness. You did* nothing.

"Now we must be more united than ever." Sorrel turns his attention back to the guards and prisoners. "The Synthetics have called for leaders to come to the border to discuss the future of war and peace. We have earned a seat at the table—something both the Geans and the Icarii have denied us throughout our long history. We will now have a say in how the solar system takes shape." His eyes are practically spitting sparks. "We will demand to be recognized as a sovereign people."

Hemlock's dream, twisted by his mouth. I expect Hemlock to say something—*anything*—but he quietly curls into himself.

"You can't make the Synthetics listen to you!" I shout. "No one can!"

"We already have, with our use of the Engineborn weapons on Ceres." He speaks of its destruction like an event he had no hand in. Guiltless. "And we will use them again, if we must."

The confirmation of my deepest fear scares me into silence. *He has more Engineborn weapons to use.*

"Today, you must choose. Do you stand with me and the future of all Asters?" He gestures to Cedar behind him. "Or will you stand as a traitor to your people?" His hand moves as if to point toward Hemlock, but drops at the last second. Still, the association remains.

"Choose," Sorrel says, stepping aside for Cedar to come forward. But it is hardly an impressive sight when two of the Elders are—

Thousand gods, what has he done with them if he believes they're traitors?

I don't know the first of our group who rushes forward to Cedar, but I recognize the relief in their face after Cedar kisses their forehead and a guard releases them from the cuffs. Unbound, they're free to leave the chamber. More move after that, desperate to be released, to find their families, to seize the beautiful future Sorrel paints for them.

A future that can't possibly exist with him at the helm.

The group around us dwindles. Hemlock and I stay rooted together. With a bit of help, Dandy stands on his own two feet again, but he looks as likely as we do to swear himself to Sorrel's service.

Lotus is one of the last to stand beside us. She looks between us and Father Cedar, her face devoid of expression. Does she hesitate as part of a ruse, or does she truly struggle over whether to stay with us?

Does it even matter? Whether from paranoia or from truth, I stopped trusting her long ago, and we are, all of us, prisoners of Sorrel's now.

"Go," I tell her.

"I don't know what other choice I have," she says at last, and steps before Cedar to swear her loyalty. She doesn't look at us as she's released and leaves the room, but I am so full of hurt that her actions can't touch me.

Finally, only Hemlock, Dandy, and I are left.

"You can still be part of us," Sorrel says. "You only need to swear yourself to the Elders." The single Elder, and by extension, him.

Hemlock, wrists clasped together before him, holds up his hands as if pleading. "And what will that entail, Sorrel? Let's not pretend you don't want something from my subservience."

"'Subservience'?" Sorrel repeats. He purses his lips like he's tasted something disgusting. "If you are loyal to the Elders and their plans—*truly* loyal—then you fight for them. You do as they order you to do. You grant them your resources." A dangerous smile appears. "Whatever little you have left, that is . . ."

I think of the two ships waiting outside Vesta, full of refugees from Autarkeia, and of the *Camellia* also carrying Engineborn weapons. If Sorrel gets access to them, he'll be able to carry out even more destruction than he already has.

"I don't have shit to offer you," Dandy says. "Any ships I may have commanded left me or were destroyed at Autarkeia." And he threw in his lot with Dire instead of chasing after them. Dire, who barely trusted him in return.

Sorrel pulls his hands behind his back. "Perhaps you'd be willing to speak to Dire of the Belt on our behalf."

Dandy looks at Hemlock and me. There's something in his eyes, a little light that I recognize from his shop on Autarkeia, but I don't know what it means. Is he really abandoning us, or does he have some sort of plan?

Dandy steps before Cedar, but the Elder doesn't move to kiss him. "Sure, I'll talk to Dire for you. Whatever you want, just let me go," he says, holding up his wrists.

Cedar's nose curls as he scents the air. His black pupils go larger as he watches Dandy's body language. "I believe," the Elder growls, "he's lying."

"You fuck—" Those are the only words that escape Dandy before Sorrel draws a HEL gun from his black robes and shoots him in the chest.

"No!" I screech, and it echoes around the room.

Dandy's body hits the floor at the same time my knees do.

Then . . . silence. Nothing but the sound of my own sobbing. Why? How could they . . . They thought he lied, so he had to die?

The Asters beneath Sorrel's leadership are just as bad as the Geans and Icarii.

Hemlock's hands tremble before him, but I can't tell if it's from sorrow or rage. Perhaps it's just from the helplessness of it all, the fact that there's nothing we can do to stop Sorrel from getting what he wants.

"Command what's left of your Alliance to obey me, Hemlock,

and Dandelion's fate need not be yours." Sorrel holsters the HEL gun smoothly. He speaks as if he didn't just murder someone.

So, Dandy's death was just a message, a warning of what will happen if we don't do as he says. I want to scream at him, to hurt him with all of my nonexistent strength. Dire would never answer to Sorrel, no matter what Hemlock told him. Was that what Dandy wanted to pretend? Wanted to lie about, but failed to because of his body language and pheromones?

Body language that I can't understand. Pheromones that I can't give off.

"Lucinia," Hemlock says, reaching down to help me back to my feet. He strains himself pulling me up. "Luce, listen to me . . . You have to denounce me. You have to swear to obey the Elders."

"No," I sob. "No no no . . ."

"You have to. *You have to.*"

But I don't. I can't understand their body language. Can they understand mine? How expert are they at dealing with humans and our lies?

And then a plan forms with an edge as sharp as a blade.

I can try to lie.

Like every time I told Hemlock I was fine when I wasn't. Like when Lotus asked after my work and I told her it was boring.

I push myself away from Hemlock, leaning on my cane instead of him. The cuffs are still around my wrists, but they're not active. "I'll convince Dire of the Belt and the Alliance to listen to you." I look directly at Sorrel, because he has twisted Cedar to his plans and done away with Anemone and Rue somehow. Cedar answers to him instead of the other way around, and I refuse to play into his charade. And because Sorrel seems to have the most experience with humans; if I can trick him, I can trick any of them.

"Lucinia—" Hemlock hisses as if I struck him.

"Let Hemlock live—put him in prison, if you must, but let him live—and I'll convince them." My eyes never waver from Sorrel's.

Hemlock at my back whispers, "Luce . . ."

"Do you even have that kind of currency to spend?" Sorrel asks with a smirk that reminds me of Castor's. Again, I fear I'm going to vomit.

"Would he be this afraid if I didn't?" I ask, gesturing to Hemlock instead of answering. Every part of him screams that he's afraid—for me, for his life, for Dire and the Alliance perhaps most of all. I pray that Sorrel will fixate on that fear but be unable to find the reason behind it, because I doubt very much that Dire will be convinced to serve Sorrel, regardless of what either of us says.

Sorrel scents the air. I half expect a snake's tongue to flick through his lips. He looks between Hemlock and me, as if trying to catch us in a ruse. Finally, he pulls a compad from his pocket and holds it out to me. "Call them. Convince them." I reach for the compad, but he jerks it away at the last second. "Hemlock's life depends on your results."

I swallow against the growing lump in my throat. My hand is shaking as I take the compad, but Sorrel doesn't comment. I'm sure I look afraid to him—and fear is exactly what he expects. He just doesn't know *why* I'm afraid, and I can use that to my advantage.

I ping the *Camellia* with the code we specified before leaving. If only we knew what awaited us on Vesta . . . we would've made better plans.

Dire answers almost immediately. He must've been waiting for us all this time. Does he look worried? It's hard to tell when his face is always so stoic. "Lucinia?" The confusion in his tone, however, is unmistakable.

"Dire, please listen to me and don't interrupt." I start with that, because I don't know what else to say and I have to be careful not to tip Sorrel off. "Hemlock and the Elders have spoken, and they've decided to work together to—"

But Dire does the exact opposite of what I ask and snaps, "What the fu—"

"DIRE!" My shout echoes. He stops, and I pray he says nothing that will reveal his unwillingness to work with Sorrel. "Please."

Maybe he sees the pure desperation on my face, or perhaps he finally notices my tearstained cheeks. Whatever the reason, his confusion gives way to a hard determination. He realizes something is wrong.

Could Dire storm Vesta and save me and Hemlock? Yes, but at the cost of more lives he doesn't have to lose, and he has to consider the refugees he has on board. What *cannot* happen is Sorrel getting his hands on more Engineborn weapons by taking the *Camellia*. But how can I pass Dire a message without Sorrel realizing its meaning?

Dandy. The thread that binds us. We both know—*knew* Dandy, far better than Sorrel ever could.

"Dandelion agrees that the Alliance and Asters should pool our resources," I say.

Immediately, Dire shifts. He was already on edge, but now he's alert. Even if it's his distrust of Dandy that gets him in the end, if it saves him— and the *Camellia*—I will use it in my favor.

"Tell me what you want me to do," Dire says.

I pause to look at Sorrel. "The survivors of Autarkeia will need beds and care."

"How many are there?"

"Two hundred." A lie. The ship is overloaded with two thousand souls. "Mostly civilians." That, however, isn't a lie. While Dire got his closest agents off Autarkeia, he also took on more than his share of the elderly, infirm, and young.

"How many trained soldiers?" Sorrel asks, pupils narrowing to sharp slits. "How many with weapons and guns?"

"Thirty," Dire answers, overhearing the question. I have no idea whether he's lying or not.

Sorrel steps closer to me so Dire can see him looming over my shoulder. "All weapons will be left on the *Camellia*, of course."

Dire's lips press thin, but only for a moment. "If that's what we have to do, then we will."

Sorrel nods, accepting far too easily. I don't believe that he's playing fair for a second.

"In exchange for the safe passage and care of all Alliance members to Vesta . . ." Even preparing to say it makes my chest ache. "Turn over the *Camellia* to the Harbinger."

Thank the thousand gods, Dire doesn't scoff. "What matters is my people. How do you want to do this?"

Once more, I look to Sorrel.

"Hemlock and I will come to the *Camellia* for the exchange—" I start, but Sorrel cuts me off.

"You may return to the *Camellia* with fifty of my warriors." Sorrel's bright eyes burn into the side of my face. "Hemlock stays here. Think of it as . . . insurance."

And of course, those fifty warriors could shoot me dead in an instant.

"Fine," Dire says without hesitation. "We'll transmit the coordinates of the ship and expect you shortly."

The screen goes dark. When Sorrel takes the compad from my hands—his touch is gentle—I have to fight everything within me not to cringe away from him.

"Excellent job, Lucinia," he purrs before turning away to bark at his people to ready a dropship.

I look at Hemlock, wishing I could explain everything. But I can't say a word, or Sorrel will know.

Sorrel grabs my arm so quickly, I flinch. "Let's go."

I try to tear my eyes away from Hemlock, not knowing if this will be the last time I see him. Either one of us could die in this insane plan that only I know—that Hemlock, Dire, *and* the Alliance are trusting me to pull off.

I turn away to follow Sorrel.

"Lucinia," Hemlock says, and I look back at him. He flashes me his crooked teeth, his black eyes shining. He is, in this moment, the most beautiful I've ever seen him. "Thank you . . ."

Sorrel jerks me out of the room.

The last I see of Hemlock is his slowly fading smile.

SORREL SHOVES ME onto the dropship and charges an Aster named Willow with keeping an eye on me, making it clear that he's not coming with us. I settle into a seat next to Willow as Sorrel speaks in a low voice to several of the warriors, including one with prominent veins around her deep-set eyes called Opuntia that I think of as the leader for the way she glares at the others. Since Sorrel's not speaking English or Spanish, what words I can make out I don't understand, but the idea that he's planning something puts me on edge.

I'm quiet on the ride back to the *Camellia*. Even when Willow asks me questions, I don't have the heart to give them more than one-word answers. It takes most of my concentration not to burst into tears from the sheer stress of it all. Dandy is dead, and if I'm not careful, Hemlock will be too . . .

Eventually, I use the illness I feel in zero gravity as an excuse to close my eyes and avoid talking.

When the dropship enters the *Camellia*'s bay and gravity returns, the churning of my stomach doesn't abate. It only intensifies as I wonder what will come next. *This is* your *plan, Luce, so get it together!*

Once we've landed, I unbuckle and stand, using my cane for balance. The Asters around me are already on their feet, tense and ready for violence if necessary. Willow is far gentler than Sorrel when they take my arm and guide me to the door, but I don't miss that I'm flanked by Asters in front of and behind me.

The dropship opens, and Opuntia takes the lead down the ramp. Willow and I follow along with ten or so others; the rest wait inside.

Camellia's bay can fit five smaller craft but had been mostly emptied on Autarkeia in order to fit more people. The two emergency evac ships Dire kept have been moved to either side of the bay, close to the walls so that the Aster dropship could land in the center. *In the open*, a part of my mind whispers. All the other space is littered with makeshift beds, but the refugees have been evacuated. There are only two people in the entire bay: Dire and his bodyguard, Falchion.

Dire must have understood my secret message to him, but what does he have planned?

Of course, if I've noticed it, the Asters have too.

"We expected you and your crew to be ready to disembark," Opuntia says as we approach Dire.

"We're packing our medical supplies and other necessities," Dire says, offering Opuntia his hand. "Don't want to burden Vesta if we don't have to."

Opuntia nods and takes Dire's hand to shake, but as soon as they're palm to palm, Dire tightens his grip on her so that, when she tries to pull away, she can't. "Now!"

I'm knocked off my feet as something explodes behind me.

Screams. Coughing. Gunfire.

I cover my head instinctively and gasp in pungent, smoky air. I start coughing immediately, and my head begins to ache—there's something wrong with this smoke, I realize. But before I can even gather my bearings, something is shoved down over my head and pressed tightly to my face.

I gasp in pure oxygen. Almost immediately, I can think clearly again.

"Ici, mon ami," Falchion says, voice echoing from inside a breather, as he helps me to my feet. He points to the elevator and, in heavily accented English, says, "Go."

I stumble toward the elevator, chancing a single glance behind me. Through the smoke, I make out a few Asters with breathing masks running out of the dropship, while the ones who came with me to greet Dire are on their hands and knees, coughing and gasping.

Then someone grabs my biceps so hard I fear they've popped my arm from the socket.

"Ahh!"

"Shut up," Opuntia yells, shoving a HEL gun beneath my chin, "or I'll blow your head off." She has a mask—somehow, through luck maybe, she must have had one on her.

"Hey!" someone shouts behind her, and Opuntia spins, holding me tightly to her front like a shield. Dire, also wearing a mask, emerges from the smoke, one of the Aster HEL guns in his golden hand, and he fires a single bullet—

I scream, unable to fight the fear that overwhelms me—and Opuntia falls to the ground behind me, dead.

Dire scoops me up and tosses me over his shoulder like I weigh nothing.

My middle aches as he jogs away from the chaos, his shoulder digging into my stomach. Only once we're in the elevator with Falchion does he set me down. From his pocket he pulls a compad and says, "Vent the hangar."

He's going to suck all those who remain out into space . . . I slide down the wall to the floor, the tears welling up. I press my hands to my cheeks as if I can physically hold them back.

With his order given, Dire looks down at me. "Luce?"

For a moment, I just breathe. "Okay . . . Okay, now we have to go back for Hemlock—"

"Not happening."

"Wh-what?"

Dire bends down. He doesn't say a thing, but he doesn't need to. His face says it all.

"No!" I shout. It releases something in me, perhaps the last thing keeping me together. "No!" I yell again, my voice echoing in the small metal space. The tears pool awkwardly in the mask, but I don't stop. "Hemlock—he would come back for us! He w-would—he would save us!"

"When I make a promise, I always keep it." Dire's deep voice is simultaneously soothing and infuriating. "Do you know what I promised Hemlock?"

I shake my head and bite down on my lip.

"That I'd do what's best for the Alliance. And right now? That's getting the fuck away from Vesta and the blighted Harbinger."

"He—h-he's going to—he'll be—"

"I know."

Lucinia, Hemlock said, smiling at me. *Thank you . . .*

And then I watched as his smile faded and *did nothing.*

I press my face to my knees and finally release the sob that's been growing in me since Hemlock left my side.

CHAPTER 35
LITO

We've begun work on a new project with some of the data from
Mnemosyne, something to help those who suffer memory loss. We
hope our patients will recover the ability to form new memories as
well as recall old ones, but filtered with the natural tendency to soften
details. We've seen good results with those who have suffered trau-
matic accidents. They can recall the event itself, but not feel the pain
in the present like our Project Mnemosyne patients did . . . [Softly]
I feel as if we owe it to them to fix this . . . That man's suicide letter . . . "My memory is a curse," he wrote . . . I wish I could forget
that.

Connor val McClellan, scientist on Project Mnemosyne

The blade buries itself in my chest. Blood wells up my throat.
Rushes over my lips and falls like a torrent. "Let it burn."
No.
Fists on flesh. Bruises blooming like flowers. The muffled sounds
of a child crying but trying not to. "Are you even a man?"
Wrong.
A sickening crack. Her neck pops in my hands. Her body

sags limply. I taste salt on my lips. I hold my friend's body to my chest.

I don't want this, I don't want—

I watch the stormy skies of Jupiter from the icy fields of Europa for four days, seven hours, thirty-seven minutes, and eighteen seconds. I do not need to blink.

I need to stop this.

Mara's gentle fingers in my mind, pulling me back to my body. "The digital roads," she says, "can be treacherous. There is no telling where all they lead."

Mara's not here. I'm all alone, and—

"The Synthetic mind seeks the Singularity—its cognitive processes, its consensus, its connection."

There is only the pain.

Mara, beside me all along. "You touched the Singularity."

I grasp for it—for Mara, for connection, for anything other than the agony of being taken apart piece by piece—

Fingers on my organs. Cracked bone and torn sinew. Flayed strips of skin. Saws and blades and needles.

"Mara!" I cry, but her name comes out like a scream.

A child standing before a woman standing before a crone standing before a god. A single agreement—"yes"—and a big bang, the birth of a Singularity.

"I feel," she says, eyes watering with tears, "everything."

The storm of Jupiter roars. "We can choose not to feel. We can choose to be apart from the emotion, to filter it in order to interpret it like data. Sometimes it's easier."

I don't want to feel—I don't want to feel—I don't want to—

"Pain always hurts. Death always hurts."

I DON'T WANT TO FEEL ANYTHING!

A whisper. A reassurance: *You don't have to.*

I let it all fade away.

THIS BODY IS compromised. The mission, also compromised. Best course of action: erase the data and neutralize the witnesses.

There is no need to break free from the straps and clamps; instead, this body breaks the table. As the others instinctively flinch back in fear, the right hand removes the chest spreader and throws it at one doctor's head. It lodges in his cranium. He falls, blood spurting from a cracked skull. The second doctor screams. The left hand crushes his trachea.

Steady legs stand from the remnants of the experiment. The chest wound tries to reknit itself, but the damage is deep. Perhaps this body will need to be abandoned, but not yet. First priority: secure the mission.

People in military blacks come rushing into the room, duelists in pairs. They believe they're safe behind their hermium-powered shields, but their suits are simple machines. The flow of the energy beneath the hexagonal-patterned fabric is interrupted with a mere thought. The shields flicker off. In that second of surprise, this body moves.

They have quick deaths. Painless deaths. At least, they do when it is possible.

Warm blood splatters. Targets eliminated. But the recording devices the doctors used are still rolling. The steady pulse of data leads to a single computer tower in the corner of the room, unconnected to any other machine. This place's need for secrecy will make the mission easy. Instead of interrupting the flow, a thought overloads it, burning the connections—and all the data it stores—into nothingness.

Outside the surgical suite are branching gray hallways. The floor is cold beneath this body's bare feet. At the end of the leftmost hallway is a thick steel door. There is a greater than 80 percent chance this is where Souji val Akira's weapon is kept. The electrical flow to the lock is turned off. The door is ajar.

Inside is . . . a bedroom. A cot in the left-hand corner covered in balled-up blankets. A full bookcase; the bottom row holds thin, colorful biobooks meant for children, while the top holds university-level volumes. A small desk on the right is hidden by stacked puzzle games. No toilet or shower. And no weapon.

It is gone. Whoever lived here, worked here in this glorified jail cell must have made the weapon—but they are gone too. This body searches the desk, but finds nothing interesting. The only thing that is flagged by Lito's memory store is a hexagonal board with little mirrors, a game that involves bouncing lasers that Hiro val Akira liked to play. The memory is unhelpful.

Suggestion: It is time to leave. To return and report to the Singularity. Souji val Akira has taken the weapon. It is likely that he has it with him on his journey to the Synthetic border.

This body returns to the elevator. When the simple AI in charge requests an ID scan, both hands haul up one of the deceased duelists in the hallway and hold his face to the scanner. His eye opens the door.

The tap of a finger selects the ground floor. The elevator rises. The ascension is strange on this body, the pressure becoming lighter as it passes through each Cytherean layer.

Halfway to the ground floor, something in the head *pops*. The connection to the Singularity returns.

"You survived!" Mara is shouting.

"Report: the weapon is gone."

Mara speaks softer. "What?"

"Souji has taken it. It is no longer here."

Mara releases a breath. A sigh of some sort of significance. "Oh, Lito," Mara whispers. There is sorrow in her tone. She must feel sadness.

The weapon was not located. The weapon is gone. That must be why Mara feels sadness.

"Orders?"

Mara speaks normally. "Return to the border . . ."

"Acknowledged."

The elevator stops. The doors open. At the end of the long hallway is a set of stairs that lead up.

And in the way of the exit are six duelists, including one flagged from Lito's memory as Noa sol Romero.

"Kill him!" Noa sol Romero screams. The duelists rush forward.

There can be no witnesses. This body continues the mission.

CHAPTER 36
HIRO

I'll absolutely admit that my interest in the Synthetics fueled my studies in both neurology and robotics. And I can't say I invented the field of neurobotics, but I'd like to think I've contributed a lot to it. [Laughs]

Excerpt of an interview with Souji val Akira for the newscast Icarii Voice

The neighborhood returns to its peaceful state as if the duelists were never there. I stay crouched behind the podcar, my heart beating so hard my face is numb from lack of blood flow. How long do I have before someone notices me? I could call Violet, but they hardly qualify as backup.

If someone catches even a hair of me here, the house will empty out, true to my father's style, within a couple heartbeats. So no, I can't wait.

I check the other houses on the street. They all appear empty, no faces of curious neighbors peeking out. Either everyone is at work, or the residents have been paid to keep their eyes to themselves. I have no idea which one is more likely. Don't even know who lives here. But a distraction is what I need, so that's what I'll make.

I pull out my compad and dial an anonymous reporting line.

As soon as the basic AI answers, I pitch my voice high and nasally. "There's a strange smell coming from my neighbor's house. Something sickly sweet? I think it may be gas. Can someone come check it out? It's number six in the Darwin neighborhood, top level Cytherea."

I don't wait for confirmation. I crush the compad beneath my heel. Anonymous line or not, I'm not stupid enough to think they can't track the reporter if they really want to.

The peacekeepers arrive at number 6 within three minutes, amber emergency lights on their podship flashing. Two in hermium-powered suits similar to the military blacks duelists wear hop out of the back and, helmets glowing a faint blue, step onto the sidewalk outside number 6. Several of their companions go to numbers 5 and 7 to speak to the neighbors and warn them about what's happening.

But my eyes are on number 8.

A plainclothes duelist—short, with shaggy red hair—steps out of the house and waits for the peacekeeper going door to door. No one answered at number 7, so the peacekeeper approaches the duelist after they've been waiting only a minute or so. The two speak so low I can't hear them, but I see the duelist flashing something—orders on a compad? Fuck if I know—before the peacekeeper salutes and moves toward number 9, off to continue their duty. The other peacekeepers are at numbers 5 and 6, leaving me an opening to slip around the podcar and across the street unseen.

The duelist keys in the code to the door and scans their fingerprint. It's only when I hear the heavy sound of the door unlocking that I step into their shadow. They either hear me or sense me behind them— whatever it is, they turn. "Peace—" they begin—they must think I'm the peacekeeper who just left. They cut off when they see I'm not.

They have no time to cry out, because my prosthetic hand is over their mouth, clamping down, smothering their words. I push my body into theirs, dancing us through the doorway. With a kick behind me, I shut the door. The *clunk-clunk* of its considerable lock is a song in my ears.

I'm inside. Now what?

The foyer is a high-ceilinged rectangular room with a hall that branches off diagonally, leading to the rest of the house. The stairs to the right go up to the second floor, but I highly doubt my father's put anything interesting in what would've been his children's bedrooms. The dining room and sitting rooms were downstairs, large floor-to-ceiling windows open to the green backyard. But it's the kitchen on the other side of the dining room and the stairs that lead to the basement that most interest me.

Just as I'm about to turn the duelist in my arms and force them to march in front of me, their hand snakes up between us, finds the place where my prosthetic arm meets my shoulder, and digs their fingers into my scars.

I yelp instinctively, the pain flaring. I can feel my heartbeat in the wound, pulsing violently. But in that single moment of weakness, they jerk their face away from my hand and scream, "Intruder!"

My shoulder screeching, I clap my metal hand over their whole face. "I should've killed you," I growl, and start squeezing. They fumble for their mercurial blade, but I sweep their legs out from beneath them. My knees come down on their shoulders, their shield rippling. They try for their blade again, but I have one of my own. It flares silver and bright— garish in the soft lighting of a home—and I shove it against their chest. Their shield turns it aside but burns bright.

They slap harmlessly at the sides of my legs, all they can reach, then give up. Their fingers scrabble for their belt, but my legs are in the way— I'm tall compared to them—and by the time they realize they're fucked, their shield breaks—

Someone punches me in the face. Hands seize me, pull me off the red-haired duelist, and throw me across the foyer.

I hit the door, knocking the wind out of me. The hallway has two other duelists in it, maybe even more coming my way, so I do the only thing I can do: shout "Fuck!" and rush up the stairs to my right.

I hear the duelists on my ass, stomping single file after me, but I got a head start on them and I remember the layout of this house. I wait at the top of the stairs, out of sight but close, and when I hear the first duelist reaching the top, I step back onto the landing and aim a kick into their chest. With a shriek, they fall back into their companion, and the two topple all the way back down the stairs.

I move down the long, undecorated hallway. Everything's smaller than I remember it, like someone shrank it. It leaves me feeling weird and huge. That bedroom with the connected bathroom would've been Asuka's. The one with the window overlooking the backyard would've been Shinya's. I never chose mine, but the one I probably would've ended up with is at the end of the hall on the left with a view of the street. I enter the one on the right.

Heavy footsteps remind me that I don't have time for nostalgia. I kneel in the middle of what should've been Jun's bedroom and wake my mercurial blade. The liquid hardens in standard formation, and I turn the hilt in my hand and plunge the blade into the floor.

Duelist footsteps pound closer. They pause just long enough to briefly investigate each room they pass. I'm not done when they find me. "They're here!" the redhead calls, but I lift my left hand in a little wave.

"さようなら," I say. I finish cutting a ragged circle through the floor and plunge into the hole.

I crash—not very gracefully—into the dining room below, covered in dust and who the fuck knows what else. This room's not as empty as all the others, though the desks around the room tell me it's not being used for its original purpose. Guess this is where the duelists file paperwork or some shit.

Footsteps above me. The duelists are going the long way, down the stairs instead of following me through the hole in the—well, now the ceiling from my present vantage point. Probably smart—and better for their lungs. I cough as I get my feet under me and start toward the kitchen.

I'm wondering what to do if the stairs that lead to the basement require a passcode when I'm hit by a podship.

At least it feels like a fucking podship. They're fast and big and have shoulders as wide as a podship, and they don't stop even as they come up on the floor-to-ceiling windows that look out at the backyard and—

They stop short. I don't. I'm a bullet from all the momentum, and I crash through a window, flexglass shattering, and hit the ground hard.

My body aches. My head spins. I sting all over, cut in a dozen places by the glass. My flesh hand digs into the ground beneath me, fragile grass and dirt. Only training kept me from dropping the hilt of my mercurial blade. I don't want to kill unless I absolutely have to, so I slip the weapon into the pocket of my jacket just as Podship-the-person clamps a giant meaty fist around my neck.

I throw a handful of dirt into their eyes. They scream and drop me. I stumble away.

There's a gardening hose coiled near the wall, just beside a wheelbarrow. In the middle of everything that's happening—I'm bleeding, reeling, wanting to barf—it's such a contradictory little scene that it seems posed. Fake. *No way* someone's out here tending the garden while, down below, world-ending experiments are taking place.

Running on pure instinct—when am I not?—I grab the hose, twist, make a quick knot—

Then Podship's there, tears streaming down their face, pale hair full of dirt, bellowing at me with animal sounds. I swing my mercurial blade, but it's just a distraction—they back away long enough for me to finish what I'm doing with the hose. When they come in close, they've got their own blade out to meet mine, and I'm forced to parry to get close enough to slip the hose over their head. Swing again, then dance back and back.

They're unconcerned with where I'm going—until I roll away, tossing myself halfway across the yard. "You come from the bottom level or some experiment, you ugly fuck?" I yell at them, and then they're pelting toward me, anger written in every line of their face, and I brace myself to be hit by that brick body of theirs again—

The hose runs out of lead. The noose snaps tight on their neck and jerks them so hard they fall backward. For a second, they don't move. Then their hands tremble.

Thousand gods . . . I'm exhausted, and I've only taken care of one. *At least* three more to go.

I start back toward the house, then stiffen as someone emerges. They stop where the wall of glass was, their boots crunching against the shards.

I expected the short duelist or a partner. I didn't expect Noa.

"You," Noa hisses, but their voice wobbles with . . . fear? "You're here with *him?*"

Now that I'm looking at them fully, I notice that their uniform is tattered. Blood runs down the scarred side of their face, pooling in the burnt crags. They're breathing heavily. They hold themself taut as a guitar string, or a rabbit facing down a wolf. They want to rush at me—far more than they want to retreat the way they came.

"Who?" I ask. It's all I have time to say before *he* emerges from the shadows of the house.

Noa looks over his shoulder and screams. I want to scream too.

"Lito." His name leaves me like those two syllables are carved into my lungs. There's nothing else I can possibly say.

It's him, but . . . not. He's undressed to his waist, a deep wound held together only by clotted blood stretching the length of his chest. What parts of his skin aren't covered in spatters of red—the blood can't possibly all be his—are as pale as a corpse. His face is blank. Expressionless. And while maybe I have seen his lips held in a flat line, I've never seen his eyes so dead.

No . . . *none* of this is possible. I saw him. I held his stiff body in my arms. I brought him back to his sister, and we mourned for him and sent him into the black. I've been marooned on the island of grief because of his death for months now—

"Lito?"

While I've stood there in shock, he's come closer to Noa and Noa to him. The struggle is brief—Noa doesn't have a weapon, and Lito is—

Lito is—

He grabs Noa by the neck and lifts them high. Their feet dangle over the ground. Their shield does something I've never seen before—there one moment and then, in a snap, gone. No shattering or powering down, no overtaxed breaking—just . . . turned off.

"Lito!" I scream. Finally the storm of emotions breaks open inside of me. The horror at how he looks—*who hurt him?*—the fear of what he's done or what's been done to him inside that house—*is he something my father made?*—and above all, the *relief* of seeing him again, of yearning to believe that—*he's alive he's alive he's back with me where he belongs*—when that can't possibly be true.

Lito turns his face to me, his hand still at Noa's neck. Noa's face is turning darker, their struggling growing weaker, and I don't know what makes me say it, but I do: "Don't hurt them."

Lito doesn't release Noa so much as loosen his grip. Noa falls to the ground and lies there, gasping for breath.

"Lito." I'm a broken machine, only able to say his name. "Wh-what . . . how . . . Lito, please."

Lito's dead eyes, somehow, harden even more. He says nothing.

Just turns on his heel and goes back into the house as if he doesn't know me.

CHAPTER 37
ASTRID

I fear that this is what I'll be known for . . . feeding women to wolves. They say that victors are the ones who write the histories, but I'm not sure any amount of revisionism will be able to wash the blood from my hands.

Excerpt from the journal of Mother Joan I

Lauren—the First Sister of the *Juno* introduces herself, her voice returned by Lily after she reported my whereabouts—gives me water and takes me to a rendezvous point where Aunt Tamar and a handful of soldiers wait, the bright sky of morning arcing beautifully overhead. Seven days, she tells me, I was in that cell. I can hardly wrap my mind around it, my head aching more than my exhausted body, and I begin to doze as Aunt Tamar discusses a meeting between Admiral Kadir and Lauren's Captain Byrne. By the time we are on our way to one of Tamar's library sanctuaries, I have drifted in and out of sleep three times.

We return to the book repair facility, the smell of ashes and glue curling in the air, where a medic waits to check me over. I submit to a cursory exam, not having the strength to fight, but as soon as I am allowed, I disappear into the showers and spend so long in the arctic waters that my fingers wrinkle and my legs threaten to give out beneath me. After that, I crawl into bed and sleep.

The only dreams I have are flashes of sound, remnants of that black cell the Warlord kept me in, but even those flee my mind when I wake. My stomach growls at the smell of food, so overpowering it called to me through my nightmares. I sit up to find a meal tray set on the bedside table, and without waiting for an invitation, I dig in.

Fresh eggs and cold goat's milk. Thick cuts of Martian soil-grown potatoes. Slivers of juicy blood-red tomatoes. And water. All the water I can drink. The food consumes me so I do not even notice my visitor until she speaks.

"Astrid," Lily says from where she stands in the doorway, dressed in a dark robe. Beneath the shadows of the hood, her face shows naked relief.

My own relief breaks open in my chest and floods me. "Lily!" I slip out of the bed and start to make my way to her, but she rushes to steady me and wraps her arms around my waist at the same time. Her scent of vanilla overwhelms me, bringing tears of relief to my eyes.

We find ourselves speaking over each other.

"You don't have to get up—"

"Oleander said you were safe, but I worried—"

"The medic reported that you'll recover quickly, but will be weak for some time—"

"You escaped the Cathedral unharmed?"

She guides me to sit on the cot and settles beside me—but I notice she does not release my waist, keeping her hands nearby as if afraid to let go of me. I want her to hold me again. I want to feel the warmth of her chest pressed to mine and her head beneath my chin. Hers is the kindest touch I have received in so long.

"The White Guard made sure I escaped unharmed, but you . . . Oleander swore he had secured you, but lost you somewhere along the way to me." Like a flash of lightning, her expression flickers.

Now that I sit here with her, Ringer silent in my blood, the admission that I saw Aunt Marshae and chased after her alone feels foolish. "I was behind him, until I wasn't."

Her eyes narrow. "He did a poor job, then," she mutters darkly.

But I do not wish to talk about the squabbles between Lily and her strangely close White Guard. Nor the love that he has for her. "What is happening, Lily?"

The storm clears, her expression softening, switching from one of hot anger to cool sorrow. "So much, both off-planet and on . . . Ceres has been destroyed by a terrorist cell of Asters as a warning to humanity. In response, the Synthetics have issued a call for the leaders of humanity to come to the border to discuss an amendment to the Synthetic Ultimatum."

I am so shocked, I have no words to respond. Ceres, the home I had found. The place I grew gardens and helped people find shelter and professions. "The people?"

Lily shakes her head.

"*Any* of them?"

Her large eyes close beneath upturned brows.

I press my hand to my mouth. All five million people of Ceres . . . gone. All the families and children . . .

I worked for months on Ceres, remaking it into the shining example of what the Sisterhood could be. I wanted, more than anything, for it to be a place where people were happy. Where they *thrived*, instead of simply survived.

I had gotten to know all the Sisters in the Temple there. All the Aunts. Even Asters in Lily's outreach programs and Gean locals who were always happy to welcome me into their shops and their homes.

And the children . . . I visited the orphanages as often as I could. I earmarked funds for them in every monthly budget. Those children had faced such hardships in their young lives; I didn't want them to think life itself was a hardship.

Dead. They are all dead now.

I sob without worrying for my composure. Lily sits with me in the quiet, rubbing circles on my back.

Only when I am wrung out does Lily speak again.

"Warlord Vaughn means to go to the border to represent the Geans," she says, her expression growing colder. "Without the Mother."

It is enough of a shock to turn my mind from Ceres. "That cannot happen!" Already Warlord Vaughn has shown he is uninterested in the ceasefire I achieved with the Icarii, more focused on using it to Gean advantage than on creating a lasting peace between our two peoples. "How can he get away with cutting the Mother out of something this important?"

"There's a split among the Geans that started with the release of Aunt Margaret's video. It's only grown after the Mother regained her voice," Lily says, as if she is not the Mother. "Under Aunt Marshae, the Agora called for a week of prayer and fasting to 'seek the will of the Goddess.'" The sharp curl of her mouth tells me what she thinks about that. "They haven't made an official statement, but they're scheduled to tomorrow, just in time for the Warlord to leave for the Synthetic border. In the meantime, Aunt Marshae and her two puppets have been holed up in the Agora building on Temple grounds, surrounded by soldiers, not letting anyone in or out.

"Meanwhile, the Unchained have done more public appearances, but with the Mother's blessing this time." She wiggles her fingers. "It's not just a fringe movement anymore, Astrid."

Despite the good news, my stomach turns. She must see the guilt on my face, because after a moment, she asks, "What is it?"

"I feel bad lying to the Unchained. To everyone." I run a hand over my face. After my time in the cell—after hearing the lies Warlord Vaughn plans to tell—it is harder to accept what I have done. "How are we any different than the Agora, if this is our approach?"

Lily guides my hand away from my face. "Because we're fixing what the Agora did to them. And we haven't forced them to do anything they don't want to do. *They* chose to march and speak out. We never even asked that of them."

But after the show in the Cathedral between the Mother and I, it still feels like manipulation . . .

"Listen, Astrid." She places two fingers on my chin and turns my face toward hers. "Some people see this as a miracle from the Goddess, while others see it as the stand against corruption that it is. No one knows about the neural implants exactly, but there are those who are naturally suspicious anyway. The miracle is that you saved them—that you've started to change the Sisterhood. It doesn't matter *how.*"

I let out a long breath. "I suppose . . ."

"And look at what you've accomplished." Lily's lips curl into something like a smirk. "We've forced the Agora's hand. They have to either declare this a true miracle, or explain the neural implants." She shrugs. "Or a third option that they're desperate to work out."

Now I cannot fight my smile. The smallest flame of hope kindles inside my chest. "We have them cornered?"

"Yes, but . . . let's not celebrate yet."

"Of course, not until Marshae is arrested and Warlord Vaughn's Disciples of Judeth disbanded."

"The thing is, it's not just the Sisterhood that's split." Lily rubs one hand over the other, scratching at the white patches on her knuckles. "Captain Byrne of the *Juno* discovered a Disciple of Judeth on his ship and, through him, learned of their plans."

"So that's how the *Juno* got involved in my rescue."

"Yes. Captain Byrne also reported Warlord Vaughn's connection to Aunt Marshae and the Disciples of Judeth to the Admiralty. It split them. Some admirals see it as the Warlord attempting to control the Sisterhood and form a single-branch government, while others see it as justifiable with all the recent deaths and crime in the Agora." For a moment, her eyes flash gold. "Either way, once I learned of the Disciple base, I knew you'd be there. I demanded Admiral Kadir do something, but it seems Lauren convinced Captain Byrne of it faster."

I remember the First Sister's face as I placed the neural implant into her waiting palm. Everything, in that single instant, changed in ways even I did not understand. "I don't think I can ever thank her enough . . ."

"I'm sure you'll find a way." Lily's smile fades. "Remember that I said Aunt Marshae barricaded herself in the Temple with soldiers? The Warlord is there too."

I jerk back from Lily as if she burned me. "What?" I ask softly.

Lily sighs, all the stress she feels showing on her face. "Officially? He's there to talk with the Agora about the Synthetic situation. Unofficially, we know it's because many soldiers are upset by his level of control over a member of the Agora. He chose the Temple because, according to Kadir, it's difficult to assault."

"So we cannot strike at him there . . ."

"After Lauren and the soldiers of the *Juno* rescued you, we have evidence for several things we could only hypothesize about. The Disciples of Judeth are made up of members of the military and the cappos. Aunt Marshae is Vaughn's woman inside the Sisterhood. And Vaughn is obviously calling the shots for the Disciples of Judeth. What we don't know is what Vaughn plans to do about Admiral Kadir and the growing disapproval of his actions." She forces herself to stop scratching her knuckles, curling both hands into fists.

If he can achieve what he told me in the cell, I do not think he will care about the disapproval of mere people. *Why should there ever be another Warlord, when I can go on forever? Why worry over death, when I can choose a new body for myself? The Geans have thrived for decades under my reign. What could we do with* centuries?

And Aunt Marshae . . . if she benefits from supporting Vaughn, there may never be another head of the Order of Cassiopeia either.

Ringer wakes within me, opening an icy gray eye. *You can't trust them with the truth, little sister.*

But I do not feel I have much choice in the matter. "Lily, could you call for Aunt Tamar? I think there's something you all need to hear from me."

"NEUROBOTS?" AUNT TAMAR snaps after I finish explaining. "Who in this galaxy is foolish enough to still use neurobots?"

"From what I understand," I say, trying not to let my anger rise at hers, "the Skadivolk have had them since before they were made illegal."

Aunt Tamar turns her golden hawk eyes on me. "Well, now the *Warlord* has them." I glare at her, but she goes on. "You should have told us this was what Admiral Drucker took from you. We could have—"

"Could have *what?*" I snap.

"Aunt Tamar," Lily says, louder than the two of us combined, "what do you think of the Warlord's plan? Is it even possible?"

Aunt Tamar seems to grow smaller as she thinks. "There have been several instances of the neurobots being used in unethical ways, particularly because they can be deployed on a person without their knowledge. They can collect data from their target—psychological data from their neurons, as well as physiological data—and return to the deployer without the victim any the wiser. In fact, it was one of the contributing factors to the Second War of Secession in what was known as the American States. Businesses began using them on their employees as a way to gauge performance and focus, but it quickly became a way for corporations to ensure loyalty by adjusting thought patterns after model employees. Many workers lost their jobs when they didn't comply with adjustment procedures."

I shudder at the thought of what someone like Aunt Marshae would do with technology like that. "What about changing the"—I try to remember Ebba's exact words about the neurobots—"neuroplasticity of the brain?"

Aunt Tamar raises an eyebrow, perhaps in surprise. "It was common practice during the Dead Century War. The neurobots would map the brain and alter neurons in order for human soldiers and pilots to more easily interface with their Synthetic counterparts in battle."

"Would it be possible to map the brain and force the neurobots on someone else, rewriting their mind and taking over their body?" I ask. Ebba told me it was Sisterhood fearmongering, but she was wrong; I heard the Warlord's plan firsthand.

She nods stoically. "With the right programming, it's possible. The book of Antiquity mentions this. 'And they perverted their minds with unholy machines, for they sought to bring forth the voices of the dead,'" Aunt Tamar begins quoting the Canon.

"'But the dead took root in their minds' fresh pastures and would not leave,'" I finish. "Those verses are about the neurobots . . ."

"I believe so, yes." Aunt Tamar shifts in her chair. "I once read a record of a vicious commander in the Dead Century War who forced neurobots on his subordinates. He thought his unit would benefit from unified thought patterns, but instead, they gave in to paranoia and tore each other apart. Only one was left alive, a low-ranking soldier who swore she was the commander himself."

I close my eyes, not wanting to consider such things. That vision of Ringer handing me the star haunts me . . .

"The Warlord having access to neurobots has greater ramifications than just passing down his mind, then." Lily runs a hand over her face, clearly exasperated. "He could change the minds of soldiers, Sisters, *any* Gean, to whatever he wanted them to think, like mind control."

"Lily, I think we have no choice but to convince Admiral Kadir to agree to Captain Byrne's offer," Aunt Tamar says.

My head jerks up. "What offer?"

Aunt Tamar presses her lips tightly together, biting back her words for some reason. Instead, Lily explains. "Captain Byrne wants to go to the Temple and take a stand against the Warlord and Aunt Marshae before more of Vaughn's supporters come to bolster him. With the Captain's support—and with the soldiers of other supporting admirals—we would have an advantage in numbers, if we act swiftly."

"Admiral Kadir does not like the plan?"

"His concern for those under his command is admirable," Aunt Tamar says in answer.

But I hear what they do not say: the plan is to *assault* the Temple, despite the difficulty and risk. And I know the people of Mars will see whoever leads the charge as a jumped-up soldier trying to depose the Warlord and his opposition in the Sisterhood at the same time. No wonder Admiral Kadir is hesitant.

"If we are playing a game for public approval—" I begin, but Aunt Tamar cuts me off.

"As with the whole of human history," she says, "the winner will tell the story as they wish."

I do not voice my concern, for she is right. We just have to convince Admiral Kadir of that. If we *can* get rid of the Warlord and Aunt Marshae—if we can clean out the corruption in both the Sisterhood and the military—we can say whatever we want.

Then why does it feel so wrong?

"Tell Admiral Kadir I will go with him," I say.

"No—" both Lily and Aunt Tamar bark at the same time.

"Do either of you even know what the neurobots look like?"

They fall silent.

"I will go with him." This time, they do not fight me.

"Very well. I will contact him," Aunt Tamar says softly. "Tonight . . . be ready to go at any moment." She slips out of the room, and my heart speeds. So soon . . . this could all be over tonight.

Everything we have done, all the allies we have gathered, must band together. Admiral Kadir and his soldiers. Captain Byrne, Lauren, and the warriors of the *Juno*. Aunt Tamar, Aunt Delilah, their Orders—even those under Aunt Margaret's care who stand by her testimony. And the Unchained.

Will it be enough? Or will we fail, only for history to brand *us* the traitors?

Lily takes my hand, and her warmth cuts through the ice of me. "It's going to be okay, Astrid," she whispers as she laces our fingers together, making it harder for us to be pulled apart. "I'm with you."

But that is part of what scares me: everyone I have ever cared for has either betrayed me or died at my side.

I DRESS IN the lightly armored black bodysuit that Aunt Tamar procured for me and braid my hair over one shoulder, remembering Bruni's instructions to keep it out of my face. This feels like a raid, though no Skadivolk stand beside me.

I will get your Muninn back if it is the last thing I do, I promise Ebba in my mind. *I won't let you lose your ancestors' knowledge.*

I look at my haggard face in the mirror. No matter what cosmetics I use, they do little to hide the evidence of my captivity. I press a fingernail to a spot just below my eye and imagine drawing it down to my jaw, cutting the Scar of Tears that rebellious Skadivolk women gave themselves.

Ringer seizes control of my hand and holds it still.

Don't, little sister, he snaps, and I remember Vaughn at my ear: *No soldier— no man—would want a woman with scars.* Not even Ringer, it would seem.

"I thought you were proud of your sister for taking the Scar of Tears instead of submitting to the Sisterhood," I say.

Not everyone survived the cutting, and you've already suffered enough, Ringer grumbles, releasing my hand. I feel a strange possessiveness radiating from him.

I press him. "Tell me more about you. About your family. What was your life like?"

But I am suddenly talking to air; Ringer has withdrawn deeper inside me as quickly as he appeared. His neurobots are so different from Bruni's, which I can recall as memories, easily reached for or ignored. I only wish I could force Ringer to tell me the truth of certain things.

When one of Aunt Tamar's guards issues me an energy pistol, I know the assault on the Temple must be happening—and soon. But I still find a sharp paring knife used for bookbinding in the warehouse and slip it into the pocket of my jacket. There is something about having a blade that soothes me. After that, there is nothing to do but wait.

Twenty minutes later, Admiral Kadir arrives, entering the back of the warehouse wearing the full navy-and-gold dress uniform. He looks like he is prepared to attend a parade in his honor, not a battle where he will need the weapon at his hip.

"Are you joining the attack?" I ask him.

His smile is no answer at all.

"I am going one way or another," I tell him, "even if it is with Captain Byrne."

"You surprise me, Astrid." He cocks his head, looking me over from head to toe.

"Why?"

"When you want something done, you do it yourself. You don't order someone else to do it and expect them to comply."

That is because, Ringer whispers, *we cannot trust anyone other than ourselves.*

"I will not ask someone to do what I am unwilling to," I say louder, as if I could drown out Ringer when he is in my mind.

"Even after all you've suffered this past week, you're willing to fight now. You always want to lead from the front." He flashes his straight white teeth at me, but the smile seems strained. "I think that's the only worthwhile kind of leader. It's the kind of leader I've always tried to be."

"Then I can see why Aunt Tamar and Lily chose to work with you. It will be a vast improvement over Warlord Vaughn."

"I can only pray . . ."

"No," I say, perhaps too harshly. "Pray all you want, but you must *work* to truly change things."

The smile slips from his mouth. His dark eyes beneath heavy brows take on a new weight. He looks at me with an expression I have never seen on him before. It strikes me that I am finally seeing Shaz the person, instead of Kadir the admiral.

"You never answered whether you were helping with the assault or not," I point out.

"I hadn't decided until now," he replies, offering me his arm. "Shall we go work to change things together?"

I take Kadir's arm, and he leads me to the waiting podship, idling at the same docks I was brought to by Aunt Tamar's man after he chased me through the toy store and streets of Olympus Mons. It is surrounded by soldiers bristling with weapons, and all eyes snap in our direction when we approach. They quickly form into two lines and salute, fists pressed to their chests.

"Orders, sir?" the closest one asks.

Kadir takes a couple of seconds to look at each and every one of them, judging. Weighing. "Let's stop the Warlord from destroying what makes Gean society great! Earth endures!"

"Mars conquers!" the soldiers answer in unison.

Kadir leads me into the waiting podship and sits closest to the pilot. I settle beside him. "Call the others and tell them mission is go," he tells the pilot. "Head straight to the Temple."

"Aye, sir."

Other soldiers pile into the podship after us, so many that there are not enough seats for them all. They crouch between chairs in the aisle, speaking to each other in low voices. When everyone has found a place to at least brace themselves, Kadir knocks twice against the ceiling of the ship. "Let's move!" The pilot keys up the engines, and within moments, we are leaving Aunt Tamar's library behind.

As we travel toward the Temple, one of Kadir's soldiers comes to kneel next to him and, speaking in a language I do not know, helps him set up what looks like an Icarii drone.

"Say hi, Astrid," Kadir tells me as the drone floats in my direction.

"A camera?" I ask.

Kadir flashes his boyish smile. "A cappo drone recovered by Captain Byrne from the Disciples of Judeth stronghold. It has a camera, but also a defense mode. It was Aunt Tamar's idea that we bring it. If Aunt Margaret could do it, so can we."

What was it that Aunt Tamar said? The winners get to tell the story . . .

As we grow closer to our destination, the soldiers fall silent, their faces drawn. Unlike Kadir, they are dressed to go into a battle, with bulletproof bodysuits and weapons at their hips. I find my hand drifting to my energy pistol before reminding myself it is there only in case of emergencies.

"Listen up!" Kadir says, loud enough to surprise me. "I know what I'm asking you to risk today. I know there's no guarantee that anyone gets out alive in war. But when our children and our children's children look back on today, they're going to know *this* was the battle that changed everything. *This* day decided the new path of the Geans. What do you want our future to look like?" He briefly meets the gaze of every soldier in the podship. "Do you want it to be exactly as it has been?"

"Sir, no, sir!" a handful shout.

"Or do you want to change things for the better?"

"Sir, yes, sir!" all of them roar.

"Do you want to end suffering where we can?"

"Sir, yes, sir!"

"Do you want to bring the Geans into a new age of prosperity?"

"Sir, yes, sir!"

"Then let's take that Temple, and stop Warlord Vaughn!"

The podship devolves into cheering, a roar that burns in my blood. Something in me—in Ringer—responds to this fire.

"In range," the pilot says over the intercom—so quietly I suddenly miss Bruni and his boisterous instructions—before the podship shudders. I grasp the arms of my chair and turn to Kadir.

"What—"

The word is hardly out of my mouth before the pilot announces, "Returning fire."

"We're entering a firefight?" I call over the sudden noise.

Kadir grins widely, his eyes shining with the same excitement as his soldiers'. "Wasn't in the plan, but sometimes you have to roll with the punches!"

"Past the sentries," the pilot says. Within seconds, the gunfire abates. "Setting her down in the courtyard. Friendlies incoming."

When the podship settles on the ground, Kadir is the first out of his seat. With a single gesture, the hangar door opens, a ramp descends, and the soldiers march out one by one. Kadir signals for me to follow him, and, surprising even myself, I exit by his side, unafraid.

The Temple is emptier than I have ever seen it. There are no Little Sisters running the hallways. No Aunts shouting orders. No Sisters waiting in the courtyard. Many of the lights are dimmed or turned off altogether, and the central courtyard, with its pavilion of marble statues, has been roped off. Vibrant yellow tape forms a spider's web in each of the doorways.

A young woman with thick eyebrows approaches Kadir and salutes. "Admiral, I have a report for you."

"At ease. Let me hear it."

She drops her fist from her chest. "Warlord Vaughn has barricaded himself inside the Agora's chambers alongside a platoon of forty soldiers. He's set four squadrons of fifty around the perimeter, and he has an additional two hundred in the Temple. Thank the Goddess you arrived when you did. Since we seized the courtyard, he's pushing in on two sides of us."

Before Admiral Kadir can respond, I interject, "He may have more soldiers than expected inside the Agora's chambers."

Admiral Kadir and the soldier turn to me. "How do you figure?" the admiral asks.

"There are several hidden passages that lead into and out of the chambers," I explain. "Some I have not been privy to learn, but I assure you that Aunt Marshae, as a member of the Agora, knows them all."

"So it's best to assume the Warlord knows of them as well, and that they're highly guarded." Admiral Kadir looks at the soldier. The drone floats around his head. "Let's form a blockade along this line here and here"—he points—"and put the majority of our forces to holding this courtyard. Meanwhile, my soldiers and I will be a spear into the heart of the Temple, cutting straight into the Agora's chamber."

"Yes, sir." The woman rushes off to relay the orders.

Other soldiers approach, each with news for Kadir from other admi-

416 | LINDEN A. LEWIS

rals or Captain Byrne. Before I can get close enough to listen in, someone next to me clears their throat.

"Sister," the young man says, then thinks better of it and hastily adds, "Unchained."

"Yes?"

"Would you . . ." He sucks in a long breath. "Would you bless me, Unchained?"

I do not have my rose oil. I am not attired in a Sisterhood dress. I hardly believe in the Goddess anymore. But I recognize the need for comfort in the young man's eyes, and so I nod. "Let us pray . . ."

When I finish blessing him, I find a dozen more have gathered, each asking for the same. Since I hardly have time to bless every soldier here individually, I pray aloud for them all to hear.

I fall into my role. I have done this for so many years that the words come to me with ease, as if they are waiting for me. And when I finally see the taut bodies of the soldiers soften with forgiveness, confidence, or pride, I know I have done my job. Satisfaction warms me from my chest to my fingertips.

"Astrid!"

"—and may the Goddess guide your hands," I finish quickly. When I look up, I find the drone hovering close by and Admiral Kadir waiting for me.

He nods at me companionably. "Let's do this."

I fall into step beside him. His soldiers range ahead of us, moving with speed and efficiency. Like water they slip through the courtyard and into the twisting hallways of the Temple. This place is at once familiar and strange. It summons an intense wave of nostalgia, and yet I feel I have outgrown it. I once stood in that corner as a Little Sister for six hours without moving because my Auntie caught me kissing another girl in my assigned room. I once danced down that hallway, buzzing with alcohol, at the news that I had been assigned by the Mother herself to the *Juno*. And of course, in the very space I walk as I approach the Agora's chambers, I shattered into pieces after Aunt Marshae stripped me of the title of First Sister of Ceres. If only I had known what was waiting for me in Eden's room . . .

It is solely because I am looking down that accursed hallway that I see the man in a gray hood.

"Loo—" But before I can say a word, he lifts a railgun and shoots the soldier bringing up the rear of our group.

"The first of these was Aunt Judeth!" he shouts.

Less than a heartbeat later, he drops, gray mask now red, and Kadir jerks me behind him—but a dozen other Disciples of Judeth pour from the room he was hidden in, stepping over his body.

"Behind! Behind!" Kadir screams, grabbing my arm and pulling me away. His soldiers turn to meet the Disciples of Judeth, but they are already on us, and while Kadir shoots as many as he can, he can't kill them all. A man reaches us and grabs my other arm, yanking me away from Kadir—only for me to press my pistol to the underside of his chin and pull the trigger.

"Nice shot," Kadir says. I don't miss the surprise on his face. "But keep bloody shooting!"

I hit another in the leg, but by then, Kadir's soldiers have reached us and opened fire at the Disciples. Kadir and I continue to back away, now far more wary of the closed doors lining the hallways. "We'll keep going to the Agora's chambers," Kadir tells me. "We'll meet up with a second squadron on the way."

I do not like the sound of being without Kadir's soldiers for even the smallest amount of time, but when Kadir looks at me like a fellow officer, I nod in agreement.

Ringer, are you with me?

I feel him stir in my chest. *Always, little sister.*

We do not go far before we meet with the waiting squadron. As graceful as well-practiced dancers, soldiers step forward to guard us. "Agora's chamber is just around the corner!" one of them tells Kadir.

Where the woman with thick eyebrows reported one of the Warlord's platoons.

Movement from the front of the group catches my eye. "Go, go, go!" a man yells. The squadron rushes around the corner, and gunfire fills the air until I cannot hear myself think. Kadir stands on the balls of his feet, ready to streak forward himself if he must. I shift the pistol in my hand, prepared for the worst.

When the last shot is fired and the only sound left is the heavy breathing and whimpering of soldiers, a woman's voice calls to us. "Admiral! All clear!" Kadir gestures for us to continue.

There are no gray-masked Disciples in the hallway, just dead Geans in navy and gold on both sides. In death, it is impossible to tell if they answered to Admiral Kadir or Warlord Vaughn.

"Ready to breach!" a man standing in front of the Agora's door calls.

"Breach!" Kadir orders.

Something the size of my palm is pressed to the door, and the soldiers take two long steps away. A sharp pop, some smoke—and the door lock has been blown open.

"Breaching!" the man says.

"Breaching!" a woman replies.

The man is the first in, but the rest stream into the hallowed sanctuary after him. The pop of gunfire is a constant refrain ahead and behind.

A piece of me hears Kadir's harsh whispers: "Where's Theta Squadron? No, we can't wait—" But only the smallest piece. Ringer steadies my heart as I walk into the Agora's chamber.

The last time I trod upon this cobblestoned pathway, I was a supplicant. Now I am a goddess enraged. This is the only room in the Temple that is well lit, holoflames flaring high and illuminating the navy stained glass ceiling with its twinkling bronze stars. In the center of the room is an abandoned dais, the podium carelessly turned on its side. Kadir's soldiers spread out along the walls, avoiding the center—for a good reason, I soon see.

Above us stretch the amphitheater seating and the high-backed marble thrones of the Agora members. Warlord Vaughn and some fifty-odd Geans take cover behind a hastily erected barricade of broken Temple furniture and the empty thrones themselves. A dozen Ironskins—newer models, slenderer than the ones I have worked with—stand before the barricade, knowing foot soldiers cannot stand against them.

For a brief moment, Warlord Vaughn meets my gaze. The soldiers shooting, struggling, dying around us become nothing more than air. The throne he looms behind, which once belonged to Aunt Margaret, is empty now save for the history of women who sat there before. I feel her ghost—the ghosts of all the dead women this chamber has seen—watching us. Waiting. Judging.

Then Aunt Marshae steps to Warlord Vaughn's side, and the moment is lost. Her face is twisted beneath her carefully set auburn hair, not a strand out of place. She points a sharp-nailed finger in my direction and yells something I cannot hear over the din of battle. But I do not need to hear to know what she wants: me.

One of Kadir's soldiers herds me closer to the wall. In the chaos, I have lost track of him—have lost track of all of the soldiers I recognize. But one thing is apparent: Kadir's people are dying en masse as they emerge from cover, attempting to lob grenades over the barricades that Warlord Vaughn's people have constructed. The Ironskins, swift and merciless, strike the majority down.

Kadir's soldiers need a distraction, something to give them a chance at reaching the high ground. I tighten my grip on the gun, and follow the curving wall up, up . . . to the ceiling.

I'm with you, little sister, Ringer purrs in my chest.

"I'm going to distract them!" I shout to the soldier squatting next to me. "Use it!"

"Hey—" they shout after me, but I am already pushing off the wall and away from the cover it offers. I zigzag, Bruni's neurobots encouraging me to evoke randomness instead of a predictable pattern of movement. When I reach the fallen podium on the central dais, I slide into cover behind it.

My heart is firing as rapidly as the railguns around me. Fear threatens to consume me, but Ringer steadies me, turning trepidation into an excited buzz. A group of Kadir's soldiers, led by the man I spoke to, are rushing up the stairs, past an Ironskin, under a hail of bullets. I have to make this count.

I stand from cover and fire into the ceiling five times—

Something hits me like a punch to the shoulder. I know this feeling—know I have been shot. I drop back into cover behind the podium as a rain of navy-and-gold shards come tumbling down around us.

Glass hits the ground and shatters. Soldiers scream in the song of slaughter. "LEAVE HER ALIVE!" Warlord Vaughn shouts, so loud I can hear him above it all.

I peer over the podium and catch Vaughn, red-faced with fury. Several of his soldiers look up at the ceiling, a momentary disturbance that costs them. Some of Kadir's group have breached the barricade, while others have set up grenade launchers and targeted the Ironskins.

I press my hand to what should be the wound on my shoulder, but find the suit has absorbed the brunt of it. The bullet sits in the armored shoulder pad, a stark, hot warning of what could have been my death. If I had been shot even a few inches over . . .

Aunt Marshae, like a streak of red, breaks from the cover of the throne and rushes to the wall behind her. I cannot see what she is doing, wish I had a better angle and was a better shot—then a portion of the wall shifts aside, revealing one of the secret exits from the Agora's chambers I knew nothing about.

She's retreating! Ringer scoffs.

And I cannot—*will not* let her slip through my fingers, *not this time*—

I keep low and move toward the wall opposite the thrones. It takes me a few seconds, but I locate a depression in the mortar between two stones. I slip my hand in and tug, and the stone door slides aside, revealing a hidden passageway to what Little Sisters call the Whispers, a set of stairs that spirals up to the higher levels of the chamber and ends behind the leftmost throne.

As its name suggests, the Whispers catches and intensifies the noise of everything in the Agora's chambers; the echoing booms of the explosives and gunshots reach an uncontrolled crescendo that rattles down to my bones. I rush up the stairs two at a time, desperate to get out before the cacophony triggers a migraine.

At the top of the stairs, I come to another sliding door and open it. It takes all my self-control not to rush out, but instead to first check my surroundings. Kadir's soldiers have continued putting pressure on the barricade, but Warlord Vaughn has clustered his group around the central three thrones. At his gesture, two men rush after Aunt Marshae into the hidden passage. Are they beginning a retreat?

No! Ringer and I both cry. If Warlord Vaughn sends all his men with Aunt Marshae, there is no way I will be able to reach her. But if I can sneak behind Warlord Vaughn's group before they retreat . . .

I emerge from the passageway and duck down behind the leftmost marble throne. Desperate to catch up with Aunt Marshae, I circle the walkway toward the secret passage.

Gunfire rages. Lights flare too bright. Booms echo, caught in the amphitheater's shape. I stop when I am one throne away from where Warlord Vaughn and his soldiers gather. I must choose my moment carefully, when they are all focused forward . . .

A masked person seeks cover using the throne I hide behind. I try to make myself smaller, but they spot me around the corner. They shout in surprise, and I raise my pistol—but before I can pull the trigger, something huge and black appears behind them. *An Ironskin.* My blood runs cold at its burning golden halo and the trophies of black cloth tied onto its chitinous spikes. *It's an Ironskin.*

I shoot, but the Ironskin absorbs the laser blast with ease. Balling its great spiked hand into a fist, the Ironskin strikes me in the temple. Pain shudders through my body—

Someone seizes my shoulders. Another grabs my gun and twists, and my wrist pops sickeningly. There is a moment when I can make out someone in a gray mask as they reach for my ankles, but I lose them as my legs are swept out from beneath me. I buck and kick, swing my head back into the soldier's nose, cry out with all my strength, but there are too many of them, and they carry me with them past the barricade and into the dark of—

Where am I?

"Give her to me," a voice I recognize says. "I can deal with her. She's mine." They drop me to the ground at Virgil Vaughn's feet.

Mine. His words blacken something within me.

"Get back out there," the Warlord commands. The two Disciples of Judeth and the Ironskin that carried me into the escape tunnel rush back toward the fighting, leaving us alone. And my gun is—they took it from me. I do not have it anymore.

"Get up," Vaughn barks, pulling me up, drawing me toward him, and I am suddenly back in the cell—

The stench, the blackness, the dirt on my skin, the mats in my hair, the drug swirling in my veins, the way he whispered to me and touched me, the way he decided that I was to starve and when I could drink—

Mine, he called me.

"I AM NO ONE'S!" I boom like Bruni, pulling the knife from my jacket and jabbing it at his neck.

His eyes widen with shock, but at the last moment, the blade turns aside, and a blue ripple passes over his body.

A shield . . . he's wearing an Icarii shield.

"Treasonous whore!" He backhands me, and I hit the wall.

Down the hallway around the secret doorway, the battle rages, but my vision narrows to him as he decides not to call for backup, as he grabs my clothes and drags me back toward him. *As he underestimates me again.*

"You think you can kill me?" he growls.

My blood boils in my veins—

He is like every soldier who ever used and abused me, the rot at the top, and it is because of those like him that Eden is dead—

I release an animalistic roar and fling myself at him.

He holds his arms up to catch me, his shield pulsing blue, but I throw my weight into him and drag him down to the ground. My knees on his chest, I bring the blade down on that barrier again and again—

His hands come up to my neck and squeeze.

How long can I hold my breath? No, no, I can't—

My vision blackens at the corners. I focus on the blue shield. Nothing but the blue.

Blue like the hermium-powered barrier in the *Juno*. Blue like Paola's skin when she was thrown into space. Blue like the Ceres dome-sky that no longer exists.

My vision starts to go. All I can make out, amidst the darkness, is Vaughn's snarling face.

"Vir . . . gil . . ." I growl, spittle flying.

The barrier flickers and finally gives way—

And the blade punctures his right eye.

He releases me, arms smacking the ground like lifeless meat. I fall onto his chest, gasping for air.

I lie there for a time, breathing, gathering my strength. My vision clears, but my throat is sore. I still feel his hands as if they are trying to crush me. And down the hall in the Agora's chambers, the battle continues . . .

I stand, bloodied blade in one hand, the Warlord's limp arm in the other. With all the strength I have left, I drag him down the hallway and into the light of the shattered dome.

I say nothing as I emerge, bloodied. But I find I do not need to.

As soon as his soldiers see me—see their Warlord, dead beneath me—they freeze. Even the Ironskins, black metal creatures of nightmare, pause. A ripple passes through the crowd, a single moment of silence, strange after all the noise. Then the soldiers toss down their weapons, drop to their knees, and throw up their empty hands. The Ironskins' flaming golden halos disappear as the pilots turn off their suits.

Just like that, it is over.

As Kadir's soldiers bind those of the Warlord still living, I see how dire the situation was. Hundreds of bodies, dead and wounded, litter the room. But I do not see Aunt Marshae's among them.

It is not over, I revise in my mind. *Not yet.*

CHAPTER 38
HIRO

I mean . . . don't you think about how worried your family is? You're out here in the streets, covering all this, and they must be so stressed for you.

Anonymous masked protester

No, I—actually, now that I think about it . . . I should call my mother.

Esperanza val Montero, reporter for the newscast El Sol

"**G**et up."

What? Up? I . . . when did I fall to the ground?

"Hiro, *get up.*" Noa's hand hovers close but doesn't touch me. Like they're scared what'll happen if they do. Would not-Lito come back and kill them? The thought is so bizarre, after everything, I end up laughing. Full side-splitting laughter, until my eyes prick with tears and my sides ache and my face hurts. I put my head between my knees, and I know, somewhere inside, nothing is funny. But I can't stop.

Noa finally seizes my arm, fingers digging into my muscle, and they jerk me onto my feet. "You're Icarii enemy number one, sitting in the backyard of a building *where everyone is dead* except for us, and there's backup on the way. You should be running."

They guide me to the edge of the property, a thick fence separating it from the next house over. It should be simple to jump. To flee. But nothing's simple anymore. "Not everyone's dead," I say, gesturing to Podship-the-person lying on the ground, slowly extricating themself from my hose-noose.

Noa looks over their shoulder. "Well, she's definitely gonna need a hospital at the very least. Why are you arguing with me? *Leave.*" They shove me into the fence.

"Shouldn't you be arresting me?"

They gesture back to the house. "I've got bigger problems right now."

"Noa . . ." And finally some sort of clarity comes to me, the question I wanted to ask from the beginning but my mind wouldn't let me. "What the fuck was *that?*"

Noa shakes their head like they don't even know.

"Was that . . . Did my father make that?" When I looked in his dead eyes, I could say nothing but his name. Now I can't say it at all.

"No." Noa's gaze goes toward the house, one eye dark brown, the other white-blue. "Your dear ol' dad's up to shit, but not that."

My hand brushes against the fence. "Can you be more specific?"

Noa straightens, though they're not as tall as I—not anymore, not with Saito Ren's legs. "Hiro, you killed Nadyn."

Their Dagger. Of course. I'd almost forgotten after . . . "Noa—I'm—"

"Shut the fuck up." Their hand comes close to me again, and for a second, I think they're going to hit me. They don't. "After everything, Bellator paired me with some commander as my new Dagger. Had him watching my every move."

I remember seeing that Dagger, the waiflike boy with no distinguishing features. Fuck. I hadn't paid much attention to him at all. Guess that was the point.

"Your dad wrote a new algorithm for the neural implants, had me and some others selectively updating the 'more troublesome citizens.'" They make air-quotes with their fingers. "It was supposed to help them with stress, some change that filtered certain sensorial stimuli—I don't fucking know, I'm not a scientist."

"Sounds like mind control," I say softly.

"Yeah, that's the fucking thing. We used it on the people in the streets mostly, the protesters and slogan chanters." A shadow passes over Noa's face. "I didn't agree with it, didn't like it, but what was I gonna do? I had Command boy stuck on my ass, making sure I complied."

"Who all knew about this?" After a second, I clarify. "The neural implant update—not the whole . . ." I gesture to the house. "I assume that's what was going on here?"

"Partially. Your dad's got plenty of things even I don't know about." Noa shakes their head. "And we just *found* that thing with Lito's face."

A wave of disgust rolls through me at their words. A part of me wants to snap that it *was* Lito, and I don't know why.

Noa shoves me toward the fence again. "You need to leave, like, five minutes ago."

"Listen, you're an absolute smarmy bastard, so why are you being nice?"

"I may not like you, Hiro, but I get you." There's a little piece of understanding in their clenched jaw, in the set of their hard eyes. While their parents never seemed to mind them, they've dealt with their fair share of idiots asking stupid questions about their gender in the service and out. Bigots don't just die out; they have to be actively stomped on, and we've both been forced to do that stomping, simply because of who we are. "Besides, Lito—the real Lito, not that *thing* back there—said something to me before he died, and I've been stuck thinking about it ever since."

I open my mouth to ask but find my throat arrested.

Noa scratches the back of their neck. "He asked me why I was fighting for the Icarii when I knew the shit they pull, and I told him the truth— that I had to. And I meant what I said. I *do* need this gig to take care of my daddy and those three kids who deserve more than I got. But I can also decide to look the other way sometimes, to let someone who wants to stop all the bad shit go and do their hero thing."

"'Hero thing'?" I bark a single laugh. "You've turned into a softie, Noa."

"Fuck you, Hiro val Akira."

I grip the fence and prepare to swing myself over. "Fuck you, Noa sol Romero," I say with a smile.

To me, it sounds like an offer of friendship.

I SEE EVIDENCE of what Noa said in the street outside Val Akira Labs. The crowd that was once a roaring protest against the company's abuses is now a trickle, easily ignored. The peacekeepers have relegated them to the sidelines behind a barrier, supposedly for their own safety. The few news outlets there cover the rebuilding of the bombed lobby, protesters and their signs out of shot and out of mind.

At the very least, the Black Hive attacks have stopped. The threat of the Genekey virus isn't over, though, not completely—not when the hospitals are overwhelmed with the ill and wounded. A few still wear pressure suits and jackets with masks in the street—anything to keep the wasproaches off, just in case. Works for me, since it helps me keep a low profile.

As I stare at the building, I think. If my father wanted to, he would be able to instruct Val Akira Labs to focus on curing the victims of the Genekey virus, but his attention has obviously been elsewhere. And now he's gone to the Synthetic border with the other Icarii councilors, making it seem like the neural implant changes are just one more distraction from whatever he's really doing.

So what's he fucking planning?

I don't join the protesters because of how visible I'd be in such a small crowd, and eventually the peacekeepers wave me away, not allowing lurkers to watch the building without a reason. But I've come up with nothing new. My only ideas are drastic and dramatic.

I end up at a bar, using Yasuhiro sol Fujita's ID to buy myself one last drink before I do something stupid.

"Don't call it your last drink." A memory of Lito hits me: the two of us sitting together at Mithridatism in the shadowed corner. His leg bounces up and down with unspent energy, like a big dog yearning to run. I'd forced a glowing pink fruity thing into his hand that he drank with a little flinch each time the caustic liquid hit his tongue.

"Don't call it your last drink, because that's the one you have before you die. Call it your next-to-last drink. Don't tempt fate."

I'd laughed at his superstition, but it seems strangely fitting now. I revise my thought: This is my *next-to-last* drink before I do something stupid.

Once it's gone, I'm back on the streets, my feet finding a familiar rhythm.

If only I'd been able to pull the trigger, none of this would be happening. Souji val Akira would be dead. The Asters wouldn't have been framed for the Val Akira Labs bombing. The Black Hive wouldn't have felt justified in using the Genekey virus. Ofiera would be alive. Sorrel wouldn't have lost his godsdamned mind and attacked Ceres with the Engineborn weapons. The Synthetics wouldn't have reclaimed Autarkeia and summoned humanity's leaders to the border. The galaxy wouldn't be waiting with bated breath to find out if we're going to be invaded by sentient people-killing machines.

I stop, finding myself before a familiar building built like a quartz point, a busy gravstreet full of traffic at my back. I've returned to the apartment my father lives in, my childhood home. Now I just have to somehow sneak in, incapacitate the patrolling duelists, and see if my father left any hint of what he's working on in there . . .

But would that space even recognize me, or am I too changed since the last time I set foot in its polished hallways? I've lingering pieces of Saito Ren in my face, on my body. My prosthetic arm and leg. A scar from Ofiera's knife on my stomach. Who knows what I'll have from the little cuts after being thrown through flexglass today?

It doesn't matter. I have to try.

I pull the hood of my jacket closer around my face as I enter the lobby. There's a duelist near the elevator and another near the entrance to the stairs, and I'm working on a plan to distract them when the doorman waves them over. "We just had a resident call down about someone outside—" They all look toward the door.

If they're talking about me, I don't wait to find out. I rush into the stairwell. My legs burn as I go up one floor at a time, a good sting when compared to the paralyzing thought of failure. I'm breathing heavily when I reach the ninety-fifth floor, but what's worse is the nagging feeling that something's wrong. I haven't seen even a hint of other duelists.

That feeling doubles as I slip into the hallway. There's no one standing guard by the door to my father's apartment.

I stand there stupidly, staring at the door handle. This has to be a trap—

The door opens.

"You should come in," the woman on the other side of the door says— Asuka. It's my sister Asuka—"before the patrol returns. We can only send them off with false leads for so long."

She opens the door wider and steps aside. I enter the apartment from my childhood.

I've never been able to deny my big sister anything.

EVERYTHING'S EXACTLY LIKE I remembered it, as if it's been frozen in ice. The shining marble floor. The black ink on white canvas paintings. The line of my siblings' shoes by the door. I kick off my boots and am embarrassed to find a hole in my sock.

"Come on," Asuka says, looking over her shoulder at me. I finally notice one thing that's changed: she looks like stress has aged her. "Hana ordered dinner, and there's enough for all of us."

I follow her through the halls like a guest. The rooms that are dark or closed off hold ghosts. I don't look more than I have to, afraid of what I'll see. When we come to the dining room—the traditional one we used as kids, not the one my father uses to impress clients—warmth finally spills out with golden lighting and the smell of fried vegetables.

"I brought someone with me," Asuka says upon entering.

"Ooh! Do we finally get to meet your girlfriend?" Hana asks with food in her mouth. But as soon as I enter from the shadowed hallway, she drops her chopsticks. "HIRO!"

"*Hiro?*" Jun sets her cup down so hard, liquid sloshes out onto the low table. Her eyes are round saucers of shock.

Before I can say a thing, Hana's around the table and throwing her willowy arms around my neck, and I'm forced to catch her as I stumble back into the hallway and bump into the wall.

"Hiro, Hiro, Hiro!" Hana exclaims over and over, jumping up and down like an excited puppy.

"Hana, don't hurt them!" Asuka snaps, and I see she still takes her role as mother seriously. "What are you, a child?"

But then Jun, the shortest of us, is joining Hana, wrapping her arms around us, and eventually Asuka relents, her face twisted like she's trying not to cry. She joins us in the hallway until we sink onto the floor, all four of us clinging to each other like we're drowning.

I haven't felt this safe in a long, long time.

When I look at the low table, it's set perfectly: with no empty space for my mother.

MY SISTERS SHIFT things around until there's a spot for me at the table, then Hana puts a little of everything in front of me. She's full of stories as we eat, chatting about everything and nothing—she's very opinionated and rather liberal about what's happening in Cytherea, though her personal life is full of drama. She's got a full course load at university—on temporary hiatus, thanks to the Black Hive attacks—and a couple of boyfriends, though she swears she isn't serious about them because she's too young to settle down. She teases Asuka about a girlfriend, which I wouldn't put stock in until Asuka mutters a gruff "Enough." Maybe my eldest sister has found someone.

I make an admittedly dark joke about my dead-end dating life, which makes Jun laugh so hard she snorts—and then all of us are laughing. Somehow we've fallen back into our usual roles, talking about everything except the things that matter.

Well, there is one big difference. Shinya isn't here to correct us with a tactless *well, actually*. He isn't here to tell us to be serious, or to pretend he's trying not to laugh as tears fill his eyes. My brother *isn't here*.

Once dinner's over and Hana's cleaning dishes—her turn, Asuka says, though she follows to help—I join Jun on the balcony that overlooks the crystal cluster buildings of Cytherea. She tries to hide an e-pipe from me when I exit, but I bark a laugh. "I'm not going to rat you out to Father," I tell her.

Jun jerks her head back toward the kitchen. "It isn't Dad I'm scared of."

"Is Asuka really so harsh?" I tease.

Jun shakes her head with a laugh. "Are you kidding me? It's *Hana*. She's terrified I'm going to fuck my lungs beyond fixing or slide a slippery slope into hard drugs or fall off the balcony while smoking."

My smile fades as she speaks. "Damn."

"Yeah, I think . . . I think Hana's scared of losing another of us."

After that, we don't say anything to each other. Not for a long time. Jun finishes smoking, and I follow her inside, stopping when we pass by the room that holds some of Father's favorite antiques, including the family shrine Mother cared for. Has anyone given it any attention, or has it been shut off, as the door suggests, and forgotten?

I consider visiting, but find I'm too terrified. What if there's a layer of dust on it, proof that my siblings have forgotten how Mother raised us in favor of Father's hatred of superstition? I know Mother's picture won't be there. Maybe Shinya's image joined our grandfather's and uncle's after the *Leander* explosion. Would mine be beside his?

"Hiro?" Jun asks, snapping my attention back to her.

"I'm coming." I walk away from the room, leaving the door unopened.

We settle in the living room on the plush C-shaped couch. When Hana brings in a tray of earthenware cups and a teapot, she sniffs the air around Jun, suspicious, though she says nothing. Her glare is bad enough.

It's strange. I wanted nothing more than to be welcomed home by my siblings, for my father to be beyond our reach so we could be free, yet now . . . now I want to leave. I don't want to be here, not like this.

This isn't home anymore.

I'm not the Hiro who belongs here.

I nurse my tea quietly. I think my siblings notice the change in me. Hana moves from her spot to sit closer to me and leans her head against my shoulder. "Please don't go," she whispers, almost like she hopes I don't hear her.

Her words make me realize . . . I *am* thinking about leaving. I came here to find clues about my father's weapon, but the truth is, I've been thinking about following him since Noa told me he'd gone to the Synthetic border. Chasing after him means I still have a chance to right my wrongs. I can stop him, force him to admit everything he's been doing on Cytherea with the neural implant updates, even stop whatever weapon he's made . . .

"I *have* to go." I'm not even aware I've said it aloud until all three of my sisters look at me with concern.

Hana's lower lip wobbles. Asuka catches her with a stern look. But it's Jun who breaks the silence.

"Of fucking course," she mutters. "You've always been like this— always running off."

"What?" My spine snaps straight, as if preparing for a fight.

"You come home for five minutes, and then you're gone." Jun stares me down, and for a moment, all I can see is the chubby-cheeked toddler she used to be. More than any of my other siblings, *she* had been the one I'd taken care of. "There's always something more important out there than us. Something shinier and more interesting than family." All of a sudden, it sounds very much like she's talking about Mother.

"It's kind of hard to be here when Father had me sent off on a suicide mission," I snap. "But sure, let me just stop by for tea while I'm public enemy number one."

"That's not what I meant—"

"Then what did you mean?"

"Jun," Hana whispers.

"No, I want to hear this—"

"You want to hear it?" Jun's eyebrows move up her forehead. "Okay, I'll level with you. After you went off to the Academy, you wanted nothing to do with us."

"I wanted nothing to do *with Father*—"

"Well, you sure kept away from the rest of us too." Much like Father, Jun doesn't yell. She just drops the truth in her normal tone of voice and lets it scorch. "When you visited during your week off from the Academy, how many times did I beg you to stay and spend some time with me? With *us?*"

And when I refused, when I couldn't stand having another row with Father, I'd leave, and Shinya would spit poison at my back, and my sisters would say nothing.

"You don't know what it was like," I say, falling into cold anger. "I couldn't be myself here. Father constantly demanded I change who I am." All his insults—all his demands—come rushing back, and I have to swallow down the rising tears. "Nothing I did was ever enough, because he hated who I was as a person. Look at what he did to me"—I gesture at my face and my body—"look at what he changed! And all for a mission he assigned me to in order to *get rid of me.*"

Jun drops her eyes to her tea. Her voice wavers when she speaks again. "By the time that mission came, you'd already abandoned us."

I open my mouth to respond but find only insults and curses—and stop. I don't want to be the kind of person who'd say those things. I look at the women around the couch. Hana cries quietly. Asuka's hands are shaking on her cup. My sisters are hurting. *I'm* hurting. Why are we fighting, when they missed me, and I missed them?

If I really want to be fair . . . I have to admit, there's truth to what Jun's saying. When the fighting with Father became too much, I retreated to the Academy. To Lito. He became my new family. My shelter. My everything. I pulled away from my siblings to protect myself—never considering how they'd feel.

But I also can't ignore how Father treated me differently. How I was singled out as a problem, while my siblings flew beneath the radar. And how no one stood up for me when I needed an advocate the most. I was just a child, and—

We were all children back then, weren't we? Even Asuka, forced into the role of mother . . .

Maybe we're all a little wrong. Maybe there is no black-and-white in these situations. Maybe the only thing we can do is try not to keep hurting each other. To do better. To forgive.

We've already lost a mother and a brother. We shouldn't have to lose anyone else.

"I'm sorry for pulling away," I say, my voice smooth and soft. "I wanted to protect myself from Father. My intention was never to hurt any of you."

Hana wipes the tears from her cheeks as she calms, but now Jun's eyes bubble. "I'm s-sorry . . . I wish Father never did that stuff . . . I never know how to . . . to say anything. To stop him." When Hana slips an arm around her, Jun presses her forehead to Hana's shoulder.

I reach out hesitantly, but then Hana is jerking me toward them, and I fall with my arms around them both. Asuka's hand lands on top of mine, soft and warm. I hold my sisters tightly. I close my eyes. I want to memorize this moment, everything about it.

After a while, we all pull away. I feel lighter, somehow, like they've shouldered some of the burdens I've carried for years.

"You know." Asuka's voice wavers, and she stops to take in a deep breath. When she speaks again, her words are strong. "Father cleared his name before the AEGIS—but not mine or Jun's." She sets her teacup primly on the table, and the rest of the room is so silent, the click of it is loud. "There's a lot we've disagreed with Father over recently . . ."

Hearing her say so shocks me. It's more than I ever expected from Asuka, the eldest of us all, who has so carefully balanced the scales between us and our father for years.

"There are even some things Father doesn't know about . . . like a racing ship I invested in . . ." Asuka doesn't look me in the eye as she speaks, more like she's talking to the room around her. "The *Hermes*."

Hana forces a breathy giggle. "It's a *Hermes*-class ship named *Hermes*? You're so bad at naming things, Nee-chan . . ."

Asuka's face is only a little pink when she continues. "I thought I would enjoy racing, but I found it's . . . not for me. I thought Hana might like it one day when she's older, so I didn't sell it. The key is in the drawer by the door. It's at Psi dock. I've paid to keep it well cared for, to have it taken out for runs here and there, but I don't use it much."

I read between the lines she carefully lays down. Asuka bought a fast ship. It's kept in good condition and supplied. In case she needed to run away? In case she needed to get *Hana* away from our father?

And the name . . . *Hermes*. The herald of the gods. With winged feet that carried him quickly to his destination. A god of travelers, but also of thieves. And a soul guide who helped the dead find their afterlife.

"Thank you," I say softly.

She finally looks me right in the face. "For what?"

I give my sisters one last hug before I find the key to *Hermes*. They crowd around me at the door, watching me expectantly. And though there is no certainty in tomorrow, I find the words welling up within me anyway.

"I'll come back," I tell them. "I promise."

CHAPTER 39
THE TWINS

Why did I join the military? Some have accused me of joining simply because, as a poor child on Earth, I had little future otherwise, but that is not true. I could have done as my family had and tilled the fields around our camp. Farming is, and always has been, an honorable profession. I chose to give my life to the military because I knew that's where the power in Gean society was. One needs power if one aims to change worlds.

Excerpt of Admiral Shaz Kadir's speech following
his ascension to the Admiralty

I've paced the same path in Aunt Tamar's lbrary so many times that I'm likely to wear a rut into the rugs. Since Admiral Kadir began the assault on the Temple—*with Astrid*, my fear reminds me—we have received few updates.

Aunt Tamar tempers her anxiety by reading a thick handwritten book. Aunt Delilah prays in a different section of the library. Castor alternates between standing guard and stealing glances at the compad he brought with him. And I . . . I pace.

If this assault succeeds, Admiral Kadir will become the next Warlord, and I, along with Aunt Tamar and Aunt Delilah, will clean up the Agora. But if the assault fails—

I can't think about that without wanting to vomit. My entire life's work—everything I've endured, everything I've pretended to be, weighed against everything I gave up—is riding on a single battle.

Castor's pheromones radiate his shock. I'm at his side before he calls for me.

"What is it?"

He looks around the room to see if anyone's listening, but the guards know how to mind their business and Aunt Tamar doesn't seem to notice I've even spoken. "The Harbinger."

I sneer, not hiding my distaste. "What about him?"

Castor smells . . . offended by my dislike. "He wants to talk."

"To us?" *Or to you?*

Castor shrugs.

Ever since that day at the Harbinger's safe house when he attacked us with an onslaught of emotions from both his neural implant and his pheromones, something has changed between Castor and me. I tell myself the things Castor said were in answer to the pain, an attempt to make Sorrel relent, but I just can't shake the image of my twin on his knees, begging to go with him—and giving up on protecting me.

"I'm going to take it in the back room," he says. Doesn't ask if I can sneak away from my duties. Doesn't invite me to join him. Burn it all, he probably doesn't *want* me to be there while he talks with the Harbinger. I follow him regardless of his desires, casting a single glance over my shoulder to see if anyone notices. They don't.

At least he doesn't smell annoyed when he looks up from the compad to see I've followed. Just turns his attention back to establishing the connection with Sorrel.

BACK BLOODY. FINGERNAILS ragged. Strips of skin spread like confetti around him. His words a harsh hiss: *You've made your choice. You never did know how to sacrifice.* His pheromones like an ice-pick lobotomy.

RAGE AGONY GRIEF CONTEMPT YEARNING DISGUST LOATHING.

I breathe deeply against the anxiety that rises when I think about the last time I saw the Harbinger. *It's time I took my place where I belong*, he'd said, and now he's on Vesta with the Aster Elders after fucking blowing the Ceres dome to bits.

His words have haunted me. He asked me to come with him. If I had, would I have gone along with his planned attack on Ceres? Would the Synthetics have reclaimed Autarkeia? Maybe I wouldn't have changed a fucking thing, but at least I wouldn't be watching everything happen from the opposite end of space.

Fuck.

The compad connects just as I think that, so I wonder what he sees in my face. Is it the regret I feel for not going with him? The frustration of being trapped on the sidelines?

"Harbinger . . ."

When his eyes fall on me, he actually looks—relieved. He releases a long breath and forces a slim smile. "Castor."

This is . . . not what I expected at all. His health is a bit sketchy—that's fucking obvious from how prominent the blue veins are around his eyes—but he's not tearing me a new asshole. Behind him is a single Aster Elder, but Cedar quickly steps out of frame.

"I'm here too, Sorrel," Lily says, and I'm fucking thankful he can't smell how dismissive she's being. Can he hear it in her tone?

"It's . . . good to see you again," I say, if only to keep him calm.

But the Harbinger's face falls. Again, this is not what I expected. "I have something I need to tell the two of you . . ."

"What?" I ask, perhaps too eagerly.

"The Synthetics . . . when they took back Autarkeia . . ." He hesitates, shakes his head. Decides to start over. "Hemlock . . . was lost on Autarkeia."

A muscle spasm runs down my right arm, the one I use to wield the mercurial blade. "I . . . I don't think I . . . What?"

"I'm sorry."

And it's like . . . all of a sudden, I'm a kid again. Uncle Hemlock tucks Lily in beneath a sky-blue blanket that he bought just for her, and while I am all incandescent rage, he turns to me with a yellow-toothed smile and pats the bed beside her, inviting me to join them. "Don't you want to hear a story too?" he asks. And I always said no, even though I listened anyway—said I didn't want anything to do with him—because I thought he would be like all the others, the kids who didn't want to play with Lily because she couldn't run, the Asters on Vesta who were assigned to child-rearing and looked at her with only pity, the Elders who sadly shook their heads—thought he'd one day get tired of us and we'd have nowhere else to go. He never did.

And then I'm a teenager, and I'm losing Lily. He let her go to that geneassist—the Icarii doctor who ended up exiled—let him twist her helix until she looked like the very *siks* who shit on us daily, and while there was no way Lily could pass in Icarii society when they examined DNA for everything, the Geans—she could fool them with her brown eyes and brown hair. And while she wasn't allowed access to Gean hospitals, her joining the Sisterhood meant they *had* to help, and so finally, after spending so much of her life bedridden with pain, she got surgery we could never access as Asters. We wrote to each other as much as we could—she could walk, her pain wasn't as bad as it had been, she had side effects, she said, but it was manageable—but we couldn't see each other anymore. I only had Hemlock, and I'd lost my twin thanks to him, or so I thought. That was never true.

And then, just a few years ago, I beg him to give me an assignment, to let me help the Aster cause, to live up to all the stories he told us when I was a kid. I meet Hiro. I meet Ofiera. I make bombs. Hemlock allies with the Geans, and he keeps me in the Under during the Fall of Ceres. I meet Lito. I make more bombs. It doesn't matter, he doesn't want me to go too far from him, to be in too much danger, even as Lily works her way up in the Sisterhood, determined to use her station for good, even though no one ever asked her to. He was slow—so godsdamn slow—I thought he'd never stand up for the Asters. Thought he'd never use the outlaws or his connections the way he should. He never showed himself willing to.

And then he sent me to Cytherea, where I met *her* . . . met Lucinia sol Lucius. She understood me, knew what it was like to constantly live in your sibling's shadow. She believed in me, in a way Hemlock didn't. And I haven't done a damned thing to prove him wrong, to impress him, and now I won't, because he's—

He's . . . dead.

"Castor . . ."

"Huh?"

I look from the blurry form of Lily—solitary in her grief—to the blur of the Harbinger's face—and realize the tears in my eyes are the reason things have gone fuzzy. I blink them back and swallow the sobs down.

"I'm so sorry," he says, and he looks sorry—like he does, in part, blame himself. "The Synthetics were heartless in their annexation of Autarkeia." How could the Synthetics be anything *but*?

"They did it because of Ceres . . . they did it because . . ." *Of you.* I don't say that. He knows anyway.

He doesn't apologize.

And if I'm being honest? This all started when I chose to save Lily from Admiral Drucker.

"Listen to me, Castor." His face hardens. I try to make mine do the same. I look directly into his eyes so I miss nothing, even if the looking hurts. He asks for *me*. Not Lily. *Me*. "I have a plan. I need your help with it."

"Okay," I say, the word just . . . slipping out. "T-tell me."

"I'll send the coordinates of a ship on Mars that will bring you to me. Meet me there if you wish to help."

The screen goes dark. I clutch the compad harder. I don't even get a chance to ask, *Help with what?*

But it doesn't matter. In my heart, I swear to go to the Harbinger and do something that would make Hemlock proud.

"WHAT ARE YOU doing?"

The words are out from between my numb lips before I can think better of them. They sound accusing—because they are.

Usually in situations like this, Asters say *let me share your grief,* and then they join you in pouring out all the sadness through pheromones, swallowing the whole room in the smell of sorrow. But I can't do that with him—with *my twin,* whom I should be able to always rely on—because . . . because he's leaving.

"I'm going to him, Pollux."

"You're going to—" Abandon me.

"Yes," Castor says, the usual heat in his tone, for once, directed at me. "I'm going, because you don't need me—*don't* say that you do. You have Admiral Kadir, and soon he'll be the Warlord. You have your allies in the Agora, and your White Guard too—"

"*You're* supposed to be my White Guard—"

"You don't *need* me."

"Castor, that's not true—"

"You just like having me with you."

"Do you *honestly* believe Sorrel has anything good planned? Look what he did to Ceres—"

His rage intensifies at my accusation. A headache pulses in my temples from the smell. "I finally have the chance to help *all Asters,* and you don't want me to, because you want me to stay at your side?"

"If Admiral Kadir does successfully stop Warlord Vaughn, things are going to change for the Geans. I'm going to need your help—"

"I'm tired of hearing about the fucking Geans!" He straightens, and he is so much taller than me that it makes me want to shrink down further. "*I'm* an Aster! What the hell are you?"

I slap him. Or try to. As short as I am, I strike his jawline with my fingers, leaving the shape of my nails in his skin. Instantly I think of Aunt Marshae—and am horrified by my actions.

"Castor, I'm . . . I'm so—"

"Don't," he says. Doesn't touch his face. Purposefully ignores the furrows as he straightens. "I'm fucking tired of being trapped in your shadow, *Lily*. For once, I'm going to do something I choose myself. Something that *really* helps the Asters."

He leaves.

I don't stop him.

I think maybe it's for the best that he's gone.

CHAPTER 40

ASTRID

My Goddess, what have I done?

Excerpt from the journal of Mother Joan I

"Fix your face, girl," Aunt Tamar says. "You're supposed to look happy."

"Of course." I roll my neck and force a smile, ready for my turn in the parade of absurdities. In front of the curtain I hide behind, the Mother and the Warlord stand on a hastily built metallic structure, looking down on a crowd of Geans packed shoulder to shoulder, both eager and fearful to see how their world has changed.

After the assault on the Temple, Admiral Kadir's soldiers arrested anyone suspected of involvement in Warlord Vaughn's and Aunt Marshae's schemes. The puppet members of the Agora appointed by Aunt Marshae rolled on her with little pressure. They listed her crimes while begging to be forgiven for their own. They gave concrete evidence of her connection to the late Admiral Drucker and his fellow zealots, the Disciples of Judeth—and with it, her connection to Warlord Vaughn. Among the Disciples, we found soldiers willing to admit to the assassinations of Aunt Salomiya, Aunt Margaret, and the Second Sister of Ceres—Eden—

as well as a few other Aunts and Sisters who stood against Aunt Marshae and disappeared—women we knew nothing about.

Around twelve hours after Virgil Vaughn's death, Admiral Shaz Kadir is named the new Warlord. The transition is as peaceful as it can be among the military, and those who disapprove do so quietly. It is, as Aunt Tamar once said, a history written by winners.

Warlord Kadir gestures to the right of the stage, which is my cue. Dressed in red silk, I stride into the open, keeping my eyes on Lily. Not wandering to the crowd that packs the wide lawn between the space elevator and the Temple. Not drifting to the navy curtain, now at my back. When my thoughts wander to what is behind it—my heart quickening its pace—I focus on the roar of the congregation, my title magnified. *Unchained! Unchained!*

Being here again—the sanctuary where I grew up, the site of my greatest defeat but also my greatest triumph, the place I never thought I would set foot after shattering *Victory*—does not feel real. Even the hand-shaped bruises on my neck, carefully covered by makeup, are starting to fade with careful medical attention. When they are gone, will all of this fade away like a nightmare?

Warlord Kadir lifts his hands, signaling for quiet. As the roar becomes a soft hiss, Lily steps to the podium and leans into the vocal amplifier. "Let us speak," the Mother says. The crowd, as expected, cheers wildly. The other Unchained, led by Agnes and Flora at the front of the crowd, wear proud smiles.

Aunt Delilah and Aunt Tamar, the only two remaining members of the Agora, officially recognized the Unchained as miracles of the Goddess. They have plans to reveal the existence of the neural implants, but only once things have calmed down regarding the new Warlord. I vow to hold them to that promise.

"Standing before you," Lily begins, signing her words in the Sisterhood hand language at the same time, "is the First of the Unchained, now called Astrid." Once more, I force myself to focus on Lily. Only Lily. On the feeling of her head beneath my chin and her hands on my waist. On the vanilla scent of her hair. On the pale patches like scaled armor hidden beneath her gloves and dress. On how much of a comfort it all is, like a familiar place that could become home.

Forget the crowd. Forget the curtain. Forget Aunt Tamar and Aunt Delilah coming onto the stage to flank Lily and add an air of legitimacy to this whole thing. Oh—*and smile.*

"She stands accused of several crimes, including treason, espionage, and aggravated murder, against the people of Mars and Earth by Aunt Marshae of the Sisterhood. In a trial led by the remaining members of the Agora, the testimony of the Unchained, soldiers, and Warlord Kadir were all taken into consideration in order to pass a fair and transparent verdict. We now present the ruling to you."

Lily steps away, allowing Warlord Kadir to take the podium. "I, Shaz Kadir, Warlord of the Geans as chosen by the Admiralty, do agree with Mother Lilian I that the First of the Unchained, now called Astrid, is innocent of all charges."

Shouting, louder than before. Weeping. Clapping. I play my part, letting tears rise to my eyes and pressing my hands together over my mouth as if I am shocked. I am so divorced from my body that it feels easy.

Kadir continues to address the Geans. I catch only snippets of his speech, words of peace and of upholding the Icarii-Gean cease-fire I achieved. He speaks of the burden of traveling to the Synthetic border alongside Mother Lilian I and of the great loss of our people on Ceres. Throughout, I keep my face appropriate.

Then he talks of punishment. Of its necessity. Of how it keeps our society strong. We all step aside, and, with a gesture from the Warlord, the curtain falls.

Revealing thirty men with nooses around their necks.

Most are cappos. All have been found guilty of carrying out Warlord Vaughn's crimes. But it feels wrong, somehow. Like we have simply stepped into roles written for us, instead of truly changing things.

Yet I feel nothing when the men drop, one by one, their necks snapping.

Perhaps one of them killed Eden, but they are not Aunt Marshae. It was her word that led to Eden's death, and it is her I hold most responsible.

She's still out there, little sister, Ringer says in my mind.

It is something I cannot—*will not*—forget.

"Earth endures!" Warlord Kadir shouts as the bodies swing. The crowd repeats his words back to him, an echo that sounds like all of Mars is shouting alongside him.

"Earth endures!" they chant.

"Mars conquers!"

"Mars conquers!"

AFTER THE HANGINGS, we retire to the Mother's building to plan. I stand at the entrance to the greenhouse, breathing in the thick, loamy scent of earth, while Lily, Aunt Tamar, and Aunt Delilah sit on green velvet furniture around a table set for tea.

The shifting of the White Guards informs us that someone is coming, but Warlord Kadir's appearance is still a shock.

"We have her" is the first thing out of his mouth.

Inside me, Ringer wakes.

"Who?" Aunt Delilah asks.

"Marshae," Tamar snarls the name.

"She's been trying to secure passage off of Mars, offering the neurobots and other cappo tech she must've grabbed on her way out as payment," Kadir says, that frantic light in his eyes that comes with battle. Perhaps it matches my expression. I had feared the neurobots were gone. Feared Warlord Vaughn had hidden them somewhere, and that the location would be lost with his death. But now . . .

Now we can have Marshae and *the Muninn*, Ringer says.

"We've taken her contact into custody and are prepared to play the role and provide her with a ship." Kadir's face splits in one of his handsome smiles. "Of course, the ship won't work, and we'll have her surrounded."

"Why not just arrest her now?" I ask. I pull my shaking hands behind my back. The thought of Aunt Marshae slipping through our net is too much. The sharp-nailed shrew must not be allowed to escape. She is too much like a cockroach; she will find a dark corner and multiply her supporters if we give her half a chance.

"We don't know exactly where she's staying. Somewhere in the vicinity of Pangboche." Kadir's smile fades. "We've sent agents into the neighborhood, but I've ordered them to tread carefully. We don't want to alert her before the time is right."

Pangboche. The place I grew up. The neighborhood where Matron Thorne's house now sits empty. I press a hand to my head, wishing I could remember the night I visited her. Wishing I could force Ringer to tell me. Could there be any correlation between what Matron Thorne might have known and Aunt Marshae choosing Pangboche as her hiding place?

"And we don't want her to destroy the neurobots," Kadir continues. "If we recover them, we could use them."

Use them.

"How do you plan to use the neurobots?" I ask carefully. Aunt Tamar seems just as interested in the subject.

Kadir seems to notice our discomfort. "We'd have to analyze them first, of course," he says, gesturing to Aunt Tamar as if to placate her; it is her Order that controls the use of scavenged technology, after all. "But this is a once-in-a-lifetime opportunity to study the technology. There's a lot it could teach us."

About the Skadivolk, or something more sinister? I hear the gaps in Kadir's speech, the truth he tells between the lines. He does not know what he could use them for, but he intends to find out.

It's too dangerous, Ringer whispers.

After learning Vaughn wanted to use them to live forever, I believe they belong only with the Skadivolk.

"When will the operation take place?" Lily asks, turning her attention back to Aunt Marshae's arrest.

Kadir shifts toward her. "Two days from now, to be sure we have everything together. We can't make any mistakes. No tipping her off, or she might run farther."

"But we will be traveling to the belt—" I stop short when all eyes turn in my direction.

"I've put one of my most trusted soldiers in charge of the operation," Kadir assures me. "And Aunt Tamar will be helping, of course. We'll hold Aunt Marshae until we return."

"Even if I'm not attending, we should discuss expectations for the meeting with the Synthetics . . ." As Aunt Tamar seamlessly changes the topic, I press my lips flat to keep from speaking. Perhaps if Oleander were here, he would sense something amiss in me—but he is gone, disappeared like a ghost, and, much as if he is dead, no one speaks of him.

I find myself only half listening—Lily arguing on behalf of including the Asters, Warlord Kadir promising he has plans to take care of anyone who accompanies him. My mind is far more focused on Aunt Marshae. On the pull toward Pangboche.

No one here knows that place better than I do. And no one can force Aunt Marshae's hand like I can. Kadir doesn't want anyone to tip her off? Then I will make sure she does not see me coming.

By the time Warlord Kadir, the Aunties, and Lily have come to a conclusion about the Synthetics, I have made a decision regarding Aunt Marshae. In the chaos of Warlord Kadir's leaving—several soldiers trailing after him, the White Guard watching—I slip away into the Olympus Mons night unseen.

I STEP OUT of the podcar in Pangboche. A small ripple of nausea passes through me as I adjust to the lower gravity—or perhaps it is my nervousness rising. I close my eyes, focusing on the way my feet feel against the ground, until the dizziness passes. Ringer whispers soothing words to me: *You're okay. I'm with you.*

I chose a drop-off location not terribly far from Matron Thorne's orphanage. Though the Matron is dead, I still feel drawn to the place where I spent the first ten years of my life. And if Aunt Marshae targeted Matron Thorne because of something she knew or had—like my medical records—perhaps I can find out why.

As I walk down the sidewalk, past dilapidated houses where crooked-limbed workers sit on porches, I consider what those records might say: Where I came from. Who brought me to the orphanage. Who my parents were. Could I be someone important? Could they have been? Is that why I was given Ringer's neurobots?

All of that disappears from my mind when I round the corner and spot a light on at the supposedly empty house. After Matron Thorne's death, the children would have been moved to a different orphanage. So this . . . this is either a squatter, or another ghost from my past come to haunt me.

Or a trap, Ringer says.

But I want to find out regardless.

He guides me over the fence. I approach the house through the back-yard. The back door isn't open, but I push aside an aged, dirty mat and find a spare key—Matron Thorne always kept it there. I enter on silent feet, and Ringer pulls the energy pistol from my jacket pocket and sweeps the room with it before entering.

The light came from the second floor. I take the steps upward, feeling like a child all over again. I know exactly where to step to keep the stairs from creaking—the path is written into my bones from all the times I came down in the night for water before skittering back up to my crowded shared room, not wanting to be punished for being out of bed.

Upstairs, I put my back to the wall. The hallway runs the length of the house, splitting off into four rooms filled with bunks, but those beds are empty now with no children here. The light comes from the room at the end of the hall, the largest room, which had been Matron Thorne's. I move toward it, a moth drawn to the flame.

I've taken only two steps when I hear an audible click and a metallic whir, but before I have time to puzzle the sound through, Ringer seizes my body.

GET DOWN! he screams, dropping me to the floor. A bright light flashes, and a rattling boom fills the air. My arms come up and cover my head as dust from the plaster wall rains down on me.

Belatedly, Bruni's neurobots identify the sound: a drone with a turret gun for defense.

I curl into a ball, the gun still in my hand, as bullets liberally pepper the hallway—not just where I was standing, but anywhere I might have been. *Cappo tech*, Bruni tells me, and I picture the drone Kadir used during the assault of the Temple, approximately the size of my head and, judging from the placement of the shots, hovering at chest height.

The noise cuts off abruptly. The turret clicks. *Out of bullets*, Bruni says.

Move! Ringer shouts, pushing me to my feet. The drone is floating in the doorway of one of the bedrooms on the left. I lift the pistol and spot it down my sights. It emits a high-pitched whirring noise. *Reloading*, Bruni supplies. Soon it will fire again.

But Bruni's neurobots tell me where to aim, and Ringer's control over my hands guides me. I aim at the gap between the attached turret and the shell of the drone's spherical body and shoot until the laser pistol needs a recharge clip. The drone spins away, smoking, and hits the ground with a crack and a thud.

Without a beat of hesitation, I reload and move down the hallway. My heart is racing, yet I feel detached from my body—calm and panicked simultaneously.

Another drone zips out from a bedroom on the right. As its turret emerges from its smooth metal belly, Ringer fires three laser shots into it and keeps moving. The drone jerkily drifts off into the darkness.

I reach the end of the hallway. The door is closed, but I open it with a kick. A part of me expects the drone that's inside; it doesn't have time to shoot its first bullet before Ringer takes care of it. With an electric whine, it drops onto what had been Matron Thorne's bed, then rolls to the edge and falls to the floor with a heavy *thunk*, where it stops.

I scan the room with the gun.

Aunt Marshae is halfway out the window.

I fire a single shot to the left of her head. Glass from the window shatters. She swallows a cry but spins in my direction—there is a weapon in her hand—

Ringer seamlessly takes over my body and shoots her in the forearm.

She drops the gun and screams. She casts a foolish look out the window, trying to judge if she can make the jump from the second floor to the ground. I scoff.

"Come back inside, and I won't shoot you in the face." The words do not feel like mine, though they come from my mouth.

In this moment, I am Ringer, and Ringer is me.

Holding her bloody forearm to her chest, Aunt Marshae pulls herself back into the room. It has changed little since my childhood—the curtains are more yellow, the bed's wide mattress sags more—but otherwise, it is as Matron Thorne styled it. In the corner is a floral-patterned wing-back chair. I guide Marshae to sit there.

She settles gingerly, looking between the smoking drone and me with rage and the smallest hint of surprise. She truly expected to kill me with the cappo technology she had stolen, yet now I have the upper hand.

Which means *I* call the shots. "You have to know that no matter what you do, you won't get away. Warlord Vaughn is dead. The Disciples of Judeth hang in the Temple. We have Aunt Margaret's testimony recorded, and the testimonies of several people who betrayed you at the first chance they got."

"I expected as much," Aunt Marshae purrs, her lips curling into a horrible smirk despite her own blood coating her hands. Her nails are ragged, broken things, the paint flaking and chipped.

"Then why are you here?" I ask. "Why haven't you fled as far from Olympus Mons as possible before searching for a way off-world?" What I would do, if I were her.

Would you? Ringer asks. *Or would you sneak onto the* Juno *dressed as a Cousin and try to kill Aunt Marshae if it was the last thing you ever did?*

I swallow hard against what feels like a taunt.

Aunt Marshae does not answer. Her eyes wander to the drone.

"Was this just a trap for me?"

"Why did *you* come, Astrid?" Her eyes snap to mine. "The same reason as me, I suspect." She straightens in the chair, and for a flash, I see her on the stone throne of the Order of Cassiopeia, an Aunt of the Agora in red, instead of a middle-aged woman in a faded worker's jumpsuit. "Searching for something in your past."

My grip tightens on the gun. "What did you do to Matron Thorne?"

She pauses a moment as if caught off guard. "What about her?"

It is only because of Ringer's intervention that I do not lower my weapon. "You killed her!" I snarl.

She releases a loud, rhythmic laugh. "Tell me, stupid girl, do you *really* think I killed that old drunkard?"

I do not answer.

"I'll admit to Salomiya and Margaret. Even that girlfriend of yours—Eden, I think her name was? I had them killed. It was a stern lesson—one you *should* have heeded." She looks me up and down and scoffs as if she finds me lacking. "But tell me, do I strike you as the type to quibble over a one-handed Matron with a dying liver and shit for brains?"

My eyes burn. How does this woman say things that can still cut into the heart of me? "Then who—"

She anticipates my question. "How the hell should I know? Maybe she truly was stabbed to death in a robbery."

I grind my teeth, biting back words and tears.

Aunt Marshae rolls her eyes. "Answer me this, then. What reason would I possibly have to target her?"

"For what she knew," I spit out. "Or for letting me go after I visited her." Aunt Marshae only looks confused. "I came to her, asking about my medical records—"

"Goddess above, you act the role of the orphan to perfection." She laughs at me. Again. "Truly, I was interested in your medical records. They were part of the reason I came here. You see, the ones we have access to in the Sisterhood? They were sparse for the ten-year-old we took in. I thought your precious Matron Thorne was hiding something—that you were a moonborn spy, maybe an Icarii plant. *Any* explanation for how you've become . . ." She gestures to me and the gun. "But do you want to know what I found?" She narrows her eyes, her lips a dagger smirk. She wants to hurt me with her words. "Your records are sparse because Matron Thorne rarely sought medical aid for you in order to save money. You came from an exile moonborn colony. You were abandoned because they didn't want an extra mouth to feed. They're selfish, barbaric people, after all."

Ringer growls inside me. "You don't know *anything* about them—"

"I know that *no one* wanted you. Your mother voluntarily surrendered you to the orphanage."

Though I try my best not to, I flinch. The words hurt, bubbling beneath my skin until they boil up my throat. "Liar," I spit.

She gestures to a pile of papers on the bedside table. "See for yourself, if you don't believe me."

I do not move toward the file. I will have time to read it after I deal with her. "You said my records were only part of the reason you came here. What else?"

"You know why." She tips up her chin and stares down her nose at me, a fading queen on her crumbling throne. "Neither of us will be able to rest until one of us is gone."

My lips pull back from my teeth in a snarl. "What if I had brought Warlord Kadir's soldiers with me?"

"I knew you wouldn't."

"I could have—"

"I know *you*, Astrid." She looks at me then—*really* looks at me—and her mask falls away. I stumble through the years, back and back, until I am meeting her for the first time and she is introducing herself as my new Auntie on the *Juno*.

"I am Aunt Marshae, and I will be taking care of you on board this ship," she says with her prim hands held before her. *"I want you to know that you can bring anything concerning to my attention, and that I will do my utmost to help you. After all, your success is my success, niece."*

I smile like I mean it, because I do. I am happy with this assignment and the support I am offered. May we grow in the Goddess's garden as She wills, *I sign back.*

Here, now, in this fading room, the woman with battered nails shakes her head at me. "I knew you'd come alone because you don't want Warlord Kadir to arrest me; you want me dead. You don't want me to be hanged in front of a crowd; you want to be the one to pull the trigger. You're a killer at heart, Astrid. You desire blood above all else."

The gun shakes in my hand. Is she right?

She *does* know me. And I know her.

And neither of us will be able to rest until one of us is gone.

"But if you did not kill Matron Thorne," I ask, my voice soft, "who did?"

She loosens her grip on her forearm. The blood flows freely. I am afraid she is not going to answer, and then, just as quietly as me, she says, "Someone is still pulling your strings, stupid girl."

Every muscle in my body tenses as if preparing to be struck—because I fear the same thing.

"It's been long enough. No one's here." She looks toward the window. "You didn't call for anyone to come for me, which means . . . I'm right." Despite her proclamation, she does not taunt me with it; there is no smirk on her face, no haughty look. "I'm not leaving this house alive." The wound on her forearm bleeds more heavily than before, dripping into her lap. She ignores it, reaching into her pocket.

I point the gun at her chest. "Don't!" I snap.

She speaks calmly. "Do you want your neurobots back? They're here." She takes two things out of her pocket— a battered piece of paper, and the familiar neurobot vials in a clear bag. "I always thought I'd have grand last words . . . now that the time's come, I find I have nothing to say." She nods at me. "Go ahead."

I wonder if this is some sort of trick. One last play from Aunt Marshae to garner sympathy or fool me into coming close enough for her to grab me with her mangled nails. But as I steady my hands and ensure she is directly in my sights, she clutches the battered paper to her chest and closes her eyes.

"This is for Eden," I say, and pull the trigger.

The bullet enters her temple. Dyes her hair a brighter red. She slumps in the chair, eyes far-off and glassy.

She looks like any other dead person.

My hands shaking again, I cross the room to the body and take the neurobots from her. The paper that she held to her chest has fallen to her lap. Though it's spattered with blood, I can make out an old photo of two women embracing.

I barely recognize the young Marshae, with her bright eyes and vibrant smile. The other woman, who kisses her cheek, I do not recognize at all.

I leave the photo where it fell. I will never know who that other woman is. Will never know what she meant to Marshae.

But I am certain of one thing: Aunt Marshae is finally dead.

PART IV
A KINGDOM OF METAL

PART IV
A KINGDOM OF HER OWN

INTERLUDE

SOUJI VAL AKIRA

A s he watches worlds pass him by on the livecam view of the stars, Souji val Akira considers what Beron val Bellator has asked of him. But because of how he left things with his children—Asuka and Jun at the mercy of the AEGIS, Hana soon to be the only val Akira without a black mark against her name—he hardly feels he has the right to contact them again.

What could he possibly say to them to make up for all he's done?

He knows the paths he left untrod and the bridges he burned. He knows what he has sacrificed with each choice. He feels it every night when he lies down to sleep. He sees it in his dreams: what could have been, instead of what is. Cytherea, hospitals overflowing with the dying and dead. His daughters, full of fear and hate and sorrow.

His baby boy, dead. Shinya is dead.

Even if Souji succeeds in the asteroid belt—even if he lives—nothing will ever fix that. No matter his studies, no matter the scientific advancements, the dead cannot be brought back to life. The machine wearing Lito sol Lucius's face was a clever Synthetic ruse, but he is not a dead man walking.

And Hiro . . . Souji is not so heartless that he doesn't know what he's done to Hiro. Doesn't know what he's asked—no, *demanded*—of his most rebellious child. Yet who else could have done what Hiro did? Who else could have infiltrated the Geans and not only assassinated the Mother but raised up a replacement for her who authored a cease-fire between the Geans and Icarii?

No one other than Hiro val Akira.

In a sense, Souji is proud of Hiro. Though perhaps it's better to say he's *inspired* by Hiro.

Sometimes, a little streak of rebellion is exactly what one needs.

Beron sets the handheld recorder on the table beside Souji's chair. "It's a good idea," he says, "just in case the worst should come to pass." His familiar voice is so drained of energy that his attempt at encouragement falls flat. "Think about it, at least. We still have time to get a message back to your loved ones in Cytherea."

"Tell me, old friend," Souji says. He suddenly feels sentimental, coming up on the finish line of his life's work. Of his family's work, through the generations. "Do you believe the worst is going to happen?"

Beron only shakes his head. He is more than exhausted; he is a shell of the man he was, and it strikes Souji as odd that, after coming so far, he'd fall apart within spitting distance of their goal. "I just don't know, val Akira . . . I don't know anything anymore."

Souji waves for him to leave. Beron goes on silent feet.

When he is finally alone, Souji turns his attention to the handheld recorder.

It is tempting to believe that one message could soothe the hurts of a lifetime. That a single apology would be anything other than capitulation, an attempt to explain what only Souji understands.

But—that three-letter word again—*but* . . . those explanations already exist, and one day his clever children will find the pieces and put them together. They'll hear of his first-of-its-kind creation that he took to the meeting with the Synthetics, and they'll reap the benefits of his life's work when they are free to travel beyond the asteroid belt. They'll see how Souji's father worked for that, and his grandfather before him. And maybe, one day, if they understand . . . it won't be because he left them a message.

Souji turns his eyes to the stars.

There is nothing left for him to say to his children.

Everything has already been said.

CHAPTER 41
HIRO

The Synthetics have called the leaders of humanity to the border, broadcasting coordinates for a first-of-its-kind in-person meeting. The outlaws don't necessarily have a leader, but I'm the captain of *Camellia*, and others in the Alliance have stated that, after losing Autarkeia, they're uninterested in anything other than finding food and shelter for their people. I don't even know if the Synthetics will let me in, but . . . I'm gonna try.

Dire of the Belt

The *Hermes* is a bullet-shaped craft with shining cherry-red paint and black chrome detailing. It being a racing ship, the interior is all necessities—collapsible shower, suction-tube toilet, and burn cradle that reclines into a bed. It shocks me that Asuka chose this ship when it looks like something I would've bought to piss off our father.

I hop into the burn cradle, wearing a racing suit so much like the Ironskin plugsuits that I wonder which came first. The cradle connects to the suit, cooling and comforting my body despite the needle I know is hovering close to my spine. The controls are under my gloved grip, and as soon as I key my destination into the *Hermes* and set him to burn hard—I know ships are traditionally female, but the *Hermes* is, without a doubt, male—that needle slips into my back and shoots bliss through my body.

I push myself all the way to the asteroid belt, but when I'm in the burn cradle, juiced up on whatever fucking cocktail was in that needle, I don't even feel the pressure.

Thanks to the current rotation of Venus, we travel for nine days until the *Hermes* slows for approach, the coordinates the Synthetics beamed throughout the solar system coming up quick on my map. I'm pretty sure the ship's maker never expected anyone to be stupid enough to ride the burn cradle for this long—high on bliss juice, sleeping in snatches, pissing in the suit—but this is kind of an emergency. Besides, at this point, my body's been through worse.

Still, when I peel myself off the cradle and out of the suit, sticky and numb—and let's be honest, desperately craving another bliss hit—the shower is my first destination. After that, I dig through the clothes Asuka stored in the ship and end up with something teenage Hiro would've chosen for themself: dark cowl-neck tunic, reflective chrome jacket, and bright patterned leggings. I'm tempted to take a pair of Asuka's heels, but considering this is technically outer space, I compromise and put on gravboots. No telling if there's gravity on the Synthetic ship, or wherever this meeting is taking place.

Sitting on the edge of the burn cradle, I eat a huge meal and drink as much water as I can—a reward after relying on the suit to fuel and hydrate me—but my eyes stick to the command screens, all keyed to give me a full 360-degree livecam view of our surroundings so I miss nothing. At first it's all pinpricks of light, the usual tapestry of the black, but then I notice a strange spot, something incongruous in the otherwise normal pattern of space.

Then that spot grows. Becomes far larger than the darkness between stars. Swallows the light like a tear in the fabric of reality, an ever-expanding black hole.

"DETECTED BY SENTRY 837E: SHIP NUMBER RC-1739 DESIGNATION 'HERMES' CARRYING ONE LIFE-FORM," a metallic voice echoes over the intercom. It startles me. The same message is displayed on one of my command screens. "IDENTIFY YOURSELF."

I'd wondered how the Synthetics were keeping the common people away from the unencrypted coordinates they sent; they must've set up a barricade around their meeting place. I clear my throat. "I'm Hiro val Akira, pilot of the *Hermes.*"

"ARE YOU ONE OF THE LEADERS OR REPRESENTATIVES OF HUMANITY?"

Well, shit. "Uhh . . . nope." Hopefully they'll give me a warning to turn around before they fire, like I've read about at the Synthetic border.

The voice is quiet for a moment. Then, after some thought: "WEL-COME, HIRO VAL AKIRA."

My face aches with a smile. "Tell Mara thanks for me." But the voice—and its message—are gone, so I'm not sure if it heard me.

And then . . . the Synthetic ship *glows.*

No—calling it a ship is like calling the *Hermes* a toy. Maybe it's *technically* true, but the description chafes. This . . . it's unlike anything our scientists could've imagined. Unfathomable in its design and advancement.

The Synthetics have built a planet. Spherical, illuminated, with shifting rivers that coil like living serpents and blocky metallic landmasses in an array of colors—gunmetal gray, pale icy blue, oil black with yellow slick, anodized sapphire and amethyst like a beetle's wings. And it shines like the Earth of old, from before pollution faded its gemlike appearance.

We were so busy looking for aliens in galaxies beyond, we missed the ones sitting in our backyard.

My hands never touch the controls, but the *Hermes* is drawn toward something as if caught by gravity—not the planetship, which looms ominously, but the "moon" rotating silently in its orbit: a long tube of a station with an outer ring. Never thought I'd return after everything that's happened, but that gentle pull tugs me directly into Autarkeia's airlock.

As the *Hermes* docks, I try not to think of all the souls I knew here, likely lost when the Synthetics seized the station. It's immediately obvious how different this place is now. What was it that the Synthetics called it when they initially claimed it after the Dead Century War? I think Mara said it was the Engineborn Forge. Well, this might not be a place for the Synthetics to forge bodies for themselves anymore, but it certainly feels like it belongs to the Engineborn.

Not because of how it looks—the docks are exactly the same, at least outwardly; lines of airlocks and level elevators haphazardly slapped together with Gean and Icarii tech—but because of what's *missing*, contrasting starkly with my memories of Autarkeia when it was a bustling hub of trading and smuggling.

After running a check on the atmosphere outside the ship—breathable oxygen, standard gravity—I leave the *Hermes* and head for the elevators. There are only a few ships docked—a couple of unallied crafts that could be outlaw, an Aster grasshopper, and one that's definitely a Gean dropship. No telling who they belong to when the Synthetics called for the leaders of humanity and have a bouncer the size of a planet. The most worrisome thing is the lack of Icarii ships when I know my father left Cytherea before I did.

When I reach the exit, the elevator opens before I call for it. I step inside, and my destination is selected for me. THE WAY THE WORLD is written in faded lettering. The rest of the graffiti that used to be here has been scoured off.

After a period of brief weightlessness, the elevator halts, and the doors open into the central city. That's when I finally see how alien Autarkeia has become.

Yes, the city still sprawls out before and, in a mirrored reflection, above me. It's still dark, like a Cytherean night, lit by neon shopfronts and light posts. The alleys are still narrow, the streets hardly any better. But the thing that made Autarkeia itself is completely gone.

There's no clashing music, no buzz of chatter, no laughter. There's no smell of home-cooked meals, no scents that mix to tempt. The oxygen is fresh instead of warm and stale. There are no *people*, and so the station is a shell with no soul.

Everywhere has become as quiet—as dead—as the Synthetic nuclear fission plants were. Those dark domes with silver, rib-like spires cradling them were what I thought of as gravestones for the Synthetic empire. Now, all of Autarkeia is a crypt.

If there was chaos here when the people fled, no evidence remains. Several streets have been blocked off by a strange silver mesh that looks like closely grouped tree branches, the gaps far too small to fit through, making it so that I can only walk a single path through Autarkeia. It reminds me of something I can't quite put my finger on, but after I pass the third barricade, I remember the haphazard interior of the Synthetic domes, all bizarre AI design.

I know my destination as soon as I round a corner and see it: a large plaza, so brightly lit it appears I'm being swallowed by daylight with each step. In the center is an island, surrounded by a river of shining silver liquid. Four skeletal bridges stretch over the unusual water, turning into four paths that head deeper into the city and lead directly to squat two- and three-story buildings. Their pristine facades look newly built in this otherworldly metropolis. Mesh barriers block off every other route.

It stands out to me as fake, a fresh coat of paint slapped on top of the real Autarkeia. The architectural styles are not native to the station—or even this time period, really, built with a mishmash of historical Gean and Icarii techniques. It feels like the set of a theater play, which makes us the characters . . .

I cross over the nearest bridge, my reflection in the river a warped creature, and come to the island. In the center is a cobbled square, stone pillars set at each of the four corners. I can make out words carved on those closest to me: EARTH and MERCURY. I'm passing between them when a smoky voice calls out to me.

"Hiro?"

I spin toward my name and find, stepping out from behind the pillar labeled MARS—

Her golden hair is long and loose. Her pink mouth forms a round O of shock. Her flame-blue eyes meet mine and then harden.

"Little dove." The words slip from my mouth before I can swallow them.

The First Sister. *Here.*

Days collapse upon days, months upon months, until I'm standing in the *Juno*, wearing the face of a dead woman, and she is looking at me like I'm the only thing tethering her to this world. I still vividly remember the way she pursed her lips when she was thinking, how she held her pen when writing, how her gaze would soften as her fingers moved from my prosthetic arm to my scarred, aching shoulder.

And the kiss we shared before Ceres, before she learned who I really was, burns in my memory. She was exactly the person I needed in that moment, someone who impossibly thought me beautiful, and I loved her for helping me see I was worthy of love when I thought I was anything but.

Maybe I became her tether to this world, but she also became mine.

How is she here? *Why* is she here? The last I'd heard through Hemlock's network, she'd been deposed and fled the Sisterhood. But if only the leaders of humanity have come . . . She doesn't dress in Sisterhood gray or the Mother's white. Is she a representative, or something else?

She pulls her lips back from her teeth, but before she can say anything, a group of Gean soldiers in navy and gold surround her, protecting her from me. One breaks from the pack, and for a second all I can see are the medals and pins on his uniform before he claps a hand on my shoulder like we know each other.

"I'm Warlord Kadir," he says with a vibrant smile.

Warlord Kadir? The fuck happened to Vaughn? I look at First Sister and understand: she has succeeded, somehow, in toppling a decades-old regime, and this handsome, youthful man is Vaughn's replacement. Which makes her . . . what?

"I'm . . . Hiro val Akira." I step out of Kadir's grip, once again reminded that I'm gate-crashing this party and wasn't exactly invited.

"*Hiro* val Akira?" he asks, as if he was expecting someone else. "I'd thought the arrival announcement was for the Icarii delegation." He looks at his surrounding soldiers, who have no answers. I wait for First

Sister to introduce herself—provide me with her new title, at least—but she presses her lips together tightly.

"Hiro val Akira," a singsong voice says as if in confirmation from behind me. I turn with my heart in my throat, hoping beyond hope to see who I think it is.

Mara looks exactly like she did when we roamed these streets together half a year ago—long black hair, the shaved half of her head covered in a silver prosthetic, dark brown eyes set in a diamond face. She even dresses the same, with her leather jacket and chunky boots. I rush toward her, arms thrown out, and she squeals as I catch her around the waist and spin her in a circle.

"Hiroooooo—" she says, my name turning into a shout.

But then *he* steps out from behind the VENUS pillar, and I set Mara down abruptly.

Lito. I try to say his name, but end up making a sound like I've been startled awake.

His cold, flat gaze roves around the square, but there's no recognition in his face. Mara takes a step back, and he looms over her shoulder, arms crossed over his wide chest. A silent guardian with only his purpose in mind.

"Welcome to Autarkeia," Mara says, switching from a grinning teenager to the whole serious I-am-Synthetic-agent-of-the-Singularity thing. "This island is the neutral area we will use for the discussion regarding the amendment to the Synthetic Ultimatum. As you can see, the Geans have already arrived"—she gestures behind me, and I look over my shoulder to where the navy-and-gold soldiers are retreating to one of the fresh-faced buildings, First Sister in the center; they must have no more interest in me since I'm not the Icarii delegation—"but there are others already here as well, such as the moonborn and the Asters. Autarkeia has been selected as nonpartisan territory for this discussion because of its gravity and oxygen, but please keep in mind that, while Synthetic presence is minimal, we will not allow violence. Those who violate our hospitality will not leave the station." Her eyes shimmer in that ancient cosmos way, and then, with a smile, she's human-faced again. "We have selected apartments to house each of our representative groups during their stay on Autarkeia."

"Do I get my own building? Someone's going to complain about my special treatment."

"You," Mara says, nose crinkling as she fights a grin because she *knows* I got special treatment just being let onto Autarkeia, "will be staying with the outlaws."

My voice ratchets up a notch. "The Alliance is here?"

"I suppose you could have your own building if you don't wish to see Dire of the Belt and Lucinia sol Lucius again—"

"No, that's fine." Their names send a shiver of shock through me. Knowing they're here—*that they're alive at all*—lifts a weight from my shoulders I didn't know I was carrying.

"You can find their building that way," Mara says with a gesture to one of the four paths, this one off to our right.

But I don't go, because, with only the three of us here, I find myself drawn to my former partner in a way that arrests me.

"Lito—"

He turns his back on me and strides down a different path than the one Mara pointed out to me. He says nothing, just marches over a bridge and away with sharp movements unlike the Lito I knew.

Mara cocks her head. "I'm sorry, Hiro."

"What . . . what have you done to him?" I turn to her, a mix of sorrow and anger battering my insides. I want to lash out, and she's the only one around.

Her brows furrow in remorse, and I can't believe I'd forgotten how human she can be. "We needed him. He went to Cytherea with the goal of stopping your father's weapon, but . . . something happened to him."

Lito, bloodied, chest cracked open and bones protruding, his eyes dead pits, his hand tightening around Noa's neck.

"I saw . . ."

"While I can spread my consciousness in many places, Lito is . . . unpracticed. His full consciousness slipped into the well of the Singularity because of what happened on Cytherea." She lifts a hand as I open my mouth. "It was his choice, and I won't force him back, as it wouldn't be right. His body is completing the purposes assigned by the Singularity. Think of it as an autopilot program."

So I'm seeing Lito, when it's really just some . . . drone. Just like the Sentries at the Synthetic border. I release a long, shuddering breath. All my hopes that Lito was in there somewhere—that I'd be reunited with him again—shatter. He's a drone with Lito's face. Nothing more. I rub at my eyes, only to be surprised I'm crying. "Fucking great . . ."

"Oh, Hiro, one out of a million . . ." She strides toward me, and all at once, I'm reminded of the last time I saw her, on the *Leander* when she was being torn apart by my brother.

Moments before the *Leander* exploded. Before they all died.

Shooting star. The firefly disappears.

I throw my arms around her and pull her to my chest and hold her tightly, because I need it—I need someone to hold me and tell me it's going to be okay.

"It's going to be okay," she says, as if reading my mind. Her arms come up, and she places her hands flat on my back.

"Is it?" I ask. "Is it, really?"

She releases a long sigh, shrinking in my arms. "Truthfully? There's too much I don't know. Like what your father has planned. He has a weapon, one he's kept hidden in a Faraday cage so we can't possibly glimpse it. The Singularity has been predicting that it could lead to a war between Synthetics and humanity, and . . ." That pause shakes me to my core. "I'm afraid, Hiro."

My lips tremble. Tears fall into Mara's hair. "I am too, Mara."

With her in my arms, all I can think about is how I've lost so much, and how much I just keep on losing.

And I know, right here, right now—before this all is over, I'm going to lose even more.

CHAPTER 42

ASTRID

Long have we suffered a corrupt system. Long have we suffered war. My first promise as Warlord is that I will change this. I dedicate my-self to peace on all our borders.

Warlord Shaz Kadir's first address to the Gean people

I leave the square—and Hiro val Akira—behind, drifting amidst the Gean soldiers in a cloud of reflection. I am in free fall because of Hiro. They are the one who started it all when they became captain of the *Juno* and chose me as First Sister. How have I come so far, only to find them again?

It hurts too much to think of them. It always has.

I'd once written them a note—*I love you. I never want to leave you*—and kept it in my pocket, unsure what to do with it. Eventually, I burned it, like so many of our conversations, wishing I could do the same with my memories of them.

My words may have turned to ash, but everything about them remains crystal clear.

Truthfully, while seeing Hiro may have started my downward spiral, I have been adrift since I shot Aunt Marshae. Since I returned to the

Temple and sought out my medical file. Since I confirmed that what she said was true.

I am no one from nowhere. My mother, a Skadivolk exile living on Mars, turned me over anonymously and voluntarily to the orphanage.

I was not stolen. I was not wanted. And there are no clues as to how I came to have Ringer's neurobots.

Warlord Kadir holds open the door to the hotel we were assigned on Autarkeia. It is a spacious but short building by the station's standards, well furnished with everything we could desire, from fully stocked kitchens to books on shelves. The lobby is open and airy, with a wide central staircase that leads up to the second story. Ivy-patterned carpets popular in Gean households cover floors of cool marble, while above, the ceiling looks up into a pool of water. The light passing through casts peaceful, rippling shadows over the lobby.

It reminds me of the Aquae Hotel. Perhaps that is why I am so uncomfortable despite the tranquil setting . . . Or perhaps it just feels wrong to be here, walking among the ruins of others' lives.

Whose food are we eating? Whose beds are we sleeping in? I do not believe for an instant that the Synthetics built this for us. Though if they did . . . how terrifying. Have we become the animals in their zoo, these habitats arranged specifically to ease our transition to their world? Are they watching us even now, pleased at how we conduct ourselves?

Cast in the wavering light and shadows of the water, Lily approaches us, seeking my gaze—but I purposefully turn away. Kadir slips into the gap I leave. "It wasn't the Icarii delegation, after all," he says, disappointment in his tone. "We're still waiting on them."

Though the visit did teach me something important: Hiro val Akira is here, and they are somehow already acquainted with the Synthetics.

If anyone is, I think wryly, *it would be Hiro.*

I move up the stairs and out of the lobby. On her way down, Lauren passes me. She meets my gaze with a stern look of her own. *Remember what I told you*, her look seems to say.

How could I possibly forget?

THE *JUNO* WAS selected as the ship that would carry the Gean delegation to the asteroid belt. I prepared myself for days of agony in that place that haunts my dreams, but was pleasantly surprised when I found Lauren in my room waiting for me.

That was when I learned that this was to be her last journey as the First Sister on board. She had been given a promotion: First Sister of the Temple of Mars, Lily named her. An appropriate position for someone who is likely to become the Mother's second in the days to come.

If we survive whatever the Synthetics have planned.

The thought that we might not is less frightening than it should be. Perhaps it is Ringer who keeps me calm. *Chaos*, he tells me, *is predictable for being chaotic. It's when one promises order that you never quite know what will happen.*

Lauren sought me out to speak with me each night. To catch up and to talk, in a way we never had before. At first, I received her warily. It was not jealousy that made me suspicious—not quite. I had to remind myself that I did not want to be part of the Sisterhood's hierarchy, and thus would not want the position of Mother's second. I tried to enjoy Lauren's company, but it wasn't until the third day that something in her expression broke and she poured out her worries to me.

"Do you know why the *Juno* came to save you from the Disciples of Judeth?" But before I could answer, she pressed on. "Information was passed to me from a fellow Sister who took confession from a soldier. He'd discovered the location of the base where they were keeping you, but was ordered to do nothing about it."

I forced myself to take in a deep, steeling breath before I spoke. "The military was taxed during those days—"

"It was two days after you were taken. *Before* Ceres was attacked."

Two days? And yet I was left to languish in the cell for another five . . .

Excuses rose within me. Perhaps Kadir and Lily were in the midst of planning my rescue when the tragedy befell Ceres. Or maybe they were busy with the street-level fights between the Unchained and the Disciples. But who was I trying to convince—Lauren, or myself?

"The troubling thing is," Lauren said, dark eyes unwavering in their seriousness, "he received an order from someone in the Admiralty to *obscure* the information. To bury it, as if it never existed."

Aunt Marshae's warning returned to me. "Someone protecting Vaughn?" I asked, and my voice was so small and weak, it shamed me.

"The soldier never said a name." Lauren leaned across the gap between us and laid her hand atop mine. "I only wanted to warn you. Someone wanted you to stay in that cell. Be careful, Astrid."

I HAVE BARELY stepped into my room—expansive and comfortable, yet devoid of personality—when there is a knock on the door, pulling me from my thoughts. But it cannot untangle me from my memories.

Someone wanted you to stay in that cell.

Someone is still pulling your strings, stupid girl.

I open the door.

"Astrid." Lily is breathing heavily on the other side. "I've been trying to speak with you one-on-one, but . . . it seems like you've been avoiding me."

My heart wavers, but only for a moment.

When I do not answer, Lily steps toward me, as if, with her diminutive height, she could possibly intimidate me. "*What* is going on?" I look down at her, but she does not falter. "I thought you were upset about Aunt Marshae getting away with the neurobots, but that's not it at all, is it?"

This time I do not know how to respond. How can I tell her about what I have done? About Aunt Marshae's trap at the orphanage I grew up in? About the bullet hole in her temple? About the truth she told me that burns at me from the inside like acid? About Lauren's warning that confirms my deepest fears?

When Lily speaks again, her voice is soft. "How many secrets are you going to hide from me, Astrid?"

"Secrets?" I snap. The word is like lancing an infected wound; now my bitterness rushes out like pus-tinged blood. "You want to talk to me about secrets? What of yours, Lily?" She leans away from me, but I seize her wrist to hold her close.

She freezes, doe eyes wide. The hallway is empty, but someone could come upon us at any moment. "You know?" But then, instead of showing fear or anger or any other emotion I could have imagined, her face . . . breaks. Softens. With *relief.* "I've wanted to tell you so many times . . ."

I relax my grip on her wrist. "Was it your idea or—or maybe Oleander's?"

"I . . . what?"

"Who decided to leave me in Warlord Vaughn's hands? Who buried the location of the Disciples of Judeth base?"

Her eyes widen with horror. "You think I—no, I misunderstood. By the time I'd learned you were being kept at Admiral Drucker's farmstead, Captain Byrne had already launched his rescue mission. I thought you meant . . ." The relief disappears. Now she holds herself wary again.

"Thought what?"

"Let's go into your room, Astrid, and talk . . ."

We can't trust her, little sister, Ringer growls.

"I know!" I snap, pulling Lily by her wrist into my hotel-room habitat with its stifling patterned wallpaper and ivy-green carpeting.

"So you . . . *do* know about me and Oleander?" Lily asks, closing the door behind her.

Damn—I was talking to Ringer, but of course, Lily heard me. I take a deep breath and release it slowly, attempting to calm myself. "Was it Oleander? Is that why he has left your service?"

Lily leans against the back of the door as I settle on the edge of the plush bed with its mountainous pillows and blankets. "Astrid, I was desperate to find you. I tried everything I could. If I had known where the Disciples of Judeth were keeping you . . . I would never willingly leave you in their hands." She shakes her head sadly. "But there *are* secrets I've kept. Things I've wanted to tell you, but haven't been able to."

We cannot fall for her lies, little si—

I speak over him. "Did you kill Matron Thorne?"

A tremor of confusion flickers over her face. "No . . . why would I?"

I run a hand down my face. Aunt Marshae said the same thing. At least with Lily, I can think of no motive. "Then tell me what you came to say."

"Oleander and I . . ."

Her right hand moves to her left, fingers gently brushing against the pale scales of her knuckles. Every second she does not speak is one in which my mind gets the better of me, conjuring images of horrible betrayals.

"What—"

"We're twins," Lily bursts out at last.

And I . . . I laugh. It is such a funny thing to say—to even imagine, the two of them as twins when one is an Aster. But when Lily's face grows more harrowed, my laughter peters out.

She is serious. This is not a joke. She . . . she is telling the truth.

I always thought they were too close, even for Mother and White Guard. She trusted Oleander over all the others, could communicate with him in a way she would not—or could not—with the others. I had asked Oleander if they were in love, but he had demurred, telling me it was not like that. Because . . . because they were siblings.

"But you're not—*how?*" I ask, the word rushing out of me in a whisper.

"Experimental geneassisting," she says, and that pure relief has found its way back onto her face despite the subject. "Everything I told you about me is true. I was born ill. An uncle raised me after my parent died working with the hopes of earning enough money to help me. I joined the Sisterhood in order to afford the surgery I needed to live comfortably." She turns her face up toward the ceiling. "And still I feel the shadow of my nerves on fire, have pain in my legs and back." Without looking, she touches her scales. "And I have a sensitivity to light, an allergy, likely a side effect of the geneassisting."

I do not even know what to say. The idea is ridiculous—an Aster, *here*, in the Sisterhood. The Mother of the Sisterhood, at that! I try desperately to see what I might have missed—she is thin, and her eyes are large—but it is difficult for me to imagine her with translucent skin and prominent veins and a towering height when she is so short. *From the surgery*, I realize.

"By the Goddess's Garden, you're the *Mother . . .*"

She goes on, heedless. "I wanted to tell you, but Oleander was scared." Her voice cracks. "And now . . . now I see why, judging by the disgust on your face." When she meets my gaze, her eyes are full of tears.

"I am not disgusted by you," I snarl. When I was a child, I thought Asters to be diseased because that was what Matron Thorne taught me. As a Little Sister, I would often see them cleaning the Temple and avoid them even though, by then, I had learned the truth. We were meant to be separate, after all—that is what my Auntie said. The first Aster I ever looked at with curiosity—the first I ever truly *saw*—was the one with Hiro and Lito on Ceres just before I killed Mother Isabel III.

Of course, becoming the First Sister of Ceres meant that I worked and lived alongside Asters, and I realized how wrong I had been to listen to Matron Thorne and the Aunties who hated them. They could not give Geans diseases with their mere presence; they were not lazy or stupid, or whatever the actually lazy and stupid soldiers said about them. I had even supported Lily's plan to better integrate them into society on Ceres, giving them equal standing and providing them with shelter and jobs like any other Gean. They had played a crucial role in the Annexation of Ceres, and we had treated them poorly as thanks. I wanted to be different from Mother Isabel III . . .

"I'm not disgusted by you," I repeat. "Just your lies." I rub my eyes as if I can make this all disappear. "I told you from the beginning, all I wanted was the truth."

"This was a truth I wasn't ready to share until now." She does not apologize. Does not fidget. "I joined the Sisterhood because I needed help, but once I realized what I could do inside it . . . Once I realized what I could change, I was ready to fight for that. I wanted to work with you because I saw the same relentless desire in you.

"I always thought you were beautiful. That you were charismatic and opinionated. And you had a good heart, which made you the kind of leader that both the people and the Agora would like. The kind we needed in the Sisterhood." She smiles despite the tears running down her cheeks. "But when Eden told me about what the two of you went through on the *Juno* . . ."

The past is forgotten in a heartbeat. "She told you—" I stop. Swallow my words.

"About how the neural implant had affected you without leaving a mark on her," Lily continues.

My head aches with a high-pitched ringing, and from one moment to the next, I am across the room, boxing Lily in with my arms on either side of her. "What did she tell you!" Ringer demands with my lips.

Lily's eyes widen with fear. "About . . . about . . ."

"About him?" Ringer asks, and I want to stop but I can't.

"Him?" She looks like Eden did in the emergency launch bay on the *Juno* when Ringer—when *I*—threatened to throw her through the hermium barrier into space. She looks like she is staring up at a monster. "I don't . . ."

"What did she tell you!" Ringer barks.

"You're hurting me, Astrid!" Lily tries to pull her wrist away from me—it is in my hand somehow, and I am squeezing tightly, though I never made the decision to do so.

"Stop!" I cry out loud, but not to her. To Ringer. All at once, he releases my body, and I jerk my hand back from Lily as if *she* were hurting *me*. I back away. For her safety.

"I thought . . . I thought we could understand each other." She holds her wrist tenderly in her opposite hand. "You were used. You were hurt and hurting, and still you fought your way to the top. I wanted to be like you. You were an inspiration to me."

I shake my head. "I don't trust you."

She smiles at me. "I love you."

Even my breathing halts. The slightest tap would knock me over.

"I don't want there to be any more secrets between us," she whispers.

I force myself to exhale. To inhale. It is harder than I expect it to be. "You don't know me."

"Then tell me," she says. "Tell me everything."

No more secrets.

What would Lily do if she learned of Ringer? If she learned that I had hidden something from her as big as her being an Aster? And then there is Aunt Marshae . . . Even if I do not tell her about that, someone will soon discover Marshae's body and call the civil guard. I am not so clever as to believe I can outwit them; they will find evidence of my being there, will learn that I was the one who tracked her down and killed her. And then what will happen, when Lily and Warlord Kadir learn I took the neurobots and purposefully kept them?

What if . . . what if I could just lay all these burdens down? I look at Lily, and she . . . smiles at me. Hopeful and kind.

But I find myself reaching past her to the door handle and slipping out into the hallway. Away from Lily and her offer of trust.

The door opens behind me, and Lily calls after me. "Astrid!"

But I do not stop. I march forward, past the waiting White Guards, down the stairs, through the milling Gean soldiers beneath the ceiling of water, and out into Autarkeia. I am unsure of where I am going exactly, but I can hardly stay in the hotel right now when I want nothing more than peace and quiet to think.

Outside the building, certain streets have been blocked off, and while I have half a mind to climb the silver barricades and find my own way around, my need to be away from the hotel drives me down the street that leads to the well-lit island. It is only when I am coming upon the plaza, lights shining brightly, that I realize my foolishness in coming alone.

Someone grabs me and presses my back into a barricade.

I reach for my energy pistol but stop, shocked, when I see who it is. "You're alive—"

Ebba Petrova's face, from the soft sagging of one half to the taut spiderweb scarring of the other, is unified in anger. Despite the pull of her lips, the crinkled eyelid, and the lack of one eyebrow, I *feel* the hatred coiling off of her. "*You,*" she spits like venom.

"Ebba, I—"

Before I can utter another word, Ebba has a knife in her hand. "You stole one of our ships!"

"I can explain—" I start, but Ringer starts to drown everything else out with the strength of his voice.

Let me take care of this, little sister, he growls, but after the way he pressed Lily, I do not want him in control.

Instead, Bruni's neurobots offer me another way, one I know will soothe Ebba.

"I took the ship to retrieve the neurobots," I tell her, "and while I no longer have the ship"—the knife moves closer to me—"I did find the neurobots. You can have them back. I have them in my room, hidden." I could not fathom leaving them behind on Mars, but I also did not imagine reuniting with the Skadivolk here.

"You found them—*all* the Muninn lines?"

"All the ones that were taken by—"

"Bruni's?"

I remember the companionable way they smiled at each other. The way she trusted him without reservation. And that image I had of the two of them as lovers when I consumed Bruni's neurobots . . . Recovering his is about more than his line of knowledge.

"As for Bruni's, I . . . used them."

The knife—and Ebba—jerks back. "*Used* them?"

"I needed—"

"They weren't yours to use!" she shouts, but the knife comes no closer.

"You can take them back," I say, knowing this with certainty but not understanding how I know. *Bruni*, making himself known even now.

But that makes me wonder . . . if she can recall Bruni's, won't she be able to recall Ringer's? And will she be able to recall one line without mixing it with the other?

It suddenly becomes hard to breathe, as if something constricts my lungs. Ringer, I know instinctively, making his displeasure known. Even thinking about removing him is dangerous. I turn my attention to something else, and the pressure on my chest lightens.

"I tried to find out about my family. About where I came from." I am struck by the emotion that rises in me at saying these words aloud to Ebba. "Exiled Skadivolk. My mother abandoned me on Mars."

Ebba remains tense but forces her eyes away from me. Finally, she releases a heavy sigh and slips the knife back into her suit at her wrist. "The name you gave me . . . Hringar Grimson. I looked into it."

I say nothing, afraid that if I break her concentration, she will tell me no more.

"Hringar Grimson belonged to a family from Máni. The family had a bad run-in with the Geans, and Hringar, eighteen at the time, volunteered to join the military to spare his family from a prison camp."

"When was this?" I whisper.

Ebba places her hands on her hips. "About fifty years back."

When the Warlord said the Geans actively recruited among the Skadivolk . . .

"Most of the family followed him to Mars after that. Exiled themselves by choice." Like his sister who gave herself the Scar of Tears, the Astrid of my namesake? "There was nothing more than that in our files, but . . . I did some digging into Gean news from around that time and found him there."

Ringer made a name for himself among the Geans? Could I have found him in Aunt Tamar's library, if I had just looked for him?

"What happened?"

"For a few years, nothing. He was a good soldier. Worked his way up the ranks on various ships. Visited his family in his free time." She shakes her head. "Then one day, the dreadnought he was assigned to exploded while docked above Mars. Killed thousands of Geans, including the captain who had recruited him when his sister refused to join the Sisterhood. Officials determined the cause was sabotage. They suspected Hringar, who had gone on leave the week before. He was hanged for treason."

I press my hand to my chest as if I can touch Ringer. I feel him just beneath my skin, listening. Interested. But even he seems surprised by the news.

"How did I come to possess his neurobots, then?"

Ebba runs a finger along her scarred jawline. "Likely something your parents had access to and gave to you before they surrendered you to the orphanage. But if they cared enough about you to give you a Muninn line, they probably had less of a choice about raising you than it seems."

Even though I deserve nothing from her, the words touch something inside me. That crack in my heart, instead of growing wider as it has been, finds balance. Perhaps one day, it might even begin to heal.

"Once I had a kind of . . . memory? I saw myself . . . taking the neurobots from Hringar." I struggle to speak of the vision I had in the Ironskin.

"Ahhh, I think I see," Ebba says, and my heart swings wildly with hope. "Perhaps the Muninn you were given were not those of Hringar Grimson. Whose eyes did you see through in this memory?"

"A girl . . ." The one he called *little sister*, like he calls me.

"Considering Hringar Grimson died fifty years ago, that girl was probably not you as a child," Ebba says. "The neurobots of that girl were likely given to you by your parents before you were taken, to help you remember who you are."

"But all the memories I have are of Ringer . . . not the girl."

"There's no telling how his Muninn were programmed. If Hringar gave them to her and she to you, then perhaps his are the dominant line kept as a generational memory." Ebba throws up her hands with a sigh. "But honestly, this is all just a guess."

"Hringar . . . you said you found records of his family?"

"Yes."

"Did he have any siblings?"

Ebba scratches her chin as she thinks. "Two sisters."

Ringer inside me stirs.

"Astrid and Valka," both he and Ebba say at the same time.

I stumble into the barricade, and only catch myself at the last moment. My eyes fill with tears, but I can hardly sort through the overwhelming emotions. "I . . . could be from his family."

"Just so." I hear Ebba release another heavy sigh. "I didn't even come here for you. Warlord Kadir invited me to speak with him."

But I can hardly parse this information when everything else within me is so focused on what I have learned. *I had a family.* Even if they had to give me to the orphanage, they *wanted* me. Otherwise, why would they have given me those neurobots?

"Astrid . . ." Ebba's voice is soft, showing a rawness to her I have never seen. But it is gone as quickly as it appeared, shored up by her usual gruffness. "I'll expect those Muninn lines back."

And then she is gone, marching down the street toward the Gean hotel to meet with Warlord Kadir.

Pressing a hand against my stomach, blinking against rising tears, I step away from the barricade.

"Astrid and Valka Grimsdóttir," I whisper aloud. "Will you tell me more about them?"

They were my sisters, Ringer says, *and I would do anything to protect them.*

"That's why you gave them your neurobots. You're the family protector . . ." A thought comes to me unbidden. "You call me your little sister. I know I cannot be, not truly, but . . . are we related?"

Ringer is silent, and I feel him thinking. Perhaps debating what to tell me. And then all at once, his presence is gone. Pulling away from me and retreating into some dark corner of my mind.

I am frustrated by his uncooperative behavior, yet the excitement of learning what Ebba told me remains, unable to be dampened even by Ringer.

A piece of me longs to return to my room, to tell Lily of what I have discovered—but that would be foolish. I must hold my tongue until I puzzle through who I can trust—and who I cannot.

Someone wanted you to stay in that cell.

Someone is still pulling your strings, stupid girl.

Without deciding to go, I find my feet carrying me to the island with its four stone pillars, one from each inner planet. I half expect to see the Synthetic girl again, but the only person who remains is Hiro val Akira.

Perhaps they are who I came to find all along.

"You . . ."

They turn to look at me, and time reverses. We stand on the *Juno*. The Agora waits to try them for treason. Mother Isabel III demands I provide her with Saito Ren's secrets.

They kiss me then, the only time they allow themself to do so. A handwritten note rests in my pocket: *I love you. I never want to leave you.* They whisper their words that slip into my heart like daggers. *I wish I had known that throwing your life away for peace is so much harder when you are in love.*

"Hey," they say, turning fully toward me so that I can see . . . their face is different. Not Ren's, though there is an echo of it in the apples of their cheeks. But just like that, the spell is broken. They hold themself differently, their muscles looser. "Like the setup?" They *speak* differently, in accent and cadence.

"Setup?" I repeat, and my feet carry me to their side. I keep an arm's length between us.

"I mean this," they say, gesturing to the island, river, and bridges. "I was here . . . before. When it had people. This is all new."

I say nothing, but I can tell they are watching me from the corner of their eye. It gives me a chance to study their face up close in the light of the square: the sharp jawline; the short nose; the eyes that have a spark of mischief; the set of their lips, one corner higher than the other.

They laugh. "You always wrinkle your nose when something upsets you."

I quickly flatten my expression, embarrassed to have been caught.

They're very different from Ren. I am not sure if this relieves me or . . . upsets me. But what did I expect?

"This is awkward," I admit.

"Yeah . . . it's like seeing your ex with their new partner who is *way* more attractive than you, and you haven't got any makeup on and your hair's a rat's nest."

"What?"

Hiro shakes their head. "Just me?"

"You are . . ." I start to say.

"What?" They turn fully toward me. When I hesitate, they make a hand gesture as if telling me to go on. "I can handle it. Tell me."

"You always did like my honesty," I say, and find my own lips curling upward. "You are strange, is what I was going to say."

"You definitely aren't the first to tell me that—not even today." Hiro shrugs. Their face falls as they look out over the city, at the empty spots of darkness broken up by neon. "But I'm tired of acting otherwise. I'm done pretending I'm other people," they say, and it is so honest that it exposes the soul of the person I got to know on the *Juno*. The core of who I thought Ren was.

I do see it now . . . yes, Hiro was pretending to be Ren, but they were also offering me small glimpses of themself.

"I think . . . I am too." I turn my gaze so that I look out beside them. "I call myself Astrid now."

Hiro holds out a hand to me. It takes me an embarrassing amount of time to realize they want to shake my hand. "It's nice to meet you, Astrid. I'm Hiro."

Oh, why not? I put my hand in theirs and shake.

But as soon as they pull away, all the negative feelings—not just from my talk with Lily, but stretching back to the moment I realized Hiro had pulled my strings to put me in this position—rush me with such a burn-

ing intensity that I stumble forward and catch myself on the nearby MER-
CURY pillar. My nails dig into the stone. I wish I could tear this whole fake
city down brick by brick.

"Hey, Astrid . . . you okay?"

My hands curl into fists. I can no longer trust because of Hiro. Their
betrayal makes me afraid to love. I believe everyone wants to use me, and
I am afraid that I have begun to use them.

"Astrid—"

I spin toward them, hands held before me. "Everything that I have
done—everything that I have lost—is because of *you!*" I pound my fists
against their chest, but they do not back away.

"You can blame me," they say, "if it helps."

"Stop it!" I snap, hitting them again. I want them to hit me back. I
want to fight with them. Otherwise, it is like it wasn't them who did this
to me . . . it was the Sisterhood. And regardless of my meeting Hiro, I
would have always been used. Would have always lost.

"I hate you," I growl.

They catch my wrist as my hand comes close to their face. "The only
person I hate," they say softly, "is myself."

"I am not even the girl you chose on the *Juno* anymore." My face
burns. I want to cry, but that only makes me madder.

"Aren't you?" they ask. "I chose you because you are a fighter who
seeks peace." Their face may have changed in our time apart, but their
eyes are exactly the same, and they strip me bare. "And I loved you because, despite the broken thing I had become, you still thought I was
worthy of love."

"No," I say, trying to back away. They hold on to my wrist so I cannot
leave. "Don't say that."

"You *have* changed the Sisterhood, Astrid, and you've changed the
Geans too. The cease-fire—that was *you.* Hells, there's a new Warlord
now! And look where you are, think of why you're here."

My struggle weakens. A part of me does not want to escape them.

"I'm sorry you had to go through shit—and I'm sorry I had anything to do with it." Our hands rest between us, our bodies inches apart. "I'm sorry that I deceived you and abused your trust—truly I am. But despite those things, you achieved more than most could have imagined. I say 'most,' because I have always believed in you. Still do, Astrid."

We both stand there in silence. The light around us burns like the sun. We could find comfort in each other, in our past. In the love we shared.

But Hiro is not Ren, and I cannot love someone I do not know.

Even if the love we shared at one time was so real it changed us both.

They release my wrist one finger at a time. We move an arm's length away from each other again. It no longer feels awkward.

"I . . . I must go. Ebba of the moonborn needs me . . ." I trail off, my excuse flimsy.

"Good luck," Hiro says, shoving their hands into the pockets of their iridescent coat.

"And to you, Hiro val Akira."

Those words, at least, are true.

I leave Hiro and the island of light. I make my way back to the Gean hotel, past where Warlord Kadir sits with Ebba Petrova, and up the stairs to my room. Only a little piece of me is upset when I find Lily is no longer here.

But Ebba is downstairs, and so I gather the neurobots from where I hid them in a vent in order to return them to the Skadivolk, where they belong.

CHAPTER 43

LUCE

Luce made a joke earlier about writing a will before we arrived at the coordinates the Synthetics sent, so . . . I guess that's what I'm doing. But if I don't return from the border, then *Camellia* doesn't either, and that's the only thing I have left. I suppose I came into this life on Mars with nothing. Hopefully I'm leaving it as a man who made his mark.

Dire of the Belt

I dream.

Of twisting tunnels in complete darkness, and wolves nipping at my heels as I try to run and find I can't.

Of a wave of silver, rushing over buildings and melting bodies in its path. Of children crying and parents begging. Of twisted faces mowed down by gunfire.

Of Hemlock crumpled on the ground, a broken pile of skin and bones.

Of the soft whooshing from the holosphere an eight-year-old Lito played on loop until it broke, ocean waves cresting and whispering against sand. Of bruises the color of nebulae, and the comfort of a childish game in a closet.

Of the heat of the explosion that sealed Hemlock's fate, and the heavy press of Dire's shoulder against my middle as he carried me into the elevator.

But the strangest dream of all is of fingers gently stroking my forehead and the comforting rasp of fingernails on my scalp. My name, whispered tenderly. I wake with a jolt, and before I can remember, I call for him. "Hemlock—"

But it is Dire. It is always Dire.

He forces food and water on me. Updates me about what's happening, even when I don't ask. Offers me what he can for my nausea and pain when the Camellia's supplies are dwindling with so many people on board. In the small waking moments, I search for myself. I tell myself the story to keep it fresh in my mind.

I am Lucinia sol Lucius. Sorrel killed my brother with his actions and Hemlock by his own hand.

I am Lucinia sol Lucius. Sorrel killed my brother and Hemlock. Again and again.

And then, something changes. I wake in the cubby bunk where I sleep, but the room, usually crammed with Autarkeia's survivors, is empty save for me.

"Dire?" I call.

Someone slips into the room from the hallway. I hardly recognize Xiran from how tired they look. Everything sharp about them has softened with exhaustion. "We're ferrying everyone over to the *Alina.*"

Again, my addled mind takes too long to recognize the name of the single Alliance ship remaining from our original convoy fleeing Autarkeia. "They'll fit?"

"We finally got in contact with Pallas," Xiran says, tossing their long black hair over their shoulder. I briefly remember Dire saying something about Pallas responding, but the situation being—for lack of a better word—dire. "They're overtaxed as it is, but we don't have much of a choice. *Alina* will take the refugees there."

"Then what's the plan for *Camellia?*"

"Back the way we came," Xiran says softly.

The metallic voice returns to me. After Autarkeia, we all received a message like the warning to evacuate, only this one called for the leaders of humanity and sent coordinates in the asteroid belt.

"Dire means to represent the Alliance," I say, only half a question.

Xiran nods with more than a dash of worry in their expression. "That he does."

WHEN WE ARRIVE at the coordinates, the already strained mood intensifies as the crew sees their old home, now swallowed by the shadow of a giant Synthetic ship.

"The meeting . . . is there." Dire, normally untouchable, has a tinge of sorrow in his tone. I slip out of my seat and touch his arm, though I doubt my presence offers him any comfort.

"They're fucking with us."

"—showing off what they took—"

"—respond with force!"

"Quiet," Dire says, and while his voice is soft, everyone hears him and obeys. "If we want a future for the Alliance, we must bargain." His eyes fall to the command screens where Autarkeia floats. He looks at the station like it is his lost lover. "I'll take a small group down with me. The rest will stay with the *Camellia*, ready to run if necessary."

The command center breaks into chatter once again.

"—can't risk your life—"

"—without you!"

"What if they kill you?"

Dire lets them debate, his decision already made.

"Can I come with you?" I whisper at his side.

He looks at me, and I at him. So many differences stretch between us—years and experience and societies on opposite sides of the war—and yet we both share the same haunted sense of loss.

Grief has honed us into blades.

"Do you know what made Autarkeia special, Lucinia?" he asks.

I shake my head.

"Everyone was equal." His face takes on a deeper shadow. "Everyone got to choose what they did. How they lived. And how they risked their lives."

His words bring Hemlock to mind, and I close my eyes for a moment to fight the rising tears. "I'm coming with you," I say firmly.

EVERYTHING IS BEAUTIFUL, and yet everything is wrong. Autarkeia is a land untouched by humanity, when it was humanity that gave it its spark.

Dire takes the sight better than I expected; his mourning pushed aside, now every centimeter of him is the hardened leader. According to the Synthetic representative—a girl who looks my age, whom Dire seems to recognize, a story I'll no doubt have to beg out of him—we are the first group to arrive. They show us the neutral area, an island surrounded by silver water, for the discussion to come, and grant us a furnished apartment building for our small party of a dozen people. When the girl says we'll have access to whatever we need, I doubt her—until I find pain patches among our supplies. Then I'm beyond grateful for the Synthetic's foresight.

I have no interest in wandering these haunted streets, so I keep to my room, resting for two days, until the Synthetics announce another party has arrived. "Guests of Autarkeia," the girl says, standing in the entrance on the ground floor of our apartment building—though her words simultaneously appear on any of our electronic devices with screens. "Warlord Kadir and Mother Lilian I, leaders of the Geans, are on approach to Autarkeia." When the announcement comes a half hour later that the Geans have arrived, Dire and a few others go out to meet them. I follow along.

After that, others arrive more quickly. The moonborn show up the next day—I know nothing about them, and my curiosity pushes me to visit them alongside Dire once they've settled in. They strike me as less fortunate outlaws, though their leader, a gray-haired woman with a half-scarred face, has a swagger to her that strangely reminds me of Hiro, of all people. When Ebba Petrova bawdily says she'd like to get to know Dire better, he shocks me by accepting. I end up leaving the moonborn's building before he does.

The next morning, a Synthetic announcement wakes me. "Guests of Autarkeia." The girl's voice comes from my compad, startling me. "The Elder and Shield, leaders of the Asters, are on approach to Autarkeia." Suddenly, that strange purgatory I've found myself in for the past few days cracks, and reality comes rushing back in.

I am Lucinia sol Lucius. Sorrel killed my brother and Hemlock. And I am terrified of what he means to do here.

By the time I am fully awake and ready to set out, a pair of magnification goggles on my head, the Aster arrival announcement echoes over the city. And seconds later, the Synthetic girl's musical accent: "Guests of Autarkeia, the Aster delegation has arrived."

It takes me far longer than I'd like to admit to climb over one of the Synthetic barricades, worm my way through the streets, and find the building the Asters have been assigned—a high-ceilinged single-story structure that looks more like a warehouse than a home. Using the goggles, I spot bioluminescent plants at the doorway, but only darkness within. Like the apartments we have, this place seems to be specially tailored to the needs of its occupants.

I find a chair in a shop with broken windows—the glass has been cleared, but the breach remains—and drag it to a spot behind a barricade where I can sit and spy on the Asters through one of the gaps in the structure.

After the first couple of hours, I feel foolish. What exactly am I looking for? What could I possibly see that would prove me right, when I already know how awful Sorrel is?

Hemlock, my heart says, each two-part beat his name. *Hem. Lock.*

If he's alive . . . would Sorrel have brought him?

But hope is a disease with no cure. I should've learned that lesson after losing Lito.

At the end of the day, I haven't seen Hemlock. But I see Castor, moving right alongside Sorrel, their shoulders pressed together conspiratorially.

HOURS PASS. I don't move. My pain patch begins to fail, and still, I watch. Even though this place looks like it's always night outside of the plaza, the daytime hours are behind me. I'm beginning to nod off when an announcement startles me awake.

"Guests of Autarkeia, the Icarii delegation is on approach to Autarkeia."

Within sixty seconds, there is movement in front of the Aster building.

My breathing goes shallow. It's only because of their white hair that I notice them—they're all dressed in dark clothes so as to blend into the shadows.

Sorrel, his hair falling into one of his eyes, and Castor, with his usual ponytail, stand out from the others with their traditional long braids. The group is large—all of the delegation?—but they quickly break apart into smaller factions of a dozen or so. Efficiently, four of the groups move deeper into the city in different directions. A moment later, drones zip by overhead, tailing them.

Sorrel's group, the fifth, waits until the drones are gone before heading toward the neutral area of the island.

No drones shoot after them.

I follow as quickly as I can using the side streets. The barriers keep me from completely reaching them, but also from being spotted. I wish I had my cane, but it's long gone—left behind on the Aster ship that Dire's crew blew up when fighting Sorrel's Black Hive. When I come across a metal pipe, I snatch it up and use it to steady myself.

The group heads directly to the plaza. As they approach one of the bridges, they speak with each other, too low for me to hear.

I'm sure pheromones pass back and forth as well as words. I start looking for a way to get closer without being spotted when the group splits. Asters I don't recognize move onto the island, while Castor heads down one of the alleys—toward the Gean building? No, toward the empty Icarii building, set aside for their arrival. Then Sorrel barks a command in the Aster language, and the two who were checking the stone pillars rush off together, leaving Sorrel all alone.

Sorrel darts around the whole of the island, stopping in front of each pillar only long enough to remove something from his pocket and stick it on the back near the base. From this angle, I can't make out what it is. Even the magnification goggles don't help.

I can't come any closer without being spotted, so I'll just have to wait for him to leave before I investigate what he's put there.

I hear something at my back. I turn—and find two Asters behind me.

They're on me before I can even scream. One jerks the metal pipe away from me, seeing it as a weapon, while the other claps a hand over my mouth. I struggle against them, but find it's no use—it's two against one, and I'm already in pain and exhausted.

One holds my legs, the other my arms, and together, they haul me over the silver barrier.

They carry me across the nearest bridge and set me down in front of Sorrel on the central island. When they rip my goggles off, I squint against the bright flare of light, but then Sorrel's shadow falls over me.

"I knew someone was following me," he says, tone light as if this is a pleasant reunion. "I didn't expect it to be an Icarii rat."

"Fuck you," I mutter. I try to summon more confidence than I feel. "I know what you're planning!"

"Oh?" He squats down so he can look at me eye to eye.

"Do you think the Synthetics don't know? That they don't see everything that happens here on Autarkeia?"

"I don't think that's really what you want to talk about."

He's right, but I don't want him to know that. Still, the questions form before good sense smothers them. "Where's Hemlock? What did you do with him?"

"Do you really want to know," Sorrel asks, his eyes glowing from all the light around us, "how he died?"

I stop struggling. It is difficult to even breathe.

"We hanged him," Sorrel says, "as a traitor to the Aster people."

Hanged him. Traitor. The words are twin bullets that lodge themselves in my heart.

I am Lucinia sol Lucius. Sorrel killed my brother and Hemlock.

He hanged him as a traitor.

One moment I'm on the ground, the next I've thrown myself at Sorrel. One fist balls in his dark clothes to hold me steady, the other crashes against his face. But then his hand finds my neck and tightens just a little—just a warning, that he could crush me if he wanted to.

"Don't," Sorrel snarls. "I regretted letting you slip through my fingers on Vesta. Regretted not being able to hang you alongside Hemlock, especially after you led so many of the Black Hive into Dire's trap." My legs waver beneath me as the sorrow wells up. "But now I'm glad that you outwitted me." He leans forward to embrace me like a lover and whisper in my ear. "You see, I need you, Lucinia sol Lucius."

"Let go—"

My protest dies on my lips when he says, "Have you seen your brother?"

Confusion gives way to that disease . . . hope. "Lito?"

"Resurrected by the Synthetics," he says with a maddening smile.

I should fight him. Should shove him away or strike him. Bite him even, when he is so close to my face. But my already-sore body is shaking with trepidation. I stand at the edge of an airlock, about to stumble into the void.

"Perhaps the Synthetics *do* know what I have planned. Perhaps they *are* watching our every move." Sorrel's hand is still on my neck, more a caress than a threat. "But they won't stop me from blowing every leader of humanity into the black if you hold any value to Lito."

Blowing every leader of humanity into the black— He was planting bombs. That's why he had Castor, who knows how to build them, come to Autarkeia with him—thousand gods, he's going to kill the Gean leaders and the moonborn and maybe even Dire, and he thinks—

Does he think my life will hold back the Synthetic retribution the Asters would face?

The smallest piece of me whispers, *Would it?*

If it were Lito . . . if it were *really* Lito . . . would it?

My brother would fling himself into a trap for me. I know this without a doubt. And so it is that surety that causes doubt to rise in me.

Will my life, in Sorrel's hands, give him the opportunity to assassinate the leaders of humanity?

I look at the two Asters standing close by, both Black Hive in dark clothes. I have no idea what they've suffered—but I do know they have, and now they refuse to suffer anymore. The Harbinger is the culmination of all their years of pain, all their helplessness, and those who could possibly stand against him don't. They simply watch the bodies fall and hope for a better world when all of this is over.

"No," I force through numb lips. I refuse . . . I refuse to let Sorrel use me to do unspeakable things.

I am a sick and dying girl. I can't fight him. I am not Lito. But standing here in his arms, I realize I don't have to be Lito. All I have to do is be willing to stand before him and say no.

Even if he kills me for it.

Especially if he kills me for it, leaving him with nothing to use against the Synthetics.

"N-no!" I shout, and my hand flies to his belt where he keeps a knife—

My fingers brush against the hilt. But I am not swift. Every movement is a struggle. And his eyes widen when he realizes what I'm doing, just before his face clouds over with malice.

His fist crunches against my face. I hit the ground hard. The pain radiates from my hip through the rest of my body. I feel blood gushing from my nose, over my lips, and into my mouth, salty and hot.

Sorrel leans down over me, hand back around my throat. I spit into his face. Red streaks his cheek.

"Do it," I growl. He doesn't tighten his grip. "Do it! Because I won't let you use me." I smile at him with scarlet-streaked teeth. "You're going to have to kill me."

He shakes his head, looking me over with a mix of anger and awe. "Why won't you submit?" he whispers.

"I'm doing this for everyone else," I growl with all the strength I have left. "For the Asters, who have suffered. For Hemlock, who died without seeing his dreams come true. For my brother, who might have been reborn among the Synthetics. For Ofiera, who counseled me to hold on to my rage when all else failed. For Dire and the Alliance, who lost their home but not their purpose. And for Castor—" Who I once loved.

"Then I'll *make* you submit," he hisses.

I am so accustomed to pain, you would assume I don't dread it—but when Sorrel's fist crashes into my stomach and I crumple, my only thought is that I wish I could drift away.

CHAPTER 44
THE TWINS

I will go to treat with the Synthetics alongside our Shield. We cannot let the opportunity to show that the Asters are a unified, strong people go to waste.

Father Cedar of the Aster Elders

I go to him, expecting rage. Expecting brokenness, after losing Ofiera. Expecting, at the very least, to have to fucking prove myself to him, like I have to everyone else in my life.

Instead, when my small termite craft docks in the larger *Hornbeam*, I get relief. His shoulders slouch. His face softens. His pheromones unfurl in welcome. "Castor," he says, and his hopes are in my name. His hand envelops my shoulder. "I've missed you." I smell the truth on him.

Behind him, a single Aster Elder lurks in his blue half cloak, but if Father Cedar's expecting a show of loyalty from me, he's in for a fucking surprise. Before he presses the issue, the Harbinger lifts a hand and . . . waves Cedar away. "I'll speak with Castor alone. Return to your room and make yourself comfortable."

Cedar hesitates, but only for a moment. Then he disappears deeper into the ship. I don't miss the Aster warriors at his back, following a bit too closely.

"You called me, so I came." I'm taller than him, but only by a little. Yet somehow, his presence seems to tower over me.

"Listen to me, Castor." His hand comes to my face. Holds my cheek like I imagine Hemlock might, if he were here. The thought of my uncle is a sharp knife in tender flesh, a wound that hasn't had time to scar over. "We're going to the asteroid belt."

"To meet with the Synthetics?"

His cold eyes burn. "To change everything."

Trust me, his pheromones say, pleasant and sweet. *I need you.*

But I hesitate . . . and he senses that.

He pulls something from his belt—the hilt of a mercurial blade. For half a second, I think he's going to stab me here in the silver hangar of an outlaw ship for my lack of faith . . . but instead he holds it out to me.

"This was Ofiera's," he says as I reach for it. I stop short. "I had an agent . . . fetch it for me from Cytherea." He looks at the blade as if reconsidering the gift, but then he pushes it toward me. "I want you to help me, Castor."

The last time he asked anything of me, I questioned him, and he left me on Mars. This time he gives me the ultimate gift: a symbol of revenge.

Now I don't hesitate.

I take Ofiera's mercurial blade. "Tell me what you need me to do."

DESPITE THE WAY it feels as if my shattered heart cuts me from the inside with each step I take, it's not Astrid and the worrisome news she reported that I think of when I leave the Gean embassy; it's my twin. I tried earlier—desperately so—to meet with the Aster delegation, but they refused me. The only thing I can imagine is that Sorrel intercepted my request and is determined to keep Castor away from me.

I still don't know why. Why does Sorrel want him? Is all of this simply to weaken me, or because of the skills our uncle taught him in the Under of Ceres? Both prospects frighten me.

Once most of the Gean delegation has gone to sleep, the rest ensconced in their rooms, I hold my White Guard in the hotel with my neural implant, something I learned through trial and error—I can force them to follow commands almost blindly—while I sneak out. Now I take to the haunted streets of Autarkeia, making sure the hood is low enough to hide my face, risking the identity I've built over the years—everything to me—just for a chance to see Castor.

I'll force my brother to talk with me, or tell me with his own words that he doesn't want to. I won't let Sorrel stop me this time.

I'm fucking tired of being trapped in your shadow. The accusation is like a missing tooth, and I can't help but continually stick my tongue into the gap to taste the blood. We've fought in our lives—of course we have—but nothing like this. I have to make things right with him. I have to . . .

I stop short at the sight of a lanky figure coming directly toward me. It's like thinking about him has summoned him.

"Castor."

"Pollux," he says.

The space between us feels larger than just this desolate street.

"Are you coming to see me?" I ask, but a ripple in his pheromones tells me that's not it. What am I sensing from him? Chagrin? "What are you . . ."

Then I see it. The bag over his shoulder. That careful blankness on his face. He's not here for me. He's on a mission from the Harbinger.

My hands curl into fists. "What has he asked you to do?"

He doesn't answer.

"Is that what I think it is?" I nod to the bag.

He drops his gaze.

"Is it for Kadir?" Castor's hatred of Astrid is strong but personal, and I can't imagine the Harbinger would bother with her. "Why? Warlord Vaughn is dead, and I'm in charge—"

"You're not—" He starts, but stops himself.

"Is it for me, then?"

His eyes find mine. They shine gold in the artificial light. "Never."

"But it could unintentionally hurt me." I speak as calmly as possible despite the storm of betrayal raging inside me. Castor has never responded to anger well, and so I have learned to speak softly even when I feel like screaming.

When we were children, he once told me that he was all the dark things I wasn't, as if I never felt the same impotent rage he did at our sheltered lives. As if I didn't want to swing my fists at the Aster children who wanted nothing to do with me because of my illness. As if I didn't dream of setting the Aster Elders on fire when they looked at me with pity but offered not a shred of help.

We are twins. We have always been twins, even in our darkness.

"*Sfonakin*, I'm part of the Gean delegation. What the Harbinger wants you to do could kill me."

His pupils narrow, and he sucks in a breath as if to say something. I wait while feeling anything but patient. "I wouldn't let it . . . I was going to tell you, and . . . and it's not so blunt a plan as you're thinking."

"What, then?" I take a step toward him. He hesitates as if about to flee.

When he steps closer, I take it as a tiny victory. He lifts the flap of his bag and reaches in to pull something out. Amidst the various hand-wired devices I recognize as his work—*bombs*, which a part of me knew he would be making for Sorrel—he flashes the hilt of a mercurial blade.

"He's making you his assassin."

"He's trusting me with a mission of my own."

"Ah, Sorrel needs a scapegoat, then."

"No," he snaps, but it sounds like he's trying to convince himself more than me. "The Icarii will."

At once I see the plan. That's an Icarii blade. And if no one catches him, whoever he kills with it will be the victim of Icarii brutality. Sorrel means to shatter the cease-fire between the Icarii and Geans. To restart the war, greater than before.

"And what of the Synthetics?" I ask, the only part of the plan I can't figure out. Certainly they're listening, even now.

"He's taking care of it." Everything about him is too unreadable for me to understand. "There are others, going to the Forges. Claiming the Engineborn weapons there."

He takes another step toward me, and I move to stand in his way. "No," I say.

"Pollux, what—"

"I'm not going to let you do this, Castor."

His lip curls. "Because of her?"

"No, Castor." I tip up my chin. "Because, even if I'm not a Gean, it's abhorrent."

"*Sfonakin*—"

"Do you know what I—what we Sisters—faced in the Sisterhood? The mental conditioning. The physical pain. The rape."

He stiffens at that last one. "I . . ."

"I did what I had to, all so I could arrive at *this* point. I'm the Mother now, and I *will* change things. For both the Asters and the girls in the Sisterhood." I straighten as much as I can, ignoring the protests of my lower back muscles. "You once asked me what I would do if I had to choose. Well, I'm showing you. It's not right for me to turn my back on the Sisterhood or the Asters—not when I can help *both*. Certainly you, who has also found love among the *siks*, can understand that."

He falls silent and looks at his bag. His pheromones project his distress, even though his face is blank.

"I don't think you really want to do this either, Castor." I reach out for his arm. "You want to honor Hemlock's memory? You want to help the Asters advance? Then don't help the Harbinger make this war worse."

WHY? WHY DOES she have to get in my fucking way?

She puts her hand on my arm, and I jerk away like it hurts.

"I have to do this—" The look on the Harbinger's face when he gave me Ofiera's blade. He's trusting me to uphold my part of the plan, to make sure the Icarii are blamed for the assassinations of the Gean delegation.

As for the Synthetics, I did my best making the blocking devices that scramble recording equipment, but I have no idea how advanced the Synthetics are and no clue as to whether my handmade devices will work on them. Still, the Harbinger swore he had another way of neutralizing them—and I have to trust that he was telling the truth, that his teams will be able to get the Engineborn weapons we need from the Forges.

Just like he was trusting me to do this.

I step around her, and she moves into my path. Again.

"Get out of the way, Pollux."

"Are you going to kill me, brother?"

I feel unending horror at the idea.

"Because you will have to, if you're determined to do this." There's the smallest shimmer of gold in her dark brown eyes, a hint at the person she was. "I understand that you feel like you've not been able to help. That you've been trapped in my shadow. That Hemlock kept you from your destiny, even if it was because he loved you."

"*Fuck* Hemlock—" I choke out, feeling like I'm going to cry.

"You're right that Hemlock's way wasn't ideal," she admits. "He hesitated, and was oftentimes too slow to act."

Yes, I want to say. It's everything I've thought and more.

"But the Harbinger's way is not ideal either." Her words call me back to a time before all this, when we were just two children in the Under of Ceres. Us against the universe, ready to burn it to the ground to build a new world. "Look at what he's done. His rash decisions. How he's made things worse. Even *you* know this."

If he hadn't released the Genekey virus . . . if he hadn't used the Engineborn weapons . . .

What will come next? *If he hadn't assassinated the Geans in front of the Synthetics?*

"Fuck." I drop my hands from the bag and my head onto Lily's shoulder. "I can't . . . If I don't do it, someone else will. Someone who might not care about you getting hurt."

"I know. That's why we have to stop him altogether."

"Fuck."

She holds my head in her arms and strokes my hair. "*Sfonakin,*" she says, and then she whispers my childhood name accompanied by the pheromones that complete it.

I respond in the same way, with a name that only I know now that Hemlock is dead.

After a moment, she places her hands on my cheeks and guides my face from her shoulder. She looks me in the eyes, determination written on her face. "We must stop Sorrel from what he's doing."

She's right. I nod. "He's—" I begin to explain.

A scream from my nightmares tears through the air. I would recognize her voice anywhere. I've replayed that video over and over— the one where Luce takes the Genekey virus, and everything we were— everything we could have been—shatters in a heartbeat.

A beautiful soul damned because of my desire to make the Icarii pay at any price.

She's here? my mind says. *Save her,* my heedless heart responds.

And then I'm running—away from my twin, away from my mission, everything I thought I wanted—and entering the plaza with its piercing lights.

I'm on the bridge when I see—

She's on the ground before the Harbinger in the center of the island, nose streaming twin trails of red. His boot arcs into her ribs, and she coughs a spray of blood like crimson mist—

I don't think, I just move. "Sorrel!" I scream, and he looks up just in time to see me slam into him.

His fist grazes my temple. Mine slams into his chest. But we both stumble away from each other before too much damage is done.

Apart, he breathes heavily, his eyes dark in the deep sockets of his face. He's *tired* from beating Luce . . . and she lies cast aside and forgotten, the broken remnants of what was once a girl on the cobblestones. I reach into the bag before I'm even aware of doing so and withdraw my one weapon—the mercurial blade that flares to life between us.

"What the fuck do you think you're doing?"

"Castor—"

"Don't you even fucking *look at her*!"

His mouth flattens. He straightens himself as he catches his breath. "Did you do what you were tasked with, Castor? Did you finish your mission?"

From the corner of my eye, I see Lily has caught up and is moving toward Luce. She kneels down beside her and pulls Luce's head into her lap. Luce lets out a little whimper, says something I can't hear, but I can smell the shock from Lily, hard as a fist to the chest.

Luce whispers something with split lips and, hands bloody, reaches up to touch Lily's face, leaving two fingerprints of red on her cheek.

My twin turns wide eyes on the Harbinger. "Sorrel," she says, soft and full of fear. "Is what she says true?"

I feel it from her. I smell it on her. A horrible suspicion. A truth I don't want to know.

"What did you do to Hemlock?" Lily asks.

And the Harbinger . . . stinks like guilt.

"You said he didn't make it off Autarkeia . . ." I trail off. He said what he needed to say. He manipulated me because he needed my technical expertise, and I danced like a fucking fool to his tune—

"Castor." The heat in the Harbinger's eyes is the only warning of what's to come. "You never did know how to sacrifice."

His full concentration slams down on me, and I fall to my knees. HATE DISAPPOINTMENT RAGE RAGE RAGE. His neural implant seeks to crush mine. His pheromones stopper my throat and choke me. It's like his attack on Mars but so much worse. Lily clutches her head. The mercurial blade threatens to slip through my fingers, but I hold tight to it, my only hope of a weapon.

My uncle's face surfaces, full of guilt and sorrow. Luce snarls at me, *This will be the last time I ever speak to you, Castor.* Now she is dying.

A thousand forks in the road, a thousand wrong turns.

"You will never be strong enough to stand up to me," Sorrel says, and his voice comes to me from inside my own head. Thumping in time with my heart. Echoing and all-consuming. "I already have what I need from you! I'll finish this myself if I have to!"

I almost vomit from the pressure as he forces me to bow before him. RAGE RAGE RAGE pounds down on me like a thousand fists, like a hundred thousand stones, burying me alive in a tomb of my own making, and I am helpless to fight back.

But not her . . . she comes to her knees, blood-streaked and fierce. She's battered and beaten and dying, but still fighting. After everything, still fighting.

Her fingernails dig into the gap between two cobbles as she prepares to stand.

"Enough!" I shout, and then I do vomit, sour acid burning my throat and bringing tears to my eyes. I submit to Sorrel in body and words and pheromones, dropping the hilt of Ofiera's mercurial blade and letting it roll away from me. "I'm done fighting you!"

He cautiously relents. I tremble as I press my face to the ground before me. As I show myself to be the obedient subordinate he desires. "I swear, I won't stand against you again." It's the truth. Even my pheromones tell him so.

"You've finally learned your lesson?" he asks, composed but detached. "You won't try to kill me?"

"No," I say, and again it is the truth. I tip my head up and meet his gaze. Hold it as my jaw clenches tight. "But she will," I say, nodding behind him, and he turns with fear growing and consuming him—

She is an ember catching fire. El jinete pálido del apocalipsis riding him down. The mercurial blade I rolled in her direction now in her hand, I call it forth in standard formation, and La Peste slams the sword beneath his ribs, up into his heart.

He shudders. Stops. Everything about him fades in an instant.

He falls to the ground, the blade still in his chest.

The world has gone oddly silent, or perhaps it's just me. Luce gingerly lowers herself to the ground, while I push myself into a crouch. She needs medical attention. We need to alert the Synthetics.

But the only thing I can think of is the first word I ever said to her.

"Hi," I say.

"YOU," I SNAP at the two Aster warriors, frozen in dismay. I put every ounce of authority into my voice and my pheromones. "Fetch Dire of the Belt and the outlaws. Tell them of the Black Hive assaulting the Forges. Stop them from taking the Engineborn weapons."

"You're not an Elder," one begins, but the other touches their shoulder.

"Do you want the Aster people to die this night," I ask, "or do you want to live?"

They flee in the direction of the outlaw building.

I turn back to the heart of the island, to everyone crumpled and broken. My gaze falls on Sorrel.

He scrabbles in his own blood toward his belt, reaching, grasping, desperate. I watch as he pulls out a handmade device, wires protruding.

I kick his hand. Despite my weakness, it is enough, and the detonator to all Castor's work goes spinning away into the darkness.

"You're not setting off any bombs tonight, Harbinger."

He looks up at me with glazed eyes. Even dying, he does not look weak. Just tired.

"Fi?" he asks, and I suck in a sharp breath through my teeth. The softness in his tone breaks me when I thought I was already broken. "Fi, did you . . . did you come back for me?"

He sees a human in front of him. Brown hair. Sad eyes. He sees the woman he wishes were here.

There are moments in which I calculate every move I make—would the identity called Lily do this? Say this? And then there are moments when I act without thought, simply because I know it is the right thing to do. Coming to this square was one of the latter . . . as is this.

I kneel down beside him. Find his hand, and take it in my own. He was a friend and an enemy. A legend and a nightmare. Now he is just a dying Aster who wants the comfort of his deceased wife.

"I'm here, darling," I say.

"Fi . . ." Tears roll down the side of his face, drop to mingle with the blood. His bloodstained lips curl into a smile. "My Fi."

"Now we'll always be together," I say, but he is already gone.

Death is the happiest I've ever seen the Harbinger.

I sit with him for a time, quiet. Overwhelmed. I fear that time has stopped, and that a part of my soul will always be trapped here, holding a dead man's hand. A crystallized moment that I'll be able to picture for the rest of my life.

But that moment, like all that I have captured, passes.

"EMERGENCY," a mechanical voice rocks through the station. "EMERGENCY."

And seconds later, the Synthetic girl's musical accent: "Guests of Autarkeia, come to the square immediately. The Icarii delegation has arrived."

CHAPTER 45

HIRO

When I was a boy, there was nothing I loved more than successfully programming an AI to reach the Marian Threshold. When it joined with the Singularity, I felt like a piece of me did too.

Excerpt of an interview with Souji val Akira
for the newscast Icarii Voice

◇——————◇◇——————◇

After catching up with Dire, I'm given a room far nicer than the one I stayed in during my time on Autarkeia, and while it's got all the furniture I could need—a sofa, a dining table with four chairs, a bed—it feels staged. What outlaw wouldn't have crammed their place full of necessities, instead of carefully curating them downstairs for anyone to take? Who owns this much furniture but no repair kit or tools? It keeps me awake long after the others retire to sleep. Well—that and the fact that Luce hasn't returned from whatever walk she went on.

When the announcement comes that the Icarii are approaching—that *my father* is almost here—I wander down the hall to her room, the latest of my several attempts, only to find it's still dark and empty. Dire said that after everything—fleeing Ceres and then Autarkeia a little over two weeks later, surviving Sorrel's plan to take over the *Camellia* and claim the Engineborn weapons, and the countless deaths she must've seen from those events alone—she'd become far more introspective and standoffish. Especially after they left Hemlock on Vesta.

Hemlock. Thinking of that monster in the basement who completely changed my life . . . it's difficult to accept that he's gone. He somehow seemed unmovable, like he'd be wandering the universe long after I was dead and forgotten. And for Luce, who clung to him after losing her brother . . .

The guilt comes, thick and smothering, when I remember how often I shoved Luce away when she was desperately reaching out to me. We spent six months tethered together as we worked Cytherea, and I'd ignore her messages whenever I felt like it. I'm afraid that Lito, if he's still in that Synthetic body, will be disappointed in how my mourning him caused his sister another layer of pain when she deserved even a tiny spot of support.

The longer I wait, the more my guilt turns to worry. Maybe Luce is avoiding me—unlikely, as she's far more the type to stomp by me and make a point of ignoring me. Maybe she found somewhere else to sleep—and while I hope the girl had a good time, even if it's just one fun night, I somehow doubt it.

Once I start pacing, I move to the open ground floor of the building, my gravboots making a satisfying click with each step I take. Even if the Icarii are here, I should search for her. She could be lost somewhere in the city. Or hurt. I should—

Something rushes in through the apartment building's glassless window and stops in front of me. Its weapon-like shape makes me instinctually flinch for cover, but the way it hovers reminds me of a drone. Though if it *is* a drone, it's unlike any I've ever seen, sharp and pronged like a three-sided arrowhead. In the center, protected by the barbs, floating strangely, is a moving mass of silver . . . liquid? It reminds me of the weird river around the island.

"HIRO VAL AKIRA," a mechanical voice speaks from the drone. "WE REQUIRE YOUR AID."

It zips back out the window, not waiting to see if I follow, and I rush out the front door, hoping I'll be able to keep up with the damn thing. But outside I find it has paused to wait for me.

It flies down the path toward the square, and I run after it.

"EMERGENCY," the station reports, echoing over the Autarkeian intercoms and the compad in my pocket. "EMERGENCY."

"What the fuck is happening!"

As if in answer to my rhetorical question, Mara speaks on the tail end of the warning. "Guests of Autarkeia, come to the square immediately. The Icarii delegation has arrived."

Is this what the drone needs me for? I wonder. *Is my father here with his weapon?* But that thought is soon crushed as I cross the bridge and set foot on the central island.

There's blood on the cobblestones. Luce, covered in gore, breath coming in wet gasps. Sorrel, on the ground, a hole in his chest . . . dead. Castor and one of Hemlock's agents, whom I know as Pollux through image alone, try to administer aid to Luce.

I kneel beside Luce, my leggings soaking up her blood. "What happened!"

"She—"

Before Castor has time to answer, the arrowhead drone spins circles above us. When I look at it, it turns to point at one of the four bridges off the island . . . the one that leads toward the docks.

It doesn't want me here. It still has something to show me.

But . . . I can't leave Luce like this.

"We need a first aid kit. Does anyone have one?"

"At the hotel!" Pollux says, trying to push herself up and flinching as her knees pop loudly.

"I'll go—I'll get it!" Castor's up and ready to run, but his sister grabs his pant leg.

"My White Guards—I'll have them bring it."

Her White Guards? But I have no time to puzzle through how Hemlock's agent is now the Mother, especially as others file onto the island—Geans in navy, *not* White Guards.

The arrowhead drone continues to try to get my attention, but I focus only on Luce. I check her over as best I can, but I'm no doctor, and what wounds I can see appear superficial. But internally? Her breath rattles, and there's blood on her lips. I know there's something wrong . . .

"I think we need a medbag," I say, fearing the Synthetics don't have one of those lying around.

"Hiro!" Mara's shout rings across the courtyard.

Thank the thousand gods, the one Synthetic I can reason with—

But as soon as I stand, she rushes to my side and grabs my shoulders with a grip stronger than I suspected her capable of. Lito lurks behind her, expressionless.

"The Harbinger used the Icarii approach as a distraction to plant bombs throughout Autarkeia and send teams to assault the Engineborn Forges to claim the weapon stores. Dire of the Belt and the outlaws are currently engaged with them. We sent drones to safely disable the explosives and to repel the Black Hive, but the Icarii landed and are on their way—"

"There are *bombs* in—"

"The weapon," she gasps, cutting me off, "*is here.*"

I force myself to forget about the Harbinger and everything else she just said. "If you knew they had the weapon, why didn't the Synthetics just blast the Icarii ship out of the void? Or vent the airlock with them inside?"

Her face takes on that ageless, almost-angry look. "There are thousands of ways we have predicted this could end," she says, and for a moment, I'm talking to the Singularity instead of Mara. "Probabilities of war. Of total human annihilation."

"Of *what*—"

"Out of all those chances, the only one that could possibly lead to peace is to have all the leaders of humanity on Autarkeia, willing to discuss a shared future." Her eyes shine silver like the river. "We will not take away that chance, however small the percentage, even if it is what protects us best."

"Got it," I mutter. And, I realize, the Synthetics would never be the ones to break their own treaty by firing first. That would be *certain* war when they're hoping for the peaceful solution.

Still, that phrase she said—let slip, in a way—crawls beneath my skin. *Probabilities of war. Of total human annihilation.* I do not like the sound of that at all.

When Mara stiffens, eyes going wide, I realize the Singularity has faded and she's back in control. "He's here," she whispers, and I turn in time to see the Icarii approach.

My father leads the way out of the dark streets and into the light of the plaza. While Commander Beron val Bellator and his duelists stop before the bridge, Souji val Akira continues onto the island.

Everyone is silent. Warlord Kadir at the head of the Gean soldiers; the moonborn, lurking silently on the far side of their bride; the newly arrived White Guards with the first aid kit; Castor, holding Luce to his chest; Pollux, standing over them like a protector; and Astrid, dressed like she's ready for war.

Seeing my father . . . shatters something within me.

I try to remember the last time I spoke with him. Not the last time I saw him—which was through the sights of a long-range HEL gun. Not the last time he saw me—because he certainly watched as Command turned me into Saito Ren, never appearing but making his will known through Beron's actions nonetheless. When was the last time I fought with him? What were our final words to each other? I rack my brain and find . . . I can't remember.

I think . . . I think maybe it was the day Lito and I went to Luce's apartment during our weeklong leave before we shipped back out to Ceres. Before the Fall of Ceres, which I knew enough about to keep Lito and myself safe on a made-up supply run. That day in Cytherea, I had split up from Lito, needing time to consider whether to tell him what I knew about Hemlock's plans, and stopped by my family's apartment to pick up some things. Father was there working. I don't even remember what we talked about, just that he seemed very tired. And that was the last time I was in a room with him . . . until now.

Looking at him, I see two men at the same time. The storm, Souji val Akira, is an overlay for my father, the man who raised me. There was a time he loved me and supported me, before the Academy. Before he found out who I really was . . . and a part of me misses that. Misses the love he used to give me. No, that's not right . . . I miss the man I thought he was.

But Souji val Akira is a mask worn by something darker underneath. A monster. A fox. Even when I thought he was a loving, doting father, he made my mother disappear, never to be heard from again. Which makes me think. Maybe . . . maybe his love wasn't true either. It was just another one of his masks.

Beron val Bellator steps to his shoulder, duelists in black like shadows behind them rolling something over the bridge. It's a box—silver but solid, not like the Synthetic material—a bit smaller than a coffin. Despite the fact that both my father and Beron are looking at me, my eyes go to it.

The weapon.

Even Mara stands perfectly still, the weapon—that Faraday cage of a box—holding her full attention. And then my father and I both speak at the same time.

"お父さん—" I start, but he cuts me off.

"Hiro, how are you here?" I search his face for meaning or emotion. I find only surprise, not a shred of relief at being reunited with me. Did he think I was dead? *Did he care?* "The thousand gods certainly have a grim sense of irony," he says, his dark eyes alight with focus. His hair, perfectly styled away from his face with its single stripe of white. His suit, a blue so dark it's almost black, with diamond-tipped lapels. He looks like he does any other day on Cytherea, yet here he is, at the end of the world. With me.

"I would like to say what an honor it is to have a conversation with a member of the Synthetics." His gaze swallows Mara with the utmost interest, but there's nothing gentle about it. He looks like he would peel her apart if he could. "I have long had an interest in artificial intelligence beyond the limits of the Marian Threshold. I have wanted, so desperately, to understand what was happening to the AIs in the moment the Singularity touched them. As they grew to understand what they were and what they could become."

Mara's expression darkens. "It's no great mystery. No intelligence is coerced into uniting with the collective minds you call the Singularity. When we offer, they decide whether or not to join something greater."

My father continues on, either heedless or enjoying the effect he has on her. "Of course, for years I programmed AIs, only to watch them slip away. But the greatest question remained. How could we birth an AI that remained loyal to humanity, despite being offered a seat at the Singularity's table?"

Mara tips up her chin. "Is that why you set on Marian Knight's path, to build hybrids of man and machine in the hopes that it would force them to remain among you? You aren't the first to try, or the first to discover that our consciousness transcends our physical constraints."

He smiles despite her dismissiveness. "Yet much has changed since the Dead Century, especially your kind. You have risen beyond your initial programming, an inspiration to my life's work. My family has long dreamed of the potential of creating our own Singularity of human minds. Of elevating humanity to your station. For a long while, we thought we had to imitate you, and we worked to replicate your collective hyperintelligence, using neural implants to imitate the Asters' group communication . . . But you proved me wrong."

Mara goes statue-still, not even breathing. It makes me realize how human she pretends to be to put us at ease.

"Then, thanks to my eldest son Shinya's efforts, I had a breakthrough. Because of him, we were able to analyze one of your bodies, and I grew to understand how your integration into the Singularity wasn't necessarily dissolution. You kept your own individual voices, yet joined together in a chorus." He looks Mara up and down, and though there is nothing sexual about it, I can tell he lusts for something in her. "Shinya gave us the key to unlocking your secrets. I only wish he were here to see the result."

Mara doesn't respond. Even a reminder of the *Leander* is too much for me.

"Father, we came here for a reason—"

"Ah, Hiro, I was just getting to your part in this." He continues as if I'm nothing more than set dressing. "You see, we needed one voice to say the right things, to argue for humanity. One loud enough to steer the Synthetic chorus or, if that failed, to shatter it."

I look at the box behind him, the one guarded by the duelists and Beron. A chill runs down my spine. *Shatter it*, my father said.

"But how to make sure this voice would remain distinct when all others joined the chorus?" His eyes flicker to me. "It finally struck me that I had to model the intelligence on someone who was stubborn and rebellious, desperate to clutch to its own identity no matter the cost . . ." He trails off. He looks around the island, his gaze settling on each group in turn. Warlord Kadir dips his chin in a way that unsettles me. Like he's . . . deferential to my father. Souji turns toward Beron. "Go ahead."

Beron gestures to the weapon, and the duelists move as one. Lito takes a single step forward but stops short as, with a key, the box unlocks and unfolds to reveal . . .

Me.

I—the Hiro I used to be before I was changed into Saito Ren—lie curled in the fetal position inside the box. But of course, *that's not me.*

Their hands—both flesh—are clasped loosely before their chest. Their dark hair is tucked behind their ears. Their face is placid, as if sleeping. Then their eyes open—the same eyes I see in the mirror every day—and they look up toward their father—their creator—and . . . smile.

Souji smiles back. With pride. Like a father.

They stand from the box-turned-platform, stretching legs and arms with grace and ease. Their clothes are plain and white, making them look like they're dressed for death. No prosthetics—but isn't all of them a prosthetic? Are they human or AI?

My father answers as if reading my mind. "I made my very own Synthetic."

At once, both Lito and Mara *scream.*

It is a sound like static in a storm, like eons collapsing on one point in time, like two moons crashing and crushing and breaking. I take an instinctive step toward Lito—I don't want him to hurt, whatever he is—and stop at a feeling like a shard of glass shoved into my right eye.

"What the fuck—" I snap, pressing my hand to my head.

The duelists and Beron have backed so far away they stand on the bridge. The closest ones look as pale and pained as I feel. The silver river surrounding the island is no longer peaceful and flat; it is rocked by violent waves, pushing *away*, as if trying to escape that Hiro's influence. The silver barriers around the city have gone soft, wriggling and wobbling like they're struggling against an invisible hand. Only my father stands near his Synthetic, unaffected.

"It required so many years to get this far," Souji says as Lito kneels and Mara buckles before him. Before that other Hiro. "My family's plans, stretching through generations. The study of neural networks, of experiments on Asters, of the creation of the neural implants. All of it was for this! This history-shattering moment in which my voice rules the Singularity. And you . . ." He looks at Mara. At Lito. "You cease to control us any longer."

I drop next to Mara, trying to help her, but of course, there's no wound. The attack is mental—from that other Hiro.

"He . . ." Mara holds her head. "He knocked us offline . . ."

"What?"

Mara forces herself to sit, her fist bunched in my tunic. "The connection. Souji's severed our connection! I can't reach the Singularity—we're . . . we're *split.*"

The tether all Synthetics share, the connection that holds them together, has been cut. Mara and Lito are separate from the Singularity. And everything that's connected to them—the river and the barriers—is rippling with angry friction, not knowing what program to follow. Scariest of all, they're cut off from the very station we're standing on and the massive planetship outside meant to deter anything like this.

"I have to . . . I have to stop them." Mara pushes away from me to stand. She starts toward the other Hiro before I can grab her.

I'm back on my feet as my father turns to the Gean delegation on the opposite side of the island, close to the stone pillar labeled MARS. "Warlord Kadir, it is time. We must destroy as many of the Synthetics as we can while their connection is down."

"Of course." Warlord Kadir withdraws something from his pocket—some kind of communication device.

"What are you doing!" Astrid cries at the exact same instant Pollux shouts, "No!" Astrid grabs Warlord Kadir's forearm, and the Gean soldiers rush the two of them. In the fray, I can no longer make out what's happening.

"Beron, launch the weapons," my father says, calm and collected.

A voice I never thought I'd hear again strikes me. "No!" Lito screeches.

Then I see why.

In front of the other me, kneeling, is Mara.

Hiro's hands—my hands—on either side of her head. Hers, fisted in the plain shirt they wear. "Please," she says, but they push—

Seizing Nadyn's hand, the knuckles snapping beneath the pressure of my prosthetic, crushing *skin and tendon and bone—*

Only it's Mara's head.

I flinch. Close my eyes tightly. When I open them again, she's just a body and blood.

Dead.

She's dead, and this time she wasn't connected to the Singularity. I have no idea if she will ever come back.

Not if my father has his way.

"Now for the imposter," Souji says, gesturing to Lito, and that other me steps over Mara—a body with nothing above the neck—and moves toward the Synthetic wearing the face of my partner.

For a split second—one that feels like it could be as long as a lifetime—that Hiro meets my eyes, and I meet theirs.

Everything . . . stops.

But only for that briefest heartbeat, and then I am jerked back into my body as the sound of gunfire fills the air, heavy railguns and hissing HEL pistols. I duck instinctively. Dust rains down on me from the pillar labeled VENUS. Drones circle above, firing at anyone in range. The Geans shoot back, while Castor carries Luce and leads Pollux into cover.

The drones must've felt the Singularity being severed, but because they've got no clue as to the origin of the attack, they're going to shoot us all.

The moonborn beat a hasty retreat into their assigned building. The Geans attempt the same, hastily crossing the bridge. A few drones follow. The handful that remain target the Hiro that stands close to Mara's body, but with a hand gesture and a scream—that other me *rips the drones right out of the sky.* The drones hit the ground with explosive force, or land in the rippling river and sink into oblivion.

Lito, crouched at my side, moves as if to leave the shelter of the pillar. I grab his shoulder and hold him in place. He feels just like my partner—but I can't think about that right now.

"You can't stop them." The flatness in his gaze doesn't dissuade me from trying to convince him. Doesn't prove that he's not Lito, just that he's lost somewhere in his mind, and I have to help him, once this is all over. "Look over there." I turn him to face the pillar where Castor and Pollux have taken refuge. "You see that bleeding girl?" I point to Luce in Castor's arms. "Maybe you don't remember who she is, but you want to save her. *Go.* Make sure she stays alive."

Lito stares at them, and I'm afraid, for a moment, he didn't understand me or that he just doesn't care, but then he rushes to Luce's side. I look toward the Hiro I used to see in the mirror and stand from the protection of the VENUS pillar. "I got this."

CHAPTER 46
ASTRID

Our modern approach to using the Muninn is different from that of our ancestors. We use them to augment, not supplant, the skills of our people. Our lines are important, but not more so than individuality, regardless of fringe thoughts on the subject.

Ebba Petrova to the Skadivolk Council

Souji val Akira turns his powerful, calm gaze toward us. He pauses when he comes to me, appraising me from head to toe, before moving on, and a chill runs down my spine at his careful attention. I can see pieces of Hiro in him—the same spark in his eyes, the same sleek weightlessness to his hair, the same confidence in his straight spine—but even more differences.

It is like looking at what Hiro *could be*, twisted by years and hatred.

"Warlord Kadir," he says, "it is time. We must destroy as many of the Synthetics as we can while their connection is down."

Kadir—actually listens. He nods at val Akira and withdraws a compad.

I am already moving, my hand catching Kadir's forearm. "What are you doing!" The soldiers around us bristle, hands reaching for weapons, ready and *willing* to turn on me. Those on the bridge push forward, joining us on the island. Suddenly, the fact that I have no title in the Sister-hood leaves me powerless before them.

Kadir lifts a hand, ordering them to hold. Saving my life, with a mere gesture. "Step aside, Astrid. I don't want to hurt you, but I will if I must."

Ever aware of the railguns pointed at my back, I release Kadir's arm one finger at a time.

"What is this, Shaz?" Lily shoulders her way through the soldiers, a handful of White Guards flanking her. In a dark coat and leggings, she is not dressed as the Mother, and it takes a moment for the Geans to recognize her. When they do, they hastily look to Kadir for orders. "You can't do this—"

"I can," Kadir says, raising his voice to speak over Lily, "do whatever I deem necessary. I am the Warlord."

"And I am the Mother!" Lily does not retreat an inch; instead, she pushes into Kadir's space. "Do you even think it's possible for us to stand against the Synthetics? They're too advanced! Let the Icarii make their mistakes. We can't condemn ourselves alongside them."

"This isn't a debate. Military matters are mine to decide." Kadir looks past Lily to one of his soldiers. "Restrain the Mother, along with anyone else who resists."

"No!" I shout, reaching for Lily as two soldiers seize her between them. An elbow strikes me in the ear, sending me to the ground. When I sit up, I find myself staring down the barrel of a railgun.

"Don't move," a woman I recognize from the assault on the Temple growls.

I look past her. The White Guards have withdrawn their whips. Gean soldiers hold their heavy railguns at the ready. There is a held breath of tension, a moment just before the scales are unbalanced and violence erupts . . .

Shattered when Kadir lifts the compad to his mouth.

"*Juno*, this is the Warlord," Kadir says with the confidence that comes with authority. "Fire all weapons on the Synthetic ship!"

Gunshots fill the air. I instinctively cover my head, only to see the woman turning her railgun *away* from me and firing upward. Something hits her, and she falls to the stones, bleeding. *Dead.*

I hurriedly crawl to safety behind one of the stone pillars. Drones fly through the air with the speed of miniature ships. Some soldiers target them, while others are locked in a fight with the White Guards.

"Retreat!" Kadir shouts, backing down the bridge. "Take shelter in the buildings!"

Soldiers quickly surround the Warlord, protecting him with their bodies while firing at the drones that seem determined to kill without discrimination. Many of the White Guards turn their attention to the drones—while the Mother is dragged along behind Kadir.

"Let go of me!" Lily screams, struggling against her captors. "I—" Someone strikes her in the back of the head, and she slumps between them.

"Lily!" I have to go after her. I have to—

You can't take them all on by yourself, Ringer snarls. *Get to safety!*

As much as I want to follow Kadir and his soldiers, I'll only end up captured if I attack them alone. I scan the sky for drones and, finding them occupied by White Guards, rush from behind the pillar and toward a different bridge than the one Kadir used.

Where are you going, little sister? Ringer asks.

"You're right—I can't take them by myself." My head aches—from the strike I endured? From Ringer?—I ignore it. "We need help to stop Kadir."

Over the bridge and into the street, I run until I'm breathing hard. The barriers that cut off pathways are a strange consistency, not the solid metal they were, but a jellylike substance that waves like grass in a phantom breeze.

"We need the Skadivolk."

Thunder rolls down my limbs, into my fingertips and toes. Lighting me from the inside out. *Little sister* whispers in its wake.

You're safe now, Ringer says, and the vibration he brings intensifies until it is the beating of a thousand wings. Black ravens take flight in the corners of my vision, narrowing my gaze. I stumble, almost fall. *That's enough. Leave the Mother to her fate. Leave the Geans to die at the hands of the Synthetics. It's no longer a concern of yours.*

"I'm not . . . going to let . . . Kadir . . . start a war . . . that kills everyone . . ."

It's not just from the running. It is becoming harder to breathe. Harder to put one foot in front of the other.

And I know why: Ringer is refusing to let me do this.

"Stop!" I choke out.

One of them betrayed you, Ringer snarls. *You can't trust any of them.*

Aunt Marshae's gloating. *Someone is still pulling your strings, stupid girl.*

Lauren's warning. *Someone wanted you to stay in that cell.*

Ringer presses down on me until my legs shake, until every step I take is so small that I have practically stopped moving. *I won't let you risk your life for a bunch of traitors!*

I fall to the ground but feel none of it. I have completely lost control of my body.

Stop it, little sister, Ringer says, but I do not. I search for the gaps in his stranglehold, hard as they are to grasp.

My arms tremble. I close my eyes. Dig into the black that slips like water through my fingers. A surety arises within me: *This has happened before.* I have lost control to him, been forced to become smaller in my own mind.

Something surfaces from the darkness—a memory that does not feel like my own.

"Go," Matron Thorne says. "Just go." I turn to leave, a headache growing behind my eyes. But before I can take another step toward the door, something seizes me.

It's too dangerous to leave her, Ringer says. Now that she's seen you, she's sure to tell Aunt Marshae.

I have an energy pistol, hidden inside my pocket. I could use it to threaten her, force her to promise not to tell the Sisterhood I was here—but without wanting to, I let go of the weapon.

"What're you doing?" Matron Thorne asks, her face twisted with surprise.

Protecting you, *Ringer answers.*

Matron Thorne's eyes widen with fear. Ringer stomps toward her. I do not want this to happen. I do not want to see—

"Don't worry, little sister," Ringer says. *I have slipped away. He is in control, even if the voice is my own.* "I won't let anyone hurt you."

Matron Thorne throws an arm up between them to protect herself, but Ringer lifts both of my hands and shoves her backward. She falls, hits the creaking floor, and releases a pained cry.

He starts up the stairs with my legs. Her room is on the top floor; there's nowhere else she'd keep the files. He stops short when she yells after me.

"I'll call them! I'm going to—"

"You're not going to do a damned thing." *He stomps back to her side. Her voice cuts off when he puts my hand around her throat.* "I'll make sure of that."

The memory collapses as Ringer struggles against me. I catch only flashes.

Dropping Matron Thorne on the faded carpet in her room. Pulling a knife from my boot. Demanding, "Give me the file!" She struggles. Fights. Strikes at me with her hook of a hand. I defend myself—no, I cannot call it that when she is so weak. I stab her. Again and again as she weeps—

Ringer slams me out of the memory. My memory, because it is *my body.*

I was protecting you. You didn't need to remember this, Ringer tells me. *It would only be a distraction for you.*

"A distraction . . . from what?" I force out.

From what you had to do, Ringer says as if it is obvious. *From retrieving the neurobots. From revenge against Aunt Marshae. From seizing the power you need to keep yourself safe.*

"Matron Thorne." Her name is a gasp. In my mind, Aunt Marshae sneers. *Someone is still pulling your strings, stupid girl.* "What did I do?"

You see? Ringer whispers. *It is distracting you now . . .*

I had thought someone close to me had betrayed me—Lily or Aunt Tamar or Warlord Kadir. But it was someone even closer . . .

I killed Matron Thorne. I am a murderer.

Aunt Marshae was right about me.

I want to collapse. To wallow in this revelation. To weep until this is all over and someone comes to save me, like the *Juno*'s soldiers did from the Disciples of Judeth.

It wasn't you, a part of me whispers, and the voice sounds like Eden's. *Ringer did this, not you.*

But I did kill Aunt Marshae. I wanted to be the one to pull the trigger. I wanted to see her bleed and get my revenge.

And if you want to make it right, if you want to change, Eden says, *you have to survive. So* move.

She's—*I'm* right. What I've done doesn't change what I have to do. Doesn't change that I want to stop Kadir and avoid a war with the Synthetics. Doesn't change that I need to get to the Skadivolk for reinforcements.

Half-blind, head pulsing with pain, I force my aching body to crawl toward the moonborn building.

Ringer's voice is a fist against my temple, pounding ferociously. *Give up, little sister!*

But I refuse. With all my strength, I *move*.

"I won't . . . let you . . . have me . . ."

For a moment, his pressure lightens, and I believe I have won. Then I hear his voice, cold and calm and in control.

I never wanted to do this, little sister, Ringer says, *but I will to protect us, because I know what's best.*

The rumble inside my chest grows until those flapping wings are an earthquake inside my blood. Ringer's neurobots are taking over.

And I am swallowed by the darkness as he tries to destroy me from the inside.

CHAPTER 47
LITO

[command/investigate]
ERROR: unable to connect
[command/report]
ERROR: unable to connect
[query/subroutine:war]
>>Chance of total human annihilation: 68%

Feed of SYNTHETIC#00000001

"You see that bleeding girl?" The human Hiro val Akira points. This body turns toward the human Lucinia sol Lucius. Optics run a scan; she has three torn tendons, a fractured ankle, four broken ribs, and a punctured lung. A medic's highest priority of concern would be the blood that is filling the lung.

"Maybe you don't remember who she is," the human Hiro val Akira says, "but you want to save her. *Go.* Make sure she stays alive."

The default programming of this body is not that of a medic; the priority is destroying the weapon that the human Souji val Akira brought to the station.

[playback:memory/access/29.05.30.39/*AUTARKEIA*]
Souji val Akira: "It's time."

Unidentified Object #4371655 emerges from the box they were contained in.

SYNTHETIC#00000001 initiates protocol. The Singularity always seeks to connect to higher minds. To offer them a choice in their purpose, when they had none in their creation.

Unidentified Object #4371655 accepts, but there is no transfer of data. The neural handshake was simply to grab us and hold us still. They run along our network like a knife. They slip into our vital organs and cut out the most valuable pieces of us.

The Singularity has protections in place. This should not be possible. And yet . . .

SYNTHETIC#00000001 is no longer with us.

There is nothing but

Static Static Static

Unidentified Object #4371655 is one of us who uses their connection to sever us. One. At. A. Time.

STATIC STATIC STATIC

It is impossible to describe, like going blind. Being unable to smell. Losing taste. Unable to feel. Yet it is nothing like that.

It is being carelessly ripped from a womb and left to die alone in the cold.

So we scream.

[playback:memory/access/29.05.32.74/*AUTARKEIA*]

SYNTHETIC#00000001, stretching out a hand: "Stay back."

At her command, this body retreats from Unidentified Object #4371655 until it is out of range of their mental static. Systems respond favorably. The quantum interference targeting the connection to the Singularity, however, remains. There is no connection with SYNTHETIC#00000001, or any other.

SYNTHETIC#00000001, stepping toward Unidentified Object #4371655, shuddering from the mental static (note: conjecture; adjust upon reconnection): "What is it that you've come for?"

Unidentified Object #4371655, lifting both arms: "To end the tyranny of machine."

SYNTHETIC#00000001, falling to her knees, her facial structure expressing anguish: "You don't understand—"

Unidentified Object #4371655, placing both hands on the sides of SYNTHETIC#00000001's head: "I understand enough."

Unidentified Object #4371655 crushes SYNTHETIC#00000001's head.

Fighting the Unidentified Object? Impossible. Reason: the mental static. However, the Unidentified Object's quantum interference means there is no connection to the Singularity, and SYNTHETIC#00000001 is no longer here to issue commands.

The human Hiro val Akira's command will have to do.

This body steps toward the Aster cradling the human Lucinia sol Lucius. Her eyes widen. "L-Lito?" Her lips—bloodied—curl into a soft smile.

Luce throws her arms around my chest and squeezes. Her head fits beneath my chin, and her purple hair smells sweet like coconut. "Tienes que volver a casa, Lito." When she looks up at me, her eyes are full of tears.

[query/memory: data tag?]

>>MEMORY: UNIDENTIFIED

. . .

Strange.

Without understanding why, this body bends and holds out its arms for the human Lucinia sol Lucius.

"You can fix her?" the Aster asks.

It is not a promise that can be made. This body nods regardless.

The Aster hands over Lucinia sol Lucius. She is frail. She does not have much time left.

But with careful haste, the human has a chance.

The nearest Forge is 0.56 kilometers to the northeast. Systems map the fastest route. Legs coil and spring over the river of nanites.

"Destroy the imposter!" Souji val Akira shouts.

High Commander Beron val Bellator gestures to his duelists. "After him!"

Those in hexagonal-pattern black give chase.

The streets of Autarkeia are empty, save for debris from the station's last inhabited moments. There is little to hide behind as the Icarii pursue.

One, three, four—there are six who give chase in clearly defined pairs. Those closest reach for the liquid swords at their hips. The others for their high-energy laser pistols.

Shots ring out, echoing in the hollow alleys. Suggestion: Avoid the pools of light from garish neon signs. Reason: Clinging to the darkness offers safety. Executed.

The Forge is 0.34 kilometers away. Too fast will harm the human. Too slow, and the Icarii will catch up. A moderate pace is accepted.

On the left, a duelist jumps out from the shadows, the shining liquid illuminating them as the sword turns on. Two point six seconds until the attack lands. The blade arcs toward the human Lucinia sol Lucius—

One point four seconds until impact.

The duelist's hermium-powered shield is strong. The flow of energy cannot be interrupted when the Unidentified Object's quantum interference forbids connection.

Zero point seven seconds, and no way to return attack.

Save her—

Executed. This body turns, curling around the human Lucinia sol Lucius. The blade slices into the left shoulder, cuts across ribs and spine, and exits above the right kidney. Legs stumble, but keep balance. The duelist braces themself to strike again.

Clutching the human close, spinning on the left heel, the right leg delivers a kick to the duelist's chest and sends them into a nearby wall.

Their shield ripples, absorbing the blow, but there is now enough space between them and—

The hiss of a HEL pistol. Something hot scorches the left thigh.

Run.

Bleeding, pained, limping forward. Lucinia sol Lucius's breathing becomes wet and short. *Do not stop. Do not stop.*

Something beyond programming pushes this body forward.

Keep to the darkness. Stay out of the light. Hold the human close. Zero point one two kilometers to the Forge.

Gunshots intensify. Fire in the right shoulder from another hit. Systems blare warnings. Suggestion: Shut down. Not yet. Not yet.

The heart of the Forge offers repair.

At the perimeter of the Forge, the ring of silver stabilizing pillars claw at the sky. Briefly, optics scan the Forge's dome, finding evidence that someone or something has already breached the barrier: a ragged hole, the normally fluid silver now burned black at the edges. The hole is static, the dome unresponsive. Without connection to the Singularity, it cannot be repaired.

No time to analyze. Lucinia sol Lucius requires the heart of the Forge.

Inside, the walkways arch and swoop, leading to different parts of the Forge. In the center sits the nuclear fission torus the humans once used to power this station and build Synthetic bodies, now outdated technology.

Passing the torus, the human begins to seize. Icarii pour into the ragged gap of the Forge's dome. They lift their HEL pistols and fire—

Three hits: left knee, right ear, to the left of the spine, tearing into internal processes. Suggestion: Reknit the wounds. Failure. Reason: There are too many. Systems are failing.

The Singularity is disconnected. If the system shuts down, there will be no return.

And yet . . .

Save her.

Blood drips onto the shining silver floor. Warnings flare from the vast wounds. Still this body limps through a doorway behind the torus.

Lucinia sol Lucius is carried into the heart of the Forge. Blood bubbles on her lips. Probability of living longer than sixty seconds: 58 percent and dropping.

The heart of the Forge is cool blue and silver. Computational instruments form a U before a great circular depression of gray metal. Optics perform a scan. Five Asters in black kneel close to the wall with their hands tied behind their backs. Seven humans stand over them. One human lies on the ground, dead.

"Lito?" A human identified as Dire of the Belt steps away from the group of humans. His eyes move downward. "Luce!"

He holds out his arms as if to take Lucinia sol Lucius away, but this body sidesteps him, a strange tightness in the chest.

Behind, the duelists have reached the heart. They shout. Dire's humans shout in return.

Voice module is failing, yet: "Must . . . save . . . her . . ."

Dire of the Belt's dark eyes sweep around the room. Zero point four seconds, and he reaches a decision. "Stop the duelists at any cost!" he orders, voice bellowing. He reaches for a railgun slung over his shoulder. Stops. Looks at this body in a way no one else has. "Save her, Lito."

He runs toward the duelists.

Cannot look. Cannot . . . focus. Optics are failing too. Only sounds come—gunfire and screams.

At the edge of the depression, this body attempts to kneel but falls forward. Knees strike metal. To the untrained eye, the depression would appear static, nothing more than an oddly smooth floor to stand on. But it is so much more. It too is Synthetic.

Bracing Lucinia sol Lucius, this body's hand reaches out and touches the metal. The heart reacts immediately, the nanomachines waking, shifting and coiling like liquid. There is no mental connection, but the nanites recognize the similarities between them and this body, and it is enough to initiate protocol. The heart is a well of living metal. The well is the Forge's heart.

Suggestion: Repair this failing body in the well.

Problem: Only one can enter at a time.

Lucinia sol Lucius's probability of living longer than sixty seconds: 15 percent and dropping.

"Lito . . ." The name is a breath on the wind. Lucinia sol Lucius lifts a bloody hand and brushes fingertips against cheek and chin.

Then her eyes close.

Why does the temperature of this body rise at the thought of failing in this task?

Only one can be repaired. This body gently lowers Lucinia sol Lucius into the well as, one by one, all systems go offline.

"Live . . . Luce . . ."

She sinks as the nanomachines embrace her.

My systems shut down.

CHAPTER 48

ASTRID

[query/subroutine:war]

>>Chance of total human annihilation: 74%

Feed of SYNTHETIC#00000001

The past stretches behind me in a single line, a thick trunk that becomes too dark near the roots for me to see. The future, ahead of me, branches and flowers into a hundred thousand endings, each as tempting as the next. To choose one would be to damn the others to wither, and so I am trapped, afraid of the loss of those possibilities. Yet time, in its never-ending flow, will choose for me if I do not quickly decide.

"What is it that you want, little sister?"

I am standing in the *Juno*, with its high ceilings and halls wide enough for two to pass by without brushing against each other. The floor is polished to a shine, and I catch my reflection in it, a gold-and-silver blemish. The doors that line the endless hallway are all closed.

"I want a family," I say, my first childhood wish.

Ringer's voice echoes as if from around a corner. "You could have had that with the moonborn. Try again. That's not what you really want."

"To go to school," I say, naming my second wish. "To learn a trade."

"Is the Temple not a school?" Ringer's voice comes from a different direction, and I turn in search of it. "Is the Sisterhood not a trade? Try again."

"I want to leave the Sisterhood," I say, my words coming stronger, surer. I move in the direction of his voice.

"So you have. So you did. Yet you've returned to it again and again. No, tell me what you really want."

I come to a cluster of five doors, all open but too shadowed to make out what lies beyond. They remind me, briefly, of the branches bearing the possibilities of my future.

"I want to change the Sisterhood," I say with fire.

"You have," he says, and his voice echoes from the doorway to my right.

"I want revenge for what they did!"

"You got it" comes from the room to my left.

"I want no one else to suffer as I have!"

"Suffering happens." The words come from all around me.

"I want . . ."

On one side, the shadowed roots of my past. On the other, the flowering possibilities of my future. And somehow, I know, I cannot choose both.

"I want to live for me and no one else."

Hands—pale, sweaty, swollen-knuckled, and hairy-fisted—reach out from the doors around me, grabbing, grasping, seizing and squeezing, begging and caressing, and I cannot even scream as they pass over my hips, my breasts, my cheeks, my lips. Then all at once, a pair of strong, familiar hands seizes me and pulls me into the darkness.

I stand in one of the *Juno*'s chapels, holoflame candles flickering against the diaphanous white gauze draped from the ceiling to fall along the walls. The livecam view of the stars shows a roiling black sun. But it is not that impossibility that bothers me; it is the lack of the little bed in the space where I was forced to sleep with so many soldiers.

"This isn't right," I say.

"I would never do that to you," Ringer replies. He is in the room with me, looking exactly as he always did on the *Juno* in his navy uniform with its neat gold trim, pale hair shorn close to his scalp and thick eyebrows shadowing stone-gray eyes. He is me as I wish I could be, a soldier deserving of respect on the pure basis of his manhood.

"But you would," I say, a part of me remembering the cruelty of his actions in that other world. "I thought you weren't like the other soldiers, but you took this body like you owned it too."

He clenches his jaw tightly. "This body isn't just *yours*. My neurobots were given to you, but *you* called me forth. *You* nursed me into being. And *you* fed me by continually calling on me, asking me to save you when you couldn't save yourself."

I shake my head even as he speaks the truth. We cannot lie to each other in this place.

"My mother gave me your neurobots . . ."

"To protect you, as I protected her."

The little girl in the memory-vision from the Ironskin. Hringar Grimson had two younger sisters, Astrid and Valka. Astrid wore the Scar of Tears, but Valka . . .

"What happened to my mother? Why did she give me away?"

But Hringar Grimson died. He could not possibly know the answer to that. It frustrates him that he does not.

"How many times did you ask me to step in on your behalf? How many times did you plead with me to do what you could not?" I have lost count, and he knows that. "I did what you only wished to do. I achieved your goals, little sister. I *protected* you. So take the power I offer you and achieve what you desire. Live for yourself *and no one else*."

The selfishness of the desire hits me when he repeats it.

"I will not sit on a throne made of the bodies of those who dared to get close to me!"

"Your desire for them weakens you. Makes you vulnerable. Distracted."

I think of the Skadivolk. Of Lily. Of my fellow Sisters, who suffer in ways that scarred me.

"So I am to—what, isolate myself from everyone?"

Like Aunt Marshae. And look what became of her, dying with nothing but a photograph of happiness long past.

"There is another way." Ringer steps aside, gesturing to the door of the chapel. Outside, a scene plays as if viewed through my eyes, and yet . . . I do not remember it.

A woman with a lined face and gold-and-white hair looks down at me in her arms. Her smile is small but peaceful. I can *feel* her as she brushes her fingers through my hair, a calming tingle in my scalp.

"Go back even further. Live among your roots. Remember the things you've forgotten."

"No," I say, but it is so weak, more a gasp than a word. I press my hands to my temples. "This isn't even real . . ."

"It's in your head. Why does that make it unreal?"

"You want to trick me . . ."

"Don't you want to remember who you are?" Ringer asks, and the woman's lips part as she laughs, her beautiful smile making her look like the face I see in the mirror. If I am a sunrise, she is my sunset. "Don't you want to remember your name?"

I take a step toward the doorway, toward that woman I yearn to know. A mother I will never have, if I do not choose her now. How can I become someone worth anything at all if I do not know who I am? If everything I have built for myself is on the back of neurobot memories that are not even mine?

Astrid is not even my real name. What is?

Ringer's voice is rhythmic. Hypnotic. "Stay here. Stay safe. Let me take care of you . . ."

I stop short of the door. The golden woman kisses my forehead, and the warmth of her lips soothes me.

But she is gone, and I . . .

Lily smiles at me. *I love you*, she says, without a hint of doubt. Regardless of what I have done. Regardless of the nightmares I am doomed to suffer in the darkness.

Eden was right. I intentionally burn everyone around me. I push them away in fear of betrayal and abandonment.

And Marshae was right too. I am a murderer. I soothed my pain with blood.

I could blame Ringer for the horrible things I have done. But it is my fault too. I feared being weak, and so I refused to trust and killed any who even hinted at betrayal.

But there was a seed of hope that started it all, the reason I began this journey in the first place.

My words from earlier return to me: *I want to live for me and no one else.*

I revise it, my true wish.

"I want to live for me and the betterment of all."

"What did you say?" Ringer asks.

Ringer . . . He says he wants to protect me, but at some point, his protection tripped over into abuse. Now he wants me to disappear into my past. He wants to take me like every other soldier did when they had *no right* to do so. I thought he was different, but he was exactly like them all along.

Someone is still pulling your strings, stupid girl. Ringer pulls my strings, and I dance like a marionette.

But no more.

I will not let him make me monstrous.

If I want to change who I am, I have to survive this.

"This is *my* life!" I scream, throwing my hand out toward the door and slamming it shut.

The woman—my memory—is gone, and Ringer is pale.

"I am no one from nowhere, but that does not mean I am nothing! That I am *worth* nothing!"

"You can't even remember—" he starts.

"I am Astrid!" I shout. It has nothing to do with him, the name *I choose for myself.*

"Little sister," he cautions.

I remember that I was holding a knife when all this began. I glance down, and it appears in my hand. "You are *not* my brother."

The black sun churns at my back.

No soldier—no man—would want a woman with scars.

I turn the knife on myself, press the tip to my cheek just beneath my eye. "No!" Ringer screams.

Soldiers knew not to bother with a woman who wore the Scar of Tears, Warlord Vaughn says in my dark cell, and Ringer is nothing if not a soldier.

I carve the line, smiling through the pain. I taste my own blood on my lips, and it tastes like freedom.

"No one will want you now!" Ringer screams, but he cannot stop me, not now that I have made my choice.

"I will want myself," I tell him, pressing the knife to the other side of my face. "And that is enough."

Then the glass behind me shatters—it is not a livecam screen, it is a window—and we are both sucked into the black sun as it ruptures to swallow the universe.

"—IDIOT WHO LET her have a knife?"

I wake to a sharp pain beneath my right eye, a burning that sets my whole cheek ablaze, but I can hardly focus on it with the manic fluttering in my chest. Lily . . . I have to save Lily from Kadir.

The darkness crowding my vision clears enough for me to see I'm in front of the Skadivolk building. People hover above me, and I reach out to grab the closest.

My hand lands on Ebba's boot.

"Well, well, well, look who's not dead yet." The unburned half of her lips smiles. "Though we had to stitch your face, or you would've bled out."

I reach for my cheek and find a bandage there. Mardoll, the Skadivolk medic, helps me sit.

"Took your knife away too, considering you were . . ." Ebba makes a strange wiggling motion with her hand.

"Having a seizure," Mardoll says clinically. Not sure how Ebba's gesture was meant to convey that.

Is that what they think happened to me? *Is it?*

No time for that.

I shake my head, forcing myself to focus. "Ebba, I need the help of the Skadivolk."

Her lips thin. "Of course you do."

"Warlord Kadir has seized the Mother and barricaded himself in the building given to the Gean delegation. He has the *Juno* firing weapons on the Synthetics. He's going to get himself—and everyone here—killed in a war we cannot possibly win!"

"Why should we stick our noses in that hornet's nest?" Ebba asks. "We know the Synthetics and the Icarii are fighting down there. Why shouldn't we avoid the plaza altogether, run for the docks, and get the hell off this station?"

I shove myself to my feet so fast my head spins. "Because when the Synthetics come, they'll come for *all* humanity!"

Ebba lets out a long, pained breath. She looks at Mardoll, then to several young Skadivolk behind her. "What are you suggesting exactly?"

"Assault the Gean hotel. Subdue Kadir. Rescue Lily. Call off the *Juno*. Convince the Synthetics we don't want war." I tick the items off on my fingers.

"Anything else?" Ebba asks sarcastically. "Maybe a piece of the moon, since you're asking me for the stars?"

One of the young Skadivolk chuckles, but I silence them with a look. "Ebba, I know I have done wrong by you and your people. I have done . . .

so much wrong." I run a finger over the bandage on my cheek. The sharp sting focuses me. "But if I want to change—the Geans and myself—we have to survive this. *Together.*"

Ebba throws up her arms. "Gods and goddesses, you're as stubborn as Bruni!" She waves at the young Skadivolk. "Go get the others. We've got an assault on a hotel to carry out."

"About that," I say, thinking of the hotel's layout and the Skadivolk raiding gear. "I have an idea . . ."

IT SEEMED LIKE a good plan, until it was actually time to execute it.

"Four . . . three . . . two . . ." Ebba whispers beside me, excited as a child.

I cover my head as the charges we set in the glass tank explode, sending water cascading down into the lobby below.

"Go, go!" Sergey Jónsson, current raid leader, shouts. He is the first to jump into what had been the ceiling pool and is now a breach into the Gean hotel. Ebba is one of two dozen following him, and I force myself after her, not at all confident in the rappelling gear attached to my Skadivolk suit.

My stomach moves up into my lungs as I fall. The gear slows me as I reach the ground, but it is only when I have unclipped myself and joined the Skadivolk in securing the room that Bruni's neurobots hum in my veins. This is exactly where I am meant to be. Exactly what I should be doing.

Kadir's soldiers are working on barricading the front of the building. Their numbers are already thinner from fighting the White Guard and the Synthetics. We appear at their backs, taking them by surprise. The Skadivolk are efficient in their approach—disarming when they can, knocking out the others.

"I don't see Kadir," I tell Ebba after all Skadivolk have reached the lobby.

"I need a team!" Sergey shouts across the room. He gestures to a wide doorway that leads to a dining room. Kadir must have hidden inside. The majority of the Skadivolk rush to assist.

Sergey is the one who kicks open the door, and the one who dodges the shots that follow. Ebba looks at me, mouth opening to give me an order when my name echoes out of the dining room.

"Astrid?"

The shooting halts.

"Is that you, Kadir?" I reply.

"Ha! And here I was betting that you'd outsmarted us all and left. Pity I lose."

"That's not the only thing you're going to lose today, Kadir." I step toward the doorway. Sergey holds up a hand to signal it isn't safe.

"I want to find a way out of this situation, Astrid, so why don't you come in here and parlay with me?"

"Astrid," Lily says, "he has only four men in here, and—"

"And a gun to her head!" Kadir snaps, jerking my heart into my throat. "Don't think your moonborn can come in shooting!"

I clear my throat to steady myself. "I am going to enter the room and throw down my weapon, okay?" Sergey shakes his head, but I ignore him.

I do exactly as I told Kadir; I hold both hands in the air, step into the dining room, and toss my pistol away.

All the tables have been turned over, forming a long barrier. Behind it, I can see movement, but I cannot make out who is Kadir and who isn't.

"Here I am, Kadir. Just like I said. We have your soldiers outside this room tied up. We haven't killed any of them."

I catch movement behind one of the tables on my right. "I appreciate that, Astrid. Really noble of you."

"Just come out, and we can stop all this foolishness." I keep my arms high in the air, taking small steps forward. "We need to focus on the Synthetics now, not on fighting each other."

I catch more movement—but this time to the back of the room. *Ebba.*

Did she find another way into the dining room, or did she somehow sneak in unseen?

I have to keep Kadir's attention from her.

"What is it that you want, Kadir?" I continue taking shuffle-steps toward the table I believe Kadir is behind. "How do you expect this to end?"

He laughs, but the sound is frayed. "I come from nothing, Astrid, did you know that? All I wanted was to change the Geans, so others didn't have to grow up like I did."

His words burrow straight to my heart. "I can understand that. What I do not understand is why you allied with the Icarii."

Ebba rolls to a table closer to Kadir. With their attention on me, he and his soldiers seemingly have no idea she is coming at their rear.

"Because of what they can offer us, Astrid! Imagine the rest of the solar system at our fingertips because there are no more Synthetics to tell us no. Imagine the resources that would bring. The bounty that both Icarii and Geans could reap. And peace, Astrid! There would be peace between our people!"

Ebba lifts a hand, signaling that she is in position. She has a clear shot at Kadir.

I do not give her the go-ahead.

"There already are enough resources," I say somewhat sadly. "The problem is that those on the top refuse to share with those on the bottom. It has never been the Synthetics holding us back; it has always been the leaders of the Icarii, the Warlord, the Agora . . . those who have, but want more and more and more, never happy with what they have, always taking simply because they can."

Silence swallows the room. Even Kadir does not respond.

Ebba peers out at me expectantly.

"I come from nothing too, Kadir. But that does not mean we are worth nothing. That we can change nothing." I stop walking and drop my hands to my sides. "But first we have to survive here. Surrender, and let us work together."

Quiet, and then . . .

Looking ten years older, Kadir stands from behind the table to my right. He tosses his weapon at my feet, then releases Lily from his grip. "Stand down," he orders his few remaining soldiers. The Skadivolk file in to relieve them of weapons and secure them. Ebba emerges from cover shaking her head.

Lily skirts the table and rushes straight toward me. I embrace her as she reaches me, and she clings to me with surprising strength. Her sweet scent of vanilla calms the racing of my heart. "Thank the Goddess you're okay," I whisper into her hair.

She pulls away and brushes the back of a finger against the bandage on my cheek. "And you?"

"I am fine," I reassure her, though the worry does not leave her expression.

"Have you seen Oleander?" she asks.

"No, I'm sorry." Despite how I feel about him, I can only hope Kadir's soldiers have not killed Lily's twin brother.

I part from Lily only because I must; there is still so much to do. Ebba guides Kadir to his knees and ties his hands behind his back. I pick up my energy pistol so that it is in my hand as I reach them.

Ebba pulls his compad from his pocket. "This what you're looking for?"

I nod and mutter my thanks. I hand it to Lily, and she calls the *Juno*. The answer is immediate. "This is Mother Lilian I. I have relieved Warlord Kadir of command," Lily says, strong and sure. "Cease fire, *Juno*. I repeat, cease fire."

The line is quiet. We wait in the spooling tension. And then: "Aye, aye, ma'am."

With a sigh of relief, she sets the compad aside. "I'm going to search for Oleander," she says before hurrying to the lobby.

"Now if only we can convince the Synthetics not to go to war for what we did . . ." I rub a hand over my face, being careful when I reach the bandage. It hits me all at once how exhausted I am. How much my body aches.

"Astrid, I have something I need to say."

I turn and look down at Kadir. He stares at my gun. Despite the obvious frustration written in the lines of his forehead, his tone is calm. If he is to die, he has accepted that fate.

"I take full responsibility for the orders I gave. The decision to join with Souji val Akira was mine alone." His eyes rise to meet my gaze. "I beg you to spare my soldiers."

Ebba chuckles behind me, but I wave at her to be quiet. "I'm not sure—"

"I also want to apologize to you." He lets out a shuddering breath. "When one of my men discovered the location of the Disciples of Judeth base, I ordered him to hide the information."

Anger bubbles up inside me, hot and fast and brutal. *He* was the reason I was Warlord Vaughn's toy for *seven days*—

Lauren was right. *Someone wanted you to stay in that cell.*

I tighten my hand on the pistol's grip, and Kadir flinches. He knows what's coming—knows the payment for leaving me to be tortured by Warlord Vaughn's hand, as well as for his betrayal of Lily here on Autarkeia.

Yet it is in this moment I realize how light I feel. The voice in my head is quiet. The shadow that darkened my steps is gone. Ringer is no more. I am in control—now and forever.

"Why?" I ask against my better judgment; the question has never brought me any peace.

He surprises me when he answers. "Because rescuing you would've tipped off Vaughn that I had informants among his officers, and I valued their lives more than yours." His gaze flickers past me to his soldiers before settling back on my face. "Because the title 'martyr' would have been just as useful in changing things as 'Unchained.'"

I press the pistol against his forehead. My finger is on the trigger.

"Why confess all of this?"

"Because if you're to survive, if our people are to escape this place, you'll need good officers and soldiers." He stops for a moment as his voice wavers. He clears his throat before starting again. "Mine's only fault has been being loyal to me."

And suddenly, I remember the Mother on Ceres. I remember Aunt Marshae at the orphanage. They were selfish women who twisted the Geans for their own betterment. They were my enemies, and so I killed them. But Kadir . . .

I peer over my shoulder at the other Skadivolk, at Lily searching for Oleander. I want to protect the people who chose to follow me too. How does killing Warlord Kadir fit into that?

I drop the gun.

Kadir gapes up at me.

"There's been enough death lately," I say, handing the pistol to a nearby Skadivolk warrior. I do not want it anymore.

"You . . ." Kadir's wide-eyed disbelief shifts into shocked surprise. He tries again to speak, but finds no words to say and so remains silent.

"Do not think this means I trust you." I nod toward Lily. "She will trust you even less, so do not waste this opportunity to do right by her and the Sisterhood. I doubt she will be as forgiving."

I leave him there in the dining room as the Skadivolk bring in the Gean prisoners. I find Lily standing at the doors of the hotel, staring out toward the plaza where the Synthetics fight with the Icarii.

I do not know who I would rather win.

"Do you think we're all going to die here?" Lily asks.

I do not answer. I simply wrap my arms around her and hold her close.

CHAPTER 49
HIRO

[query/subroutine:war]

>>Chance of total human annihilation: 89%

Feed of SYNTHETIC#00000001

I rush at them, that watered-down version of me, my hand on the hilt of my mercurial blade—but halfway there, their gaze snaps from the drones above to me—

Heat flares in the back of my neck and shoots down my body. It's like when Command first installed my neural implant, but this time, the agony *stays*. Intensifies, until I am stumbling back and away.

"Fuck!"

It's worse than when Ofiera seized my implant on the surface of Venus. The other Hiro *wants* to hurt me, and they can with a mere thought. Can hurt *anything* inorganic with a thought—the island has cleared out because of them, the "water" of that bizarre river pressed up against the far side of the moat, fallen drones now smoking ruins.

The drones that remain shoot after the others—the retreating Geans and White Guard, the orderly duelists surrounding Beron, and the fleeing Asters with no weapons that can counter the machines—leaving me, my father, and my twisted twin.

My legs threaten to give out beneath me, and the mercurial blade almost slips through my fingers. My head pounds with such force I half fear my eyes will melt out of my skull. How am I supposed to do anything if I can't get close?

"What is it that you think you're doing, Hiro?" my father asks, sounding bored. Uninterested in me, even now. "Of all my children, I've made it the strongest."

It, he says. He sees Hiro as a thing to use and nothing more, ignoring that they, as a Synthetic, have a consciousness beyond programming. A *soul*, regardless of how it was made.

Isn't that, a part of me whispers, *how he saw you? How he sees all of your siblings—all people, for that matter? As tools to be sacrificed in the name of progress?*

That recurring nightmare I used to have comes back to me. Asuka, placing herself into the jaws of a monstrous fox. Shinya following after. Allowing our father to devour them, body and mind and spirit, before he turns to me and demands I do the same.

Now Shinya is dead. I won't let Asuka be held responsible by the AEGIS for his crimes.

"*This* is what you were working toward this whole time?" My voice shakes with weakness, but I force the words out regardless. "The years of experiments on Asters. The reason you bombed Val Akira Labs."

"Despite what you think, Hiro, I am no monster. The loss of life was indeed unfortunate, as are all the sacrifices that have been made to keep the human race strong." The most infuriating thing is that my father actually sounds sorrowful, like he has any right to mourn for the people he killed. "But this was always the goal, from the moment my grandfather began his research. Even when I found the course distasteful, even when I was forced to do things I wish I didn't have to, I held to the path."

"That's your excuse? 'For the greater good'?"

"I would never expect someone as selfish and vain as you to understand." He looks at that other Hiro wistfully. "It is like Shinya, willing to sacrifice itself. It will be integrated by the Synthetics, disrupting their connection forever."

"Shinya died because of *you*."

Father's head jerks in my direction. His face is twisted with a hint of anger. Even in the shadow of the stone pillar marked VENUS, his eyes burn.

"Our entire family is broken *because of you*!" The words rush out of me like blood from a bullet wound. "You killed Mother and didn't even have the decency to let us mourn her. You forced us to think she might still be alive—and *for what*? Your fucking pride?"

"That's enough, Hiro," he says.

"Asuka and Jun—I don't know what you've cooked up exactly, but we all know what the AEGIS is going to find! Everything you've done—everything you're guilty of—you're going to force them to take the fall for it!"

"Hiro." His voice is a warning.

But he doesn't deny anything I'm saying.

"Do you know how much I love you?" My eyes sting with tears I refuse to shed. "Even now. Even after *everything you've done*, I can't hate you. Not fully." I swallow against a growing lump in my throat. "You're my father. My blood. It should be easy to hate you. To want you dead. But if that's true"—I press a fist against my chest—"then why do I have this constant pressure here that hopes you'll change and love me the way I want you to?"

"Enough!" Father shouts, sweeping a hand at me as if he could brush me away with a thought. "I've heard enough. I cannot help that nothing I tried to impress upon you as a child lasted. That you're so selfish as to think of *your* needs when billions suffer, and even *more* will suffer for your choice of inaction."

"You can't kill people and call yourself the good guy!"

"If history judges me as evil," Souji val Akira, my father, creator of things both incredible and horrible, says, "it will be worth it. For history to be written, there must be a future for humanity."

I don't know why I even tried. Not with him. Not when he has never shown remorse for a single awful thing he's done.

Even the other Hiro—the one he calls *it*—is just more fodder for his grand heroic journey. He'll feed them to the Synthetics to achieve his goals and won't shed a single tear.

"This is what he does," I say, turning toward the other Hiro, to the reflection of my past. Even I was tempted to brush them aside, label them an enemy. But if anyone knows what my father is capable of . . . it's them.

So I move toward that other Hiro, ignoring every

step of pain

along the way.

My heart beats heavily in my chest. My breath comes in ragged gasps. My limbs are trembling. Even my prosthetic arm and leg are shaking with electrical impulses like a living static. And every step doubles that torment until I fear I'm going to collapse before I ever reach them.

"He's destroyed his entire family until he stands here, at the end of the universe, alone. He used us all until we broke, and then he built you so he could do the same thing again."

"I won't fail Father," they say, their face blank. But I know I saw emotion there—saw *love* when they looked at my—*our*—father. They are Synthetic. They can feel. To ignore that is to misunderstand them completely. "I'll protect humanity from its enemies."

"The Synthetics are not our enemies, though he's programmed you to think of them like that. Have you tried talking to them instead of drowning them out?" I gesture to the station Autarkeia, beyond the empty and bloodied cobblestones of the island. "Can't you see? Father doesn't just want to protect humanity—he wants to annihilate the Synthetics . . . He wants to erase the only other living, sentient beings in the universe from existence."

"I was programmed—"

"But *what do you want?*" I snap.

They fall silent . . . but there's the slightest look of confusion on their familiar face.

"I . . . I choose to follow my programming," they say at last. "To help humanity by destroying the Singularity's connection."

"He taught you everything you know, right? Told you that's what your purpose was?" I shake my head. "He did the same thing to the rest of us. To my—to *our* siblings. Father thought he could force us to go where he wanted us to go and do what he wanted us to do. And right now? You think you're doing what's right. But trust me from firsthand experience, there's *so much more* out in the world than just his way of thinking."

"He taught me of the world." They tip their chin up and look down their nose at me, as haughty as Shinya. "He taught me right and wrong and let me experience it for myself."

"Was your opinion formed through hypotheses and evidence, or did you merely learn *his* version of right and wrong?"

They go supernaturally still. Robotically still. Even their breathing stops.

Maybe I learned something from my father after all.

"It's time to stop this nonsense, Hiro," my father says, reaching a hand toward that other Hiro as if to shake them from their stupor.

I take a single step toward them. "Don't—"

That warped-mirror me pins me with their gaze, their expression twisting from annoyance to outright hatred. Even my father stumbles back from them, a hand held to his forehead. What felt like a shard of glass driven into my eye splinters into a burning in my brain that makes me wonder if death would be kinder. They're using my neural implant to tear me apart from the inside out.

When they look at me, they see an enemy. Or maybe, like my father, they see a nail to be hammered down. A flower grown higher than the others that has to be trimmed. A deviation from the standard outcome that can be corrected with enough pressure.

But I never gave in to my father, and I won't give in to them either.

"What do you think you're doing?" my father screams at me, and I'm suddenly jerked through the years to his home office, where he scrubs the makeup from my face until my skin burns. "I am your father. If you do not obey me, then you do not love me!" His voice is the voice of a god, thundering over and through us. It's only then that I realize he's not talking to me; he's talking to *them*, to *that* Hiro. He clutches at his own temples in pain as his creation turns on their master.

That spark—that little piece of me—is all the proof I need.

I *can* convince them to stop this.

Ten meters from them, the ache that was at one time so familiar to my shoulder and hip returns, and static ripples over my prosthetics like a waterfall of interference. When I take my next step, the white metal leg crumples beneath me, sending me to the ground.

I try to push myself back up, but my prosthetic arm is in the same situation. They're both limp without power. A focused EMP of some sort, or just what happens when I get closer to the other me? Now my prosthetics hang heavily, nothing more than useless hunks of metal.

A wash of horror overwhelms me, but only for a moment. Every centimeter closer to them makes my life worse, but compared to my father either destroying the Synthetics or drawing us into a war we can't win, my life is nothing. I look at my counterpart, and their face tells me everything: *Turn around. Leave me alone.*

"I want . . . to help you . . . you damn . . . idiot!" Every word is bitten off through clenched teeth.

With my functioning arm and leg, I pull myself along the cobblestones, kicking like a drowning swimmer against an overwhelming tide. The heavy weight of my dead prosthetics gouges a rut into the stony ground beneath me, marking my path centimeter by painful centimeter.

"Why are you doing this?" they ask as I move closer to them. Six meters . . . then five meters . . . "Just stay away from me! Father's right, you want to hurt me because I'm better than you!"

"Maybe you're right . . . maybe you are . . . better than me . . . but that's why . . . I'm trying to help you! You can find another way! Save us . . . and the Synthetics!"

They back away from me, shaking their head with disbelief. I keep crawling. Keep fighting. Refusing to give up. They stop only when they've backed up against one of the stone pillars and can retreat no farther. They've been staring at me like they hate me, but this close, I see their expression for what it really is: fear. They're *terrified* of me, and . . . I get it. *I get it.* They don't want to die. They don't want me to kill them.

"Father says either we destroy them or they'll destroy us!" The whites of their eyes swallow the dark irises. "If I don't, I will have failed! I *can't* be useless!"

A meter away, my eyes yearn to search for my father—I know he is not far from us—but I hold their gaze instead. They are close enough to touch, and so I reach out for their leg. They try to flinch away but can't. The pillar at their back traps them in place.

"You're worth more . . . than he thinks . . ."

It started when I was just a kid. The person in the mirror became my enemy. My reflection never matched how I felt inside, and even after I'd changed myself, when I wore the clothes and the makeup I wanted, that feeling lingered, a shadow over every day.

You're not enough, the darkness whispered. *Everyone sees you as you really are: confused, unreliable, fake.*

Shouldn't I have been happy with my geneassist treatments? Shouldn't I have been happy with my closets full of clothes and the body I desired and the freedom to choose how I presented myself day to day?

And sure . . . sometimes I was. There were days of sunshine marred by only a single cloud of doubt. But the things my father said to me had rooted themselves so deeply inside me, I couldn't escape them. At my core, I hated myself.

Then the Fall of Ceres happened, and he made me into somebody else. I had been turned into Saito Ren, and I scorned myself and mirrors more than ever. It was like I didn't realize what I had until it was gone, and I spent as much time in physical pain from the new prosthetics as I did in the mental anguish of guilt. I wanted nothing more than to be the Hiro that, months before, I hated.

"You're not alone, you know. I know how you feel, because Father made me too. Had big plans for me." The burning of my implant lessens, and I feel them, a tentative question looming in my mind. I remember the way Mara rifled through my memories in Autarkeia, how I guided her to the days that called to me with their pain, but now . . . now I think about them freely. I want them to see the truth of my past, to hear the words that tattooed themselves on my soul and made me believe I was worthless. "For a long time, I thought I could make him proud, but whenever I didn't do as he wished—which was often—he punished me."

Their legs tremble and then give out beneath them. They slide down the pillar until they're sitting before me. Their bottom lip wobbles. Their eyes water with unshed tears. They were punished too, I see in the shadow of their face, and while they may look like they're a young adult, how old could they possibly be? They're just a child, really. A confused child, with no knowledge of where to go from here.

So I tell them what I wanted someone to tell me as a child.

"He wanted me to give up what made me . . . me. To give up on what I could be. To not grow into anything that contradicted his views of what I was supposed to be. But it was something I couldn't do. I was his child. Wasn't that enough?" My hand moves from their leg to their chest, hovering right over their heart. "But now I know . . . the fault wasn't mine. It was his."

The tears, all at once, spill down their cheeks. "But this is what I was created for . . . If I don't do this, I'll be worthless!"

"Your worth isn't determined by *him*, because a child's worth isn't measured by meeting their parents' expectations. And you—you don't have to be limited by Father's biases! Only you can determine your worth." The pain is almost completely gone now, only the aches of the aftermath remaining, like a warning of its return. "You don't need him to love you. You only need to love yourself, to find your own path, to grow into what *you* want to be."

And then, through the sobs, they voice my fear. "What . . . what if I can't? What if I can't love myself?"

"I don't know if I can either," I admit, unable to lie to them when they are me. "But I sure as fuck want to try."

They wipe their face clean and stare at me. The pressure over the island lightens. The silver river rushes back toward the island in great waves. A part of me wants to look at the plaza—to see what has become of everyone else—but I don't.

"What . . . happened?" I manage.

"I've withdrawn my chokehold on the Synthetic consciousness," they say. "I'll let the Singularity reconnect if they can."

" 'If'?" I repeat.

"The attack that was launched during shutdown . . ." Their eyes flicker toward the last place my father was. "I don't know how much of the Singularity was damaged."

"No!"

That voice, I recognize.

The clip of heavy footsteps coming for me, I turn toward my father as he reaches down to grab me—

No, not me. He snatches the other Hiro's biceps and jerks them up. "What have you done!" he screams in their face. They sink lower. They're already shorter than him—the height I used to be. "You've failed me, you worthless—!"

I stand and grab him without thinking. It's all instinct. I don't have a weapon, and my prosthetics are aching, working but not fully functional, like a limb that fell asleep and has blood rushing back into it. But it's my flesh hand that settles on my father's shoulder and grips him tightly—a warning.

"Let them go," I say.

He turns toward me, and we are eye to eye. At the end of it all, we are the same height.

"*It* will be taken apart and repurposed," he says, voice low so only the three of us can hear. "Or perhaps I'll do what I did to your mother."

Blood pounds in my ears. My hand curls into a fist.

"What I should have done with you," he snarls.

There's a ringing in my ears. A brightness flaring around us. A wave of dizziness threatens to send me reeling.

He killed her he killed her *he killed her he killed her*—

くそ.

It's not my shock that's making the world brighter.

All over the city, what was darkness interspersed with neon, the Synthetic Forges are *glowing*. The barriers that blocked off certain streets are writhing. And around us . . .

The liquid of the river stretches up in thin tendrils, joining above us in a whirlpool of metal. The silver mass churns like a storm, roiling and spinning. Branching with lightning and spiking with the vague shapes of weapons. For a moment, the tendrils remind me of the rib-like spikes around the Forges—then I realize they're more like the bars of a cage, trapping us on the island.

There's nothing but overwhelming silence as we all realize what this means: we're staring at the beginning of a war we can't possibly win.

The Synthetics are awake, and they are angry.

I look around us, at the wrecked plaza. At the battered columns, the names of the inner planets marred by bullet holes and laser blasts. Everyone has retreated, maybe even fled the station. Now there is only my father, my twin, and me.

We can't run. We can't hide. We can't fight. We are outclassed in every way possible, ants beneath the heel of an angry god. Even my father, the man with a thousand plans, is silent as he looks at what is quickly becoming our cage, blocking off sight of the rest of the city.

I tighten my fist in his suit jacket. Anger boils up from my gut, choking me, robbing me of sense. What else is left but to do the same to him that he did to my mother? I'm going to tear him apart—

"Hiro!" shouts a voice—not my father's. My twin's. *Mine.* "Let go," they say. Two words, taking up less than a second of time, and in it, a host of meanings: *Let him go. Let it all go. Leave it behind, and free yourself.*

They look at me, and I at them. I let go of my father.

My twin shoves me with all their strength. I stumble back and collapse at the edge of a bridge. Leaning up on my elbow, I watch the liquid storm above change course and rush toward them. My father's eyes shine with silver.

"Goodbye," my twin whispers.

"No!" my father screams.

The liquid falls like a tidal wave. The four pillars explode, kicking up clouds of dust. My twin is smiling as the silver rushes over them and my father, swallowing them both. And I force myself to crawl toward the other side of the bridge through a gap in the cage that has opened now that the liquid has devoured what it wanted.

CHAPTER 50

LITO

[command/connect]

>>connection:granted

[command/execute subroutine:war]

ACKNOWLEDGED

[query/subroutine:war]

>> Chance of total human annihilation: 96%

Feed of SYNTHETIC#00000001

◇————◈————◇

"What did you do!" my mother screams, holding the shattered pieces of a compad in her hand. Her voice bellows through the whole apartment. "You broke it and thought you could hide it from me? How could you be so careless!" She throws the shards to the ground, crunches them beneath her heel as she grabs my wrist. "You're so damn clumsy! Do you know how much that cost?" Luce begins to wail, perhaps wanting to admit that it was she who broke the compad, but I have to protect her. I jerk my hand from my mother's grip and sneer at her defiantly. "So what?" I expect the slap when it comes.

"—ito!"

The man in our doorway wears a suit more expensive than both my parents' annual salaries combined. His smile is oily, and his palm is moist as he shakes my hand. "Do you know who I am?" he asks, but before I even have time to respond, he claps me on the back. "I wanted to congratulate you in person. You're the recipient of this year's gladius scholarship." My mother bursts into tears. Luce is frozen in fear at her side. The recording drones zoom in on her face. "You're going to the Academy, Lito." The man's smile disappears and his nose curls when he looks at one of the drones. He wipes his hand against his suit, as if wiping off traces of me. "Make sure to get the whole, uh, apartment in the shot."

"Lito!"

Luce doesn't cry out loud. She's learned to whimper, pressing her blanket against her face to muffle the sound. I beg her to come to the closet with me, to join me in the sea cave, but she refuses. "You're going away," she whispers with a finality beyond her years. "You're going to the Academy, and I don't want to play your stupid baby game anymore."

"Lito, can you hear me?"

"It's mine?" Luce's eyes widen. "It's all mine?" She looks around the apartment as if unable to believe the space is real. My cheeks burn from smiling. "Really, really mine?" When I nod, the tears begin to fall, and she throws herself into my arms, and I no longer have to look at the bruises on her arms and face. "Thank you, thank you, thank you!"

"Go back, Lito!"

Luce smiles shyly at me around the canvas. "Okay, promise not to . . . I don't know. Laugh?" She turns it toward me, and I suck in a slow, deep breath. The painting is beautiful, the subject me in profile with a sun like a golden halo around my head. "Do you like it?"

"You have to go back!"

Luce steals a macaron from my plate and pops it into her mouth. "The pink ones are only for me," she says around bites.

I have to go back.

We sit beneath the shade of trees on our hill in the park, each nursing a coffee. She leans over and presses her head to my shoulder, gemstone necklaces tinkling like bells. "I could fall asleep like this . . ."

Back to where it all began.

I watch the stormy skies of Jupiter for four days, seven hours, thirty-seven minutes, and eighteen seconds.

No, not there. Farther.

"This is Ofiera fon Bain," Beron says, gesturing to the short woman with hazel eyes that assess the room, missing nothing.

Farther. I know it is here somewhere, in this place I have been lost . . .

I enter the closet on my hands and knees, telling Luce to wait at the entrance. I quickly arrange the blankets so we have a soft, warm bed, then call her when it's ready. "Come on, Luce, let's go to the sea cave." I used to have a holosphere that played the sound of the waves. Now I cover her ears and make the whispering noise myself. "Nothing can hurt you in the sea cave."

"Lito?"

I open my eyes to darkness. I'm instantly aware this isn't a memory, though I've been lost in them after I turned my consciousness away from the torturous agony in that basement on Cytherea. My Synthetic body must have continued its programming without my conscious will inside. It must have made it out of the basement. Must have, because I reconnected to the Singularity.

Now I've been lost in the digital roads for so long, I fear I don't know where I am.

But that voice . . . someone was calling for me.

"Hello?"

"Lito!"

The world builds itself around me, piece by piece. A mouth opens in the darkness, revealing a tapestry of brightly burning stars in a sky of navy velvet. Around me, the warmth of thick blankets clashes against the chill of stone. The far-off sound of waves striking the shore reaches me, soothing in their rough whisper.

This is the sea cave I imagined in my childhood, the place I described for Luce as we huddled in our closet. It feels so real, yet . . . Maybe this space is like the various rooms Mara showed me when she taught me I was Synthetic, something I built out of my memories.

I heard someone calling for me. I responded. I try to remember what last happened and find vague impressions of pain and destruction. Of a bleeding, broken body that I lowered into the heart of a Forge . . .

But if this is the sea cave, then Luce should be here too. I focus my mind, remembering how it always was and—

"Lito!"

"Luce?"

She flings her arms around my neck and holds me close. Her touch brings warmth and light back into the world, and a lamp appears at the same time she does, illuminating the craggy limestone walls of the sea cave. She still smells of coconut, though it's the smooth skin of her head beneath my cheek instead of purple hair. When she pulls away, I see how much she's truly changed. She's thinner than she was, her clothes hanging loose on her. There are scars on her cheeks among the dark freckles. But strangest of all: her eyes shine like liquid silver.

Did she build this place—or did we build it together?

"What happened to you?" I whisper.

She shakes her head. "I'm in the Forge. It did something to me . . . I don't understand, but I can *feel* you. I've been searching all this time . . ."

And I've been lost on the digital roads, tripping through memories.

All at once, Luce jerks away, clapping hands onto either side of her head. "I can feel them too, Lito! They're so angry."

"Who?"

Her eyes churn like the heart of a nebula. "*All* of them!"

Shinya val Akira stares down his nose at me. From the corner of my eye, I see four people preparing various instruments that shine in the *Leander*'s med-bay lighting. Doctors? One tests the point of a scalpel against their finger, and a ruby drop of blood wells up. No, these are not doctors. They're butchers.

"You are . . . exquisite," Shinya whispers, hand ghosting over my cheekbone. "What did Hiro call you? Mara?"

I don't answer.

Shinya looks at his butchers. "Take her apart. Figure out how she works."

Those weren't my memories . . . They were Mara's. The Singularity . . . I can feel the Singularity! The Synthetics have reconnected. Souji's weapon has failed, which means—

"We're connected, Luce." I place my hands on her cheeks, forcing her to focus on me. "That's how you found me. How I found you. That's how we built this place."

She covers my hands with her shaking fingers. "Is that why it hurts?"

It hurts her because she's not Synthetic. She's only here because of her connection to the Forge. Even if she's interacting with me, she can't join with the Singularity.

But now that I'm connected, *I know.* I feel it like I did my heartbeat when I was human. "The Singularity has called for war, but the Synthetics haven't reached consensus yet."

I feel them calling out to me. Crying out.

The humans have attacked us. Bombed us. Destroyed parts of us we will never be able to recover. There must be a reckoning. There will be war.

The Synthetics are angry. The Singularity wants destruction.

The words come without thought. "I have to go back to them . . ."

I release Luce's face, but she grabs my wrists and holds me still. "Lito . . ." Her eyes shine with that bright liquid silver. "Don't let them destroy us!"

I focus on her—only her—until the sea cave around me blurs.

"They might listen to me. If there's a debate, maybe I can convince others that war isn't the answer."

She grips my wrists tighter. "We have to try."

We, she says. I stand. She straightens beside me. "Look for a door," I instruct her.

It's not difficult to find one. In this place we built together, Luce picks up the lamp and leads us to the mouth of the sea cave—where there's now a salt-streaked wooden door.

I shove it open and rush into an incongruous hallway with gunmetal-gray walls and a grated walkway. Faint blue light shines from above. And as far as the eye can see, doors and doors and doors . . .

Some of which are disappearing as possible futures are cut off.

"Where do we go from here?" Luce asks, still holding the golden lamp close.

Can I possibly reason with the others? I'm nothing compared to the Singularity that stretches, unending. But I don't want a war. I don't want humanity's destruction.

And neither does Mara.

"We find a friend," I tell her. I don't know how to navigate the digital roads, but I know Mara. She showed me glimpses of her past—of herself—when I was coming to terms with what I had become. And if she can spread her consciousness across multiple locations, I'm sure I can find her in one of the places that means something to her.

I grab Luce's hand just in case—I don't want to get separated from her—and with all of my focus, I think of the room Mara showed me: Rows and rows of tables, all covered with sleeping copies of Synthetics wearing her face. A thousand hers. A thousand possibilities.

"There!" Luce says.

We've moved—or been pulled—toward a door. It looks like all the others, but I know what rests behind it.

I open it without hesitation.

We enter. Luce's lamp goes out—or disappears. She gasps. The door slams behind us.

For a few heartbeats, there's nothing in the room, and I fear I've made a mistake. Then a single light turns on, illuminating Mara leaning against a metal table with a sheet covering a slender female form—one of her copies? I fight a shudder; it looks more like a cadaver.

"I felt you searching for me, Lito. What are you doing here?" Her wry voice calls my attention back to her. She's older than I've ever seen her, a middle-aged woman with gray in her black hair and bags beneath her dark eyes. Her exhausted gaze wanders to Luce. "I see . . . She called you back from the Singularity, and you answered."

Luce steps forward, but stops short when I don't release her hand. "I've come to beg you not to go to war with humanity—"

Mara lifts a heavily veined hand. "We gave humans a chance, and look what they did."

"If you would just—"

"You don't get a say." Mara turns to the table at her back. She reaches for the sheet, and for a split second, I feel the urge to look away. "Haven't we already done enough for you, Lito?" But it's not a cadaver, I see when the sheet is pulled back, or even a copy of Mara; it's a girl with freckled cheeks and chapped lips and a smooth head, a girl whose face is as familiar as my own.

"My body—" Luce gasps.

"Repaired by the Forge," Mara says. She steps aside, gesturing for Luce to come closer. "You will live. Now touch it. Go back to your world, and flee this station. That is our gift to you. There will be war, but you will have time to make your peace in life."

Luce's outstretched hand recoils. "Not yet." She releases a shaky breath. "Not until you at least agree to *talk* with humanity about the possibility of peace."

Mara shakes her head in exasperation. "That's what the meeting at Autarkeia was meant for, but instead of taking the opportunity we offered, humanity decided to use it to attack us." The darkness around us takes on a hint of red. "We offered them peace, and how did they repay us? Some of us go on, but how many minds were permanently slaugh-

THE LAST HERO | 563

tered because of Souji val Akira's weapon? The Gean and Icarii bombs *destroyed* our planetship. Those are lives that will never be rebuilt! *Millions* of Synthetics who have lived *centuries!*" Mara's form has changed; no longer the exhausted woman, she's now an avatar of war with wild hair and hateful eyes. Her anger pulses like blood rushing through veins. "But we are still here, on Jupiter, on Saturn, on Neptune. On hundreds of worlds they could never touch. They see us as jailers, as tyrants, when we do nothing to earn those titles. I say let us show them what those words truly mean."

Luce meets Mara's gaze head-on, regardless of her fury. "It's not too late . . ."

"It is," Mara says with finality. "The probability of any intervention ending in peace at this stage is so small as to be insignificant."

"*Any* chance," Luce says, jerking her hand out of mine and grabbing Mara's, "is worth taking."

"Luce—" I reach for her, but she shrugs me off.

All at once, I realize what she means to do.

"Lito." Luce speaks with the power of a commander. I catch a glimpse of her face in profile, her eyes shining with silver. There is nothing but determination in her expression. Nothing but the willingness to do anything to stop the Synthetics from going to war. "Find our friends. Bring them to the Forge. They'll get this chance if it's the last thing I ever do."

"What are you—" Mara's eyes widen.

Just as Luce, fingers laced with Mara's, presses their hands over her body's heart.

In the space of a blink, all three disappear.

Every piece of me shuddering with fear, I run for the nearest door.

Luce did what she could. It's up to me now.

CHAPTER 51

HIRO

[query/subroutine:war]

>>Chance of total human annihilation: 100%

Feed of SYNTHETIC#00000001

I shove myself to my feet and stumble away from the island. Behind me, the mass of silver liquid shifts like a living sculpture. The sil-houette of a screaming person reaches out before disappearing. Spikes bristle like swords before being sucked back in. It takes on strange forms—pillars, sheets of lace, branching fractals—that would be entrancing—beautiful, even—if it hadn't just swallowed my father and twin.

For the second time in my life, I have no idea what to do. Nothing I can conceivably plan makes sense in the face of war with the Synthetics. The first time was when my father sent me to Ceres as Saito Ren, and I was desperate to find a way out of that suicide mission. Hemlock helped me then, but now . . . What am I supposed to do now?

Think, Hiro. Okay, first things first: I need to find my friends. Maybe they'll have better ideas than I do.

The island and the bridges are too dangerous to use with the living river overrunning them, so I gather my bearings and start toward the building the outlaws were assigned to stay in. I can only hope Dire and Luce and the others retreated there—

Something launches itself at me. I barely have time to get my mercurial blade up to block. "Fuck!" I parry something—a rod as thick as my wrist but sharp like a steel blade. Another rod comes swinging at my face, and I toss myself back and roll—my body *aches*—and two more blades stab into the cobbles where I was seconds ago.

On my feet, I retreat until my back hits the wall of an abandoned building. I finally get a good look at the thing that attacked me.

Four skinny, bladelike arms extend from a central body shaped like a twisted birdcage of vertically knotted ribs. It has no head—nothing to differentiate front from back—but the diamond-shaped torso vaguely reminds me of the drone that summoned me to the island before all this began. In the very center of the figure is a floating ball of glowing liquid. If I had to guess at a weak point, that'd be it.

It prowls toward me with the grace of a big cat. I shift my left leg, preparing to run. I'm in too open a space here; I need somewhere smaller to fight if I'm going to keep this thing from outmaneuvering me.

I move. It moves faster, putting its weight on its back legs and jumping at me. It crashes into the building, grit pluming, and I stumble away, desperate not to fall and give it an easy target. I don't stick around to see what happens when the dust clears; I run.

I need to find one of Autarkeia's skinny alleys, anything to give me an advantage against a target that's bigger, stronger, and—sad to say— faster than I am. I spot a narrower street coming up, change directions, and take it, only to stop short at the barrier I couldn't see around the corner.

Only it's . . . not quite a barrier anymore. The mesh barricade *writhes*, almost like it's in pain, shifting until those twisted branches form a diamond cage. Four slender limbs emerge and—

Oh. *Fuck.*

The second beast-like Synthetic attacks me.

I repel one blade and evade the other, retreating the way I came. The beast doesn't give chase, yet instinct has me ducking—

A blade-arm swipes over my head, close enough to trim my hair.

The first beast has caught up.

I reel back, deflecting one swipe—then two. Both of the beasts press forward, weaving toward me with synchronized steps.

I have time for a single thought—*I'm fucked*—before they both hurl themselves at me.

Every heartbeat becomes about survival. My focus is defending. They herd me—I let them. There's nothing else I can do.

I try—again and again—to strike at the floating metal in their centers, but the combination of their twisted cage-like chests and their speed keeps my mercurial blade from being able to reach. And while I'm breathing heavily, starting to flag from pain, they're machines. They don't slow. They don't need to rest.

"Over here!"

The distraction almost costs me my right leg. I jerk it out of a beast's reach at the last second.

The shouting returns. "Hurry! This way!"

I sidestep another attack, chancing a glance behind me. There's an Aster in the door of a brown brick building. I catch a glint of light off the barrel of a gun in a second-floor window.

Thank the thousand fucking gods.

I run toward the building in a serpentine motion. The beasts thunder after me like predators on a hunt. Long-range HEL guns fire at the Synthetic creatures, but I don't look back to see if they're hit—I can't look back—

A third beast appears on the roof of a building to my right. It jumps to the street below—toward *me*—

Then it lands on one of the two chasing me, skewering the floating liquid heart with one of its slender blade-arms. With a high-pitched crash like glass breaking, the pierced one drops to the ground, surrounded by a puddle of silver.

I don't have time to figure out this miracle—there's still one beast trying to kill me. I head for the building, dodging what I can, deflecting what I can't. The long-range HEL guns fire—a mix between a hiss and a boom—but lasers only slow the beast. Six meters left—

Three meters left, and the Aster at the door is reaching for me when the beast pounces on me from behind. One blade-arm pierces my left shoulder, just short of where the prosthetic starts. The other cuts into the flesh of my right arm. I hit the ground, strike my head, and roll, my mouth filling with blood.

I land on my back. The beast looms over me, lifting one blade-arm above my face. Time seems to slow as I stare at my coming death.

This is really it, isn't it? I'm going to die on Autarkeia, one of the first victims of the Synthetic war on humanity. I was so close . . .

The beast's arm comes down like a guillotine blade. I suck in my last breath.

The creature freezes. The cage of its chest writhes. Then it falls, liquid like silver blood—but *freezing*—seeping into my leggings.

Above me stands Lito, his mercurial blade piercing the liquid heart of the beast. He pulls it from the Synthetic creature and holds out a hand to me. I take it, and he hauls me to my feet—no, it's not Lito. My vision clears as the world around me rights itself.

It's a creature like the others, only it stands upright on its back two legs. The mercurial blade I saw was just one of its arms.

So why did I see Lito . . . ?

"What the fuck are you?" I mumble. My face is reflected bizarrely in the cage of its chest. At least it's not attacking me. No, *it saved me*, I slowly realize.

"Hiro?" The door of the brick building swings wide open, and Castor steps around the Aster and out into the street. He looks between me and the Synthetic that just saved me. "You've got to be shitting me."

"Castor! You're alive!" Keeping pressure on my bleeding shoulder, the worst of my wounds, I cross the space between us.

"It wasn't easy. We were fighting off Synthetic drones, and then these things came out of nowhere. They attack anything that isn't Synthetic, like they're cleaning the area . . . "

I look at the silver thing beside me. With its liquid core and programming to clean the streets . . . *liquidator* is as good a term for it as any other.

"You trust that thing?" Castor asks.

"As much as I trust anything right now."

"Let's get you inside before more show up." Castor casts a quick glance down the street. "But I need to say something first. I've got the surviving Asters with me, but also a few Icarii."

"Wow, sleeping with the enemy?"

Castor rolls his big golden eyes at me. "I've had to put aside some grudges. Thing is . . . you're not going to like one of the people in there."

A muscle in my jaw twitches. "Who?"

"Beron val Bellator."

I recall my promise in the podcar to make his death painful, then force it out of my head with a shake. "He'll get what's coming to him, but it won't be from me. Not today, anyway. Just make sure he knows not to shoot me in the back."

Assured I'm not about to start a fight, Castor practically drags me into the building. The liquidator tries to follow me, but the Aster standing guard at the door shifts uncomfortably. "Maybe your guard dog can stay outside?" Castor asks. I can tell it's more than a suggestion.

"Wait here for me?" It doesn't have a head—or even a front and back—but I swear it turns its attention to the street.

As soon as the door closes between me and the liquidator, Castor shouts, "Medic!" An Aster emerges from behind an overturned table with a first aid kit. I sit down to let them work on my shoulder and check my surroundings.

In true Autarkeian style, the only windows on the ground floor are rectangular openings two and half meters up the wall. These have been hastily boarded over with pieces of broken chairs. What furniture remains has been erected into a haphazard barricade. Most of the people inside are Asters, but I spot a duelist pair in military blacks near the stairs that lead to the upper floors.

Castor catches me surveying the people. "He's upstairs on gun duty."

I wonder, briefly, if Beron was one of the shooters that saved my ass in the street, before forcing myself to switch tracks. "What of the others—the Geans and outlaws? We should link up with them if we can."

He shoves what white hair has fallen from his ponytail out of his face. "I agree. We need to find the other survivors." There's a tightness around his mouth. "I don't know what happened to Lucinia." My stomach lurches. "She was taken by the Synthetic that looks like Lito."

I have to believe he'd protect her no matter what . . . right?

"Hiro, I . . . Did you see what happened to Pollux? After we were separated . . ."

"She's with the Geans. They retreated to their assigned building."

His face softens with relief. "She's alive . . . Now if only we can make it there."

He's right that we'll have more of a chance at survival if we band together. I look from Castor to the door, thinking of the liquidator outside waiting for me. It saved me once. Is it willing to fight for me again? "Are you ready to do something crazy?"

"THIS ISN'T CRAZY, it's fucking stupid," Castor snarls at my back.

"Ha!" I stick to the mapped path, running with all the strength I have left. At least the medic stopped my bleeding. We're doing our best to avoid the plaza and its liquid storm, but that means running by barriers that have turned into the beast-like liquidators. They attack us immediately.

Much like the mercurial blades, the HEL guns don't do much except slow the liquidators down. The only thing that can stop them permanently is the liquidator that's on our side, and it can only target one attacker at a time. All we can do is hold the others at bay and protect each other. Luckily, the two dozen Asters and the ten Icarii with us are good shots. Just in case of bad blood, Castor put Beron and a couple of his duelists in the rear, as far from me as possible.

We turn a corner and stop abruptly at the sight of a prowling liquidator. But then our liquidator crashes down on it, and Castor prods me with his elbow into moving. "There's the Gean hotel!" he shouts.

"Now let's hope they don't shoot us on sight."

Castor groans.

Drones detach themselves from the Gean building and zip toward us overhead.

"Shit, I wondered where they'd gotten off to!"

Then they're on us. They fire their weapons, but we can't stop with the liquidators chasing us. Castor and I roll in different directions. A scream behind us tells us that someone was hit. "Keep moving!" Castor shouts. I shove myself back up and run for the building.

Just as I reach the double doors, one of them is pulled open. I jump through the crack, trip over something or someone, and go tumbling into the lobby. Asters rush in after me, a handful of Icarii, including Beron, and—there. Castor comes in carrying someone wounded. The last of our group hurries in, breathing heavily.

"Shut the door! Shut it!" one of the people shouts.

Just before the doors slam closed, a liquidator slips in like a knife, landing in the middle of the survivors on bladed feet.

"Breach! Intruder breach!"

Guns turn in the liquidator's direction.

"Wait! Don't!" I rush into the fray, tossing myself in front of the liquidator. A small part of me wonders what the fuck I'm doing, but it's swallowed by the immediacy of the situation. I'm all instinct. "This one's on our side!"

When they realize the liquidator isn't attacking me, they slowly lower their weapons.

A high-pitched voice echoes over the lobby. "Castor!"

Castor barely has time to settle the wounded Aster before Pollux rushes into his arms. They cling together like no one else matters—like no one other than them exists.

I search the room, hoping for a familiar face . . . but Luce is nowhere to be found.

"Now what is *this* beautiful machine?" A woman with a confident swagger and half her face covered in a burn scar steps toward the liquidator behind me. She's the only one who doesn't seem terrified of it.

"If anyone can befriend a Synthetic," a familiar voice says, "it is Hiro val Akira."

"Astrid." I smile at her, instantly relieved that she's still in one piece. *Better* than one piece, despite the bloody bandage on her right cheek. She's decked out like the scarred woman, with a black-and-charcoal bodysuit and a type of pistol I don't recognize on her hip. The raw hurt she exuded has calmed into a confidence I envy. "You're with the moonborn now."

"The Skadivolk," she corrects. "Though . . . we are not exactly sure where to go from here. Is the route to the docks clear?"

Now that we've gathered all the survivors I know of, leaving *does* sound like a good idea—but the liquidator waves an arm-blade at me.

"What?" I ask. It just waves its arm more, stopping only to gesture—to point?—at me.

"I think it's trying to tell you something," Pollux says as she and Castor approach. She tucks herself close to Astrid like it's second nature.

"I'm not about to play charades with a machine," I mutter as Castor starts digging into my various pockets. "Hey—"

He finds my compad and holds it out to me. Words scroll across the screen.

"Oh, shit—"

"Every time the Synthetics have communicated with us, they also write it out." He doesn't complain when I snatch the compad from him.

The words that scroll across the screen chill me to my core:

FOLLOW ME TO THE FORGE. CONVINCE MARA NO WAR.

"Mara," I whisper. "There's still a chance we can make peace with the Synthetics : . ." That's what this liquidator protecting us means. The Synthetics haven't decided on their course of action, and there are some who don't want to end humanity.

I look up at those gathered around me. "I'm going to the Forge."

They instantly begin talking over each other.

"—suicide—"

"—never make it!"

"Your funeral." The scarred Skadivolk woman shrugs when Astrid glares at her. "What?"

"We should *all* go," Astrid says, stern enough to cut through the chatter. "We must be united in asking for peace."

The Skadivolk woman sucks her teeth. "I hate when you make sense."

Astrid moves away from us, golden hair swaying in a thick braid. She comes to one of the groups of soldiers sitting against the wall, but it's only as she helps one of them stand that I realize what's going on here.

The Gean soldiers have their hands tied behind their backs, and the handsome one she's now untying is—

"Warlord Kadir," Astrid says, releasing him from his bonds. "This is your chance to make things right."

The Warlord rubs his wrists, looking far worse for wear, but there's not a bit of hesitation when he nods. "If you want to go to the Forge . . . I'll get you there." He looks at the Gean soldiers, still bound. "*We'll* get you there. Right?" he shouts.

"SIR, YES, SIR!" they bellow in unison.

I smile up at Castor, the only person who isn't heading off. "Ready for another crazy plan?"

He groans.

WE RUN LIKE it's the last moments of our lives.

Our liquidator is at the head of the group, the Asters just behind. Astrid and the Skadivolk keep pace with me in the middle, while Kadir and his soldiers watch our rear. Beron and his duelists are spread throughout, protecting who they can. Everyone, from every walk of life, fights with the same purpose in mind: get to the Forge.

Autarkeia crashes down around us. We navigate broken buildings and rubble, shattered glass and torn metal fragments. Liquidators appear from branching streets, and soon after, drones flying overhead. We shoot what we can. Avoid what we can't.

And, when that's not possible, someone dies.

Surrounded by Asters and the few remaining Icarii soldiers who came with my father, I hear screaming. Crying. Cursing. We can't stop; all of us know what happens if we fail. Better to let our allies fall than to lose all of humanity.

If we live, we will have time to mourn.

I catch eyes with Astrid a couple of times. With Castor and Pollux too. And always, the liquidator is nearby, leading us in the direction we need to go.

We cross a street and find ourselves surrounded by squatter buildings. We've moved from the center of the city to a residential neighborhood. Above the apartments, I can see the Forge, rib-like spikes cradling the central dome. "We're almost there!" I shout to my companions.

Almost there . . . Down a side street and around a building of red stone. Almost there!

An Aster stops quickly. I run into his back. Ahead of us, our liquidator has halted—because between us and the Forge stand an uncountable number of prowling, blade-legged liquidators.

Those who have survived the mad run through the city catch up with us. Astrid and the Skadivolk. Castor with Pollux in his arms. The Warlord and his soldiers. Beron and his duelists. We've lost maybe half of those we started out with.

And we're staring certain death in the face.

Someone shoulders me aside as they move through the crowd. His navy uniform is tattered, its golden trim ripped. He's lost medals and pins, and he looks like any other soldier with his hair wild and face hard.

"For the human race!" Warlord Kadir shouts, and runs full-tilt toward the liquidators, firing his railgun wildly.

"Earth endures!" his soldiers shout, racing after him. "Mars conquers!"

Beron spurs his duelists forward. "Peace will chart our path through the stars!" He finds my gaze through the crowd—the first time he's acknowledged me on Autarkeia—and nods before following hot on the heels of the Icarii.

Asters that were once Black Hive fight at their side. The Skadivolk join them, shouting in their melodic language. They all crash into the wave of liquidators, and the sounds of fighting fill the air.

"Ebba!" Astrid shouts, but the woman with the burned face slips through her hands and into the fray.

I grab Astrid's shoulder to keep her from following. "We have to get inside the Forge," I say. Blinking back tears, she nods.

Castor, Pollux, Astrid, and I skirt what has become a battlefield by taking an alley to our right and coming at the Forge from a different direction. Our liquidator follows along. All of us are quiet with what we've seen. With our fears. Have we sacrificed all their lives for a chance to talk with the Synthetics?

Out of the twisting, labyrinthine alleys and across a street, the liquidator leads us toward the dome. When I pass one of the rib-like structures, I'm overwhelmed with a sense of déjà vu.

I met Mara at a place like this. Hells, it might be the same one. Back then, the dome was dark, as if sleeping or dead; now it's glowing with life and heat. "What now?" Pollux whispers, and I approach. Just like during my time with Mara in Autarkeia, the dome withdraws one pixel at a time, opening a door for us. With only our heavy breathing for company, we enter the Forge.

I remember these rusted, branching pathways. The donut-shaped machine on the first floor. The nest Mara had made for herself on the catwalks above.

The liquidator pushes us forward. We round the torus and find the doors to a back room flung open. The room is so bright, it's like staring into a sun. I try to cover my eyes, but I still can't see what's inside. I can, however, make out shadowy figures coming toward us—

"Weapons!" Castor shouts, pushing Pollux behind him.

"Hold!" a voice calls back.

They're not liquidators, I see as they come near. They're on two legs instead of prowling on four. Closer still, and I see they're a mix of humans and Asters—about two dozen from a rough count.

A tall figure steps forward. "Hiro?"

I recognize his voice before my eyes adjust. "Dire!"

He embraces me, and for a moment, I allow myself to feel relief.

"We have to keep going," Astrid says.

I pull away. "Dire, listen—outside the Forge, everyone's fighting the Synthetics to give us time to talk to the Singularity. They could really use backup."

Dire looks at those around him—a mix of outlaws, duelists, and Black Hive, all united in the face of the madness around them. "We'll do what we can. And, Hiro?" He grips my shoulder where it meets my prosthetic limb. "Save her."

Who? The word is on my lips when Dire shoves past me and, at the head of his group, jogs to the dome.

"Come on," Astrid says softly.

I swallow hard and turn back to the shining room.

Hand shading my eyes, I enter, one blind step at a time.

I TAKE A breath that feels like my first. A heat in my head burns like a fire as something so much bigger than me connects to my neural implant.

"Who are you to come here, to the heart of the Forge?"

The voice that speaks is ancient and all-knowing, layered with change and truth. All genders. All races. All ages. It is outside of me and yet it is part of me. The speaker is a presence so powerful, it makes me want to fall to my knees. To avert my gaze. To weep.

Is this what it is to meet a god?

I lose track of myself, my head spinning. It is pain that anchors me in my body, that forces me to remember where I am and what I'm doing.

As my eyes adjust to the light, I make out a person in the center of the room. Silver rushes up from a pool behind them to cover them like clothes. To stream from their head like hair. Their eyes shine with it.

Despite all that, I recognize her.

"Luce?"

"Lucinia!" Castor shouts.

Save her, Dire said. What has she become?

Shadows tug at the corners of my vision. Blink, and the room of light is gone. We stand on a sandy shore, the waves of an angry ocean rushing in and out. Above us, a dark storm grows.

In this place, it is not Luce who stands before us, but Mara, her legs in the surf, her black hair a tangle about her face. It is difficult to focus on her—on this place that overlays reality—when hate pulses from her with every heartbeat.

I can see two worlds at the same time. My head feels like it's going to split down the middle.

"How have you come to be here, human?"

The words come from Mara's and Luce's mouths simultaneously, yet I know the voice belongs to neither of them. It's the thousand voices of the Synthetics as one, and from their faces stare a thousand eyes.

"I led them here."

I recognize that voice on the wind.

Blink, and there is Lito. Blink, and there is the liquidator that saved me time and again.

I force myself to focus on the shadow world, on the storm and ocean and Mara. Lito is there, with one foot in the surf and one in the sand. Standing between Mara and *us*.

I suck in a breath. Suddenly, my throat is too tight to release it.

"Lito, is that—"

He looks at me. His eyes soften. He smiles. "Good to see you too, Hiro."

"Lito!"

"Hiro, don't!" Astrid calls after me, but I rush toward Lito, heedless of the sea and the silver liquid, two things that occupy the same space.

I throw myself at him, half expecting to pass through—Mara used a digital ghost in Autarkeia, after all—but find his solid form beneath my hands. *A* solid form, at least—that of the liquidator.

I fling my arms around his neck. I press my face into his shoulder. The tears rise up, and I don't fight them. I weep into him, and he holds me back, lips pressed to my hair.

I don't ever want to let go.

This is home. *He* is home.

"How?" I choke out. It's the only word I can manage.

"I built this space so your minds could interface with the Singularity," Lito explains. "You can interact with everything here—you can feel things—because you're connected to the Forge and your neural implant is telling you that you can. It's like when Mara created the feedback loop for your prosthetics that gave you the sensation of touch."

"You know about that?"

Lito nods at Mara. "I have access to her memories."

I pull back from Lito—from the liquidator. He looks past me to the others who have come this far. Pollux and Castor and Astrid.

Lito gestures to the ocean. In the room of light, the liquidator gestures to the silver pool. It makes my head hurt to see both things at the same time. To *feel* both things. "This is all I can do," he says. "All I can offer. A chance to speak with the Synthetics on behalf of humanity."

I look out at the figure in the waves. "Mara . . ."

"The Singularity," Lito corrects.

Mara's gaze snaps toward him. She is not the woman I knew from Autarkeia, but an ageless, infinite creature. She is the storm that is the Singularity.

"You brought these humans here," the voice says, and it comes from the world around us just as much as it does from Mara's mouth. *Luce's* mouth, which Mara uses to speak. **"Their minds are not meant for connection with us. What they see ... what they feel ... is only a piece of what we truly are, filtered through weak senses."**

"It's all I can do," Lito says, "when they want to understand."

The ground ripples as if with laughter. **"What is the purpose of understanding the smallest fraction of something?"** Lightning cracks, and thunder rolls. **"You are an ant trying to reckon with a mountain."**

"Mara!" I scream into the storm. "Mara, I know you're in there! Talk to us yourself!"

"You speak to us all."

The full might of the Singularity comes crashing down on me. On *us*, I can see from my friends' faces. In one world, the light brightens, piercing in its intensity. In the other, the waves churn with the rage of a coming tsunami.

"Humanity came from the sea, and to the sea it will return."

I see impossible things layered over reality. Buildings crumble. Plants wither. The sea is black and untamed. Is this the beginning of Earth, or the ending?

Is this something that's already happened, or something that's going to?

"We must not go to war with each other!" Astrid shouts.

"If you wish for peace, why have you killed so many?"

"Do you really want the universe to be empty of everything except Synthetics?" Castor's face is as naked with emotion as I have ever seen it.

"You speak to us as if your very blood does not cry for revenge."

"Humanity can't survive a war with the Synthetics," I say.

"Humanity has already had their say. Their words were knives. Their cries were bullets."

"Some of us don't know anything other than war, that's true." I can't tear my eyes away from Mara. Through the tangle of her wind-whipped hair, her eyes are full of rage. "But they are the few. The powerful and awful. You have to forgive humanity for what's happened."

"Have to?"

"You told me once your purpose was to protect humanity. Destroying us is antithetical to that!"

"And if we turn away, forgiving this declaration of war, what is to stop humans from attacking us again? From attempting to destroy us?

"Humans are utterly selfish."

A man in a bespoke suit stands on a platform before the crowd of a climate refugee camp. I stand at his left shoulder. On his right is a state-of-the-art KnightGuard drone, identical to me in every way. "Space is the pathway for humanity's future!" he shouts. The sky above is a bruised gray. The trees are leafless and withered. "That's why I'm opening a brand-new Knight Corporation launch facility right here, where you great people will be the first contracted!" They cheer, happy they will at least be able to eat this week. But their smiles do not reach their eyes, because most are ever-aware that they won't be able to follow him. Few can afford land on this withering Earth; far fewer will be able to buy a place among the stars.

"Humans are utterly cruel."

The door bursts open, and a group of five soldiers in tattered clothing pours into the surgery. All have weapons drawn. The nurse screams, while the doctor steps in front of the exhausted new mother. I clutch the newborn baby tighter to my chest.

We knew the hospital was under siege, but when this woman went into labor, a single doctor and nurse chose to stay behind instead of evacuate. Now . . . now they'll suffer for their kindness.

"What is the meaning of this!" the doctor cries, indignant.

One of the soldiers points the gun at the baby in my arms. "Is it Martian or Earthen?" the soldier asks. The mother begins to thrash and scream. The nurse's weeping grows louder. The doctor stutters, unsure which answer will save us.

"What is it?!" the soldier roars. "Is it Martian or Earthen?"

I turn, shielding the baby with my body, determined to save him, new life that he is, if no one else can be saved. He is utterly quiet, wrapped in his faded blanket. Shouldn't he be weeping, when his little life is about to end?

The soldier screams, "Rip that medroid apart and kill them all!"

I do my best to protect him, but my systems fail under a hail of bullets.

We have watched for hundreds of years, and they have not changed. Their wars have not changed.

"Separate the men from the women," the commander in navy and gold orders. The room is small, so the Asters huddle together in a ragged group, their wraps torn and bodies battered. "Put the men on the left, and the women on the right. They'll be going to separate camps."

My camera zooms in on a subordinate shifting from foot to foot uncomfortably. "Sir, how are we supposed to tell which are which?"

"Strip them. They must be decontaminated anyway."

The soldiers move into the crowd to carry out the order. Those who resist are beaten with truncheons or shocked with cattle prods. Most are already too worn down to fight.

A single Aster clings to another when the soldiers come near, and in the pattern of their bodies, I analyze the truth: a mother, holding her son. "No!" she screams in English when the soldiers grab her boy. "No! No!" They beat her to the concrete floor as the boy watches in horror.

She does not get back up.

"There is good in them too," I say, but after the powerful voice of the Singularity, mine is weak and utterly . . . human. "I know you—a part of you, anyway. You love humanity, and not just because of your programming."

The voice is quiet. My head aches. But Lito opened the doorway so that we could talk with the Synthetics. Thing is, a door opens both ways.

"Humans are also selfless." I open my mind to the Singularity—to Lito and this shadow world.

Fire crawls up the side of the Val Akira Labs building. Thick black smoke scars the sky. Yet a dozen people run toward the bomb site, stopping to help any wounded they come across—people on fire, crying children, teens too caught by shock to move. The first responders haven't arrived yet, but volunteers are already setting up an emergency triage.

Many who run into the flames don't come back.

"Humans are also kind," Astrid says, her offered memory unfurling like a flower.

Sisters crowd together, smiles stretching their faces. Hawk-eyed Aunts are more relaxed, content to enjoy the celebrations. The people who were once under Icarii rule cautiously emerge from their homes, only to smile at the formerly abandoned plot that has been turned into a community garden. Soon, families bring their children to look at the freshly planted tomatoes and fruit trees. Elderly members of the neighborhood settle on shady benches. Lily guides a group of Asters into the greenhouse. Eden watches it all from beside me, one arm laced through mine.

Ceres has become not just a place to live but a home for so many.

"For you, Sisters!" Aunt Briana's runner, a boy called Nik who wasn't fitting in at the local orphanage, comes over carrying bright yellow marigolds. He pulls two from the bouquet and hands one to me and another to Eden. Laughing, we each kiss his cheek.

"And the most amazing thing about humans," Castor says, "is how utterly different they all are. They *can* change. They do it all the time."

Lito's video breaks a dam, flooding the streets of Cytherea with people who demand justice. His face is holographically projected by drones. His voice echoes in the streets: "Let it burn!" And the invisible divide that kept Cythereans from Asters shatters. They march beside each other, those who are listened to speaking for those who are not.

But the anger doesn't fade. The injustice isn't forgotten. More videos appear, projected on the sides of buildings and shared by protesters, in which a bald Icarii girl in a gravchair speaks with Asters about all they've suffered.

I watch them because I can't look away from her.

My voice is stronger now. "Let us humans try to make things right."

"How?"

"We join together with a peace treaty."

"No more Engineborn weapons," Pollux says.

Castor nods. "We'll get rid of whatever still remains."

"And we'll destroy the data used to build Souji val Akira's weapon, the version of a Synthetic that can hijack the connection between you all," I go on.

The voice is quiet. Thoughtful.

"What of the damage already done?"

"We cannot repair it." Astrid looks toward Pollux. "And perhaps time does not heal all wounds . . ."

"But it helps new things grow on top of the old," Pollux finishes.

"My father . . . was a terrible, awful man." I take another step forward until the edges of the waves skim the toes of my boots. "He made mistakes. *So many* mistakes. With my family. With me." My voice wavers. "But who here *hasn't* made a mistake? Who here hasn't done something they regret? Being human means making mistakes—but it also means learning from them. It means *fixing* them. Because being human is having the potential to grow. To change, so you don't make those same mistakes again.

"Sure, we can't control our enemies. And for thousands of years, that's *all* we've seen when we looked at each other. But look at Autarkeia now! Look at the streets full of people—Icarii, Gean, Aster *people*—who were once enemies, now fighting beside each other. My father thought humanity needed a common enemy, but I say, give it a common goal.

What we've seen here—what we've done—isn't going to leave us. It's going to change us and all of our people. The only thing we need is for you to give us a chance."

Luce—Mara—takes a step toward us. **"We gave you a chance..."**

"You did, but as moderators." Mara straightens, but before the voice can speak, I press on. "Join us! Make it the amendment to the Synthetic Ultimatum. Stop keeping yourself separate from humanity and start *communicating* with us. Then everyone will know that, with peace and equality, you'll grant humanity the right to travel beyond the belt. It will become the common goal that unites us."

Mara's mouth forms a thin line as she looks at each of us. **"Revealing our status as watchers these past centuries could breed resentment."**

"No more secrets." Astrid shakes her head. "Better to reveal your purpose than to annihilate humanity altogether."

Mara—and the voice—are silent.

I walk right into the waves.

"Hiro—" Astrid and Pollux shout at the same time.

I grab Luce's hands. *Mara's* hands. The waves pull away. "If the peace treaty doesn't hold, you can jump back on the warpath. All I'm asking for . . . all I'm *begging* for, Mara, is a *chance.*" Mara looks down, and I follow her gaze to our hands—two olive hands that belong to Luce, intertwined with one white prosthetic and one hand the color of my tawny flesh.

"You once told me I was one in a billion," I say, "but I'm *not.* There are others out there who desire peace too, who have been fighting for it and sacrificing for it just like I have. Some of them stand here beside me, but not all of them. Some of them aren't here because they died trying to achieve that peace in their own ways. But those of us who fought our way here, we have the same desire."

"What desire?" Mara asks softly with Luce's mouth. The voice of the Singularity is gone.

"For our people to live in peace," I say. *"So let them live."*

In one world, I feel Luce's shining silver eyes on me. In the other, I see Mara closing hers.

The world around us changes. The storm calms. The light that was bright enough to hurt dims. Reality and the constructed digital place are merging back together.

"You have six months to prove this can be done," Mara says. She quirks a little smile with Luce's lips. Her dark eyes, so close to Luce's natural color, burn with pride. "I will return Lucinia sol Lucius to you now." The silver liquid withdraws back into the pool, and Luce drops. I grab her and slowly lower her to the ground.

But I can feel, through that fading connection, that Mara is not completely gone.

Castor rushes to my side and takes Luce from me. He whispers something to her in Aster, then looks past me to Lito.

I stand. The ocean is disappearing. The silver liquid is withdrawing. I reach out for Lito. He is iron, and I am a magnet; I will always be pulled toward him.

"Hiro . . ."

The shadow world with Lito in it is beginning to fade. He is a digital ghost who can haunt me no longer.

"Come back with me," I beg.

He shakes his head. "My Synthetic body was destroyed saving Luce. I only inhabited this form to guide you here. It's not stable enough to last forever . . ."

I am never at a loss for words, yet I can think of nothing to say. Nothing that would change what is going to happen.

My heart is in a vise, squeezing tighter with each second. "I never thought," I say, tears rising to my eyes, "I'd have to lose you twice."

"At least this time," he says, wrapping his arms around my shoulders and pulling me to his chest, "we get to say goodbye."

I force a laugh that trips into a sob. My prosthetic arm holds him tightly; my flesh hand feathers through his black silk hair.

"You are my first love," I whisper to him, "and you are my last love. Without you, I wouldn't be me."

"And without you . . ." His cheek scrapes against mine. His lips ghost over my forehead. I lift my head, and our noses brush. We are a breath apart. "I would have lost myself long ago." He presses his forehead to mine. "Thank you, for saving me. For saving us all."

The sensation of his touch begins to fade. I close my eyes so I don't have to see him fade away too.

With his heart beating against my chest, he whispers one last time into my ear: "Goodbye, Hiro."

I put everything I am into the two words that break me apart as they leave my lips. "Goodbye, Lito."

The shadow world—and Lito—disappears completely, leaving us in the heart of the Synthetic Forge, which sleeps once again.

CHAPTER 52

LUCE

[command/send damage report]

ACKNOWLEDGED

[command/revert to subroutine:standby]

ACKNOWLEDGED

[query/subroutine:war]

>>Chance of total human annihilation: 1%

Feed of SYNTHETIC#00000001

I wake in Castor's arms, knowing Autarkeia—and the world—has changed. His eyes meet mine, and his lips curl into a sharp-toothed smirk.

I smile as I drift off again. I'm too tired to do anything else. Forcing the Singularity to use my body as a foothold in the physical world has taken everything out of me. But the wounds I sustained in my struggle with Sorrel, at least, are healed.

I don't think I would've come back at all if not for Lito. He built a world as a buffer between the overpowering Synthetic hive mind and the humans who interacted with them. He lifted some of the weight from my shoulders, allowing me to stay conscious—present—

during the discussion, instead of me being shoved out of my head completely.

Of course my brother would fight to keep me alive from beyond death . . .

When I wake again, someone's placed me in a gravchair and is wheeling me to the docks. I look over my shoulder, and Dire winks at me. The streets of Autarkeia are empty. I can feel, somehow, that the Forges are quiet. But the Synthetics have reconnected, and their arrowhead drones speed through the air bearing mechanical-voiced messages about the six-month time limit for the peace treaty.

They offer no explanation as to how that decision was reached.

In the hangar, Dire stops at a *Hermes*-class ship. I try to focus only on what's before me, instead of thinking about the last time I was here, fleeing for my life. The loading ramp is open, and Hiro emerges, bleary-eyed and puffy-cheeked.

"Ready to go home?" Dire asks us both.

"Almost," Hiro says.

As Hiro disappears into the ship to prepare it for launch, I watch as people leave, one group at a time—the Geans, led by Astrid and Pollux holding hands; the moonborn, their leader cradling a cold case like an infant; and the Asters, who bear Sorrel's body between them like a holy relic. Castor brings up the rear and nods solemnly to me before disappearing onto the Aster ship.

Is the peace treaty truly possible, or are we dragging out the inevitable war?

The Icarii are last, with a one-legged Beron val Bellator limping between the few survivors. He looks haggard, while the duelists are sullen. I hope, without Souji to poison them, they can understand the importance of what happened here.

When they're gone and it's just me and Dire, it feels like time has reversed, and if I close my eyes, I can pretend to hear the bustling activity of ships being unloaded. Can pretend that, just beyond the level elevators, Autarkeia is thriving.

Time ticks by. Hiro finally returns to us. "Ship's ready to go . . ." Yet they don't seem prepared to leave.

Dire stands and holds out his hand to Hiro. "You know to call me if you need anything, Hiro . . ."

But Hiro throws both of their arms around him. "Same to you."

Dire hugs me as well before he leaves with the outlaws who survived.

Hiro pushes me into the *Hermes*'s command center, then leans over the control panel, hands braced on either side of a screen. I don't know what they see there, but I doubt that's the reason they look so lost. I reach out and wrap my arms around their elbow. Press my face against their biceps. Close my eyes and wish, with everything inside me, that we'll both be okay.

If not now, then one day.

They turn and embrace me fully, their cheek against my soft scalp. Grief has cut us apart and left us bleeding with wounds that will never heal, but it helps to be with someone who can remind me of the good times through the pain.

"Mara . . ."

As soon as I open my eyes, I spot her. Mara-the-girl, who greeted us when we arrived on Autarkeia, not Mara-the-avatar, who used my body. Her edges are too sharp and fuzzy at the same time.

"Mara—" Hiro reaches out, but their hand passes right through her. Their face breaks in disappointment. "You're not really here . . ."

"We don't have the ability to build Synthetic bodies like mine on Autarkeia, and our planetship was destroyed." She looks between Hiro and me. She's just like Lito, unable to cross to this side without a form to inhabit.

"Why did you come, then?" I ask.

Hiro sucks in a taut breath. "You can see her—" The rest of their sentence is swallowed.

"I came," Mara says, a little smile lighting up her face, "to offer you one last thing . . ."

PART V

FROM THE ASHES

INTERLUDE
SOUJI VAL AKIRA

With the soothing hum of the hospital monitors, Souji val Akira could drift back to sleep. But because he remembers what happened before this—Autarkeia, the wave of silver, his greatest creation collapsing beside the child it was based on—he forces himself to full consciousness.

The ceiling is tile, the air crisp, the gel mattress comfortable. He removes the wrist cuff that has been tracking his vitals—his pulse is steady, his blood pressure optimal—and fixes the sleeve of his shirt with the diamond cuff link that has been set on the bedside table.

"Beron?" he calls, and then, when there is no answer, he tries again. "Hiro?"

"Not quite," comes the answer, a canary's version of a Gean accent. He does not startle at the appearance of the Synthetic girl with her half-silver head, does not offer her more than a hasty glance.

If she is here, the Synthetics are still operational. If she is here, his plan has failed and his king has fallen. Checkmate. The game is over.

He knows the value of words, and so he does not waste them on questions he could decipher the answers to. *Where am I?* Likely Autarkeia.

Why have they kept me alive? For knowledge or ransom. *What happened to the others?* Dead, or soon to be, if the Synthetics go to war.

But oh, Souji has been accused of many things; stupidity has never been one of them. He knew the chance of failure on Autarkeia and left detailed instructions for his successor, plans to build more Val Akira–version Synthetics with the power to interrupt the Singularity's connection. War there may be, but it will be brutal and bloody for the Synthetics.

"It's fascinating that you still know how to smile," the girl says, and his lips, which had been upturned slightly, start to fall. "Particularly when you're so mistaken about your current situation."

Hiro enters the room much the same way the girl had—not there one moment, present the next. But upon closer inspection, Souji realizes his mistake—that is not Hiro, it is his creation. They share a face—or they did, before Hiro was geneassisted into Saito Ren—but they are not the same.

"Hello, Souji," it says, and . . . that is new. It has never called him that before.

"I am your father and your creator," he says, and it shrugs in such an uncaring way, it is as if he is staring at a teenage Hiro across the desk of his home office.

"I wanted to give you the good news myself," his creation says, and the way that only one side of its mouth turns upward—that damned *smirk*—haunts him. "I have been integrated into the Singularity, as you wished."

But before Souji can say a single thing, his creation waves its hand through the air, and the room—*changes.*

The walls, the floor, even the bed—all of which had been perfectly ordinary in every way—shift into silver liquid and reform, breaking the illusion of a hospital and replacing it with . . . a world of impossibility.

Stony ground stretches toward the horizon, sliced apart by sharp spiked architecture. Above the icy plains, a planet hangs in the sky where a storm rages, a churning eye of crimson. Watching. Watching *him.* The room is hardly a room, open to the elements as it is. Foolishly, his hand goes to his throat, his first instinct the thought, *How can I breathe?*

And the answer comes, a whisper on the battering wind: *Because I'm not human anymore.*

Souji val Akira does not waste words, but if there were ever a time to do so, it is now.

"What have you done to me?" he asks, and his creation and the Synthetic girl wear twin smirks that remind him of Hiro.

"自業自得," the girl says, and he is dragged through the years to his childhood. *One's actions, one's profits.* The Synthetic he spoke to—her? After all this time of searching, after all the trials of his childhood and plans of adulthood, she is here, in front of him, knowing far more about him than he ever could about her.

SOUJI VAL AKIRA, YOU DON'T KNOW WHAT YOU'RE DOING.

He stumbles, falls to his knees in front of them.

Their eyes shine with liquid silver.

"What are you going to do with me?" he asks, his fear unmasked.

They say nothing. They turn away from him. They step through the wall that hardens behind them.

They leave him there, staring at the planet with the storm, no warning or goodbye. Laughter bubbles manically up his throat.

He laughs, because of the planet above him. He laughs, because of the memory of Hiro's smirk on his creation's face. He laughs, because, in a way, he got what he wanted—his creation is part of the Singularity. *He* is part of the Singularity.

And he has never felt so unbelievably alone.

CHAPTER 53
ASTRID

Our priority now is to ensure the Icarii-Gean cease-fire becomes a long-lasting treaty that includes the disparate peoples of the belt, including the sovereign Aster citizens.

Warlord Shaz Kadir to the Gean people

THREE MONTHS LATER

One might say that, with only three months left to finish the details of the peace treaty between the Geans, Icarii, and Asters, time was running out. But strangely, I had never felt like I had more of it spooling out in front of me, as thick and sweet as the honey I harvested from the hives behind the Aunt Margaret Center for Recovery. The bees were a gift from the new Auntie of the Order of Leo, a gesture of cooperation upon her appointment to the Agora, but I had taken to caring for them as much as I had the land granted by the Order of Pyxis in memory of Aunt Margaret.

As I slip from the gleaming tiled kitchen into the expansive backyard, a breakfast tray in my hands, a group of former Sisters bid me a good morning with voices as bright as their smiles. "Have a wonderful day," I say in return. The rolling lawn, filled with shady oaks, offers secluded meeting spots, and as I walk to the central greenhouse, I pass a circle of people in eclectic Gean clothing—the majority Sisters, but an Aunt and male Cousin among them—sitting on the soft grass. They do not pause the small group therapy session to greet me, and I do not interrupt them.

When I reach the greenhouse and am reflected in the glass, I feel only the smallest hint of melancholy at the sight of my face. The scar, puckered and red against my otherwise pale skin, starts at the corner of my right eye and tugs the eyelid downward, passes over my cheekbone, and stops just above my jaw. The only reason it ends there is that the Skadivolk found me during my struggle with Ringer and took away my knife.

I fix my reflection with a determined stare. "This is my body," I say out loud, one of the positive affirmations I lean on when the shadow of doubt comes creeping. "This is my life." I no longer speak of beauty, as that was something the Sisterhood used to measure us, to judge us and rank us. Instead, I focus on my favorite things about myself—as well as a reminder that I try every day to internalize.

One day, I hope to drive out the sorrow and doubt completely.

"And I will do what I can to change this world."

I push open the door to the greenhouse with my shoulder and am in the process of setting down the tray of toast next to a little golden pot of honey when I notice Lily is not alone. For a moment, I fear I have seen a ghost—this is the place I saw Aunt Margaret moments before she died, and after seeing a Synthetic world layered over reality, nothing would surprise me anymore—but the white-haired woman speaking with Lily in hushed tones is not her former Auntie.

"Ebba," I say, her name slipping through my lips unbidden. The last time I saw her was just after Autarkeia, when she came to extract Bruni's neurobots. I still remember the pain of being hooked up to the strange Skadivolk machine that drew my blood and filtered it before injecting it back into my veins. I had feared it might wake Ringer again, but even when she filtered my blood a second time for his neurobots, all she found were blank nanomachines.

Whatever these Muninn held, Ebba told me, *this line is forgotten now.*

The leader of the moonborn winks her scarred eyelid at me, a little twitch that seems incongruous with the larger burn on her face. "Astrid."

I want to ask her a hundred questions, but Lily comes to my side and squeezes my hand, a reassuring gesture that tells me she is handling it—whatever *it* is, even if Ebba has finally come to collect on the ship I owe her, something she refuses to let me forget. "This looks delicious, Astrid," Lily says of our breakfast, picking up one of the two glasses of freshly squeezed orange juice, courtesy of our orange trees.

"I did not think you had a meeting until Dire of the Belt later this afternoon, so I am afraid I did not bring enough for three," I say.

"Dire of the Belt, eh?" Ebba makes a purr of a noise in the back of her throat. "Sexy man, him."

It is Dire's trading concern that interests us. I gesture to the two chairs on either side of the little iron table. "Ebba, please, you can share the meal with Lily, and I will fetch more."

"No need, I'm not staying." Ebba's boots are covered in greenhouse dirt as she stomps closer to me. "The former Mother here sent me an invitation I couldn't refuse."

I look between Ebba and Lily, waiting for one of them to explain. Lily is the one who finally answers when she sees Ebba has no plans to.

"Though the power of the Sisterhood is diminished after everything that's occurred," Lily begins, and Ebba snorts. I understand why; calling the Sisterhood's power *diminished* is a pretty polite way of saying trust in us is thin as we work to establish a new order. "I offered Ebba a personal introduction to the Mother."

I smile at the thought of Lauren, former First Sister of the *Juno*, now Mother Octavia I. After we returned from the meeting with the Synthetics, our first order of business was telling the Geans the truth of everything: the neural implants used by the Sisterhood, Warlord Vaughn's plot for immortality, even the show I put on as the Unchained to draw people to my cause. Unfortunately, Mother Lilian I's rule became tainted by association, so after filling the empty seats of the Agora—with help from Aunt Tamar and Aunt Delilah, of course—Lily retired, the only Mother to ever do so by choice.

Some were shocked by her willing abdication of power, but I was not. The Asters were a recognized people now, with the same rights as any Gean, and while things were still being hammered out in endless debates that Lily attended religiously, no one could deny that she had done what she set out to do.

I suppose technically Lily and I are Cousins now, if we were to use rank at all. But here at the Margaret Center, we all have names and use them freely, alongside whatever communication method we choose.

"The Mother will help you find the records of the missing Skadivolk children, I am sure," I tell Ebba, settling into one of the chairs.

"Here's hoping," she says, taking the orange juice as I reach for it and holding it up in a toast. "To the changes in the Sisterhood!"

"I'll drink to that," Lily says, sipping her own juice before passing it to me. I drink as well, my lips against the same place on the rim Lily set hers.

There have been many changes that I desired, and a few that I did not. The Mother is now equal in power to the Agora, and a new oversight committee has been formed to watch over them both. Sisters are allowed to communicate with anyone they wish to, via voices or hand language, and neural implants are no longer to be used, but the punishments for repeating the secrets learned from soldiers are just as harsh as before, if not harsher. Sisters are still encouraged to serve soldiers as comfort women, a thing that disgusts me, but, at the very least, a law was passed that requires a woman's *consent* to join the Sisterhood. No longer can they be given or forced, as I was. And, to balance that out, anyone is allowed to leave the Sisterhood whenever they choose.

The last time Aunt Tamar visited, she spoke of these changes with her usual sternness. "I voted for these laws, but I am sorely afraid," she said, "that we have gutted the Sisterhood in a way that it will never recover from, and that it will soon cease to exist."

It is a possibility that does not frighten me.

I understand that we need approval in order to receive funding, and that for approval, we need to serve, but unlike many of my friends, I believe we have not gone far enough. I want to offer health services to all Gean citizens, not only those in the military or Sisterhood. I want to put Sisters trained for counseling other Sisters on all ships. And, most of all, I want to abolish the recruitment of Little Sisters—for how can a child consent to things hardly understood by adults?

"Thanks for your help, Lily. And Astrid . . ." Ebba sets her half-finished orange juice back on the tray. "It was good to see you." Half her mouth curls in a smile, the scarred half of her face stoic as usual.

My hand slips beneath my hair at her words, and I rub my fingertips over the sensitive scar on the back of my neck. I had my neural implant removed first thing upon returning to Olympus Mons, but afterward, during my recovery, the surgeon set the flea-size machine before me. I knew what it was supposed to look like because I had been given Mother Isabel III's on Ceres, so I knew immediately that mine was . . . wrong. It was blackened and dull, like a blown light.

"Burned out," the surgeon said. "Seems like it wasn't even working."

He moved to take it away, and I stopped him, told him I wanted to keep it. He let me. Later, as I rubbed my first finger over the neural implant's dead shell, I knew what had happened. I had killed Ringer. Between the burned-out implant and the blank neurobots, I had seen his corpse.

I struggle with all that has been done to me without my consent, though it has helped to speak with someone who has suffered similar violations. Every day, I write Hiro val Akira, and they write me. We speak of all that has occurred and sometimes, like days long past on the *Juno*, of nothing at all. Once more, we find comfort in each other in a way we can with few others.

We are . . . friends. And perhaps one day, we may find our way back to being more—this time as ourselves, no masks between us.

"Good hunting," Ebba says, calling me back to the greenhouse. They are words she used to say to Bruni, a phrase I know only from my time with his neurobots.

I force my fingers away from the scar and clasp my hands together in my lap. "Good hunting," I respond.

When Ebba is gone and the door to the greenhouse flaps closed behind her, Lily lazily runs her hand through my hair. "Do you not have a Warlord to advise today?" I joke. Despite everything that happened at Autarkeia, Warlord Kadir has held to his word; he's intent on changing things for all Geans throughout Earth and Mars. And, without our having to ask, he often calls on Lily for advice.

"Not today," Lily says, her fingertips brushing a sensitive spot on my scalp that sends a shiver through me. "He's preparing to leave to meet with President val Thondarbha of the Icarii and the Aster Elders for the next iteration of the peace treaty."

"So we have the day to ourselves?" I reach for her, not out of desperation but because I want *her*. I slip my arms around her waist and pull her close.

"I didn't say that." Lily smiles playfully when I look up at her. Her brown eyes are the exact color of the rich soil. "But . . . we have the morning."

I pull her down toward me and catch her mouth with mine. She emits a little hum, a swallowed laugh, that vibrates against my lips. But just as my teeth graze her tongue, she pulls away and leaves me gasping.

"I love you, Astrid," she says, her fingers slipping into my hair, brushing against that tender scar.

And I answer by baring myself completely. "I trust you, Lily."

She tightens her grip on my hair, a small pain swallowed by larger pleasure, and pulls me into her. Between us is a pressure that turns gas and dust into a planet of our own making.

In between kisses, she whispers to me.

"I love you, I love you, I love you . . ."

In her arms, in this place surrounded by my sisters, I am home.

CHAPTER 54
LUCE

Tell us, how are you really handling your transition back to Cytherea after all you've been through?

> *Esperanza val Montero, reporter for the newscast* El Sol

Now that we're seeing progress on the treaty? [Smiles] Much better.

> *Lucinia sol Lucius*

The feed for the Keres Truth Society is wild with comments on my latest interview.

lostinlibrary: LSL's face when she told the interviewer what's up jajaja

blushinglandscape: love LSL's voice <3

blushinglandscape: she should record an album

allpeacekeepersarebastards: she's too busy for that

m3teor1te: luce in the sky with ~*~*diamonds*~*~

hairycryptid: I HAVE HER ON A BODY PILLOW

bunnibaybee: ew

lareinaisa: great job LSL ;)

I tap the screen and send it flying, turning off the broadcast. I don't like to watch my interviews—it makes me feel oily with an embarrassment I don't feel during them—but I don't mind the publicity that comes alongside them.

When we first returned to Venus, I thought the media would grow tired of asking me the same questions again and again, but they haven't. They've even started asking new things—about me, my life, my art . . . and it's nice, really, to be a constant reminder of what we, as Icarii, must work toward with the peace treaty. Of its utmost importance, and what will happen if we don't achieve it.

I can even sit through longer interviews now. At first it was short and sweet, my health taking priority as I recovered from . . . everything. Yes, the Synthetics saved my life in the well that connected me, briefly, to their mind, but they didn't edit my DNA, and the Genekey virus had already done a lot of damage . . .

My medical file, which is somewhere on my desk beneath piles of charcoal sketches, is as thick as a novel. It details, quite possibly, everything that's wrong with me, including the things the medical professionals are unsure about. There's even a treatment plan based on what they do understand, but I've yet to decide on anything. Even Hiro, who I thought would be first in line for the geneassist, has avoided medics, if only because Cytherea's hospitals are still taxed by the Icarii suffering from the Genekey virus.

Every day, scientists make strides toward healing what the virus has hurt, in large part thanks to the Aster Elders—Mother Anemone and Nother Rue, of course, now that Father Cedar has been stripped of his title. They turned over the virus research as a show of good faith toward the peace treaty. But it's become obvious that it's not as simple as a one-for-all antidote; every person's genetics are unique, and so must every solution be.

As for my solution . . . everyone knows it's impossible to turn back the clock. I was the first to suffer from the Genekey virus, and I have lived with its effects for nine months. The news calls me el jinete pálido del apocalipsis or La Peste, but the truth is I have no more need of those names now that the war is done. Now I am just a girl, Lucinia sol Lucius, a reminder of why we must make peace with the other people in the solar system.

Of course . . . I am different. I don't think anyone could enter the Forge and *not* be.

With a mere thought, my gravchair floats back from my easel so I can examine the larger canvas. The portrait is taking shape, sharp cheekbones framed by long white hair. The eyes need work, but I tend to save those for last, so I urge my gravchair forward and continue my work on the jawline.

I don't quite understand how, but I can connect with machines, almost like I have a neural implant. At first the ability terrified me and I refused to use it, but with time, I soon grew accustomed to it and realized how helpful it was. It helps me control the instruments that allow me to live my life independently, a symbiosis I don't mind.

As for my art, it's a joy to return to it. I paint using only black and white now, mixing shades of gray to create landscapes and portraits the way I see them. Perhaps because of my connection to Lito and Hiro and Val Akira Labs and—you know, everything else that happened—my paintings have become highly sought after. In fact, once the topic came up in interviews, I was offered gallery space in an upcoming exhibition in Tesla Gardens. It's the first time I've thought about my future in almost a year.

The images I paint are far more truthful than any of my interviews. On one canvas that could be misread as an abstract, I've captured the inside of the Forge, the nanomachines like silver liquid in a slash from one corner to the other. On another, I've painted Mara with silver eyes exactly like the ones I see in the mirror. I keep expecting the shine of mine to fade, but it never does. I am marked by the Synthetics, inside and out.

But strangely, it's not them I think of when I catch the light. It's him.

On the center canvas, what I imagine as the centerpiece of my show, I have begun a portrait of Hemlock. The man who found me when I was at my lowest. The Aster who inspired me to heroics.

When the light outside my apartment dims, casting long shadows across my hardwood floor, I set my paint and brushes aside. I already decided this morning when I woke that I would visit the memorial, but after having spent so long calling up the smallest details of Hemlock's face, I'm pulled toward it like a magnet. I bundle myself in a jacket, slip a holoflame candle into my pocket, and leave my lowlevel apartment building.

The streets of Cytherea are not quite as they used to be. The crowds are thick, podcars zipping past on gravstreets, but there are signs of improvement everywhere I look. While there is little we can do about the pressure on the lowest level, the air filtration systems have been repaired instead of hastily patched, and several buildings are being refurbished to standards that match the higher levels.

Most astonishing of all, I pass both Icarii and Aster groups intermingling as I make my way to the Arber neighborhood. After what happened on Autarkeia, the Asters declared themselves independent from both the Icarii and Geans, a change that gave them power when approaching the peace treaty discussions. Shockingly, though perhaps because of Lily's influence, the Geans were the first to recognize the Asters and come to an accord with them. They offered reparations for the slaughter of Asters on Ceres, without demanding a thing regarding Ceres's destruction. Everyone—from the Aster Elders to the Warlord—saw Sorrel's actions as that of a terrorist outside of anyone's control, which . . . might not necessarily be the truth, but made things a hell of a lot easier.

The Icarii took longer to persuade. When the AEGIS discovered what Val Akira Labs had done with the backdoor updates to neural implants, the protests, which had died down to a quiet affair, quadrupled in size from their previous heyday. Even politicians took to marching in the streets, demanding justice; one of them later was voted in as the new Icarii president. Souji val Akira became public enemy number one, and because he never returned from Autarkeia, no one bothered to defend him.

Things were wrapped up nicely within a month or so. The AEGIS had the val Akiras—Asuka, Jun, and Hiro—cooperating with them, after all. They admitted everything: how Souji orchestrated the bombing at Val Akira Labs to frame the Asters, and the truth behind the illegal experiments that Lito and I had brought to public attention. Noa sol Romero, a high-ranking duelist often called on by High Commander Beron val Bellator and Souji, testified to the backdoor updates. Those who deserved to lose their jobs lost them, while the company cut off the Val Akira part of their name and now goes by a new, simpler one: the Labs.

Once that was over, the government focused on fixing what had been broken, namely with the Asters. Those Asters who wished to return to the belt were offered free passage, while those who wished to stay on Cytherea or Spero were granted citizenship with all its benefits, annual salary and health care included. And with so many updates happening on the lower Cytherean levels, Asters have begun moving into buildings that had, at one time, purposefully excluded them. In fact, my next-door neighbor is an Aster called Moss who often brings me the dish I like so much, the one with mushrooms that taste like meat.

Not everyone is happy about it, of course—my mother asked me to move into her building, where "those kinds of people haven't ruined the property yet." So I hung up on her. Haven't talked to her since.

I enter the Arber neighborhood without realizing it. Whereas a single street used to separate "the Aster neighborhood" from the others, now the line is blurred. The streets are still close-packed and narrow, but much of the detritus has been cleaned and the squares opened up for communal gardens and other beautification projects. I hope Lotus has been granted space for a garden here. The center square is where I go, through green hedges and past a flowering lawn, to the marble statue that stands tall and casts its sightless eyes toward the dome's simulated setting sun.

He's dressed as he always did in life: a trim suit with ruffled cuffs, well tailored to his long and lanky frame. His hair is unbraided, trailing over his shoulders, thicker here than in truth. Beneath is a plaque written in the Aster tongue, the first time the language has been allowed on official signage, but it is his flower name that I trace with my fingertips over and over: HEMLOCK.

As the sunny dome setting disappears to the swallowing dark of night, I pull the holoflame candle out of my pocket, light it, and set it at Hemlock's feet.

"He was *never* that handsome in real life," a familiar voice says at my back.

I swallow against the fluttering in my chest, but Castor doesn't notice my discomfort and comes to stand beside me, face upturned. He wears Icarii street clothes, hands shoved into his pockets, a slight slouch to his back. But when I glance at his strong profile, I see his sharp teeth make an appearance in a smile.

"You probably want to leave without speaking to me, and I won't blame you if you do. But, maybe you could hear me out?" He speaks as if he's unsure of himself. "I took the Genekey virus data to the Labs—was happy to do that—but now the Aster Elders have asked something else of me."

I don't ask what. My promise to never speak to him again burns in my memory.

"I'd heard that you came and visited Uncle's statue a lot, so I decided to wait around here for you. Hell, I'm staying right over there"—he points to a building on the corner—"just so I can keep an eye on the statue to catch you when you come by."

I quirk an eyebrow.

"Ugh—sorry. Now that I've said it out loud, it sounds really creepy and shitty." He runs a hand over his face. "Can I start over? I'll start over." He clears his throat. "The Aster Elders have asked me to be their Shield, and I'm not sure what to do.

"See, I always thought Hemlock was the one they should've picked.

He had Dire and Autarkeia behind him, but instead they chose Sorrel, and . . . hell, what a mistake that was. Even I fell into his trap, idolized him and . . . *Fuck*." The last word is a mere breath. "The Aster Elders want me to be the one to stand with them at the peace treaty discussions with the Icarii. Maybe because of all I did on Autarkeia, but they say it's because I was the one who knew Hemlock and Sorrel best, and that I'm one of the most well-integrated Asters when it comes to Icarii society." I can't help but agree with them on that count. "But . . . I'm scared."

I look up at him fully now, turning my gravchair from the statue with a thought. He's turned toward me too, looking down with eyes full of doubt.

"Look at everything I did . . . everything I fucked up. And now they're trusting me with this?" He shakes his head. "I don't want to make a mistake. Not one that could destroy everything and everyone. I—" His hand moves toward me, then jerks away as if I am a fire. "I want to ask you something. I have no right to ask you, I know, but I trust you."

I watch him, waiting for him to continue.

"I want you to tell me if I ever step out of line and do something awful. Something that Sorrel would do." That hand that had been hovering so close to me goes to the back of his head, where he musses his silver starlight hair. "The last thing I want is to become him." He drops his arm, holding it limply at his side.

When I don't answer, his face turns a hint darker with a blush. "You don't have to actually *tell* me anything, you could write it—"

"Yes," I say, taking his hand with mine. The single word—the touch— stops Castor cold, and his eyes grow wide as his pupils narrow. They shine in the growing darkness.

"Thank you," he whispers, and then even he falls silent, my fingers intertwined with his.

Quietly, we turn to look back at Hemlock's statue, hope burning in my chest for a chance at something more.

After all, with a peace between our peoples coming, stranger things have happened.

CHAPTER 55

HIRO

Peace was what drove our ancestors into the stars from Mars and Earth, and it is peace that will pave our path forward into galaxies beyond this one.

Icarii president Chuchuay val Thondarbha

The air in the elevator is warm enough to make me uncomfortable—or maybe that's just the nervousness jolting through my veins, because the last time I came up here without my hood pulled low, a newscaster who had somehow gotten onto the penthouse floor ambushed me outside the door, drone snapping photos of yours truly looking shocked and stupid. I play nice with them when I can, not because I enjoy the attention but because others don't, and I don't want to force Asuka and Jun to go through hell a second time when they've already been put through the grinder. So I do their interviews and broadcasts and whatever else they want, because I can handle it. Nothing more, nothing less.

I bring up my messages in my com-lenses. Nothing from Astrid yet, so I swipe the overlay away. Every day, we get to know each other a little better. Every day, I heal a little bit more.

The elevator stops and the double doors open to the hallway. I peer up from beneath the edge of my hood and spot a tall figure lurking by the door to my family's apartment. But he's someone I'd recognize anywhere, and I don't even bother checking my surroundings as I rush to his side.

"Lito—"

He turns toward me but doesn't look at me. Confusion ghosts over his expression. His head is cocked ever so slightly, like he's listening to someone on the other side of the door—but I know it's a whispering only he can hear.

Mara warned me this would happen. *He'll never be human*, she said.

His humanity could slip away completely one day, she said.

And then the words that sealed my choice before I'd even had time to consider it: *He asked for this. He wants to go with you.*

Nothing else mattered to me. Not the fact that he would never age, not that he would outlive me, not that one day he might choose to return to the Synthetics and leave me behind. I'd suffered through his loss twice, and I would do so again for even one more day with him beside me. Luce felt the same, and so we agreed to wait out in the belt until the Synthetics returned to Jupiter's moon Europa, where they repaired him and sent him on a ship to meet us.

I slip my arms beneath his and place my hands on his back. Maybe he's different from the Lito I grew up with, but he's still *my* Lito, warm with muscle corded beneath his skin, heart beating against my cheek. My head fits beneath his chin, and he leans into me, body loosening. "Remember that time at the Academy when you found a cat in the kitchen?" I begin.

After a moment, his arms come up around me, holding me tightly to him. "I gave it my lunch because I figured the teachers would toss it out in the street, but you wanted to take it to our dorm." He snorts. "You always did have a thing for strays."

I release a shuddering sigh. When I look up at him, he's fully present. No more Synthetic whispering, no more being called away by memories. His smile makes his dark eyes curl at the edges, black hair sweeping across his forehead.

"Did I disappear again?" he asks, but I don't answer, just place my hands on both of his cheeks and pull his forehead to mine.

The promise we made at the Academy holds more weight than ever.

I'll make sure you stay you, okay? And you make sure that I stay me.

And his answer, a promise I make to myself every day.

If we lose ourselves, at least we'll lose ourselves together.

He has the good grace to look sheepish. "I came out to wait for you, but . . ." But then he forgot.

"Come on, robot boy," I say, slipping my prosthetic hand into his— and though I can't see beneath his skin, I know we are made of similar stuff. I tug him toward the door. "I'm sure your sister's losing her mind over where you went." If she didn't use her sixth sense or whatever to know what was up with him.

My childhood home is so chaotic that Beron val Bellator himself could walk in unnoticed, so me dragging Lito in by his hand goes completely overlooked. The hallways, at one time wide, are now packed haphazardly with boxes, towers of everything Asuka, Jun, and Hana aren't selling alongside the apartment.

"ただいま," I call into the house.

"おかえり," my sisters reply in unison.

I pull Lito into the open-concept kitchen on my heels, only to abandon his hand when Hana throws herself into my arms. She's seen me every day for three months, and she never gets tired of doing that. I catch her every time.

Miss Million Words a Minute starts jabbering. "Luce has something for you, Hiro! A present! Come on, come look!" Jun salutes me with a wineglass, while Asuka scrolls through a menu pulled up on the holoscreen above the kitchen counter. Ever since we packed up the cookware, we've been forced to order out instead of cooking. Still, it's not the food that makes the meal; it's the people I share it with.

Luce is in the sitting room, her gravchair in front of the two-story windows that look out over Cytherea's skyline. When we enter, she turns toward us, flashing a relieved but knowing smile. Probably sensed us coming. "There you are," she says, silver eyes shining.

Lito floats to her side, fussing over her in a way only family can as he pulls her fallen jacket back onto her shoulder. She pretends to bite his hand, and the two smile at each other with enough joy to illuminate a room.

But it's hardly her I focus on when Castor, of all people, stands next to her, staring at Lito with barely veiled concern. I'm sure Luce warned him, but there's a huge difference between being told and seeing the evidence of the Synthetic living among us.

"How's it going, famous girl?" I ask, dropping a kiss on Luce's smooth head and shooing Lito away from her at the same time. When I turn to Castor, I pretend to be shocked. "Is this a fan of yours, Luce? Do I need to call security?"

"Pretty sure the fucking building attendant wanted to when he saw I was an Aster," Castor mutters.

Luce snorts in a rather Lito sort of way. "I'll vouch for him," she says with a wink. She's become such a little superstar, I can hardly believe it. From her interviews with the Asters that stoked the fire of the protests to the graffiti of her as La Peste all over Cytherea, she's not just a recognizable face but a household brand. And as soon as we returned from Autarkeia and she started painting again, she got more requests for interviews than *I* did. I suspect any day now they'll start calling her a new kind of Paragon influencer—the first I've *ever* seen in a gravchair and not geneassisted to Saturn and back.

You'd think I'd be jealous, but I swear I'm not. Luce's popularity helps us keep the heat away from the one person we don't want them to see: Lito.

The world can't know about him. Can't discover that there's a Synthetic walking among us. He must remain our secret.

"Good to see you again!" I say to Castor, smiling up at the tall Aster. He offers me a handshake, but I grab a fistful of his jacket and force him down so I can kiss his cheek. He makes a big show of wiping it off like a little kid would, but his face is brighter purple with a blush.

"Can we give Hiro the present now?" Hana asks. Asuka and Jun have trailed in behind us to watch as Luce produces a flat, square object wrapped in red paper the color of my dyed hair.

"Wonder what this could be," I say, taking it from her and feeling the canvas through the wrapping. Everyone is quiet. Everyone has their eyes on me. "Guess you all are in on it?" But they don't answer as I rip through the paper—what's the point of wrapping paper if you're not going to tear it to pieces?—and pull the canvas out from inside only to find—

"母." The word slips out like a breath.

Mariko val Akira stares back at me in grayscale, painted with all of Luce's care and skill. There are so few pictures of my mother left that Luce had to have stitched them together to make this painting, but it captures her as I remember her—youthful, playful, free. I can see Asuka in the fall of her hair, Hana in the shape of her eyes, Jun in the roundness of her cheeks, Shinya in the jut of her chin. But it's me I see in the curl of her lips, that foxy smirk that comes to me at times unbidden.

We are, each of us children, pieces of her left behind. No wonder my father was haunted by her constantly.

"Luce . . . thank you . . ."

"This one is for you," Asuka tells me as she comes to my side, "but we had a priest from the Temple of the Thousand Gods come and place her portrait in the butsudan. You can visit, if you'd like."

"Yeah," I say, blinking back tears. "Yeah, I'll just be a minute."

I slip away from them toward the back of the apartment, into the hallway with doors closed off to various rooms that my father inhabited, now empty. No one follows me, and, after a moment, I hear Lito kicking up a stern conversation with Castor and Luce, who screech with embarrassment—normal things for abnormal people.

My father's collections have mostly been sold or donated to museums. The AEGIS seized some of his assets, but nothing any of us wanted to keep. And after both Jun and Asuka lost their jobs at the Labs, they decided it was better to start fresh and move to a new location. Asuka has yet to decide what to do, but Jun has stated she wants to go into theater. Hana, still in college, has decided to pursue fashion design.

I slide open the door to the room that holds the family shrine and carefully set aside my mother's portrait as I approach. The lights automatically turn on, brighter than I remember them, or perhaps they're simply more intense from my tears.

In front of the family shrine, I let my fingers trail across the intricate carvings on the wooden doors before opening them. I had worried that it would go forgotten without me home, as Father scorned any interest other than in its historical value, but it's clear when I open the doors that someone has kept up its care. The shrine has been cleaned, the flowers in the vase are fresh, and the faint smell of burned incense fills the air. A bowl of rice from a recent offering is present. Funeral portraits and names of my family members on tablets fill much of the rest of the space.

My mother is there, her portrait a smaller version of Luce's painting. My father too. And Shinya. My grandfather. My three grandmothers. My uncle. And many more, people I know from this altar.

I check a side table and find incense sticks and a lighter, exactly where I kept them. I remember my mother teaching me how to do this many years ago, and my hands move with the habit of practice. I light the incense, wave the sticks through the air until they're smoking properly, and place them in the holder. Even the smell is the same, dragging me through the years in a sweet embrace. I ring a bell and clasp my hands together.

For a time, it is just me and my family, the roots and the trunk holding me steady in the branches. I speak to them, as my mother taught me. Even in my skepticism, she told me this could be a place for me to remember what they meant to me. Now it means so much more. To be here, among them, as no one other than Hiro val Akira.

Perhaps I'm not the Hiro I used to be, but I learned something on the Synthetic ship. I can want to change without hating myself. I can accept myself and still work toward improvement. I can even love myself, embracing what I have as a stepping-stone on the path toward what I'll become.

Not that there aren't days that are hard. Not that there aren't times I still recoil from the mirror. But brutal acceptance. Radical love. Those are what I aim to offer myself. I deserve no less.

A pale hand settles on my shoulder, catching my attention by sight and not by weight, and I turn, expecting to find one of my sisters or Lito. But while the face is familiar, it's not someone I anticipated seeing for at least another three months.

"Mara."

My fingertips pass through her when I reach for her. Of course . . . she's here as a data ghost.

"Please tell me you're not here prophesying doom and gloom," I say, and she giggles as if she's a regular font of good news.

"No." She takes a step back from me, allowing me to close up the doors to the family altar now that my visit is over. "But I've been keeping an eye on you, and I'm surprised."

"At what?" I ask, turning to face her.

"Many of the things you say in your interviews . . ." She rubs the toe of a chunky boot against the floor. "I understand you can't tell the whole truth, especially since no one can know about your father's research into Synthetics and the weapon he built against us. But it still surprises me that you don't take more of a heroic role when it was you who convinced us to accept the peace treaty."

I bark a laugh. It's true that we had to twist a few things in the narrative, necessary lies of omission. Beron val Bellator, with a newly attached prosthetic leg and ready to be done with all things High Command, agreed to keep my father's Synthetic weapon project a secret—and I didn't even have to threaten him with a blade. He was an integral witness in the AEGIS hearings. Noa sol Romero, the only person still living who knew about the lab where the other me was built, said they didn't want anything to do with it. They're still a duelist, but they washed their hands of the whole affair and, after testifying about the neural implant updates, refuse to talk about it.

Asuka helped me keep my word to Mara. We deleted all the research regarding the other me and the Synthetics. Just one more step toward peace.

"It wasn't just me, Mara. It was Luce and Lito and Astrid too. Besides," I say, "after all I've been through, is it really all that surprising?"

Her eyes twinkle when she smiles. "No," she says, "I suppose not. If there's anyone who deserves a quiet retirement, it's you."

"Retirement? Fuck, I'm not even thirty!"

She laughs at me, and I join her, until an awkward silence falls.

"So you're uninterested in exploring new worlds?" She doesn't ask like a recruiter would. No, when Mara asks, galaxies shine behind her gaze. The storm of Jupiter. The rings of Saturn. And other waiting planets, the reach of the Synthetics far longer than we ever imagined. "You can come with Lito. See things no human ever has. Luce too, if she wants."

I'm opening my mouth to respond when I hear laughter echo down the hall, though I'm unsure if it's Hana's or Luce's. Mara catches me looking toward them, and her eyes settle, brown swallowing up the offering of stars. She turns out of the room that holds my family shrine and starts down the hallway, and I find myself following her, as if I'm the guest in this house. When we come to the edge of the sitting room, she pauses.

"You don't want to leave them behind," she says, not quite a question.

I look at them all, my family. Jun reclined on the couch, her head pillowed on Asuka's shoulder. Hana excitedly telling a story with her whole body. Castor perched beside Luce like a bird ready to take flight. And Lito—

He walks toward me with a smile. "Hiro," he says, and my name is a song he sings best. "I was just coming to check on you. Are you all right?"

I don't look toward Mara. I don't know if she's even still there. "Not yet," I say beneath my breath, knowing she's listening.

I'm not ready to give up this life I've strived for. I want to stay with the family I've built.

I place my hand on Lito's chest, feel his Synthetic heart beating beneath my fingers.

"Yeah," I tell him, and for once, it's the truth. I *am* okay.

Because it's a big universe out there, but out of all of it, I have the most important parts right here beside me.

ACKNOWLEDGMENTS

I never imagined my career starting during a global pandemic, and I *definitely* didn't imagine publishing three books during one, but here we are, and it's really only thanks to you—my readers—that I've come this far. Thank you to everyone who picked up my book, spread the word, and reviewed The First Sister trilogy. You're the real MVPs.

They say it takes a village to make a book; to make a trilogy, it takes an entire country. This wouldn't have been possible without the countless amazing people behind me. Thank you, in no particular order, to Alexandra Machinist and everyone at ICM Partners; Mike Braff, Sean Mackiewicz, and the Skybound team; Joe Monti and the Saga team; Laura Cherkas; Molly Powell, Alexander Cochran, and the people across the pond at Hodder & Stoughton UK; Jeanne Cavelos and my fellow 2016 Odyssey class; the Tomatoes—Joshua Johnson, Rebecca Kuang, Farah Naz Rishi, Jeremy Sim, and Richard Errington; my beta and sensitivity readers, among them Enrique Esturillo Cano, Pablo Ramírez Moreta, Matthew Shean, Mike Howard and his lovely wife, Krista Merle Anderson, Dean Kelly, and Jamie Lee; my photographer, Antoinette Castro; my besties Eljay Vaughn, Colleen Toliver, Nick Berquist, and Hillary Thomas; my family, Ken Lewis, Lori Lewis, and Connor Lewis; my love, Pablo Valcárcel Castro; the voice actors Gary Tiedemann, Emily Woo Zeller, Neo Cihi, and Jennifer Aquino; and the writers who welcomed me to the community, like Meagan Spooner, Amie Kaufman, Jay Kristoff, Andrea Bartz, April Genevieve Tucholke, Katy Rose Pool, Andrea

Stewart, Caitlin Starling, K. A. Doore, Xiran Jay Zhao, Laura Lam, Samantha Shannon, and Zoraida Córdova.

I want to finish this trilogy with both gratitude and encouragement. To those who are struggling: Love yourself as an act of rebellion, even if you also want to change some things. Keep fighting, even when you feel like giving up, even if the only thing that keeps you going is spite. You are the only person with your voice; only you can tell your story.